BIG
BREASTS
&
WIDE
HIPS

ALSO BY MO YAN

The Garlic Ballads
The Republic of Wine
Shifu, You'll Do Anything for a Laugh
Life and Death are Wearing Me Out

BIG
BREASTS
& | a novel | Mo Yan
WIDE
HIPS

Arcade Publishing • New York

Arcade Publishing books may be purchased in bulk at special discounts for
sales promotion, corporate gifts, fund-raising, or educational purposes. Special
editions can also be created to specifications. For details, contact the Special Sales
Department, Arcade Publishing, 307 West 36th Street, 11th Floor, New York, NY
10018 or arcade@skyhorsepublishing.com.

Arcade Publishing® is a registered trademark of Skyhorse Publishing, Inc.®, a
Delaware corporation.

This is a work of fiction. Names, places, characters, and incidents are either the
products of the author's imagination or are used fictitiously.

Visit our website at www.arcadepub.com.

10 9 8 7 6 5 4 3 2

Library of Congress Cataloging-in-Publication Data is available on file.

ISBN: 978-1-61145-343-0

Printed in the United States of America

To the spirit of my mother

First Sister was stunned. "Mother," she said, "you've changed."

"Yes, I've changed," Mother said, "and yet I'm still the same. Over the years, members of the Shangguan family have died off like stalks of chives, and others have been born to take their place. Where there's life, death is inevitable. Dying's easy; it's living that's hard. The harder it gets, the stronger the will to live. And the greater the fear of death, the greater the struggle to keep on living."

—from *Big Breasts and Wide Hips*

Introduction

No writer in recent memory has contributed more to the imagination of historical space in China or a reevaluation of Chinese society, past and present, than Mo Yan, whose *Red Sorghum* changed the literary landscape when it was published in 1987,[1] and was the first Chinese film to reap critical and box-office rewards in the West.[2] In the process of probing China's myths, official and popular, and some of the darker corners of Chinese society, Mo Yan has become the most controversial writer in China; loved by readers in many countries, he is the bane of China's official establishment, which has stopped the sale of more than one of his novels, only to relent when they are acclaimed outside the country.

Born in 1955 into a peasant family in northern China, where a hardscrabble existence was the norm, Mo Yan received little formal schooling before being sent out into the fields to tend livestock and then into factories during the disastrous decade of the Cultural Revolution (1966–1976). His hometown, in quasi-fictional Northeast Gaomi County, is the setting for virtually all his novels; the stories he heard as a child from his grandfather and other relatives stoked his fertile imagination, and have found an outlet in a series of big, lusty, and always controversial novels, the earliest of which, in a delicious quirk of irony, were written while Mo Yan was serving as an officer in the People's Liberation Army.

Mo Yan styles himself as a writer of realist, often historical fiction, which is certainly true, as far as it goes. Like the Latin American creators of magic realism (whose works Mo Yan has read and enjoyed, but, he insists, have exerted no influence on his own writing), he stretches the boundaries of "realism" and "historicism" in new, and frequently maligned, directions. Official histories and recorded "facts" are of little interest to this writer, who routinely blends folk beliefs, bizarre animal imagery, and a variety of imaginative narrative techniques with historical

---

[1] An English translation appeared in 1993. Dates of subsequent translations appear after the original publishing date.
[2] This was the film that launched director Zhang Yimou's international career.

realities — national and local, official and popular — to create unique and uniquely satisfying literature, writing of such universally engaging themes and visceral imagery that it easily crosses national borders.

Following the success of *Red Sorghum*, a fictional autobiography of three generations of Gaomi Township freedom fighters during the War of Resistance against Japan (1937–1945), Mo Yan wrote (in less than a month) a political, if not polemical, novel in the wake of a 1987 incident that pitted impoverished garlic farmers against the mendacity of corrupt officials. And yet the unmistakable rage that permeates the pages of *The Garlic Ballads* (1988; 1995) is tempered by traces of satire, which will blossom in later works, and a lacerating parody of official discourse. Viewed by the government as likely to stir up emotions during the vast popular demonstrations in 1989 that led to the Tiananmen massacre, the novel was pulled from the shelves for several months. That the peasant uprising was crushed, both in the real world and in Mo Yan's novel, surely gave the leaders of China little comfort as they faced students, workers, and ordinary citizens in the square where a million frenzied citizens once hailed the vision of Chairman Mao.

Mo Yan's next offering was *Thirteen Steps* (1989), a heavily sardonic novel whose insane, caged protagonist begs for chalk from his listeners to write out a series of bizarre tales and miraculous happenings; in the process, the reader is caught up in the role of mediator. In narrative terms, it is a tour de force, a tortuous journey into the mind of contemporary China.

In a speech given at Denver's The Tattered Cover bookstore in 2000, Mo Yan made the following claim: "I can boast that while many contemporary Chinese writers can produce good books of their own, no one but me could write a novel like *The Republic of Wine*" (1992; 2000).[3] Compared by critics to the likes of Lawrence Stern's *Tristram Shandy*,[4] this Swiftian satire chronicles the adventures of a government detective who is sent out to investigate claims that residents of a certain provincial city are raising children for food, in order to satisfy the jaded palates of local officials. The narrative, interrupted by increasingly outlandish

---

[3] Sylvia Li-chun Lin, tr., "My Three American Books," *World Literature Today* 74, no. 3 (summer 2000): 476. This issue of *WLT* includes several essays on novels by Mo Yan.
[4] M. Thomas Inge, "Mo Yan Through Western Eyes," *World Literature Today* 74, no. 3 (summer 2000): 504.

short stories by one of the novel's least sympathetic characters, gradually incorporates "Mo Yan" into its unfolding drama, until all the disparate story lines merge in a darkly carnivalesque ending. Indeed, no other contemporary novelist could have written this satirical masterpiece, and few could have gotten away with such blatant attacks on China's love affair with exotic foods and predilection for excessive consumption, not to mention egregious exploitation of the peasantry.

As the new millennium approached, Mo Yan once again undertook to inscribe his idiosyncratic interpretation of China's modern history, this time incorporating nearly all of the twentieth century, a bloody century in China by any standard. Had he been a writer of lesser renown, one bereft of the standing, talent, and international visibility that served as a protective shield, he might well not have been able to withstand the withering criticism that followed the 1996 publication of his biggest novel to date (nearly a half million words in the original version, a "book as thick as a brick," in his own words), *Big Breasts and Wide Hips*. This novel, with its eroticism and, in the eyes of some, inaccurate portrayal of modern China's political landscape, would have sparked considerable controversy had it simply appeared in the bookstores. But when, after its serialized publication (1995) in a major literary magazine, *Dajia*, it was awarded the first Dajia Prize of 100,000 renminbi (roughly $12,000), the outcry from conservative critics was immediate and shrill. The judges for this nongovernmental prize had the following to say about a novel that its supporters have called a "somber historical epic":

> *Big Breasts and Wide Hips* is a sumptuous literary feast with a simple, straightforward title. In it, with undaunted perseverance and passion, Mo Yan has narrated the historical evolution of Chinese society in a work that covers nearly the entire twentieth century. . . . It is a literary masterpiece in the author's distinctive style.

The judges took note of the author's skillful alternation of first- and third-person narration and his use of flashback and other deft writing techniques. As for the arresting title, Mo Yan wrote in a 1995 essay that the "creative urge came from his deep admiration for his mother and . . . the inspiration [for] the title was derived from his experience of seeing an ancient stone sculpture of a female figure with protruding breasts and buttocks."[5] That did not still his critics, for whom concerns over his evocation of the female anatomy were of lesser consequence than his treatment of China's modern history.

While the novel opens on the eve of the Sino-Japanese War (1936), with the birth of the central male character, Shangguan Jintong, and his twin sister, the narration actually begins in time (chapter 2) at the turn of the century, in the wake of the failed Boxer Rebellion, in which troops from eight foreign nations crushed an indigenous, anti-foreign rebellion and solidified their presence in China. As in Mo Yan's earlier novel, *Red Sorghum*, the central, and in many ways defining, events occur during the eight years of war with Japan, all on Chinese soil. For Mo Yan, the earlier decades, while not peaceful by any means, are notable for personal, rather than national, events. It is the time of Mother's childhood, marriage, and the birth of her first seven children — all daughters and all by men other than her sterile husband. The national implications become clear when Mother's only son, Jintong, arrives, the offspring of Swedish Malory, the alien "Other."

The bulk of the novel then takes the reader through six turbulent decades, from the Sino-Japanese War, in which two defending factions (Mao's Communists and Chiang Kai-shek's Nationalists) fought one another almost as much as they fought, and usually succumbed to, the Japanese. It is here that Mo Yan has particularly angered his critics, in that he has created heroes and turncoats that defy conventional views, resulting in a "sycophantic, shameless work that turns history upside down, fabricates lies, and glorifies the Japanese fascists and the Land-lord Restoration Corps [groups of landed individuals who went over to Nationalist-controlled areas after the War when their land was redistributed by the Communists]," in the words of one critic. Of the several male figures in the novel, excluding the foreigner, whose "potency" cannot save him and stigmatizes his offspring, one is a patriot-turned-collaborator, another is a leader of Nationalist forces, and two are Communists (a commander and a soldier); all marry one or more of Mother's daughters, but only one, the Nationalist, earns Mother's praise: "He's a bastard," she says, "but he's also a man worthy of the

---

[5] Rong Cai, *The Subject in Crisis in Contemporary Chinese Literature* (Honolulu: University of Hawaii Press, 2004), 159. Mo Yan further noted "that his purpose in creating the novel [was] to explore the essence of humanity, to glorify the mother, and to link maternity and earth in a symbolic representation."

name. In days past, a man like that would come around once every eight or ten years. I'm afraid we've seen the last of his kind."

Big Breasts and Wide Hips is, of course, fiction, and while it deals with historical events (selectively, to be sure), it is a work that probes and reveals broader aspects of society and humanity, those that transcend or refute specific occurrences or canonized political interpretations of history. Following Japan's defeat in Asia in 1945, China slipped into a bloody civil war between Mao's and Chiang's forces, ending in 1949 with a Communist victory and the creation of the People's Republic of China. Unfortunately for the Shangguan family, as for citizens throughout the country, peace and stability proved to be as elusive in "New China" as in the old. The first seventeen years of the People's Republic witnessed a bloody involvement in the Korean War (1950–53), a period of savage instances of score-settling and political realignments, the disastrous "Great Leap Forward," which led to three years of famine that claimed millions of lives, and the Cultural Revolution. In defiance of more standard historical fiction in China, which tends to foreground major historical events, in Mo Yan's novel they are mere backdrops to the lives of Jintong, his surviving sisters, his nieces and nephews, and, of course, Mother. It is here that the significance of Shangguan Jintong's oedipal tendencies and impotence become apparent.[6] In a relentlessly unflattering portrait of his male protagonist, Mo Yan draws attention to what he sees as a regression of the human species and a dilution of the Chinese character (echoing sentiments first encountered in *Red Sorghum*); in other words, a failed patriarchy. Ultimately, it is the strength of character of (most, but not all) the women that lends hope to the author's gloomy vision.

In the post-Mao years (Mao died in 1976), Jintong's deterioration occurs in the context of national reforms and an economic boom. Weaned of the breast, finally, he represents, to some at least, a "manifestation of Chinese intellectuals' anxiety over the country's potency in the modern world."[7] Whatever he may symbolize, he remains a member of one of the most intriguing casts of characters in fiction, in a novel about which Mo Yan himself has said: "If you like, you can skip my other novels [I wouldn't recommend it — tr.], but you must read

---

[6] David Der-wei Wang's study deals superbly with this aspect of Mo Yan's writing. See "The Literary World of Mo Yan," *WLT* 74, no. 3 (summer 2000): 487–94.

[7] Rong Cai, *Subject in Crisis*, 175.

Big Breasts and Wide Hips. In it I wrote about history, war, politics, hunger, religion, love, and sex."[8]

Big Breasts and Wide Hips was first published in book form by Writers Publishing House (1996); a Taiwan edition (Hong-fan) appeared later the same year. A shortened edition was then published by China Workers Publishing House in 2003. The current translation was undertaken from a further shortened, computer-generated manuscript supplied by the author. Some changes and rearrangements were effected during the translation and editing process, all with the approval of the author. As translator, I have been uncommonly fortunate to have been aided along the way by the author, by my frequent cotranslator, Sylvia Li-chun Lin,[9] and by our publisher and editor, Dick Seaver.

---

[8] Li-Chun Lin, "My Three American Books," 476. Mo Yan is also justifiably proud of his shorter fiction, a sampling of which has been published in English under the title *Shifu, You'll Do Anything for a Laugh* (New York: Arcade, 2001).

[9] We have collaborated on four novels, three from Taiwan and one, Alai's *Red Poppies*, from China.

List of Principal Characters

In Chinese, the family name comes first. In families, proper names are used far less often than relational terms (First Sister, Younger Brother, "Old Three," etc.). In this novel, some of the characters change names, a few more than once, for a variety of reasons. Nicknames, including numbers, are common.

Mother	Shangguan Lu; childhood name Xuan'er. Motherless from childhood, raised to adulthood by aunt and uncle, Big Paw. Married to blacksmith Shangguan Shouxi. A convert to Christianity in her late years.
Eldest Sister	Laidi, daughter of Mother and Big Paw. Married to Sha Yueliang, mother of Sha Zaohua. After the founding of the People's Republic, forced to marry crippled mute soldier Speechless Sun. Later has a son with Birdman Han, named Parrot Han.
Second Sister	Zhaodi, daughter of Mother and Big Paw. Married to commander of anti-Japanese forces Sima Ku; mother of twins, Sima Feng and Sima Huang.
Third Sister	Lingdi. Also known as Bird Fairy, daughter of Mother and a peddler of ducklings. First wife of Speechless Sun, mother of Big Mute and Little Mute.
Fourth Sister	Xiangdi, daughter of Mother and an itinerant herb doctor.
Fifth Sister	Pandi, daughter of Mother and a dog butcher. Married to Lu Liren, political commissar of the Demolition Battalion, mother of Lu Shengli. Holds several official positions, changing her name to Ma Ruilian after the founding of the People's Republic.
Sixth Sister	Niandi, daughter of Mother and wise monk of the Tianqi Monastery. Married to American bomber pilot Babbitt.

Seventh Sister	Qiudi, offspring of a rape of Mother by four deserters. Sold to a Russian woman as an orphan, changes her name to Qiao Qisha.
Eighth Sister	Yunü, a twin born to Mother and Swedish missionary Malory. Born blind.
I (narrator)	Jintong, Mother's only son, born together with Eighth Sister.
Shangguan Shouxi	Blacksmith; Mother's impotent husband.
Shangguan Fulu	Blacksmith, Shangguan Shouxi's father.
Shangguan Lü	Shangguan Fulu's wife, "Mother's" mother.
Sima Ting	Steward of Dalan Town's Felicity Manor; later serves as mayor.
Sima Ku	Younger brother of Sima Ting, husband of Zhaodi (Second Sister). A patriot, linked to the Nationalists during the War of Resistance (1937–1945).
Sima Liang	Son of Sima Ku and Zhaodi (Second Sister).
Sha Yueliang	Husband of Laidi (Eldest Sister), commander of the Black Donkey Musket Band during the War of Resistance (1937–1945). Goes over to the Japanese as a turncoat.
Sha Zaohua	Daughter of Sha Yueliang and Laidi (Eldest Sister). Grows up together with Jintong and Sima Liang.
Birdman Han	Lingdi (Third Sister)'s lover.
Pastor Malory	Swedish missionary; has illicit affair with Shangguan Lu, and fathers twins Jintong and Yünü.
Parrot Han	Son of Birdman Han and Laidi.
Lu Liren	Also known as Jiang Liren and, later, Li Du. Serves in many official capacities for Communists.
Lu Shengli	Daughter of Lu Liren and Shangguan Pandi (Fifth Sister). Becomes mayor of Dalan.
Speechless Sun	Eldest son of Aunty Sun, neighbor of the Shangguan family. Born a mute. Engaged to Laidi (Eldest Sister), is crippled in battle, and returns to marry Laidi.
Ji Qiongzhi	Jintong's inspiring teacher.

BIG
BREASTS
&
WIDE
HIPS

Chapter One

1

From where he lay quietly on the brick-and-tamped-earth sleeping platform, his *kang*, Pastor Malory saw a bright red beam of light shining down on the Virgin Mary's pink breast and on the pudgy face of the bare-bottomed Blessed Infant in her arms. Water from last summer's rains had left yellow stains on the oil tableau, investing the Virgin Mary and Blessed Infant with a vacant look. A long-legged spider hung from a silvery thread in the bright window, swaying in a light breeze. "Morning spiders bring happiness, evening spiders promise wealth." That's what the pale yet beautiful woman had said one day when she saw one of the eight-legged creatures. But what happiness am I entitled to? All those heavenly breasts and buttocks in his dream flashed through his head. He heard the rumble of carts outside and the cries of red-crowned cranes from the distant marsh, plus the angry bleats of his milk goat. Sparrows banged noisily into the paper window covering. Magpies, the so-called happiness birds, chattered in poplar trees outside. By the look of things, happiness could well be in the air today. Then suddenly his head cleared, and the beautiful woman with the astonishingly big belly made a violent appearance, haloed in blinding light. Her nervous lips quivered, as if she were about to say something. She was in her eleventh month, so today must be the day. In a flash Pastor Malory understood the significance of the spider and magpies. He sat up and got down off the *kang*.

After picking up a black earthenware jug, he walked out to the street behind the church, where he saw Shangguan Lü, wife of

Shangguan Fulu, the blacksmith, bent over to sweep the street in front of the shop. His heart skipped a beat, his lips quivered. "Dear Lord," he muttered, "almighty God . . ." He crossed himself with a stiff finger and backed slowly into a corner to silently observe the tall, heavyset Shangguan Lü as she silently and single-mindedly swept the dew-soaked dust into her dustpan, carefully picking out pieces of trash and tossing them aside. Her movements were clumsy but vigorous; her broom, woven from golden millet tassels, was like a toy in her hand. After filling the dustpan and tamping down the dust, she straightened up.

Just as Shangguan Lü reached the head of her lane, she heard a commotion behind her and turned to see what it was. Some women came running through the black gate of Felicity Manor, home of the town's leading gentry family. They were dressed in rags, their faces smeared with soot. Why are these women, who normally dress in silks and satins, and are never seen without rouge and lipstick, dressed like that? Just then, a wagon master known to all as "Old Titmouse" emerged from the compound across the way on his new wagon, with its dark green canopy and rubber tires. The women clambered aboard even before it came to a complete stop. The wagon master jumped down and sat on one of the still damp stone lions to silently smoke his pipe. Sima Ting, steward of Felicity Manor, strode out from the compound with his fowling piece, his movements as quick and nimble as a young man. Jumping to his feet, the wagon master glanced at the steward, who snatched the pipe out of his hand, took several noisy puffs, then looked up at the early-morning rosy sky and yawned grandly. "Time to go," he said. "Wait for me at the Black Water River Bridge. I'll be along shortly."

With the reins in one hand and his whip in the other, the wagon master turned the wagon around. The women in the bed behind him shouted and chattered. The whip snapped in the air, and the horses trotted off. Brass bells around the horses' necks sang out crisply, the wagon wheels crunched on the dirt road, and clouds of dust rose in the wagon's wake.

After taking a piss in the middle of the road, Sima Ting shouted out at the now distant wagon, then cradled his fowling piece and climbed the watchtower, a thirty-foot platform supported by ninety-nine thick logs and topped by a red flag that hung limply in the damp morning air. Shangguan Lü watched him as he gazed off to the northwest. With his long neck and pointy mouth, he looked a little like a goose at a watering trough.

A cloud of feathery mist rolled through the sky and swallowed up Sima Ting, then spat him back out. Bloody hues of sunrise dyed his face red. To Shangguan Lü, the face seemed covered by a dazzling layer of sticky syrup. By the time he raised the fowling piece over his head, his face was red as a cockscomb. She heard a faint metallic click. It was the trigger sending the firing pin forward. Resting the butt of the piece against his shoulder, he stood waiting solemnly. So did Shangguan Lü, as the heavy dustpan numbed her hands, and her neck was sore from cocking it at such a rakish angle. Sima Ting lowered his fowling piece and puckered like a pouting little boy. She heard him curse the gun: "You little bastard, how dare you not fire!" He raised it again and pulled the trigger. *Crack!* Flames followed the crisp sound out of the barrel, simultaneously darkening the sun's rays and lighting up his red face. Then an explosion shattered the silence hanging over the village; sunlight filled the sky with brilliant colors as if a fairy standing on the tip of a cloud were showering the land below with radiant flower petals. Shangguan Lü's heart raced from excitement. Though only a blacksmith's wife, she was much better with a hammer and anvil than her husband could ever hope to be. The mere sight of steel and fire sent blood running hot through her veins. The muscles of her arms rippled like knotted horsewhips. Black steel striking against red, sparks flying, a sweat-soaked shirt, rivulets of salty water flowing down the valley between pendulous breasts, the biting smell of steel and blood filling the space between heaven and earth. She watched Sima Ting jerk backward on his perch, the damp morning air around him soaked with the smell of gunpowder. As he circled the tiny platform, he broadcast a warning to all of Northeast Gaomi Township:

"All you elders, fellow townsmen, the Japs are coming!"

2

Shangguan Lü emptied her dustpan onto the exposed surface of the *kang*, whose grass mat and bedding had been rolled up and put to one side, then cast a worried look at her daughter-in-law, Shangguan Lu, who moaned as she gripped the edge of the *kang*. After tamping the dirt down with both hands, she said softly to her daughter-in-law, "You can climb back up now."

Shangguan Lu trembled under the gentle gaze of her mother-in-law. As she stared sadly at the older woman's kind face, her ashen lips quivered, as if she wanted to say something.

"The devil's gotten back into that old bastard Sima, firing his gun so early in the morning!" Shangguan Lü announced.

"Mother . . ." Shangguan Lu said.

Clapping her hands to loosen the dirt, Shangguan Lü muttered softly, "My good daughter-in-law, try your best! If this one's a girl, too, I'd be a fool to keep defending you."

Tears trickled from Shangguan Lu's eyes as she bit down on her lip; holding up her sagging belly, she climbed back onto the dirt-covered *kang*.

"You've been down this road before," Shangguan Lü said as she laid a roll of white cotton and a pair of scissors on the *kang*. "Go ahead and have your baby." Then, with an impatient frown, she said, "Your father-in-law and Laidi's daddy are in the barn tending to the black donkey. This will be her first foal, so I should be out there giving them a hand."

Shangguan Lu nodded. Another explosion flew in on the wind, setting off a round of barking by frightened dogs. Sima Ting's booming voice came in fits: "Fellow townsmen, flee for your lives, don't wait another minute . . ." She felt the baby inside her kick, as if in response to Sima Ting's shouts, the stabbing pains forcing drops of rancid sweat out of every pore in her body. She clenched her teeth to keep the scream inside her from bursting out. Through the mist of tears she saw the lush black hair of her mother-in-law as she knelt at the altar and placed three sandalwood joss sticks in Guanyin's burner. Fragrant smoke curled up and quickly filled the room.

"Merciful Bodhisattva Guanyin, who succors the downtrodden and the distressed, protect and take pity on me, deliver a son to this family . . ." Pressing down on her arched, swollen belly with both hands, cold to the touch, Shangguan Lu gazed up at the enigmatic, glossy face of the ceramic Guanyin in her altar, and said a silent prayer as fresh tears began to flow. Removing her wet trousers and rolling up the shirt to expose her belly and her breasts, she gripped the edge of the *kang*. In between contractions she ran her fingers through her matted hair and leaned against the rolled-up grass mat and millet stalks.

The chipped quicksilver surface of a mirror in the window lattice reflected her profile: sweat-soaked hair, long, slanted, lusterless eyes, a pale high-bridged nose, and full but chapped lips that never stopped quaking. Moisture-laden sunbeams streamed in through the window and fell on her belly. Its twisting, swollen blue veins and white, pitted skin looked hideous to her; mixed feelings, dark and light, like the clear blue of a summer sky in Northeast Gaomi with dark rain clouds rolling past, gripped her. She could hardly bear to look at that enormous, strangely taut belly.

She had once dreamed that her fetus was actually a chunk of cold steel. Another time she'd dreamed that it was a large, warty toad. She could bear the thought of a chunk of steel, but the image of the toad made her shudder. "Lord in Heaven, protect me . . . Worthy Ancestors, protect me . . . gods and demons everywhere, protect me, spare me, let me deliver a healthy baby boy . . . my very own son, come to Mother . . . Father of Heaven, Mother of Earth, yellow spirits and fox fairies, help me, please . . ." And so she prayed and pleaded, assaulted by wrenching contractions. As she clung to the mat beneath her, her muscles twitched and jumped, her eyes bulged. Mixed in with the wash of red light were white-hot threads that twisted and curled and shrank in front of her like silver melting in a furnace. In the end, willpower alone could not keep the scream from bursting through her lips; it flew through the window lattice and bounced up and down the streets and byways, where it met Sima Ting's shout and entwined with it, a braid of sound that snaked through the hairy ears of the tall, husky, stooped-over Swedish pastor Malory, with his large head and scraggly red hair. He stopped on his way up the rotting boards of the steeple stairs. His deep blue ovine eyes, always moist and teary, and capable of moving you to the depths of your soul, suddenly emitted dancing sparks of startled glee. Crossing himself with his pudgy red fingers, he uttered in a thick Gaomi accent: "Almighty God . . ." He began climbing again, and when he reached the top, he rang a rusty bronze bell. The desolate sound spread through the mist-enshrouded, rosy dawn.

At the precise moment when the first peal of the bell rang out, and the shouted warning of a Jap attack hung in the air, a flood of amniotic fluid gushed from between the legs of Shangguan Lu. The muttony smell of a milk goat rose in the air, as did the sometimes pungent, sometimes subtle aroma of locust blossoms. The scene of making love with Pastor Malory beneath the locust tree last year flashed before her eyes with remarkable clarity, but before she gained any pleasure from the recollection, her mother-in-law ran into the room with blood-spattered hands, throwing fear into her, as she saw green sparks dancing off those hands.

"Has the baby come yet?" her mother-in-law asked, nearly shouting.

She shook her head, feeling ashamed.

Her mother-in-law's head quaked brilliantly in the sunlight, and she noted with amazement that the older woman's hair had turned gray.

"I thought you'd have had it by now." Shangguan Lü reached out to touch her belly. Those hands — large knuckles, hard nails, rough skin, covered with blood — made her cringe; but she lacked the strength to move away from them as they settled unceremoniously onto her swollen belly, making her heart skip a beat and sending an icy current racing through her guts. Screams emerged unchecked, from terror, not pain. The hands probed and pressed and, finally, thumped, like testing a melon for ripeness. At last, they fell away and hung in the sun's rays, heavy, despondent, as if she'd come away with an unripe melon. Her mother-in-law floated ethereally before her eyes, except for those hands, which were solid, awesome, autonomous, free to roam where they pleased. Her mother-in-law's voice seemed to come from far away, from the depths of a pond, carried on the stench of mud and the bubbles of a crab: ". . . a melon falls to the ground when it's time, and nothing will stop it . . . you have to tough it out, za-za hu-hu . . . want people to mock you? Doesn't it bother you that your seven precious daughters will laugh at you . . ." She watched one of those hands descend weakly and, disgustingly, thump her belly again, producing soft hollow thuds, like a wet goatskin drum. "All you young women are spoiled. When your husband came into this world, I was sewing shoe soles the whole time . . ."

Finally, the thumping stopped and the hand pulled back into the shadows, where its hazy outline looked like the claws of a wild beast. Her mother-in-law's voice glimmered in the darkness, the redolence of locust flowers wafted over. "Look at that belly, it's huge, and it's covered with strange markings. It must be a boy. That's your good fortune, and mine, and the whole Shangguan family, for that matter. Bodhisattva, be here with her, Lord in Heaven, come to her side. Without a son, you'll be no better than a slave as long as you live, but with one, you'll be the mistress. Believe me or not, it's up to you. Actually, it isn't . . ."

"I believe, Mother, I believe you!" Shangguan Lu said reverently. Her gaze fell on the dark stains on the wall, grief filling her heart as memories of what had happened three years before surfaced. She had just delivered her seventh daughter, Shangguan Qiudi, driving her husband, Shangguan Shouxi, into such a blind rage that he'd flung a hammer at her, hitting her squarely in the head and staining the wall with her blood.

Her mother-in-law laid a basket upside down next to her. Her voice burned through the darkness like the flames of a wildfire: "Say this, 'The child in my belly is a princely little boy.' Say it!" The basket was filled with peanuts. The woman's face was suffused with a somber kindness; she was part deity, part loving parent, and Shangguan Lu was moved to tears.

"The child I'm carrying is a princely little boy. I'm carrying a prince . . . my own son . . ."

Her mother-in-law thrust some peanuts into her hand and told her to say, "Peanuts peanuts peanuts, boys and girls, the balance of yin and yang."

Gratefully wrapping her hand around the peanuts, she repeated the mantra: "Peanuts peanuts peanuts, boys and girls, the balance of yin and yang."

Shangguan Lü bent down, her tears falling unchecked. "Bodhisattva, be with her, Lord in Heaven, come to her side. Great joy will soon befall the Shangguan family! Laidi's mother, lie here and shuck peanuts until it's time. Our donkey's about to foal. It's her first, so I cannot stay with you."

"You go on, Mother," Shangguan Lu said emotionally. "Lord in Heaven, keep the Shangguan family's black donkey safe, let her foal without incident . . ."

With a sigh, Shangguan Lü reeled out the door.

3

The dim light of a filthy bean-oil lamp on a millstone in the barn flickered uneasily, wisps of black smoke curling from the tip of its flame. The smell of lamp oil merged with the stink of donkey droppings and urine. The air was foul. The black animal lay on the ground between the millstone and a dark green stone trough. All Shangguan Lü could see when she walked in was the flickering light of the lamp, but she heard the anxious voice of Shangguan Fulu: "What did she have?"

She turned toward the sound and curled her lip, then crossed the room, past the donkey and Shangguan Shouxi, who was massaging the animal's belly; she walked over to the window and ripped away the paper covering. A dozen rays of golden sunlight lit up the far wall. She then went to the millstone and blew out the lamp, releasing the smell of burned oil to snuff out the other rank odors. Shangguan Shouxi's dark oily face took on a golden sheen; his tiny black eyes sparkled like burning coals. "Mother," he said fearfully, "let's leave. Everybody at Felicity Manor has fled, the Japanese will be here soon . . ."

Shangguan Lü stared at her son with a look that said, Why can't you be a man? Avoiding her eyes, he lowered his sweaty face.

"Who told you they're coming?" Shangguan Lü demanded angrily.

"The steward at Felicity Manor has been firing his gun and sounding the alarm," Shangguan Shouxi muttered as he wiped his sweaty face with an arm covered with donkey hairs. It was puny alongside the muscular arm of his mother. His lips, which had been quivering like a baby at the tit, grew steady, as his head jerked up. Pricking up his tiny ears to listen for sounds, he said, "Mother, Father, do you hear that?"

The hoarse voice of Sima Ting drifted lazily into the barn. "Elders, mothers, uncles, aunts — brothers, sisters-in-law — brothers and sisters — run for your lives, flee while you can, hide in the fields till the danger passes — the Japanese are on their way — this is not a false alarm, it's real. Fellow villagers, don't waste another minute, run, don't trade your lives for a few broken-down shacks. While you live, the mountains stay green, while you live, the world keeps turning — fellow villagers, run while you can, do not wait until it's too late . . ."

Shangguan Shouxi jumped to his feet. "Did you hear that, Mother? Let's go!"

"Go? Go where?" Shangguan Lü said unhappily. "Of course the people at Felicity Manor have run off. But why should we join them? We are blacksmiths and farmers. We owe no tariff to the emperor or taxes to the nation. We are loyal citizens, whoever is in charge. The Japanese are human, too, aren't they? They've occupied the Northeast, but where would they be without common folk to till the fields and pay the rent? You're his father, the head of the family, tell me, am I right?"

Shangguan Fulu's lips parted to reveal two rows of strong, yellow teeth. It was hard to tell if he was smiling or frowning.

"I asked you a question!" she shouted angrily. "What do you gain by showing me those yellow teeth? I can't get a fart out of you, even with a stone roller!"

With a long face, Shangguan Fulu said, "Why ask me? If you say leave, we leave, if you say stay, we stay."

Shangguan Lü sighed. "If the signs are good, we'll be all right. If not, there's nothing we can do about it. So get to work and push down on her belly!"

Opening and closing his mouth to build up his courage, Shangguan Shouxi asked loudly, but without much confidence, "Has the baby come?"

"Any man worth his salt focuses on what he's doing," Shangguan Lü said. "You take care of the donkey, and leave women's business to me."

"She's my wife," Shangguan Shouxi muttered.

"No one says she isn't."

"My guess is this time it's a boy," Shangguan Shouxi said as he pressed down on the donkey's belly. "I've never seen her that big before."

"You're worthless . . ." Shangguan Lü was losing spirit. "Protect us, Bodhisattva."

Shangguan Shouxi wanted to say more, but his mother's sad face sealed his lips.

"You two keep at it here," Shangguan Fulu said, "while I go see what's going on out there."

"Where do you think you're going?" Shangguan Lü demanded as she grabbed her husband's shoulders and dragged him back to where the donkey lay. "What's going on out there is none of your business! Just keep massaging the donkey's belly. The sooner she foals, the better. Dear Bodhisattva, Lord in Heaven. The Shangguan ancestors were men of iron and steel, so how did I wind up with two such worthless specimens?"

Shangguan Fulu bent over, reached out with hands that were as dainty as his son's, and pressed down on the donkey's twitching belly. The donkey lay between him and his son; pressing down one after the other, they seemed to be on opposite ends of a teeter-totter. Up and down they went, massaging the animal's hide. Weak father, weak son, accomplishing little with their soft hands — limp wicks, fluffy cotton, always careless and given to cutting corners. Standing behind them, Shangguan Lü could only shake her head in frustration, before reaching out, grabbing her husband by the neck, and jerking him to his feet. "Go on," she demanded, "out of my way!" She sent her husband, a blacksmith hardly worthy of the name, reeling into the corner, where he sprawled atop a sack of hay. "And you, get up!" she ordered her son. "You're just underfoot. You never eat less than your share, and you're never around when there's work to be done. Lord in Heaven, what did I do to deserve this?"

Shangguan Shouxi jumped to his feet as if his life had been spared and ran over to join his father in the corner. Their dark little eyes rolled in their sockets, their expressions were a mixture of cunning and stupidity. The silence in the barn was broken once again by the shouts of Sima Ting, setting father and son squirming, as if their bowels or bladders were about to betray them.

Shangguan Lü knelt on the ground in front of the donkey's belly, oblivious of the filth, a look of solemn concentration on her face. Rolling up her sleeves, she rubbed her hands together, creating a grating noise like scraping the soles of two shoes together. Laying her cheek against the animal's belly, she listened attentively with her eyes narrowed. Then she stroked the donkey's face. "Donkey," she said, "go on, get it over with. It's the curse of all females." Then she straddled the donkey's neck, bent over, and laid her hands on its belly. As if planing a board, she pushed down and out. A pitiful bray tore from the donkey's mouth and its legs shot out stiffly, four hooves quaking violently, as if beating a violent tattoo on four drums, the jagged rhythm bouncing off the walls. It raised its head, left it suspended in the air for a moment, then brought it crashing back to earth with a moist, sticky thud. "Donkey, endure it a while longer," she murmured. "Who made us female in the first place? Clench your teeth, push . . . push harder . . ." Holding her hands up to her chest to draw strength into them, she took a deep breath, held it, and pushed down slowly, firmly.

The donkey struggled, yellow liquid shot out of its nostrils as its head jerked around and banged on the ground. Down at the other end, amniotic fluid and wet, sticky feces sprayed the area. In their horror, father and son covered their eyes.

"Fellow villagers, the Jap horse soldiers have already set out from the county seat. I've heard eyewitness accounts, this is not a false alarm, run for your lives before it's too late . . ." Sima Ting's shouts entered their ears with remarkable clarity.

Shangguan Fulu and his son opened their eyes and saw Shangguan Lü sitting beside the donkey's head, her own head lowered as she gasped for breath. Her white shirt was soaked with sweat, throwing her solid, hard shoulder blades into prominent relief. Fresh blood pooled between the donkey's legs as the spindly leg of its foal poked out from the birth canal; it looked unreal, as if someone had stuck it up there as a prank.

Once again, Shangguan Lü laid her twitching cheek against the donkey's belly and listened. To Shangguan Shouxi, his mother's face looked like an overripe apricot, a serene golden color. Sima Ting's persistent shouts floated in the air, like a fly in pursuit of rotting meat, sticking first to the wall, then buzzing over to the donkey's hide. Pangs of fear struck Shangguan Shouxi's heart and made his skin crawl; a sense of impending doom wracked him. He lacked the courage to run out of the barn, for a vague sense of foreboding told him that the minute he stepped out the door, he'd fall into the hands of Jap soldiers — those squat little men with short, stubby limbs, noses like cloves of garlic, and bulging eyes, who ate human hearts and livers and drank their victims' blood. They'd kill and eat him, leaving nothing behind, not even bone scraps. And at this very moment, he knew, they were massing in nearby lanes to get their hands on local women and children, all the while bucking and kicking and snorting like wild horses. He turned to look at his father in hopes of gaining solace. What he saw was an ashen-faced Shangguan Fulu, a blacksmith who was a disgrace to the trade, sitting on a sack of hay, arms wrapped around his knees as he rocked back and forth, his back and head banging against the wall. Shangguan Shouxi's nose began to ache, he wasn't sure why, and tears flowed from his eyes.

With a cough, Shangguan Lü slowly raised her head. Stroking the donkey's face, she sighed. "Donkey, oh donkey," she said, "what have you done? How could you push its leg out like that? Don't you know the head has to come out first?" Water spilled from the animal's lackluster eyes. She dried them with her hand, blew her nose loudly, then turned to her son. "Go get Third Master Fan. I was hoping we wouldn't have to buy two bottles of liquor and a pig's head for him, but we'll just have to spend the money. Go get him!"

Shangguan Shouxi shrank up against the wall in terror, his eyes glued to the door, which led to the lanes outside. "The l-lanes are f-filled with J-Japanese," he stammered, "all those J-Japanese . . ."

Enraged, Shangguan Lü stood up, stormed over to the door, and jerked it open, letting in an early-summer southwest wind that carried the pungent smell of ripe wheat. The lane was still, absolutely quiet. A cluster of butterflies, looking somehow unreal, flitted past, etching a picture of colorful wings on Shangguan Shouxi's heart; he was sure it was a bad omen.

4

The local veterinarian and master archer, Third Master Fan, lived at the eastern end of town, on the edge of a pasture that ran all the way to Black Water River. The Flood Dragon riverbank wound directly behind his house. At his mother's insistence, Shangguan Shouxi walked out of the house, but on rubbery legs. He saw that the sun was a blazing ball of white above the treetops, and that the dozen or so stained glass windows in the church steeple shone brilliantly. The Felicity Manor steward, Sima Ting, was hopping around atop the watchtower, which was roughly the same height as the steeple. He was still shouting his warning that the Japanese were on their way, but his voice had grown hoarse and raspy. A few idlers were gaping up at him with their arms crossed. Shangguan Shouxi stood in the middle of the lane, trying to decide on the best way to go to Third Master Fan's place.

Two routes were available to him, one straight through town, the other along the riverbank. The drawback of the riverbank route was the likelihood of startling the Sun family's big black dogs. The Suns lived in a ramshackle compound at the northern end of the lane, encircled by a low, crumbling wall that was a favorite perch for chickens. The head of the family, Aunty Sun, had a brood of five grandsons, all mutes. The parents seemed not to have ever existed. The five of them were forever playing on the wall, in which they'd created breaches, like saddles, so they could ride imaginary horses. Holding clubs or slingshots or rifles carved from sticks, they glared at passersby, human and animal, the whites of their eyes truly menacing. People got off relatively easy, but not the animals; it made no difference if it was a stray calf or a raccoon, a goose, a duck, a chicken, or a dog, the minute they spotted it, they took out after it, along with their big black dogs, converting the village into their private hunting ground.

The year before, they had chased down a Felicity Manor donkey that had broken free of its halter; after killing it, they'd skinned and butchered it out in the open. People stood by watching, waiting to see how the folks at Felicity Manor, a powerful and rich family in which the uncle was a regimental commander who kept a company of armed bodyguards, would deal with someone openly slaughtering one of its donkeys. When the steward stamped his foot, half the county quaked. Now here were all these wild kids, slaughtering a Felicity Manor donkey in broad daylight, which was hardly less than asking to be slaughtered themselves. Imagine the people's surprise when the assistant steward, Sima Ku — a marksman with a large red birthmark on his face — handed a silver dollar to each of the mutes instead of drawing his pistol. From that day on, they were incorrigible tyrants, and any animal that encountered them could only curse its parents for not giving it wings.

While the boys were in their saddles, their five jet black dogs, which could have been scooped out of a pond of ink, sprawled lazily at the base of the wall, eyes closed to mere slits, seemingly dreaming peaceful dreams. The five mutes and their dogs had a particular dislike for Shangguan Shouxi, who lived in the same lane, although he could not recall where or when he had managed to offend these ten fearsome demons. But whenever he came across them, he was in for a bad time. He would flash them a smile, but that never kept the dogs from flying at him like five black arrows, and even though the attacks stopped short of physical contact, and he was never bitten, he'd be so rattled his heart would nearly stop. The mere thought of it made him shudder.

Or he could head south, across the town's main street, and get to Third Master Fan's that way. But that meant he would have to pass by the church, and at this hour, the tall, heavyset, redheaded, blue-eyed Pastor Malory would be squatting beneath the prickly ash tree, with its pungent aroma, milking his old goat, the one with the scraggly chin whiskers, squeezing her red, swollen teats with large, soft, hairy hands, and sending milk so white it seemed almost blue splashing into a rusty enamel bowl. Swarms of redheaded flies always buzzed around Pastor Malory and his goat. The pungency of the prickly ash, the muttony smell of the goat, and the man's rank body odor blended into a foul miasma that swelled in the sunlit air and polluted half the block. Nothing bothered Shangguan Shouxi more than the prospect of Pastor Malory looking up from behind his goat, both of them stinking to high heaven, and casting one of those ambiguous glances his way, even though the hint of a compassionate smile showed that it was given in friendship. When he smiled, Pastor Malory displayed teeth as white as those of a horse. He was forever dragging his dirty finger back and forth across his chest — Amen! And every time that happened, Shangguan Shouxi's stomach lurched amid a flood of mixed feelings, until he turned tail and ran like a whipped dog. He avoided the vicious dogs at the mutes' house out of fear; he avoided Pastor Malory and his milk goat out of disgust. What irritated him most was that his wife, Shangguan Lu, had special feelings for this redheaded devil. She was his devout follower, he was her god.

After wrestling with his thoughts for a long moment, Shangguan Shouxi decided to take the north and east route, even though the watchtower, with Sima Ting standing on its perch, and the scene below had him in its thrall. Everything seemed normal down here, except, of course, for the steward, who was acting like a monkey. No longer petrified by the prospect of encountering Jap devils, he had to admire his mother's ability to size up a situation. But just to be on the safe side, he bent down and picked up a couple of bricks. He heard the braying of a little donkey somewhere and a mother calling to her children.

As he walked past the Sun compound, he was relieved to see that the wall was deserted: no mutes saddled in the breaches, no chickens perched on top, and, most importantly, no dogs sprawled lazily at the base. A low wall to begin with, the breaches brought it even closer to the ground, and that gave him an unobstructed view of the yard, where a slaughtering was in progress. The victims were the family's proud but lonely chickens; the butcher was Aunty Sun, a woman of ample martial talents. People said that when she was young, she was a renowned bandit who could leap over eaves and walk on walls. But when she fell afoul of the law, she had no choice but to marry a stove repairman named Sun.

Shangguan Shouxi counted the corpses of seven chickens, glossy white, with splotches of blood here and there the only traces of their death struggles. An eighth chicken, its throat cut, flew out of Aunty Sun's hand and thudded to the ground, where it tucked in its neck, flapped its wings, and ran around in circles. The five mutes, stripped to the waist, hunkered down beneath the house eaves, staring blankly at the struggling chicken one minute and at the razor-sharp knife in their grandmother's hand the next. Their expressions and movements were alarmingly identical; even the shifting of their eyes seemed orchestrated. For all her renown in the village, Aunty Sun had been reduced to a skinny, wrinkled old woman, although her face and her expression, her figure and her bearing, carried evocative remnants of her former self. The five dogs sat in a huddle, heads raised, blank, mysterious looks in their eyes, bleak gazes that defied attempts to guess what they meant.

Shangguan Shouxi was so mesmerized by the scene in the Suns' yard that he stopped to watch, his mind purged of anxieties and, more significantly, his mother's orders. He was now a forty-two-year-old shrimp of a man leaning up against a wall, a rapt audience of one. Feeling the icy glare of Aunty Sun sweep past him like a knife, yielding as water and sharp as the wind, he felt scalped. The mutes and their dogs also turned to look at him. Evil, restless glares emerged from the eyes of the mutes; the dogs cocked their heads, bared their fangs, and growled as the hair on the back of their necks stood up. Five dogs, like arrows on a taut string, ready to fly. Time to get moving, he was thinking, when he heard Aunty Sun cough threateningly. The mutes abruptly lowered their heads, swollen from excitement, and all five dogs hit the ground obediently, legs splayed in front of them.

"Worthy nephew Shangguan, what's your mother up to?" Aunty Sun asked calmly.

He was stuck for a good answer; there was so much he wanted to say, and not a word would come out. As his face reddened, he just stammered, like a thief caught in the act.

Aunty Sun smiled. Reaching down, she pinned a black-and-red rooster by the neck and stroked its silky feathers. The rooster cackled nervously, while she plucked the stubborn tail feathers and stuffed them into a woven rush sack. The rooster fought like a demon, madly clawing the muddy ground with its talons.

"Do your daughters know how to kick shuttlecocks? The best ones are made from the tail feathers of a live rooster. Ai, when I think back . . ."

She stopped in midsentence and glared at him as she sank into the oblivion of reverie. Her gaze seemed to bounce off the wall then bore through it. Shangguan Shouxi's eyeballs didn't flicker, and he held his breath, fearfully. Finally, Aunty Sun seemed to deflate in front of his eyes, like a punctured ball; her eyes went from blazing to mournfully gentle. She stepped down on the rooster's legs, wrapped her left hand around the base of its wings, and pinched its neck. Unable to move, it gave up the struggle. Then, with her right hand, she began plucking the fine throat feathers until its reddish purple skin showed. Finally, after flicking the rooster's throat with her index finger, she picked up the shiny knife, shaped like a willow leaf, made a single swipe, and the throat opened up, releasing a torrent of inky red blood, large drops pushing smaller ones ahead of them. Aunty Sun slowly got to her feet, still holding the bleeding rooster, and looked around wistfully. She squinted in the bright sunlight. Shangguan Shouxi felt lightheaded. The smell of poplars was heavy in the air. Scat! He heard Aunty Sun's voice and watched as the black rooster tumbled through the air and thudded to the ground in the middle of the yard. With a sigh, he let his hands drop from the wall.

Suddenly, he remembered that he was supposed to be getting Third Master Fan to help with the donkey. But as he was turning to leave, the rooster, bloody but fighting to stay alive, struggled miraculously to its feet, propped up by its wings. Shorn of feathers, its tail stood up in all its strange, hideous nakedness, frightening Shangguan Shouxi. Blood still streamed from its open throat, but the head and comb, bled dry, were turning a deathly white. Yet it kept fighting to hold it up. Struggle! It held its head high, but then it sagged and hung limply. Again it rose in the air, then drooped, and rose one more time, this time, it seemed, to stay. It shook from side to side, as the rooster sat down, blood and foamy bubbles seeping from its beak and then from the opening in its neck. Its eyes glittered like gold nuggets. Distressed by the sight, Aunty Sun wiped her hands with straw and seemed to be chewing on something, even though her mouth was empty. She spat out a mouthful of saliva and yelled at the five dogs, "Go!"

Shangguan Shouxi fell flat on his backside.

When he pulled himself back to his feet, black feathers were flying all over the yard; the arrogant rooster was being torn apart, splattering the ground with raw meat and fresh blood. Like a pack of wolves, the dogs fought over the entrails. The mutes clapped their hands and laughed — *guh-guh*. Aunty Sun sat on the doorstep holding a long pipe, smoking like a woman deep in thought.

5

The seven daughters of the Shangguan family — Laidi (Brother Coming), Zhaodi (Brother Hailed), Lingdi (Brother Ushered), Xiangdi (Brother Desired), Pandi (Brother Anticipated), Niandi (Brother Wanted), and Qiudi (Brother Sought) — drawn by a subtle fragrance, came out of the side room to the east and huddled under Shangguan Lu's window. Seven little heads, pieces of straw stuck in their hair, crowded up to see what was happening inside. They saw their mother sitting on the *kang* leisurely shucking peanuts, as if nothing were amiss. But the fragrance continued to seep through their mother's window. Eighteen-year-old Laidi, first to comprehend what Mother was doing, could see the sweaty hair and bloody lips, and noted the frightening spasms of her swollen belly and the flies flitting around the room. The peanuts were being crushed into crumbs.

Laidi's voice cracked as she cried out, "Mother!" Her six younger sisters followed her lead. Tears washed all seven girls' cheeks. The youngest, Qiudi, cried pitifully; her little legs, covered with bedbug and mosquito bites, began to churn, and she broke for the door. But Laidi ran over and swept her up in her arms. Still bawling, the little girl pummeled her sister's face.

"I want Mommy, I want my Mommy . . ."

Laidi's nose began to ache, and there was a lump in her throat. Hot tears streamed down her face. "Don't cry, Qiudi," she coaxed her little sister as she patted her on the back, "don't cry. Mommy's going to give us a baby brother, a fair-skinned, roly-poly baby brother."

Shangguan Lu's moans emerged from the room. "Laidi," she said weakly, "take your sisters away. They're too small to understand what's going on. You should know better." Then a shriek of pain tore from her mouth, and the remaining five girls crowded up to the window again.

"Mommy," fourteen-year-old Lingdi cried out, "Mommy . . ."

Laidi put her sister down and ran to the door on feet that had been bound briefly then liberated. She tripped on the doorsill's rotting boards and crashed into the bellows, smashing a large dark green ceramic bowl filled with chicken feed. When she clambered to her feet, she spotted her grandmother, who was kneeling at the Guanyin altar, where incense smoke was curling into the air.

Quaking from head to toe, she righted the bellows, then bent down to pick up the pieces of the broken bowl, as if by somehow putting it back together she could lessen the severity of her blunder. Her grandmother stood up quickly, like an overfed horse, swaying from side to side, her head shaking crazily, as a string of strange sounds spilled from her mouth. Shrinking into herself and holding her head in her hands, Laidi braced for the anticipated blow. But instead of hitting her, her grandmother pinched her thin, pale earlobe and pulled her up, then propelled her toward the door. With a screech, she stumbled into the yard and fell on the brick path. From there she watched her grandmother bend down to scrutinize the broken bowl, her posture now resembling a cow drinking from a river. After what seemed like a very long time, she straightened up, holding some of the pieces in her hand and tapping them with her finger to produce a pleasantly crisp sound. Her wrinkled face had a pinched quality; the corners of her mouth turned down, where they merged with two deep creases running straight to her chin, making it seem as if it had been added to her face as an afterthought.

Kneeling on the path, Laidi sobbed, "Grandma, you can come beat me to death."

"Beat you to death?" Shangguan Lü said sorrowfully. "Will that make this bowl whole again? It comes from the Yongle reign of the Ming dynasty, and was part of your great-grandmother's dowry. It was worth the price of a new donkey!"

Her face ashen, Laidi begged her grandmother for forgiveness.

"It's time for you to get married!" Shangguan Lü sighed. "Instead of getting up early to do your chores, you're out here causing a scene. Your mother doesn't even have the good fortune to die!"

Laidi buried her face in her hands and wailed.

"Do you expect me to thank you for smashing one of our best utensils?" Shangguan Lü complained. "Now quit pestering me, and take those fine sisters of yours, who aren't good for anything but stuffing their faces, down to Flood Dragon River to catch some shrimp. And don't come home until you've got a basketful!"

Laidi clambered to her feet, scooped up her baby sister Qiudi, and ran outside.

After shooing Niandi and the other girls out the door like a brood of chickens, Shangguan Lü picked up a willow shrimping basket and flung it to Lingdi. Holding Qiudi in one arm, Laidi reached out with her free hand and took the hand of Niandi, who took the hand of

Xiangdi, who took the hand of Pandi. Lingdi, shrimping basket in one hand, took Pandi's free hand with her own, and the seven sisters, tugging and being tugged, crying and sniffling, walked down the sun-drenched, windswept lane, heading for Flood Dragon River.

As they passed by Aunty Sun's yard, they noticed a heavy fragrance hanging in the air and saw white smoke billowing out of the chimney. The five mutes were carrying kindling into the house, like a column of ants; the black dogs, tongues lolling, kept guard at the door, expectantly.

When the girls climbed the bank of the Flood Dragon River, they had a clear view of the compound. The five mutes spotted them. The oldest boy curled his upper lip, with its greasy mustache, and smiled at Laidi, whose cheeks suddenly burned. She recalled the time when she'd gone to the river to fetch water, and the mute had tossed a cucumber into her bucket. He had grinned at her, like a sly fox, but with no sinister intent, and her heart had leapt, for the first time in her life. With blood rushing to her cheeks, she'd gazed down at the glassy surface of the water and seen how flushed her face had become. Afterwards, she'd eaten the cucumber, and the taste had lingered long after it was gone. She looked up at the colorful church steeple and the watchtower. A man at the top was dancing around like a golden monkey and shouting:

"Fellow villagers, the Japanese horse soldiers have already set out from the city!"

People gathered below the tower and gazed up at the platform, where the man grabbed the railing from time to time and looked down, as if answering their unasked questions. Then he'd straighten up again, make another turn around the platform, cupping his hands like a megaphone to warn one and all that the Japanese would soon be entering the village.

Suddenly, the rumble of a horse-drawn wagon emerged from the main street. Where it had come from was a mystery; it was as if it had simply dropped from the sky or risen out of the ground. Three fine horses were pulling the large, rubber-wheeled wagon, the clip-clopping of twelve hooves racing along, leaving clouds of yellow dust in their wake. One of the horses was apricot yellow, one date red, the other the green of fresh leeks. Fat, sleek, and fascinating, they seemed made of wax. A dark-skinned little man stood spread-legged on the shafts behind the lead horse, and from a distance, it looked as if he were straddling the horse itself. His red-tasseled whip danced in the air — *pa pa pa* — as he sang out, *haw haw haw*. Without warning, he jerked the reins, the horses whinnied as they stiffened their legs, and the wagon skidded to a halt. Clouds of dust that had followed them quickly swallowed up the wagon, the horse, and the driver. Once the dust had settled, Laidi saw the Felicity Manor servants run out with baskets of liquor and bales of straw, which they loaded onto the wagon. One burly fellow stood on the steps of the Felicity Manor gateway, shouting at the top of his lungs. One of the baskets fell to the ground with a thud, the pig-bladder stopper fell out, and the fine liquor began to spread on the ground. When a pair of servants rushed over to pick up the basket, the man in the gateway jumped down off the step, swirled his glossy whip in the air, and brought the tip down on their backs. They covered their heads and hunkered down in the middle of the street to take the whipping they deserved. The whip danced like a snake coiling in the sun. The smell of liquor rose in the air. The wilderness was vast and still, wheat in the fields bent before the wind, waves of gold. On the watchtower the man shouted, "Run, run for your lives . . ."

People emerged from their houses, like ants scurrying around aimlessly. Some walked, others ran, and still others stood frozen to a spot; some headed east, others headed west, and still others went in circles, looking first in one direction, then another. The aroma drifting across the Sun compound was heavier than ever, as a cloud of opaque steam rolled out through the front door. The mutes were nowhere to be seen, and silence spread throughout the yard, broken only by an occasional chicken bone sailing out the door, where it was fought over by the five black dogs. The victor would take its prize over to the wall, to huddle in the corner and gnaw on it, while the losers glared red-eyed into the house and growled softly.

Lingdi tugged at her sister. "Let's go home, okay?"

Laidi shook her head. "No, we're going down to the river to catch shrimp. Mommy will need shrimp soup after our baby brother is born."

So they walked single file down to the river's edge, where the placid surface reflected the delicate faces of the Shangguan girls. They all had their mother's high nose and fair, full earlobes. Laidi took a mahogany comb out of a pocket and combed each of her sisters' hair; pieces of straw and dust fluttered to the ground. They grimaced and complained when the comb pulled through the tangles. Finished with her sisters, Laidi then ran the comb through her own hair and twisted it into a single braid, which she tossed over her back; the tip fell to her rounded hip. After putting away the comb, she rolled up her pant legs, revealing a pair of fair, shapely calves. Then she took off her blue satin shoes, with their red embroidered flowers; her sisters all stared at her bare feet, which had been partially crippled from the bindings. "What are you gawking at?" she demanded angrily. "If we don't bring home lots of shrimp, the old witch will never forgive us!"

Her sisters hurriedly took off their shoes and rolled up their pant legs; Qiudi, the youngest, stripped naked. Laidi stood on the muddy bank looking down at water grasses swaying gently at the bottom of the slow-flowing river. Fish frolicked there, while swallows skimmed the surface of the water. She stepped into the river and shouted, "Qiudi, you stay up there to catch the shrimp. The rest of you, into the water."

Giggling and squealing, the girls stepped into the river.

As her heels, accentuated by the bindings she'd worn as a little girl, sank into the mud, and the underwater grasses gently stroked her calves, Laidi experienced an indescribable sensation. Bending over at the waist, she carefully dug her fingers into the mud around the roots of the grasses, since that was the best place to find shrimp. Without warning, something leaped up between her fingers, sending shivers of delight through her. A nearly transparent, coiled freshwater shrimp the thickness of her finger, each of its feelers a work of art, lay squirming in her hand. She flung it up onto the riverbank. With a whoop of joy, Qiudi ran over and scooped it up.

"First Sister, I got one, too!"

"I got one, First Sister!"

"So did I!"

The task of retrieving all the shrimp was too much for two-year-old Qiudi, who stumbled and fell, then sat on the dike and bawled. Several of the shrimp were able to spring back into the river and disappear in the water. So Laidi went up and took her sister down to the water's edge, where she washed her muddy backside. Each splash of water on bare skin resulted in a spasm and a shriek mixed with a string of meaningless foul words. With a swat on her sister's bottom, Laidi let go of the younger girl, who nearly flew to the top of the dike, where she picked a stick out of some shrubbery, pointed it at her big sister, and cursed like a shrewish old woman. Laidi laughed.

By then, her sisters had made their way upriver. Dozens of shrimp leaped and squirmed on the sunlit bank. "Scoop them up, First Sister!" Qiudi shouted.

She began putting them into the basket. "I'll get you when we get home, you little imp!" Then she bent down, a smile on her face, and continued scooping up the shrimp, enough to wipe her mind clear of worries. She opened her mouth, and out came a little song — where it had come from, she didn't know: "Mommy, Mommy, you are so mean, marrying me to an oil vendor, sight unseen . . ."

She quickly caught up with her sisters, who stood shoulder to shoulder in the shallows, their rumps sticking up in the air, chins nearly touching the water. They moved ahead slowly, hands buried in the water, opening and closing, opening and closing. Yellow leaves that had snapped off the plants floated in the muddy water they left in their wake. Each time one of them stood up meant another shrimp caught. Lingdi, then Pandi, then Xiangdi, one after another they straightened up and tossed shrimp in the direction of their big sister, who ran around, scooping them up, while Qiudi tried to keep up.

Before they realized it, they had nearly reached the arched footbridge spanning the river. "Come out of there," Laidi shouted, "all of you. The basket's full, we're going home." Reluctantly, the girls waded out of the water and stood on the dike, hands bleached by the water, calves coated with purplish mud. "How come there are so many shrimp in the river today, Sis?" "Has Mommy already given us a baby brother, Sis?" "What do the Japs look like, Sis?" "Do they really eat children, Sis?" "How come the mutes killed all their chickens, Sis?" "How come Grandma's always yelling at us, Sis?" "I dreamed there was a big, fat loach in Mommy's belly, Sis . . ." One question after another, and not a single response from Laidi, whose eyes were fixed on the bridge, its stones glittering in the sunlight. The rubber-wheeled wagon, with its three horses, had driven up and stopped at the bridgehead.

When the squat wagon master flicked the reins, the horses stepped restlessly onto the bridge flooring. Sparks and a loud clatter rose from the stones. Some men were standing nearby; they were stripped to the waist, wide leather belts cinching up their trousers, brass belt buckles glinting in the sun. Laidi knew the men: they were Felicity Manor servants. Several of them jumped up onto the wagon and tossed down the rice straw, then unloaded the liquor baskets, twenty altogether. The wagon master tugged on the reins to back the shaft horse over to a vacant piece of ground beside the bridgehead, just as the assistant steward, Sima Ku, rode out of the village on a black German-made bicycle, the first ever seen in Northeast Gaomi Township. Laidi's granddad, Shangguan Fulu, who could never keep his hands to himself, had once reached out, when he thought no one was looking, to fondle the handlebar; but that had been back in the spring. Blue flames nearly shot out of Sima Ku's angry eyes. He was wearing a long silk robe over white imported cotton trousers, tied at the ankles with blue bands and black tassels, and white-soled rubber shoes. His trouser legs billowed, as if pumped full of air; the hem of his robe was tucked into a belt woven of white silk tied at the front, with one long end and one short one. A narrow leather belt over his left shoulder crossed his chest like a sash, and was connected to a leather pouch with a piece of flaming red silk. The German bicycle bell rang out, heralding his arrival, as if on the wind. He jumped off the bicycle and removed his wide-brimmed straw hat to fan himself; the red mole on his face looked like a hot cinder. "Get moving!" he ordered the servants. "Pile the straw on the bridge and soak it with liquor. We'll incinerate those fucking dogs!"

The servants busily carried the straw onto the bridge until it stood waist high. White moths carried along with the straw flitted around the area; some fell into the water and wound up in the bellies of fish, others were snapped up by swallows.

"Douse the straw with the liquor!" Sima Ku ordered.

The servants picked up the baskets and, struggling mightily, carried them up onto the bridge. After pulling out the stoppers, they poured the liquor onto the straw, beautiful, high-octane liquor whose fragrance intoxicated an entire section of river. The straw rustled. Rivulets of liquor spread across the bridge and down to the stone facing, where it puddled before showering into the river, becoming a cascade by the time all twelve baskets were empty, and washing the stone facing clean. The straw changed color, a transparent sheet of liquor falling into the water below, and before long, little white fish were popping up on the surface. Laidi's sisters wanted to wade out into the river and scoop up the drunken fish, but she stopped them: "Stay away from there! We're going home!"

But they were mesmerized by the activity on the bridge. In fact, Laidi was as curious as they were, and even as she tried to drag her sisters away, her gaze kept returning to the bridge, where Sima Ku stood, smugly clapping his hands; his eyes lit up and a smile creased his face.

"Who else could have devised such a brilliant strategy?" he crowed to the servants. "No one but me, damn it! Come on, you little Nips, get a taste of my might!"

The servants roared in response. "Second Steward, shall we light it now?" one asked.

"No, not until they arrive."

The servants escorted Sima Ku over to the bridgehead and the Felicity Manor wagon headed back to the village. The only sound was of liquor dripping into the river.

Shrimp basket in hand, Laidi led her sisters to the top of the dike, parting the shrubbery that grew on the slope on her way up. Suddenly, a skinny, black face materialized in the brush in front of her. With a shriek, she dropped the basket, which bounced on the springy shrubbery and rolled all the way down to the edge of the water, spilling the shrimp, a shimmering, squirming mass. Lingdi ran down to pick up the basket, while her sisters went after the shrimp. As Laidi retreated toward the river, she kept her eyes fixed on that black face, on which an apologetic smile appeared, exposing two rows of teeth that shone like pearls. "Don't be afraid, little sister," she heard him say softly. "We're guerrilla fighters. Don't scream. Just get away from here as fast as you can."

Looking around, she spotted dozens of men in green clothing hiding in the shrubs, hard looks in their staring eyes; some were armed with rifles, others held grenades, and others still carried rusty swords. The man behind the dirty, smiling face held a steel blue pistol in his right hand and a shiny, ticking object in his left. It wasn't until much later that she learned that the object was a pocket-sized timepiece; by that time, she was already sharing her bed with the dark-faced man.

6

Third Master Fan, drunk as a lord, walked grumbling into the Shangguan house. "The Japanese are on their way. Bad timing by this donkey of yours. But what can I say, since it was my horse that impregnated her? Whoever hangs the bell on the tiger's neck must take it off. Shangguan Shouxi, I see you've got enough face to pull this off, oh shit, what face do you have? I'm only here because of your mother. She and I . . . ha ha . . . she made a hoof-scraper for my horses . . ." Shangguan Shouxi, his face covered with sweat, followed Third Master Fan in the door.

"Fan Three!" Shangguan Lü cried out. "You bastard, the local god makes a rare appearance!"

Feigning sobriety, Third Master Fan announced, "Fan Three has arrived." But the sight of the donkey lying on the floor turned him from completely drunk to half sober. "My god, would you look at that! Why didn't you send for me earlier?" He tossed his leather saddlebag to the floor, bent down to stroke the donkey's ears, and patted its belly. Then he went around to the animal's rear, where he tugged on the leg protruding from the birth canal. Straightening up, he shook his head sadly, and said, "I'm too late, it's a lost cause. Last year, when your son brought the donkey over for mating, I told him the donkey was too scrawny, and that you should mate it with one of its own. But he insisted on mating it with a horse. That horse of mine is a thoroughbred Japanese stallion. His hoof is bigger than your donkey's head, and when he mounted your animal, she nearly crumpled under the weight. Like a rooster and a house sparrow. But he's a good stud horse, so he just closed his eyes and humped away. If it'd been another horse, shit! See, the foal won't come out. Your donkey isn't made to have a mule. All she's good for is producing donkeys, a scrawny donkey . . ."

"Are you finished, Fan Three?" Shangguan Lü interrupted his monologue angrily.

"Finished, yes, I've said what I wanted to say." He picked up his leather bag, flung it over his shoulder, and, returning from half sober to completely drunk, stumbled toward the door.

Shangguan Lü grabbed him by the arm. "You're leaving?" she said.

Fan Three smiled grimly. "Old sister-in-law," he said, "haven't you been listening to the Felicity Manor steward? The village is almost deserted. Who's more important, that donkey or me?"

"Three, you're afraid I won't make it worth your while, is that it? Well, you'll get your two bottles of fine liquor and a fat pig's head. And don't forget, in this family, what I say goes."

Fan Three glanced at father and son. "I'm well aware of that," he said with a smile. "You're probably the only old woman anywhere in this country who's a true blacksmith. The strength in that bare back of yours . . ." A strange smile creased his face.

"Up your mother's ass!" Shangguan Lü cursed as she thumped

him on the back. "Don't go, Three. We're talking about not just one, but two lives here. That stud horse is your son, which makes this donkey your daughter-in-law, and the mule in her belly your grandson. Do what you can. If the mule lives, I'll thank you *and* reward you. If it dies, I'll blame my own meager fate, not you."

"You've gone and made these four-legged creatures my family," Fan Three said unhappily, "so what can I say? I'll see if I can bring this half-dead donkey back to the land of the living."

"That's right, why listen to the ravings of that crazy Sima? What would the Japanese want with a backwater village like ours? Besides, by doing this, you'll be storing up virtues, and the ghosts always steer clear of the virtuous."

Fan Three opened his bag and took out a bottle filled with an oily green liquid. "This is a secret family tonic, handed down for generations. It works miraculously on breech births and other obstetric irregularities in animals. If this doesn't do it, even the magical Monkey couldn't bring that animal into the world. Sir," he summoned Shangguan Shouxi, "come over here and lend a hand."

"I'll do it," Shangguan Lü said. "He's a clumsy oaf."

Fan Three said, "The Shangguan hen goes and blames the rooster for not laying eggs."

"If you have to insult someone, Third Younger Brother," Shangguan Fulu said, "do it to my face, and don't beat around the bush."

"Is that anger I hear?" Fan Three asked.

"This is no time to bicker," Shangguan Lü said. "What shall I do?"

"Raise the donkey's head," he said. "I'm going to give it the tonic."

Shangguan Lü spread her legs, mustered her strength, and picked up the donkey's head. The animal stirred; bursts of air snorted from its nostrils.

"Higher!" Fan Three said.

She strained to lift it higher; bursts of air were now snorting from her nostrils, too.

"Are you two dead or alive?" Fan Three complained.

The two Shangguan men rushed up to help, and nearly tripped over the donkey's legs. Shangguan Lü rolled her eyes; Fan Three shook his head. Finally, they got the donkey's head up high enough. It curled its lips back and showed its teeth. Fan Three stuck a funnel made of an ox horn into the animal's mouth and emptied the contents of the bottle into it. "That'll do it," Fan said. "You can lower its head."

As Shangguan Lü tried to catch her breath, Fan Three took out his pipe, filled it, and hunkered down to smoke. Two streams of white smoke quickly exited through his nostrils. "The Japanese took the county town and murdered the county chief, Zhang Weihan, then raped all the women in his family."

"Did you hear that from the Simas?" Shangguan Lü asked him.

"No, my sworn brother told me. He lives near Eastgate in the county seat."

Shangguan Lü said, "The truth never travels more than ten li."

"Sima Ku took the family servants to set fires on the bridge," Shangguan Shouxi said. "That's more than a rumor."

Shangguan Lü looked at her son angrily. "I never hear an encouraging, proper sentence from that mouth of yours, and you never tire of spouting nonsense and rumors. Fancy you, a man and the father of a large brood of children, and I can't tell if that thing on your shoulders is a head or an empty gourd. Haven't any of you considered the fact that Japanese have mothers and fathers, just like everybody else? There's no bad blood between them and us common folk, so what are they going to do with us? Run off? Do you think you can outrun a bullet? Hide out? Until when?"

In response to her chiding, the Shangguan men could only bow their heads and hold their tongues. But Fan Three knocked the ashes from his pipe and tried to save the situation. "In the long run, our sister here sees things more clearly than we do. I feel better after what she said. She's right. Go where? Hide where? I might be able to run and hide, but what about my donkey and my stud horse. They're like a couple of mountains, and where can you hide a mountain? You might stay hidden past the first of the month, but you'll never make it through the fifteenth. Up their mother, I say. Let's get that baby mule out of there, and then figure out what to do next."

"That's the attitude!" Shangguan Lü said happily.

Fan took off his jacket, cinched up his belt, and cleared his throat, like a martial arts master about to take on an opponent. Shangguan Lü nodded approvingly. "That's what I like to see, Three. A man leaves behind his good name, a wild goose leaves behind its call. If you bring this mule into the world, I'll give you an extra bottle of liquor and beat a drum to sing your praises."

"That's pure shit," Fan said. "Whose idea was it to make your donkey pregnant by my stud horse, anyway? This is what's called doing the sowing *and* the harvesting." He circled the donkey, tugged at the mule's leg, and muttered, "Donkey, my little in-law, you're standing at the gate of Hell, and you're going to have to tough it out. My reputation hangs in the balance. Gentlemen," he said as he patted the donkey's head, "get a rope and a stout carrying pole. She can't get it done lying there. We need to get her to her feet."

The Shangguan men looked over at Shangguan Lü, who said, "Do as he says." Once father and son had done as they were told, Fan ran the rope under the donkey just behind its front legs, then tied a knot, and had Shangguan Fulu stick the pole through the hole made by the rope.

"Stand over there," he ordered Shangguan Shouxi.

"Bend down and lift the pole with your shoulders!"

The Shangguan men began lifting the pole, which dug deeply into their shoulders.

"That's it," Fan said. "Now there's no hurry. Straighten up when I tell you, and put some shoulder into it. You'll only get one chance. This animal can't take much more suffering. Sister-in-law, your spot is behind the donkey. It's up to you to keep the foal from dropping to the ground." He went around to the donkey's rear, where he rubbed his hands, took the lamp from the millstone, poured oil over his palms and rubbed them together, and then blew on them. When he tried sticking one of his hands up the birth canal, the little leg flailed wildly. By this time, his entire arm was inside the animal, up to the shoulder, his cheek pressed up against the mule's purple hoof. Shangguan Lü's eyes were glued to him; her lips were quivering. "Okay, gentlemen," Fan said in a muffled voice, "on the count of three, lift with all your might. It's life or death, so don't cave in on me. All right?" His chin rested against the animal's rump; his hand appeared to be grasping something deep inside. "One — two — three!" With a loud grunt, the Shangguan men made a rare display of mettle, straining under their load. Taking a cue from the effort around her, the donkey rolled over, tucked her front legs under her, and raised her head. Her rear legs shifted and curled up beneath her. Fan Three rolled with the donkey, until he was nearly lying facedown on the ground. His head disappeared from view, but his shouts continued: "Lift! Keep lifting!" The two men struggled up onto the balls of their feet, while Shangguan Lü slid beneath the donkey and pressed her back against its belly. With a loud bray, it planted its feet and stood up, and at that moment, a large, slippery object slid out from the birth canal, along with a great deal of blood and a sticky fluid, right into Fan Three's arms, and from there to the ground.

Fan quickly cleared the little mule's mouth of the fluid, cut the umbilical cord with his knife, and tied off the end, then carried the animal over to a clean spot on the floor, where he wiped down its body with a rag. With tears in her eyes, Shangguan Lü muttered over and over, "Thanks to heaven and earth, and to Fan Three."

The baby mule staggered unsteadily to its feet, but quickly fell back down. Its hide was satiny smooth, its mouth the purplish red of a rose petal. Fan Three helped it to its feet. "Good girl," he said. "A chip off the old block. The horse is my son and you, little one, you're my granddaughter. Sister-in-law, bring some watery rice for my donkey daughter, returned from the dead."

7

Shangguan Laidi hadn't led her sisters more than a few dozen paces when she heard a series of sharp noises that sounded like strange bird cries. She looked into the sky to see what it was, just in time to hear an explosion in the middle of the river. Her ears rang, her brain clouded. A shattered catfish came on the air and landed at her feet. Threads of blood seeped from its split orange head; its feelers twitched, and its guts were spread all over its back. When it landed, a spray of muddy hot river water drenched Laidi and her sisters. Numbed and sort of dreamy, she turned to look at her sisters, who returned the look. She saw a gob of sticky stuff in Niandi's hair, like a wad of chewed grass; seven or eight silvery fish scales were stuck to Xiangdi's cheek. Dark waves churned in the river no more than a few dozen paces from where they stood, forming a whirlpool; heated water rose into the air, then fell back down into the whirlpool. A thin layer of mist hovered above the surface, and she could smell the pleasant odor of gunpowder. She struggled to figure out what had just happened, gripped by a foreboding that something was very wrong. Wanting to scream, all she could manage was a shower of tears that fell noisily to the ground. What am I crying for? No, I'm not really crying, she was thinking, and why should I? Maybe they were drops of river water, not tears at all. Chaos reigned inside her head. The scene arrayed before her — the sun glinting off the bridge beams, the churning, muddy river, densely packed shrubbery, all the startled swallows, and her stunned sisters — enveloped her in a chaotic mix of images, like a tangled skein of string. Her eyes fell on her baby sister, Qiudi, whose mouth hung slack and whose eyes were squeezed shut; tears ran down her cheeks. A sizzle filled the air around them, like beans popping in the sun. Secrets hidden amid the riverbank bushes produced a rustling sound like skittering little critters, but no sound from the men in green she'd seen in the bushes a few minutes before. The shrub branches pointed silently upward and their gold-coin-like leaves shimmied slightly. Were they still there? If so, what were they doing? Then she heard a flat, distant shout: "Little sisters, hit the ground . . . little sisters . . . down on your bellies . . ."

She searched the landscape to locate the source of the shouts. Deep down in her brain a crab crawled around, and it hurt terribly. She saw something black and shiny fall from the sky. A pillar of water as thick as an ox rose slowly out of river just east of the stone bridge, and spread out once it reached the height of the dike, like the branches of a weeping willow. Within seconds the smells of gunpowder, river mud, and shattered fish and shrimp rushed into her nostrils. Her ears stung so badly she couldn't hear a thing, but she thought she saw sound waves spreading through the air.

Another black object fell into the river, sending a second pillar of water skyward. Something blue slammed into the riverbank, its edges curled outward like a dog's tooth. When she bent down to pick it up, a wisp of yellow smoke rose from the tip of her finger, and a sharp pain shot through her body. In a flash, the crashing noises of the world rushed at her again, as if the now searing pain in her finger came from her ear, breaking up the blockage. The water was lapping noisily, smoke was rolling upwards. Explosions rumbled in the air. Three of her sisters were howling, the other three were lying on the ground with their hands over their ears, their fannies sticking up, like those stupid, awkward birds that bury their heads in the sand when they're pursued, forgetting all about their hindquarters.

"Little sisters!" Again she heard a voice in the bushes. "Down on your bellies, hit the ground and crawl over here . . ."

She lay on her belly and searched for the man in the bushes. Finally, she spotted him amid the lithe branches of a red willow. The dark-faced stranger with the white teeth was waving her over. "Hurry!" he shouted. "Crawl over here."

A crack opened up in her confused mind and let in rays of light. Hearing the whinny of a horse, she turned to look behind her and saw a gold-colored colt, its fiery mane flying as it galloped onto the stone bridge from the southern end. The lovely, halterless colt was unruly, lively, reveling in its youth. The son of Third Master Fan's Japanese stud horse, it belonged to Felicity Manor; in other words, the golden colt was another of his grandsons. She knew that lovable colt, and she liked it. She often saw it galloping up and down the lane, throwing Aunty Sun's dogs into a frenzy. When it reached the middle of the bridge, it stopped as if brought up short by the wall of straw, or made woozy by the liquor it was soaked in. It cocked its head and scrutinized the straw. What could it be thinking? she wondered. Another shriek tore through the air as a lump of blinding molten metal crashed into the bridge with a thunderous roar, seemingly having traveled a great distance. The colt disintegrated before her eyes; one of its charred legs landed in the bushes nearby. A wave of nausea drove a sour, bitter liquid up from her stomach into her throat, and at that moment, she understood everything. The colt's severed leg showed her what death was all about, and a sense of horror made her quake, made her teeth chatter. Jumping to her feet, she dragged her sisters into the bushes.

All six younger sisters huddled around her, holding on to each other like stalks of garlic wrapped around the stem. Laidi heard that now familiar hoarse voice shouting at her, but the seething waters of the river swallowed up the sound.

Folding her baby sister into her arms, she felt the searing heat of the little girl's face. A calmness returned to the river for the moment, giving the layer of smoke a chance to dissipate. More of those hissing black objects flew over the Flood Dragon River, dragging long tails behind them before landing in the village with muffled explosions, followed by faint screams from women and the thud of collapsing structures. Not a soul in sight on the opposite dike, nothing but a solitary locust tree. On the riverbank below stood a line of weeping willows whose branches touched the surface of the water. Where were these strange, scary flying objects coming from? she wondered stubbornly. A shout — *Ai ya ya* — broke her concentration. The sight of the Felicity Manor assistant steward, Sima Ku, riding his bicycle up onto the bridge appeared through the branches. What's he doing? she wondered. It must be because of the horse. But he was holding a lit torch, so it wasn't the horse, whose corpse was splattered all over the bridge and whose blood stained the water below.

Sima Ku slammed on the brakes and flung the torch into the

liquor-soaked straw, sending blue flames into the sky. Jerking his bicycle around, but too rushed to climb onto it, he ran it down the bridge, the blue flames licking at his heels. The eerie *Ai ya ya* shouts kept spilling from his mouth. When a sudden loud crack sent his wide-brimmed straw hat flying into the river, he let go of his bicycle, bent low at the waist, stumbled, and fell face-first onto the bridge flooring. *Crack, crack, crack,* a string of noises like firecrackers. Sima Ku hugged the bridge flooring and crawled like a lizard. Suddenly he was gone, and the cracking noises stopped. The bridge all but disappeared in blue, smokeless flames, those in the center rising higher than the others and turning the water below blue. Laidi's chest constricted in the stifling air and waves of heat; her nostrils were hot and dry. The waves of heat changed into gusting, whistling winds. The bushes were wet, sort of sweaty; the leaves of trees curled up and withered. Then she heard the high-pitched voice of Sima Ku emerge from behind the dike:

"Fuck your sisters, you little Nips. You may have crossed Marco Polo Bridge, but you'll never cross Fiery Dragon Bridge!"

Then he laughed:

"Ah ha ha ha, ah ha ha ha, ah ha ha ha . . ."

Sima Ku's laughter seemed endless. On the opposite bank, a line of yellow caps popped up over the top of the dike, followed by the heads of horses and the yellow uniforms of their riders. Dozens of horse soldiers were now perched atop the dike, and though they were still hundreds of meters away, Laidi saw that the horses looked exactly like Third Master Fan's stud horse. The Japs! The Japs are here! The Japs have come . . .

Avoiding the stone bridge, which was engulfed in blue flames, the Japanese soldiers eased their horses down the dike sideways, dozens of them bumping clumsily into each other all the way down to the riverbed. She could hear the men's grunts and shouts and the horses' snorts as they entered the river. The water quickly swallowed up the horses' legs, until their bellies rested on the surface. The riders sat their mounts comfortably, sitting straight, heads high, their faces white in the bright sunlight, which blurred their features. With their heads up, the horses appeared to be galloping, which in fact was impossible. The water, like thick syrup, had a sticky, sweet smell. Struggling to move ahead, the massive horses raised blue ripples on the surface; to Laidi, they looked like little tongues of fire singeing the animals' hides, which was why they were holding their large heads so high, and why they kept moving forward, their tails floating behind them. The Japanese riders, holding the reins with both hands, bobbed up and down, their legs in a rigid inverted V. She watched a chestnut-colored horse stop in the middle of the river, lift its tail, and release a string of droppings. Its anxious rider dug his heels into the horse's flanks to get it going again. But the horse, refusing to move, shook its head and chewed noisily on the bit.

"Attack, comrades!" came a yell from the bushes to her left, followed by a muted sound like tearing silk. Then the rattle of gunfire — crisp and dull, thick and thin. A black object, trailing white smoke, hit the water with a loud *thunk* and sent a pillar of water into the air. The Japanese soldier on the chestnut horse was thrown forward at a bizarre angle, then sprang back, his arms flailing wildly in the air. Fresh black blood gushing from his chest soaked the head of his horse and stained the water. The horse reared, exposing its muddy forelegs and its broad, shiny chest. By the time its front hooves crashed through the surface of the water again, the Japanese soldier was draped face-up across the animal's rump. A second Japanese soldier, this one on a black mount, flew headfirst into the river. Another, riding a blue horse, was thrown forward out of his saddle, but wrapped his arms around the animal's neck and hung there, capless, a trickle of blood dripping from his ear into the river.

Chaos reigned on the river, where riderless horses whinnied and spun around to struggle back to the far bank. All the other Japanese soldiers lay forward in their saddles, clamping down with their legs as they aimed their shiny rifles at the bushes and opened fire. Dozens of snorting horses made their way to the shoals the best they could. With beads of water dripping from their bellies and mud covering their purple hooves, they dragged long glistening threads all the way out to the middle of the river.

A sorrel with a white forehead, a pale-faced Japanese soldier on its back, jumped and leaped toward the dike, its hooves thudding clumsily and noisily into the shoals. The squinting, tight-lipped soldier on its back smacked its rump with his left hand and brandished a silvery sword in his right, as he charged the bushes. Laidi saw beads of sweat on the tip of his nose and the thick lashes of his mount, and she could hear the air forced out through the horse's nostrils; she could also smell the sour stench of horse sweat. All of a sudden, red smoke emerged from the sorrel's forehead, and all four of its churning legs stiffened. Its hide was creased with more wrinkles than she could count, its legs turned to rubber, and before its rider knew what was happening, both he and the horse fell crashing into the bushes.

The Japanese cavalry unit headed south along the riverbank all the way up to where Laidi and her sisters had left their shoes. There they reined in their horses and cut through the bushes up to the dike. Laidi kept looking, but they were gone. She then turned to look down at the dead sorrel, its head bloody, its big, lifeless blue eyes staring sadly into the deep blue sky. The Japanese rider lay facedown in the mud, pinned beneath the horse, his head cocked at an awkward angle, one bloodless hand stretched out to the riverbank, as if fishing for something. The horses' hooves had chewed up the smooth, sun-drenched mud of the shoals. The body of a white horse lay on its side in the river, rolling slowly in the shifting water, until it flipped over and its legs, tipped by hooves the size of clay jugs, rose terrifyingly into the air. A moment later, the water churned and the legs slipped back into the water to wait for the next opportunity to point to the sky. The chestnut horse that had made such an impression on Laidi was already far downriver, dragging its dead rider with it, and she wondered if it might be off looking for its mate, imagining it to be the long-separated wife of Third Master Fan's stud horse.

Fires continued to burn on the bridge, the now yellow flames sending thick white smoke out of the piles of straw. The green bridge flooring arched high in the air as it groaned and gasped and moaned. In her mind, the burning bridge was transformed into a giant snake writhing in agony, trying desperately to fly up into the sky with both its head and tail nailed down. The poor bridge, she thought sadly. And that poor German bicycle, the only modern machine in Gaomi, was now nothing but charred, twisted metal. Her nose was assailed by the smells of gunpowder, rubber, blood, and mud that turned the heated air sticky and thick, and her breast was suffused with a foul miasma that seemed about to explode. Worse yet, a layer of grease had formed on the roasted bushes in front of them, and a wave of sparking heat rushed toward her, igniting crackling fires in the bushes. Scooping Qiudi up in her arms, she screamed for her sisters to leave the bushes. Then, standing on the dike, she counted until they were all there with her, grimy-faced and barefoot, their eyes staring blankly, their earlobes roasted red. They scampered down the dike and ran toward an abandoned patch of ground that everyone said was once the foundation and crumbled walls of a Muslim woman's house that had since been reclaimed by wild hemp and cocklebur. As she ran into the tangle of undergrowth, her legs felt as if they were made of dough, and the nettles pricked her feet painfully. Her sisters, crying and complaining, stumbled along behind her. So they all sat down amid the hemp and wrapped their arms around each other, the younger girls burying their faces in Laidi's clothing; only she kept her head up, gazing fearfully at the fire raging over the dike.

The men in green uniforms she'd seen before trouble arrived came running out of the sea of flames, shrieking like demons. Their clothes were on fire. She heard the now familiar voice shout, "Roll on the ground!" He was the first to hit the ground and roll down the dike, like a fireball. A dozen or more fireballs followed him. The flames were extinguished, but green smoke rose from the men's clothes and hair. Their uniforms, which only moments earlier had been the same eye-catching green as the shrubbery in which they were hiding, were now little more than black rags that clung to their bodies.

One of the men, not heeding the order to roll on the ground, screamed in agony as he ran like the wind, carrying the flames with him all the way up to the wild hemp where the girls were hiding, heading straight for a big puddle of filthy water; it was covered by a profusion of wild grasses and water plants, with thick red stems and fat, tender leaves the color of goose down, and pink, cottony flower buds. The flaming man threw himself into the puddle, sending water splashing in all directions and a host of baby frogs leaping out of their hiding places. White egg-laying butterflies fluttered into the air and disappeared into the sunlight as if consumed by the heat. Now that the flames had sputtered out, the man lay there, black as coal, gobs of mud stuck to his head and face, a tiny worm wriggling on his cheek. She could not see his nose or his eyes, only his mouth, which spread open to release tortured screams: "Mother, dear Mother, I'm going to die . . ." A golden loach accompanied the screams out of his mouth. His pitiful writhing stirred up mud that had accumulated over the years and sent an awful stench into the air.

His comrades lay on the ground, moaning and cursing, their rifles and clubs scattered about — except for the thin man with the dark face, who still held his pistol. "Comrades," he said, "let's get out of here. The Japanese will be back!"

As if they hadn't heard him, the charred soldiers stayed where they were on the ground. A couple of them climbed shakily to their feet and took a few wobbly steps before their legs gave out. "Comrades, let's get out of here!" he bellowed, kicking the man nearest him.

The man crawled forward and struggled into a kneeling position. "Commander," he cried out pitifully, "my eyes, I can't see anything . . ."

Now she knew that the dark-faced man was called Commander. "Comrades," he said anxiously, "the Japs are coming. We must be ready for them . . ."

Off to the east, she saw twenty or more Japanese horse soldiers in two columns on the top of the dike, riding down like a tide in tight formation in spite of the flames around them, the horses trotting across the ridge, heads thrust out, one close on the heels of the other. When they reached Chen Family Lane, the lead horse turned and negotiated the slope, the others quickly falling in behind it. They skirted a broad expanse of open land (the land, which served as a grain-drying ground for the Sima family, was flat and smooth, covered by golden sand), then picked up speed, galloping in a straight line. All the Japanese horsemen brandished long, narrow swords that glinted in the sun as they bore down on the enemy like the wind, their war whoops shattering the silence.

The commander raised his pistol and fired at the onrushing cavalry troops, a single puff of white smoke emerging from the mouth of the barrel. Then he threw down the pistol and limped as fast he could toward where Laidi and her sisters were hiding. A speeding apricot-colored horse brushed past him, its rider leaning over in the saddle as he slashed the air with his sword. The commander hit the ground in time to keep his head from being struck by the sword, but not quickly enough to avoid having a chunk of his right shoulder sliced off; it sailed through the air and landed nearby. Laidi saw the palm-sized piece of flesh twitch like a skinned frog. With a scream of pain, the commander rolled on the ground, then crawled up against a large cocklebur and lay there without moving. The Japanese soldier spun his mount around and headed straight for a big man who was standing up holding a sword. With fear written on his face, the man swung his sword weakly, as if aiming for the horse's head, but he was knocked to the ground by the animal's hooves, and before he knew it, the rider leaned over and split his head open with his sword, splattering the Japanese soldier's pants with his brains. In no time at all, a dozen or more men who had escaped from the burning bushes lay on the ground in eternal rest. The Japanese riders, still in the grip of frenzied excitement, trampled the bodies beneath their horses' hooves.

Just then, another cavalry unit, followed by a huge contingent of khaki-clad foot soldiers, emerged from the pine grove west of the village and joined up with the first unit; the reinforced cavalry forces then turned and headed toward the village along the north-south highway. The helmeted foot soldiers, rifles in hand, fell in behind their mounted comrades and stormed the village like locusts.

On the dike the fires had died out; thick black smoke rose into the sky. Laidi could see only blackness where the dike was, while the ruined bushes gave off a pleasant charred odor. Swarms of flies, seemingly dropping out of the sky, fell upon the battered corpses and the puddles of blood near them, and on the scarred branches and leaves of the shrubs, and on the commander's body. The flies seemed to blot out everything within sight.

Her eyes felt dull and heavy, her lids sticky, in the presence of a world of strange sights she'd never seen before: there were the severed legs of horses, horses with knives stuck in their heads, naked men with huge members hanging between their legs, human heads rolling around on the ground clucking like mother hens, and little fish with skinny legs hopping on hemp plants in front of her. But what frightened her most was the commander, whom she thought was long dead; climbing slowly to his knees, he crawled over to the chunk of flesh from his shoulder, flattened it out, and stuck it onto the spot where it had been cut off. But it immediately hopped back off and burrowed into a patch of weeds. So he snatched it up and smashed it on the ground, over and over, until it was dead. Then he plucked a tattered piece of cloth from his body and wrapped the flesh in it.

8

An uproar in the yard startled Shangguan Lu awake. She was crestfallen when she saw that her belly was as swollen as ever, even now that half the *kang* was stained with her blood. The fresh dirt her mother-in-law had spread over the *kang* had turned into sticky, blood-soaked mud, and what had been only a vague feeling suddenly turned crystal-clear. She watched as a bat with pink wing membranes flew down from the rafters, and a purple face materialized on the black wall across from her; it was the face of a dead baby boy. A gut-wrenching, heartrending pain became a dull ache. Then her curiosity was piqued by the sight of a tiny foot with bright toenails poking out from between her legs. It's all over, she thought, my life is all over. The thought of death brought feelings of deep sadness, and she saw herself being placed in a cheap coffin, with her mother-in-law looking on with an angry frown and her husband standing nearby, gloomy but silent. The only ones wailing were her seven daughters, who stood in a circle around the coffin . . .

Her mother-in-law's stentorian voice overwhelmed the girl's wails. She opened her eyes, and the hallucination vanished. The window was suffused with daylight; the heavy fragrance of locust blossoms gusted in. A bee banged into the paper window covering. "Fan Three, don't worry about washing your hands," she heard her mother-in-law say. "That precious daughter-in-law of mine still hasn't had her baby. The best she can do is one leg. Can you come help out?"

"Elder sister-in-law, don't be foolish. Just think what you're saying. I'm a horse doctor, I can't deliver a human baby."

"People and animals aren't that different."

"That's nonsense, elder sister-in-law. Now get me some water so I can wash up. I say forget the expense and go get Aunty Sun."

Her mother-in-law's voice exploded like a clap of thunder: "Stop pretending you don't know I can't stand that old witch! Last year she stole one of my little hens."

"That's up to you," Fan Three said. "It's your daughter-in-law who's in labor, after all, not my wife. All right, I'll do it, but don't forget the liquor and the pig's head, because I'll be saving two lives for your family!"

Her mother-in-law changed her tone of voice from anger to melancholy: "Fan Three, show some kindness. Besides, with all that fighting out there, if you went out and ran into Japanese . . ."

"That's enough!" Fan said. "In all the years we've been friends and neighbors, this is the first time I've done anything like this. But let's get something straight first. People and animals may not be that different, but a human life matters more . . ."

The clatter of footsteps, mixed with the sound of someone blowing his nose, came toward her. Don't tell me that my father-in-law and husband and that slick character Fan Three are coming in while I'm lying here naked. The thought of it angered and shamed her. Puffy white clouds floated before her eyes. When she strained to sit up and find something to cover her nakedness, the pool of blood she lay in made that impossible. The intermittent rumble of explosions from the edge of the village came on the air, punctuated by a mysterious yet somehow familiar clamor, like the magnified noise made by a horde of tiny crawling critters, or the gnashing of countless teeth . . . I've heard that sound before, but what is it? She thought and she thought. Then a flash of recognition quickly transformed itself into a bright light that brought into focus the plague of locusts she'd witnessed a decade or more earlier. The red swarms had blocked out the sun; it was a raging flood of insects that stripped every tree bare, even the bark of willows. The sickening gnawing sound ate its way into the marrow of her bones. The locusts have returned! she thought to her horror, as she sank into the mire of despair. "Heavenly Master, just let me die, I can't take it anymore . . . God in Heaven, Blessed Virgin! Send down your grace and bounty to save my soul . . ." she prayed hopefully even in the throes of despair, sending prayers both to China's supreme deity and to the paramount god of the West. When she had finished, her mental anguish and physical agonies had lessened a bit, and she thought back to that late spring day when she and the redheaded, blue-eyed Pastor Malory had lain in the grass, and he had told her that China's Heavenly Master and the West's God were one and the same, like the two sides of your hand, or just as the *lianhua* and *hehua* are both lotus flowers. Or, she thought bashfully, like a cock and a dick are the same thing. He stood amid the locust trees, as spring was giving way to summer, that thing of his standing up proudly . . . the surrounding trees in full bloom with white flowers, and red flowers, and yellow flowers, a rainbow of colors dancing in the air, their rich fragrance thoroughly intoxicating her. She felt herself rise in the air, like a cloud, like a feather. With gratitude filling her breast, she gazed at the somber and sacred, friendly and kindly smile on Pastor Malory's face, and her eyes filled with tears.

When she closed her eyes, the tears spilled into the creases all the way to her ears. The door was pushed open, and her mother-in-law said meekly, "Laidi's mother, what's wrong? You must hold out, child. Our donkey's had a lively little mule. Now, if you have this baby, the Shangguan family can be content at last. You might be able to hide the truth from your parents, but not from a doctor. Since it doesn't matter whether a midwife is male or female, I've asked Third Master Fan to come over . . ."

The rare note of tenderness moved her. Opening her eyes, she looked up into the golden aura of the older woman's face and nodded weakly. Her mother-in-law turned and summoned Fan Three. "You can come in now."

He entered with a long face, trying hard to look dignified. But he averted his eyes, as if he'd seen something so terrifying it drained the blood from his cheeks. "Elder sister-in-law," he said softly as he backed to the door, his gaze resting fearfully on the body of Shangguan Lu, "raise your merciful hand and spare me. Threaten to kill me if you want, but I cannot do what you ask." He turned and ran out the door, only to bump into Shangguan Shouxi, who was craning his neck to see what was going on inside. With disgust, Shangguan Lu noted her husband's gaunt, pointy face, looking more like a rat than ever, as her mother-in-law ran out on the heels of Fan Three.

"Fan Three, you fucking dog!"

When her husband stuck his head in the door a second time, she mustered the strength to raise an arm to signal him and say icily — she couldn't be sure if the words actually emerged from her mouth: "Come over here, you son of a bitch!" By this time, she'd forgotten her hatred and enmity toward her husband. Why take it out on him? He may be a son of a bitch, but it's my mother-in-law who's the bitch, an old bitch . . .

"Are you talking to me?" Shangguan Shouxi asked from where he stood beside the *kang*, looking out the window in embarrassment. "What do you want?" She gazed up sympathetically at this man with whom she'd lived for twenty-one years, and felt pangs of remorse. A sea of locust blossoms rippled in the wind . . . in a voice as thin as a single hair, she said:

"This child . . . it's not yours . . ."

In tears, Shangguan Shouxi said, "Mother of my children . . . don't die on me . . . I'll go get Aunty Sun . . ."

"No . . ." She looked into her husband's eyes and implored him, "Go beg Pastor Malory to come . . ."

Out in the yard, Shangguan Lü, sensing a pain worse than having her skin flayed, took an oilpaper bundle from her pocket and peeled it back to reveal a shiny silver dollar; she clutched it tightly as the corners of her mouth curled in a grimace and her eyes glowed red. The sun shone down on her gray head; black smoke drifted over in the hot air. She heard a loud disturbance to the north, near the Flood Dragon River; bullets whistled through the air. "Fan Three," she sobbed, "can you just stand by and watch someone die? 'There is nothing more poisonous than a hornet's sting and nothing more ruthless than a physician's heart.' They say 'money can make the devil turn a millstone.'

Well, this silver dollar has rested against my skin for twenty years, but it's yours in return for my daughter-in-law's life."

She laid the silver dollar in Fan Three's hand, but he flung it to the ground, as if it were a piece of hot metal. A film of sweat covered his oily face, and his cheeks twitched so violently they distorted his features. Slinging his bag over his shoulder, he shouted, "Elder sister-in-law, please let me go . . . I'll get down on my knees and bang my head against the ground for you . . ."

He had nearly reached the gate when Shangguan Fulu, stripped to the waist, came barging through. He was wearing only one shoe, and his bare, scrawny chest was smeared with something green, like axle grease, like a gaping, festering wound. "Where have you been, you walking corpse?" Shangguan Lü cursed angrily.

"Elder brother, what's going on out there?" Fan Three asked anxiously. Ignoring both the curse and the question, Shangguan Fulu stood there with an idiotic smile on his face, a string of *duh-duh-duhs* streaming from his mouth, like chickens pecking the bottom of an earthenware dish.

Shangguan Lü grabbed her husband by the chin and shook him hard, wrenched his mouth up one minute and down the next, stretching it horizontally and then vertically. A dribble of saliva emerged from one corner. He coughed, then spat up, and finally settled down. "What's going on out there" He looked at his wife with deep sorrow.

As his mouth twisted, he sobbed. "The Japanese horse soldiers have reached the river . . ."

The dull thuds of approaching horse hooves froze them in their tracks. A flock of magpies with white tail feathers flew overhead, their cries settling over the compound. Then the stained glass in the church steeple shattered noiselessly, splintered glass glinting in the sunlight. But immediately after the glass began flying, the crisp sound of an explosion engulfed the steeple, sending dull sound waves like the rumble of iron wheels spreading in all directions. A powerful wave of heat toppled Fan Three and Shangguan Fulu like harvested wheat. It sent Shangguan Lü reeling backward into the wall. A black earthenware chimney with ornamental carvings rolled off the roof and landed on the brick path in front of her, where, with a loud crash, it crumbled into pieces.

Shangguan Shouxi ran out of the house. "Mother," he sobbed, "she's dying, she's going to die. Go get Aunty Sun . . ."

She glared at her son. "If it's your time to die, then you die. If it isn't, you don't. Nothing can change that."

Listening but not quite grasping her meaning, the three men looked at her with tears in their eyes. "Fan Three," she said, "do you have any more of that secret potion that speeds the delivery process? If you do, give a bottle to my daughter-in-law. If not, then to hell with it, and with you." Without waiting for his answer, she tottered in the direction of the gate, head high, chest thrown out, not looking at any of them.

9

On the morning of the fifth day of the fifth lunar month, 1939, in the largest village of Northeast Gaomi Township, Shangguan Lü led her mortal enemy, Aunty Sun, into her house, ignoring the bullets whizzing overhead, to help deliver her daughter-in-law's baby. At the very moment they walked through the door, out on the open field near the bridgehead, Japanese horse soldiers were trampling the corpses of guerrilla fighters.

Shangguan Fulu and his son were milling in the yard with the horse doctor, Fan Three, who proudly held up a bottle filled with a viscous green liquid. The three men had been in the same spot when Shangguan Lü left to find Aunty Sun, but were now joined by the red-headed Pastor Malory. Wearing a loose Chinese robe, with a heavy brass crucifix around his neck, he was standing beneath Shangguan Lu's window, head up, facing the morning sun, as he intoned a prayer in the local dialect: "Dear Jesus, Lord in Heaven. Merciful God, reach out to touch the heads of me, Your devoted servant, and the friends gathered here, give us the strength and the courage to face this challenge. Let the woman inside safely deliver her infant, give the goat plenty of milk and the laying hens plenty of eggs, throw a sheet of black before the eyes of the evil invaders, let their bullets jam in their weapons, and let their horses lose their way and perish in bogs and marshes. Dear Lord, send all Your punishments down on my head, let me take unto myself the suffering of all living creatures." The other men stood silently listening to his prayer. The looks on their faces showed the depths to which they were moved.

With a sneer, Aunty Sun pushed Pastor Malory aside and walked in the door. His "Amen" came as he stumbled wide-eyed to keep his balance, hurriedly crossing himself to bring his prayer to an end.

Aunty Sun's silvery hair was combed into a bun held in place by a shiny silver ornament; her sideburns were pinned with mugwort spikes. She was wearing a starched white cotton jacket with a slanted lapel that buttoned down the side; a white handkerchief was tucked in between two of the buttons. Her black cotton trousers were tied around the ankles above a pair of green cotton slippers with black embroidery and white soles. The fresh smell of soap clung to her body. She had prominent cheekbones, a high nose, and lips that formed a tight line above her chin. Bright, piercing eyes were set deeply in lovely sockets. Her poise and confident bearing stood in stark contrast to the prosperous, well-fed Shangguan Lü. Taking the bottle of green liquid from Fan Three, Shangguan Lü walked up to Aunty Sun and said softly, "Aunty, this is Fan Three's potion to hasten childbirth. Will you use it?"

"My dear lady Shangguan," Aunty Sun said with obvious displeasure, her gaze covering Shangguan Lü with icy beauty, then shifting to the men in the yard, "who have you asked to help with the delivery, me or Fan Three?"

"Don't be angry, Aunty. As they say, 'When a patient is dying, find doctors where you can,' and 'Anyone with breasts is a mother.'" Forcing herself to be congenial, she kept her voice low and controlled. "I'm asking you, of course. I wouldn't have disturbed such an eminent personage if I hadn't reached the end of my rope."

"Didn't you once accuse me of stealing your chickens?" Aunty Sun remarked. "If you want me as the midwife, tell everyone else to stand clear!"

"If that's how you want it, that's how you shall have it," Shangguan Lü said.

Aunty Sun removed a thin piece of red cloth from around her waist and tied it to the window lattice. She then strode purposefully into the house, and when she reached the door of the inside room, she stopped, turned, and said to Shangguan Lü, "Lady Shangguan, come with me."

Fan Three ran up to the window to retrieve the bottle of green liquid Shangguan Lü had left there. He stuffed it into his bag and headed quickly toward the gate, without so much as a backward glance at the Shangguan father and son.

"Amen!" Pastor Malory repeated, making another sign of the cross. Then he nodded to the Shangguan father and son in a show of friendship.

A shriek from Aunty Sun tore from inside the room, followed by horrible wails from Shangguan Lu.

Shangguan Shouxi hunkered down on the ground and covered his ears with his hands. His father began pacing the yard, hands clasped behind his back, head down, as if he were looking for something he'd lost.

Pastor Malory repeated his prayer in a muted voice, eyes cast to the misty blue sky.

Just then the newborn mule emerged from the barn on shaky legs. Its damp hide shone like satin. Its weary mother followed it outside to the accompaniment of Shangguan Lu's agonizing wails. With its ears standing straight up and its tail tucked between its legs, the donkey wobbled over to the water trough under a pomegranate tree, casting a fearful glance at the men in the yard. They ignored it. Shangguan Shouxi, his ears covered, was weeping loudly. Shangguan Fulu was still pacing the yard. Pastor Malory was praying with his eyes closed. The donkey buried its mouth in the water and drank noisily. When it had drunk its fill, it walked slowly over to the peanut vines held up by stalks of sorghum and began nibbling at the stalks.

Meanwhile, inside the house, Aunty Sun stuck her hand up the birth canal to extract the baby's other leg. The pregnant mother screeched once before passing out. Then, after inserting some yellow powder into Shangguan Lu's nostrils, Aunty Sun grabbed the baby's legs and waited calmly. Shangguan Lu moaned as she regained consciousness, then sneezed, causing a series of violent spasms. Her back arched, then settled back down heavily. That was what Aunty Sun had been waiting for: she pulled the baby out of the birth canal, and as its long, flat head cleared the mother's body, it made a loud popping sound, as if shot from a cannon. Aunty Sun's white jacket was spattered with blood.

Hanging upside down in Aunty Sun's hand was a purplish baby girl.

Shangguan Lü began beating her chest and wailing.

"Stop crying! There's another one in there!" Aunty Sun demanded angrily.

Shangguan Lu's belly was jerking and twitching horribly; blood gushing from between her legs washed out another down-covered infant.

When she spotted the little wormlike object between the baby's legs, Shangguan Lü fell to her knees beside the *kang*.

"What a shame," Aunty Sun said pensively, "another stillborn."

Suddenly dizzy, Shangguan Lü fell forward and banged her head on the *kang*. She stood with difficulty, propping herself up by the *kang*, and gazed at her daughter-in-law, whose face was stone gray. Then, with a moan of despair, she shuffled out of the room.

A pall of death hung over the yard. Her son was on his knees, the bloody stump of his neck resting on the ground, a stream of fresh blood snaking along the ground; his head, a look of fear frozen on the face, sat perfectly upright in front of his torso. Her husband was gnawing a brick on the path; one of his arms was tucked under his abdomen, the other stretched out in front of him. A mixture of gray matter and bright red blood from a gaping wound in the back of his head stained the path around him. Pastor Malory was on his knees, making the sign of the cross and mumbling something in a foreign tongue. Two massive horses, reins draped across their backs, were eating the sorghum stalks supporting the peanut vines, while the donkey and her newborn mule huddled in a corner of the wall, the young animal's head tucked under one of its mother's legs, its tail writhing like a snake. Two Japanese men in khaki stood there, one cleaning his sword with a handkerchief, the other hacking down sorghum stalks with his sword, sending peanuts to the ground, where they were eaten by the two horses, whose tails swished happily.

Suddenly feeling the earth wheel on its axis, Shangguan Lü had a single thought: to rescue her son and her husband. Instead, she crumpled heavily to the ground like a toppled wall.

Aunty Sun quickly skirted Shangguan Lü's body and strode steadily out of the yard. But one of the Japanese soldiers, who had remarkably wide-set eyes and short eyebrows, threw down his handkerchief and moved to block her way, standing rigidly between her and the gate. Pointing the tip of his sword at her heart, he said something that was only gibberish to her, a loutish expression on his face. She looked at him calmly, the hint of a sneer on her lips. She took a step backward; the Japanese soldier took a step forward. She retreated two more steps, he took two steps forward, the tip of the sword still pressed up against her breast. As he bore relentlessly down on her, Aunty Sun reached up and brushed his sword to the side. Then one of her feet flashed through the air and landed precisely on his wrist, knocking the sword out of his hand. She rushed up and slapped him across the face. With a yelp of pain, he covered his face. His comrade ran up, sword in hand,

and aimed it at Aunty Sun's head. She spun out of the way and grabbed his wrist, shaking it until he too dropped his sword. Then she boxed his ear, and although it didn't seem to be much of a slap, his face began to swell immediately.

Without so much as looking back, Aunty Sun strode out of the yard, as one of the soldiers raised his rifle and fired. Her body stiffened for a moment, then sprawled forward in the gateway of the Shangguan house.

At that moment, the two youngest mute grandsons, who had come looking for her, were felled by the same bullet on the steps leading up to the Shangguan gate. The three older grandsons were, at the time, occupied with cutting up the rump of a dead horse on the riverbank, where the smell of gunpowder thickened the air.

At around noon, a swarm of Japanese soldiers filled the Shangguan compound. The horse soldiers found a basket in the barn, into which they scooped the loose peanuts and carried them out into the lane to feed their weary horses. Two of the soldiers took Pastor Malory captive. Then a military doctor, eyeglasses perched on the pale bridge of his nose, followed his commander into the room where Shangguan Lu lay. With a frown, he opened his medical kit, donned a pair of surgical gloves, and cut the babies' umbilical cords with a stainless steel knife. Picking up the infant boy by the feet, he slapped it on the backside until a hoarse cry emerged from the other end. He then picked up the baby girl and repeated the procedure until there were signs of life. After cleaning the cuts on the umbilical cords with iodine, he wrapped the babies in white gauzy cotton and gave Shangguan Lu injections to stop the bleeding. All the while the doctor was performing his lifesaving procedures on mother and children, a journalist was taking photographs from various angles. A month later, these photographs would appear in a Japanese newspaper back home to bear witness to the friendship between China and Japan.

Chapter Two

1

The twenty-sixth year of the Guangxu reign of the Great Qing, the Manchu dynasty, the year 1900 in the Western calendar.

My maternal grandfather, Lu Wuluan, was a martial arts practitioner who barely left footprints when he walked. As a leader of the Red Spears, he was active in training and arming troops and in building bunkers and moats to ward off attacks by foreign troops. But after several months of uneventful waiting, the local forces' vigilance had slackened, and on the foggy seventh morning of the eighth lunar month, German forces under the leadership of County Magistrate Ji Guifen surrounded Sandy Nest Village in Northeast Gaomi Township. When the day's battle was over, nearly four hundred Sandy Nest residents lay dead. That included my grandfather, who was killed by German soldiers after burying his spear in the belly of their comrade, and his wife, who had hidden her daughter, Xuan'er, in a large flour vat before hanging herself from the rafter to preserve her chastity. My mother, now an orphan, was six months old on that day.

On the following day, my aunt and uncle found my mother in the flour vat, barely alive, her body coated with flour. After clearing the baby's mouth and nose and patting her on the back, my aunt was relieved to hear her little niece cough and begin to cry.

2

When Lu Xuan'er reached the age of five, her aunt fetched some bamboo strips, a wooden mallet, and some heavy white cloth. "Xuan'er," she said to her niece, "you're five years old, time to have your feet bound."

"Why do I have to do that?"

"A woman without bound feet cannot find a husband."

"Why do I have to find a husband?"

"You don't expect me to look after you for the rest of your life, do you?" her aunt replied.

Mother's uncle, Big Paw Yu, was an easygoing gambling man. Fearless and swaggering out in society, at home he was docile as a kitten. He was sitting in front of a fire roasting some tiny fish to go with what he was drinking. His huge hands were not nearly as clumsy as they looked. The tantalizing aroma of the sizzling fish drifted into Xuan'er's nostrils. She was particularly fond of this lazy uncle, because every time her aunt went out to work, he stayed home to eat what and when he wasn't supposed to. Sometimes he'd fry eggs, at other times it was dried meat, but there was always something for Xuan'er, on condition that she didn't say a word to her aunt.

After scaling the little fish with his fingernails, he peeled off a strip, placed it on his tongue, and washed it down with a drink. "Your aunt's right," he said. "Girls who don't bind their feet grow up to be big-footed spinsters that nobody wants."

"Did you hear what he said?"

"Xuan'er, do you know why I married your aunt?"

"Because she's a good person."

"No," Big Paw Yu said, "it's because she has such tiny feet."

Xuan'er looked down at her aunt's feet and then her own. "Will my feet look like yours?"

"That depends on you. If you do as I say, yours will be even smaller."

Every time Mother talked about having her feet bound, it was a mixture of blood-and-tears indictment and personal glory.

She told us that her aunt's steely resolve and dexterity were renowned throughout Northeast Gaomi Township. Everyone knew she was the head of the household, and that Big Paw Yu was good for gambling and bird-hunting only. The fifty acres of land, the two donkeys that worked it, the household chores, and the hiring of workers all fell to Mother's aunt, who was barely five feet tall and never weighed more than ninety pounds. That such a small person could get so much done was a mystery to everyone. When she promised to raise her niece into a fine young lady, she certainly was not about to cut corners on foot binding. First she bent the toes back with bamboo strips and wrapped them tightly, wrenching loud squeals of protest from her niece. Then she wrapped the feet tightly with the alum-treated white cloth, one layer after another. Once that was done, she pounded the toes with her wooden mallet. Mother said the pain was like banging her head against the wall.

"Please, not so tight," Mother beseeched her aunt.

"It's tight because I love you," her aunt said with a piercing glare. "If I didn't, I wouldn't care how loose they were. One day, when you have a perfect pair of golden lotuses, you'll thank me."

"Then I won't get married, all right?" Mother pleaded tearfully. "I'll take care of you and Uncle for the rest of your lives."

Hearing this, her uncle softened. "Maybe you can loosen them a little, don't you think?"

"Get out of here, you lazy dog!" her aunt said as she picked up a broom and threw it at him.

He jumped to his feet, picked up a string of coins, and ran out of the house.

In what seemed like the blink of an eye, the Great Qing fell and was replaced by a republic. Xuan'er was now sixteen and the possessor of perfect lotus feet.

Her uncle, who took great pride in Xuan'er's tiny bound feet and viewed his uncommonly beautiful niece as a truly marketable treasure, hung a plaque over the front gate. "Fragrant Lotus Hall," it read. "Our Xuan'er will marry a *zhuangyuan*, top scholar at the Imperial Examination," he announced. "Big Paw," they said, "the Manchu dynasty has fallen. There are no more *zhuangyuan*." "Then she'll marry a provincial military governor, and if not that, a county magistrate."

It was the summer of 1917. Upon taking office, the newly appointed magistrate of Gaomi, Niu Tengxiao, banned the smoking of and trade in opium, outlawed gambling, vowed to annihilate bandits, and prohibited foot binding. The sale of opium went underground, gambling continued unabated, and annihilating bandits proved impossible. That left only foot binding, which hardly anyone opposed. So County Magistrate Niu personally went down into the villages to promote the ban, which earned him considerable prestige.

It happened during the seventh month, on one of those rare clear days. An open sedan drove into the town of Dalan. The county magistrate summoned the town head, who summoned the community heads, who summoned the neighborhood heads, who summoned the residents, all of whom were to gather at the threshing ground — men, women, young, and old. Nonattendees would be fined a peck of grain.

As the crowd gathered, Magistrate Niu spotted the plaque above Uncle Big Paw's gate. "I'm surprised to see such sentiments at a peasant's house," he said. "There is a perfect pair of golden lotuses at that house, Magistrate," the town head said fawningly. "Depraved tastes have become a national illness. Those so-called fragrant lotuses were once nothing but stinky feet."

Eventually, the crowd settled down to hear what Magistrate Niu had to say. Mother told us that he was wearing a black high-collar tunic and a brown top hat. He had a dark mustache and wore gold-rimmed eyeglasses. A pocket watch chain dangled in front of his tunic, and he carried a walking stick. His voice was raspy, almost ducklike, but even though she had no idea what he was saying, she was sure he spoke with great eloquence.

Shy and timid, Mother clung to her aunt's clothes. Once the foot binding process had begun, she'd stopped going outside, spending nearly all her time weaving nets or doing embroidery. She had never seen so many people before, and was too frightened to look around. She felt that everyone's eyes were on her tiny bound feet. Mother told us she was wearing a leek green satin jacket, with wide sleeves and borders of fine silk. Her glossy black braid hung down nearly to her knees. Her trousers were cerise, also with hand-sewn borders. On her feet a pair of high-heeled red-embroidered shoes with wooden soles peeked out from beneath her trousers from time to time and clicked on the roadway when she walked. Since she had trouble standing, she had to hold on to her aunt.

During his oration, the magistrate singled out Fragrant Lotus Hall in his exhortation against the evils of foot binding. "It is a poisonous legacy of a feudal system," he said, "a morbid aspect of life." Everyone turned to gape at Mother's feet; she didn't dare look up. The magistrate then read the anti–foot binding proclamation, after which he summoned the women he'd brought along to perform the "Natural Foot Olio." Six young women jumped spryly out of the open car, chattering as they showed off their fine figures. "Fellow villagers and elders, boys and girls, open your eyes wide and watch this!" the magistrate said. Everyone stared at the women, who wore their hair short, with bangs across the forehead, and were dressed in long-sleeved sky blue blouses with turn-down collars over short white skirts that showed a lot of leg. Short white socks and white sneakers completed the outfit.

A breath of fresh air had blown into the bosom of Northeast Gaomi Township.

After lining up and bowing to the crowd, the young women raised their brows and began to recite in unison: "We have natural feet, no abnormal fads, our bodies are precious, they came from moms and dads" — they bounced up and down, raising their feet high in the air to show their natural beauty — "we can run and jump and play in the rain, not like crippled feet that bring so much pain" — more bouncing and running around — "the feudal system is bad for a woman, who is only a toy, but we have natural feet, so take off your wrappings, girls, and share in our joy."

As the "natural feet" girls hopped and bounced away, their place was taken by an orthopedic surgeon who brought an oversized model of the foot to demonstrate how the broken bones of bound feet forever altered the shape of the foot.

Just before the meeting ended, Magistrate Niu had a brainstorm. He ordered that Northeast Gaomi's number one golden lotus come up and bear witness to how disgusting bound feet can be.

Mother nearly passed out from fright and hid behind her aunt. "The county magistrate's orders are not to be ignored," the town head said. But Mother wrapped her arms tightly around her aunt's waist and begged her not to make her go up there.

"Go on, Xuan'er," her aunt coaxed. "Show them your feet. As long as they know what they're looking for, you'll do fine. Don't tell me that golden lotuses I personally created won't compete favorably with the hooves on those six donkeys."

So her aunt escorted her up front, and then stepped aside. Xuan'er swayed as she walked, like a willow in the wind, and in the eyes of tradition-bound Northeast Gaomi men, that was the mark of true beauty. They stared at her, desperately wishing that by raising their eyelashes they could lift a leg of her trousers for a good view of one of those tiny feet. Like a moth drawn to a flame, the magistrate's gaze flew to that spot beneath her trouser hem, and he just stood there for a moment, mouth agape, before regaining his composure. "Just look," he announced. "Such a lovely girl turned into a freak incapable of manual labor."

Unmindful of the consequences, Mother's aunt refuted the magistrate's comment. "A golden lotus girl is meant to be pampered. Manual labor is what servants are for!"

With her aunt's gaze boring into him, the magistrate asked, "Are you the girl's mother?"

"What if I am?"

"Are her bound feet your handiwork?"

"What if they are?"

"Take this shrewish woman into custody," he ordered, "and keep her there as long as her daughter's feet remain bound."

"I'd like to see any of you try!" Big Paw Yu thundered as he leaped out from the crowd, fists clenched, to protect his wife.

"Who are you?" the magistrate asked.

"I'm your elder," he said defiantly.

"Seize him!" the enraged magistrate demanded.

Some of his underlings stepped up warily and reached out to restrain Big Paw, who brushed them aside with a swipe of his arm.

Now the crowd got involved, and amid the flurry of opinions, some people picked up dirt clods and threw them in the direction of the six natural feet girls.

The people of Northeast Gaomi have always been known for their boldness, something the magistrate must have been aware of. "I have important business to take care of today, so I'll let you off this time. But unbinding women's feet is national policy, and anyone who defies that policy can expect to be severely punished."

The magistrate threaded his way through the crowd and climbed into his car. "Let's go," he told his chauffeur, who went to the front of the car and turned the crank until the engine started with a loud cough. The natural feet girls and other hangers-on piled in as the chauffeur ran around to the driver's seat, grabbed the steering wheel, and drove off, leaving a trail of smoke behind.

A youngster in the crowd clapped. "Our Big Paw Yu scared off the county magistrate!"

That night, Shangguan Lü, wife of the local blacksmith Shang-guan Fulu, presented a bolt of white cloth to a matchmaker called Big Mouth Yuan with a request that she approach the Yu family with a marriage proposal on behalf of her only son, Shangguan Shouxi.

"Elder sister-in-law," Big Mouth said to Mother's aunt as she tapped her feet with a rush fan, "if the Manchu dynasty hadn't fallen, I wouldn't dare cross your threshold, even if someone shoved a drill up my backside. But we now live in the Republic of China, and girls with bound feet are out of favor. The sons of well-to-do families have taken up new ways of thinking. They wear uniforms, they smoke cigarettes, and they chase after girls educated in foreign schools, girls with big feet, who can run and jump and chat and laugh and giggle when a boy puts his arm around her. I'm afraid your niece is a fallen phoenix, which is worse than a common chicken. The Shangguan family is willing to overlook that, and I think it's time to burn the incense. Shangguan Shouxi is a good-looking, well-mannered boy, and the family owns both a donkey and a mule. Running their own blacksmith shop doesn't make them rich, but they're not badly off. Xuan'er could do worse than a family like that."

"Have I raised a proper young lady just so she can marry the son of a blacksmith?"

"Haven't you heard that the wife of the Xuantong emperor was sent up to the city of Harbin to polish shoes? Life is unpredictable, elder sister-in-law."

"Tell the Shangguans to come see me in person."

On the following morning, Mother peeked through a crack in the door to get her first glimpse of the robust woman who was to be her mother-in-law, Shangguan Lü. She also watched as her aunt and Shangguan Lü argued over the betrothal gifts until they were both red in the face. "Go home and talk it over," Mother's aunt said. "Either the mule or two acres of arable land. Raising the girl for seventeen years has to be worth something."

"All right," Shangguan Lü said. "You win. The mule is yours, and we'll take your wooden-wheeled wagon."

With a clap of the hands, the deal between the two women was struck. "Xuan'er," Mother's aunt called to her. "Come out and meet your mother-in-law."

3

Three years into her marriage to Shangguan Shouxi, Xuan'er remained childless. Her mother-in-law railed at the family hen, "All you do is eat, and we still haven't seen a single egg." Her meaning was clear.

The weather that spring could not have been better, and business at the blacksmith shop reaped the benefits, selling new scythes and repairing broken ones for a steady stream of peasants. The furnace was in the middle of the yard, under a sheet of oilcloth to keep out the sun. The pleasant smell of burning coal hung over the yard, and dark red tongues of flame crackled in the sunlight. Shangguan Fulu handled the tongs, his son, Shouxi, worked the bellows. Shangguan Lü, wearing a tattered robe cinched at the waist by an oilcloth apron spotted with black marks from burning sparks, and an old straw hat on her head, handled the hammer. With sweat and soot streaking her face, the only way anyone could tell she was a woman was by the two protuberances on her chest. The clang of hammer on hot steel resounded from morning to night. As a rule, the family ate only two meals a day; Xuan'er was responsible for preparing the meals and tending the family livestock, pigs included, chores that kept her hopping all day long. And still her mother-in-law found fault, keeping an eye on her even as she hammered the red-hot steel, and muttering nonstop. When she ran out of complaints about her daughter-in-law, she'd turn her attention to her son, and from there to her husband. They were all used to being harangued by the head of the household and the best blacksmith in the family. Xuan'er both hated and feared her mother-in-law, but she admired her as well. Standing around watching Shangguan Lü work was a bit of a holiday at the end of the day, and the compound was frequently filled with people coming and going.

Her son, Shouxi, was small everywhere — nose, eyes, head, arms, hands — and one would be hard pressed to spot any resemblance to his burly mother, who often sighed and said, "If the seed's no good, fertile soil is wasted." He worked the bellows while she pounded the steel into shape.

On this particular day, as the last scythe was tempered, she raised it to her nose, as if its smell could determine its quality. Finally, she shrugged her shoulders and said in a voice that revealed her exhaustion, "Serve dinner."

Like a foot soldier receiving a general's command, Shangguan Lu ran on tiny bound feet, back and forth, setting the table under the pear tree, where a single hanging lantern produced a murky yellow light and drew hordes of moths that flew noisily into the lantern shade. Shangguan Lu had prepared a platter of buns stuffed with ground-up pork bone and radish filling, a bowl of mung bean soup for each person, and a bunch of leeks and a paste to dip them in. She cast an uneasy look at her mother-in-law to gauge her reaction. If there was plenty of food, she'd pull a long face and complain about wastefulness; if it was a simple meal, she'd toss down her bowl and chopsticks and complain angrily that it was tasteless. Being her daughter-in-law was not easy. Steam rose from the buns and the rice porridge. This was the time that the family, deluged by the clang of metal on metal during the day, fell silent. Xuan'er's mother-in-law sat in the center, her son on one side, husband on the other, while Xuan'er stood beside the table awaiting her mother-in-law's instructions.

"Have you fed the animals?"

"Yes, Mother."

"Closed up the chicken coop?"

"Yes, Mother."

Shangguan Lü bent down and slurped a mouthful of soup.

Shangguan Shouxi spat out a sliver of bone and grumbled, "Other people eat pork-filled buns, but all we get are the bones. Like dogs . . ."

His mother slammed down her chopsticks. "You," she cursed, "what gives you the right to be picky about what you eat?"

"We've got all that wheat in the bin and plenty of money in the cupboard," Shouxi said. "What are we saving it for?"

"He's right," his father pitched in. "We deserve a reward for all our hard work."

"That wheat in the bin and money in the cupboard, who does it belong to?" Xuan'er's mother-in-law asked. "When I finally stretch out my legs for the last time and journey to the Western Heaven, do you think I'm going to take it with me? No, I'm leaving it for you."

Xuan'er hung her head and held her breath.

Shangguan Lü exploded to her feet and stormed off. "Listen to me," she shouted from inside the house. "Tomorrow we'll fry fritters, braise pork strips, hard-boil some eggs, kill a chicken, bake some flat-cakes, and make dumplings! Why spread it out? One of our ancestors must have done something to make us suffer. We bring a barren woman into the family, and all she can do is eat. Well, since our family line is coming to an end, who are we saving for? Let's finish it all off and be done with it!"

Xuan'er covered her face with her hands and burst out crying.

"You should be goddamned ashamed of yourself, crying like that!" Shangguan Lü shouted. "You've eaten our food for three years and haven't even presented us with a daughter, let alone a son! You're eating us out of house and home! Tomorrow you can go back where you came from. I won't let this family line die out all because of you!"

Not a minute passed that night when Xuan'er's tears didn't flow. When Shouxi wanted to have his way with her, she submitted weakly. "Nothing is wrong with me," she said through her tears. "Maybe it's you."

Without climbing off, he growled, "A hen can't lay an egg, so she blames it on the rooster!"

4

The harvest was in, and the rainy season was about to begin. Local custom demanded that new brides return to their parents' home to pass the hottest days of the year. Most of those who had been married three years returned proudly holding the hand of one child, suckling a second, and carrying a third inside, plus a bundle filled with patterns for shoes to be made. Poor Xuan'er. All she brought home, besides her sadness, were scars and bruises bestowed upon her by her husband, the echoes of her mother-in-law's curses, a pathetic little bundle, and eyes red and puffy from crying. Now, the most caring aunt is still no match for your own mother, so even though she returned with a bellyful of bitter complaints, she had to keep them to herself and put on the best face possible.

As soon as she stepped through the doorway, her keen-eyed aunt saw right through her. "Nothing yet, I see."

That simple comment brought tears of pain gushing from Xuan'er's eyes.

"Strange," her aunt muttered. "You'd think three years would be long enough to produce something."

At dinnertime that evening, Big Paw Yu spotted the bruises on Xuan'er's arm. "That sort of wife-beating has no place in a modern republic," he said angrily. "I'd like to burn that turtles' nest of theirs to the ground!"

"I see that not even rice can stop up that foul mouth of yours!" her aunt said as she glared at her husband.

For a change, there was plenty of food in front of Xuan'er, but she forced herself not to overeat. Her uncle placed a large piece of fish in her bowl.

"You know," her aunt said, "you can't blame your in-laws. Why does anyone take a wife? To continue the family line."

"You didn't continue my family line," her husband said, "and I've been good to you, haven't I?"

"Who asked you? Get the donkey ready so you can take Xuan'er into town to see a woman's doctor."

Sitting astride the donkey, Xuan'er passed through the fields of Northeast Gaomi Township, which were crisscrossed with rivers and streams. The sun sent down blistering rays of heat, raising steam from the ground and drawing groans from the foliage around her. A pair of dragonflies, connected at the rear, darted past; a pair of swallows mated in the sky above. Baby frogs that had just shed their tails hopped across the roadway; locusts that had just emerged from eggs perched on the tips of roadside grass. A litter of newborn rabbits followed their mother in a hunt for food. Baby ducks paddled behind their mother, their tiny pink webbed feet sending ripples to the edge of a pond . . . rabbits and locusts can produce offspring, so why can't I? She felt empty inside, and was reminded of the legend regarding a child-rearing bag that existed in the bellies of all women, all but hers, it seemed. Please, Matron of Sons, I beg you, give me a child . . .

Even though her uncle was nearly forty, he had not lost his playfulness. Instead of holding the donkey's halter, he let the animal trot along on its own while he ran up and down the roadside picking wildflowers, which he made into a wreath for Xuan'er — to keep out the sun, he said. After chasing birds until he was out of breath, he went deep into the field, where he found a fist-sized wild melon, which he handed to Xuan'er. "It's sweet," he said, but when she bit into it, it was so bitter it nearly paralyzed her tongue. Then he rolled up his pant cuffs and jumped into a pond, quickly catching a pair of insects the size of melon seeds and shaking them in his hand. "Change!" he shouted. Holding his closed hand up to Xuan'er's nose, he asked her, "What do they smell like?" She shook her head and said she didn't know. "Like watermelons," he said. "They're watermelon bugs. They come from watermelon seeds."

Xuan'er couldn't help thinking that her uncle was really just an overgrown, playful child.

The results of the doctor's examination? There was nothing wrong with Xuan'er.

"The Shangguan family will pay for this!" Xuan'er's aunt said indignantly. "They've got a sterile mule of a son, and have no right to take out their frustrations on Xuan'er!"

But she only made it as far as the door.

Ten days later, during a pouring rain, the aunt prepared a sumptuous meal, complete with some of her husband's strong liquor. With her niece seated across from her, she placed one green cup in front of each of them. Candlelight cast her shadow on the wall behind as she filled both cups with liquor. Xuan'er saw that her hand was shaking.

"Why are we drinking liquor, Aunty?" Xuan'er asked. She had the uneasy feeling that something was about to happen.

"No reason. It's a rainy, sultry day, and I thought we could stay inside and talk, just the two of us." She raised her cup. "Drink up."

Xuan'er held out her cup and looked at her aunt with fear in her eyes. The older woman clinked glasses with her before tipping her head back and draining the cup.

Xuan'er emptied her cup.

"What do you plan to do?" Xuan'er's aunt asked.

With a sorrowful look, Xuan'er just shook her head.

Her aunt refilled both cups. "I'm afraid we're going to have to accept things the way they are," she said. "The fact that their son is sterile is something we have to keep in mind. They owe us; we don't owe them. Girl, I want you to understand that in this world, some of the finest deeds are accomplished in the dark, out of sight. Do you know what I'm getting at?"

Xuan'er shook her head, completely mystified. Her head was already spinning from the two cups of strong liquor.

That night, Big Paw Yu visited Xuan'er's bed.

When she awoke the next morning, suffering a splitting headache, she was surprised to hear someone snoring loudly beside her. With difficulty she opened her eyes, and there, lying naked beside her, was her uncle, one of his big paws cupping her breast. With a shriek, she pulled the blanket up to cover herself and burst out crying, waking Big Paw from his sleep. Like a child who's gotten himself into trouble, he jumped out of bed, grasping his clothes around him, and stammered, "Your aunt . . . made me do it . . ."

The following spring, shortly after the Grave-Sweeping Festival, Xuan'er gave birth to a scrawny, dark-eyed daughter. Her mother-in-law knelt before the Bodhisattva's ceramic icon and kowtowed three times. "Thanks to heaven and earth," she announced gratefully. "The seam has finally split. Now I ask the Bodhisattva to look over us and deliver a grandson next year."

She went into the kitchen and fried some eggs, which she brought in to her daughter-in-law's room. "Here," she said, "eat these."

As Xuan'er looked into her mother-in-law's face, her eyes filled with tears of gratitude.

Her mother-in-law looked down at the infant lying in the tattered cloth wrapping and said, "We'll call her Laidi — Brother Coming."

5

My second sister, Zhaodi — Brother Hailed — also came from Big Paw Yu's seed.

After Xuan'er delivered two daughters in as many years, Grandmother's unhappiness showed clearly. It didn't take Mother long to realize the cruel reality that for a woman, not getting married was not an option, not having children was not acceptable, and having only daughters was nothing to be proud of. The only road to status in a family was to produce sons.

Mother's third child was conceived in a reedy marsh. It happened at noon on a day shortly after Zhaodi was born. Grandmother had sent Mother to the reed pond southwest of the village to catch snails for the ducks. That spring a man had come to the village selling ducklings. A tall, husky stranger with a piece of blue cloth over his shoulder and hemp sandals on his feet, he carried two baskets filled with downy yellow baby ducks. A crowd quickly gathered to gawp at the furry little animals, with their pink beaks and tiny quacks, as they tumbled all over each other in the baskets. Shangguan Lü stepped up and bought a dozen; others followed her lead, quickly snapping up the rest. The peddler took a turn around the village and left. That evening, as it turned out, Sima Ting was taken from Felicity Manor by bandits and not returned until the family had paid a ransom of several thousand silver dollars. People said that the duck peddler had really been an informer for the bandits, who wanted a detailed report on the layout of Felicity Manor.

But those were good ducks he sold. In five months they had grown to the size of tiny boats. Shangguan Lü, who loved those ducks, sent her daughter-in-law out to look for snails, anticipating the day when the ducks would begin laying eggs.

So Mother took an earthenware jar and a wire strainer on a pole wherever her mother-in-law told her to go. The ditches and ponds near the village had been picked clean of snails by villagers who were raising ducks, but on her way to the market at a place called Liaolan the day before, Shangguan Lü had seen that the shallows in a nearby pond were alive with snails.

When Mother got there, however, the surface of the pond was covered with green-feathered ducks that had eaten all the snails. Knowing she would be yelled at if she returned empty-handed, she decided to follow a muddy path that skirted the pond to see if she could find some water that hadn't been visited by ducks, where there still might be snails she could take home. Sensing a heaviness in her breasts, she thought about her two small daughters at home. Laidi had just begun to walk and Zhaodi was barely a month old. But her mother-in-law placed greater value on her ducks than on her granddaughters, whom she refused to even pick up when they were crying. And as for Shangguan Shouxi, well, to call him a man was a terrible exaggeration. He was as useless as a gob of snot outside the house and totally subservient in front of his mother. But abject cruelty characterized his treatment of his wife. He had no use for either of the children, and whenever he abused Mother, she mused angrily, "Go ahead, you ass, beat me. Neither one of those girls is yours, and if I have another thousand babies, not one of them will have a drop of Shangguan blood running through their veins." In the wake of her intimacy with Big Paw Yu, she did not know how she could face her aunt again. So that year she did not go home. "They're all dead," she said when her mother-in-law pressed her to return home for a visit, "so there's nothing to go home to." Big Paw, obviously, could give her only daughters, so she began the search for a better donor. Go ahead, Mother-in-law, Husband, beat me and curse me all you want. Just you wait, I'll have my son one of these days, but he won't be a Shangguan, and to hell with you!

Caught up in these thoughts, she walked on, parting the reeds that all but sealed off the path. The scraping sound and chilled, mildew-laden odor of water plants evoked a pale fear in her. Water birds cried out from the surrounding foliage as breezy gusts swirled among the plants. Up ahead, no more than a few paces, a wild boar blocked her path. Mean-looking horns poked out from the sides of its long snout; tiny staring eyes, surrounded by bristly brows, glared hatefully at her, accompanied by snorts of intimidation. Mother shuddered and awoke to unknown surroundings. How did I get here? she wondered. Everyone in Northeast Gaomi knows that the bandit hideouts are somewhere deep among the reeds. No one, not even armed troops, dares to set foot here.

Anxiously, Mother turned to head back, but she quickly discovered that human and animal traffic had formed a checkerboard of footpaths, and she couldn't tell which one had brought her this far. Panic-stricken, she tried several of the paths, but they led nowhere, and she wound up crying over her predicament. Scattered shards of sunlight shone down on the ground, where years of fallen leaves rotted. Mother stepped into a pile of loose excrement, which, though foul-smelling, actually boosted her spirits; it could only mean there were, or had been, people in the vicinity. "Hello!" she shouted. "Is there anyone out there?" She listened as her shouts careened off of densely packed reed stalks before being swallowed up. When she looked down at her feet, she saw coarse vegetation amid the squashed pile of excrement, which meant it wasn't human after all, but the droppings of a boar or other wild animal. Once again she headed down a footpath, but soon lost heart and sat on the ground, where she cried tears of despair.

Suddenly she felt something cold on her back, as if sinister eyes were watching from a hiding place behind her. She spun around to look — nothing but interlaced leaves of reed stalks, the top ones pointing straight up into the sky. A light breeze was born and died among the reeds, leaving behind only a soft rustle. Birdcalls from deep in the patch had an eerie quality, as if made by humans. Danger lurked everywhere. All those green eyes hidden amid the reeds, whose tips played host to will-o'-the-wisps. Her nerves were shattered, the hair on her arms stood on edge, her breasts hardened. As all rational thoughts fled, she shut her eyes and took off running, until her feet sank into the shallow water of a pond, startling clouds of dark mosquitoes into the air, and from there straight back to her, stinging her mercilessly; a sticky sweat oozed from her pores, attracting even more mosquitoes. At some point she'd lost her earthenware jar and wire strainer; now she was running to escape the mosquito onslaught and screeching pitifully. As she was about to give up hope altogether, her God sent a savior in the person of the duck peddler.

With a palm rain cape over his shoulders and a conical rain hat on his head, he grabbed Mother and led her to a high spot in the field, where the reed plants weren't nearly as dense, and into an awaiting tent. A metal pot hung from a rack over a fire outside; millet was cooking inside.

"Please, kindly brother," Mother said as she fell to her knees in the tent, "help me find my way out of here. I am the wife of blacksmith Shangguan."

"What's your hurry?" the man said with a smile. "I don't get many visitors out here, so at least allow me to play the host."

A waterproof dog pelt covered the bed on a wooden platform. "You've got mosquito bites all over," the man said as he blew on a smoldering wick of repellent made of mugwort. "Mosquitoes around here can bring down an ox, so it's no wonder they did such a job on your fair skin."

Fragrant wispy smoke from the mugwort filled the tent as he reached into a basket hanging from one of the supports and took out a little red metal box filled with orange salve, which he rubbed on the swelling bites on Mother's face and arms. The coolness penetrated deeply. He then took out a piece of rock candy and forced it into her mouth. What was about to happen, given the remote setting in which a man and a woman were alone, was inevitable, Mother was certain of that. With tears in her eyes, she said, "Kindly brother, do with me what you will, but please lead me out of this place as soon as you can. There are nursing children waiting for me at home."

Mother gave herself to the man without a struggle, feeling neither pain nor joy. Her only hope was that he would give her a son.

6

After Lingdi, my third sister, came Xiangdi, the daughter of a quack doctor.

He was a rail-thin, hawk-nosed, vulture-eyed young man who

roamed the streets and byways ringing a brass bell and chanting, "My grandfather was a court physician, my father ran a pharmacy, but I am penniless and in deep sorrow, which is why I must wander to and fro with my bell."

As she was returning home from the fields with a load of grass on her back, Mother spotted him using tweezers to remove little white "tooth worms" from the mouth of an old man. When she got home she told her mother-in-law, who was suffering from a toothache, what she had seen.

After summoning the physician to the house, Mother held the lantern while he poked at Shangguan Lü's aching tooth. "Madam," he said, "your problem is what we call 'fire tooth,' not tooth worms." So he stuck some silver needles into Shangguan Lü's hand and cheek, then reached behind him and removed some medicinal powder from a sack, blowing it into her mouth. That did it, the pain vanished.

His treatment finished, he asked to be put up for the night in the family's eastern side room. The following morning, he offered them a silver dollar to let him use the room to treat patients. Since he had cured her toothache and was offering a shiny silver dollar, Grandmother was happy to accommodate him.

The man lived in the Shangguan household for three months, paying for his room and board on the first of each month. He was like a member of the family.

One day, Shangguan Lü asked if he had any sort of fertility drug. He did, writing out a prescription for Mother, which consisted of ten hen's eggs fried in sesame oil and honey.

"I'd like to try some of that myself," Shangguan Shouxi said.

One day Mother, who had developed a fondness for the mysterious physician, slipped into his quarters and revealed the fact that her husband was sterile.

"Those tooth worms," he revealed to her, "were in my little metal box all along."

Once he was sure that Mother was pregnant, it was time to be on his way. But before he left, not only did he hand Shangguan Lü all the money he'd earned treating patients at their house, but formally declared her to be his adoptive mother.

7

During dinner, Mother dropped a bowl and broke it. An explosion went off in her head, and she knew she was in for more misery.

Following the birth of my fourth sister, a pall settled over the Shangguan household. A permanent frown adorned my grandmother's face, which had the hardened look of a sickle ready to lop off Mother's head at the slightest provocation.

The age-old tradition of a lying-in month was abolished at the house. Before she even had time to clean up the mess between her legs after the birth of the baby, Mother heard the clang of tongs on the window frame and the voice of her mother-in-law: "You think you've made another contribution, don't you? One fucking daughter after another, and you think you've earned the right to have your mother-in-law wait on you hand and foot! Is this the sort of training you got at the house of Big Paw Yu? You're supposed to be the daughter-in-law of this family, but you act like you're the mother-in-law. Maybe I disturbed some heavenly order by slaughtering an old ox in a previous life, and this is my retribution. I must have been out of my mind, blind as a bat, to find a woman like you to marry my son!" She banged the tongs against the window again. "I'm talking to you! Are you playing deaf or dumb or what? You haven't heard a word I said!" "I heard you," Mother sobbed. "Then what are you waiting for? Your father-in-law and your husband are out threshing grain, and I've swapped a broom for a hoe, so damned busy I wish I could be in four places at once. But you, like a pampered princess, lie there in luxurious comfort. Now, if you could bring a son into this family, I would personally wash your feet in a gold basin!"

So Mother got out of bed, put on a pair of trousers, and wrapped her head in a filthy scarf; casting a longing glance at her baby, still covered with blood and muck, she dried her eyes with her sleeve and walked out into the yard on rubbery legs, putting up with the shooting pains the best she could. The glare of the midsummer sun nearly blinded her as she scooped up a ladleful of water from the vat and gulped it down. Why can't I just die? she was thinking. Living like this is sheer torture. I could end it myself! But then she saw her mother-in-law was pinching Laidi on the leg with her tongs, while Zhaodi and Lingdi huddled fearfully in a pile of straw, not making a sound and wishing they could hide their little bodies by burrowing out of sight.

Laidi howled like a pig being slaughtered and rolled around on the ground. "I'll give you something to cry about!" Shangguan Lü growled as she pinched the girl's legs over and over, putting her years of practice and strength as a blacksmith to work.

Mother ran up and grabbed her mother-in-law's arm. "Mother," she pleaded, "let her go. She's just a child, she doesn't know anything." She knelt weakly in front of her mother-in-law. "If you must pinch someone, pinch me . . ." Flinging her tongs to the ground in an explosion of anger, her mother-in-law paused for a second before pounding her own chest and crying, "My god, this woman will be the death of me!"

Mother had no sooner dragged herself out to the field than Shangguan Shouxi hit her with a rake. "What took you so long, you lazy ass? Thanks to you, I'm about to die from all this work!" She fell to the ground in a seated position, and heard her husband, who had been baked in the sun until he looked like a bird roasted on a spit, yell hoarsely, "Quit faking. Get up and rake some of this grain!" He threw the rake down in front of her and wove his way over to a locust tree to cool off.

With both hands on the ground, Mother managed to get to her feet, but when she bent over to pick up the rake, she nearly passed out. She propped herself up with the rake, as the blue sky and yellow earth whirled like gigantic wheels, wanting to topple her dizzily back to the ground. Somehow she managed to remain upright, in spite of the tearing pains in her belly and the excruciating contractions in her womb. Chilled, nauseating fluids kept leaking from between her legs, soiling her thighs.

The sun's diabolical rays burned their way across the land like white-hot flames; stalks of grain and the tassels that topped them happily gave up the last remaining moisture in the form of evaporation. Bearing up as best she could with the pain racking her body, Mother turned over the tassels on the threshing floor to speed up the drying process. She was reminded of what her mother-in-law had said: There's water on the hoe, but fire on the rake.

An emerald green locust that had ridden a tassel to the threshing floor spread its pink wings and flew onto Mother's hand. She noticed the delicate little insect's jadelike compound eyes, then saw that half of its abdomen had been lost to the sickle. And yet it lived on and could still fly. Mother found that indomitable will to live extremely moving. She shook her wrist to get the locust to fly away, but it stayed where it was, and Mother sighed over the sensation of the tiny insect's feet resting on her skin. That reminded her of the time her second daughter, Zhaodi, was conceived, in her aunt's tent in the melon field, where breezes from the Black Water River cooled purple melons as they grew amid the silver leaves of vines. Laidi was still nursing at the time. Hordes of locusts, with pink wings just like this one, raised a din all around the melon shelter. Her uncle, Big Paw Yu, knelt in front of her, pounding his own head. "Your aunt tricked me into this," he said, "and I've not been able to live with myself since. I've given up the right to call myself a man. Xuan'er, take that knife and put me out of my misery." He pointed to a gleaming melon knife on a shelf, as tears sluiced down his cheeks. Mother experienced a welter of emotions. She reached out to stroke the man's bald head. "Uncle," she said, "I don't blame you a bit. It's them, they drove me to this." At that point, her voice turned shrill and she pointed to the melons on the ground outside the tent, as if they were people. "Listen to me! Go ahead, laugh! Uncle, life is full of twists and turns. I did my best to remain chaste and upright, and how was I rewarded? I was yelled at, beaten, and sent back to my childhood home. So what must I do to gain their respect? Get pregnant by other men! Sooner or later, Uncle, my boat is going to capsize, if not here, then somewhere else." A wry smile twisted her mouth. "What is it they say, Uncle — Do not fertilize other people's fields?" Her uncle stood up anxiously. She reached out, un-ladylike, and jerked his pants down.

Father and son rested in the cool shade near the Shangguan threshing ground; the family dog was sprawled out at the base of the crumbling wall, its pink tongue lolling to the side as the animal panted from the oppressive heat. Mother's body was covered with rancid-smelling, sticky sweat. Her throat was on fire, her head ached, she was nauseous, and the veins on her forehead throbbed so violently they seemed about to burst. The lower half of her body felt as if it were cotton packed in a tub. Thoroughly prepared to die there on the threshing ground, she summoned up an astonishing amount of strength to keep working. Golden flashes of light on the floor made the tassels seem to come alive, like schools of tiny goldfish, or millions of squirming snakes. As she turned over the grain, Mother experienced a sense of tragic sorrow. Heaven, open your eyes and look around! All you neighbors, open your

eyes and look around. Feast your eyes on this member of the Shangguan family, working on a threshing floor with the sun blazing overhead, after just giving birth, the blood not even dry on my legs. And
what about my husband and father-in-law? Those two little men are
resting in the shade. Pore over three thousand years of imperial history,
and you'll not find more bitter suffering! Finally, as tears slid down her
cheeks, she passed out, overcome by the heat and her own emotions.

When she came to, she was lying in the thin shade at the foot of
the crumbling wall, covered with mud that attracted swarms of flies,
thrown there like a dead dog. The family mule was standing at the
edge of the threshing floor, near Shangguan Lü, who was just then
whipping her lazy husband and son. Covering their heads with their
arms, those two little darlings filled the air with screeches as they tried,
unsuccessfully, to avoid being hit.

"Stop hitting me, stop . . ." Mother's father-in-law pleaded. "Venerable wife, we're working, what else do you want?"

"And you, you little bastard!" she screamed as she turned her
whip on Shangguan Shouxi. "Every time you two pull something off, I
know it's your idea!"

"Don't hit me, Mother," Shangguan Shouxi said, tucking his
head between his shoulders. "Who would look after you in your old
age or handle the funeral arrangements if you accidentally killed me?"

"Do you really think I'm depending on you to do that?" she said
sadly. "I expect they'll use my bones for kindling before anyone comes
out to bury me!"

Father and son struggled to harness the mule; once that was
done, they picked up their tools and headed out into the field.

Whip in hand, Shangguan Lü walked over to the wall. "Get up
and go inside, my fine little daughter-in-law," she said accusingly.
"Why lie out here like that, just to make me look bad? To make it easy
for neighbors to curse me behind my back, saying I don't know the
proper way to treat my daughter-in-law? I said, get up! Or are you waiting for me to hire an eight-man sedan chair to carry you inside? I don't
know what the times have come to when a daughter-in-law thinks
she's better than her mother-in-law. I hope you have a son one of these
days, so you'll get a chance to see what it means to be someone's
mother-in-law."

After Mother rose unsteadily to her feet, her mother-in-law took
off her conical hat and put it on the younger woman's head. "Go on,

now. Pick some cucumbers in the garden. Tonight you can cook them with eggs for the two men. And if you think you've got the strength, go draw some water to wash the vegetables. I don't know how I get through the days anymore. I guess it's as they say, I carry the rest of you on my back."

She turned and headed over to the threshing floor, muttering to herself.

Thunder crashed and rolled that night, threatening the grain on the threshing floor, a whole year's blood and sweat. So, her body still racked with pain, Mother dragged herself outside with the rest of the family to move the grain inside. By the time they'd finished, she looked like a drenched chicken, and when she was finally able to crawl into bed, she was convinced she'd wandered into the doorway of Yama, the King of Hell, and that his little demons had looped a chain around her neck to drag her inside.

Instinctively, Mother bent down to pick up the pieces of the smashed bowl. She heard a bellowing roar that sounded like an ox as it raises its head out of water. That was followed by a blow on the head that knocked her to the floor. "Go ahead, smash it!" her mother-in-law screamed, the words exploding from her mouth as she flung away the now bloodstained garlic pestle. "Smash everything, since this family is falling apart anyway!"

Mother struggled to her feet after the pestle had smacked the back of her head. Warm blood ran down her neck. "Mother," she wept, "it was an accident."

"How dare you talk back to me!"

"I'm not talking back."

With a sidelong glance at her son, the older woman said, "I can't handle her, you worthless turd. Why not just put her on a pedestal and worship her?"

Understanding exactly what she was getting at, Shouxi picked up a club lying in a corner and drove it into Mother's waist; she crumpled to the ground. Then he began hitting her, over and over, as his mother looked on approvingly. "Shouxi," his father intervened, "stop that. If you kill her, the law will be on us."

"Women are worthless creatures," Shangguan Lü said, "so you have to beat them. You beat a woman into submission the way you knead dough into noodles."

"Then why are you always beating me?" Shangguan Fulu asked.

Worn out from swinging the club, Shouxi dropped it to the floor and stood there gasping for air.

Mother's waist and hips were wet and sticky. "Damn, that stinks!" her mother-in-law exclaimed, sniffing the air. "A few swats and she shits her pants!"

Propping herself up on her elbows, Mother raised her head and said, an unprecedented malicious edge to her voice, "Go ahead, Shangguan Shouxi, kill me while you're at it. You're a son of a bitch if you don't . . ."

The words were barely out of her mouth when she lost consciousness.

She awoke in the middle of the night and saw a star-filled sky. And there, in the glittering Milky Way, on that night in the year 1924, a comet streaked across the heavens, ushering in an age of upheaval and unrest.

Three helpless little creatures lay alongside her — Laidi, Zhaodi, and Lingdi, while Xiangdi lay at the head of the *kang* crying hoarsely. Worms were crawling in and around the eyes and ears of the newborn baby, the larvae of greenbottle flies laid earlier that day.

8

Filled with loathing for the Shangguan family, for three straight days Mother gave herself to a bachelor named Gao Dabiao, a dog butcher. A man with bovine eyes and upturned lips, Gao was never seen, regardless of the season, without his padded jacket, so smeared with dog grease it looked like armor. Any dog, no matter how vicious, gave him a wide berth, then turned and barked at him from a safe distance. Mother went to see him one day when she was on the northern bank of the Flood Dragon River, where she had gone to look for wild herbs. He was, at the time, stewing a pot of dog meat. "Here to buy some dog meat?" he asked when she barged in the door. "It's not ready yet." "No, Dabiao, I've brought some meat for you this time. Remember that time at the open-air opera when you touched me when no one was looking?" Gao Dabiao blushed. "Well, today you don't have to worry if anyone's looking or not."

Once she was sure she was pregnant, Mother went to the Matron's shrine at the Tan family tent, where she burned incense, kowtowed, made her vows, and handed over the little bit of money she'd brought with her when she was married. But that changed nothing — she had another girl, whom she named Pandi.

Not until much later was Mother able to determine whether the father of her sixth daughter, Niandi, was Gao Dabiao or the skinny little monk at the Tianqi Temple. When Niandi was seven or eight years old, Mother could tell by the shape of her face, her long nose, and long eyebrows.

In the spring of that year, Shangguan Lü contracted a strange illness, with itchy silvery scales erupting all over her body from her neck down; in order to keep her from scratching her skin raw, her husband and son were forced to tie her hands behind her back. The illness had this iron woman howling day and night; out in the yard, the wall and the stiff bark of the plum tree were blood-specked where she had rubbed her back to relieve the terrible itch. "I can't stand it, this itching is killing me . . . I've offended the heavens, help me, please help me . . ."

The two Shangguan men were so incompetent that a stone roller couldn't get them to fart and an awl couldn't draw blood, so the responsibility of finding help for her mother-in-law naturally fell to Mother. All in all, after riding the family mule from one end of Northeast Gaomi to the other, she engaged a dozen or more physicians, employing both Chinese and Western methods; some left after writing a prescription, others just left. So Mother brought in a shaman and then a sorcerer, but their magic potions and spirit waters also ended in failure. Shangguan Lü's condition actually worsened daily.

One day, her mother-in-law called Mother to her bedside. "Shouxi's wife," she said, "as the saying goes, fathers and sons are bound by kindness, mothers and daughters-in-law are linked by enmity. After I die, this family's existence will depend upon you, because those two are a pair of asses who'll never grow up."

"Don't talk like that, Mother," my mother said. "I heard from Third Master Fan that there is a wise monk at the Tianqi Temple in Madian Township who possesses remarkable medical powers. I'll bring him to see you."

"It's a waste of money," her mother-in-law said. "I know the source of my illness. Back when I was first married, I killed a damned cat by pouring scalding water on it. That hateful animal kept stealing our chickens, and I only wanted to teach it a lesson. I never thought it would die, and now it's wreaking its vengeance."

But Mother made the thirty-li trip on their mule.

The pasty-faced, effetely handsome, fragrant-smelling monk counted the beads on his rosary as he listened to Mother. "Madam patron," he said at last, "this unworthy monk sees patients here in the temple. I never make house calls. So you go back and bring your mother-in-law to see me."

And that is precisely what Mother did. She harnessed the mule to a cart and took her mother-in-law to Tianqi Temple, where the wise monk wrote out two prescriptions, one liquid to be ingested and another for washing the skin. "If these do not work," he told them, "there is no need to see me again. If they do, then return and I will give you a new prescription."

Mother went immediately to a pharmacy, bought the medication, and returned home to prepare and administer them. After her mother-in-law ingested one of the potions three times and was bathed twice with the other, almost miraculously, the itching stopped.

Deliriously happy, the patient withdrew some money from the family chest and sent Mother back to thank the monk and fetch the new prescription.

While she waited for the new prescription, Mother asked the wise monk if there were some way he could help her bear sons rather than daughters. As their conversation grew more intimate — a passionate monk and a woman eager to produce a son — they became lovers.

As for Gao Dabiao, the dog butcher at Sandy Mouth Village, his brief affair with Mother had whetted his appetite. So on the evening that Mother rode her mule home from Tianqi Temple, passing by the Black Water River as the moon was replacing the sun in the sky, Gao Dabiao leaped out from among the sorghum stalks and blocked her way.

"Lu Xuan'er, you are a fickle woman!"

"Dabiao," Mother said, "I felt sorry for you, and that is why I closed my eyes and let you have your way a time or two. That is as far as it goes."

"You can't toss me aside just because you got a piece of that little monk!"

"That's nonsense!"

"You can't fool me. Do as I say, or I'll spread the word all over

Northeast Gaomi Township that you had an affair with the little monk on the pretense of seeking a cure for your mother-in-law."

Mother let Gao Dabiao carry her into the sorghum.

Her mother-in-law's illness was completely cured, but word of Mother's illicit relationship with the monk reached the older woman's ears anyway.

So when Niandi was born, and her mother-in-law saw it was another girl, she picked the baby up by her legs and was about to drown her in the chamber pot.

Mother jumped out of bed, wrapped her arms around her mother-in-law's legs, and pleaded, "Mother, be merciful, please. For my sake, after taking care of you all these months, spare the little one . . ."

"That makes sense," her mother-in-law said, lowering her voice. "But this business with the monk, is it true?"

Mother said nothing.

"Tell me! Is this a bastard I'm holding?"

Mother shook her head resolutely.

Her mother-in-law tossed the baby onto the bed.

9

In the fall of 1935, while Mother was on the bank of the Flood Dragon River cutting grass, she was gang-raped by four armed soldiers fleeing from a rout.

When it was over, she looked out at the river and decided to drown herself. But just as she was about to walk to her death, she saw the reflection of Northeast Gaomi's beautiful blue sky in the clear water. Cool breezes swallowed up the feelings of humiliation in her breast, so she scooped up handfuls of water to wash her sweaty, tear-streaked face, straightened her clothes, and walked home.

In the early summer of the next year, eight years after the birth of her previous child, Mother gave birth to her seventh, Qiudi. The birth of yet another daughter threw her mother-in-law into despair. Stumbling as she walked, she retrieved a bottle from a trunk in her room and gulped down great mouthfuls of the strong liquor before dissolving into loud wails. Mother, too, was dejected, and as she looked with disgust into the wrinkled face of her newborn child, her only thought was: God in Heaven, why are you so stingy? All you had to do was add a smidgeon of clay to this child to make it a son.

Her husband then stormed into the room, pulled back the blanket, and staggered backward. The first thing he did after recovering from the shock was reach behind the door, pick up the club for pounding wet clothes, and bring it down on his wife's head. Blood splattered on the wall as the crazed little man turned and ran outside, fuming. Snatching a pair of red-hot tongs out of the blacksmith furnace, he ran back to his wife's room and branded her on the inside of her thigh.

Wisps of yellow smoke and the stench of burning flesh quickly filled the room. With a shriek of pain, Mother fell out of bed and curled into a ball on the floor, her body twitching.

When Big Paw Yu heard that Lu Xuan'er had been branded, he rushed over to the Shangguan home with a hunting rifle, and without saying a word, aimed it at the chest of Shangguan Lü and pulled the trigger. The rifle misfired. By the time he'd readied the weapon for a second try, Shangguan Lü had run into the house and slammed the door behind her. His anger building, he fired at the closed door, blowing a hole in it with buckshot and drawing a fearful shriek from Shangguan Lü on the other side.

Big Paw Yu then began battering the door with the butt of his rifle, breathing heavily but saying nothing. He looked like a bear, his burly figure rocking back and forth. Mother's daughters huddled fearfully in the side room as they watched what was happening out in the yard.

Mother's husband and father-in-law, one brandishing a steel-headed hammer, the other the pair of tongs, cautiously approached Big Paw. Shouxi was the first to act, rushing up and hitting Big Paw in the back with his tongs. Big Paw turned and roared at his attacker. The tongs fell from Shouxi's hand, and he would have run away, if only his rubbery legs had let him. He tried to force a smile. "I'll kill you, you son of a bitch!" Big Paw bellowed as he knocked Shouxi to the ground with his rifle, with such force that it snapped in two. Shouxi's father rushed Big Paw with his hammer, but missed his target altogether, and nearly lost his footing in the process. Big Paw helped him along with a swat on the man's shoulder, sending him sprawling alongside his son. Big Paw took turns kicking both men, then picked up the hammer, raised it over his head, and cursed, "Now I'm going to crack that melon head wide open, you son of a bitch!" just as Mother hobbled out into the yard. "Uncle," she shouted, "this is family business. I don't need your help."

Letting the hammer drop to the ground, Big Paw, a pained

expression on his face, looked at his niece standing there like a dried-out tree. "Xuan'er," he said, "how you've suffered . . ."

"When I left the Yu home," Mother said, "I became a member of the Shangguan family, and whether I live or die because of it is not your concern."

Big Paw Yu's rampage succeeded in deflating the arrogance of the Shangguan family. Realizing how she had mistreated her daughter-in-law, Shangguan Lü finally began treating her more humanely. Shangguan Shouxi, having barely escaped death, also began to see his wife in a different light, and subjected her to less abuse.

Meanwhile, Mother's scalded flesh began to fester and smell. This time, she thought, I won't survive, so she moved into the side room.

Early one morning, she was awakened from a half-sleep by the church bell. Although the bell was rung daily, on this day it seemed to be talking to her, the enchanting peal of bronze on bronze stirring her soul and sending ripples through her heart. Why haven't I heard that sound before? What was stopping up my ears? As she pondered this change, the pain racking her body slowly went away. Her thoughts weren't interrupted until some rats climbed up and began nibbling at her putrefying flesh. The old mule that had brought her over from her aunt's house gave her a melancholic look, consoling her, inspiring her, encouraging her.

Mother stood up with the help of a cane and dragged her festering body out onto the road, one faltering step at a time, all the way up to the church's gate.

It was a Sunday. Pastor Malory stood at the dusty pulpit, Bible in hand, intoning a passage from Matthew for the benefit of a handful of gray-haired old women:

"When as his mother Mary was espoused to Joseph, before they came together, she was found with child of the Holy Ghost. Then Joseph her husband, being a just man, and not wanting to make her a public example, was minded to divorce her privately. But while he thought on these things, behold, the angel of the Lord appeared unto him in a dream, saying, 'Joseph, son of David, fear not to take unto thee Mary thy wife, for that which is conceived in her is of the Holy Ghost. And she shall bring forth a son, and thou shall call His name Jesus; for He shall save his people from their sins.'"

This passage brought tears to Mother's eyes, tears that fell on her collar. She tossed away her cane and fell to her knees. Looking up into the face of the cracked jujube Jesus on the iron cross, she sobbed, "Lord, I've come to You late . . ."

The old women stared uncomprehendingly at Shangguan Lu, the stench from her rotting flesh crinkling their noses.

Pastor Malory laid down his Bible and stepped down off the raised platform to lift Lu Xuan'er up off her knees. Crystalline tears filled his gentle blue eyes. "Little sister," he said, "I have been waiting for you for a very long time."

In the early summer of 1938, in the dense grove of locusts in a remote corner of Sandy Ridge Village, Pastor Malory knelt reverently beside Mother, whose injury had begun to heal, and gently rubbed her body with trembling reddened hands. His moist lips quivered, his limpid blue eyes blended in with the fragments of Northeast Gaomi Township's deep blue sky that filtered in through the gaps between the flowering locusts. "Little sister," he stammered, "my lovely mate . . . my little dove . . . my perfect woman, your thighs are as glossy as fine jade, formed by a master craftsman, your navel is like a perfectly round cup filled with a mixed drink . . . your waist is like a sheaf of wheat tied with a string of lilies . . . your breasts are like twin fawns, like the sagging fruit of a palm tree. Your nose is as fragrant as an apple, your mouth smells like fine liquor. My love, you are beautiful, a sheer delight. You make me deliriously happy!"

Basking in the approving words and gentle fondling of Pastor Malory, Mother felt as light as goose down floating in the deep blue skies of Northeast Gaomi and in Pastor Malory's blue eyes, as the subtle perfume of red and white locust blossoms flowed over her like waves.

Chapter  Three

1

After getting an injection to stop the bleeding, Mother slowly came around. I was the first thing she saw — more specifically, what she saw was the little pecker standing up like a silkworm chrysalis between my legs — and the dullness in her eyes was replaced by light. She picked me up and kissed me, like a hen pecking rice. Crying hoarsely, I sought out the nipple, which she stuck in my mouth. I began to suck, but instead of milk, all I got was a taste of blood. I was bawling, Eighth Sister — the girl born just before me — was whimpering. Mother laid me alongside my sister and struggled to get down off the *kang*. She walked unsteadily over to the water vat, bent over, and drank a ladleful of water. Numbly she looked out at the corpses in the yard. The adult donkey and her baby mule stood trembling beside the bed of peanuts. My older sisters walked into the yard, cutting a sorry figure. They ran to Mother and wept weakly before crumpling to the floor.

White smoke billowed out of our chimney for the first time since the catastrophe. Mother broke open Grandma's trunk and removed some preserved eggs, dates, rock candy, and a piece of old ginseng that had lain there for years. She threw it all into the wok, and when the water began to sizzle, it set the eggs in rapid motion. Finally, Mother called all the girls in and sat them around a large platter. "All right, children," she said, "eat."

My sisters scooped the hot food out of the platter and ate ravenously. Mother only drank the broth, three bowlfuls, until there was nothing left. They were quiet for a while, but then threw their arms around each other and wailed. Mother waited until they had cried themselves out before announcing, "Girls, you have a little brother, and another little sister."

Mother suckled me. Her milk tasted like dates, rock candy, and preserved eggs, a magnificent liquid. I opened my eyes. My sisters looked at me excitedly. I returned their looks bleary-eyed. After draining Mother's breast of its milk, surrounded by the cries of my baby sister, I closed my eyes. I heard Mother pick up Eighth Sister and sigh. "You're one I didn't need."

Early the next morning, the clang of a gong shattered the quiet of the lane. Sima Ting, the Felicity Manor steward, called out hoarsely: "Fellow villagers, carry out your dead, bring them all out."

Mother stood in the yard holding Eighth Sister and me in her arms and wailing loudly; there were no tears on her cheeks. She was surrounded by her daughters, some crying, some not; there were no tears on their cheeks either.

Sima Ting walked into the yard with his brass gong, looking like a dried-out gourd, a man of inestimable age, his face deeply wrinkled. He had a nose like a strawberry, deep black eyes that kept rolling in their sockets, the eyes of a little boy. His aging stooped shoulders gave him the look of a candle guttering in the wind, but his hands were fair and plump, the palms nicely dimpled. He walked up to Mother and struck his gong with all his might. A gravelly *klong wah-wah-wah-wah* emerged from the cracked gong. Mother swallowed a sob, straightened her neck, and held her breath for at least a full minute. "What a tragedy!" Sima Ting said with an exaggerated sigh. Desperate grief was written on his lips, in the corners of his mouth, on his cheeks, even on his earlobes. And yet, despite the obvious sense of righteous indignation, there was an unmistakable hint of a smirk hidden in the space between his nose and eyes, a look of furtive glee. He walked up to the rigid body of Shangguan Fulu and stood woodenly beside it for a moment. Then he went over to the headless body of Shangguan Shouxi, where he bent down and looked into the dead eyes of the severed head, as if wanting to establish an emotional link. Saliva dribbled from the corner of his mouth. In contrast to the peaceful expression on Shangguan Shouxi's face, Sima looked somewhat stupid, and savage. "You people wouldn't listen to me, why wouldn't you listen to me? . . ." He was scolding the dead men in a low voice, talking to himself. He walked back up to Mother: "Shouxi's wife, I'll get someone to take them away. In this weather . . . well, you see." He looked heavenward, and so did Mother. The sky was an oppressive leaden gray, and off to the east, the sunrise, blood red, was being beaten back by dark clouds. Our stone lions were damp. "The rain, it's coming. If we don't carry them away, once it starts raining, and then the sun comes out, you can imagine what it will do to them." Mother held my sister and me in her arms and knelt in front of Sima Ting. "Steward," she said, "I am a widow with a brood of orphaned children, so we will have to rely on you from now on. Children, come bow to your uncle." All my older sisters knelt in front of Sima Ting, who hit the gong — *bong bong* — with all his might. "Fuck his ancestors!" he cursed, as tears streamed down his face. "It's all the fault of that bastard Sha Yueliang. His ambush infuriated the Japanese, who went on a murderous rampage against us common people. Get up, girls, all of you, and stop crying. Yours is not the only family that has suffered. Just my luck that the county head put me in charge of this town. He fled for his life, but I'm still here. Fuck his ancestors! Hey there, Gou San, Yao Si, quit your dawdling. Are you waiting for me to send a sedan chair for you?"

Gou San and Yao Si came running into the yard bent at the waist, followed by some of the town idlers. They were Sima Ting's errand boys, his honor guard and his followers, his prestige and his authority, the means by which he carried out his duties. Yao Si held a notebook with a ragged-edged straw-paper cover under his arm and had a pencil stuck behind his ear. Gou San strained to roll Shangguan Fulu over, so he could look up into the red morning clouds. He sang out: "Shangguan Fulu — head crushed in — head of the family." Yao Si wetted a finger, opened the household registration notebook, and thumbed his way through it until he found the Shangguan page. Then he took the pencil from behind his ear, knelt on one knee, and rested his notebook on the other; after touching the tip of his pencil to his tongue, he struck out Shangguan Fulu's name. "Shangguan Shouxi" — Gou San's voice suddenly lost its crispness — "head separated from body." A wail tore from Mother's throat. Sima Ting turned to Yao Si: "Go ahead, record it, you hear me?" Yao Si drew a small circle over Shangguan Shouxi's name, without listing the cause of death. Sima Ting raised the mallet in his hand and thumped Yao Si in the head. "Your mother's legs! How dare you cut corners with the dead, thinking you can take advantage of me because I can't read, is that it?" With a drawn look on his face, Yao Si pleaded: "Don't hit me, old master. It's all right up here." He pointed to his head. "I'll not forget any of it, not in a thousand years." Sima Ting glared at him. "And what makes you think you'll live that long? A thousand years, you must be some sort of turtle spawn." "Old master, it was only a figure of speech. Why start a fight?" "Who's starting a fight?" Sima Ting thumped him on the head again. "Shangguan" — Gou San, who was standing in front of Shangguan Lü, turned to Mother and asked, "What was your mother-in-law's maiden name?" Mother shook her head. Yao Si tapped the notebook with the tip of his pencil and said, "It was Lü." "Shangguan née Lü," Gou San shouted as he bent down to look at the corpse. "That's strange, there are no wounds," he muttered, turning Shangguan Lü's gray head this way and that. A thin moan escaped from between her lips, straightening Gou San up in a hurry. He backed off, gaping in astonishment and stammering, "She's come back . . . back to life." Shangguan Lü opened her eyes slowly, like a newborn baby, glazed and lacking focus. Mother shouted, "Ma!" She handed me and my eighth sister to two of the older girls and ran up to her mother-in-law, stopping abruptly when she noticed that the old woman's eyes had settled on me as I lay in First Sister's arms. "Everyone," Sima Ting said, "the old woman has returned briefly from death to see the child. Is it a boy?" The gaze in Shangguan Lü's eyes made me squirm, and I began to cry. "Let her look at her grandchild," Sima Ting said, "so she can leave us in peace." Mother took me from First Sister, got down on her knees, and shuffled up to the old woman, where she held me up close to her. "Ma," she said tearfully, "I had no choice" . . . A light flashed into Shangguan Lü's eyes when her gaze alit on that spot between my legs. A rumble emerged from her abdomen, followed by a rank odor. "That's it," Sima Ting said, "this time she's really gone." Mother stood up with me in her arms and, in front of a crowd of men, opened her blouse and stuffed a nipple into my mouth. With my face nestled against her heavy breast, I stopped crying. Sima Ting announced, "Shangguan née Lü, wife of Shangguan Fulu, mother of Shangguan Shouxi, has died of a broken heart over the deaths of her husband and her son. All right, take her away!"

The corpse detail walked up to Shangguan Lü with metal hooks, but before they could place them under her, she stood up slowly, like an ancient tortoise. With the sun shining down, her puffy face looked like a lemon, or a New Year's cake. She had a sneer on her face as she sat with her back against the wall, like a miniature mountain.

"Elder sister-in-law," Sima Ting said, "you have a tight grip on life."

Covering their mouths with towels sprayed with sorghum liquor to ward off the smell of rotting corpses, the town head's followers carried up a door plank on which the remnants of a New Year's couplet could nearly be made out. After laying the plank on the ground, four town idlers — now designated as the official town corpse detail — quickly picked Shangguan Fulu up by his arms and legs and laid him out on the plank. Then two of them carried the plank out the gate. One of Shangguan Fulu's rigid arms hung off the side of the plank and swung like a pendulum. "Drag the old lady away from the gate!" one of the idlers shouted. Two men rushed over. "It's old Aunty Sun. How could she have died there?" someone in the lane wondered aloud. "Put her on the cart." The lane was buzzing with comments.

The door plank was laid out beside Shangguan Shouxi, who lay in the position in which he died. Transparent bubbles floated skyward from his mouth, opened in his screams to the heavens, as if a crab were hidden inside. The corpse detail hesitated, not sure what to do. "Oh, hell," one of them said, "let's get on with it." He picked up his metal hook, but was stopped short by Mother's shout: "Don't use hooks on him!" She handed me to Shangguan Laidi, then, with a loud wail, threw herself on the headless corpse of her husband. She reached out to drag the head over, but drew her hand back when it touched flesh. "Let it go, sister-in-law!" one of the idlers said, his voice muffled by the towel covering it. "That head cannot be reattached. Go take a look in the cart out there. All that's left of some of those bodies is a leg, after the dogs got to them. He could be in worse shape. Step aside, you girls. Turn your heads and don't look." He wrapped his arms around Mother and half-carried, half-pushed her to one side, along with my sisters. "Close your eyes, all of you!" he warned us once more.

By the time Mother and my sisters opened their eyes again, all the bodies had been removed from the yard.

We fell in behind the horse cart, piled high with corpses, dust rising in its wake. There were three horses, like the ones my sister Laidi saw that other morning: one apricot yellow, one date red, and one leek green. But now they plodded on dejectedly, their heads drooping, their coats dull. The apricot yellow lead horse had a gimp leg, and thrust its neck out with each step. The driver dragged his whip along the ground, his free hand resting on the shaft. The sides of his hair were black, the middle completely white, like a titmouse. A dozen or more dogs on the sides of the road stared hungrily at the corpses on the cart. A procession of survivors followed the cart, all but hidden in the dust; we in turn were followed by our town head, Sima Ting, and his underlings, led by Gou San and Yao Si. Some had hoes over their shoulders, others carried metal hooks; one man shouldered a bamboo pole with strips of red cloth tied to the end. Sima Ting was still holding his gong, which he struck every few dozen steps. And with every clang, the families of the deceased wailed. But they seemed reluctant to cry, and no sooner had the sound of the gong trailed off than the crying stopped. Rather than grieve for their family members, it appeared, they were carrying out duties given them by the town head.

And so it went, us following the horse cart, crying from time to time, past the church, with its collapsed bell tower, and the flour mill where Sima Ting and his younger brother, Sima Ku, had harnessed the wind five years earlier. A dozen or more rickety windmills still rose above the mill, creaking in the wind. On the right, we passed the site of a company created twenty years before by a Japanese businessman to grow American cotton. Then we passed the podium on the drying floor of the Sima compound where Niu Tengxiao, Gaomi's county magistrate, had gotten the women to unbind their feet. Finally, the cart turned left, following the Black Water River, and drove into a field that extended all the way to the marshland. Gusts of moist air from the south carried the odor of decay. Toads in roadside ditches and in the shallows of the river croaked weakly. Swarms of fat tadpoles changed the color of the water.

The cart sped up once it entered the field. The "Old Titmouse" driver used his whip on the lead horse, gimp leg or no. The cart bounced around wildly on the uneven road, the corpses giving off a terrible stench. Something wet dripped through the cracks in the bed of the cart. By then, the crying had stopped altogether, and family members were covering their mouths and noses with their sleeves. Sima Ting and his followers brushed past us and rushed up to the cart, bent at the waist as they ran, leaving us and the cart behind, that and the stench. A dozen mad dogs set up a cacophony of howls as they leapt all over the wheat fields on either side of the road. They kept appearing and disappearing amid the wheat stalks, like seals leaping through the waves. It was a day set aside for crows and hawks. All the crows in Northeast Gaomi descended on the township's basin, like a dark cloud settling over the horse cart. They circled the area, their ex-

cited screeches filling the air as they formed a myriad of patterns before going into nosedives. Older crows went straight for the corpses'
eyes, pecking them out with their hard, pointed beaks; younger, less
experienced birds attacked the skulls, setting up a loud tattoo. "Old
Titmouse" flicked his whip at them, each time bringing down at least
one bird, which was turned to mush under the wheels of the cart.
Seven or eight hawks circled high in the sky, sometimes forced by
competing air currents down below the crows. They were just as interested in the corpses, but refused to join forces with crows, over whom
they maintained smug superiority.

The sun poked its face out from behind a cloud, bestowing upon
the maturing wheat plants a resplendent glow and causing the wind to
change direction, which created a momentary stillness that put waves
of wheat to sleep, or to death. A golden platter, seemingly extending
all the way to the horizon, rose under the sun. Spikes on the ripe wheat
were like tiny golden needles that set the world aglitter. The horse cart
turned onto a narrow path in the middle of the field, forcing the driver
to thread his way between two rows of wheat stalks. The lead horses,
one apricot yellow, the other leek green, could not negotiate the path
side by side, so either the yellow horse had to walk amid the wheat
stalks or the green horse was forced to plod through the layer of gold.
Like pouting little boys, one would push the other off the path, only to
be pushed right back. And so the cart slowed, which sent the crows
into a frenzy. Dozens of them landed on the heads of corpses and began pecking away, their wings drooping. "Old Titmouse" had his
hands too full to worry about the birds. The crop that year was sure to
be a good one, since the stalks were thick, the tassels full, and the kernels plump. Wheat spikes brushing against the horses' bellies and
scraping against the cart and its tires produced a skin-tingling scratchy
sound. Dogs poked their heads out from between stalks, eyes shut to
protect them from the spikes. Tracking the cart was easy; they just followed their noses.

Our procession thinned out and grew longer once we were in the
wheat field. No one was wailing any longer, not even sobbing softly.
Every once in a while a child would stumble and fall, and someone,
usually a family member, would reach out a friendly hand and help
him to his feet. In the midst of this solemn unity, children refused to
cry even with a split lip. Silence reigned, but it was a tense, uneasy silence. The passing cart and mad dogs startled partridges in the field,

sending them flapping into the air only to settle once again into a sea of gold. Wheat snakes, those poisonous red vipers unique to Northeast Gaomi, slithered among the wheat like lightning bolts, causing the horses to shudder; dogs crept along the ruts, not daring to look up. The sun was partially hidden behind dark clouds, the revealed half sending down scorching rays of light. Cloud shadows seemed to fly above the wheat field, momentarily extinguishing the golden flames that engulfed the sunlit stalks. As the wind changed direction, millions of spiked tassels set up wind currents; kernels of wheat, their voices hushed, relayed their frightful news.

At first, warm gusts of wind from the northeast brushed the tips of the stalks, shaped by the tassels through which they passed, and opened up tiny gurgling currents amid the tranquil sea of wheat. Then the wind picked up in intensity, cleaving its way through the wheat stalks. The red banner carried by a man up front began to flutter; clouds overhead rumbled. A golden serpent writhed in the northeastern sky, which was dyed blood red; peals of thunder rolled earthward. Another momentary hush, during which hawks circling high above wheeled toward the field and disappeared among the stalks of wheat. Crows, on the other hand, exploded skyward, trailing loud caws behind them. The storm burst, sending the wheat reeling, some of the stalks swerving from north to west and others from east to south. Long, flowing waves pushing and being pushed by short, choppy ones formed a yellow whirlpool. It looked as if the sea of wheat was boiling over a vast cauldron. Crows scattered. Pale, flimsy raindrops brought with them hailstones the size of apricot pits. Chilled air immediately cut to the bone. The hailstones pelted the wheat tassels and spikes, the horses' rumps and ears, the exposed bellies of the dead and the bare scalps of the living. An occasional crow, its head cracked by a hailstone, fell like a stone right in front of us.

Mother held me tightly, shielding my fragile head by burying it in the warm valley between her ample breasts. She had left Eighth Sister, a superfluous human being from the moment she was born, on the *kang* to accompany the now mindless Shangguan Lü, who crawled into the western side room and gobbled down handfuls of donkey turds.

My sisters took off their shirts and covered their heads with them. All except Laidi, since the little green apples that were her girlish breasts showed beneath her shirt; she covered her head with her hands, but got soaked anyway. The wind plastered her shirt up against her body.

Finally, our exhausting trudging brought us to the public cemetery, ten acres of open land surrounded by wheat fields. Rotting wooden markers stood at dozens of overgrown grave mounds.

The rainsquall passed and splintered clouds skittered out of sight, giving way to a dazzling blue sky and blistering sunlight. Steam rose from the melting hailstones. Some of the damaged wheat stalks straightened up; others would never stand erect again. Cold winds abruptly turned hot, warming the ripening kernels of wheat, which were turning bright yellow.

As we massed at the edge of the cemetery, we watched our town head, Sima Ting, pace the area, scattering locusts with each step, their soft green outer wings revealing the pink wings beneath. He stopped beside a wild chrysanthemum bush, covered with little yellow blooms. Stomping on the ground, he called out: "Right here, here's where I want you to dig."

Seven swarthy men with spades over their shoulders walked up listlessly, casting looks back and forth, as if wanting to commit all the other faces to memory. Finally, they turned to look at Sima Ting. "What are you gawking at me for?" Sima bellowed. "Dig!" He tossed away his gong and mallet. The gong landed in a clump of white-tasseled weeds, where it startled a lizard; the mallet landed atop some dogweed. Grabbing one of the spades, he jammed the blade into the ground and stomped down with his foot, listing slightly to the side as the spade bit deeply into the earth. Straining mightily, he lifted up a spadeful of earth and grass and turned ninety degrees, holding the spade out in front of him. He then spun a hundred-eighty degrees and, with a loud grunt, sent the dirt flying, tumbling in the air like a dead rooster and landing in a clump of yellow dandelions. Handing the spade back to its owner, he said, somewhat breathlessly: "Now dig. I'm sure you can smell the stench by now."

The men began to dig, sending dirt flying. Slowly, a ditch took shape, deeper and deeper.

By then it was noon. The sun turned the earth a shimmering white; the stench from the cart grew stronger, and even though we were upwind, the gut-wrenching odor followed us. Then the crows returned. Their wings were bathed a shiny blue-black. Sima Ting retrieved his gong and mallet and, braving the stench, ran up to the cart. "You feathered bastards, let's see which of you has the guts to come down here! I'll tear you limb from limb!" He banged his gong and began jumping around, shouting curses into the air. Crows circled a good fifty feet above the cart, their caws tumbling earthward along with droppings and worn-out feathers. "Old Titmouse" picked up the red-bannered staff and shook it at the crows, which separated into groups that went into steep, screeching dives, circling the heads of Sima Ting and "Old Titmouse," with their tiny oval eyes, powerful stiff wings, and hideously filthy talons. The men fought them off, but the unyielding beaks kept finding their mark. So the men used the gong and mallet and the staff as weapons, increasing the sounds of battle. Wounded crows folded their wings and thudded into the velvet grass amid the white flowers, then limped off into the field, dragging their wings behind them. Mad dogs hidden among the stalks were on them like a shot, quickly tearing them to pieces. In no time, sticky feathers littered the ground, while the dogs retreated to the edge of the field to crouch in readiness, panting noisily, scarlet tongues lolling to the sides of their mouths. Some of the uninjured crows kept up their assault on Sima Ting and "Old Titmouse," but the bulk of their force attacked the cart — noisily, excitedly, repulsively — their necks like springs, their beaks like awls, as they feasted on delicious human carrion, a demonic feast. Sima Ting and "Old Titmouse" fell to the ground, exhausted, runnels of sweat cobwebbed on their dusty exposed faces.

The pit by then was more than shoulder-deep, and all we could see were the occasional top of someone's head and soaring clumps of wet, white mud; the air was suffused with the cool, fresh smell of raw earth.

One of the men climbed out of the pit and walked up alongside Sima Ting. "Town Head," he said, "we've struck water." Sima looked at him with glazed eyes and slowly raised his arm. "Come take a look," the man said. "It's deep enough." Sima crooked a finger at the man, who was puzzled by the sign. "Idiot!" Sima growled. "Help me up." The man bent down and helped Sima to his feet. Moaning, Sima thumped his waist with his fists and, with the other man's help, hobbled over to the ridge of the pit. "Goddamn it," Sima Ting cursed. "Get up here, you bastards, you'll dig all the way down to Hell before you know it."

The men climbed out of the pit and were pelted by the corrupt stench of the dead. Sima kicked the carter. "On your feet," he demanded, "and get your cart over there." The carter didn't budge. "Gou San, Yao Si," Sima bellowed, "toss this son of a bitch in first!"

Gou San, who was standing with the other men, grunted a reply.

"Where's Yao Si?" Sima asked. "The itchy-footed prick slipped away already," Gou San said angrily. "Smash that bastard's rice bowl when we get back," Sima said as he gave the carter another kick. "Let's see if this one's dead."

The carter climbed to his feet, a hangdog look on his face, and cast a fearful glance at his cart standing at the edge of the graveyard. The crows were clustered on the bed, hopping up and down with loud, piercing cries. The horses were lying on the ground, their noses buried in the grass, crows perched on their backs. The rest of the crows were on the grassy ground, feasting. Two of them were fighting over a large morsel, one backing up, the other reluctantly surging forward and forcing the other to keep retreating. From time to time, neither would budge, as they dug in their talons, flapped their wings frantically, thrust out their heads, neck feathers standing straight up to reveal the purple skin beneath, both necks seemingly about to detach themselves from the torsos behind. A dog came out of nowhere and snapped up the entrails, dragging the two birds tumbling through the grass.

"Spare me, Town Head," the carter implored as he fell to his knees in front of Sima Ting, who picked up a dirt clod and hurled it at the crows. They barely noticed. He then walked up to the families of the deceased and muttered, "That's it, that will do it. You folks go home."

Mother was the first of the stunned crowd to get down on her knees, followed by the others, who raised a piteous howl. "Elder Sima, lay them to rest," Mother begged. The rest of the crowd pleaded with him, "Please, please, lay them to rest. Father, Mother, our children . . ."

Sweat poured down Sima's neck from his bowed head. With an exasperated gesture, he walked back to where his men were standing, and said softly, "Brothers, I have tolerated your bullying tactics, your thievery, your fights, your taking advantage of widows, your grave-robbing, and all the other sins against heaven and earth. One trains soldiers for a thousand days, all for a single battle. And now, today, we have a job to do, even if the crows gouge out our eyes and peck out our brains. I, the town head, will take the lead, and I will fuck eighteen generations of women in the families of any one of you who tries to slack off! After we've finished, I'll take you back and get you all drunk. Now on your feet," he said to the carter, pulling him up by his ear, "and get that cart over here! Men, pick up your weapons, the battle is on!"

At that moment, three dark-skinned youngsters swam up through the waves of wheat. It was Aunty Sun's mute grandsons. They were all wearing the same colored shorts, and nothing else. The tallest of the three was brandishing a sword that whipped in the air, making a whistling sound. The second was carrying a wood-handled dagger; and the shortest brought up the rear dragging a long-handled sword. With wide, staring eyes, they grunted and made a series of gestures describing their anguish. As a light flickered in Sima Ting's eyes, he patted each of them on the head. "Youngsters," he said, "your grandma and your brothers are there on the cart. We are going to bury them. Those damned crows have gone too far. They are the Japs, so let's take the fight to them! Do you understand what I'm saying?" Yao Si, who had reappeared from somewhere, made some signs to the boys. Tears and flames of outrage spewed from the eyes of the mutes, who charged the crows, their knives and swords flashing in the air.

"You slippery devil, where the hell have you been?" Sima demanded of Yao Si, grabbing him by the shoulders and shaking him violently.

"I went to get those three."

The mutes jumped up onto the back of the cart, quickly bloodying their flashing knives and swords, sending dismembered crows thudding to the ground. "Charge!" Sima Ting shouted. The men swarmed up to the cart to fight the crows. Curses, the sounds of battle, the screeches of crows, and the flapping of wings created a sheet of noise that joined a convergence of fetid smells — death, sweat, blood, mud, wheat, and wildflowers.

The torn and broken bodies were laid out pell-mell in the pit. Pastor Malory stood atop the new earth beside the pit and intoned, "Dear Lord, deliver the souls of these unfortunate victims . . ." Tears streamed from his blue eyes down through the purplish scars from the whip; from there they dripped onto his ripped black robe and the heavy bronze crucifix on his chest.

Sima Ting pulled him down off the ridge of the pit. "Malory," he said, "go over there and take it easy. Don't forget that you barely escaped the jaws of death yourself."

As the men shoveled dirt into the pit, Pastor Malory cast a long shadow under the setting sun. Mother stood there watching him and feeling her heart race beneath her heavy left breast. By the time the sun's rays had turned red, a massive grave mound had risen in the middle of the cemetery. Sima Ting led the survivors in kowtowing before the mound and discharging several obligatory but feeble wails. Mother urged the family members of the victims to kowtow to Sima Ting and his funeral detail to show their gratitude. "There's no need for that," Sima said.

The members of the funeral detail walked toward the sunset on their way home. Mother and my sisters were well behind the ragged column of people, which stretched for at least a quarter of a mile, with Pastor Malory bringing up the rear on unsteady legs. Thick human shadows lay across the fields of wheat. Under the sun's blood-red rays, the seemingly endless expanse of quiet was broken by the tramping of feet, the whistling of the wind past the stalks of wheat, the hoarse sounds of my crying, and the first drawn-out mournful hoot of a fat owl as it woke from a day's sleep in the canopy of a mulberry tree in the cemetery. It had a heart-stopping effect on everyone who heard it. Mother stopped to look back at the cemetery, where purple mist rose from the ground. Pastor Malory bent down to pick up my seventh sister, Qiudi. "You poor things," he said.

His words hung in the air when a chorus of millions of chirping insects rose all around him.

2

It was on the morning of the Mid-Autumn Festival, a hundred days after my sister and I were born, when Mother took us to see Pastor Malory. The church gate facing the street was tightly shut and marred by blasphemous, antireligious graffiti. We took the path to the rear of the church, where our raps on the door echoed in the wilderness. The emaciated goat was tied to a stake beside the door. She had such a long face that she looked more like a donkey or a camel or an old woman than a goat. She raised her head to look gloomily at Mother, who clipped her on the chin with the toe of her shoe. After a lingering complaint, she lowered her head to continue grazing. A rumbling noise was accompanied by the sound of Pastor Malory's coughs. Mother rang the bell. "Who is it?" Pastor Malory asked. "Me," Mother replied softly. The squeaky door opened a crack, and Mother slipped inside with us in her arms. Pastor Malory shut the door behind her, then turned, reached out and embraced us with his long arms. "My adorable little ones, the fruit of my loins . . ."

Sha Yueliang and his newly formed band of men, the Black Donkey Musket Band, walked spiritedly up the road we'd just taken on the funeral procession, heading straight for our village. On one side of the road, sorghum grew tall amid the wheat; reeds stretched to the edge of the Black Water River on the other side. A sun-drenched summer, with plenty of sweet rain, had made it a wildly fruitful growing season. The leaves were fat and the stalks thick, even before there were silks atop the head-high sorghum; river reeds were lush and black, the stems and leaves covered by white fuzz. Even though it was already mid-autumn, there wasn't a hint of autumn in the air. And yet, the sky was the rich blue of autumn, the sun autumnally beautiful.

Sha Yueliang had a band of twenty-eight men, all riding identical black donkeys from the hilly south country of Wulian County. With their thick, muscular bodies and stumpy legs, the donkeys were easily outrun by horses; but they had amazing stamina and could be ridden for long distances. Sha had selected these twenty-eight donkeys from over eight hundred: not gelded, blessed with loud, strident voices, young, black, and energetic. Those were their mounts. The twenty-eight animals formed a black line, like a flowing stream. A milky white mist floated about the road; sunbeams were reflected off the donkeys' backs. When he spotted the battered clock tower and watchtower, Sha reined in his lead donkey. The ones behind kept coming stubbornly. Looking back into the faces of his band, he told the men to dismount, then ordered them to wash up and clean their donkeys. A look of sobriety and seriousness adorned his dark, gaunt face as he dressed down his band of men, who lazed around after dismounting. He had elevated washing up and cleaning mounts to glorious heights. He told his men that the anti-Japanese guerrillas were popping up everywhere, like mushrooms, and that the Black Donkey Musket Band was going to take its place ahead of all others, owing to its unique style, until it became the sole occupying force of Northeast Gaomi Township. In order to impress the villagers, they needed to carefully watch what they said and did. Under his mobilization, the band's morale surged; after taking off their shirts and spreading them on the ground, they stood in the shallows of the river and sent water spraying as they washed up. Their newly shaved heads glinted in the sunlight. Sha Yueliang took a bar of soap from his knapsack and cut it into strips, which he handed out to his men, telling them to wash every speck of dust off their bodies. Joining them in the river, he bent down until his scarred shoulder nearly touched the water, so he could scrub his dirty neck. While their riders were washing up, the donkeys grazed among the leafy water reeds or chewed the leaves of sorghum stalks or nibbled at one another's rumps; some just stood there deep in thought or slipped the meaty clubs out of their sheaths and beat them against their bellies. As the donkeys busied themselves with whatever pleased them, Mother struggled free of Pastor Malory's embrace. "You're crushing the babies, you foolish donkey!"

Pastor Malory smiled apologetically, revealing two neat rows of white teeth; he reached out to us with one of his big red hands, paused for a second, then reached out with the other. Grabbing hold of one of his fingers, I began to gurgle. But Eighth Sister lay there like a log, neither crying nor squirming nor making any noise at all. She had been born blind. Cradling me in one arm, Mother said, "Look at him, he's laughing." She then deposited me into those big, sweaty waiting hands. He put his head down next to mine, so close I could see every strand of red hair on his head, the brown whiskers on his chin, his hawkish nose, and the benevolent gleam in his eyes. Suddenly I felt sharp pains up and down my back; taking my thumb out of my mouth, I let out a howl and a gusher of tears as the pain seemed to penetrate the marrow of my bones. I felt his whiskery lips on my forehead — they seemed to be trembling — and got a powerful whiff of his goat's milk and oniony breath.

He handed me back to Mother. "I frightened him," he said sheepishly.

Mother handed Eighth Sister to Pastor Malory after taking me from him. She patted and rocked me. "Don't cry," she purred. "Do you know who he is? Are you afraid of him? Don't be, he's a good man, your very own . . . very own godfather . . ."

The pains in my back continued, and I cried myself hoarse. So Mother pulled open her blouse and stuck a nipple into my mouth. I seized it like a drowning man clutching at a straw and sucked desperately. Her milk had a grassy taste as it poured down my throat. But the shooting pains in my back forced me to let go so I could cry some more. Wringing his hands anxiously, Pastor Malory ran over to the base of the wall, where he pulled up a tasseled weed and flicked it back and forth in front of me to stop me from crying. It didn't work. So he ran back and pulled up a sunflower, as big as the moon and ringed with golden petals, then brought it over to wave in the air for me. I was drawn to the flower's smell. All during Pastor Malory's frantic running back and forth, Eighth Sister slept peacefully in his arms. "Look at that, darling," Mother said. "Your godfather plucked the moon out of the sky for you." I reached out for the moon, but was stopped short by more shooting pains. "What's wrong with him?" Mother asked, her lips pale, her face bathed in sweat. Pastor Malory said, "Maybe something's pricking him."

With Pastor Malory's help, Mother took off the red outfit she'd made for me in celebration of my hundredth day in this world, and discovered a needle caught in one of the folds. It had drawn dozens of bloody pinpricks on my back. She flung it over the wall. "My poor baby," she said tearfully, "it's all my fault! My fault!" She slapped herself, hard. Then a second time. Two crisp smacks. Pastor Malory grabbed her hand, then walked behind her and put his arms around both of us. He kissed Mother on her cheeks, her ears, and her hair with his moist lips. "It's not your fault," he said. "It's mine. Blame me." His tenderness had a calming effect on Mother, who sat in the doorway and stuffed the nipple back into my mouth. Her sweet milk moistened my throat, as the pain in my back gradually disappeared. With my lips around a nipple and my hands cupping one breast, I kneaded and protected the other one with my foot. Mother pushed my foot away, but as soon as she let go, it sprang right back up there.

"I checked the clothes when I put them on him," she said uncertainly, "so where did that needle come from? The old witch must have put it there! She hates all the females in this family!"

"Does she know? About us, I mean," Pastor Malory asked.

"I told her," Mother said. "She kept pressuring me, until I could no longer take her abuse. She is an outrageous old witch."

Pastor Malory handed Eighth Sister back to mother. "Feed her," he said. "They are both gifts from God, and you should not play favorites."

Mother's face colored as she took the baby from him. But when she tried to give her the nipple, I kicked my sister in the belly. She started bawling.

"Did you see that?" Mother said. "What a little tyrant! Go get her some goat's milk."

After Pastor Malory had fed Eighth Sister, he laid her down on the *kang*. She didn't cry and she didn't squirm. He then studied the downy fuzz on my head. Mother noticed his quizzical look. "What are you looking at? Do we look like strangers to you?" "No," he said with a shake of his head, a foolish smile on his face. "The little wretch suckles like a wolf." "Like someone else I know." Mother replied mischievously. He smiled even more foolishly. "You don't mean me, do you? What sort of child was I?" His eyes grew clouded as he thought back to his youth, which he'd spent in a place spent many thousands of miles away. Two teardrops fell from those eyes. "What's wrong?" Mother asked. He tried to hide his embarrassment with a dry laugh as he wiped his eyes with thickly knuckled fingers. "It's nothing," he said. "I've been in China . . . how long now?" A note of displeasure crept into Mother's voice: "I can't remember a time when you weren't here. You're a local, just like me." "No," he said, "I have roots in another country. I was sent by the archbishop as one of God's messengers, and I once owned a document to prove it." Mother laughed. "Old man," she said, "my uncle says you're a fake foreign devil, and that your so-called document was a forgery from an artisan in Pingdu County." "Nonsense!" Pastor Malory jerked upright, as if deeply offended. "That Big Paw Yu is a stupid ass!" "Don't talk like that about my uncle," Mother said unhappily. "I'll forever be in his debt." "If he weren't your uncle," Pastor Malory said, "I'd relieve him of his manhood." Mother laughed. "He can fell a mule with his fist." "If you won't believe I'm Swedish," he said dejectedly, "then no one will." He took out his pipe, filled it with tobacco, and began smoking silently. Mother sighed. "Isn't it enough that I admit you're an authentic foreigner? Why be angry with me? Have you ever seen a Chinese as hairy as you?" A childlike smile appeared on Pastor Malory's face. "I'll return to my home someday," he said. Then, after a thoughtful pause, he added, "But if I really had the opportunity to do it, maybe I wouldn't go. Not unless you came with me." "You'll never leave here," she said, "and neither will I. So why not make the best of it? Besides, don't you always say that it doesn't make any difference what color hair a person has — blond, black, or red — that we're all God's lambs? And that all any lamb needs is a green pasture. Isn't a pasture the size of Northeast Gaomi enough for you?" "It's enough," Pastor Malory replied emotionally. "Why would I go anywhere else when you, my grass of miracles, are right here?"

Seeing that Mother and Pastor Malory were otherwise occupied, the donkey at the millstone began nibbling the flour on the stone.

Pastor Malory walked up and gave it a loud smack, sending it quickly and noisily back to work. "The babies are asleep," Mother said, "so I'll help you sift the flour. Go get a straw mat, and I'll spread it out in the shade." Pastor Malory brought a mat over and spread it under a parasol tree; yet even as Mother was laying me on the cool mat, my mouth was clamped defiantly around her nipple. "This child is like a bottomless pit," she said. "He'll suck the marrow right out of my bones before I know it."

Pastor Malory kept the donkey moving: the donkey turned the millstone, the millstone crushed the kernels of wheat, which turned to coarse powder and fanned out atop the stone. As she sat beneath the parasol tree, Mother put a willow basket on the mat and fixed the rack atop it. She then poured the coarse powder into her sieve and began shaking it back and forth rhythmically at an even pace; the snow white flour floated down into the basket, leaving the broken husks behind at the bottom of the sieve. Bright sunlight filtered through the leafy cover and fell on her face and shoulders. An air of domesticity hung over the courtyard, as Pastor Malory followed the donkey round and round the millstone to keep it from slacking off. It was our donkey; Pastor Malory had borrowed it that morning to help mill the wheat. The sweat on its back darkened its hide as it trotted to avoid the sting of the switch. The bleat of a goat beyond the wall heralded the arrival at the gate of the mule that had entered the world the same day I had. The donkey kicked out with its rear hooves. "Let the mule in," Mother said, "and hurry." Malory ran over to the gate and shoved the young animal's lovely head backward to put some slack in the tethering chain. He then unhooked it from the post and jumped back as the mule burst through the gate, ran up to its mother, and grabbed a nipple in its mouth. That calmed the donkey. "Humans and animals are so much alike," Mother said with a sigh. Malory nodded in agreement.

While our donkey was nursing its bastard offspring around the open-air millstone in Malory's compound, Sha Yueliang and his band of men were scrubbing their mounts. After brushing the mane and sparse hair of their tails, they dried the donkeys' hides with fine cotton cloths and waxed them. The twenty-eight donkeys emerged from the grooming like new animals; twenty-eight riders stood proud and energetic and twenty-eight muskets shone brightly. Each man had two gourds tied to his belt, one large and one small. The larger one held gunpowder, the smaller one held birdshot. Each gourd had been treated with three coats of tung oil. All fifty-six polished gourds glinted in the sunlight. The men wore khaki trousers and black jackets, their heads covered by coolie hats woven from sorghum stalks. As squad leader, Sha Yueliang wore a red tassel in his hat. With a satisfied look at his men and their mounts, he said, "Stand tall, brothers. We'll show those people what a band of men with shiny black donkeys and muskets is made of." He mounted his donkey, smacked it on the rump, and rode off. Now, horses may be swift, but donkeys are model parade animals; men on horses ride with an air of majesty, while men on donkeys ride with a sense of fulfillment. Before long, the squad appeared on the streets of Dalan. After being pounded by a summer of rain, the streets were hard and sleek, unlike the harvest season, when they would be so dry and dusty that a galloping horse would raise a cloud of dust. Sha's band of men left a trail of white hoofprints and, of course, the clopping sounds that formed them. Sha's donkeys were all shod, just like horses. A stroke of genius, thanks to Sha. The crisp clatter first attracted neighborhood children, then Yao Si, the township's bookkeeper, who came out in a Mandarin robe that belonged to an earlier age, a pencil tucked behind his ear, and planted himself in front of Sha Yueliang's donkey. Bowing deeply and smiling broadly, he asked, "What troops do you command? Will you take up residence here or are you just passing through? I am at your service."

Sha leaped down off his donkey and replied, "We're the Black Donkey Musket Band, an anti-Japanese commando unit. We have been ordered to set up a resistance in Dalan. For that we need quarters, feed for our mounts, and a kitchen. Simple food, like eggs and flatbread, will do just fine for us. But our donkeys are resistance troop mounts, and must be fed well. The hay must be fine and free of impurities, the fodder made of crumbled bean cakes and well water. Not a drop of muddy water from the Flood Dragon River."

"Sir," Yao Si said, "duties of this magnitude cannot be entrusted to the likes of me. I must seek instructions from the venerable township head, who has recently been appointed head of the Peace Preservation Corps by the Imperial Army."

"That cocksucker!" Sha Yueliang cursed darkly. "Anyone who serves the Japanese is a traitorous dog!"

"Sir," Yao Si explained, "he did not accept the assignment willingly. As the owner of vast acres of land and many draft animals, he wants for nothing. The duty was forced upon him. Besides, someone has to do it, and who better than our steward. . . ."

"Take me to him!" Sha demanded. His men dismounted to rest at the township office while Yao Si escorted Sha to the gate of the township head's residence, a compound with seven rows of fifteen rooms, each with a connecting garden and separate gate, one leading to the next like a maze. Sha Yueliang's first sight of Sima Ting was in the midst of an argument with Sima Ku, who was lying in bed nursing wounds sustained in a fire on the fifth day of the fifth month. He had burned down a bridge, but instead of immolating the Japanese, had managed only to burn the skin off his own backside. Taking far too long to heal, his injuries were now compounded by bedsores, which forced him to lie on his belly with his backside elevated.

"Elder brother," Sima Ku said as he propped himself up on his elbows and raised his head high, "you bastard, you stupid bastard." His eyes were blazing. "The head of the Peace Preservation Corps is a running dog of the Japanese, a donkey belonging to the guerrilla forces, a rat hiding in a bellows, a person hated by both sides. Why did you accept the job?"

"That's shit! What you're saying is pure shit!" Sima Ting defended himself. "Only a damned idiot would take on the job willingly. The Japanese stuck a bayonet up against my belly. Through Ma Jinlong, the interpreter, their commander said, 'Your younger brother Sima Ku joined the bandit Sha Yueliang to burn a bridge and launch an ambush. They inflicted heavy casualties on the Imperial Army. At first we planned to burn down your residence, Felicity Manor, but since you seem like a reasonable man, we have spared you.' So you are one of the reasons I am the new head of the Peace Preservation Corps."

Sima Ku, having lost the argument, cursed angrily, "This goddamned ass of mine, I wonder if it will ever heal."

"I'd be happy if it never healed," Sima Ting said heatedly. "You'll give me a lot less trouble that way." Turning to leave, he spotted a smiling Sha Yueliang standing at the door. Yao Si stepped forward, but before he could make the introductions, Sha announced, "Corps Head Sima, I am Sha Yueliang."

Sima Ku rolled over in bed before his brother could react. "I'll be damned, so you're Sha Yueliang, nicknamed Sha the Monk."

"At present I am the commander of the Black Donkey Musket Band," Sha replied. "My thanks to the Sima brothers for setting the bridge on fire. You and I, hand in glove."

"So you're still alive, are you? What sort of birdshit battles are you fighting these days?"

"Ambushes!" Sha said.

"Ambushes, is it? If not for me and my torch, you'd have been trampled into the mud!" Sima Ku said.

"I have a salve for treating burns," Sha said with a broad smile. "I'll have one of my men bring it over."

"Lay out some food," Sima Ting instructed Yao Si, "to welcome Commander Sha."

Yao Si replied timidly, "All our money went to set up the Peace Preservation Corps."

"How stupid can you be?" Sima Ting said. "The Imperial Army doesn't serve our family alone, it serves eight hundred households. And the musket band was raised not for our family, but for all the citizens of the township. Get every family to contribute some food and money, since these men are the people's guests. We'll supply the wine and liquor."

"Corps Head Sima serves two masters well, and gains equally from both."

"What can I do?" Sima Ting pleaded. "As old Pastor Malory said, 'Who will go to Hell, if not me?'"

Pastor Malory took the lid of his pot and dumped noodles made of the new flour into the boiling water, then stirred them with chopsticks before replacing the lid. "The fire needs to be a little hotter," he shouted to Mother, who nodded and stuffed more golden, fragrant wheat stalks into the belly of the stove. Without letting go of the nipple, I looked down at the flames licking out of the stove and listened to the stalks crackle and pop as I thought back to what had just happened: They had laid me in the basket — on my back at first, although I quickly rolled over onto my belly, so I could watch Mother roll the noodles. As her body moved up and down, those two full gourds on her chest bounced around, summoning me, passing me a secret sign. Sometimes they threw the two datelike heads together, as if kissing or whispering to one another. But most of the time they were bouncing up and down, bouncing and calling out, like a pair of happy white doves. I reached out to touch them, saliva oozing from my mouth. Then, all of a sudden, they turned bashful and edgy, as a blush fell over their faces and delicate pearls of sweat streamed down the valley between them. I saw a pair of blue lights dancing on them; they were spots of light from Pastor Malory's eyes. Then two hands with blond hair reached out from the blue eyes to take my food from me, sending yellow flames leaping from my heart. I opened my mouth to cry, but that only made things worse. The tiny hands retreated back into Malory's eyes, but the big hands attached to his arms reached out to Mother's chest. He stood tall and massive behind her; those ugly hands reached around and covered the two white doves. He stroked their feathers with his coarse fingers, then pinched and scissored their heads. My poor gourds! My precious doves! They struggled to free their wings, then tucked them close to their bodies, close and tight, until they were as small as they were ever going to get, before pumping themselves up and spreading their wings, as if wanting desperately to fly away, all the way to the far ends of the wilderness, to the edge of the sky, floating gently up to be with the clouds, bathed by the winds and stroked by the sun, then to moan with the wind and sing with the sun, and finally to sink silently earthward and disappear into the depths of a lake. Loud wails burst from my throat; a river of tears clouded my eyes. Mother and Malory's bodies writhed in unison, Mother moaned softly. "Let me go, you donkey. The baby's crying." "The little bastard," Malory said resentfully.

Mother picked me up and rocked me nervously. "Precious," she said sheepishly, "my son, what have I done to my own flesh and blood?" She stuck the white doves up under my nose, and I urgently, cruelly grabbed one of their heads with my lips. Big as my mouth was, I wished it were bigger still. It was like the mouth of a snake, and all I could think of was how to wrap it around my very own dove to keep it away from others. "Slow down, my baby." Mother gently patted my bottom. I had one of them in my mouth and was grasping the other in my hands. It was a little red-eyed white rabbit, and when I pinched its ear, I felt its frantic heartbeat. "The little bastard," Malory said with a sigh.

"Stop calling him a little bastard," Mother said.

"That's what he is," Malory said.

"I'd like you to baptize him, then give him a name. This is his hundredth day."

As he prepared the dough with a practiced hand, Malory said, "Baptize him? I've forgotten how. I'm making you noodles the way I learned from that Muslim woman."

"How close were you two?" Mother asked him.

"We were just friends."

"I don't believe you!" Mother said.

Malory laughed hoarsely as he stretched and pulled the soft dough, then smacked it down on the chopping board. "Tell me!" Mother insisted. He smacked the dough again, then stretched and pulled it some more. Some of the time he pulled it like a bowstring and some of the time it looked as if he were pulling a snake out of its hole. Even Mother was surprised that a Westerner with such coarse hands could manage this Chinese action with such practiced dexterity. "Maybe," he said, "I'm not Swedish after all, and my so-called past has been nothing but a dream. What do you think?" Mother smiled coldly. "I asked about you and that dark-eyed woman. Don't change the subject." Pastor Malory laid the dough out straight, as if this were all a childish game, then began waving it in and out, taut one moment and slack the next. The strawlike dough began to spiral and form a bundle; then, with a flick of his wrists, it fanned out like a horse's tail. Mother praised his display of skill: "It takes a good woman to make noodles like that." "All right," Malory said, "young mother, stop those crazy thoughts. Once you get the fire going, I'll cook these for you." "And after we're finished eating?" "After we're finished, I'll baptize the little bastard and give him a name."

With a feigned show of anger, Mother said, "The real bastards are the sons you had with that Muslim woman."

Mother's words hung in the air as, in another place, Sha Yueliang and Sima Ting made a toast. They had reached the following agreement during the banquet: The donkeys belonging to the musket band would be stabled at the church; the men would be quartered with local families; and Sha Yueliang would personally choose a headquarters site after the meal.

Sha and four bodyguards followed Yao Si into our compound. My eldest sister, Laidi, caught his eye immediately as she stood beside the water vat casually combing her hair and gazing at her reflection in the water, white clouds in the blue sky as her backdrop. Having just passed through a peaceful summer with plenty to eat and nice clothes to wear, she had matured dramatically. Her breasts jutted out proudly, her once dry, brittle hair now had a dark sheen, her waist had narrowed and become soft and springy, and her buttocks curved upwards. In a hundred days she had shed the skin of a scrawny adolescent and been transformed into a lovely young woman, like a butterfly emerging from a cocoon. She had Mother's high, fair nose, as well as her full breasts and lively buttocks. Rays of melancholy issued from the eyes of the lovely yet bashful young virgin as she gazed into the water vat and stroked her silken locks with a wooden comb, her graceful reflection displaying myriad melancholies. Sha Yueliang was shaken to the depths of his soul. "This will be the headquarters of the Black Donkey Musket Band," he said decisively to Yao Si. "Shangguan Laidi," Yao Si called out, "where's your mother?" Sha dismissed Yao with a wave of his hand before the girl could answer. He walked up to the water vat and looked long and hard at Laidi. She returned the look. "Remember me, girl?" he asked. She nodded, her cheeks reddening.

My sister then turned and ran into the house. After the fifth day of the fifth month, my seven sisters had moved into the room once occupied by Shangguan Lü and Shangguan Fulu. Their former room was now being used to store three thousand catties of millet. Sha Yueliang followed Laidi into the house, where he saw the other six girls asleep on the *kang*. With a friendly smile, he said, "Don't be afraid, we're anti-Japanese fighters who bring no harm to the local populace. You have seen how we fight. That was a heroic battle, heroic and tragic, fiercely fought, the glory of the ages, and the day will come when people act out our exploits and sing our praises." Eldest Sister lowered her head and twisted the tip of her braid as she recalled the uncommon events of the fifth day of the fifth month, how the man standing in front of her now had peeled away, strip by strip, the tattered remnants of his uniform. "Little girl — no, young mistress, we are linked by fate!" he announced before walking back outside. My sister followed him as far as the doorway and watched him first enter the side room to the east, then the room to the west. In the west room he was startled by the green light in the eyes of Shangguan Lü. Holding his nose, he quickly backed out of the room and gave an order to his troops: "Make some room by stacking the grain and find me a place to sleep." My sister leaned up against the doorframe as she observed this skinny, stooped, dark-skinned man who looked like a scholar tree that had been struck by lightning. "Where is your father?" he asked her. Yao Si, who was lying low next to the wall, replied solicitously, "Her father was killed on the fifth day of the fifth month by the Jap devils — no, I mean the Imperial Army. Her grandfather, Shangguan Fulu, died the same day."

"Imperial Army, did you say? Japs! Little Jap devils!" Sha

Yueliang roared, stomping his foot to express his loathing. "Young mistress," he said, "your debt of vengeance, deep as a sea of blood, is our debt, and we will exact it one day, that I promise you. Who is the head of your family now?"

"Shangguan Lu," Yao Si answered for her.

Meanwhile, Eighth Sister and I were being baptized.

The door of Pastor Malory's residence opened directly onto the church, where faded oil paintings hung on the wall. Most were of naked winged infants, plump as fat yams. It wasn't until later that I learned they were called angels. At the far end stood a brick pulpit, a carving from a heavy piece of jujube of a bare-chested man hanging in front. Owing either to the poor skills of the carver or to the hardness of the wood, the hanging man didn't look much like a man at all. I later learned that it was our Lord Jesus, an amazing hero, a true saint. A dozen or so dusty pews, replete with bird droppings, were scattered here and there in front of the pulpit. Mother walked in with me in one arm and Eighth Sister in the other, startling the resident sparrows, which flew off and banged into the windows. The church's front door opened onto the street. Through the cracks in the door, Mother could see a number of black donkeys shuttling back and forth outside.

Pastor Malory was holding a large wooden basin half filled with hot water in which a loofah floated. Steam rose from the basin, through which his slitted eyes showed. Bent over by the weight of the basin, he walked unsteadily, his neck thrust out. When he stumbled, water splashed into his face. But he regained his balance and shuffled on, until he was able to place the baptismal basin on the pulpit.

Mother walked up and handed us to him. He placed me in the basin, my feet curling inward the moment they touched the hot water. My tearful cries reverberated in the dreary emptiness of the church. Baby swallows in a white nest in the rafters craned their necks over the edge to watch me with their black, beady eyes; just then their parents flew in through one of the broken windows with worms in their broad beaks. After handing me back to Mother, Malory knelt and stirred the water with one of his large hands. The jujube Lord Jesus observed us warmly from where he hung. The angels on the walls were chasing the sparrows from the beams to the crossbeams, from the eastern wall to the western wall, from the spiral wooden staircase up to the rickety bell tower, and from the bell tower back down to the walls, where they

rested. Crystalline beads of sweat oozed from their glistening buttocks. The water swirled in the basin, creating a little eddy in the center. Malory tested the water with his hand. "Okay," he said, "it has
cooled down. Put him in."

They had taken off my clothes; Mother's plentiful, nutritious
milk had made me fat and fair-skinned. If I'd changed my look of sadness into one of anger or I'd worn a solemn smile, and if I'd had a pair
of wings on my back, I'd have been an angel, and those fat little infants
on the walls would have been my brothers. I stopped crying as soon as
Mother laid me in the basin, because the water was so comfortably
warm. I sat up and played in the water, shrieking happily as it splashed
all over the place. Malory fished his bronze crucifix out of the water
and pressed it down on my head. "From this moment on," he said,
"you are one of God's beloved sons. Hallelujah!" Then he picked up
the water-laden loofah and squeezed it over my head. "Hallelujah!"
Mother parroted Malory: "Hallelujah!" she said, and I laughed joyfully as the holy water bathed my head.

Mother was beaming as she laid Eighth Sister in the basin with
me, then picked up the loofah and gently washed us both as Pastor
Malory ladled water over our heads. I shrieked happily with each ladleful, while Eighth Sister sobbed hoarsely. I kept grabbing my dark,
scrawny twin.

"They don't have names yet," Mother said. "That's your job."

Pastor Malory put down his ladle. "This is nothing to be taken
lightly. I need time to think."

"My mother-in-law said that if I have a boy I should call him
Little Dog Shangguan," Mother said. "He would grow up better with
a humble name."

Pastor Malory shook his head vigorously. "No, that's no good.
Names like dog or cat are an affront to God. They also go against the
teachings of Confucius, who said, 'Without proper names, language
cannot speak the truth.'"

"I have one," Mother said. "See what you think. We can call him
Shangguan Amen."

Malory laughed. "That is even worse. Stop trying, and let me
think."

Pastor Malory stood up, clasped his hands behind his back, and began pacing feverishly in the rank atmosphere of the run-down church.

His quick steps were the outward manifestation of the churning in his head, through which all manner of names and symbols — ancient and modern, Chinese and Western, heavenly and mundane — flowed. As she observed his pacing, Mother smiled and said to me, "Look at your godfather. That's no way to think up a name. He looks like he's about to declare a death." Humming to herself, Mother picked up Malory's ladle, scooped up some water, and poured it over our heads.

"I've got it!" he announced loudly as he stopped in his twenty-ninth trip to the closed front door of the church. "What will it be?" Mother asked excitedly. But before he could tell her, there was a clamor at the door. The noise of a crowd erupted, making the door rattle. Someone out there was shouting and carrying on. Mother stood up, seized with terror, the ladle still in her hand. Malory put his eye up to the crack in the door. At the time we didn't know what was happening, but we saw his face redden, either from anger or nervousness, we didn't know which. He turned to Mother. "Leave, quickly. To the courtyard out front."

Mother bent down to pick me up. She first threw away the ladle, of course, which bounced around noisily on the floor, like a bullfrog in mating season. Left behind in the basin, Eighth Sister began to bawl. The bolt snapped in two and clattered to the floor as the double doors burst open, and a shaven-headed young man holding a musket exploded into the church. He butted Malory in the chest, sending him reeling back all the way to the rear wall. A bare-bottomed angel was suspended above his head. When the door bolt clattered to the floor, I tumbled out of Mother's arms and thudded back into the basin, sending a spray of water skyward and nearly crushing the life out of Eighth Sister.

Altogether five musket soldiers swarmed in, but their brutal arrogance dissolved as they took in the sights of the church. The one who had nearly butted Pastor Malory into the next world scratched his head. "There are people here. Why is that?" He glanced at his four comrades. "Didn't they say the church had been abandoned years ago? How come there are people here?"

Covering his chest with his hands, Malory walked up to the soldiers, who were frightened and embarrassed by his dignified appearance. If he had spewed forth a string of foreign words and made a flurry of hand gestures, the soldiers might well have turned on their heels and run out of the church. Even speaking Chinese with a heavy foreign accent would have stopped them from turning violent. But the unfortunate Pastor Malory spoke to them in perfect Northeast Gaomi Chinese: "What do you want, my brothers?" He bowed deeply to them.

As I lay there crying — Eighth Sister had stopped crying by then — the soldiers burst out laughing. Sizing up Pastor Malory as if he were a performing monkey, a soldier with a crooked mouth reached out and tickled the hairs in Malory's ear with his finger.

"A monkey, ha ha, he's a monkey." His comrades joined in: "Look, this monkey's even hiding a woman in here!"

"I object!" Malory shouted. "I object! I am a foreigner!"

"A foreigner, did you all hear that?" the crooked-mouthed soldier said. "Are you telling me a foreigner can speak perfect Northeast Gaomi Chinese? I think you're the bastard offspring of a monkey and a human. Bring in one of the donkeys, men."

Holding Eighth Sister and me in her arms, Mother came up and grabbed Malory's arm. "Let's go, we don't want to anger them."

Malory pulled his arm free and ran up to push the donkey back out of the church. The animal bared its teeth, like an angry dog, and brayed loudly.

"Back off!" one of the soldiers demanded as he pushed Malory out of the way.

"The church is a holy place, belonging to God. You can't stable a donkey in here," Pastor Malory said defiantly.

"You phony foreign devil!" cursed one of the soldiers, a man with a pale face and purple lips. "My old mother told me that that man," he said as he pointed to the jujube Jesus hanging up front, "was born in a horse stable. Donkeys are cousins to horses, so if your god owes a debt to horses, he also owes one to donkeys. If a horse stable can serve as a delivery room, then why can't a church serve as a donkey's pen?"

The soldier, obviously pleased with his powers of logic, stared at Malory with a smug grin.

Malory made the sign of the cross and began to weep. "Punish these evil men, Lord. Strike them down with lightning, let them be bitten by poisonous vipers, let them perish at the hands of the Japanese . . ."

"Traitorous dog!" the crooked-mouthed soldier snarled, giving Malory a resounding slap. Intending to slap him in the mouth, he was slightly off target, hitting his hooked nose instead, and releasing a gush of fresh blood. With a painful cry, Malory raised his hands toward the jujube Jesus. "Lord," he intoned, "almighty God . . ."

The soldiers looked first at the jujube Jesus, which was covered with dust and bird droppings, then at the bloodied face of Pastor Malory. Finally, they let their eyes roam over Mother's body, which was covered with slimy marks that looked like the trails of snails. The soldier who knew about Jesus' birthplace stuck out his tongue, like a footed clam, and licked his purplish lips. By then, twenty-eight black donkeys had been crowded into the church. Some moved around aimlessly, others scratched their backs on the walls or relieved themselves or misbehaved themselves, and some nibbled at the clay walls. "Lord!" Malory implored. But his Lord was unmoved.

In their anger they ripped Eighth Sister and me out of Mother's arms and tossed us among the donkeys. Mother ran to us like a she-wolf, but was stopped by the soldiers before she reached us. That is when they began fooling around with Mother, starting with crooked mouth, who reached out and grabbed one of her breasts. Purple lips crowded up and pushed crooked mouth out of the way to wrap his hands around my doves, my precious gourds. With a loud screech, Mother clawed his face; unfazed and grinning his evil grin, he ripped off her clothes.

What happened after that will remain my secret anguish for the rest of my life. Out in the yard, Sha Yueliang was cozying up to my eldest sister, while in the eastern side room, Gou San and his pack of mongrels spread out a bunch of straw in a corner for beds; all five of the musket soldiers — the team assigned to watch the donkeys — threw Mother down on top of it. On the floor among the donkeys, Eighth Sister and I had by then cried ourselves hoarse. Malory jumped up, grabbed one of the broken halves of the door bolt, and brought it down on a soldier's head. One of his comrades aimed at Malory's legs and fired. An explosion tore through the room as a swarm of buckshot thudded into Malory's legs, spraying pearls of blood into the air. The broken bolt fell from his hands and he slumped to the floor; he looked up at the bird-splattered jujube Jesus and began to murmur something in his long-forgotten Swedish tongue, the words fluttering from his mouth like butterflies. The soldiers took turns ravaging Mother; the donkeys took turns sniffing Eighth Sister and me. Their loud brays crashed through the ceiling of the church and flew up into the bleak sky. Sweat beaded the face of the jujube Jesus. Satisfied, the soldiers tossed Mother, Eighth Sister, and me out into the street; the donkeys followed us outside, but ran off following the scent of female donkeys.

While the soldiers were trying to run down their mounts, Pastor Malory dragged his buckshot-honeycombed legs up the familiar, foot-worn
stairs to the bell tower. He managed to prop himself up by holding on
to the windowsill so he could gaze out through the broken stained
glass and see the panorama of Dalan, the municipal seat of Northeast
Gaomi, where he had lived and left his mark for decades: neat rows of
thatch-roofed cottages; wide, gray-colored lanes; misty green treetops;
shimmering rivers and streams circling tiny villages; the mirrorlike surface of the lake; the swaying thickets of reeds; pools of water rimmed
by wild grasses; the red marsh that was a playground for passing birds;
an expanse of open country that scrolled all the way to the edge of
heaven; the golden yellow Reclining Ox mountain range; the sandy
hills, with their flowering locusts . . . as his gaze traveled down to the
street, where Mother lay like a dead fish, her naked belly exposed to
the sky, deep sorrow filled his heart and tears clouded his eyes. Dip-
ping his finger in the blood oozing from his legs, he wrote four words
on the gray wall of the bell tower:

Golden Boy Jade Girl.

Then he shouted at the top of his lungs, "Forgive me, dear Lord!"

Pastor Malory flung himself off the bell tower and plummeted
like a gigantic bird with broken wings, splattering his brains like so
much bird shit when he hit the street below.

3

Winter was approaching, and Mother began wearing her mother-in-
law's blue satin–lined jacket. Four old village women, who were blessed
with many sons and grandsons, had come over on Grandmother's sixti-
eth birthday to sew this jacket, which she would one day wear in her
coffin. But now it was Mother's winter jacket. Mother cut two holes in
the top, so she could free her breasts anytime I was hungry. They had
been ravaged during that infuriating autumn, when Pastor Malory
leaped to his death, but the calamity would pass, and her fine breasts
would prove to be indestructible. They were like people who are forever young or evergreen pines. To keep them from prying eyes and,
more importantly, to protect them from the chill winds and keep their
milk warm, Mother sewed red flaps over the holes. Her inventiveness
started a tradition; flapped lined jackets are still worn in Dalan to this

day, although the holes now are rounder, the flaps made of softer material, and they are embroidered with bright flowers.

My winter clothing was a thick pouch fashioned from durable canvas and lined with a drawstring at the top and two straps from which it hung just beneath Mother's bosom. When it was feeding time, she would suck in her belly and shift the pouch until I was perfectly positioned: cradled in a kneeling position, my head nestled up against her breasts. Then, by turning my head to the right, I could put my mouth around her left nipple; by turning it to the left, I could nurse from her right nipple. It was a double-sided advantage worthy of the name. But my pouch wasn't perfect, for it bound up my hands, and made it impossible to hold one breast while I was nursing at the other, as I had done in the past. By then I had completely stripped Eighth Sister of her right to nurse, and anytime she came near one of Mother's breasts, I clawed and kicked until the poor blind thing cried her eyes out. She survived on a thin gruel, and this made my other sisters very unhappy.

My nursing process over the long winter months was shrouded in anxiety, for when my lips were wrapped around the left nipple, all I could think about was the right one. I felt as if a hairy hand would suddenly reach into the cavernous opening and take the temporarily idle breast away with it. Falling under the control of that feeling, I'd quickly switch nipples, leaving the left one, from which milk had just begun to flow, for the right one; but I'd no sooner begun to suck there than I'd switch back to the left. Mother would give me a puzzled look, seeing how I would suck from the left but never take my greedy eyes off the right, and quickly guessing what I was up to. Showering my face with kisses from her chilled lips, she would say softly, Jintong, Golden Boy, my little treasure, all Mama's milk belongs to you, and no one can take it away from you. Her words lessened my anxiety, but didn't drive it away altogether, for I could sense those hairy hands all around her, just waiting for an opening.

One morning, as a light snow fell, Mother put on her nursing blouse and strapped me onto her back, where I was kept warm in the cotton wrap. She told my sisters to move the red-skinned turnips into the cellar. Not knowing, or caring, where those turnips had come from, what attracted me to them was their shape: pointy tips that swelled out to the base made me hungry for the tit. And so, large red turnips were added to oily gourds, with their shiny skins, and sleek, white little doves. Each had its unique color, its aura, and its degree of warmth, and each was like a woman's breast in one way or another. They came to symbolize breasts, each belonging to a different season and a different mood.

The sky was clear one minute and cloudy the next; snowflakes swirled one second and disappeared the next. My sisters, all wearing thin clothing, scrunched their necks down between their shoulders as chilled northern winds blew past them. My eldest sister was responsible for putting the turnips into baskets; Second and Third Sisters were responsible for carrying the baskets; Fourth and Fifth Sisters were responsible for stacking them in the cellar; Sixth and Seventh Sisters were free to help out here and there; and Eighth Sister, not yet old enough to do any work, sat alone on the *kang* deep in thought. Sixth Sister stacked the turnips four at a time, all the way to the cellar opening; Seventh Sister did the same, but two at a time. Meanwhile, Mother and her little Golden Boy toured the area among the piles of turnips, ordering the girls around, criticizing them for less-than-perfect work, and heaving sighs of emotion. Mother's commands were intended to raise the quality of work, to keep the turnips healthy and allow them to get safely through the winter. Her sighs represented the central thought in her head: Life is hard, and the only way to survive is through hard work. My sisters reacted passively to Mother's commands, unhappily to her criticisms, and apathetically to her sighs. To this day I'm not sure how so many turnips appeared in our compound, as if by magic; but what I eventually came to understand was why Mother took such pains to stockpile that winter.

When the stacking work was finished, a dozen or so small turnips of varying shapes, all resembling human breasts, remained on the floor. Mother knelt down at the cellar opening, bent over, reached down, and pulled Xiangdi and Pandi up through the hole, one at a time. During the process, I was turned upside down twice; each time I looked out under Mother's armpit and caught a glimpse of snowflakes swirling in the hazy, gray sunlight. The last thing Mother did was move a cracked water vat — now filled with cotton batting and grain husks — to cover the cellar hole. My sisters formed a line against the wall, beneath an overhead beam, as if awaiting Mother's next command. But she just sighed. "What am I supposed to use to make padded clothes for you girls?" My third sister, Lingdi, said, "Cotton shells lined with cotton batting." "You think I don't know that?" Mother said. "What I mean is money — where am I going to get the money to buy the stuff?" My second sister, Zhaodi, said some-what gloomily, "Sell the black donkey and the little mule." "If I do that," Mother said reproachfully, "how will we till the field next year?"

My eldest sister, Laidi, held her tongue the whole time, and when Mother glanced at her, she lowered her head. "Tomorrow," Mother said to her anxiously, "you and Zhaodi can take the little mule into town and sell it." My fifth sister, Pandi, said with a pout, "But it's still nursing. Why don't we sell some grain instead? We have plenty." Mother glanced over at the open door of the eastern side room. A pair of cotton stockings belonging to Sha Yueliang, the leader of the band of soldiers, was drying on a clothesline.

The little mule bounded into the yard. It had been born on the same day as I, and it too was a male. But I could only stand up in the carrying cloth on my mother's back, while it was already as tall as its mother. "Here's what we'll do," Mother said before turning to walk back inside. "We'll sell it tomorrow." But from behind us came a crisp shout: "Adoptive mother!"

Sha Yueliang, who had been missing for three days, walked into the yard, leading his black donkey. A pair of bulging purple bundles lay across the donkey's back, something colorful poking through the seams. "Adoptive mother!" he called out again, a tone of intimacy in his voice. Mother turned to see an awkward smile on the dark, gaunt face of the crooked-shouldered man. "Commander Sha," Mother said insistently, "how many times have I told you I'm not your adoptive mother?" With the smile creasing his face unyieldingly, Sha replied, "No, you're not, you're more than that. I may not measure up in your eyes, but my filial obligations to you know no bounds." He turned and ordered two of his soldiers to take the donkey over to the churchyard to feed it after unloading the bundles from its back. Mother stared ven-omously at the black donkey, and so did I. It flared its nostrils to take in the smell of our female donkey emanating from the western side room.

Sha opened one of the bundles and took out a foxskin overcoat. It shimmered when he shook it out in the falling snow, which melted from the garment's heat as far away as three feet. "Adoptive mother," he said as he walked up to Mother with the coat. "Please accept this gift from your adoptive son." Mother shrank back hastily, but there was no way she could successfully avoid being wrapped in the foxskin coat. Darkness closed around me. The stink of the animal hide and the pungent odor of mothballs nearly suffocated me.

By the time I could see again, the yard had turned into an animal world. A purple marten coat was draped over the shoulders of my eldest sister, Laidi, and a bright-eyed fox was wrapped around her neck. My second sister, Zhaodi, was wrapped in a weasel coat. A black bear coat was draped over the shoulders of my third sister, Lingdi; a dark yellow roe deer coat was draped over the shoulders of my fourth sister, Xiangdi; a dogskin coat was draped over the shoulders of my fifth sister, Pandi; a lambskin coat was draped over the shoulders of my sixth sister, Niandi; and a rabbitskin coat was draped over the shoulders of my seventh sister, Qiudi. Mother's foxskin coat lay on the ground. "Take those off, all of you!" she shouted. "Take them off!" My sisters acted as if they hadn't heard her; with their heads swaying in the warmth of their collars, they reached out to touch the fur of one another's coats. The looks on their faces showed that they were delighted to be immersed in such warmth, and that they felt warmed by their delight. As she stood there shivering, Mother said weakly, "Have you all turned deaf?"

Sha Yueliang removed the last two overcoats from one of the bundles and gently rubbed the black fur covering the brown satiny-sleek hide. "Adoptive mother," he said emotionally, "these are lynx hides. There was only a single pair of them anywhere in a hundred-li radius of Northeast Gaomi. It took old man Geng and his son three years to catch them. This is the male, and this is the female. Have you ever seen a lynx?" His eyes swept the fur-clad girls. Since they didn't answer, he told them about lynxes, like a schoolteacher lecturing his class. "The lynx is a cat, only larger, and resembles a leopard, only smaller. It can climb trees and it can swim. It can leap several feet in the air and is capable of snatching birds off the limbs of trees. It's a very clever animal. This particular pair of lynxes lived amid Northeast Gaomi's unmarked burial mounds, which made it harder to catch them than climbing to the sky. But, eventually, they were caught. Adoptive mother, these two jackets are my gifts to young brother Jintong and his twin sister." With that, he laid out the two tiny jackets made from the lynxes, animals that when alive could climb trees, could swim, and could leap several feet in the air. He then bent over, picked up the flame-red foxskin coat, shook it out, and laid it too in the crook of Mother's arm. "Adoptive mother," he said with a catch in his voice, "please don't make me lose face."

After night fell, Mother bolted the door and called Laidi into our room. She laid me down at the head of the *kang*, alongside my twin sister. I reached out and scratched her face. She cried out and curled up in the corner, as far away from me as possible. Mother was too busy bolting the bedroom door to concern herself with us. My eldest sister was standing at the head of the *kang*, bundled in her purple marten coat, the fox stole around her neck, looking bashful and proud at the same time. Mother climbed onto the *kang*. Taking a silver hairpin from the bun at the back of her head, she picked the knot out of the lamp wick to make it shine brightly. Then she sat up straight and said in a taunting voice, "Sit down, young mistress. Don't be afraid you'll soil your new coat." Laidi blushed and sat on a stool beside the *kang*, pouting to show she felt hurt. Her fur stole raised its sly chin; oily green lights shot out from her eyes.

The yard was Sha Yueliang's world. Ever since he'd set up a bivouac in our eastern side room, our main gate was never closed all the way. On this particular night, there was a lot more going on in the eastern side room than usual. The bright light of a gas lantern shone through the paper covering of the window, lighting up the whole yard and adding a radiance to the snowflakes swirling in the air. People were running around; the gate kept creaking open and shut; and the crisp sound of donkey hooves clattered up and down the lane. Inside the room, husky male laughter burst into the night between shouts of their finger gambling: Three peach gardens! Five stalwart leaders! Seven plum blossoms and eight horses! The aroma of meat and fish drew my six sisters up to the window in the eastern room, where they leaned against the windowsill and drooled hungrily. Mother watched my eldest sister like a hawk, eyes blazing; Laidi returned the look with unyielding defiance. Blue sparks flew from the clash of gazes. "What are you thinking?" Mother demanded.

"What do you mean?" Laidi asked as she stroked the lush tail of the fox.

"Don't play dumb with me," Mother said.

"Mother," Laidi said, "I don't know what you're getting at."

Changing her tone to one of sadness, Mother said, "Laidi, you're the oldest of nine children, and if you get into trouble, who am I going to rely on?"

My sister jumped to her feet and, in an indignant tone I'd never heard from her before, said, "Just what do you expect of me, Mother? All you care about is Jintong. As far as you're concerned, we girls aren't worth as much as a pile of dog turds!"

"Laidi," Mother said, "don't change the subject. Jintong may be gold, but you girls are silver. So no more talk about dog turds! It's time for mother and daughter to have a heart-to-heart talk. That fellow Sha is a weasel coming to the chickens with New Year's greetings. He does not have good intentions. He has his eye on you for sure."

Laidi lowered her head and stroked the foxtail again as tears glistened in her eyes. "Mother," she said, "I'd be happy to marry a man like him."

Mother reacted as if struck by lightning. "Laidi," she said, "you have my blessings no matter whom you marry, just so long as it isn't that Sha fellow."

"Why?"

"Don't you worry about why."

With a hateful edge to her voice that seemed out of place for a girl her age, Laidi said, "The Shangguan family has worked me like a beast of burden long enough!"

The shrillness of her comment stunned Mother. Scrutinizing her daughter's face, red with anger, she then glanced down at the hand stroking the foxtail. I felt her reach for something close by; it was the whiskbroom used to keep the *kang* neat. Raising it over her head, she screamed hysterically, "How dare you talk to me like that! Just see if I don't beat you to death!"

Mother jumped off the *kang*, holding the whiskbroom high in the air. But instead of getting ready to duck the blow that was sure to come, Laidi raised her head defiantly, and Mother's hand froze in midair; when it finally came down, there was no steam behind it. Letting the whiskbroom fall to the floor, Mother threw her arms around my sister's neck and sobbed, "Laidi, we and that fellow Sha live in two different worlds. I can't sit by and watch my own daughter throw herself into a burning pyre . . ."

By then, Laidi was sobbing too.

Once they'd cried themselves out, Mother dried my sister's face with the back of her hand and implored her, "Laidi, give me your word you won't have anything to do with that Sha fellow."

But Laidi stood her ground. "Mother," she said, "this is something I really want, and not just for me, but for the good of the family." Out of the corner of her eye, Laidi looked down at the foxskin overcoat and the two little lynx jackets lying on the *kang*.

Mother too stood her ground. "I want you all to take off those coats tomorrow."

"Don't you even care if we freeze to death?" my sister said.

"A damned fur coat peddler is what he is," Mother complained.

My sister unbolted the door and strode to her room without a backward glance.

Mother sat down feebly on the edge of the *kang*, and I heard raspy breaths coming up from her chest.

Then I heard Sha Yueliang's hesitant footsteps outside the window. His tongue was thick and his lips seemed paralyzed; I knew he wanted to knock against the window frame and, in a tender voice, raise the subject of marriage. But alcohol had dulled his senses and made it impossible for his actions to match his desires. He banged on our window frame so loud and so hard that his hand tore through the paper covering, letting cold air from the outside pour in, along with the stench of alcohol on his breath. In the tone of voice so common to drunks — disgusting yet at the same time somehow endearing — he bellowed, "Mother —"

Mother jumped down off the *kang* and stood there sort of dazed for a moment, before climbing back up on the *kang* and dragging me over from beneath the window, where I'd been lying. "Mother," Sha said, "Laidi and me, when can we be married . . . I'm not a patient man . . ."

Mother clenched her teeth. "You there, Sha," she said, "like the toad who wants to feast on a swan, you can just dream on!"

"What did you say?" Sha Yueliang asked her.

"I said, dream on!"

As if he'd suddenly turned sober, Sha said without a trace of slurring, "Adoptive mother, I have never in my life begged anyone for anything."

"Nobody's asking you to beg me for anything."

With a snicker, he said, "Adoptive mother, I tell you that Sha Yueliang gets and does exactly what he wants . . ."

"You'll have to kill me first."

"Given that I want to marry your daughter," Sha said with a laugh, "how could I kill you, my future mother-in-law?"

"Then you can forget about marrying my daughter."

Another laugh. "Your daughter is a grown woman, and you can

no longer decide her fate. We shall see what happens, my dear mother-in-law."

Sha walked up to the eastern window, poked a hole in the paper covering, and flung a handful of candy into the room. "Little sisters-in-law," he shouted, "have some candy. As long as Sha Yueliang is around, you'll eat sweets and drink spicy drinks along with me. . . ."

Sha Yueliang did not sleep that night. Instead he walked around the yard and, except for an occasional cough or an outburst of whistling, which he did quite well, since he could imitate the voices of a dozen different birds, he sang arias from old operas or contemporary anti-Japanese songs at the top of his lungs. One minute he'd sing about Chen Shimei, the evil husband beheaded on the order of the angry Kaifeng magistrate, the next he'd bring his sword down on the neck of a Jap soldier. To keep this resistance hero, drunk on alcohol and love, from breaking into the room, Mother added a second bolt to the door, way up high, and, if that weren't enough, stacked anything she could move, from a bellows to a wardrobe to a pile of broken bricks, up against the door. Then, after putting me safely on her back, she picked up a cleaver and paced the room from one end to the other, back and forth. None of my sisters took off her new fur coat; they huddled together, sweat beading the tips of their noses, as they slept amid the noise created by Sha. Drool from Qiudi's mouth wetted Zhaodi's marten coat; Niandi slept nestled up against Lingdi's bear-skin coat like a lamb. Now that I think back, Mother never stood a chance in her struggle with Sha Yueliang. He won over my sisters with his fur coats, and they formed a united front with him; having lost the support of the masses, Mother became a lone warrior.

The next day, with me on her back, Mother ran over to tell Third Master Fan that she'd decided that the best way to repay Aunty Sun for her midwifery was to marry Laidi to one of the mute sons of the Sun family — the hero of the battle with the crows. The day the decision was announced would begin their engagement; the dowry would be presented the next day; and the wedding would take place the day after that. Third Master Fan stared at Mother with a look of confusion in his eyes. "Uncle," Mother said, "don't worry about the details. I'll take care of Matchmaker Xie." "But this is doing things backward." "Yes, it is," Mother replied. "Why do it this way?" "Please, Uncle, don't ask. Just have the mute come to our house at noon with his engagement gifts." "What can he possibly have as gifts?" Third Master Fan asked. "Tell him to bring what he can," Mother replied.

On the way home, I sensed Mother's fear and deep anxiety. She'd been right to be worried. The minute we walked into the yard, we were confronted by a pack of animals, dancing and singing: a weasel, a black bear, a roe deer, a dog, a sheep, and a rabbit; the only one missing was a marten. The purple marten, a fox wrapped around its neck, was seated on sacks of grain in the eastern side room, staring at the commander, who was sitting on the floor cleaning his powder gourd and musket.

Mother dragged Laidi off the sacks of grain and announced icily, "Commander Sha, she has been promised to another. You resistance fighters aren't the type to take another man's wife, I presume."

"That goes without saying," Sha replied evenly.

Mother dragged my eldest sister out of the eastern side room.

At noon, the mute son of the Sun family showed up at our door carrying a wild rabbit. He was wearing a tiny padded jacket, with his belly showing below and his neck above; the sleeves barely covered half his thick arms. All the buttons were missing, so he used a hemp rope to hold up his trousers. He nodded and bowed to Mother, an idiotic grin creasing his face. He held the rabbit up to Mother in both hands. Third Master Fan, who had come with the mute, said, "Shangguan Shouxi's widow, I've done as you asked."

Mother looked down at the wild rabbit, a trickle of blood congealing at the corner of its mouth, and stood frozen to the spot. Then she pointed to the mute son of the Sun family and said, "Uncle, I'd like the two of you to stick around. Don't go home yet. We'll stew the rabbit with some carrots for an engagement dinner."

Laidi's wails erupted in the eastern room. At first she sounded like a little girl crying, shrill and childish. That lasted a few minutes, and was quickly replaced by throaty, jagged wails wrapped around a succession of frightful, filthy curses. After about ten minutes, when the moisture was gone, those gave way to arid, brittle cries.

Laidi was sitting on the dirt floor of the eastern room, in front of the *kang*, soiling her precious coat, and not caring. She was staring straight ahead, no tears on her face, her mouth hanging slack and looking like a dried-up well. Arid-brittle cries were emerging from that dried-up well, endlessly. My six other sisters were sobbing softly, tears rolling over a bear hide, dancing atop a roe deer hide, shimmering on a weasel hide, wetting a sheep hide, and soiling a rabbit hide.

Third Master Fan stuck his head in the door; as if he'd seen a ghost, his eyes bugged out and his lips twitched. He backed out of the room, turned, and stumbled off as fast as he could.

The mute son of the Sun family stood in our living room, twisting his neck to gaze curiously at everything within eyesight. Besides the idiotic grin, the expression on his face revealed a host of impenetrable thoughts, a fossilized bleakness, a numb sorrow. Eventually, I even spotted a fearful expression of rage on that face.

Mother ran a wire through the rabbit's mouth and hung it from a rafter. The wails of terror from my eldest sister fell on deaf ears. The mute's strange expression did not register with Mother, who attacked the rabbit with her chipped, rusty cleaver. Sha Yueliang walked out of the eastern side room, his musket slung over his back. Without even looking up, Mother said icily, "Commander Sha, today is my eldest daughter's engagement day, and this rabbit is the engagement gift."

"What an extravagant gift," Sha Yueliang said with a laugh. Mother chopped down on the rabbit's head. "Today she is engaged, tomorrow the dowry will be settled, and the day after that she will be married." Mother turned and stared at Sha Yueliang. "Don't forget to join us at the wedding banquet!" "How could I forget?" Sha replied. "I definitely will not forget." He then turned and walked out through the gate with his musket, whistling a loud tune.

Mother continued skinning the rabbit, although it was clear her heart was not in it. When she finished, she hung it over the doorway and went inside, with me on her back and the cleaver in her hand. "Laidi!" she shouted. "The bonds between parent and child are formed by enmity and kindness. Go ahead, hate me!" This angry outburst was barely out of her mouth when she began to weep silently. As tears wet her face and her shoulders heaved, she sliced the turnips. *Ke-chunk*! The first turnip separated into two white, greenish halves. *Ke-chunk*! Four halves. *Ke-chunk*! *Ke-chunk*! *Ke-chunk*! Faster and faster Mother sliced, her actions more and more exaggerated. The now dismembered turnips lay on the cutting board. Mother raised her cleaver one more time; it nearly floated down as it left her hand and landed on the pile of dismembered turnips. The room was suffused with their acrid smell.

The mute son of the Sun family gave Mother a respectful thumbs-up along with a series of grunts. Mother dried her eyes with her sleeve and said to him, "You can leave now." He waved his arms and kicked out with his feet. Raising her voice, Mother pointed in the direction of his home. "You can leave now. I want you to leave!"

Finally grasping Mother's meaning, he made a face at me; the mustache atop his puffy upper lip looked like a swipe of green paint. First he made as if to climb a tree, then he made as if to fly like a bird, and finally he made as if he had a struggling little bird in his hand. He smiled as he pointed to me, and then pointed to his chest, over his heart.

Once again, Mother pointed in the direction of his home. He froze for a moment, then nodded in understanding. Falling to his knees before Mother — who quickly backed out of the way, so that he was now facing the sliced turnips on the cutting board — he banged his head against the floor in a kowtow. He then got to his feet and walked off proudly.

Worn out by all the activity of the day, Mother slept soundly that night. When she awoke the next morning, she saw wild rabbits hanging from the parasol tree, the cedar tree, and the apricot tree in the yard, as if laden with exotic fruits.

Holding on to the frame of the door, she sat down slowly on the threshold.

Wearing her marten coat, the red foxskin wrapped around her neck, eighteen-year-old Shangguan Laidi ran off with the leader of the Black Donkey Musket Band, Sha Yueliang, taking the black mule with them. Those wild rabbits were Sha Yueliang's engagement gift to my mother, as well as a display of his arrogance. My second, third, and fourth sisters were accomplices in First Sister's plan to run away. It was carried out in the middle of the night, while Mother was snoring loudly, deep in an exhausted sleep, and my fifth, sixth, and seventh sisters were fast asleep. Second Sister climbed out of bed; walking barefoot, she groped her away over to the door and removed the objects Mother had piled up behind it, after which my third and fourth sisters opened the double doors. Earlier that evening, Sha Yueliang had oiled the hinges with rifle grease, so the doors swung open without a sound. Standing under the cold, late-night moonbeams, the girls hugged each other and said their good-byes. Sha Yueliang grinned furtively at the rabbits hanging from the trees.

The day after that was to be the mute's and my eldest sister's wedding day. Mother sat on the edge of the *kang*, silently patching clothes with needle and thread. Just before noon, the mute, unable to curb his impatience, showed up. Using hand gestures and facial expressions, he signaled Mother that he had come to fetch his woman. Mother stepped down off the *kang*, pointed to the eastern side room, then to the trees in the yard, where the rabbits, now frozen stiff, still hung. She didn't have to say a word — the mute understood exactly what had happened.

That evening, we all sat around the *kang* eating turnip slices and slurping wheat congee, when we heard someone pounding on the gate. Second Sister, who had gone over to the western side room to take food to Shangguan Lü, ran in and announced breathlessly, "Mother, there's trouble. The mute and his brothers are at the gate, and they've brought a pack of dogs with them." My sisters were thrown into a panic, but Mother sat there calmly feeding my twin sister Yunü — Jade Girl — then turned her attention back to the turnip slices, which she chewed loudly. She looked as calm as a pregnant rabbit. The commotion outside the gate died out as suddenly as it had arisen. In about the time it takes to smoke a pipeful, three dark, red-faced figures clambered over the wall on the south edge of the yard. It was the three mute brothers of the Sun family. Three black dogs, their glistening coats looking as if they had been smeared with lard, entered the yard with them. They glided over the wall like black rainbows and landed noiselessly on the ground. The mutes and their dogs froze for a moment in the deep red sunset, like statues. The eldest held a glistening Burmese sword; the second wore a blue steel hunting knife at his waist; and the third carried a large, rusty short-handled sword. They all had little cotton bundles — blue with white flowers — over their shoulders, like men about to set off on a long journey. My sisters sucked in their breath fearfully, but Mother sat calmly slurping her congee. Without warning, the eldest mute roared, followed by his two brothers, and then the dogs. Spittle from human and canine mouths danced in the dying rays of the sun like glowing insects. The mutes then made a show of their skill with their knives and swords, a reprise of their battle with the crows during the funeral in the wheat field. On that winter evening, knives and swords flashed as three stocky men, looking a bit like hunting dogs, leaped into the air, stretching their bodies as far as they'd go to hack at dozens of dead rabbits hanging from the trees in our yard. Their frenzied dogs howled and swung their big heads around as they flung the rabbits' broken corpses right and left. When the men finished, our yard was littered with dismembered rabbits. A few lonely rabbit heads still hung from branches, like unpicked, wind-dried fruit. Leading their dogs, the satisfied mutes strutted around the yard a few times in a show of authority before skimming over the wall like swallows, the same way they'd entered, and disappearing in the gloom of falling night.

Holding her bowl out in front of her, Mother smiled slightly. That singular smile burned its way into our heads.

4

The first signs of aging in a woman appear on her breasts and work their way from the nipples backward. After our sister eloped, Mother's pink nipples, which had always jutted out playfully, suddenly sagged, like ripe tassels of grain. At the same time, the pink turned to date red. During those days, her output of milk fell off, and it wasn't nearly as fresh or fragrant or sweet as it had been. In fact, the now anemic milk tasted a little like rotting wood. Happily, the passage of time gradually improved her mood, especially after eating a big eel, which sparked a resurgent rise in her sagging nipples and a lightening of the color. But the deep wrinkles that appeared at the base of each nipple, like creases in the pages of a book, were disturbing; granted they were now smoothed out, yet an indelible trace of the indentation remained. This sounded a warning to me; thanks to instinct, or maybe divine intervention, a change in my reckless, indulgent attitude toward breasts occurred. I knew I must treasure them, conserve and protect them, treat them with the care due to the exquisite containers they were.

The winter that year was unusually bitter, but we moved safely and confidently toward spring, thanks to half a room filled with wheat and a cellar piled high with turnips. During the coldest days, heavy snowfalls sealed us inside, while outside, tree branches snapped under the wet accumulation. Wearing the fur coats Sha Yueliang had given us, we huddled around Mother and fell into a sort of hibernation. Then the sun came out one day and began to melt the snow; as large icicles formed beneath the eaves and sparrows reappeared, chirping for us from branches in the yard, we stirred from our wintry slumber. My sisters experienced deep revulsion over the melted snow on which we had relied for so long, and the same meal of turnips boiled in snow water, over and over, hundreds of times. My second sister, Zhaodi, was the first to mention that the snow this year carried the smell of raw blood, and if we didn't hurry down to the river to draw fresh water, we might all come down with some strange illness, and that not even Jintong, who survived on mother's milk, would be spared. By this time, Zhaodi had quite naturally taken over Laidi's leadership role. This particular sister had thick, fleshy lips and spoke with a husky voice that oozed appeal. She became the voice of authority, since she'd assumed complete responsibility for meal preparation as soon as winter closed in, while Mother sat on the *kang* shy as a wounded milk cow, occasionally wrapping herself in the precious fox fur, as she should, so as to stay warm and ensure the continued flow of high-quality milk in her breasts. With a look at Mother, my second sister said imperiously, "Starting today, we will fetch our water from the river." Mother did not object. My third sister, Lingdi, frowned and complained about the taste of the turnips boiled in snow water, and repeated her suggestion that we sell the donkey and use the money to buy some meat. "We're surrounded by ice and snow," Mother said sarcastically, "so where do you suggest we go to sell it?" "Then let's go catch some wild rabbits," Third Sister said. "With all this ice and snow they're so cold they can hardly move." Mother blanched in anger. "Children, remember one thing. I don't ever want to see another wild rabbit as long as I live."

In fact, there were many people in the village who grew tired of eating wild rabbit over that bitter winter. The plump little rabbits crawled across the snowy ground like maggots, so lethargic even women with bound feet easily caught them. These were golden days for foxes. Owing to the ongoing battles, all the hunting rifles had been confiscated by guerrillas of one stripe or another, depriving the villagers of their most effective weapons; the battles also had a debilitating effect on the villagers' mood, so that during the peak hunting season, the foxes did not have to fear for their lives as they had in years past. Over the long, seemingly endless nights, every female was pregnant, as the foxes cavorted freely in the marshes. Their mournful cries had people constantly on edge.

Using a pole, my third and fourth sisters lugged a big wooden bucket down to the Flood Dragon River, followed by my second sister carrying a sledgehammer. As they passed the home of Aunty Sun, their eyes were drawn to the yard, which was dreary beyond imagining, with no sign of life. A flock of crows lined the wall, a reminder of all that had happened there. The excitement back then was long gone, as were the mutes, to destinations unknown. The girls walked through knee-deep snow to the riverbank, observed by several raccoon dogs in the scrub brush. The sun was in the southeastern sky, its slanting rays glistening on the riverbed. Ice near the bank was white, and walking on it was like stepping on crispy flatcakes, crackling under their feet — *ge-ge zha-zha*. Out in the center the ice was light blue, hard, smooth, and glossy. My sisters walked gingerly across it, and when my fourth sister slipped and fell, she pulled my second sister, who was holding her hand, down with her. The bucket and hammer crashed loudly on the ice, which made the girls giggle.

Second Sister picked out a clean patch of ice and attacked it with the sledgehammer, which had been in the Shangguan family for generations, raising it high over her head with her thin arms and bringing it down hard; the sharp, hollow sounds of steel on ice flew through the air and made the paper covering of our window quiver. Mother rubbed the top of my head, with its yellow fuzz, and then stroked the fur of my coat. "Little Jintong," she said, "little Jintong, sister's making a big hole in the ice. She'll bring back a bucket of water and pour out half a bucket of fish." My eighth sister, wrapped in her lynx coat, lay huddled in a corner of the *kang*, smiling awkwardly, like a furry little Goddess of Mercy. Second Sister's first hit produced a white dot the size of a walnut; several splinters of ice stuck to the head of the hammer. She raised it again, straining to get it over her head, then brought it down unsteadily. Another white dot appeared on the ice, this one several feet away from the first one. By the time twenty or more white dots covered the patch of ice, Zhaodi was gasping for breath, as long, dense puffs of white mist shot from her mouth. She raised the hammer once more, but in using the last bit of strength to bring it down, she fell headlong onto the ice. Her face was ashen, her thick lips were now bright red; her eyes misted up, and the tip of her nose was dotted with crystalline beads of sweat.

By then my third and fourth sisters were muttering, voicing discontent over their elder sister as gusts of wind from the north swept across the riverbed and sliced into their faces like knives. Second Sister stood up, spit in her hands, picked up the sledgehammer again, and brought it down on the ice. But the next swing sent her sprawling on the ice a second time.

Just as they were gathering up the bucket and carrying pole and were about to head home dejected, resigned to the fact that they would have to continue using melted snow or ice to cook, a dozen or so horses pulling sleighs and leaving trails of icy mist galloped up on the frozen river. Owing to the bright rays of sunlight glancing off the ice and the fact that the horsemen rode in from the southeast, at first Second Sister thought they had coasted down to earth on those very rays of sunlight. They shone like golden sunbeams and were lightning quick. The horses' hooves flashed like silver as they pummeled the ice, iron horseshoes filling the air with loud cracks and sending shards of ice flying into the faces of my sisters, who stood there gaping, too stupefied to even think about running away. The horses skirted them at a gallop before coming to a staggering halt on the slick ice. My sisters noticed that the sleighs were coated with thick yellow tung oil that shone like stained glass. Four men sat in each sleigh, all wearing hats made of fluffy fox fur. White frost coated their beards, their eyebrows, their eyelashes, and the fronts of their hats. Dense puffs of steamy mist emerged from their mouths and nostrils. Their horses were small and delicate, their legs covered with long hair. From their calm attitude, Second Sister guessed that they were legendary Mongol ponies. A tall, husky fellow jumped down off the second sleigh. He was wearing a sleek lambskin coat, open in front to reveal a leopardskin vest. The vest was girded by a wide leather belt, from which a holstered revolver hung on one side and a hatchet on the other. He alone was wearing a felt hat with flaps instead of a leather cap. Rabbit fur earmuffs covered his exposed ears. "Are you the daughters of the Shangguan family?" he asked.

The man standing before them was Sima Ku, assistant steward of Felicity Manor. "What are you doing out here?" He supplied his own answer before they could reply. "Ah, trying to break a hole in the ice. That's no job for girls!" He turned and shouted to the men in the sleighs, "Climb down off there, all of you, and help my neighbors chop a hole in the ice. We'll water these Mongol ponies while we're at it."

Dozens of bloated-looking men climbed down off the sleighs, coughing and spitting. Several of them knelt down, took out hatchets, and attacked the ice — *pa pa*. Splinters flew as cracks opened up. One of the men, whose face sported whiskers, felt the edge of his hatchet and, after blowing his nose, said, "Brother Sima, at this rate, we could work till it was dark and not break through the ice." Sima Ku knelt down, took out his own hatchet, and attempted a few tentative whacks on the ice. "Damn!" he cursed. "It's like steel plate." The whiskered man said, "Elder brother, if we all empty our bladders on one spot, it'll

melt open a hole." "You dumb prick!" Sima Ku cursed just as exhila-
ration swept over him. He smacked himself on his rear end — his lips
cracked open, for the wound in his backside hadn't yet completely
healed — and said, "I've got it. Technician Jiang, come over here." A
bony little man walked up and looked into Sima Ku's face, not saying
a word. But his expression made it clear that he was waiting for orders.
"Can that thing you've got cut through ice?" Jiang grinned contemptuously and said in a squeaky, ladylike voice, "Like smashing an egg
with an iron hammer."

"Hurry up, then," Sima Ku said excitedly, "and give me sixty-
four — that's eight times eight — holes in this river of ice. Let my fellow villagers benefit from the presence of Sima Ku." He turned to my
sisters. "You girls stay put."

Technician Jiang pulled back the canvas tarp covering the third
sleigh, revealing two iron objects, painted green, in the shape of enormous artillery shells. With practiced movements, he freed a long plastic tube and wrapped it around the head of one of the objects. Then he
looked at the round clock face; two pencil-thin red hands were ticking
rhythmically. Finally, he put on a pair of canvas gloves, clicked a metal
object that looked like a big opium pipe, attached to two rubber tubes,
and gave it a twist. The thing sputtered into life. The technician's
helper, a skinny boy who could not have been more than fifteen, lit a
match and touched it to the sputtering ends of the tubes. Blue flames
the thickness of silkworm chrysalises shot out with a loud *whoosh*. He
shouted an order to the youngster, who climbed onto the sleigh and
twisted the heads of the two objects, quickly turning the blue flames
blindingly white, brighter than sunlight. Technician Jiang picked
up one of the intimidating objects and looked over at Sima Ku, who
squinted as he raised his hand high, then sliced it down. "Start cutting!" he shouted.

Jiang bent over at the waist and aimed the white flame at the
frozen surface. Milky white steam jetted a foot or more into the air, accompanied by loud sizzles. His arm controlled the action of his wrist;
his wrist controlled the direction of the enormous opium pipe; and the
opium pipe spat out white flames that burned a hole in the ice. He
looked up. "There's your hole," he announced.

Somewhat doubtfully, Sima Ku bent down to look at the ice, and,
sure enough, a chunk of ice the size of a millstone, surrounded by little
chips, had been burned out of the surface, with river water swirling

around it. Jiang then burned a cross in the chunk of ice with the white flame, dividing it into four pieces. When he stepped down on the detached pieces, each was carried away by the river below. Blue water gushed up from the neat hole.

"Neat," Sima Ku praised the man, who was also the beneficiary of congratulatory looks from the men standing around him. "Now make some more holes for us," Sima ordered.

Putting all his skills to work, Technician Jiang burned dozens of holes in the two-foot-thick ice covering the Flood Dragon River. They emerged in a variety of shapes: circles, squares, rectangles, triangles, trapezoids, octagons, and pear-blossom, all laid out like a page in a geometry textbook.

"Technician Jiang," Sima Ku said, "you've tasted success! All right, men, back up on the sleds. We need to reach the bridge before dark. But first we'll water the horses from the Flood Dragon River!"

The men led their horses up to the holes to drink from the river, as Sima Ku turned to Second Sister. "You're the second daughter, aren't you? Well, go home and tell your mother that one of these days I'm going to crush that donkey bastard Sha Yueliang and return your elder sister to the mute."

"Do you know where she is?" my sister asked boldly.

"Sha Yueliang took her with him to sell opium. Him and that donkey-shit band of his."

Not daring to ask any more, Second Sister watched as Sima Ku climbed up on his sled and headed off toward the west at full speed, followed by the other eleven sleds. They made a turn at the stone bridge over the Flood Dragon River and shot out of sight.

My sisters, still immersed in the miraculous sight they had just witnessed, no longer felt the cold. They stared at all the holes in the ice, from triangles to ovals, from ovals to squares, and from squares to rectangles . . . as the river water soaked their shoes and quickly turned to ice. The fresh air rising out of the holes filled their lungs. Feelings of reverence for Sima Ku washed over my second, third, and fourth sisters. Now that my eldest sister had served as a glorious model, a thought began to form in Second Sister's immature brain — she would marry Sima Ku! But someone, it seemed, had warned her coldly that Sima Ku had three wives. All right, then, she thought, I'll be his fourth! Just then Fourth Sister shouted: "Sister, a big meat stick!"

The so-called meat stick was in fact a silver-skinned eel that had risen to the surface and was writhing clumsily in the water. Its snake-like head was the size of a fist, its eyes cold and menacing, like those of a ferocious snake. As its head broke the surface, bubbles oozing from its mouth popped in the air. "It's an eel!" Second Sister shouted, picking up her bamboo carrying pole and crashing it down on the head, the hook on the end sending water splashing. The eel's head fell below the surface, but floated right back up. Its eyes were smashed. Second Sister swung again; this time the eel's movements slowed and it stretched out stiffly. Throwing down her pole, Second Sister grabbed the head and dragged the eel out of the water. By then it was frozen stiff; it had indeed turned into a meat stick. The girls trudged home, with Third and Fourth Sisters carrying water and Second Sister carrying the hammer in one hand and the eel in the other.

Mother sawed off the eel's tail and cut the body into eighteen parts, each severed chunk hitting the floor with a thunk. Then she boiled the Flood Dragon River eel in Flood Dragon River water and produced a mouthwatering soup. Beginning that day, Mother's breasts were youthful again, though scars from the wrinkles mentioned earlier remained on the tips, like the crumpled pages of a book.

That night the delicious soup also lightened Mother's mood and put a saintly look back on her face, like the merciful expression of the Guanyin Bodhisattva or the Virgin Mary, with my sisters seated around her lotus perch. Her loving children were with her on that peaceful night. Northern winds howled over the Flood Dragon River, turning our chimney into a whistle. Ice-covered branches of the trees in the yard cracked as they swayed in the wind; an icicle broke free of the house eave and shattered crisply on the laundry stone below.

On that same wonderful night, Sima Ku was crossing the metal railroad bridge over the Flood Dragon River, some thirty li from the village, and on the verge of adding a new chapter to the history of Northeast Gaomi Township. That rail line was the Jiaoji Line, built by the Germans. The Wolf and Tiger Brigade warriors had fought a heroic, bloody battle, employing every conceivable tactic to slow down the construction, but in the end they'd been unable to stop the unyielding steel road from slicing through the soft underbelly of Northeast Gaomi Township, dividing it in two. In the words of their forebear Sima the Urn: Goddamn it, that's the same as slicing open the bellies of our women! The metal dragon had belched thick black smoke as it rolled through Northeast Gaomi, as if rolling right across our chests. Now the rail line was in the hands of the Japanese, who turned it to transport coal and cotton, ultimately for weapons and gunpowder to be turned on us.

Orion's Belt was drifting west; a crescent moon hung just above the treetops. A punishing west wind swept over the frozen river, evoking creaks and groans from the steel bridge as it swayed. It was a bitterly, almost demonically, cold night, so cold that the ice kept cracking to create cobwebs over the surface of the river. The cracks were louder than gunfire. Sima Ku's sled brigade reached the foot of the bridge and stopped at the river's edge. Sima Ku jumped down off his sled, his backside feeling as if it had been clawed by a cat. Dim starlight made the river glimmer slightly, but the sky between the stars and the ice was so black you couldn't see the fingers of your hand. He clapped his hands, the sound echoing around him from other clapping hands. The mysterious darkness energized and excited him. Later, when asked how he'd felt before destroying the bridge, he'd said, "Great, just like New Year's."

His troops groped hand in hand up to the bridge, where Sima Ku climbed onto one of the stanchions, took a pickax from his belt, and hacked away at one of the supports. Sparks flew and loud clangs rang out. "Legs of a whore!" he cursed. " Nothing but steel." A shooting star streaked across the sky, trailing a long tail and hissing as it filled the sky with lovely blue sparks, momentarily lighting up the space between heaven and earth. Thanks to the light of the shooting star, he had a good look at the cement stanchion and steel supports. "Technician Jiang," he shouted, "come up here!" With a boost from his comrades, Jiang climbed onto the stanchion, followed by his young apprentice. Clumps of ice clung to the stanchion like mushrooms, and as Sima Ku reached out to take the boy's hand, he slipped on the ice and crashed to the ground; the boy managed to stay atop the stanchion. Sima fell right on his backside, from which blood and pus had never stopped seeping out. "Oh, mother —" he screamed. "Dear mother, that hurts like hell!" His men ran up and helped him up off the ice. But that did not stop the screams of pain, screams loud enough to reach the heavens. "Elder brother," one of them said, "you're going to have to bear it as best you can. Don't expose yourself." That brought an end to the screams. As he stood there shuddering, Sima barked out an order: "Get on with it, Technician Jiang. Just make cuts in a few of them and we'll leave. The painkilling medication that damned Sha Yueliang gave me is only making it worse." One of his men said, "Elder brother, I think that's what he had in mind, and you fell for it." Sima replied testily, "Don't tell me you've never heard the saying that 'when you're sick, any doctor will do'?" "Bear it the best you can, elder brother," the man repeated. "I'll take care of the problem once we get home. There's nothing better for burns than badger oil. Works every time."

Whoosh. An explosion of blue sparks, white around the edges, erupted amid the bridge supports, so bright it brought tears to the men's eyes. Gaps in the bridge, bridge stanchions, steel supports, dogskin overcoats, foxskin caps, yellow sleds and Mongol ponies, and everything around the bridge came into full view, even a single hair that had fallen onto the ice. The two people on the bridge, Technician Jiang and the young apprentice, were hunkering down on the steel support like a pair of monkeys, their "big opium pipe" spewing white-hot flames as it cut into the metal. White smoke curled upward as the riverbed gave off the strangely fragrant odor of burning metal. Sima Ku watched the sparks and arc lights in rapt fascination, forgetting the pain in his backside. The sparking flames ate through the metal like silkworms consuming mulberry leaves. In hardly any time at all, a piece of the support fell from the bridge and stuck at an angle in the thick ice below. "Cut, cut, cut the fucking thing to pieces!" Sima Ku bellowed.

"It's nearly time, elder brother," the man applying the badger oil to Sima Ku's injured backside said. "The train is due just before dawn." A dozen or more randomly located steel bridge supports had been cut with the torch, which was still spewing blue and white flames under the bridge. "Those fuckers are getting off easy!" Sima Ku cursed. "Are you sure the bridge will collapse under the weight of the train?" "If I cut any more, I'm afraid the bridge might collapse of its own weight before the train even reaches it." "All right, you can come down now. As for you men," he said to the others, "help those two hardy fellows down and reward them each with a bottle of our liquor." The blue sparks died out. The brigade members helped Technician Jiang and his apprentice down off the stanchion and onto one of the sleds. In the darkness just before dawn, the winds died out, turning the air bone-chilling cold. The Mongol ponies pulled the sleds tentatively through the darkness across the ice. Before they'd gone a mile, Sima Ku called them to a halt. "After a hard night's work," he said, "it's time to sit back and watch the show."

The sun had barely turned the edge of the sky red when the cargo train steamed up. The river glistened, the trees on both banks were glazed with gold and silver, the steel bridge sprawled silently across the river. Sima Ku rubbed his hands nervously as curses dripped from his mouth. The train clanged menacingly as it pressed down on them; when it neared the bridge, a loud whistle resounded between heaven and earth. Black smoke spewed from the engine, white mist flew from its wheels, the grinding of steel on steel made the men shudder in fear as the icy surface of the river trembled. The brigade members watched the train fitfully, the horses' ears pressed back against the mane on their necks. The loutish, vulgar train rushed up onto the bridge, which seemed to stand there loftish and unyielding. In a matter of seconds, the faces of Sima Ku and his men turned ashen, but seconds later, they were jumping up and down on the ice, whooping it up. Sima Ku's joyous shouts were the loudest of all, his jumps the highest, even given the seriousness of the injuries to his backside. The bridge collapsed in a matter of seconds, sending the engine and the load of railroad ties, steel rails, sand, and mud straight down. The engine hit one of the pilings, which also collapsed. The sound was deafening as chunks of ice bathed in the morning light, along with huge rocks, twisted metal, and shattered ties, flew high into the sky. Dozens of loaded rail cars accordioned up behind the engine with a roar; some fell into the river below, others sprawled across the tracks at rakish angles. Explosions began to erupt, starting from a car carrying high explosives and followed by detonated ammunition. The icy surface of the river split open, sending the water beneath gushing upward. Mixed with the water were fish, shrimp, even some green-shelled turtles. A booted human leg landed on the head of one of the Mongol ponies, nearly knocking it senseless and causing its front legs to crumple. A wheel from the train, which weighed hundreds of pounds, crashed into the ice, raising a geyser of water that fell muddily back to the surface. Powerful waves of sound turned Sima Ku deaf as he watched the Mongol ponies run crazily across the ice, dragging their sleds behind them. The brigade troops stood or sat in a daze, dark blood seeping out of some of their ears. He was shouting at the top of his lungs, but he couldn't hear himself; his men's mouths were open, as if they too were shouting, but he couldn't hear them either . . .

Somehow Sima Ku managed to lead his troops back to the spot on the river where they had cut holes in the ice with their blue and white flames the morning before. My second, third, and fourth sisters had come out to fetch more water and catch some fish, but the holes had frozen over during the night, as thick as a hand. Second Sister had hacked them open again with her hammer. When Sima Ku and his men reached the spot, their horses rushed up to drink from the river. In a manner of minutes, after they'd drunk their fill, they began to shudder, their legs started to twitch, and they crumpled to the ice, every one of them suddenly dead. The freezing water had ripped their expanded lungs apart.

On that early morning, every living creature in Northeast Gaomi Township — humans, horses, donkeys, cows, chickens, dogs, geese, ducks — felt the power of the explosions off to the southwest. Hibernating snakes, thinking it was thunder announcing the Insect Waking season, slithered out of their caves and immediately froze to death.

Sima Ku led his troops into the village to rest and reorganize, and was greeted by a string of the vilest curses from Sima Ting. But since everyone's hearing had been so badly affected by the explosion, they all thought he was singing their praises — Sima Ting always had a smug, complacent look on his face when he cursed. Sima Ku's three wives had pooled every folk remedy and type of medication they had to treat the burned and frostbitten backside of the man they shared. The first wife would apply a plaster, which the second wife would remove to wash the area with a lotion prepared with a dozen rare medicinal herbs, after which the third wife would cover it with a powder composed of crushed pine and cypress leaves, ilex root, egg whites, and seared mouse whiskers. Back and forth it went, the skin on his backside wet one minute and dry the next, until the old injuries were now joined by new ones. It reached the point where Sima Ku wrapped himself in a lined jacket with two leather belts, and the moment he saw his three wives coming his way, he raised his hatchet or cocked his rifle. But while his backside injuries remained, his hearing returned.

The first thing he heard were the angry curses of his brother: "You fucking idiot, you'll kill every last soul in this village, you wait and see!" Reaching out with a hand that was as soft and as ruddy as his brother's, with fleshy fingers and thin skin, he grabbed his brother by the chin. Seeing the scraggly, yellow, ratlike whiskers above his chapped upper lip, which was normally shaved clean, he shook his head sadly and said, "You and I are from the same father's seed, so cursing me is the same as cursing yourself. Go ahead, curse, curse all you like!" He dropped his hand.

Sima Ting stood there, mouth agape, and stared at his brother's broad back. All he could do was shake his head. Picking up his gong, he walked outside, climbed clumsily up the steps of his watchtower, and gazed off to the northwest.

Some time later, Sima Ku led his men back to the bridge, where they scavenged sections of twisted track, a train wheel, painted bright red, and a bunch of nondescript chunks of brass and iron, all of which they put on display outside the gate of the church as proof of their glorious military victory. With saliva bubbling at the corners of his mouth, Sima boasted to the gathered crowd, over and over, how he had destroyed the bridge and derailed the Japanese cargo train. As he recounted the event, he spiced it up with new details, his tale growing richer and more interesting with each telling, until it had all the excitement and adventure of a popular romance. My second sister, Zhaodi, was his most ardent listener. At first just a member of the crowd, before long she bore witness to the new weapon that had been used; eventually, in her mind, she became a participant in the destruction of the bridge, as if she'd been one of Sima Ku's followers from the very beginning, climbing onto the piling with him and falling to the icy surface of the river right beside him. She grimaced each time the pain in his backside erupted, as if they shared the same wounds.

Mother had always said that the Sima men were all lunatics. By this time she had figured out what Zhaodi was thinking, and had a premonition that the drama involving Laidi was about to be replayed, and soon. With growing anxiety, she looked into her daughter's dark eyes and saw the frightful passion burning inside. How could those eyes and those thick, bright red, shameless lips belong to a seventeen-year-old girl? She was like a bovine creature in heat. "Zhaodi, my daughter," Mother said, "do you realize how old you are?" Second Sister glared at Mother. "Weren't you already married to my father when you were my age? And you said your aunt had twins when she was only sixteen, both plump as little piglets!" All Mother could do at this point was sigh. But Second Sister was not through. "I know you want to say he already has three wives. So I'll be his fourth. And I know you want to say that he's a generation older than me. Well, we don't have the same surname and we're not related, so I'm not breaking any rules."

Mother relinquished her authority over Second Sister, letting her do as she pleased. She seemed calm enough, but I could tell that it was tearing her up inside by the changed taste of her milk. During those days, when Second Sister was chasing after Sima Ku, Mother took my other six sisters down to the cellar to dig a secret path among the turnips to the stockpile of sorghum stalks out by the southern wall. Part of the dirt we dug up we dumped in the latrine and part we carried out to the donkey pen, but most of it went down the well next to the stockpile.

New Year's passed peacefully. On the night of the Lantern Festival, Mother strapped me on her back and led my six sisters outside to enjoy the lanterns. Every family in the village hung lanterns outside their doors; they were small lanterns, except for the two red lanterns the size of water vats hung by the gate of Felicity Manor, each lit by a goat tallow candle thicker than my arm. The light they gave off flickered brightly. Where was Zhaodi? Mother didn't even ask. She had become our family's guerrilla fighter, one who might stay away for three days, then show up unannounced. We were about to set off firecrackers on the last night of the year to welcome the god of wealth when Zhaodi showed up wearing a black rain cloak. She proudly showed off the leather belt wrapped tightly around her narrow waist and the silver revolver hanging heavily from it. In a sort of mocking tone, Mother said, "Who'd have guessed that the Shangguan family would one day produce another highwayman?" She seemed on the verge of crying, but Second Sister merely laughed, the laugh of a lovestruck girl, which brought a ray of hope to Mother that it was not too late to bring her to her senses. "Zhaodi," she said, "I can't let you become another of Sima Ku's concubines." But Zhaodi just sneered — this time it was the sneer of a wicked woman — and the hope that had flared briefly in Mother's heart was extinguished.

On the first day of the year, Mother went with New Year's greetings to her aunt. She told her what had happened to Laidi and Zhaodi. This elderly aunt of hers, a woman of vast experience, said, "Where the romantic affairs of sons and daughters are concerned, you must let them take their course. Besides, with sons-in-law like Sha Yueliang and Sima Ku, your worries are over. Both those men are high-flying hawks." "What worries me is that they won't die in bed," Mother said. Her aunt replied, "It's usually worthless people who die in bed." Mother tried to keep arguing her case, but her aunt waved her off impatiently, sweeping away Mother's complaints like shooing a fly. "Let me have a look at your son," she said. Mother lifted me out of the cloth pouch and laid me on the bed. I was frightened by the tiny, deeply wrinkled face of Mother's aunt, especially her radiant green eyes, set deep in their sockets. Her sharply jutting brow was completely hairless, while the spots around her eyes were covered by fine yellow hairs. She mussed my hair with a bony hand, then tweaked my ear, pinched my nose, and even reached down between my legs to feel my little pecker. Disgusted by her humiliating groping, I strained to crawl over to the corner of the bed. But she grabbed me and yelled, "Stand up, you little bastard!" Mother said, "Aunty, how can you expect him to stand up? He's only seven months old." "When I was seven months old I was already going out to the chicken coop to fetch eggs for your grandma," the old woman said. "That was you, Aunty. You're a special person." The old woman said, "I think this little devil is special too! Too bad about that fellow Malory." Mother's face reddened, then paled. I crawled to the back of the bed, grabbed hold of the window ledge, and pulled myself up onto my feet. "See there?" the old woman clapped her hands and said. "I told you he could stand, and he did! Look at me, you little bastard!" "His name is Jintong, Aunty, so why do you keep calling him little bastard?"

"Whether he's a bastard or not only his mother knows. Well, is he, my dear niece? Besides, to me that's a pet name — little bastard. So are little turtle spawn, little bunny rabbit, little beast. Walk over here, little bastard!" I turned around on shaky legs and looked at Mother's teary eyes. "Jintong, my good little boy!" Mother said as she reached out for me. I threw myself into her waiting arms. I was actually walking. "My son can walk," Mother muttered as she hugged me tightly. "My son can walk." "Sons and daughters are like birds," her aunt said. "When it's time for them to fly, you can't hold them back. And what about you? What I mean is, what would you do if they all died?"

"I'd be fine," Mother replied.

"That's what I want to hear," the old woman said. "Always let your thoughts rise up to heaven, or go down into the ocean, and if all else fails, let them climb a mountain, but never make things hard on yourself. Do you understand what I'm saying?" "I understand," Mother said. When they were saying good-bye, the old woman asked, "Is your mother-in-law still alive?" "Yes," Mother said. "She's rolling around in donkey shit." The old woman said, "That old witch was a tower of strength her whole life. I never thought she'd one day fall so low!"

If not for that private conversation on the first day of the new year, I'd never have been able to walk at seven months, and Mother wouldn't have been interested in taking us outside to look at the lanterns, which would have meant a very boring Lantern Festival for us; the history of our family might well have been very different. The streets were teeming with people, but none of them looked familiar. An air of stability and unity existed among residents. Children waved sparklers — what we called golden mouse droppings — that sizzled and popped as the children threaded their way through the crowds. We stopped in front of Felicity Manor to gaze at the gigantic red lanterns on either side of the gate, their ambiguous yellow light illuminating the gilded words "Felicity Manor" carved into a hanging signboard. Bursts of noise emerged from the brightly lit courtyard within. A crowd had gathered outside the gate, where they stood silently, their hands tucked up their sleeves, as if waiting for something. My big-mouthed third sister, Lingdi, asked the person next to her, "Are they going to hand out some porridge, uncle?" The man merely shook his head, but someone behind her said, "They don't do that till the eighth day of the twelfth month, young lady." "Then why are you all standing around here?" she turned and asked. "Because they're going to put on a modern play," he said. "We're told that a famous actor from Jinan has come to town." Mother pinched her before she could say any more.

Finally, four men emerged from the Sima compound, each carrying a black metal object on a tall bamboo pole. Flames licked out of whatever they were, turning the area around the gate from night to day — no, even brighter than daylight. Pigeons roosting in the dilapidated bell tower of the church not far from the compound were startled into flight; they cooed noisily as they flew past us into the dark night. Someone in the crowd shouted, "Gas lamps!" From that moment on, we knew that in this world, in addition to bean-oil lanterns, kerosene lamps, and firefly lanterns, there was such a thing as gas lamps, and that they were blindingly bright. The husky lamp bearers formed a square in front of the Felicity Manor gate, like four black pillars. Some more men walked noisily through the gate carrying a rolled-up straw mat. When they reached the space created by the four men with their gas lamps, they tossed down the mat, undid the ropes around it, and let it spread out on its own. They then bent down, picked up corners of the unrolled mat, and began churning their dark, hairy legs. Because their movements were so quick, and because they were in the light of gas lamps, our eyes were filled with dark blurs that made it seem as if they all had at least four legs, connected seemingly by translucent cobwebs. And that image created the appearance of beetles caught in a spider's web, struggling to break free. Once the mat was laid out the way they wanted it, they stood up, faced the crowd, and struck a pose. They all had painted faces, like shiny masks made of animal skins: a panther, a spotted deer, a lynx, and one of those raccoons that feeds on temple offerings. They then went back inside, executing a two-steps-forward, one-step-backward dance.

Amid the sizzle of four gas lamps, we waited silently; just like the new straw mat. The four men holding the lamp poles were transformed into black stones. But then the crisp sound of a gong energized us, and we turned to gaze at the gateway, though our view inside was blocked by a whitewashed wall on which the gilded word "fortune" was carved. We continued to wait, an eternity, it seemed, until the master of Felicity Manor, the onetime head of Dalan, and the current head of the Peace Preservation Corps, Sima Ting, appeared, looking downcast. He was holding a badly beaten brass gong, which he struck reluctantly as he made a circle of the area. He stopped in the center of the straw mat and announced, "Fellow township residents — grandfathers, grandmothers, uncles, aunts, brothers, sisters, boys and girls — my brother has achieved a glorious victory in bringing down the steel bridge. This news has traveled far and wide, and we have been visited by friends and relatives who have presented us with more than twenty congratulatory scrolls. To celebrate this glorious victory, my brother has invited a troop of actors to perform today. He himself will mount the stage in full costume in a new drama intended to educate all township residents. While celebrating the Lantern Festival, we must not forget our heroic war of resistance and cannot allow the Japs to occupy our town. I, Sima Ting, am a son of China, and will no longer serve as head of the puppet Peace Preservation Corps. Fellow residents, as Chinese, we cannot serve those Japanese sons of bitches." When he finished his rhythmic harrangue, he bowed to the crowd, turned, and ran back to join the musicians — a fiddler, a flutist, and a balloon guitarist — who were just then walking out with their stools.

The musicians sat near the straw mat and began tuning their instruments, led by the flutist. High notes fell, low notes coiled skyward. The coordinated sounds of the fiddle, the flute, and the balloon guitar formed a single thread with three parts, stopping once they were all in tune. Then they waited. Now out came the percussionists: drummers, gong player, and cymbalist, instruments under one arm and stools under the other; they sat across from the other musicians. A fierce drum-beat banged out the rhythm, followed by the crisp clangs of a gong and the high-pitched beats of a small drum; they were joined by a rope of notes from the fiddle, balloon guitar, and flute that tied up our legs so we couldn't move and tied up our souls so we couldn't think. The melody was soft and lingering, sad and dreary, sometimes moaning, sometimes murmuring. What kind of drama was this? Our Northeast Gaomi "cat's meow" form of singing was called by some "tying up your old lady's peg." When the cat's meow was sung, the three cardinal values of social relations were turned inside out; when you heard the cat's meow, you forgot even your own mother and father. Then, as the beat picked up, the audience began to tap their feet; our lips began to twitch, our hearts quivered. The waiting was like an arrow on the bow before firing: five, four, three, two, one — the voice reached its highest point, then trailed off, rising hoarsely, higher and higher, until it tore through the heavens.

I was once a girl, gentle and graceful, charming and coy — na! With the sound of the voice lingering in the air, my second sister, Zhaodi, floated out from the Sima compound on tiny steps, as if walking on water, a red cotton flower in her hair and wearing a blue, wide-sleeved jacket over sweeping pants that all but obscured her embroidered slippers; she carried a basket over her left arm and a wooden club in her right hand. She floated up into the light of the gas lamps and stopped in the center of the straw mat, where she struck a dramatic pose. Her eyebrows were no longer eyebrows; they were crescent moons at the edge of the sky. Her gaze washed up onto our heads; her nose was thin and angular, her thick lips were painted a red more lush than cherry blossoms in May. Absolute silence surrounded her; ten thousand unblinking eyes, ten thousand pounding hearts; pent-up power burst out in a loud roar of approval. My second sister then spread her legs, bent at the waist, and ran, making a complete circle. Her limbs were supple as willow branches, her steps like a snake moving on tassels. There was no wind that night, but it was bitter cold, and yet my sister wore only thin clothing. Mother watched in amazement; my sister's figure had developed rapidly after eating the eel; her breasts were the size of pears, beautifully shaped, and she was surely destined to carry on the glorious tradition of Shangguan women, with big breasts and wide hips. She wasn't even breathing hard after making a circle around the yard, her demeanor unchanged. She sang the second line: *I shall marry the man of courage, Sima Ku.* This line was smooth and even, no rise at the end, but it had a powerful effect on the audience. People whispered to one another, Whose daughter is this? She's a daughter in the Shangguan family. Didn't the Shangguan daughter run off with the leader of the musket band? She's their second daughter. When did she become Sima Ku's concubine? You dumb fuck, this is opera! Shut the fuck up, both of you! My third sister, Lingdi, and her other sisters shouted from the crowd to protect Second Sister's reputation. Quiet returned. *My husband, an expert at destroying bridges, threw Molotov cocktails at the Flood Dragon River Bridge. In the fifth month, during the Dragon Boat Festival, blue flames shot high into the air, incinerating the Jap devils, who screamed for their mothers and fathers. My husband was badly wounded in the backside. Last night, when a storm blanketed heaven and earth with snow, my husband led his troops to destroy the steel bridge . . .* My sister then went through the motions of breaking a hole in the ice with an ax, then pretended she was washing clothes in the water. She was quaking from head to toe, like a dead leaf on the tip of a branch in the heart of winter. People were captivated by the performance; some roared their approval, others dried their eyes with their sleeves. As a burst of drums and cymbals tore through the air, Second Sister stood up and gazed into the distance. *I hear an explosion off in the southwest, and I see flames leap into the sky. It must be my husband, who has destroyed the bridge, and the Jap devils' train has gone to meet its maker. I must run home to warm a pot of wine and kill a pair of hens for chicken stew . . .* Then my sister gathered her clothes around her and made as if to climb an embankment as her song continued: *I look up and see that I am face-to-face with four ravenous wolves . . .* The four fleet-footed men in painted faces who had laid out the mats came somersaulting through the gate. They surrounded my sister and reached out to claw her, like cats closing in on a mouse. The man whose face was painted like a raccoon sang out in a strangled voice: *I am the Japanese platoon leader Tatsuda, on the lookout for a pretty young girl. I've heard there are some real beauties in Northeast Gaomi. I look up and see a lovely face right in front of me. Hey, there, young lady, come with me, an Imperial soldier, for a good life.* The men pounced on my sister, who turned as stiff as a board. Holding her high over their heads, the four "Jap devils" took a turn around the mats. The drums and cymbals beat a frenzied rhythm, like an approaching storm. The audience crowded anxiously up to the stage. "Put my daughter down!" Mother screamed as she rushed up to

the stage. I stood up straight in my carrying pouch; the feeling that action brought would return later in life as I rode on horseback. Mother
reached out and, like an eagle swooping down on a rabbit, dug into the
eyes of "Platoon Leader Tatsuda." With a cry of alarm, he released my
sister, and so did the other three men, letting her drop hard onto the
mat. The three actors scampered off the stage, leaving "Platoon
Leader Tatsuda" in the grip of Mother, who wrapped her legs around
his waist and tore at his face and head with her fingernails. Second Sister got up and wrapped her arms around Mother. "Mother, Mother!"
she shouted. "We're just acting, it isn't real!"

Members of the audience ran up and pulled Mother off "Platoon
Leader Tatsuda." His face a mass of bloody scratches, he turned and
ran in through the gate as if his life depended on it. Gasping for breath,
her anger not yet spent, Mother said, "Who dares try to take advantage
of my daughter, which one of you dares to do that?" "Mother," Second
Sister spat out angrily, "you have ruined a perfectly good play!" "Listen to me, Zhaodi," Mother said, "let's go home. We can't take part in
plays like that." She reached out to take Second Sister's arm, but
Zhaodi shook her off. "Mother," she hissed, "don't make me lose face
in front of all these people!" "You're making *me* lose face," Mother
replied. "Come home with me right now!" "I'm not going to," Second
Sister said, just as Sima Ku came onstage singing loudly: *I'm riding my
horse home after blowing up a bridge* . . . He was wearing riding boots and
an army cap, and carrying a leather crop. Seated upon an imaginary
horse, he stomped on the ground and moved forward, rising and falling
in concert with the imaginary reins he was holding, as if galloping on
horseback. The pounding of drums and crash of cymbals shook the
heavens, string and bamboo instruments rose in harmony; above it all,
the strains of a flute tore through the clouds and firmament, driving the
soul out of the body of anyone within earshot, not from fear, inspired
but not afraid. Sima Ku's face was as cold and hard as cast iron, somber
as death, not a trace of shallow slyness: *Suddenly I hear turmoil on the
riverbank, and I whip my horse to make it go faster* — A two-string *huqin*
made the sound of a horse's whinnies: *Hui-er hui-er hui-er hui . . . my
heart's on fire, my horse runs like the wind, normal steps made in one, three
steps made in two* . . . Faster and faster the drums and cymbals, stomp-
stomp, moving ever forward, a hawk's turn, a split in the air; an old ox
gasps for air, the lion dances atop the embroidered ball — Sima Ku
performed every acrobatic trick he knew on the straw mat; hard to

believe that a heavy medicinal plaster was still stuck to his backside. Second Sister anxiously pushed Mother, who was still grumbling, back into the audience, where she belonged. Three men acting as Japanese soldiers rushed into the center of the stage, bent over at the waist, planning to lift Second Sister over their heads again. "Platoon Leader Tatsuda" was nowhere to be found, so it was up to the other three; two of them lifted her head and shoulders, the third held her feet, his painted face sticking up between her legs. It was such a funny sight that the audience couldn't help but giggle, and that turned to laughter when he made a funny face. So then he started hamming it up, and the audience exploded with boisterous guffaws, which drew a scowl from Sima Ku. But he sang on anyway: *Suddenly I hear shouts and screams. It's the Japanese soldiers in another murderous rage, and I race forward with no thought for myself — I reach out and grab the shoulders of the Japanese dog. Let go of her!* Sima Ku reached out and grabbed the head of the "Japanese soldier" sticking up between Second Sister's legs and shouts. That's when the fight commenced. The odds were now three to one, rather than four to one. The end came swiftly for the "Japanese," and Sima had rescued his "wife." Holding my sister in his arms, with the "Japanese" on their hands and knees on the mat, Sima Ku strode through the gate amid the strains of joyous music. The four men holding the kerosene lanterns abruptly came to life, following Sima through the gate, taking the light with them and leaving us staring into the darkness . . .

The next morning, the real Japanese surrounded the village. The crack of rifle fire, the thud of artillery, and the loud whinnies of war ponies startled us out of our sleep. With me in her arms, Mother led my seven sisters down into the turnip cellar, crawling through the dark, dank tunnel until we emerged into a wider space, where Mother lit an oil lantern. In the dim light, we sat on a straw mat, cocking our ears and listening to the scattered noises upstairs.

I don't know how long we sat there before we heard heavy breathing in the dark tunnel. Mother picked up a pair of blacksmith tongs, quickly blew out the lantern, returning the room to darkness. I began to cry. Mother stuffed one of her nipples into my mouth. It was cold, hard, and rigid, and it had a salty, bitter taste.

The heavy breathing drew nearer; Mother raised the tongs over her head with both hands at the very moment I heard my second sister, Zhaodi, call out in a strange voice, "Mother, it's me, don't hit me . . ." With a sigh of relief, Mother let her hands drop weakly in front of her. "Zhaodi," she said, "you scared me half to death." "Light the lantern, Mother," Zhaodi said. "There's somebody behind me."

Somehow Mother got the lantern lit; its pale light shone throughout the cave once again. Second Sister was covered with mud and had a scratch on her cheek. She carried a bundle in her arms. "What is that?" Mother asked, registering her surprise. Second Sister scrunched up her mouth, as translucent tears made tracks through the dirt on her face. "Mother," she said, her voice cracking, "this is his third wife's son." Mother froze. Then: "Take that back to wherever you found it!" she said angrily. Second Sister came up to Mother on her knees, looked up, and said, "Can't you show some mercy, Mother? His family has just been wiped out. This one is all that's left to carry on the Sima family line . . ."

Mother pulled back a corner of the bundle, revealing the dark, thin, long face of the last surviving son of the Sima family. The little tyke was fast asleep, breathing evenly; his mouth puckered up, as if suckling in his dream. My heart filled with hatred for him. I spat out the nipple and howled. Mother shoved the nipple, colder and even more bitter-tasting than before, back into my mouth.

"Tell me you'll take him, Mother, won't you?" Second Sister asked.

Mother squeezed her eyes shut and said nothing.

Second Sister stood up, thrust the bundled baby into the arms of Third Sister, Lingdi, fell back onto her knees, and banged her head on the ground in a kowtow. "Mother," she said through her tears, "I'm his woman while I'm alive, and I'll be his ghost after I die. Please save this child, and I'll never forget your kindness as long as I live!"

Second Sister stood up and turned to go back out through the tunnel. Mother reached out and stopped her. "Where are you going?" she sobbed.

Second Sister said, "Mother, he has been wounded in the leg and is hiding under the millstone. I must go to him."

The stillness outside was shattered by the clatter of horse hooves and the crackle of gunfire. Mother moved over to block the entrance to the turnip cellar. "I'll do what you say, but I won't let you risk your life out there."

"His leg won't stop bleeding, Mother," Second Sister said. "If I don't go to him, he'll bleed to death. And if he dies, what's the use of my going on living? Let me go, Mother, please . . ."

Mother let out a howl, but quickly closed her mouth again.

"Mother," Second Sister said, "I'll get down and kowtow to you again."

She fell to her knees and banged her head on the ground, then buried her face in Mother's legs. But then she parted Mother's legs and quickly crawled out of the room.

5

The nineteen heads of the Sima family hung from a rack outside the Felicity Manor gate all the way up to Qingming, the day of ancestral worship in the warmth of spring, when flowers were in full bloom. The rack, made of five thick and very straight China fir boards, looked something like a swing set. The heads were strung up with steel wire. Even though crows and sparrows and owls had pecked away most of the flesh, it still took little imagination to distinguish the heads of Sima Ting's wife; his two foolish sons; the first, second, and third wives of Sima Ku; the nine sons and daughters born to those three women; and the father, mother, and two younger brothers of Sima Ku's third wife, who were visiting at the time. The air hung heavy over the village following the massacre, the survivors taking on the appearance of living ghosts, cooping themselves up in dark rooms during the daytime, daring to emerge only after night had fallen.

There was no news at all of Second Sister after she left us that day. The baby boy she left behind caused us no end of trouble. Mother had to nurse him to keep him from starving to death during those days we spent in our cellar hideaway. With his mouth and eyes opened wide, he greedily sucked up milk that should have been mine. He had an astonishing capacity, sucking breasts dry and then bawling for more. He sounded like a crow when he cried, or a toad, or maybe an owl. And the look on his face was that of a wolf, or a dog, or maybe a wild hare. He was my sworn enemy; the world wasn't big enough for the two of us. I howled in protest when he took Mother's breasts as his own; he cried just as loud when I tried to take back what was mine. His eyes remained open when he cried. They were the eyes of a lizard. Damn Zhaodi for bringing home a demon born to a lizard!

Mother's face turned puffy and pale under this double onslaught, and I sensed dimly that little yellow buds had begun to sprout all over her body, like the turnips that had been in our cellar over the long winter. The first of them appeared on her breasts, and that resulted in a diminished supply of milk, with a sweet, turnipy taste. How about you, little Sima bastard, has that scary taste eluded you? People are supposed to treasure what's theirs, but that was getting harder and harder to do. If I didn't suckle, he would for sure. Precious gourds, little doves, enamel vases, your skin has withered, you've dried up, your blood vessels have turned purple, your nipples are nearly black; you sag impotently.

In order for both me and that little bastard to survive, Mother courageously led my sisters out of the cellar into the light of day. The grain in our family storage room was all gone, as were the mule and the donkey; the pots and pans and all the dishes had been smashed; and the Guanyin Bodhisattva in the shrine was now a headless corpse. Mother had forgotten to take her foxskin coat into the cellar with her; the lynx coats belonging to my eighth sister and me were nowhere to be seen. The fur on the other coats, which the rest of my sisters never took off, had by then fallen off, giving them the look of mangy wild animals. Shangguan Lü lay beneath the millstone in the storage room. She'd eaten all twenty or so of the turnips Mother had left for her before moving into the cellar, and had shat a pile of cobblestone-looking turds. When Mother went in to see her, she picked up a handful of the petrified turds and flung them at her. The skin of her face looked like frozen, decaying turnip peels; her white hair looked like twisted yarn, some sticking straight up, some hanging down her back. A green light emerged from her eyes. Shaking her head, Mother laid several turnips on the floor in front of her. All the Japanese — or maybe it was Chinese — had left for us was a half cellar of sugar beets that had already begun to sprout. Overcome by disappointment, Mother found an unbroken earthenware jar in which Shangguan Lü had hidden her precious arsenic. She poured the red powder into the turnip soup. Once the powder dissolved, a colored oil spread across the surface of the soup and a foul smell filled the air. Mother stirred the mixture with a wooden ladle until it was smooth, then picked it up and slowly poured it into the wok. The corner of her mouth twitched oddly. After ladling some of the turnip soup into a chipped bowl, Mother said, "Lingdi, give this soup to your grandmother." "Mother," Lingdi said, "you put poison in it, didn't you?" Mother nodded. "Are you going to poison Grandma?" "We'll all die together," Mother said, to which my sisters responded by weeping, including my blind eighth sister, whose thin cries were little more than the buzzing of a hornet. Her large, black, but sightless eyes filled with tears. Eighth Sister was the most wretched of the wretched, the saddest of the sad. "But we don't want to die, Mother," my sisters pleaded tearfully. Even I took up the chant: "Mother . . . Mother . . ." "My poor, dear little children . . ." Mother said; by then she too was crying. She cried for the longest time, all the while accompanied by her sobbing children. Finally, she blew her nose loudly, took back the chipped bowl, and flung it and its contents into the yard. "We're not going to die! If death doesn't frighten a person, then nothing can!" With that comment, she stood up and led us out into the street to find food. We were the first villagers to venture out onto the street. When they spotted the heads of the Sima family, my sisters were afraid. But in a matter of days, it was just another village sight. Mother held the little Sima bastard in her arm, so he was directly opposite me. She pointed to the heads and said to him softly, "I don't want you to ever forget that, you poor child."

Mother and my sisters walked out of the village and into a reawakened field, where they began digging up white grass roots, which they would boil after rinsing and mashing them. Third Sister, the smart one, found a nest of voles. What made that such a great find was not just the addition of meat to our diet, but that the food they'd stored away was now ours as well. After that, my sisters made a fishnet out of some hemp twine, which they used to snag some dark, thin fish and shrimp that had survived the winter in the local pond. One day, Mother put a spoonful of fish broth into my mouth; I spit it right back out and started bawling at the top of my lungs. Then she put a spoonful into the mouth of the Sima brat; the moron swallowed it right down. So Mother fed him another spoonful. He swallowed that too. "Good," Mother exclaimed excitedly. "For all the bad karma, at least this kid knows how to eat." She turned her gaze to me. "Now, what about you? It's time you got weaned too." Panic-stricken, I grabbed hold of her breast.

The village began to come back to life, once we had taken the lead. It was a calamitous time for local voles; after them came wild jackrabbits, fish, turtles, shrimp, crabs, snakes, and frogs. All across the vast land, the only creatures that survived were poisonous toads and birds on the wing. And still, if not for the timely growth of edible wild herbs, most of the villagers would have starved to death anyway. After Qingming passed, the peach blossoms began to fall, and steam rose from fallow fields that cried out for a new planting. But we had no farm animals and no seeds. By the time fat little tadpoles were swimming in the marshes, and in the oval waters of the local pond, and in the shallows of the river, the villagers had taken to the road. By the fourth month, most had left; by the fifth month, most had returned to their homes. Third Master Fan said, "Here at least there are wild grasses and edible herbs to keep us from starving. That's more than you can say about other places." By the sixth month, outsiders had begun showing up in our village. They slept in the church, and on the ground in the Sima compound, and in abandoned mills. Like dogs driven mad by hunger, they stole food out from under us. Finally, Third Master Fan organized the village men to drive the outsiders away. He was our leader; the outsiders countered with a leader of their own — a young man with bushy eyebrows and big eyes. He was a master at catching birds, always seen with a pair of slingshots hanging from his belt and, over his shoulder, a burlap bag that was filled with pellets of dried mud. Third Sister saw him in action one day. A pair of partridges was in the midst of a mating ritual up in the air. He took out one of his slingshots and fired a mud pellet into the sky, seemingly without even aiming. One of the partridges fell to the ground like a stone, landing right at Third Sister's feet. The bird's head was smashed. Its mate cried out as it circled overhead. The man took out another pellet, fired it into the air, and the second bird fell to the ground. He bent down, picked up the bird, and walked up to my sister. He looked right at her; she returned his gaze with a hateful stare of her own. By that time, Third Master Fan had been to our house to inform us of the movement to drive away the outsiders, which fired up our hatred of them. But rather than pick up the bird at Third Sister's feet, he tossed her the one in his hands, then turned and walked off without a word.

Third Sister came home with the partridges; the meat was for Mother, the broth for my sisters and the little Sima bastard, and the bones for my grandmother, who crunched them up loudly. Third Sister didn't tell anyone that the outsider had given her the partridges, which were quickly transformed into tasty juices that wound up in my stomach. On a number of occasions, Mother waited until I was asleep to stick one of her nipples into the mouth of the little Sima baby; but he refused it. He preferred to grow up on grasses and bark. Blessed with an astonishing appetite, he swallowed anything that was put into his mouth. "He's like a donkey," Mother commented. "He was born to eat grass." Even the turds that came out of him were like equine droppings. Not only that, Mother believed that he had a pair of ruminating stomachs. We often saw clumps of grass rise up from his stomach into his mouth, then watched as he closed his eyes and chewed contentedly, white foamy bubbles gathering at the corners of his mouth. After he'd chewed for a while, he'd stretch out his neck and swallow it down with a gurgling sound.

Battles between the villagers and outsiders broke out following an attempt by Third Master Fan to ask them politely to leave. The outsiders' representative — the young man who had given Third Sister the partridges — was called Birdman Han, the bird-catching specialist. With his hands on the slingshots at his waist, he argued vigorously, without giving an inch. He said that Northeast Gaomi had at one time been an unpopulated wasteland, and everyone was an outsider then. So if you can live here, why can't we? But those were fighting words, and an argument ensued; that soon led to pushing and shoving. One young villager, an impetuous fellow everyone called Consumptive Six, came bursting out from behind Third Master Fan, picked up a steel club, and swung it at the head of Birdman Han's aging mother. Her skull cracked and, leaking a gray liquid, the old woman died on the spot. Birdman let out a wail that sounded more like that of an injured wolf. Taking his slingshots from his belt, he let two pellets fly, blinding Comsumptive Six where he stood. All hell broke loose then, with the outsiders gradually getting the worst of it. With the body of his mother over his shoulder, Birdman Han retreated, fighting every step of the way, all the way back to the sandy ridge west of the village. There he laid his mother out on the ground, loaded his slingshot, and took aim at Third Master Fan. "You had better not try to kill us all, headman. Even a rabbit bites when it's cornered!" Before he'd finished, one of his pellets cut the air with a whoosh and struck Third Master Fan in his left ear. "Since we are all Chinese," Birdman Han said, "I'll spare you this time." Cupping his hand over his split ear, Third Master Fan backed off without a word.

The outsiders threw up dozens of tents on the sandy ridge, making it their own. Birdman Han buried his mother on the sandy ridge, then picked up his slingshots and walked up and down the street twice, cursing in his unfamiliar accent. What he was telling the villagers was this: I am a single man, so if I kill one of you, we're even, and if I kill two of you, I'll be one ahead. It is my hope that everyone can live in peace. With Consumptive Six's blinded eyes and Third

Master Fan's shattered ear as examples, none of the villagers was willing to take them on. "Just think," Third Sister said, "he's lost his own mother, so what else can he fear?"

From that time on, the outsiders and the villagers coexisted peacefully despite the grudges each carried. My third sister and Birdman Han met nearly every day at the spot where he had laid the partridges at her feet. At first, the meetings appeared unplanned, but before long they had turned into outdoor trysts, one waiting for the other, no matter how long it took. Third Sister's feet trampled the grass in that spot until it stopped growing altogether. As for Birdman Han, he would simply show up, toss birds at her feet, and leave without a word. Sometimes it would be a pair of turtledoves, sometimes a game hen, and once he brought a huge bird that must have weighed thirty pounds. Third Sister was barely able to carry it home on her back; even Third Master Fan, the wisest man around, had no idea what kind of bird it was. All I can say is, I'd never tasted anything quite so delicious in my life. Naturally, the taste came to me indirectly, through my mother's milk.

Taking advantage of his close relationship with our family, Third Master Fan cautioned Mother to pay heed to what was going on between my third sister and Birdman Han. His words had a demeaning, foul quality. "Young niece, your third daughter and that bird-catcher . . . ah, it's a corruption of public morals, and it's more than the villagers can stand!" Mother said, "She's just a girl." To which Third Master Fan replied, "Your daughters are different from other girls their ages." Mother sent Third Master Fan off with, "You go back and tell those gossips they can to go to hell!"

Reproaching Third Master Fan was one thing, dealing with Third Sister was another: when she came home with a half-dead red-crowned crane, Mother took her aside for a serious talk. "Lingdi," she said, "we can't keep eating somebody else's birds." "Why not?" Lingdi asked. "For him, shooting down a bird is easier than catching a flea." "But they're still his birds, no matter how easily he comes by them. Don't you know that people expect favors to be returned?" "I'll repay him one day," Third Sister said. "Repay him with what?" Mother demanded. "I'll marry him," Third Sister said lightly. "Lingdi," Mother replied somberly, "your two elder sisters have already caused this family to lose more face than anyone could imagine. This time I am not going to give in, no matter what you say." "Mother," Lingdi said with rising indignation, "that's easy for you to say. If not for Birdman Han, could he look like he does today?" She pointed to me, then pointed to the son of the Sima family. "Or him?" Mother looked into my ruddy face and then at the red-cheeked Sima baby, and didn't know what to say. After a moment, she said, "Lingdi, from today on, we won't eat any more of his birds, no matter what you say."

The next day, Third Sister came home with a string of wild pigeons and, displaying her pique, flung them down at Mother's feet.

The eighth month seemed to arrive out of nowhere. Flocks of wild geese filled the sky heading south and settled on the marshes southwest of the village. The villagers and outsiders all converged on them with hooks and nets and other time-tested methods to reap a wild goose harvest. At first it was a lush yield, and feathers floated above the village streets and lanes. But the wild geese were not to be so easily victimized forever, and they began roosting in the farthest, deepest reaches of the marshes, places even foxes found inhospitable; that cancelled out the villagers' hunting strategies. And still Third Sister came home every day with a wild goose; some dead, others still alive, and no one knew how Birdman Han managed to catch them.

Faced with cruel realities, Mother was forced to compromise. If we refused to eat the birds Birdman Han caught for us, we'd all have developed signs of malnourishment, like most of the villagers: edema, asthmatic breathing, eyes with flickering light, just like will-o'-the-wisps. Eating Han's birds meant only that to the list of sons-in-law, which included the leader of a musket band and a specialist in blowing up bridges, was now added an expert bird-catcher.

On the morning of the sixteenth day of the eighth month, Third Sister went to her usual trysting place; at home we awaited her return. By then we were getting a little tired of cooked goose, with its grassy flavor, and were hoping that Birdman Han might present us with a change in diet. We didn't dare hope that Third Sister would bring home another of those oversized, delicious birds, but a few pigeons or turtledoves or wild ducks wouldn't be asking too much, would it?

Third Sister came home empty-handed, her eyes red from crying. Mother asked what was wrong. "Birdman Han was dragged off by armed men in black uniforms on bicycles," she said.

A dozen or so young men had been taken away with him, tied up and strung together like so many locusts. Birdman Han had struggled mightily, the powerful muscles in his arms bulging as he strained to break the ropes binding him. The soldiers had hit him on his buttocks and waist with rifle butts and kicked him in the legs to keep him moving. Anger had welled up in his eyes, which were so red they seemed on the verge of spewing blood or fire. "Who said you could arrest me?" Birdman Han shouted. The squad leader scooped up a handful of mud and rubbed it in Birdman Han's face, temporarily blinding him. He howled like a trussed-up wild animal. Third Sister ran after them, then stopped and yelled, "Birdman Han —" After they'd moved off down the road, she ran after them again, stopped and yelled, "Birdman Han —" The soldiers turned to look at Third Sister and laughed maliciously. At the end, Third Sister shouted, "Birdman Han, I'll wait for you." "Who the fuck asked you to wait?" he shouted back.

That noon, as we looked down at a pot of wild herb soup so light we could see ourselves in it, we — that included Mother — realized how important Birdman Han had become in our lives.

For two days and nights Third Sister lay sprawled on the *kang*, crying without end. Nothing Mother tried to get her to stop worked.

On the third day after Birdman Han was taken away, Third Sister got up off the *kang*, barefoot, shamelessly tore open her blouse, and went outside, where she jumped up into the pomegranate tree, bending the pliant branch into a deep curve. Mother ran out to pull her down, but she leaped acrobatically from the pomegranate tree onto a parasol tree, and from there to a tall catalpa tree. From high up in the catalpa tree she jumped down onto the ridge of our thatched roof. Her movements were amazingly nimble, as if she had sprouted wings. She sat astride the roof ridge, staring straight ahead, her face suffused with a radiant smile. Mother stood on the ground below looking up and pleading pitifully, "Lingdi, Mother's good little girl, please come down. I'll never interfere in your life again, you can do whatever you please . . ." No reaction from Third Sister. It was as if she had changed into a bird, and no longer understood human language. Mother called Fourth Sister, Fifth Sister, Sixth Sister, Seventh Sister, Eighth Sister, and the little Sima brat out into the yard, where she told them all to shout up at Third Sister. My sisters called out to her tearfully, but Third Sister ignored them. Instead, she began pecking at her shoulder, as if preening feathers. Her head kept turning, as if on a swivel; not only could she peck her own shoulder, she could even reach down and nibble at her tiny nipples. I was sure she could reach her own buttocks and the heels of her feet if she wanted to. There wasn't a spot anywhere she could not reach with her mouth if she felt like it. In fact, as far as I was concerned, as she sat astride the roof ridge, Third Sister had already entered the avian realm: she thought like a bird, behaved like a bird, and wore the expression of a bird. And as far as I was concerned, if Mother hadn't asked Third Master Fan and some strong young men to drag her down with the help of some black dog's blood, Third Sister would have sprouted wings and turned into a beautiful bird — if not a phoenix, a peacock; and if not a peacock, at least a golden pheasant. But whatever kind of bird she became, she would have spread her wings and flown off in pursuit of Birdman Han. But the end result, and the most shameless outcome, was: Third Master Fan sent Zhang Maolin, a short, agile fellow everyone called The Monkey, up onto the ridge with a bucket of black dog's blood; he sneaked up behind Third Sister and drenched her with the blood. She sprang to her feet and spread her arms to soar into the sky, but merely tumbled off the roof and landed on the brick path below with a thud. Blood streamed out of a deep gash in her head, the size of an apricot, and she passed out.

Weeping uncontrollably, Mother grabbed a handful of grass and held it to Third Sister's head to staunch the flow of blood. Then, with the help of Fourth Sister and Fifth Sister, she cleaned off the dog's blood and carried her inside, laying her on the *kang*.

At around dusk Third Sister came to. With tears in her eyes, Mother asked, "Are you all right, Lingdi?" Third Sister looked up at Mother and appeared to nod her head, but maybe not. Tears seeped from her eyes. "My poor, abused child," Mother said. "They're taking him to Japan," Lingdi said frostily, "and he won't be back for eighteen years. Mother, I want you to make an altar for me. I am now a Bird Fairy."

The comment struck Mother like a thunderbolt. A welter of mixed feelings filled her heart. As she gazed into the now demonic face of Third Sister, there was so much she wanted to say; but not a single word emerged.

In the brief history of Northeast Gaomi Township, six women have been transformed into fox, hedgehog, weasel, white snake, badger, and bat fairies, all a result of love denied or a bad marriage; each lived a life of mystery, earning the fearful respect of others. Now a Bird Fairy had appeared in my house, which both terrified and disgusted Mother. But she didn't dare say anything that went against Third Sister's wishes, for a bloody precedent had been set in the past: a dozen or more years earlier, Fang Jinzhi, the wife of the donkey dealer, Yuan Jinbiao, was caught in the arms of a young man in the graveyard. Members of the Yuan family beat the man to death, and then beat Fang Jinzhi to within an inch of her life. Overwhelmed by shame and anger, she took arsenic, but was saved when someone forced human waste down her throat. When she came around, she said she was possessed by a fox fairy and asked that an altar be set up for her. The Yuan family refused. From that day on, the family's woodpile often caught fire; their pots and pans and other kitchenware frequently broke apart for no apparent reason; when the old man of the family tipped over his wine decanter, out came a lizard; when the old woman of the family sneezed, two front teeth came flying out of her nostrils; and when the family boiled a pot of meat-filled *jiaozi* dumplings, what came out of the water instead were toads. The Yuans finally gave in and set up an altar for the fox fairy and installed Fang Jinzhi in a meditation room.

The meditation room for the Bird Fairy was set up in a side room. With my fourth and fifth sisters in tow, Mother cleaned up the bits and pieces left behind by Sha Yueliang, swept the walls clean of cobwebs and the ceiling of dust, and then put fresh paper coverings in the windows. They put an incense table up against the northern wall and lit three sticks of sandalwood incense left over from that earlier year when Shangguan Lü had worshipped the Guanyin Bodhisattva. They ought to have put an image of a Bird Fairy up in front of the incense table, but they didn't know what one looked like. So Mother asked Third Sister for instructions. "Fairy," she said piously as she knelt on the floor, "where can I obtain the image of an idol for the incense table?" Third Sister sat primly in a chair, her eyes closed, her cheeks flushed, as if enjoying a wonderful erotic dream. Not daring to hurry or upset her, Mother asked again even more piously. My third sister opened her mouth in a wide yawn, her eyes still closed, and replied in a twittering voice somewhere between bird and human speech, making her words nearly impossible to understand, "There'll be one tomorrow."

The next morning, a hawk-nosed, eagle-eyed beggar came to our door. In his left hand he carried a dog-beating staff made of hollowed-out bamboo, while in his right he held a ceramic bowl with two deep chips on the rim. He was filthy, as if he'd just rolled in the dirt, or had completed a thousand-mile trudge; dirt filled his ears and was crusted in the corners of his eyes. Without a word, he walked into our parlor,

freely and casually, as if it were his own home. He removed the lid
from the pot on the stove, ladled out a bowlful of herbal soup, and began slurping it down. When he'd finished, he sat on the stove counter,
again without a word, and scraped Mother's face with his knifelike
gaze. Despite the discomfort she felt inside, she put on a calm exterior.
"Honored guest," she said, "poor as we are, we have nothing for you.
Please don't be offended if I offer you this." She handed him a clump
of wild herbs. He refused the offer. Licking his chapped and bloody
lips, he said, "Your son-in-law asked me to deliver two things to you."
But he took nothing out for us, and as we examined his thin, tattered
clothes and the filthy, scaly gray skin showing through the many holes,
we could not imagine where he could have hidden whatever it was he
had brought for us. "Which son-in-law would that be?" Mother asked,
clearly puzzled. The hawk-nosed, eagle-eyed man said, "Don't ask
me. All I know is that he's a mute, that he can write, that he's a wonderful swordsman, that he saved my life once, and that I repaid the favor. Neither of us is in debt to the other. And that is why no more than
two minutes ago, I was wondering whether I should give you these two
treasures or not. If, when I was ladling out a bowl of your soup, you, the
lady of the house, had made a single rude or impertinent comment, I'd
have kept them for myself. But not only did you say nothing rude or
impertinent, you actually offered me a handful of wild herbs. So I have
decided to give them to you." With that, he stood up, laid his chipped
bowl on the stove counter, and said, "This is a piece of fine ceramic, as
rare as unicorns and phoenixes. It may be the only piece of its kind in
the world. That mute son-in-law of yours did not know its value. All he
knew was that it was part of the loot from one of his raids, and he
wanted you to have it, maybe because it is so big. Then there is this."
He hit the floor with his bamboo staff, producing a hollow sound. "Do
you have a knife?" Mother handed him her cleaver. He used it to cut
almost invisible threads at each end, and the bamboo split into pieces,
which opened up to let fall a painted scroll. He unrolled it, releasing
the smell of mildew and decay. There in the middle of the yellowed
silk was a painting of a large bird. We were stunned. The image was an
exact replica of the big, incomparably delicious bird Third Sister had
brought home that time. In the painting, it was standing straight, head
up, looking contemptuously at us with lackluster eyes. The hawk-
nosed, eagle-eyed man told us nothing about the scroll or the bird on
it. Rather, he rolled it back up, laid it atop the ceramic bowl, turned,

and walked out the door without a backward glance. His now freed hands hung loosely at his sides and moved stiffly in concert with his long strides.

Mother was rooted to the spot like a pine tree, and I was a knot on the trunk of that tree. Five of my sisters were like willow trees; the Sima boy an oak sapling. We stood there like a little wooded area in front of the mysterious ceramic bowl and bird scroll. If Third Sister hadn't broken the silence with a mocking laugh, we might really have turned into trees.

Her prediction had come true. With extraordinary reverence, we carried the bird scroll into the meditation room and hung it in front of the incense table. And since the chipped ceramic bowl had such an extraordinary history, what mortal was worthy of using it? So Mother, feeling blessed by good fortune, placed it on the incense table and filled it with fresh water for the Bird Fairy.

Word that our family had produced a Bird Fairy quickly made the rounds in Northeast Gaomi and beyond. A steady stream of pilgrims seeking nostrums and predictions beat a path to our door, but the Bird Fairy saw no more than ten a day. They knelt on the ground outside the window of her meditation room, in which a tiny hole permitted her birdlike predictions for the curious and prescriptions for the infirm to filter through. The prescriptions Third Sister — I mean the Bird Fairy — dispensed were truly unique and filled with an aura of mischief. Here is what she prescribed for someone suffering from a stomach problem: A powdered mixture of seven bees, a pair of dung beetle's excrement balls, an ounce of peach leaves, and half a catty of crushed eggshells, taken with water. And for someone in a rabbitskin cap who was afflicted with an eye disease: A paste made of seven locusts, a pair of crickets, five praying mantises, and four earthworms, spread on the palms of the hands. When the patient caught his prescription as it floated out from the hole in the window and read it, a look of irreverence appeared on his face, and we heard him grumble, "She's a Bird Fairy, all right. Everything on this prescription is bird food." He walked off, still grumbling, and we couldn't help feeling ashamed of Third Sister. Locusts and crickets, they were all bird delicacies, so how were they supposed to cure human eye ailments? But while I was caught up in confusion, the man with the eye problem nearly flew down the road our way, fell to his knees beneath the window, banged his head on the ground as if he were mashing garlic stalks, and intoned repeatedly:

"Great Fairy, forgive me, Great Fairy, forgive me . . ." His pleas for forgiveness drew mocking laughter from Third Sister inside the room.
Eventually, we learned that when the garrulous man was on the road
home, a hawk swooped down out of the sky and dug its talons into his
head, before flying off with his cap in its clutches. Then there was a
man with mischief on his mind who knelt outside the window pretending to be suffering from urethritis. The Bird Fairy asked through the
window, "What ails you?" The man said, "When I urinate, it feels like
I'm passing ice cubes." Suddenly the room went silent, as if the Bird
Fairy had left out of embarrassment. The lewd, daring man put his
eye up to the hole in the window, but before he could see a thing, he
shrieked in agony as a monstrous scorpion fell from the window onto
his neck and stung him. His neck swelled up immediately, and then his
face, until his eyes were mere slits, like those of a salamander.

The Bird Fairy had used her mystical powers to punish that terrible man, to the boisterous delight of the good people and the en-
hancement of her own reputation. In the days that followed, the
pilgrims coming to be cured of ailments or have their fortunes told
spoke with accents from far-off places. When Mother asked around,
she learned that some had come from as far away as the Eastern Sea,
and others from the Northern Sea. When she asked how they had
heard about the mystical powers of the Bird Fairy, they stood there
wide-eyed, not knowing what to say. They emitted a salty odor, which,
Mother informed us, was the smell of the ocean. The pilgrims slept on
the ground in our compound as they waited patiently. The Bird Fairy
followed a schedule of her own devising: Once she had seen ten pilgrims, she retired for the day, bringing a deathly silence to the eastern
side room. Mother sent Fourth Sister over with fresh water; when she
entered, Third Sister came out. Then Fifth Sister went in with food,
and Fourth Sister came out. This stream of girls entering and leaving
dazzled the eyes of the pilgrims, who could not tell which of the girls
was the actual Bird Fairy.

When Third Sister separated herself from the Bird Fairy, she was
just another girl, albeit one with a number of unusual expressions and
movements. She seldom spoke, squinted most of the time, preferred
squatting to standing, drank plain water and thrust out her neck with
each swallow, just like a bird. She didn't eat any sort of grain, but then,
neither did we, since there wasn't any. The pilgrims brought offerings
suited to the habits of a bird: locusts, silkworm chrysalises, aphids,

scarab beetles, and fireflies. Some also came with vegetarian fare, such as sesame seeds, pine nuts, and sunflower seeds. Of course, we gave it all to Third Sister; what she didn't eat was divided up among Mother, my other sisters, and the little Sima heir. My sisters, wonderful daughters all, would get red in the face over trying to present their silkworm chrysalises to others. Mother's supply of milk was decreasing, though the quality remained high. It was during those squawking days that Mother tried to wean me from breast-feeding, but she abandoned the idea when it became clear that I'd cry myself into the grave before I'd give it up.

To express their gratitude for the boiled water and other conveniences we supplied and, far more importantly, for the Bird Fairy's successes in freeing them from their cares and worries, the pilgrims from the oceans left a burlap sack filled with dried fish for us upon their departure. We were moved more than words can say, and saw our visitors all the way to the river. It was then that we saw dozens of thick-masted fishing boats at anchor in the slow-flowing Flood Dragon River. In the long history of the Flood Dragon River, no more than a few wooden rafts had ever been seen on the river; they were used to cross the river when it flooded. But because of the Bird Fairy, the Flood Dragon River had become a branch of vast oceans. It was the early days of the tenth month, and strong northwestern winds sliced across the river. The seagoing people boarded their boats, raised their patched gray sails, and sailed out into the middle of the river. Their rudders stirred up so much mud that the water turned murky. Flocks of silvery gray gulls that had followed the fishing boats on their way over now followed them back the way they'd come. Their cries hung over the river as they skimmed the surface one minute and soared high above it the next. A few even entertained us by flying upside down or hovering in the air. Villagers had gathered on the riverbank, initially just to gawk; but they now added their voices to the grand send-off for pilgrims who had come so far. The boats' sails billowed in the winds, their rudders began to move back and forth, and they headed slowly down the river. They would travel down the Flood Dragon River all the way to the Great Canal, and from there to the White Horse River, which would take them to the Bohai. The trip would take twenty-one days. This information was part of a geography lesson Birdman Han gave me some eighteen years later. The visit to Northeast Gaomi Township by these pilgrims from distant lands was a virtual reenactment of the sea voyages of Zheng He and Xu Fu centuries earlier, and constituted one of the most glorious chapters in the history of Northeast Gaomi Township. And all because of a Bird Fairy in the Shangguan family. The glory dispersed the clouds of gloom in Mother's breast; maybe she was hoping that some other animal fairy would make an appearance in the house, a Fish Fairy, for instance. But then again, maybe she wasn't.

After the fishermen were back on their boats, an eminent guest showed up. She arrived in a sleek, black Chevrolet sedan, with hulking bodyguards, armed with Mausers, standing on each running board. She was escorted by clouds of dust from the village's dirt road. The poor bodyguards looked like donkeys that had been rolling in the dirt. The sedan pulled up to our doorway and stopped. One of the bodyguards opened the back door. First to appear was a pearl and jade head ornament, followed by a neck, and lastly a fat torso. Both in terms of figure and expression, the woman looked exactly like an oversized goose.

In strictest terms, a goose is also a bird. But however elevated her status, when she came calling on the Bird Fairy, courtesy and reverence were expected. Nothing escaped the Bird Fairy, who knew everything in advance, so no hypocrisy or arrogance could be tolerated. The woman knelt at the window, closed her eyes, and prayed softly. Her face was the color of rose petals, so she hadn't come for relief of an illness; jewelry sparkled from head to toe, so she hadn't come to seek riches. What could a woman like that be seeking from the Bird Fairy? A slip of white paper floated out through the hole in the window; when the woman opened it up and read it, her face turned as red as a rooster's cockscomb. She tossed several silver dollars to the ground, stood up, and walked off. What was written on the slip of paper? Only the Bird Fairy and the woman knew.

Visitors continued to throng to our place for days, and then they stopped. By the time the cold winter set in, we had eaten all the dried fish in the burlap sack, and once again Mother's milk carried the taste of grass and the bark of trees. On the seventh day of the twelfth month, we heard that the largest local Christian sect would be opening a soup kitchen in Northgate Cathedral. So Mother and we children, bowls and chopsticks in hand, walked all night with groups of starving villagers into the county seat. We left Third Sister and Shangguan Lü to watch the house; since one of them was more fairy than human and the other less human than demon, they were better prepared to put up with hunger. Before leaving, Mother tossed a handful of grass to

Shangguan Lü. "Mother," she said, "if you are able to die, do so quickly. Why suffer with us this way?"

It was the first time any of us had taken the road to the county seat. By "road" I mean only that we followed a little gray path formed by the footprints of man and beast. I couldn't tell you how that rich woman's car had made it to our village. We trudged along in cold starlight, me standing up on Mother's back, the little Sima heir on the back of Fourth Sister, Eighth Sister on the back of Fifth Sister, my sixth and seventh sisters walking by themselves. As midnight came and went, we heard the intermittent cries of children in the wilderness all around us. Seventh Sister, Eighth Sister, and the little Sima heir also started to cry. Mother shouted her disapproval, but even she was crying, and so were Fourth Sister and Fifth Sister, both of whom suddenly tottered and fell to the ground. But as soon as Mother picked up one and went for the other, the first one fell again. And so it went, back and forth. Finally, Mother sat on the cold ground, along with all the others, huddling together to keep warm. She shifted me around to the front and put her cold hand under my nose to see if I was still breathing. She must have thought that either the cold or hunger had taken me from her. I breathed weakly to show her I was still alive. So she raised the curtain over her breasts and stuffed a cold nipple into my mouth. It felt like an ice cube slowly melting in my mouth and turning it numb. Mother's breast had nothing to give; no matter how hard I sucked, all I managed to draw from it were a few wispy strands of blood. It was cold, so very cold! And in the midst of that cold, mirages floated in front of the eyes of the starving people around us: a blazing stove, a pot filled with steaming chicken and duck, plate after plate of meat-stuffed buns, all that and green grass and lovely flowers. In front of my eyes were two gourd-sized breasts, overflowing with rich liquid, lively as a pair of doves and sleek as porcelain bowls. They smelled wonderful and looked beautiful; slightly blue-tinged liquid, sweet as honey, gushed from them, filling my belly and drenching me from head to toe. I wrapped my arms around the breasts and swam in their fountains of liquid . . . overhead, millions and billions of stars swirled through the sky, round and round to form gigantic breasts: breasts on Sirius, the Dog Star; breasts on the Big Dipper; breasts on Orion the Hunter; breasts on Vega, the Girl Weaver; breasts on Altair, the Cowherd; breasts on Chang'e, the Beauty in the Moon, Mother's breasts . . . I spat out Mother's nipple and gazed up the road a ways. A man holding a tattered goatskin torch high over his head came bounding toward us. It was Third Master Fan. He was bare to the waist, and amid the acrid stench of burning animal skin and the glare of its light, he was yelling, "Fellow villagers — do not sit down, not under any circumstances. If you sit down, you will freeze to death — come, fellow villagers — keep moving forward — to keep moving is to live, to sit down is to die —"

Third Master Fan's heartfelt exhortation brought many people up from the illusory huddled warmth, a sure path to death, and onto their feet, moving through the cold that was their only chance of survival. Mother stood up, shifted me around to the back, picked up the wretched little Sima heir and held him in her arms, then grabbed Eighth Sister by the arm and began kicking Fourth Sister and Fifth Sister and Sixth Sister and Seventh Sister to get them to their feet. We fell in behind Third Master Fan, who had used his own goatskin jacket as a torch to light our way. What carried us forward wasn't our feet, but our willpower, our desire to reach the county seat, to reach Northgate Cathedral, to accept God's mercy, to accept a bowl of twelfth-month gruel.

Dozens of corpses littered the roadside on this solemn and tragic procession. Some lay with their shirts open and a beatific expression on their faces, as if to warm their chests by the passing flame.

Third Master Fan died in the first glow of sunrise.

We all ate God's twelfth-month gruel; mine came through my mother's breasts. I'll never forget the scene surrounding that meal. Magpies roosted on the cross beneath the high cathedral ceiling. A train panted its way along tracks outside. Steam rose from two huge cauldrons filled with beef stew. The black-cassocked priest stood beside the cauldrons and prayed as hundreds of starving peasants formed a queue behind him. Parishioners spooned gruel into bowls, one ladleful apiece, regardless of the size of the bowl. Loud slurping noises attended the consumption of the gruel, which was diluted by countless tears. Hundreds of pink tongues licked bowls clean, and then the queue formed again. Several burlap sacks of cracked rice and several buckets of water were dumped into the cauldrons; this time, as I could tell from the quality of the milk, the gruel consisted of cracked rice, moldy sorghum, half-rotten soybeans, and barley with chaff.

6

On our way home after eating the twelfth-month gruel, our sense of hunger was greater than ever. No one had the strength to bury the corpses lining the path through the wilderness, nor could anyone muster the energy to even go up and take a look at them. The body of Third Master Fan was the sole exception. During the height of our crisis, a man people normally steered clear of had taken off his goatskin jacket, turned it into a torch, and, with its light and his shouts, brought us to our senses. That sort of kindness, the gift of life, can never be forgotten. So, with Mother taking the lead, the people dragged the old man's sticklike figure over to the side of the road and covered it with dirt.

When we got back home, the first thing we saw was the Bird Fairy pacing back and forth in the yard, holding something bundled in a purple marten overcoat. Mother had to hold on to the doorframe to keep from falling. Third Sister walked up and handed her the bundle. "What's this?" Mother asked. In an almost completely human voice, Third Sister said, "A child." "Whose?" Mother asked, although I think she already knew. "Whose do you think?" Third Sister said.

Obviously, Laidi's purple marten coat would only be used to bundle Laidi's child.

It was a baby girl, dark as a lump of coal, with black eyes like those of a fighting cock, thin lips, and big pale ears that seemed out of place on her face. These characteristics were all the proof we needed of her origins: This was the Shangguan family's first niece, presented to us by Eldest Sister and Sha Yueliang.

Mother's disgust was written all over her face, to which the baby responded with a kittenish smile. Nearly passing out from anger, Mother forgot all about the Bird Fairy's mystical powers and kicked Third Sister in the leg.

With a yelp of pain, Third Sister stumbled forward several steps, and when she turned her head back, there was no mistaking the look of bird rage on her face. Her hardened mouth pointed upward, ready to peck someone. She raised her arms, as if to fly. Not caring if she was bird or human, Mother cursed, "Damn you, who told you to accept her child?" Third Sister's head darted this way and that, as if she were feeding on insects on a tree. "Laidi, you're a shameless little slut!" Mother cursed. "Sha Yueliang, you're a heartless thug and a bandit! All you know how to do is make a baby, not how to take care of one. You think that by sending her to me, everything will be just fine, don't you? Well, stop dreaming! I'll fling your little bastard into the river to feed the turtles, or toss her into the street to feed the dogs, or toss her into the marsh to feed the crows! Just you wait and see!"

Mother took the baby and ran up and down the lanes, repeating her threats to feed the turtles or dogs or crows. When she reached the river's edge, she turned and ran out onto the street, then turned and ran back to the river. Gradually her pace slowed and her voice softened, like a tractor running out of gas. Finally, she plopped down on the spot where Pastor Malory had leaped to his death, looked up at the ruined bell tower, and muttered, "Some are dead and others have run off, leaving me all alone. How am I supposed to survive with a brood of hungry chicks needing to be fed . . . Dear Lord, Old Man Heaven, why don't you say something? How am I supposed to survive?"

I began to cry, my tears falling on Mother's neck. Then the baby girl began to cry, her tears running into her ears. "Jintong," Mother said tenderly, "my pride and joy, please don't cry." She next turned her tenderness to the baby girl: "You poor thing, you should not have come. Grandma doesn't even have enough milk for your little uncle. If I tried to feed you too, you'd both starve to death. I'm not hard-hearted, there's just nothing I can do . . ."

Mother laid the baby girl, still wrapped in the purple marten coat, on the steps in front of the church door, then turned and started running for home as if her life depended on it. But she hadn't gone ten steps when her legs stopped moving. The baby was bawling like a pig under the knife, her cries an invisible rope that had stopped Mother in her tracks . . .

Three days later, our family now numbering nine, we were standing in the human trade section of the county seat marketplace. Mother carried me on her back and Sha Yueliang's little bastard in her arms. Fourth Sister carried the little Sima brat. Eighth Sister was carried by Fifth Sister, while Sixth Sister and Seventh Sister walked alone.

In the city dump, we scrounged up some rotten greens to eat, steeling ourselves to go over to the human trade section, where Mother hung straw tallies around the necks of my fifth, sixth, and seventh sisters, then waited for a buyer to come along.

A row of simple wooden shacks with ugly whitewashed walls and roofs stood opposite us. Tinplate chimneys sticking up over the walls sent black smoke into the air, where it was carried to us on wind currents, changing shape as it came. From time to time, prostitutes, their hair undone and hanging straight down, showing plenty of cleavage, lips painted bright red, and sleepy eyes, emerged from the shacks, some carrying basins, others with buckets. They went to a nearby well to draw water. Steam rose from the mouth of the well. As they cranked the awkward pulley with soft, white hands not used to working, the rope gave off a dull twang. When the oversized bucket appeared at the mouth of the well, they stuck out a foot to hook the rim and drag it smoothly over to the lip, where a layer of ice had formed, with bumps like steamed buns or nipples. The girls ran to their shacks with the water, then ran back for more, wooden clogs clacking noisily on the ground, their freezing, partially exposed breasts emitting a sulfurlike odor. I tried looking over Mother's shoulder, but all I could see were their dancing breasts, like opium flowers or valleys of butterflies.

We were standing on a wide street in front of a high wall that effectively kept the northwest wind away and afforded us a bit of warmth. Cowering on both sides were more people just like us — gaunt and jaundiced-looking, shivering, hungry, and cold. Men and women. Mothers and children. The men were well along in years and as shriveled as rotting wood; those who weren't blind — and many of them were — had red, puffy, suppurating eyes. A child stood or squatted on the ground beside each of them — some boys, some girls. Actually, it was nearly impossible to tell the boys from the girls, since they all looked as if they'd just climbed out of one of the chimneys across the street — human soot. All had straws sticking up out of their collars, mostly rice straw, with dry, yellow leaves; you couldn't help but think of autumn, of horses and the comforting fragrance and happy sounds as they chewed rice straw in the dead of night. Some were less choosy, using bristlegrass they'd picked up somewhere. Most of the women were like Mother, surrounded by a brood of children, although none had as many as she. With some, all the children had straw sticking up out of their collars; with others, only some had it. Again, it was mostly rice straw, with dry, yellow leaves that gave off the fragrance of cut grass and the aura of autumn. Above the children with the straw tallies, the heavy, drooping heads of horses, donkeys, and mules, their eyes as big as brass cymbals, their teeth straight and white, their thick, sensous, and bristly lips revealing glistening teeth, swayed back and forth.

At about noon, a horse-drawn wagon came down the official road from the southeast. The horse, large and white, proceeded with its head held high, threads of silvery mane covering its forehead. It had gentle eyes, a pink streak running down its nose, and purple lips. A red velvet knot hung down from its neck, on which a brass bell had been tied. The bell rang out crisply as the horse drew the wagon toward us, rocking back and forth. We saw a tall saddle on the horse as well as the brass fittings of the shafts. The wheels were decorated with white spokes. The canopy was made of white material that had been treated with many coats of tung oil to protect it from the elements. We'd never seen such a luxurious wagon before, and were confident that the passenger was far nobler than the woman who'd come to see the Bird Fairy in her Chevrolet sedan, confident too that the man sitting in front, in a top hat and sporting a handlebar mustache, was not your ordinary driver. His face was taut, glaring lights shot out of both eyes. He was more reserved than Sha Yueliang, more somber than Sima Ku; and maybe only Birdman Han could have been his equal, if he wore the man's hat and clothes.

The wagon came to a slow stop, and the handsome white horse pawed the ground in a rhythmic accompaniment to the brass bell. The driver pulled back a curtain, and the person inside emerged. She wore a purple marten overcoat and a red fox stole around her neck. How I wished it had been my oldest sister, Laidi, but it wasn't. It was a foreign woman, with a high nose, blue eyes, and a headful of golden hair. Her age? I'm afraid only her parents would know that. Following her off the wagon was a strikingly handsome, black-haired little boy in a blue student uniform and blue woolen overcoat. Everything about him said he was the foreign woman's son. Everything except for his external appearance, which was nothing like hers.

The people around us stirred and surged toward her, like a gang of robbers. But they came to a timid halt before they reached her. "Madam, honorable lady, please buy my granddaughter. Madam, grand lady, just look at this son of mine. He's tougher than any dog, there's no job he can't handle . . ." Men and women meekly attempted to sell their sons and daughters to the foreign woman. Mother alone remained where she was, mesmerized by the sight of the purple marten coat and the red fox stole. There was no doubt that she longed for Laidi. Holding Laidi's child in her arms, her heart spun and tears clouded her eyes.

The aristocratic foreign woman covered her mouth with a handkerchief as she took a turn around the human market. Her heavy perfume made me and the little Sima bastard sneeze. She knelt in front of the blind old man and took a look at his granddaughter. Frightened by the red fox stole around the foreign woman's neck, the girl wrapped her arms around her grandfather's legs and hid behind him, staring at me through terror-filled eyes. The blind old man sniffed the air and smelled the arrival of an aristocratic woman. He reached out his hand. "Madam," he said, "please save this child. If she stays with me, she'll starve to death. Madam, I don't have a cent to my name . . ." The woman stood up and muttered something to the boy in school uniform, who turned to the blind old man and asked loudly, "What is the girl to you?" "I'm her granddad, her useless granddad, a granddad who deserves to die . . ." "What about her parents?" the boy asked. "Starved, they all starved to death. Those who should have died didn't and those who shouldn't have did. Sir, be merciful and take her with you. I don't want a cent from you, if you'll only give the girl a chance for life . . ." The boy turned and muttered something to the foreign woman, who nodded. The boy bent over and tried to pull the girl away from her granddad, but when his hand touched her shoulder, she bit him on the wrist. The boy shrieked and jumped back. With an exaggerated shrug of her shoulders, a grin, and raised eyebrows, the woman took the handkerchief away from her mouth and put it around the boy's wrist.

With feelings that might have been terror and might have been delight, we waited for what seemed like a thousand years; finally, the richly bejeweled, heavily perfumed woman and the youngster with the injured wrist was standing before us. Meanwhile, off to our right, the blind old man was waving his bamboo staff, trying to hit the little girl who had bitten the boy. But she kept darting out of the way, as if playing hide-and-seek, so all he ever hit was the ground or the wall. "You damned little wretch!" the old man sighed. Greedily, I breathed in the foreign woman's fragrance; amid the fragrance of locust, I detected a trace of rose petals, and amid that fragrance, I detected the subtle fragrance of chrysanthemum blossoms. But what absolutely intoxicated me was the smell of her breasts, even with the slight but disgusting smell of lamb they exuded; I flared my nostrils and breathed in deeply. Now that the handkerchief with which she'd covered her mouth was being employed elsewhere, her mouth was exposed to view. It was a wide mouth, a Shangguan Laidi mouth, with thick, Shangguan Laidi lips. Those thick lips were covered with heavy, red, greasy paint. With its high bridge, hers somewhat resembled the

Shangguan girls' noses, but there were differences too: the tips of the Shangguan girls' noses were like little cloves of garlic, making them look foolish and cute at the same time, while the foreign woman's nose was slightly hooked, which gave her a predatory look. Her short forehead filled with deep wrinkles each time she glowered at something. I knew that everyone's eyes were fixed on her, but I can say proudly that no one's observation of her was more meticulous than mine. And no one could know the measure of my reward. My gaze passed through the thickness of her leather wrap, allowing me to witness the sight of her breasts, which were about the same size as Mother's. Their loveliness nearly made me forget how cold and hungry I was.

"Why are you selling your children?" the youngster asked as he raised his bandaged hand and pointed to my sisters.

Mother didn't answer him. Did an idiotic question like that even deserve an answer? The youngster turned and muttered something to the foreign woman, whose attention was caught by the purple marten coat in which the daughter of Laidi, who lay in Mother's arms, was wrapped. She reached out and rubbed the nap. Then she saw the pantherlike, lazily sinister gaze of the baby girl herself. She had to turn away.

I hoped that Mother would hand Laidi's baby to the foreign woman. She didn't have to pay us, we'd even give her Laidi's purple marten coat. I loathed that baby girl. She was given a share of milk that belonged to me, though she didn't deserve it. Even my twin sister, Shangguan Yunü, didn't deserve it. So who gave her the right? What about Laidi, what's wrong with her breasts?

The foreign woman looked at each of my sisters in turn, starting with Fifth Sister and Sixth Sister, who had straw tags sticking up out of their collars. Then she looked at Fourth Sister, Seventh Sister, and Eighth Sister, who did not have tags. They didn't so much as glance at the little Sima bastard, but were certainly interested in me. I figured that my greatest asset was the downy yellow hair that covered my head. The way they examined my sisters was certainly peculiar. Here is the order of commands the youngster gave my sisters: Lower your head. Bend over. Kick out your leg. Raise your arms. Now wave them, front and back. Open wide, now give me an Ah — Ah! Let's hear you laugh. Take a few steps. Now run. My sisters did everything he told them to do, while the foreign woman watched, alternating between nodding and shaking her head. Finally, she pointed to Seventh Sister and muttered something to the youngster.

The youngster told Mother — while pointing to the foreign woman — that she was Countess Rostov, a philanthropist who desired to adopt and raise a pretty Chinese girl. She has settled on this girl of yours. You are a very lucky family.

Tears nearly gushed from Mother's eyes. She handed Laidi's daughter to Fourth Sister, freed her arms, and wrapped them around Seventh Sister. "Qiudi, my daughter, fortune has smiled on you . . ." Her tears fell onto the head of Seventh Sister, who sobbed, "I don't want to go, Mother. She has a funny smell . . ." "You foolish little girl," Mother said, "that's a wonderful smell."

"All right, worthy sister," the youngster interrupted impatiently. "Now we need a figure."

"Sir," Mother said, "since we're giving her to this lady to raise, it's as if my daughter has fallen into the lap of fortune. I don't want any money . . . just hope you'll take good care of her."

The youngster translated this for the foreign woman. Then, in stiff Chinese, she said, "No, I must pay you."

Mother said, "Sir, would you ask the lady if she could take one more, so she'll have a sister with her?"

Again, he translated for the foreign woman. But Countess Rostov shook her head firmly.

The youngster stuffed a dozen or more pink bills into Mother's hand and waved to the driver, who was standing beside the wagon. The man ran over and bowed to the youngster.

The driver picked up Seventh Sister and carried her over to the wagon. Not until then did she really start crying, as she reached out to us with one of her pencil-thin arms. Her sisters joined her in crying, and even the wretched little Sima boy opened his mouth and shrieked — *wah* — followed by a brief silence. Then another *wah* and another brief silence. The driver deposited Seventh Sister inside the wagon. The foreign woman followed. As the youngster was about to board, Mother ran over, grabbed him by the arm, and asked anxiously, "Sir, where does the lady live?" "Harbin," he replied icily.

The wagon drove onto the road and quickly disappeared beyond the woods. But Seventh Sister's cries, the *ding-dong* of the horse's bell, and the woman's fragrant breasts remained fresh in my memory.

Holding those few pink bills in her hand, Mother stood like a statue, and I became part of that statue.

That night, rather than sleep out in the open, we took a room at an inn. Mother told Fourth Sister to go out and buy ten sesame cakes. She returned instead with forty steaming boiled buns and a large packet of stewed pork. "Little Four," Mother said angrily, "that was money earned from selling your sister!" "Mother," Fourth Sister said through her tears, "my sisters deserve to eat at least one decent meal, and so do you." "Xiangdi," Mother said tearfully, "how could I possibly eat these buns and this meat?" "If you don't," Fourth Sister said, "just think what that means to Jintong." This comment had the desired effect; although she was still crying, Mother ate the buns and some of the meat, in order to produce milk for me and Shangguan Laidi and Sha Yueliang's infant daughter.

Mother fell ill.

Her body was hot as steel pulled from a quenching bucket and gave off the same unpleasant steamy smell. We sat around watching her, wide-eyed. Mother's eyes were closed and blisters covered her lips, through which all sorts of frightful words emerged. She went from loud shouts to soft whispers, and from a joyful tone to a tragic one. God, Holy Mother, angels, demons, Shangguan Shouxi, Pastor Malory, Third Master Fan, Yu the Fourth, Great Aunt, Second Uncle, Grandfather, Grandmother . . . Chinese goblins and foreign deities, living people and the dead, stories we knew and some we didn't, all came pouring nonstop out of Mother's mouth; it swayed, gathered, performed, and was transformed before our eyes . . . to comprehend Mother's afflicted ravings was to have an understanding of the universe itself; to commit Mother's afflicted ravings to memory was to know the entire history of Northeast Gaomi Township.

The slack-skinned innkeeper, whose face was covered with moles, was alarmed by Mother's shouts and dragged his sagging body to our room in a panic. He reached out to touch Mother's forehead, but jerked his hand back and said anxiously, "Send for a doctor right away, or you'll lose her!" He asked Fourth Sister, "Are you the oldest?" She nodded. "Why haven't you sent for a doctor? Why don't you say something, girl?" Fourth Sister burst into tears. Falling to her knees in front of the innkeeper, she said, "I beg you, uncle, save our mother." "Girl," the innkeeper said, "let me ask you, how much money do you have left?" Fourth Sister took the remaining bills out of Mother's pocket and handed them to the innkeeper. "Here, uncle, this is the money we got from selling our seventh sister."

Once the money exchanged for Seventh Sister disappeared, Mother opened her eyes.

"Mother's eyes are open, her eyes are open!" we cried out joyously with tears in our eyes. Mother lifted a hand and stroked our cheeks, one by one. "Mother . . . Mother . . . Mother . . . Mother . . . Mother . . ." we said. "Granny, Granny," the wretched little Sima heir stammered. "Her, what about her?" Mother asked as she pointed. Fourth Sister picked her up in her purple marten coat and held her out for Mother to touch. Once she was able to touch her, Mother closed her eyes; two tears squeezed out of the corners.

Hearing the sounds from the room, the innkeeper walked in with a long face and said to Fourth Sister, "I don't want to sound cruel, girl, but I've got my own family burdens, and the money for the room over the past couple of weeks, and the food, and the candles and oil . . ."

"Uncle," Fourth Sister said, "you are this family's great benefactor. We'll pay you what we owe, but please don't throw us out now. Our mother is sick . . ."

On the morning of February 18, 1941, Xiangdi handed a packet of money to Mother, who had just recovered from her illness. "Mother," she said, "I've paid the innkeeper. This is for you."

"Xiangdi," Mother asked nervously, "where did you get this money?"

Fourth Sister laughed mournfully. "Mother, take my brother and sisters away with you. This is not our home . . ."

Mother paled, grabbing Fourth Sister's hand. "Xiangdi, tell me . . ."

"Mother," Xiangdi said, "I sold myself . . . I got a good price, thanks to the innkeeper, who bargained for me . . ."

The whorehouse madam had given Fourth Sister the sort of examination she'd have given a piece of livestock. "Too thin," she said. "Boss lady," the inkeeper said, "a sack of rice will take care of that!" The madam extended two fingers. "Two hundred, and that shows what a generous person I am." "Boss lady, the girl's mother is sick, and she has many sisters. Please give a little more . . ." "Ah," the madam said, "it's hard to do good at times like this." But the innkeeper persisted. Fourth Sister fell to her knees. "All right," the madam said, "I'm too softhearted. I'll give another twenty. That's absolutely top price."

The news rocked Mother. Slowly she fell to the floor.

Then we heard the hoarse voice of a woman outside. "Let's go, girl. I don't have all the time in the world."

Fourth Sister knelt down and kowtowed to Mother. After getting to her feet, she rubbed the head of Fifth Sister, patted the face of Sixth Sister, tugged the ear of Eighth Sister, and gave me a hurried kiss on the cheek. Then she grabbed me by the shoulders and shook me. Her emotional face looked like a plum blossom in a snowstorm.

"Jintong, my Jintong," she said. "Grow up quickly, and grow up well. The Shangguan family is in your hands now!" She then took a look around the room as sobs emerged from her throat. She covered her mouth, as if she needed to run outside and throw up. She disappeared from sight.

7

We came home expecting to find Lingdi and Shangguan Lü dead. Nothing of the sort greeted our eyes. All manner of things were going on in the yard. Two men with freshly shaved heads were sitting against the wall of the house, bent over at the work of sewing clothes. They were wizards with needle and thread. Two other men, sitting nearby, heads also freshly shaved, as caught up in their tasks as the first two, were intent on cleaning the black rifles in their hands. There were two more men under the parasol tree, one standing holding a gleaming bayonet, the other seated on a bench, his head lowered, a white cloth wrapped around his neck, white, soapy bubbles popping on his water-soaked head. The man on his feet stood with his knees bent and, from time to time, wiped his bayonet clean on his pants; he then grabbed the other man's wet, soapy head with his free hand and took aim with his bayonet, as if looking for the right spot to bury it. Laying the blade against the scalp, soapy bubbles popping right and left, he stuck his backside nearly straight up in the air and drew the blade from one end to the other, scraping off soapy hair and leaving behind a patch of pale skin. Still another man stood where we had once stored peanuts, a long-handled ax in his hands, his legs spread wide, facing the gnarled roots of an old elm tree. Firewood was stacked behind him. He raised the ax over his head, holding it steady for a moment, as sunlight glinted off the blade, then brought it sharply down and grunted as the blade buried itself deep in the gnarled roots. Then, with one foot planted against the roots, he rocked the ax handle back and forth with both hands to free the blade. He took two steps backward, resumed his early stance, spit in his hands, and again raised the ax over his head. The gnarled roots of the elm tree cracked and split loudly, one piece flying into the air as if from an explosion. It hit Fifth Sister, Shangguan Pandi, in the chest. She shrieked. The men who were sewing and those who were cleaning their rifles all looked up. The man doing the shaving and the man cutting firewood both turned to look. The one being shaved tried to lift his head, but it was immediately pushed back down by the man with the bayonet. "Don't move," he said. "We've got some beggars," the man cutting firewood exclaimed. "Old Zhang, we've got some beggars here." A man in a white apron and a gray cap, his face a mass of wrinkles, emerged from the door of our house, almost at a crouch. His sleeves were rolled up, exposing a pair of flour-coated arms. "Elder sister," the man said in a friendly tone, "go try somewhere else. We soldiers are on rations and have nothing left for you folks."

"This is my house!" Mother replied icily.

Everyone in the yard abruptly stopped what they were doing. The man with the soapy head jumped to his feet, wiped his dirt-streaked face with his sleeve, and greeted us with loud grunts. It was the mute from the Sun family. He ran over to us, grunting and waving his hands to let us in on all sorts of things we could not grasp. We looked into his coarse face with puzzled looks on ours, as fuzzy thoughts began to materialize in our minds. The mute rolled his murky yellow eyes; his blubbery jowls quivered. Turning on his heel, he ran into the side room of the house and returned with the large chipped ceramic bowl and bird scroll, holding them up in front of us, as the man with the bayonet walked up. He patted the mute on the shoulder. "Do you know these people, Speechless Sun?" he asked.

The mute put down the bowl, picked up a piece of firewood, squatted down, and wrote a line of oversized, squiggly words in the sand: "SHE IS MY MOTHER-IN-LAW."

"So, the lady of the house has returned," the shaver said warmly. "We are Squad Five of the Railway Demolition Battalion. I'm the squad leader. My name is Wang. Please accept my apologies for occupying your house. Our political commissar has given your son-in-law a new name — Speechless Sun. He's a good soldier, brave, fearless, a model for us all. We'll move out of your house right away, ma'am. Old Lu, Little Du, Big Ox Zhao, Speechless Sun, Little Seventh Qin, go in and clear your things off the *kang* for the lady of the house."

The soldiers put down what they were working on and went inside. They returned in a few minutes carrying bedding and wearing leggings and cotton shoes with padded soles, with rifles strapped over their arms and grenades draped around their necks; they lined up in formation in the yard. "Ma'am," the squad leader said to Mother, "you may go in now. My men will stay out here while I report to the political commissar." The squad of soldiers, including the man now called Speechless Sun, stood at attention, like a row of pine trees.

The squad leader ran off, rifle in hand, and we entered the house, where two bamboo and reed steamers lay atop the cookpot, and a wood fire blazed in the stove, sending steam up through the gaps in the steamers. We smelled steamed buns. The elderly cook nodded apologetically to Mother as he shoved more kindling into the stove. "I apologize for making alterations to your stove without first getting your permission." He pointed to a deep groove under the stove and said, "That groove is better than ten bellows." The flames were so hot it almost looked as if the bottom of the pot might melt. Lingdi, her cheeks flushed and ruddy, was sitting in the doorway, her eyes narrowed as she stared at the steam oozing up through the gaps in the steamers and spiraling into the air above the stove, where it formed layers.

"Lingdi!" Mother shouted tentatively.

"Sister, Third Sister!" Fifth Sister and Sixth Sister shouted.

Lingdi cast us a nonchalant glance, as if we were strangers, or as if we'd never been away.

Mother led us around the neat, tidy rooms, feeling increasingly ill at ease, walking on eggshells. She decided to go back outside.

The mute made a face at us from where he stood in formation. The little Sima heir, too small to be afraid, went over to touch the soldiers' tightly wrapped leggings.

The squad leader returned with a middle-aged, bespectacled man. "Ma'am, this is Commissar Jiang."

Commissar Jiang was a pasty-faced man with a smooth upper lip. He wore a wide leather belt and had a fountain pen in his shirt pocket.

After nodding politely to us, he took a handful of colored objects out of a little leather bag on his hip. "Here's some candy for you youngsters." He distributed the hard candy evenly among us; even the baby girl in the purple marten coat got two pieces, which Mother accepted for her. It was my very first taste of candy. "Ma'am," Commissar Jiang said, "I hope you'll agree to put this squad up in the east and west side rooms of your house."

Mother nodded numbly.

He pulled back his cuff to check his watch. "Old Zhang," he shouted, "are the steamed buns ready?"

"Just about," Old Zhang replied as he ran outside.

"Feed the children first," the commissar said. "I'll have the clerk replace the rations for the soldiers."

Old Zhang promised he would.

Then the commissar said to Mother, "Ma'am, our commander would like to meet you. Will you come with me?"

Mother was about to hand the baby to Fifth Sister when the commissar said, "No, bring her along."

We followed the commissar — actually, Mother did the following; I was on her back, the baby girl was in her arms — out the lane and across the street, all the way to the gate of Felicity Manor, where two armed sentries saluted us by clicking their heels, holding their rifles vertically in their left hands and bringing their right hands across until they touched the gleaming bayonets. We walked through one corridor after another until we were in a big hall, where two bowls of steaming food sat on a purple rectangular table: one held cooked pheasant, the other cooked rabbit. There was also a basket of steamed buns so white they were nearly blue. A bearded man walked up with a smile. "Welcome," he said, "welcome."

"Ma'am," the commissar said, "this is Commander Lu."

"I understand we have the same surname," the commander said. "We were members of the same family way back when."

"What are we guilty of, Commander?" Mother asked.

Momentarily taken aback, the commander laughed and said, "Where did you get that idea, ma'am? I didn't ask you here because you'd done anything wrong. Ten years ago, your son-in-law, Sha Yueliang, and I were close friends. So when I heard you'd returned, I ordered food and wine to welcome you back."

"He's not my son-in-law," Mother said.

"There's no need to hide the fact, ma'am," the commissar said. "Isn't that Sha Yueliang's daughter you're holding?"

"This is my granddaughter."

"Let's eat first," Commander Lu said. "You must be starving."

"Commander," Mother said, "we're going home."

"Don't hurry off," Commander Lu said. "Sha Yueliang sent me a letter asking me to look after his daughter. He knows how tough things are for you. Little Tang!"

A strikingly beautiful soldier ran into the room.

"Take the lady's baby from her so she can sit down and eat."

The soldier walked up to Mother, smiled, and reached out for the baby.

"This is not Sha Yueliang's child," Mother insisted. "She's my granddaughter."

We passed through the same corridors, crossed the same street, and walked down the same alleys on our way back home.

Over the next few days, the beautiful young soldier called Little Tang brought food and clothing to us. Included in the food were tins of animal crackers, milk powder in glass bottles, and crocks filled with honey. The clothing consisted of silks and satins, padded jackets and pants with fancy trim, even a padded cap with rabbit fur earflaps. "These," she said, "are gifts for her from Commander Lu and Commissar Jiang." She pointed to the baby in Mother's arms. "Little Brother can eat the food, of course," she said, pointing to me.

Mother gave the soldier, Miss Tang, with her apple red cheeks and apricot eyes, a look of disinterest. "Take these things away, Miss Tang. They're too good for children from poor families." Mother then stuck one nipple into my mouth and the other into the mouth of the baby daughter of the Sha family. She sucked contentedly; I sucked angrily. She touched my head with her hand; I kicked her in the rear, which made her cry. I also heard the soft, light sobs of my eighth sister, Shangguan Yunü, the sort of weeping that even the sun and the moon like to hear.

Miss Tang said that Commissar Jiang had given the baby girl a name. "He's an intellectual, a graduate of Beiping's Chaoyang University, a writer and a painter and fluent in English. Zaohua — Date Flower — how do you like that name? Please, ma'am, keep your suspicions in check. Commander Lu is doing this out of the goodness of his heart. If we wanted to simply take this child, it would be as easy as snapping our fingers." Miss Tang took a glass baby bottle fitted with a rubber nipple out of her pocket. Then she put some honey and the milk powder into a pot — I detected the odor of the foreign woman who had taken Xiangdi away with her, and knew that the milk powder had come from a foreign woman's breast — added hot water, stirred, and poured it into the bottle. "Don't let her and your son fight over your milk. They'll suck you dry sooner or later. Let me give her a bottle," she said as she took Sha Zaohua from Mother. Zaohua held on to Mother's nipple with her mouth, stretching it out like one of Birdman Han's slingshots; when finally she let go, the nipple shrank back slowly, like a leech over which boiling water has been poured, taking its own sweet time to return to normal. The pain I felt was for the nipple; the loathing I felt was for Sha Zaohua. But by then, the loathsome little demon was in Miss Tang's arms, frantically and contentedly sucking up the imitation milk from the imitation breast. I didn't envy her at all, since once again, Mother's breasts were mine alone. It had been a long time since I'd slept so soundly. In my dream, I sucked to intoxication and bliss. The dream was filled with the fragrance of milk!

I owed Miss Tang a debt of gratitude. After she'd finished feeding Zaohua, she laid down the bottle and opened up the purple marten overcoat, releasing the rank smell of fox that clung to the baby. I noticed how milky white Zaohua's skin was. I'd never imagined that someone with such a dark face could have such pale skin elsewhere. Miss Tang dressed Zaohua in the satin padded coat and the rabbit fur cap, all to transform her into a beautiful baby. She flung the purple marten coat off to the side, held Zaohua in her arms, and tossed her up in the air. Zaohua was giggling happily when Miss Tang caught her.

I felt Mother tense as she readied herself to grab Zaohua away. But Miss Tang walked over and handed her back. "This baby would make Commander Sha very happy, aunty," she said.

"Commander Sha?"

"Didn't you know? Your son-in-law is the garrison commander of Bohai City," Miss Tang said, "with a complement of more than three hundred men and his own personal American Jeep."

Miss Tang took out a red plastic comb and combed the hair of Fifth Sister and Sixth Sister. While she was combing Sixth Sister's hair, Fifth Sister stood there gaping, her gaze like a comb that moved from Miss

Tang's head down to her feet, and then back up to her head. Then when Miss Tang was combing her hair, Fifth Sister had goose bumps all over her face and neck. When the two girls' hair was combed, Miss Tang left. "Mother," Fifth Sister said, "I want to be a soldier."

Two days later, Pandi was wearing a gray army uniform. Her primary job was helping Miss Tang change and feed Sha Zaohua.

Our lives took a turn for the better. As a song from those days went:

> Little girl, little girl, your worries are done,
> If you can't find a youngster, then try an old one.
> As you follow your comrades out on the run,
> Cabbage and stewed pork await in the sun,
> While still in the pot, a hot steamy bun . . .

We saw precious little cabbage or stewed pork, and, for that matter, hot steamy buns. But turnips and salted fish were often on our table, as was cornbread.

"Garlic never dies in a drought, and a soldier never starves," Mother said with a sigh. "The army has become our benefactor. If I'd known this would happen, I'd never have had to sell my children. Xiangdi, Qiudi, my poor little girls . . ."

During those days, the quality and amount of Mother's milk were as high as they'd ever been. I finally climbed out of the pouch that had been my home and was able to take some twenty steps, then fifty, then a hundred; then, no more need to crawl. My tongue, too, took on a new life — I could curse with the best of them. When the Sun family mute squeezed my pecker, I cursed angrily: "Fuck you!"

Sixth Sister joined a literacy class that was held in the church. Once the droppings of the donkeys once housed there were swept away, the pews were repaired and put back in place. The winged angels were gone; maybe they'd flown away. The jujube Jesus was gone too; maybe he had gone to Heaven, or maybe he'd been stolen and taken home to become kindling. On one wall hung a blackboard with a line of large white characters. The angelic Miss Tang tapped the blackboard with her pointer.

Fight — Japan — Fight — Japan — Women were nursing children or sewing cloth soles, the hemp thread whistling, as they repeated what Comrade Tang was saying: Fight Japan — Fight Japan —

I wandered among the women, lingering in the presence of all those breasts. Fifth Sister jumped onto the stage and spoke to the women sitting below: "The masses are the water, our brother soldiers are the fish, right? Right! What do fish fear most? What do they fear? Do they fear hooks? Seahawks? Water snakes? No, what they fear most is nets! That's right, they fear nets! What do you have on the backs of your heads? That's right, buns. And what covers those buns? Nets." All of a sudden, the women understood, and they began buzzing and whispering, blushing one minute, paling the next. "Cut off your buns and remove your nets. Protect Commander Lu and Commissar Jiang, and protect their demolition battalion. Who will take the lead?" Pandi raised a pair of scissors over her head and operated them with her delicate fingers, turning them into a hungry crocodile. Miss Tang said, "Just think, all you suffering women, you aunties, grannies, and sisters, we women have been oppressed for three thousand years. But now we can stand tall. Hu Qinlian, tell us, does that drunkard husband of yours, Half Bottle Nie, still dare to beat you?" The frightened young woman, baby in arms, stood up, let her gaze sweep across the heroic figures of soldiers Tang and Shangguan, and quickly lowered her head. "No," she said. Soldier Tang clapped her hands. "Did you hear that? Women, even Half Bottle Nie no longer dares to beat his wife. Our Women's Salvation Society is a home for women, a place dedicated to righting wrongs against women. Women, where did this life of equality and happiness come from? Did it drop from the sky? Did it rise up out of the earth? No. There is only one true source: the arrival of the demolition battalion. In the town of Dalan, in Northeast Gaomi Township, we have built a rock-solid base area behind enemy lines. We are self-reliant, we are prepared to struggle, we will improve the people's lives, especially women's. No more feudalism, no more superstition, but we must cut through the nets, and not just for the demolition battalion, but for ourselves. Women, cut off your buns, remove your nets, and become pageboys, all of us!"

"Mother, you first!" Pandi said as she walked up to Mother, clicking the scissors.

"Yes, the head of the Shangguan family should become a pageboy," several women said in unison. "We will follow."

"Mother, you go first, and give your daughter a lot of face," Fifth Sister said.

The blood rushed to Mother's face. She leaned over and said,

"Go ahead, Pandi, cut it. If it would help the demolition battalion, I'd cut off two of my fingers, without a second thought."

Soldier Tang led the women in a round of applause.

Fifth Sister loosened Mother's black hair, which cascaded down past her neck, like a wisteria plant or a black waterfall. The look on Mother's face mirrored that on the face of the nearly naked figure of the Holy Mother, Mary, on the wall. Somber, worried, tranquil, and meek, yet willing to sacrifice. The church where I was baptized still reeked of ancient, smashed donkey droppings; memories of Pastor Malory performing the rite for Eighth Sister and me floated up out of the big wooden basin. The Holy Mother never covered her breasts, but my mother's breasts were largely hidden behind a curtain. "Go ahead, Pandi, cut it. What are you waiting for?" Mother said. And so Pandi's scissors opened wide and bit down. *Snip snip* — Mother's hair fell to the ground. She raised her head — she now sported a pageboy, her hair barely reaching her earlobes and exposing her slender neck to view. Now shorn of its weighty burden, her head seemed young and sprightly, no longer sedate, sort of impish; its movements were lively, like those of the Bird Fairy. Her face was bright red. Soldier Tang took a small oval mirror out of her pocket and held it up for Mother. Embarrassed, she cocked her head to one side; so did the image in the mirror. Shyly examining the pageboy gazing back at her, her head now several sizes smaller than before, she quickly looked away.

"Isn't it pretty?" Soldier Tang asked.

"It's hideous . . ." Mother's voice was very low.

"Now that Aunty Shangguan has a pageboy, what are the rest of you waiting for?" Soldier Tang asked loudly.

"Cut away. Go on, cut it. Every time there's a change of dynasty, hairstyles change. Cut mine. It's my turn." *Snip snip.* Yelps of surprise, sighs of regret. I bent over to pick up a lock of hair. It was all over the ground — black, dark brown, thick, fine. The thick hair was black and bristly. The fine hair was soft and dark brown. My mother's was the best. You could squeeze oil out of the tips.

Those were happy days, much livelier than when Sima Ku was displaying the rubble from the bridge. The members of the demolition battalion had a wealth of talents: some sang, others danced, while still others played instruments from flutes to lutes to harps. The sleek village walls were covered with slogans written in lime water. Every morning at sunrise, four young soldiers climbed to the top of the

Sima watchtower to face the sun and practice bugle calls. At first they sounded like cattle calls, but before long, they were more like puppy cries. Finally, however, the notes rose and fell, twisted this way and that, high and low, music that was pleasing to the ear. The young soldiers threw out their chests, held their heads high, and stood stiff-necked, their cheeks puffed out behind golden bugles with red tassels. Of the four buglers, one called Ma Tong was the handsomest: he had a delicate mouth, a dimple in each cheek, and large, protruding ears. He was lively and always on the move; his mouth was as sweet as honey. He made a big show of calling on twenty or more village women, his adoptive mothers. The moment they laid eyes on him, their breasts quivered, and they would have loved to stuff a nipple into his mouth. Ma Tong once came to our house to pass on some sort of order to the squad leader. At the time, I was squatting under the pomegranate tree watching ants climb up the trunk. Curious as to what I was doing, he squatted down and watched along with me. He was more caught up in the sight than I was, and was a lot more skillful in killing the ants. He even showed me how to piss on them. Fiery pomegranate blossoms formed a canopy over our heads. It was the fourth lunar month; the weather was warm, the sky blue, the clouds white. Flocks of swallows soared on lazy southern wind currents.

Mother's prediction: A handsome, lively young man like Ma Tong is not fated to live to a ripe old age. God has given him too much already, he has drunk deeply from the well of life, and cannot look forward to a long life, with many sons and grandsons. Her prediction came true, for on one starry night, the silence was broken by a young man's screams: Commander Lu, Commissar Jiang, spare me, I beg you, just this once . . . I am the sole heir of my family, my grandparents' only grandson and my parents' only son. If you kill me, it will be the end of my family line. Mother Sun, Mother Li, Mother Cui, all you adoptive mothers, come rescue me . . . Mother Cui, you have a special relationship with Commander Lu, please save me . . . Ma Tong's pitiful shouts accompanied him out of town, until a single crisp gunshot brought deathly silence. The fairylike young bugler was no more. Not one of his adoptive mothers could save him. His crime: stealing and selling bullets.

The next day, a red coffin appeared on the street. A squad of soldiers placed it on a horse-drawn cart. Made of four-inch-thick cypress and covered with nine coats of shellac, it was draped with nine layers of cloth. It could be submerged in water for ten years without leaking a drop. Bullets could not penetrate the coffin, which would hold up in the ground for a thousand years. It was so heavy it took more than a dozen soldiers to pick it up on the command of a squad leader.

Once the coffin was loaded onto the cart, the tension among the troops was palpable. They shuttled back and forth at a jog, their faces taut. But then an old man with a white beard rode up on a donkey and dismounted beside the cart. He beat on the coffin and wailed. His face was awash in tears, some dripping off the tips of his beard. It was Ma Tong's grandfather, a highly educated onetime official during the Manchu dynasty. Commander Lu and Commissar Jiang emerged and stood awkwardly behind the old man. Once he'd cried all he was going to, he turned and glared at Lu and Jiang. "Old Mr. Ma," Jiang said, "you have read many books and have a firm grasp of right and wrong. We punished Ma Tong with the deepest regret." "With the deepest regret," Lu echoed. The old man spat in Lu's face. "He who steals hooks is a thief. He who robs a nation is a nobleman. Fight Japan, you say, fight Japan, when all you do is engage in debauchery!" In a somber voice, Commissar Jiang said, "Sir, we are a true anti-Japanese unit that prides itself on strict military discipline. There may in fact be soldiers among us who engage in debauchery, but it isn't us!" The old man stepped around Commissar Jiang and Commander Lu, let loose a burst of loud laughter, and walked off, his donkey following him, its head bowed low. The cart carrying the coffin fell in behind the donkey. The driver's shouts to his horse were like the muted chirps of a cicada.

The Ma Tong incident rocked the foundation of the demolition battalion. The false sense of security and happiness was shattered. The gunshot that killed Ma Tong told us that in time of war, human lives were worth no more than those of ants. The Ma Tong incident, which, on the surface, appeared to be a victory for military discipline and justice, had a particularly negative effect on members of the demolition battalion. For days after, there was a rash of incidents involving drunkenness and fighting. The squad billeted at our house began to display signs of dissatisfaction. Squad Leader Wang said publicly, "Ma Tong was a scapegoat! What ammunition could a kid like that have sold? His grandfather was a high official and his family owns thousands of acres of rich farmland, with many donkeys and horses. He didn't need that little bit of money. As I see it, the youngster died at the hands of those dissolute adoptive mothers of his. No wonder the old man said, 'Fight Japan, you say, fight Japan, when all you do is engage in debauchery!'" The squad leader aired his complaints in the morning. That afternoon, Commissar Jiang showed up at our house with two military guards. "Wang Mugen," Jiang said gravely, "come with me to battalion headquarters." Wang glared at his troops. "Which one of you sons of bitches betrayed me?" The men exchanged nervous glances, their faces pale gray. All except the mute, Speechless Sun, who released a guttural laugh from deep in his throat, walked up to the commissar, and, with a flurry of hand gestures, told how Sha Yueliang had stolen a wife. The commissar said, "Speechless Sun, you are the new squad leader." Speechless Sun cocked his head and stared at the commissar, who reached out, grabbed his hand, took a fountain pen out of his pocket, and wrote something on Sun's palm. Sun bent his hand back and studied it; then he flailed his arms excitedly, as lights flashed in his brown eyes. With a contemptuous laugh, Wang Mugen said, "At this rate, the mute will be talking before long." The commissar signaled the guards, who took their places on either side of Wang Mugen. "After you've finished with the millstone," Wang shouted, "kill the donkey and eat it. You've forgotten how I blew up the armored train." Ignoring the shouts, the commissar walked up and patted the mute on the shoulder. Overwhelmed by this attention, he stuck out his chest and saluted, while the sound of Wang Mugen's shouts drifted over from the lane: "Getting me angry is the same as putting a land mine under your bed!"

The mute's first act after being promoted to squad leader was to demand that my mother hand over his woman. At the time, she was beside the millstone behind which Sima Ku had hidden after he was wounded, crushing sulfur for the demolition battalion. A hundred yards away, Pandi was showing the women how to beat scrap metal with hammers. A hundred yards beyond Pandi, a demolition battalion engineer was working with apprentices on a bellows that required four strong men to operate, sending gusts of air into the furnace. Buried in the sand at their feet were molds for land mines. Mother's mouth was covered by a bandanna as she led the donkey around the millstone. The smell of sulfur brought tears to her eyes and had the donkey sneezing. Sima Ku's son and I were hunkered down in a stand of trees, carefully watched by Niandi, on Mother's orders, who didn't want us anywhere near the millstone. The mute, a Hanyang rifle slung across his back, swaggered over to the millstone twirling a Burmese sword that had been passed down through generations of his family. We watched him block the donkey's way, raise the sword in Mother's direction, and twirl it over his head, making it sing in the air. Mother was standing behind the donkey, a nearly bald broom in her hand. Her eyes were riveted on him. He showed her the palm of his hand and laughed. She nodded, as if congratulating him. A range of expressions then swept across the mute's face. Mother shook her head, over and over and over, as if to deny whatever it was he wanted. Finally, the mute swung his arm in the air and brought his fist down on the donkey's head. The animal's front legs buckled and it fell against the millstone. "You bastard!" Mother screamed. "You godforsaken bastard!" A crooked smile spread across the mute's face. He turned and swaggered off, the same way he'd come.

On the other side, the door of the smelting furnace was opened by a long hook and white-hot molten metal spilled out of the crucible, creating beautiful sparks as some of it splashed on the ground. Mother got the donkey to its feet by pulling on its ears, then walked over to where I was playing. There she removed the yellowed bandanna that covered her mouth, lifted up her blouse, and stuffed a sulfur-smoked nipple into my mouth. I seriously considered spitting out the stinky, peppery thing when Mother abruptly pushed me away, nearly jerking out my two front baby teeth. Her nipples must have been sore, but I guess she didn't have time to worry about that. She ran toward home, the bandanna flapping in the wind. I could picture those sulfur-fouled nipples of hers rubbing against the coarse material of her blouse, the venomous liquid wetting her clothes. She seemed to radiate electricity as she ran. She was immersed in a peculiar emotion; if it was happiness, it was a decidedly painful happiness. Why was she running like that? We didn't have to wait long for the answer.

"Lingdi! My Lingdi, where are you?" Mother shouted, from the main house all the way to the side room.

Shangguan Lü crawled out from the front room, lay belly down on the pathway, and raised her head, like a gigantic frog. Soldiers had taken over her west wing room, where five of them were lying on the millstone, heads facing the center, as they studied a thread-bound book. They looked up and noted our arrival with alarm. Their rifles were lined up against the wall and land mines hung from the rafters, black, round, and oily, like spider's eggs, except a whole lot bigger. "Where's the mute?" Mother asked. The soldiers shook their heads.

Mother turned and rushed over to the west wing. The Bird Fairy scroll had been tossed carelessly across a now legless table, on which lay a half-eaten piece of cornbread and a green onion. The chipped ceramic bowl, which was also on the table, was filled with white bones — maybe a bird, maybe some small animal. The mute's rifle was leaning against the wall, his grenades hung from a rafter.

We stood in the yard, filling the air with hopeless shouts. The soldiers came running out of the house, demanding to know what had happened. Just then, the mute crawled out of the turnip cellar. His clothes were covered with yellow earth and splotches of white mildew. He wore a look of fatigue and contentment.

"What a fool I was!" Mother roared, stomping her foot.

At the far end of the path in our yard, beneath a pile of dried grass, the mute had raped my third sister, Lingdi.

We dragged her out from where she lay, carried her inside, and laid her on the *kang*. Mother wept as she soaked her sulfurous bandanna in water and meticulously cleaned Lingdi from head to toe. Her tears fell onto Lingdi's body and onto her own breast, which still showed the teeth marks; interestingly, Lingdi was smiling. A bewitching light flashed in her eyes.

As soon as she heard the news, Fifth Sister rushed home and stared down at Third Sister. Without a word, she ran outside, took a grenade from her belt, pulled the pin, and tossed it into the east wing. No sound emerged; it was a dud.

The mute was to be executed on the very spot where Ma Tong had been shot: a foul-smelling bog at the southern edge of the village, with rotting rush in the middle and lined with piles of garbage. The trussed-up mute was dragged over to the edge of the bog, facing a firing squad of a dozen or more men. After an emotional speech for the benefit of the civilians who had gathered to watch, Commissar Jiang told the soldiers to cock their rifles. Ready, the commissar ordered, Aim . . . Shangguan Lingdi, all in white, floated over before the bullets had a chance to leave the rifle barrels. She seemed to be walking on air, like a true fairy. It's the Bird Fairy! someone shouted. Memories of the Bird Fairy's legendary history and miraculous deeds flooded the minds of everyone present. The mute was forgotten. The Bird Fairy had never been more beautiful as she danced in front of the crowd, like a stork parading through the marshes. Her face was a palette of bright colors: like red lotuses, like white lotuses. Her figure was in perfect harmony, her distended lips absolutely alluring. She danced her way up to the mute; after stopping in front of him, she cocked her head and gazed into his face. He responded with a foolish grin. She reached out and stroked his nappy hair and pinched his garlic-bulb nose. Finally, to everyone's surprise, she reached down and grabbed the thing between his legs that had caused all the trouble. Turning to face the onlookers, she giggled. The women looked away; the men just stared foolishly, lecherous grins on their faces.

The commissar coughed and said, his words strained and unnatural, "Move her away from there and get on with the execution!"

The mute raised his head and let out a series of weird grunts, maybe to register his objection.

The Bird Fairy's hand kept rubbing the thing down there, her fleshy lips twisted into a greedy but natural and healthy look of pure desire. The commissar's command fell on deaf ears.

"Young lady," the commissar asked in a loud voice, "was it rape or was it consensual?"

The Bird Fairy did not reply.

"Do you like him?" the commissar asked her.

Again the Bird Fairy did not reply.

The commissar went into the crowd to find Mother. "Aunty," he said, obviously embarrassed, "in your view . . . as I see it, maybe we ought to just let them become husband and wife . . . Speechless Sun was wrong . . . but not wrong enough to forfeit his life . . ."

Without a word, Mother turned and walked back through the crowd, slowly, as if her back were weighed down by a stone tablet. The people followed her with their eyes, until they heard wails tear from her throat. They couldn't watch any longer.

"Untie him," the commissar ordered halfheartedly before turning and leaving the scene.

8

It was the seventh day of the seventh lunar month, the day when the Herder Boy and Weaving Maid meet in the Milky Way. It was hot and sticky, the air so thick with mosquitoes they crashed into one another. Mother spread out a straw mat and we lay down to listen to her feeble mutterings. A drizzle came up as dusk fell; Mother said those were the Weaving Maid's tears. The humidity was high, with only an occasional gust of wind. Above us, pomegranate leaves shimmied. Soldiers in both the east and west wings lit homemade candles. Mosquitoes feasted on us, despite Mother's attempts to drive them away with her fan. All the magpies in the world chose this date to fly up into the clear blue sky, sheets and sheets of them, all beak to tail, with no space between them, forming a bridge across the the Milky Way to let the Herder Boy and Weaving Girl meet yet another year. Raindrops and dewdrops were their tears of longing. Amid Mother's mutterings, Niandi and I, plus the little Sima heir, gazed up at the star-filled sky, trying to find those particular stars. Even though Eighth Sister, Yunü, was blind, she too tipped her face heavenward, her eyes brighter than the stars she could not see. The heavy footsteps of sentries returning from their watch sounded in the lane. Out in the fields, frogs croaked a loud chorus. On the bean trellis a katydid sang its song: *Yiya yiya dululu — yiya yiya dululu.* As the night deepened, large birds flew roughly and rashly into the air; we watched their white, fuzzy silhouettes and listened to feathery wings brushed by the wind. Bats squeaked excitedly; drops of water fell from the leaves and beat a tattoo on the ground. Sha Zaohua lay cradled in Mother's arms, breathing evenly. In the east wing, Lingdi screeched like a cat, and the mute's hulking silhouette flickered in the lamplight. They had been married. Commissar Jiang had officiated at the wedding, and now the meditation room for the Bird Fairy had become a wedding chamber where they could release their passions. The Bird Fairy ran often out into the yard half dressed, and one soldier who was driven to distraction by peeping at her exposed breasts nearly had his neck broken by the mute. "It's late, time to go to bed," Mother said. "It's hot inside, and the room is swarming with mosquitoes," Sixth Sister said. "Can't we sleep out here?" "No," Mother said, "the dampness is bad for you. Besides, there are those in the sky who pick flowers . . . I think I heard one of them say, There's a pretty little flower, let's pick it. Wait till we come back, we'll get it then. You know who they were? Spider spirits, whose only purpose is to spoil young virgins."

We lay on the *kang*, but could not sleep. Except, strangely enough, Eighth Sister, who fell fast asleep, a line of slobber in the corner of her mouth. We choked on smoke from the mosquito incense. Lamplight from the soldiers' rooms came through their windows and fell on ours, making it possible for us to see bits and pieces of what was out in the yard. A saltwater fish Laidi had sent us was smelling up the latrine outside with its rank rotting odor. She'd sent back lots of valuable things, such as satin fabrics, furniture, and antique curios, all confiscated by the demolition battalion. The bolt on the door creaked. "Who's there?" Mother shouted as she picked up the cleaver she kept at the head of the *kang*. No response. Maybe we were hearing things. Mother put the cleaver back where she kept it. From the floor at the head of the *kang* brief bursts of red light flickered at the end of the smoking mugwort rope that was supposed to keep mosquitoes away.

All of a sudden, a thin figure rose from the head of the *kang*. Mother let out a frightened shriek. So did Sixth Sister. The dark figure fell across the *kang* and clapped its hand over Mother's mouth. She struggled as she groped for the cleaver. But just as she was about to swing it, she heard the figure call out:

"Mother, it's me, Laidi . . ."

The cleaver fell from Mother's hand onto the straw mat atop the *kang*. Her eldest daughter was home! Eldest Sister was on her knees on the *kang*, sobbing. We looked into her shadowy face, and I saw it was covered with little bright spots. "Laidi . . . my first little girl . . . is it really you? You're not a ghost, are you? I'm not afraid even if you are. Let me look at you . . ." Mother groped around at the head of the *kang* for a match.

First Sister stayed her hand and said softly, "Don't light the lamp, Mother."

"Laidi, you heartless thing. Where have you and that fellow Sha been all these years? You've made things so hard on your mother."

"There's so much to tell you, Mother," she said. "But first, where's my daughter?"

Mother picked up little Sha Zaohua, who was fast asleep, and handed her to Eldest Sister. "You call yourself a mother? You may know how to have a baby, but not how to raise it. Dumb animals do better than that . . . because of her, your fourth sister and seventh sister . . ."

"One of these days, Mother, I'll repay you for all you've done for me," First Sister said. "And I'll make it up to Fourth Sister and Seventh Sister."

Just then Sixth Sister came up to us. "First Sister!" she yelled.

Laidi lifted her head away from Sha Zaohua and touched Sixth Sister's face. "Sixth Sister. Where's Jintong? And Yunü? Ah, Jintong, Yunü, do you still remember your big sister?"

"If not for the demolition battalion," Mother said, "this whole family would have starved."

"Mother," First Sister said, "the men named Jiang and Lu are no good."

"They treat us well, so we should not say bad things about them."

"That is part of their scheme. They sent Sha Yueliang a letter demanding his surrender. If he didn't, they said, they'd take our daughter hostage."

"How can that be?" Mother asked. "What does a little baby have to do with war?"

"Mother, my reason for coming home this time was to rescue my daughter. I came with a dozen or more soldiers, and we have to head back immediately. We'll let Jiang and Lu enjoy their empty victory for now. Mother, our debt to you is higher than a mountain, and I hope you'll let me repay you someday. The night is long, the dreams many. Now I must leave . . ."

But before she had a chance to finish, Mother grabbed Sha Zaohua out of her arms. "Laidi!" she said angrily. "Don't think you can win me over so easily. Think how you dumped her on me back then. Well, I spared nothing in raising her this far, so don't you think you can just come and take her away. All this stuff about Commander Lu and Commissar Jiang is a pack of lies. You want to be a mother now, now that you and Monk Sha have spent all your passion, is that it?"

"Mother, he's a brigade leader in the Japanese Imperial Forces, commanding over a thousand troops."

"I don't care how many men he has or what kind of leader he is," Mother said. "Have him claim this child in person, and tell him I've kept all those rabbits he hung from the tree for him."

"Mother," First Sister said, "this involves thousands of troops and their mounts, so don't interfere."

"I've interfered in things half my life already. Thousands of troops and their mounts or thousands of horses and their riders, it doesn't matter to me. All I know is, I raised Zaohua, and I'm not about to hand her over to somebody else."

First Sister reached out and snatched the child away, then jumped down off the *kang*. "You damned turtle spawn!" Mother cursed. "How dare you!"

Zaohua began to cry.

Mother jumped down off the *kang* and ran after them.

The crackle of gunfire erupted in the yard. Then we heard chaos on the roof above us, as someone screamed and rolled off onto the ground. A foot crashed through our ceiling, letting in clumps of mud and the glare of starlight. There was loud confusion outside, with gunfire, the clang of bayonets, and a soldier's shout: "Don't let them get away!"

A dozen or more soldiers of the demolition battalion came running with kerosene torches, turning the yard from night to day. Someone behind the house shouted, "Tie him up! Now let's see you run away, my little uncle."

Commander Lu of the demolition battalion strode into the yard and said to Laidi, who was cowering against the wall, holding tightly on to Sha Zaohua, "This is no way to act, is it, Mrs. Sha?"

Zaohua was crying.

Mother walked out into the yard.

We sprawled against the windowsill to watch.

A man lay alongside the path, his body full of holes, blood forming little puddles that snaked out in all directions. The offensive smell of warm blood. The choking smell of kerosene. Blood oozing from the bullet holes bubbled in places. He wasn't dead yet: one of his legs twitched spasmodically, he was biting the ground, and his neck was twitching. We couldn't see his face. Leaves on the trees were like gold or silver foil. The mute was standing in front of Commander Lu, waving his sword and shouting. The Bird Fairy came outside, dressed this time, wearing what could only have been one of the mute's uniform shirts, which came down to her knees but only half covered her breasts and belly. Her exposed ankles were long and snowy white, the calves sleek and muscular. Her lips were parted, her eyes glazed as she gazed at the torches. A squad of soldiers came into the yard with three bound men in olive drab uniforms. One of them, his face ashen, had been wounded in the shoulder; it was still bleeding. Another was hobbling on a gimp leg. The third man was straining to raise his head, but failing, since the men behind him were pulling it down as low as it would go by a rope around his neck. Commissar Jiang came into the yard, flashlight in hand, the lens covered by a piece of red satin, which turned the light a muted red. Mother's bare feet slapped the ground — *pa-da pa-da* — crushing the tiny mounds of dirt raised by worms.

Showing no fear at all, she demanded of Commander Lu, "What's going on here?"

"This has nothing to do with you, aunty," he said.

Commissar Jiang flashed his red-satined light in Laidi's face. She stood there like a poplar.

Mother walked up to First Sister and ripped Zaohua out of her hands. Cradling the baby in her arms, she said in a calming voice, "Good girl, don't be afraid. Granny's here."

Zaohua's cries softened until she was merely sobbing softly.

First Sister held her arms as if the baby were still in them, as if she were petrified. It was an ugly sight. Her face was ghostly white, her gaze frozen. She was wearing a green man's uniform, under which her full breasts jutted out straight.

"Mrs. Sha, you people could not have received more humane treatment than we gave you. We didn't try to force you to accept our reorganization," Commander Lu said. "But you should not have gone over to the Japs."

"That is for the menfolk to decide. I'm just the man's wife."

Commissar Jiang said, "We hear that Mrs. Sha is Commander Sha's chief of staff."

"All I know," First Sister said, "is that I've come for my daughter. If you've got the balls, go do battle with him. Taking a child hostage is not how a man worthy of the name would go about it."

"Mrs. Sha, you've got it all wrong," Commissar Jiang said. "We have nothing but affection for Miss Sha. Just ask your mother. Ask your sisters. Heaven and earth are our witnesses. I'll tell you what we're all about. We love the child, and everything we do is in her best interests. What we don't want for this lovely little girl is that she have traitors for parents."

"I have no idea what you're talking about," First Sister said. "You're wasting your breath. But do what you want with me, since I am your prisoner."

The mute swung into action. He looked particularly menacing in the light of all those torches. His skin was nearly black, and glossy, as if covered with badger fat. *Ah-ao — ah-ao ah-ao.* Eyes of a wolf, nose of a boar, ears of an ape, face of a tiger. He roared, raised his thick, powerful arms, clenched his fists, and struck a martial pose. He kicked the body of the now dead soldier alongside the path, then turned to the three prisoners. One after the other, he drove his fist into their faces, each punch accompanied by an *Ah-ao*! Then he went back and did it all over again. *Ah-ao*! *Ah-ao*! *Ah-ao*! Each punch more devastating than the one before. The last one sent the man with his head pushed down crumpling to the ground. Commissar called a halt to his frenzy: "Speechless Sun, you are not to hit our prisoners!" The mute just grinned and pointed to Shangguan Laidi, then to himself. He walked up to Laidi, grabbing her bony shoulder with his left hand and gesturing to the crowd with his right. The Bird Fairy was looking at the torches, absorbed by their light. Laidi raised her left hand and gave the mute a resounding slap on his right cheek. The mute released her shoulder and rubbed his cheek, looking puzzled, as if not knowing where the blow had come from. First Sister then raised her right hand and gave him another resounding slap on his left cheek, this one harder than the first. The mute rocked on his heels, while First Sister stumbled backward, recoiling from the slap. Her lovely brow arched, her phoenix-like eyes widened, as she said through clenched teeth, "You bastard, you ravaged my little sister!"

"Take her away!" Commander Lu ordered. "She's not only a turncoat, but a savage as well!"

Soldiers rushed up and grabbed First Sister by the arms. "How stupid can you get, Mother?" she shouted. "Third Sister is a phoenix, yet you married her to that mute!"

Just then a soldier rushed up and announced breathlessly, "Commander, Commissar, Commander Sha's troops have reached Shalingzi Township."

"Stay calm, men. I want each company commander to follow our original plan and start laying land mines."

Commissar Jiang said, "Aunty, for your and the children's protection, come with us to battalion headquarters."

"No," Mother said, shaking her head. "If we're going to die, it will be on our own *kang*."

Commissar Jiang waved a squad of soldiers over next to Mother and another squad into the house. "Dear Lord," Mother shouted, "open your eyes and see what's happening."

Our family was locked into a wing of the Sima house, with sentries at the door. Gas lanterns in the adjoining room were lit, and someone inside was shouting. Beyond the village, the popping of gunshots was endless.

Commissar Jiang walked unhurriedly into our quarters carrying a lamp with a glass shade. The black smoke choked him and made our eyes water. After putting the lamp down on the table, he said, "Why are you all standing? Please, sit, have a seat." He pointed to chairs lined against the wall. "Aunty," he said, "this is quite an extravagant place your second son-in-law owns." He sat down, resting his hands on his knees, and flashed us a sardonic grin. First Sister sat across a table from Commissar Jiang and said with a pout, "Commissar Jiang, inviting a deity in is one thing. Getting rid of it is quite another!" Jiang laughed. "Given all the trouble it took to get the deity here, why would I want to get rid of it?" "Mother," First Sister said, "go ahead, sit down. They won't do anything to you."

"We don't plan to do anything to any of you," Commissar Jiang said with a smile. "Please, aunty, have a seat."

Still cradling Zaohua, Mother sat in a chair in the corner. Eighth Sister and I, who were holding on to Mother's clothes, stood next to her. The young Sima heir leaned his head against Sixth Sister's shoulder, a ribbon of drool running down his chin. Sixth Sister was so sleepy she rocked back and forth. Mother grabbed her by the arm and told her to sit down. She opened her eyes, looked around, and immediately started to snore. Commissar Jiang took out a cigarette and tapped the end against his thumbnail. Then he searched his pockets, looking for a match. He didn't find one, and First Sister found that worth celebrating. He walked over to the lamp, stuck the cigarette in his mouth, leaned over the flame, closed his eyes, and began puffing. The flame danced, the tip of the cigarette turned red and glowed. He straightened up, took the lit cigarette out of his mouth, and squeezed his lips shut; two streams of dense smoke snaked out of his nostrils. The thud of explosions somewhere beyond the village rattled the windows. The glow of fires lit up the night sky. Every few seconds we heard the cries or shouts of men out there, sometimes clear as a bell. Commissar Jiang smiled through it all, staring at Laidi as if throwing down a challenge.

Laidi fidgeted in her seat as if she was sitting on needles, making the legs of her chair creak and groan. The blood had drained from her face and her hands shook as she gripped the arms of the chair.

"Commander Sha's cavalry troops have entered our minefield," Commissar Jiang said sympathetically. "What a pity, all those fine horses."

"You . . . you're all living in a dream world . . ." First Sister stood up with her hands on the arms of the chair, but fell back into it as an even denser series of explosions split the air.

Commissar Jiang stood up and rapped leisurely on the wooden lattice separating the room from the main house and said, as if to himself, "Korean pine, all of it. I wonder how many trees were cut down just to build the Sima manor." He raised his head to look at First Sister. "How many would you say? Support beams, crossbeams, doors and windows, flooring, walls, tables and chairs and benches . . ." She squirmed in her chair. "I'd say at least one whole forest!" Commissar Jiang remarked, a note of distress in his voice, as if a forest lay before him, reduced to stumps and scattered branches. "Sooner or later, these accounts will be settled," he said dejectedly, putting the denuded forest behind him, as he walked up to First Sister and stood, legs spread, his right hand on his hip, wrist at a sharp angle. "Of course," he said, "as we see it, Sha Yueliang is not someone dead set on being a turncoat. He was once a glorious anti-Japanese resistance fighter, and if he renounces his recent past, we are more than willing to call him comrade. Mrs. Sha, he'll soon be our prisoner, and it will be your job to make him see the light."

First Sister slumped against the back of the chair. "You'll never catch him!" she said in a high-pitched voice. "Make no mistake about that! His Jeep can outrun a horse any day!"

"Well, let's hope so," Commissar Jiang said as he dropped his angled arm and brought his legs together. He took out a cigarette and offered it to Laidi, who shrank away from it. He brought it even closer. Laidi looked up at the mysterious smile on Commissar Jiang's face and reached out with a trembling hand, taking the cigarette in two nicotine-stained fingers. Commissar Jiang raised his own lit cigarette to his mouth and blew the ashes off the tip, turning it bright red. He then held the lit end out for Laidi. She looked into his face again. He was still smiling. Laidi seemed flustered as she put the cigarette to her lips and touched the tip to the lit end of Jiang's cigarette. We heard what sounded like her lips smacking. Mother was staring woodenly at the wall, Sixth Sister and young master Sima were half asleep, Sha Zaohua wasn't making a sound. A cloud of smoke rose in front of First Sister's face. She raised her head and leaned back, her chest sagging. The fingers holding her cigarette were wet, like loaches just scooped out of the water. The fiery tip of her cigarette burned its way quickly toward her mouth. Her hair was a mess, deep lines spoked out from the corners of her mouth, and there were dark circles under her eyes. Slowly the smile on Commissar Jiang's face disappeared, like water on a piece of hot metal, shrinking in on itself, until it was a bright dot the size of a needlepoint, before disappearing with a brief sizzle. The smile on Commissar Jiang's face retreated up toward his nose and vanished with a brief snap. He flipped away his cigarette, which had nearly burned down all the way to his fingers, ground it out with the tip of his shoe, and strode out of the room.

We heard him bellow in the adjoining room, "We have to catch Sha Yueliang. If he finds his way into a rathole, we must go in and dig him out." Then we heard the sound of a telephone receiver being slammed down.

With pity in her eyes, Mother looked over at First Sister, who sprawled in the chair looking as if all the bones in her body had been removed. She walked over, took her daughter's nicotine-stained hand, and examined it; she shook her head. First Sister slid down to her knees on the floor and wrapped her arms around Mother's legs. When she looked up, her lips were twitching like a suckling infant. A strange noise emerged from between those lips. At first I thought she was laughing, but I quickly realized she was crying. She wiped her tears and snot on Mother's legs. "Mother," she said, "if you want to know the truth, not a day went by that I didn't think of you and my sisters and my brother . . ."

"Do you regret what you did?" Mother asked her.

First Sister did not react right away. Then she shook her head.

"That's good," Mother said. "The Lord points out the way for you, and regret only makes Him unhappy."

Mother handed Zaohua to First Sister. "Take a look at her."

First Sister stroked Sha Zaohua's dark little face. "Mother," she said, "if they execute me, you'll have to raise her for me."

"Even if they don't execute you," Mother said, "I'm still the one who should raise her."

First Sister handed the girl back to Mother, who said, "You hold her for a while. I need to feed Jintong."

Mother walked over to the chair and lifted up her blouse. She bent over at the waist, while I kneeled on the chair and began sucking. "In fairness, that Sha fellow is no coward, and I'm obliged to accept him as my son-in-law, if for no other reason than the fact that he hung all those rabbits from the tree. But he'll never amount to a whole lot. How do I know that? The fact that he hung all those rabbits from the tree. The two of you together are no match for that Jiang fellow. With Jiang, it's a needle hidden in downy cotton. He's got teeth in that belly of his."

In the darkness just before daybreak, a flock of exhausted magpies that had served as a bridge across the Milky Way flew down and perched on our roof ridge, where they chirped listlessly and woke me up. I saw Mother sitting in a chair holding Sha Zaohua, while I was sitting on Laidi's ice-cold knees, her long arms wrapped tightly around my waist. Sixth Sister and the Sima heir were sleeping head to head, just as before. Eighth Sister was resting against Mother's leg. There was no light in Mother's eyes, and the corners of her mouth drooped from exhaustion.

Commissar Jiang walked in, took one look at us, and said, "Mrs. Sha, would you like to go see Commander Sha?"

First Sister pushed me off and jumped to her feet. "You're lying!" she cried hoarsely.

Commissar Jiang crinkled his brow. "Lying?" he said. "Why would I lie?" He walked up to the table, bent over, and blew out the lamp. Red rays of sunlight immediately striped in through the open window. With a courteous — but maybe it wasn't meant to be courteous — wave of his hand, he said, "After you, Mrs. Sha. As I told you before, we don't want to block every single avenue. If he admits the error of his ways and sets back out on the right path, we will welcome him as vice commander of the demolition battalion."

First Sister walked stiffly to the door, but turned back to look at Mother before going outside. "You may come, too, aunty," Commissar Jiang said. "And your other children as well."

We passed under all the many gates of the Sima manor and through several identical courtyards. In the fifth courtyard, we saw a dozen or more wounded soldiers lying on the ground. The female soldier, Miss Tang, was bandaging the leg of one of the wounded men, assisted by my fifth sister, Pandi. She was so focused on the task before her, she didn't even see us. Mother whispered to First Sister, "That's your fifth sister." First Sister glanced over at her. "We paid a stiff price," Commissar Jiang said. A large wooden gate had been placed on the ground in the sixth courtyard to serve as a makeshift bier for several corpses, their faces covered with white cloth. "Our Commander

Lu heroically gave up his life. That has been an incalculable loss." He bent down and removed the cloth from a blood-spattered, whiskered face. "The men begged us to let them skin Commander Sha alive, but that goes against our policy. Mrs. Sha, our good faith is enough to move even the ghosts and spirits, wouldn't you say?" At the seventh court-yard, he led us around a screen wall, and we found ourselves standing on the high steps of the Felicity Manor main gate.

Soldiers of the demolition battalion were running back and forth on the street, their faces covered with dust. Several of them were lead-ing a dozen or more horses, from east to west, while several others were supervising several dozen civilians who were pulling a Jeep by rope, from west to east. The two groups halted when they met in front of the gate, and two men who looked like junior officers came running up. They stopped, saluted, and reported to Commissar Jiang, at a pitch that sounded like an argument. One reported that they'd captured thirteen warhorses; the other reported that they'd captured an Ameri-can Jeep. Unfortunately, the radiator was blown, so it had to be towed over. Commissar Jiang complimented them on a job well done. As their commander's praise washed over them, they stood there, chests out, heads up, lights flashing in their eyes.

Commissar Jiang then led us over to the church, the gate of which was guarded by sixteen armed sentries. Jiang raised his hand, and the sentries slapped the butts of their rifles, clicked their heels, and snapped off a rifle salute. There we were, a bunch of women and chil-dren, suddenly transformed into generals on a military inspection.

At least sixty, maybe more, prisoners in olive drab uniforms were crowded into the southeast corner of the main hall. White mushrooms sprouted on the ceiling above, which was crumbling and mildewed from rain that had leaked through. A squad of four soldiers with assault rifles guarded the prisoners. They were holding magazines of ammu-nition in their left hands, while four of the fingers of their right hands were wrapped around rifle stocks that were as smooth and glossy as a maiden's thigh; their fifth finger was on the curved trigger. They stood with their backs to us. On the floor behind them was a pile of leather belts, looking like a nest of snakes. The only way the prisoners could walk was by holding up their trousers.

The corners of Commissar Jiang's mouth turned up in a barely detectable smile. He coughed lightly, maybe to announce his pres-ence, I don't know. Lazily, the prisoners raised their heads and looked at us. In an instant, their eyes flashed — once for some, twice for others, five, six, or seven times, nine at the most, for yet others. Those will-o'-the-wisp flickers of recognition must have been intended for Shangguan Laidi, if, as Commissar Jiang asserted, she was Commander Sha's right arm. Whatever complex emotions were running through Laidi's heart turned her eyes red and her face ashen; her head slumped onto her chest.

The prisoners reminded me of the black donkeys belonging to the musket band. When they were corralled in the church yard, they too huddled together in a corner — twenty-eight individual donkeys becoming fourteen pairs: you nibble my rectum while I gently bite you in the flank. Mutual concern, mutual protection, mutual aid. Where had this intimate group of donkeys met its end? Who was it that wiped them out? At Ma'er Mountain by Sima Ku's guerrilla forces? Or was it at Biceps Mountain by Japanese secret police? Mother was brutalized on that sacred day when I was baptized. They were all members of the musket band, my mortal enemies. Now you should be punished by the Father, the Son, and the Holy Ghost, Amen.

Commissar Jiang cleared his throat. "Men of the Sha Brigade," he said. "Are you hungry?"

Again the prisoners raised their heads. Some obviously wanted to reply, but didn't dare to. Others had no desire to reply.

Commissar Jiang's bodyguard said, "What's wrong, little uncles, lost your voices? Our political commissar asked you a question."

"Be civil to them!" Commissar Jiang rebuked his bodyguard, who blushed and lowered his head. "Brothers," he continued, "I know you're hungry and thirsty, and any of you with stomach problems are probably suffering right now, seeing spots in front of your eyes and breaking out in a cold sweat. Try to hold on just a little longer. Food is on its way. We don't have a lot of the things we need here, so the food isn't very good. We've prepared a pot of mung bean soup to take care of your thirst and cool you down. At noon there'll be white flour steamed buns and fried horsemeat with chives."

Happiness was written on the prisoners' faces, and some of the men worked up the courage to talk quietly among themselves.

"There are lots of dead horses," Commissar Jiang said, "all of them fine animals. What a shame you had to stumble into our minefield. When you're eating horsemeat in a little while, who knows, you may be eating your own mounts, even though, as people say, 'mules and horses may be as fine as gentlemen, but they're still only mules and horses.' So go ahead, eat as much as you can, since man is at the top of the food chain."

He was still talking about horses when a pair of elderly soldiers carried in a large cauldron, grunting from the effort. Two younger soldiers staggered along behind, each carrying a stack of bowls from their navel all the way up under their chins. "Here's the soup! Soup!" the old soldiers shouted, as if someone were blocking their way. The young soldiers strained to see over their stacked bowls to find a place to put them down. The two old soldiers squatted down and put the cauldron on the floor, nearly sitting down in the process. The young soldiers kept their upper bodies straight as they crouched down, placed the stacks of bowls on the floor, and pulled their hands out from under them. The stacks rocked back and forth. Freed of their burden, the men stood up and mopped their sweaty brows.

Commissar Jiang picked up a large wooden ladle and stirred the soup. "Did you add brown sugar?" he asked the old soldiers. "Reporting, sir, we couldn't find brown sugar, so we went out and got a jar of granulated sugar. We took it from the Cao house. Old lady Cao didn't want to part with it, and held on to it for dear life . . ."

"That's enough. Dish it out to the men here!" Commisar Jiang said as he tossed down the ladle. Then, suddenly seeming to recall our presence, he turned and asked invitingly, "Would you each like a bowl?"

With a smirk, Laidi said, "The commissar did not invite us here to drink mung bean soup, did he?"

"Why shouldn't we?" Mother said. "Old Zhang, each of the girls and I will have a bowl."

"Mother," Laidi said, "what if it's poisoned?"

Commissar Jiang had a big laugh over that. "Mrs. Sha, you have quite an imagination." He picked up the ladle, scooped out some of the soup, held it high, and let it drip back into the vat to show off the appearance and the aroma. Then he threw down the ladle again. "We put a packet of arsenic and two packets of rat poison into this soup. One drink and your stomach will burst within five paces, you'll crumple to the ground in six, and blood will spurt from all the holes in your body. Now, anyone dare to drink it?"

Mother stepped up, picked up a bowl and dusted it with her sleeve, then reached for the ladle, with which she filled the bowl with soup and handed it to First Sister, who refused it. So Mother said,

"Then this bowl is mine." After blowing on the liquid, she took a couple of sips. After a couple more tentative sips, she filled three more bowls, which she handed to Sixth Sister, Eighth Sister, and the young Sima. "Our turn," shouted some of the prisoners. "Give us some. We'll drink three bowls of the stuff, poisoned or not."

With the two old soldiers manning the ladles, the two younger ones passed out the bowls. The armed guards moved off to the sides and faced us at an angle; we could see their eyes, which were fixed on the prisoners, now on their feet and lining up, holding up their pants with one hand and ready to take bowls of mung bean soup with the other. Once they had the bowls in hand, they looked down cautiously, fearful that the hot liquid might burn their fingers. One by one, they returned slowly to the rear of the hall, where they hunkered down, freeing up both hands to hold the soup, which they blew on to cool before starting to eat. A puff of air, followed by noisy sips, the practiced way to eat without burning the inside of your mouth. Young Sima, lacking that experience, slurped up a mouthful, which he could neither spit out nor swallow, and wound up with a burned mouth. While he was taking his bowl of soup, one of the prisoners said softly, "Second Uncle . . ." The old soldier with the ladle looked up and stared into the young face before him. "Don't you recognize me, Second Uncle? It's me, Little Chang . . ." The old soldier reached out and whacked the back of Little Chang's hand with the ladle. "Who are you calling Second Uncle?" he scolded. "You've got the wrong man. I've got no nephew who's willing to be a turncoat and wear a green uniform!" With a cry of *Aiya*, Little Chang dropped his bowl onto his foot, giving him a nasty burn. With another *Aiya*, he let go of his pants to reach down and rub his foot; his pants slipped to his knees, revealing a dirty, tattered pair of underpants. A third *Aiya* escaped as he reached down to pull up his trousers and stand up straight; tears filled his eyes.

"Old Zhang, you have your orders!" Commissar Jiang said angrily. "Who gave you the authority to strike a prisoner? Report to the sergeant-at-arms. Three days in the stockade!"

"But," Old Zhang protested, "he called me Second Uncle . . ."

"I'm betting you are his second uncle," Commissar Jiang said. "Why try to hide it? If he does what he's told, he can become a member of our demolition battalion. How's that burn, youngster? We'll have a medic put some salve on it in a little while. Meanwhile, he spilled his soup, so give him another bowl, and add a few extra beans."

The unfortunate young nephew hobbled back to the rear of the hall with his thicker-than-average soup, as the prisoners behind him in line stepped up to get their bowls.

Now all the prisoners were drinking their soup, filling the church with loud slurps. For the moment, the old and young soldiers had nothing to do; one of the young ones was standing there licking his lips, the other had his eyes fixed on me. One of the older ones was scraping the bottom of the vat with his ladle, the other had taken out a tobacco pouch and pipe and was preparing to take a smoke break. Mother put her bowl up to my lips, but I pushed it away, disgusted by its coarseness. My mouth was adapted to one thing and one thing only: her nipples.

First Sister snorted disdainfully. Commissar Jiang was looking at her, and she made sure she rewarded him with an expression of contempt. "I guess I should have a bowl of mung bean soup too," she said.

"Of course you should," Commissar Jiang said. "Just look at your face. It reminds me of a dry eggplant. Old Zhang, a bowl of soup for Mrs. Sha, and hurry. Make it thick."

"I want it thin," First Sister said.

"Then make it thin," Commissar Jiang said.

Holding the bowl up to her mouth, First Sister took a sip. "You did add sugar," she said. "Commissar Jiang, why don't you have a bowl. Your throat must be dry after all that talk."

Commissar Jiang reached up and pinched his throat. "Indeed it is. Fill up a bowl for me, Old Zhang. Thin."

With the bowl in his hands, Commissar Jiang discussed the qualities of mung beans with First Sister. He told her that in his hometown there was a sandy variety that softened as soon as the water boiled, whereas the local beans didn't even begin to soften for a couple of hours. Once they'd exhausted the subject of mung beans, they moved on to soybeans. You'd have thought they were bean experts; after they'd discussed nearly all varieties of beans, and Commissar Jiang had started in on peanuts, First Sister threw her bowl to the floor and spat out savagely, "What sort of trap are you setting, Jiang?"

"Mrs. Sha," he said, "don't overreact. Let's go, what do you say? We've kept Commander Sha waiting long enough."

"Where is he?" First Sister asked derisively.

"A place you remember only too well, of course," Jiang replied.

There were more sentries at our gate than at the church.

One group was stationed at the door to the east wing, under the command of the mute, Speechless Sun. He was sitting on a log beside the wall, playing with his sword. The Bird Fairy was perched in the crotch of the peach tree, holding a cucumber and nibbling it with her front teeth.

"Go on in," Commissar Jiang said to First Sister. "Try to talk some sense into him. We're hoping he'll abandon the dark and walk into the light."

The moment First Sister entered the east wing, she let out a shriek.

We ran in after her. Sha Yueliang was hanging from the rafters. He was wearing a green wool uniform and a pair of shiny, knee-length leather boots. I remembered him as being of average height; but hanging there, he struck me as being exceptionally tall.

9

I climbed down off the *kang* and threw myself into Mother's lap before my eyes were even fully opened. Savagely, I pulled up her blouse, grabbed the mound of her breast with both hands, and took her nipple between my lips. Something spicy filled my mouth, and tears filled my eyes. I spat out the nipple and looked up, puzzled and a bit put out. Mother patted me on the head and smiled apologetically. "Jintong," she said, "you're seven years old, almost a grown man. It's time to stop the breast-feeding." Before the echo of her words had died out, I heard a peal of crisp, bell-like laughter from Eighth Sister, Shangguan Yunü.

A curtain of darkness lowered before my eyes. I looked heavenward just before I fell to the floor. Suddenly forlorn, I noticed that Mother's breasts, their nipples covered with a peppery coating, looked like a pair of red-eyed doves arching into the sky. In order to wean me, Mother had tried smearing her nipples with the juice of raw ginger, liquified garlic, smelly fish oil, even a bit of rancid chicken droppings. This time she'd used pepper oil. Each time she'd tried to wean me in the past, she'd relented when I fell to the floor as if struck dead. This time I lay on the floor, waiting for her to go in and wash her nipples, as she always had in the past. Scenes from the scary dream I'd had during the night unfolded before my eyes: Mother had sliced off one of her breasts and tossed it to the floor. "Go ahead, suck it!" she'd said. "Suck it!" A black cat had run up, snatched it in its mouth, and run off with it.

Mother picked me up off the floor and sat me down hard next to the dining table. She wore a grave expression. "Say what you like, but this time I'm going to wean you!" she said firmly. "Do you plan to suck until you reduce me to a piece of dry kindling, is that it, Jintong?"

The young Sima, Sha Zaohua, and my eighth sister, Yunü, were sitting around the table eating noodles. They turned toward me with looks of scorn. Shangguan Lü was sitting on a pile of cinders beside the stove, sneering at me. Her windblown skin was like coarse, flaky toilet paper. Young Sima lifted a long, squirmy noodle out of the bowl with his chopsticks and held it up in the air, trying to dazzle me. Then, like a worm, the noodle squirmed into his mouth — disgusting!

Mother put a bowl of steaming noodles down on the table and handed me a pair of chopsticks. "Here, eat," she said. "Try some noodles your sixth sister made."

Sixth Sister, who was feeding Shangguan Lü beside the stove, turned and gave me a hostile look. "Still breast-feeding," she said, "at your age. You're hopeless!"

I flung the bowl of noodles at her.

She jumped up, covered with squirmy noodles. "Mother," she growled, "see how you've spoiled him!"

Mother smacked the back of my head.

I ran over and threw myself against Sixth Sister, clawing at her breasts. I could hear them cry out in protest, like baby chicks being bitten by rats. She doubled over in pain, but I held on for dear life. Her long, thin face turned yellow. "Mother," she cried out, "look at him, Mother!"

Mother attacked my head. "You swine!" she cursed. "You dirty little swine!"

I lost consciousness.

When I came to, I had a splitting headache. Young Sima was still playing with his noodles, unconcerned about what was going on around him. Sha Zaohua looked up from behind her bowl, noodles stuck to her face, and gazed timidly at me. But I couldn't help feeling that there was respect in her eyes. Sixth Sister, her breasts hurting, sat in the doorway weeping. Shangguan Lü was staring malignantly at me. My mother, seemingly ready to burst from anger, was studying the mess of noodles on the floor. "You little bastard! You think these noodles come easy?" She scooped up a handful of the noodles — no, what she scooped up was a nest of squirmy worms — then pinched my nose shut, forcing me to open my mouth, and crammed the worms inside. "Eat those, every last one of them! You've sucked the marrow out of my bones, you little monster!" I threw it all up, broke free from her grasp, and ran out into the yard.

Shangguan Laidi was out there, still wearing the ill-fitting black coat she hadn't taken off in four years, bent at the waist as she honed the edge of a knife on a whetting stone. She flashed me a friendly smile. But then her expression changed. "This time I'll kill him for sure," she said, grinding her teeth. "His time has come. I've got this knife sharper than the north wind, and cooler, and I'm going to make sure he understands that murderers pay with their lives."

I was in no mood to pay her any attention, since everyone assumed she'd gone off her rocker. But I knew she was just faking madness, I just didn't know why. That time in the west wing, where she was staying, she sat high up on top of the millstone, her legs, covered by the black robe, hanging straight down. She told me what it was like being part of Sha Yueliang's marauding band, how she'd lived like royalty, and all the strange and wonderful things she'd seen. She'd owned a box that could sing and a glass that could bring distant objects right up under her nose. At the time I thought that was all crazy talk, but it wasn't long before I saw one of those boxes that could sing. Shangguan Pandi had brought one home with her. During her stay with the demolition battalion, she'd lived a life of ease and comfort, and had gotten fat in the process, like a pregnant mare. She carefully placed the object, with its brass morning glory, on the *kang* and said proudly: "Come over here, all of you. This will open your eyes!" She removed the red cloth covering and revealed the box's secret. First she cranked a handle round and round, and then she said, with a mysterious smile, "Listen, this is what a foreigner sounds like when he laughs." The sound that came out of the box at that moment nearly frightened us out of our wits. The foreigner's laughter sounded like the crying of ghosts in tales we'd heard. "Get that thing out of here!" Mother demanded. "Right this minute! I don't want any box of ghosts in this house!" "Mother," Shangguan Pandi said, "that brain of yours is too old-fashioned. This is a gramophone, not a box of ghosts." From out in the yard, Laidi said, "The needle's worn out. It needs a new one."

"Mrs. Sha," Fifth Sister said sarcastically, "you needn't show off around us. You're a damned slut!" she added said hatefully. "They should have had you shot, and would have if not for me."

"I could have killed him, and would have if you hadn't stopped me!" First Sister said. "I want you all to look at her. Does she look like some young virgin to you? That Jiang fellow nibbled on those big breasts of hers until they looked like a pair of dried turnips."

"Dogshit turncoat! Female turncoat!" Instinctively, Fifth Sister protected her sagging breasts with her arms, as she kept the curses coming: "Stinking wife of a dogshit turncoat!"

"Get out of here, both of you!" Mother said, spitting mad. "Go out and die somewhere, and don't let me see you again!"

The episode instilled in me respect for Shangguan Laidi. She was relaxing in the donkey trough, which had been lined with straw, and said to me in a friendly voice, "You little idiot!" "I'm no idiot!" I defended myself. "But I think you are." She abruptly lifted up her black coat, raised her legs high, and said in a muffled voice, "Look here!"

A ray of sunlight lit up her thighs, her belly, and her breasts, like a sow's teats.

"Come here." I saw a smile on her face at the far end of the trough. "Come here and suckle on me. Mother let my daughter suckle on her, so I'll let you suckle on me, and that way no one owes anyone anything."

I nervously walked up to the trough, where she was now arched like a leaping carp. She reached out and grabbed my shoulders and covered my head with the lower half of her black coat. My world turned dark. And in that darkness I began to grope, curious and tense, mysterious and enthralling. "Here, over here." Her voice sounded far away. "Little idiot." She stuffed one of her nipples into my mouth. "Start sucking, you little whelp. You're not a true Shangguan. You're a little hybrid bastard." The bitter-tasting dirt on her nipple melted in my mouth. Her underarm sweat nearly smothered me. I felt I was suffocating, but she held my head in her hands and pushed her body up against mine, as if trying to cram every last bit of her large, hard breast into my mouth. When I reached the point where I could no longer stand it, I bit down on her nipple. Jumping to her feet, she sent me sliding down her body and out from under the coat, to lie huddled at her feet, waiting for the kick I knew was coming. Tears coursed down her dark, gaunt cheeks. Her breasts heaved beneath the black coat, and brought forth gorgeous feathers, until they looked like a pair of birds that had just mated.

Regretting what I'd done, I reached out to touch the back of her hand with my finger. She lifted her hand and rubbed it against my neck. "Good little brother," she said softly, "don't tell anybody what happened today."

I nodded, and meant it.

"I'm going to share a secret with you," she said. "My husband came to me in a dream and said he's not dead. His soul has attached itself to the body of a blond, light-skinned man."

My imagination ran wild over my secret encounter with Laidi as I walked down the lane, where a squad of five demolition soldiers had run out like madmen. A veil of ecstasy covered their faces. One of them, a fat man, shoved me. "Hey, little fellow, the Jap devils have surrendered! Run on home and tell your mother that Japan has surrendered. The War of Resistance is over!"

Out on the street I saw crowds of soldiers whooping and hollering and jumping around, a group of puzzled civilians among them. It was 1945; the Jap devils had surrendered, and I had been denied the breast. Laidi had given me hers, but she'd had no milk, and her nipple had been covered by a layer of cold, odorific grime; just thinking about that brought feelings of despair. My third brother-in-law, the mute, ran out from the northern entrance to the lane carrying the Bird Fairy. Mother had kicked him and the other soldiers in his unit out of our house after the death of Sha Yueliang. So he put them up in his own house, and the Bird Fairy had gone with him. But though they moved away, the Bird Fairy's shameless cries often emerged late at night from the mute's house and meandered all the way to our ears. Now he was carrying her toward us. She lay in his arms with her swollen belly, dressed in a white coat that looked to have been tailored from the same pattern as Laidi's black coat; only the color was different. Seeing the Bird Fairy's coat reminded me of Laidi's coat, which in turn reminded me of Laidi's breasts, and they reminded me of the Bird Fairy's breasts. Among Shangguan women, the Bird Fairy's breasts had to be considered top of the line. They were delicate, lovely, perky, with slightly upturned nipples as nimble as the mouth of a hedgehog. Does saying that the Bird Fairy's breasts were top of the line mean that Laidi's were not? I can only give a vague response. Since the moment I was conscious of what was going on around me, I'd discovered that the range of beauty in breasts is wide; while one should never lightly say that a particular pair is ugly, one can easily say that a pair of breasts is beautiful. Hedgehogs are beautiful sometimes; so are baby pigs.

The mute put the Bird Fairy down in front of me. "Ah-ao, ah-ao!" He waved his massive fist, which was the size of a horse hoof, under my nose, but in a friendly way. I understood him: his "Ah-ao, ah-ao!" grunts meant the same as "The Jap devils have surrendered!" He took off down the street like a bull.

The Bird Fairy cocked her head and looked at me. Her belly was terrifyingly big, like that of a gigantic spider. "What are you, a turtle-dove or a wild goose?" she chirped. Maybe she was asking me, and maybe she wasn't. "My bird flew away. My bird, it flew away!" There was a look of panic on her face. I pointed to the street. She stuck her arms out straight, pawed at the ground with her bare feet, and, with a chirp, took off running toward the street. She was moving fast. How could such a huge belly not slow her down? If not for that belly, she probably could have taken wing. She ran into the crowd on the street like a powerful ostrich.

Fifth Sister came running home; she too was pregnant, and her bulging breasts had leaked into her gray uniform. In contrast to the Bird Fairy, she was a clumsy runner. The Bird Fairy flapped her arms when she ran; Fifth Sister supported her belly when she ran. Fifth Sister was gasping for breath, like a mare that's pulled a wagon up a hill. Pandi had the fullest figure of all the Shangguan daughters, and she was also the tallest. Her breasts were fierce and intimidating; as if filled with gas, they went *peng-peng* when thumped. First Sister's face was covered by a black veil; she was wearing her black coat. In the dark of night, she climbed into the Sima compound from a nearby ditch and followed the smell of sweat to a brightly lit room. The flagstones in the yard were slippery, covered by green moss. Her heart was in her throat and about to beat its way out through her mouth. The hand in which she carried the knife cramped up, and she had a fishy taste in her mouth. She peered through the crack in a latticed door, and what she saw nearly made her soul take flight and her heart stop: a large white candle, wax dripping down its sides, shone brightly and sent fleshy shadows dancing on the walls. Scattered on the stone floor were Shangguan Pandi and Commissar Jiang's clothes; a coarse wool sock was lying alongside the apricot yellow toilet. Pandi, naked as the day she was born, was sprawled atop the dark, gaunt body of Jiang Liren. First Sister burst into the room. But she hesitated as she looked down at her sister's raised buttocks and the indentation at the base of her backbone, glistening with sweat. Her enemy, the man she wanted to kill, was protected. Raising her knife, she screamed, "I'm going to kill you two, I'm going to kill you!" Pandi rolled over and off the bed, while Jiang Liren grabbed the blanket and rushed First Sister, knocking her to the ground. Ripping the veil off her face, he laughed. "I thought it might be you!"

Fifth Sister stood in the doorway shouting, "The Japanese have surrendered!"

She dragged me way back out to the street. Her hand was sweaty — sour, salty sweat. I detected along with the smell of sour sweat the odor of tobacco. That smell came from her husband, Lu Liren. In order to commemorate the victory over the Sha Band, in which Commander Lu had heroically sacrificed his life, Jiang Liren had changed his name to Lu Liren. The smell of Lu Liren was scattered across the street via Fifth Sister's hand.

Out on the street, the demolition battalion was celebrating noisily, many of the soldiers crying openly and banging into one another. One of them climbed to the top of the shaky bell tower, as the crowd down below swelled. People came with gongs, or with milking goats, even chunks of meat bouncing around on large lotus leaves. A woman with bells tied to her breasts really caught my attention. She was performing a strange dance that made her breasts jiggle, causing the bells to ring and ring and ring. The people kicked up a cloud of dust; they shouted themselves hoarse. The Bird Fairy, who was in the middle of the crowd, darted glances back and forth; the mute raised his fist and pounded a man beside him. Eventually, a group of soldiers went into the Sima compound and reemerged carrying Lu Liren over their heads. They tossed him into the air, as high as the tips of nearby trees, and when he came down, they caught him and tossed him back into the air . . . *Hai-ya*! *Hai-ya*! *Hai-ya*! Fifth Sister, holding her belly and crying, shouted, "Liren! Liren!" She tried to squeeze in among the soldiers, but was driven back.

The sun raced across the sky, seemingly frightened by the din below, and sat on the ground, resting against the trees on the sandy ridge. More relaxed now, it was bright red, blistery, and sweaty; it steamed and panted like an old man, as it observed the crowd on the street.

At first, one man fell in the dust. Then a whole string of them fell. Slowly, the dust settled back to earth and covered the men's faces and hands and sweat-stained uniforms. A whole string of men lay stiffly in the dust under the red rays of the sun. As dusk fell, cool breezes blew over from the marshes and reed ponds; the crisp whistle of a train crossing the bridge was carried on the wind. People cocked their ears to listen. Or maybe I was the only one who did that. The War of Resistance had been won, but Shangguan Jintong had been cast off by his beloved breasts. I thought about death. I felt like jumping down a well, or into the river.

One person in the crowd, wearing a khaki jacket, rose slowly out of the dust. She was up on all fours as she began clawing at the dirt in front of her, digging out something the same color as her jacket, the same color as everything else out there on the street. She dug out one, and then another. They made sounds like giant salamanders. In the midst of the celebration over victory in the War of Resistance, Third Sister, the Bird Fairy, had brought a pair of twin boys into the world.

The Bird Fairy and her babies made me momentarily forget my own troubles. Slowly I moved up closer to her to get a look at my new nephews. I had to step over the legs of men lying in the road, and the heads of others; finally, I was close enough to see the wrinkled skin — face and body — of the two dirt-colored little guys: they were bald, like a pair of lush green gourds. Crying with their mouths wide open made for a frightening sight, and for some unfathomable reason, I imagined their bodies covered with a thick layer of fishy scales. I backed off, carelessly stepping on a soldier's hand as I did. But instead of hitting me, or yelling at me, he just grunted softly and slowly raised himself into a sitting position; from there he slowly got to his feet, and when he wiped the dust from his face, I saw it was Lu Liren, Fifth Sister's husband. He was looking for his wife, who was struggling to sit up in the grass by the wall; she rushed into his arms, wrapped her arms around his head, and rubbed it frantically. "We won, we won, victory is ours! We'll call our child Shengli — Victory," Fifth Sister said.

By this time, the sun was exhausted, like an old man about to call it a day and get some sleep. The moon spat out rays of clear light, giving it the look of an anemic yet beautiful widow. With his arm around Fifth Sister, Lu Liren started to walk off just as Sima Ku entered the village at the head of his anti-Japanese commando battalion.

The battalion included three companies. First came the cavalry company, comprised of sixty-six horses of mixed Xinjiang and Mongol breed and their riders, all armed with American submachine guns. Next came the bicycle company, comprised of sixty-six Camel brand bicycles, the riders armed with German weapons. Third in line was the mule company, comprised of sixty-six powerful, fast-moving mules and their riders, all armed with Japanese M-38 carbines. There was also a small special unit, comprised of thirteen camels carrying bicycle repair equipment and spare parts, plus weapon repair tools, spare parts, and ammunition. They also carried Sima Ku and Shangguan Zhaodi, plus their daughters, Sima Feng and Sima Huang. Riding on the back of yet another camel was an American by the name of Babbitt. Perched atop the last camel was dark-skinned Sima Ting; he was wearing army trousers, a lavender satin shirt, and a frown.

Babbitt, who had gentle blue eyes, soft blond hair, and red lips, wore a red leather jacket over heavy cotton, multipocketed trousers, and deerskin boots. Uniquely attired, he sat high up on the back of his camel, rocking back and forth as he entered the village with Sima Ku and Sima Ting.

Sima Ku's battalion swept into the village like a whirlwind. The six horses in the front rank were black, and were ridden by handsome young soldiers in woolen khakis; their brass buttons had been polished to a glittering sheen, as had their riding boots, the submachine guns in their hands, and the helmets on their heads; even their horses' black flanks shone. The horses slowed down as they approached the spot where soldiers lay sprawled in the dirt; they held their heads high and began to prance as their riders fired their weapons into the darkening sky, a sparkling, eardrum-pounding chain of tracer bullets that sent leaves fluttering to the ground. Lu Liren and Shangguan Pandi, spooked by the burst of gunfire, stepped away from one another. "Which unit are you?" Lu Liren asked, raising his voice. "Your granddad's unit," one of the riders fired back. His words still hung in the air when a fusillade of bullets nearly grazed Lu Liren's head. He sprawled inelegantly on the ground, but quickly got back to his feet and shouted, "I'm commander and political commissar of the demolition battalion, and I demand to see your commanding officer!" His shout was swallowed up by another fusillade of bullets that swept the open space around them. Soldiers of the demolition battalion staggered to their feet. The horsemen spurred their horses forward, breaking ranks to avoid the confusion in the street ahead. The horses were short and extremely nimble; as they stepped over and around the men lying on the ground and those who had barely stood up, only to be knocked down again, they looked like a pack of lithe tomcats on the prowl. As soon as the first rank passed, the others followed close on their heels, sending the standing soldiers spinning and banging into each other, accompanied by a chorus of panicky screams; they looked like trees, rooted in the ground and forced to stand and take a pounding. Even after all the horses had passed, people in the street weren't fully aware of what had just happened. Then came the mule company. Marching in orderly ranks, they too shone, their riders sitting proudly, weapons at the ready. Meanwhile, the horse company had closed up ranks and was prancing back, squeezing the raggedy ranks of people on the street between the two companies. Some of the more quick-witted soldiers tried to dart down lanes intersecting the street, but their escape routes were blocked by members of the bicycle company, men in purple civilian clothes riding Camel brand bicycles. They fired their German weapons at the feet of the thwarted escapees, throwing dust up into their faces and sending them scurrying back into the middle of the street. Before long, all the officers and men of the demolition battalion had been herded into the area in front of the Felicity Manor gate.

The mule company soldiers were ordered to dismount and move off to the side, opening up a space for the leaders to make an appearance. Demolition battalion soldiers kept their eyes riveted on the section of road, as did the hapless civilians who had been herded together with them. I had a premonition that these new arrivals would somehow be connected to the Shangguan family.

The sun had nearly disappeared below the sandy ridge, leaving only a rosy border around the dreary treetops. Golden-red crows flew rapidly back and forth above the mud huts of the outsiders, and bats put on a flying demonstration in the brilliant glow of dusk. The silence was a sign that the leaders were due any minute.

"Victory! Victory!" The mighty cry heralded the leaders' arrival. They came from the west, riding up on camels festooned with red satin.

Sima Ku was wearing an olive drab wool uniform and, on his head at a rakish angle, a fore-and-aft cap, which we called a jackass cap. A pair of medals the size of horse hooves were pinned to his chest, his waist was circled by a silver ammunition belt, and he wore a holstered revolver on his right hip. His camel raised its head, turned its lewd lips inside out, pricked up its floppy-dog ears, and squinted its long-lashed eyes. Shaking its shod cloven hooves, twisting its snaky tail, and tightening its pared buttocks, it threaded its way through the mule company like a ship riding the waves, with Sima Ku its proud skipper. He flared his legs, in their fine leather riding boots, threw out his chest, leaned back slightly, and raised a white-gloved hand to straighten his jackass cap; his burnished face was hard beyond description, the red moles on his cheek looked like maple leaves after a frost. It was a face that seemed to have been carved out of a block of red sandalwood, then varnished with three coats of anticorrosive, moisture-proof tung oil. The horse and mule soldiers slapped the butts of their weapons and shouted in unison.

Right behind Sima Ku's camel came another carrying his wife, Shangguan Zhaodi. She hadn't changed much in the years since we'd last seen her; she was as fresh and beautiful, as gentle-looking as ever. A white, silky cloak was draped over her shoulders atop a lined jacket with yellow satin piping, and red silk, loose-fitting trousers. She wore tiny brown leather shoes. A deep green jade bracelet decorated each wrist, eight rings adorned her fingers. Lush green grapes hung from her earlobes — I later learned they were made of jadeite.

I mustn't forget about my two honorable nieces. They rode up on the third camel, behind Zhaodi. Thick ropes between the humps connected two riding baskets woven from waxed boughs. The girl in the left basket, flowers in her hair, was Sima Feng; the one in the right basket, flowers also in her hair, was Sima Huang.

Next to enter my field of vision was the American, Babbitt. I couldn't tell how old he was, but the light of life in his green, catlike eyes could only belong to a young man, a rooster barely old enough to mount a hen. He wore a dazzling feather in his cap, and though he swayed with the movements of his camel, his erect posture never varied, like a wood-carved boy tied to a float and tossed into a river. I was impressed. Mystified even. Later on, when we learned who he was, I realized that he rode a camel as if he were in the cockpit of an aircraft. He was an American Air Force pilot who had landed his Camel bomber on a main street in Northeast Gaomi at twilight.

Sima Ting brought up the rear. Even though he was a member of the glorified Sima family, he hung his head, dispirited. His camel, a dusty-looking animal, had a gimp leg.

Lu Liren pulled himself together and walked up to Sima Ku's camel, where he snapped off an arrogant salute. "Commander Sima," he said, "allow me to welcome you and your men as guests of our headquarters on this day of national jubilation."

Sima laughed so hard he rocked back and forth until he was in danger of falling off. He smacked the furry hump in front of him and said to the mule troops beside him and the crowd in front and back, "Did you all hear the shit that just came out of his mouth? Headquarters? Guests? You poor country camel, this is my house, the land of my bloodline. When I was born, my mother's blood pooled on this very street! You bunch of bedbugs have sucked dry the blood of our Northeast Gaomi Township, and now it is time for you to get the hell out of here! Go on back to your rabbit warrens and let me take my house back."

It was an impassioned outburst, filled with a richness of sound. He emphasized every sentence by thumping the camel's hump, and with every thump, the camel's neck twitched and the soldiers roared. Also, with every thump, Lu Liren's face paled just a little more. Finally, the camel, provoked beyond its limits, shrank back, bared its teeth, and sent something foul and sticky through its nose and into Lu Liren's ashen face.

"I protest!" Lu Liren shouted in exasperation as he wiped the muck off his face. "I protest strongly! I'm going to register a complaint with the highest authority!"

"In this place," Sima Ku said, "that highest authority is me, and I hereby announce that you and your men have half an hour to leave Dalan. If you're still here after that, I'll turn my weapons on you."

"One of these days," Lu Liren said coldly, "you'll taste the bitter wine you've brewed."

Ignoring Lu Liren, Sima Ku ordered his troops, "Escort our friends out of the area."

The horse and mule companies closed up ranks and moved in from the east and the west. The soldiers of the demolition battalion were driven into the lane leading to our house. An armed sentry in civilian clothes stood every few meters on both sides of the lane. Others were in position on the rooftops.

A half hour later, most members of the demolition battalion were climbing soaking wet up the opposite bank of the Flood Dragon River, cold rays of moonlight shining down on their faces. The remaining troops took advantage of the confusion along the river either to escape into the nearby brush or to let the current take them far enough downriver to climb up onto the bank unobserved, wring out their clothes, and take off for home in the dark of night.

A hundred or more members of the demolition battalion stood on the opposite bank of the river like chickens dumped into the pot. As they looked around at each other, some were in tears, others were secretly pleased. After observing his disarmed and disheartened troops,

Lu Liren spun around and ran back toward the river, intending to drown himself. But his troops grabbed him and wouldn't let go. So he stood on the riverbank, deep in thought for several minutes before looking up and shouting across the river at the noisy crowd, "Sima Ku, Sima Ting, just you wait. I'll be back one day with a vengeance! Northeast Gaomi Township belongs to us, not you! You may control it today, but someday, when all is said and done, it'll be ours again!"

Well, let Lu Liren and his men go lick their wounds. I had my own problems to attend to. As to whether I'd drown myself in a river or down a well, eventually I chose the river, because I'd heard that rivers empty into the ocean. That year when the Bird Fairy had first displayed her powers, a dozen or more double-masted ships had sailed down the river.

I watched the demolition battalion soldiers struggling to cross the Flood Dragon River under the cold rays of moonlight. Splashing and tumbling and crawling, they stirred up the river, sending waves in all directions. Sima's troops were not stingy with their ammunition. They fired their weapons into the river, churning the water as if it were a boil. If they'd wanted to destroy the demolition battalion, it would have been like shooting fish in a barrel. But choosing to intimidate them instead, they only killed or wounded a dozen or so men. Years later, when the demolition battalion fought its way back as an independent unit, every officer and soldier who faced a firing squad felt that the punishment did not fit the crime.

I waded slowly out toward the deep water; the surface, calm once again, reflected shards of light, thousands of them. Water grasses ensnared my feet; fish nibbled at my knees with their warm little mouths. I kept walking forward, until the water rose above my navel. I felt spasms in my gut — unbearable hunger. Then Mother's intimate and revered, incomparably graceful breasts floated into my brain. But she had smeared hot pepper juice on her nipples, and had reminded me over and over, "You're seven years old, time to stop nursing." How come I'd had to live to the age of seven? Why hadn't I died before reaching that age? Tears slid down my cheeks and into my mouth. I really ought to die, and not allow all those unclean foods to contaminate my mouth and digestive tract. Emboldened by the thought, I took several more steps forward, and the water suddenly swallowed up my shoulders; I could sense the rush of dark currents along the riverbed. I steadied my feet on the bottom to resist the powerful current. A swirling eddy drew me to it, and I was terrified. As the mud under my feet was being swept away by the rapid current of the river I felt myself sinking deeper and deeper and being pushed forward, straight into that fearful eddy. I fought to resist the force and began to scream.

Just then I heard Mother's shouts: "Jintong — Jintong, my son, where are you . . ."

That was followed by a series of shouts from my sixth sister, Niandi, First Sister Laidi, and a familiar yet somehow alien thin voice; I guessed it was my second sister, the one with rings on all her fingers, Zhaodi.

I shrieked as I fell forward and was swallowed up by the eddy.

When I awoke, the first thing I saw was one of Mother's wonderfully erect breasts, its nipple gently observing me like a loving eye. The other one was already in my mouth, taking pains to tease my tongue and rub up against my gums, a veritable stream of sweet milk filling my mouth. I smelled the heavy fragrance of Mother's breast. I later learned that Mother had washed the pepper oil off her nipples with the rose-scented soap Second Sister, Zhaodi, had given her as an act of filial respect, and that she had also dabbed some French perfume in the cleavage between.

The room was aglow with lamplight; a dozen or more red candles had been stuck in silver candelabras on high altars. I noted that several people were seated and standing around Mother, including Sima Ku, my second brother-in-law, who was showing off his new treasure: a cigarette lighter that ignited every time he pressed the top. Young Master Sima observed his father from a distance, indifferent, no trace of intimacy.

Mother sighed. "I ought to give him back to you. The poor thing doesn't even have a name."

Sima Ku said, "Since my name, Ku, means a warehouse, let's fill it with grain — *liang*. We'll call him Sima Liang."

Mother said, "Did you hear that?" Mother said. "You are now Sima Liang."

Sima Liang cast an indifferent glance at Sima Ku.

"Good lad," Sima Ku said, "you remind me of myself when I was young. Mother-in-law, I thank you for protecting the life of our Sima heir. From this day on, you can look forward to enjoying life. Northeast Gaomi Township is our dominion."

Mother responded with a noncommital shake of her head. "If you want to be truly filial," she said to Zhaodi, "you can store up some grain for me. I don't ever want to go hungry again."

The following night, Sima Ku organized a great celebration in honor of the national victory in the War of Resistance and his own return to his homeland. Eight surrounding scholar trees were festooned with a cartload of firecrackers, then the men smashed two dozen pig iron woks and dug up a cache of explosives buried by the demolition battalion, with which they fashioned a device that would make a huge explosion. The firecrackers popped and cracked half the night, bringing down all the leaves and small branches from the eight scholar trees. The dazzling splinters of metal from the big device lit up half the sky. They slaughtered a dozen pigs and another dozen head of cattle, then dug up a dozen vats of vintage liquor. Filling large platters with the cooked meat, they laid them out on tables set up in the middle of the street; everyone could help themselves by using the bayonets stuck into the meat to cut off as much as they wanted; if you sliced off a pig's ear and tossed it to one of the dogs hanging around the table, no one said a word. The vats of liquor were placed beside the tables, each with a ladle hanging on its side. Anyone wanting a drink helped himself; if you felt like taking a bath in the stuff, no one cared. That day was made for village gluttons. The eldest son of the Zhang family, Zhang Qian'er, ate and drank himself dead right there on the street. As they were carrying off his corpse, liquor and meat sprayed from his mouth and nose.

Chapter Four

1

One late afternoon a couple of weeks after the demolition battalion had been driven out of town, Fifth Sister, Pandi, handed Mother a child wrapped in an old army uniform. "Mother," she said, "take her."

Pandi was drenched, her thin clothes sticking to her skin; I was attracted to the sight of her full, high-arching breasts. Her hair gave off the heated aroma of distiller's mash. Datelike nipples quivered under her blouse, and I could barely keep from rushing over to bite and fondle them. I didn't have the nerve. Always hot-tempered, Pandi lacked First Sister's gentle nature and needed little provocation to slap your face. Maybe it would be worth it. I went over and hid from view beneath a pear tree, biting my lip and wishing I were braver.

"Stop right there!" Mother shouted at her. "Come back here!"

"Mother," Pandi said with an angry glare, "I'm your daughter too. If you can take care of their babies, you can take care of mine."

"Am I this family's babysitter?" Mother replied just as angrily. "You no sooner have your babies than you hand them over to me. Not even dogs do that!"

"Mother," Pandi said, "when the good days came around, you shared in our good fortune. Now that we've run into a spell of bad luck, not even our children are spared, is that it? A bowl has to be held straight so the water won't spill."

First Sister's laughter emerged from the darkness and sent cold chills up my spine. "Fifth Sister," she said icily, "you can tell that fellow Jiang I'm going to kill him one day!"

"First Sister," Pandi replied, "it's too early to be celebrating! Not even death will clean the slate for your turncoat husband, Sha Yueliang. So don't go off half-cocked. If you do, no one will be able to save you."

"Stop fighting!" Mother shouted, before sitting down heavily on the ground.

A big, bright moon climbed above the ridge of our roof and shone down on the faces of the Shangguan girls, making them seem as if coated with blood. Mother shook her head sorrowfully and sobbed. "I've wasted my life raising a bunch of ingrates who only curse me for my efforts. Get out of my sight, all of you. I don't ever want to see any of you again!"

Like a specter, Laidi streaked into the west wing, where she began muttering, as if Sha Yueliang were there with her. Lingdi returned from the marshes as if in a dream, a string of croaking bullfrogs in her hand; she entered the compound by climbing over the southern wall.

"You see!" Mother grumbled. "Some have gone mad, others have turned stupid. With a life like this, why go on?"

Mother laid Fifth Sister's baby on the ground and struggled to her feet, then turned and walked toward the house without a backward glance at the bawling baby. Sima Liang was standing by the doorway watching the excitement; Mother kicked him and smacked Sha Zaohua on the head as she passed by. "Why don't all of you just go off somewhere to die?" She slammed the door behind her. We heard the sound of things being thrown and knocked around inside. The last thing we heard was a heavy thud, as if a sack of grain had been dropped on the floor, and I guessed it must have been the sound of Mother collapsing onto the *kang* after her anger was spent. I couldn't actually see her lying on the *kang*, but I could imagine it: arms spread wide, her swollen yet bony, chapped hands lying palms up; the left one resting against Lingdi's two children, who might very well be mutes; the right one resting against Zhaodi's pair of flighty and very beautiful little girls. Moonlight framed her ashen lips. Her breasts lay flattened against her ribs, thoroughly exhausted. That spot between her and the Sima girls should have been mine; but it disappeared beneath her outstretched body.

Out in the yard, the baby Pandi had wrapped in a frayed gray army uniform was bawling as it lay on the path, which had been tramped down lower than the ground beside it. No one paid her any attention.

Pandi walked around her child and shouted savagely in the direction of Mother's window, "I expect you to take good care of her. Lu Liren and I will fight our way back one day!"

Pounding the straw mat covering the *kang*, Mother shouted back, "You want me to take good care of her? I'll tell you what I'll do. I'll fling her into the river to feed the turtles or down a well to feed the toads or into the latrine to feed the flies!"

"Go ahead," Pandi said. "She's my baby, and I was yours, so she's your flesh and blood!"

With that comment, Pandi bent down for one more look at the baby lying on the path, then turned and staggered off toward the street. As she passed the west wing, she stumbled and took a bad fall. Moaning and groaning as she got to her feet, she cupped her injured breasts and aimed a curse at the door: "You slut, just you wait!" Inside the room, Laidi laughed. Pandi spit at me before walking off, her head held high.

The next morning we awoke to find Mother training the white milk goat to feed Pandi's baby girl as she lay in a basket.

On those spring mornings of 1946, there was a lot going on in the house of the Shangguan family. Before the sun had climbed above the mountains, a thin, nearly transparent misty glow drifted across the yard. The village was still asleep at such times, swallows dreamed in their nests, crickets in the heated ground behind stoves made their music, and cows chewed their cud alongside feeding troughs . . .

Mother sat up on the *kang* and, with a painful moan, rubbed her aching fingers. After a bit of a struggle, she draped her coat over her shoulders and tried to limber up her stiff joints in order to button up her dress. She yawned, rubbed her face, and opened her eyes wide as she swung her feet over the edge of the *kang* and slipped her feet into her shoes; she stepped down, wobbled a bit, and bent over to pull up the heels of her shoes, then sat down on the bench next to the *kang* to see if all the sleeping babies were all right before walking outside with a basin to fetch water. Filling the basin with four, maybe five, ladlefuls, she watered the goats in the pen.

Five milk goats, three black and two white, all had long, narrow faces, curved horns, and lengthy goatees. Five heads came together as they drank from the basin. Mother picked up a broom and swept the droppings into a pile and then out of the pen. She then went out into the lane for fresh dirt, which she spread over the ground. After brushing out the animals' coats, she returned for more water to clean their nipples, which she dried with a towel. The goats baa-ed contentedly. By this time the sun was out, a mixture of red and purple rays driving away the misty glow. Returning to the room, Mother scrubbed the wok, then filled it part way with water. "Niandi," she shouted, "time to get up." She dumped in some millet and mung beans and let them soften for a while before adding soybeans and putting the lid on the wok. She bent over and fed the stove with straw. *Whoosh*, she lit a match, spreading sulfur fumes around her. Her mother-in-law, lying on a bed of straw, rolled her eyes. "You old witch, are you still alive? Isn't it time for you to die?" Mother sighed. The bean tassels crackled in the stove, filling the air with a pleasant aroma. *Pop*! A stray bean exploded. "Niandi, are you up?"

Sima Liang emerged bleary-eyed from the east wing, heading for the toilet. Puffs of green smoke rose from the chimney. Water buckets thudded against one another; Niandi was heading to the river for water. *Baa* — goats. *Wah* — Lu Shengli's cries. Sima Feng and Sima Huang whimpered; the Bird Fairy's two kids grunted — *Ao-ya-ya*. The Bird Fairy walked lazily out the gate. Laidi was standing at the window brushing her hair. Horses out in the lane whinnied. It was Sima Ku's horse company riding over to the river to water their mounts. A throng of mules passed by; it was the mule company returning from the river. Wagon bells rang out; it was the bicycle company practicing their riding skills. "Come boil some water," Mother said to Sima Liang. "Jintong, time to get up! Go down to the river and wash your face." Mother carried five willow baskets out into the sun and filled them with five babies. "Let the goats out," she said to Sha Zaohua. The skinny girl, her hair a mess, eyes still bleary from sleep, entered the pen, where the goats greeted her with friendly tosses of their horned heads and licked the grime off her knees. Their tongues tickled her. She thumped their heads with her tiny fists and cursed them childishly, "You stump-tailed devils." After removing the tethers from their necks, she tapped one of them on the ear. "Go on," she said, "you belong to Lu Shengli." The goat wagged its tail happily and sprinted over next to Shengli, who lay in her basket, arms and legs straight up, crying urgently. The goat spread its rear legs, backed up to the basket, and pushed its udder up against Shengli's face. Its nipples sought out Shengli; Shengli sought out the goat's nipples. Both knew their task well, to each other's mutual satisfaction. Each nipple was long and swollen; like a voracious barracuda, Shengli caught it in her mouth and held fast. Big Mute and Little Mute's goats, Sima Feng and Sima Huang's goats, each went straight to its master or mistress and, in the same manner, drew up next to the child's mouth, each knowing its task well, to the mutual satisfaction of all. The goats bent over, eyes slitted, goatees quivering slightly.

"The water's boiling, Granny," Sima Liang said to Mother, who was outside washing her face. "Let it boil a while longer." Flames lapped at the bottom of the wok on the stove that had been altered for their use by Old Zhang, the demolition battalion's cook. Sima Liang, who was wearing only pants, was thin as a rail and had a melancholy look in his eyes. Lingdi returned with the water, the two full buckets swaying at the ends of her shoulder pole. Her braid fell all the way to her waist and was tied at the end by a fashionable plastic ribbon. The goats all switched nipples for their children. "Let's eat," Mother said. Sha Zaohua put the table up, Sima Liang laid out the bowls and chopsticks. Mother dished up the porridge — one two three four five six seven bowls. Zaohua and Yunü put the benches in place, while Niandi fed her grandmother. *Slurp slurp.* Laidi and Lingdi walked in with their own bowls and served themselves. Without looking at them, Mother muttered, "None of you is crazy when mealtime rolls around." Her two daughters went outside to eat their porridge in the yard. "I've heard that the independent 16th Regiment is going to fight its way back," Niandi said. "Eat," Mother said. I was kneeling in front of her, suckling. "Mother, you've spoiled him. Are you going to breast-feed him until he gets married?" "That's not unheard of," Mother said. I went from one nipple to the other. "Jintong," she said, "I'm going to keep at it until the day you've had enough." Then she turned to Niandi. "After breakfast, take the goats out to pasture and bring back some wild garlic for lunch." Mother's orders brought the morning to an end.

Shengli waddled through the grass, her backside brushing against the feltlike greenery. Her goat was grazing, nibbling only the tender grass tips, its dew-wetted face giving it the haughty look of a young noblewoman. The times may have been chaotic and noisy, but the pastureland was peacefully quiet. Flowers dotted the land, their redolence intoxicating. We were sprawled on the ground around Niandi. Sima Liang was chewing a stalk of grass, coating the corners of his mouth with green juice. His eyes were bright yellow, but with a murky cast. The expression on his face and the chewing motion made him look like a gigantic locust. Sha Zaohua was watching an ant perched atop a stalk of grass scratching its head as it looked for an escape route. The tip of my nose touched a patch of golden flowers; their fragrance tickled me, and I sneezed loudly, throwing a scare into Sixth Sister, Niandi, who was lying on her back. Her eyes snapped open and she gave me a nasty look, a bit of a scowl on her lips and a slight crinkle on her nose, before closing her eyes again. She looked comfortable, lying there in the sun. Her protruding brow was clear and shiny; not a wrinkle in sight. She had thick lashes and a bit of down on her upper lip; her chin turned up fetchingly. Among all the girls in the Shang-guan family, only her ears were fleshy with no loss of grace. She was wearing a white poplin blouse passed down by Second Sister, Zhaodi, one of those fashionable types that button down the front with so-called Mandarin Duck fasteners. Her braid lay across her breast like an eel. Now, of course, I need to discuss her breasts. Not especially large, they were hard and not yet fully developed. So they kept their shape even when the body from which they grew was flat on its back. Their sleek, fair skin peeked out from the gaps between her buttons, and I was tempted to tickle them with a stalk of grass; I didn't have the nerve. Niandi and I never had gotten along. She couldn't stomach the fact that I was still breast-feeding, and if I'd tickled her breast, it would have been the same as rubbing a tiger's ass. It was a struggle. The stalk chewer kept chewing the stalk, the ant watcher kept watching the ant; as they ate, the white goats looked like noblewomen, the black ones like widows. When there's too much food, people don't know where to start; when there's too much grass, goats have the same problem. *Ah-choo*! So goats sneeze too, and loud! Their udders drooped heavily. It was nearly noon. I picked a stalk of bristlegrass and decided to rub the tiger's ass after all. No one noticed me as I reached out stealthily with the stalk of grass, drawing nearer and nearer to a gap in her blouse, stretched open by her jutting breasts. My ears were buzzing, my heart thumped like a scared rabbit. The stalk of grass touched her fair skin. No reaction. Was she asleep? If so, why didn't I hear her breathing? I twirled the end of the stalk, making the other end shake. She reached up and scratched her chest, but didn't open her eyes. She probably thought it was an ant. I pushed the grass in farther and twisted it. She slapped her chest, caught my stalk of grass, and pulled it out. She sat up and glared at me, her face turning red. I laughed. "You little bastard!" she cursed. "Mother has spoiled you rotten!" She laid me down in the grass and swatted me on the behind — twice. "But I'm not going to!" With a fierce glare in her eyes, she added, "You're going to hang yourself to death from a nipple one of these days!"

Frightened by the outburst, Sima Liang spat out a stalk of chewed-up grass and Zaohua stopped watching the ant. They both looked at me, clearly puzzled, then gave the same look to Niandi. I managed a feeble cry, for show, since I felt I'd gotten the better of the exchange. Niandi stood up and tossed her head proudly, whipping her braid around to the back of her head. Shengli had by then waddled up to her goat, but it was trying to get away from her. So she grabbed its nipple, and it responded unhappily by knocking her over. I couldn't tell if the bleats that followed meant that she was crying or what. Sima Liang jumped to his feet and, with a series of loud grunts, ran as fast as he could, startling a dozen red-winged locusts and several dirt-colored little birds. Moving quickly on her skinny legs, Zaohua ran over to a patch where velvety purple flowers the size of fists poked up above the grass tips. I stood up, embarrassed, walked around behind Niandi, and started pounding her on the backside. "Hit me, will you?" I shouted with as much bluster as I could manage. "How dare you?" Her buttocks were so hard and so tight that hitting them hurt my hands. When her patience ran out, she turned, bent at the waist, and snarled — mouth open, teeth bared, eyes staring, releasing a scary, wolfish howl. It occurred to me how similar human and canine faces can be. She pushed my head backward, throwing me flat on my back in the grass.

The white goat put up a feeble struggle when Niandi grabbed it by the horns. Shengli rushed up, flopped over beneath the animal, and strained to turn her head so she could take the nipple into her mouth as she kicked the goat's belly with both feet. Niandi rubbed the goat's ears; it wagged its tail docilely. Mournful feelings flooded my mind. It was clear that my days of relying on mother's milk were coming to an end. So before that happened, I would have to find a substitute. The first thing that came to mind was those long, wiggly noodles. But that thought brought me disgust. And dry heaves. Niandi looked up and gave me a skeptical look. "What's wrong with you?" she asked in a tone that showed how repugnant she thought I was. I waved her off to show I couldn't answer. More dry heaves. She let go of the goat. "Jintong," she said, "what do you think you're going to be like when you grow up?"

I wasn't sure what she was getting at. "Why don't you try goat's milk?" she said. The sight of Shengli greedily feeding under her goat made an impression on me. "Are you determined to be the cause of Mother's death?" She shook me by the shoulders. "Do you know where milk comes from? That's Mother's blood you're drinking. So listen to me and start drinking goat's milk."

I nodded reluctantly.

So she reached out and grabbed the mute's black goat. "Come here," she said to me as she calmed the goat down by stroking its back. "I said, come here." Encouraged by the look of kindness, I took a tentative step toward her. Then another. "Lie down under its belly. See how she does it?"

I lay down on the grass and scooted along on my back. "Big Mute, back up a little," she said as she pushed the black goat backward. I looked up into the dazzling blue Northeast Gaomi sky. Golden birds were flying through the silvery air, soaring on the wind currents and trailing sweet-sounding cries. But my view was quickly blocked by the goat's udder, which hung over my face. Two large insectlike nipples quivered as they sought out my mouth. They rubbed up against my lips, and when they did, the quivering increased, as if they were trying to pry my lips open. They tickled my lips, like tiny charges of electricity, and I was immersed in a flood of what seemed like joy. I'd assumed that goats' teats were soft, not elastic at all, sort of cottony, and that they'd lose their shape as soon as they entered my mouth. Now I knew they were actually pliable and tough, quite springy, and in no way inferior to Mother's. As they rubbed my lips, I detected something hot and liquid. It had a muttony taste that quickly turned sweet, the flavor of buttery grass and daisies. My determination weakened, I unclenched my teeth, my lips parted, and the goat's teat rushed into my mouth, where it vibrated excitedly and released powerful spurts of liquid, some of it hitting the sides of my mouth, the remainder squirting straight down my throat. I nearly choked. I spit out the teat, but a second, more aggressive one quickly took its place.

With a flick of its tail, the goat walked away casually. Tears gushed from my eyes. My mouth was filled with a muttony taste, and I felt like throwing up. But my mouth was also filled with the taste of buttery grass and daisies, and so I stopped feeling like throwing up. Sixth Sister pulled me to my feet and ran in a circle with me in her arms. I saw freckles pop up all over her face; her eyes were like black stones dredged up from the bottom of a river, clean and bright. "My foolish little brother," she said excitedly, "this will be your salvation . . ."

"Mother," Sixth Sister shouted, "Mother, Jintong drank goat's milk! He drank goat's milk!"

The sound of clapping emerged from inside.

Mother tossed the blood-stained rolling pin down next to the wok, opened her mouth wide, and gasped for breath, her chest rising and falling violently. Shangguan Lü lay beside the haystack, a crack in her skull looking like a walnut. Eighth Sister, Yunü, was huddled near the stove, a piece of her ear missing, seemingly gnawed off by a rat, and still oozing blood. The blood stained her cheek and her neck. She was bawling loudly, a steady flow of tears emerging from her sightless eyes.

"Mother, you killed Grandma!" Sixth Sister shrieked in horror.

Mother reached out and touched Grandma's wound with her fingers, and then, as if given an electric shock, sat down hard on the ground.

2

As specially invited guests, we climbed the southeastern edge of the grassy slope on Reclining Ox Mountain to watch a demonstration by Commander Sima Ku and the young American Babbitt. A southeastern wind swept past under sunny skies as Laidi and I rode a single donkey up the mountain; Zhaodi and Sima Liang shared another one. I sat in front of Laidi, who held me from behind. Zhaodi sat in front of Sima Liang, who merely held on to her clothes, since he couldn't wrap his arms around her belly, in which the next generation of Simas was growing. Our contingent skirted the ox's tail and gradually climbed onto the ox's back, where needle-sharp grass dotted with yellow dandelions grew. Even with us on their backs, the donkeys climbed effortlessly.

Sima Ku and Babbitt rode past us on horseback, excitement showing on their faces. Sima Ku waved a fist at us as he passed. At the crest of the mountain, a group of yellow-skinned people shouted down the mountain. Sima Ku raised his riding crop and smacked the rump of his horse. The horse responded by climbing even faster, with Babbitt's horse following close behind. He rode horses the same way he rode camels, his upper body straight no matter how much he swayed from side to side. His legs were so long that his stirrups nearly touched the ground, and his horse was both to be pitied and laughed at; but it galloped along nonetheless.

"Let's speed up a bit," Second Sister said as she dug her heels into the donkey's midsection. She was the head of our delegation, the esteemed wife of the commander, and no one dared disobey her. Representatives of the masses and some local celebrities followed without a word of complaint, though they were out of breath from the climb. The donkey carrying Laidi and me was right on the tail of the one carrying Zhaodi and Sima Liang; Laidi's nipples rubbed against my back through the black cloth of her dress, which took me back to the episode in the feeding trough, and brought me great pleasure.

The wind on the mountaintop was stronger than lower down, so strong in fact that the windsock snapped loudly, its red and yellow silk ribbons dancing wildly, like a pheasant's tail feathers. A dozen or so soldiers were unloading things from the backs of camels, scowling beasts whose tails and rear leg joints were soiled by dried excrement. The rich pastureland of Northeast Gaomi had fattened up Commander Sima's horses and donkeys and the locals' cows and goats, but had had the opposite effect on the dozen or so pitiful camels, who were slow to acclimate to the place; their rumps seemed chiseled by awls, their legs were like kindling; their normally tall and angular humps looked like empty sacks hanging to one side, about to fall to the ground.

The soldiers unrolled an enormous carpet and laid it on the grass. "Lift the commander's wife down off her donkey!" Sima Ku ordered. Soldiers ran up and lifted the pregnant Zhaodi off her donkey, and then helped Sima Liang down. After that it was the commander's sister-in-law, Laidi, his brother-in-law, Jintong, and his younger sister-in-law, Yunü. As honored guests, we sat on the carpet. Everyone else stood behind us. The Bird Fairy tried to hide in the crowd, and when Second Sister signaled her to come over, she hid her face behind Sima Ting and stood behind us. Sima Ting, who was suffering from a toothache, stood there covering his swollen cheek with his hand.

The spot where we sat corresponded to the ox's head, the face directly in front of us. The ox made a point of sticking its mouth up against the chest. Its face was a hanging cliff well over a thousand feet above sea level. Winds swept over our heads on their way to the village, above which misty clouds floated like puffs of smoke. I tried to locate our house, but what I spotted was Sima Ku's neatly laid-out compound, with its seven entrances. The church bell tower and the wooden watchtower appeared small and fragile. The plain, the river, the lake, and the pastureland were ringed by a dozen or more ponds and populated by a herd of horses the size of goats and donkeys as small as dogs; they were the Sima Battalion mounts. There were six milk goats the size of rabbits, and those were our goats — the big white one was mine. Mother had requested it from Second Sister, who had requested it from her husband's aide-de-camp, who had sent someone to the Yi-Meng mountain district to buy it. A little girl stood next to my goat; her head looked like a little ball. But I knew it was a young woman, not a little girl, and that her head was actually a lot bigger than a little ball, because it was Sixth Sister, Niandi. She had taken the goats out to pasture, not for their benefit, but because she wanted to see the demonstration too.

Sima Ku and Babbitt had dismounted; their squat horses were roaming around the ox's head, searching for wild alfalfa, with its purple flowers. Babbitt walked up to the ledge and leaned over to look down, as if gauging its height. Then he looked up into the sky — nothing but blue as far as the eye could see, so no problem there. He squinted and raised a hand, apparently checking the force of the wind, even though the flag was snapping, our clothes billowed, and a hawk was being tossed around in the air like a dead leaf. Sima Ku was behind him, exaggeratedly repeating all his moves. He had the same serious look on his face, but I sensed it was all for show.

"Okay," Babbitt said stiffly, "we can begin."

"Okay," Sima Ku said in the same tone. "We can begin."

The soldiers brought up two bundles and opened one of them. Inside was a sheet of white silk that seemed bigger than the sky itself; attached to it were some white cords. Babbitt signaled the soldiers to tie the cords around Sima Ku's hips and chest. Once that was done, he tugged at them to make sure they were well fastened. He then shook out the white silk and had the soldiers stretch it out as far as it would go. As a gust of wind caught it, the soldiers let go, and it billowed out into a sweeping arc, pulling all the cords taut and dragging Sima Ku along the ground. He tried to stand, but couldn't, and began rolling along the ground like a newborn donkey. Babbitt ran up behind him and grabbed the cord around his back. "Grab it," he shouted stiffly, "grab the control cord." Sima Ku, apparently coming to his senses, cursed, "Babbitt, you fucking assassin —"

Second Sister jumped up from the carpet and ran after Sima Ku. But she hadn't gone more than a few steps before he was swept over the ledge, bringing an abrupt end to his curses. Babbitt roared, "Pull the cord on your left! Pull it, stupid!"

We ran over to the ledge, even Eighth Sister, who stumbled in the general direction until First Sister grabbed her. The sheet of silk by then had been transformed into a puffy white cloud, drifting along at an angle, with Sima Ku hanging beneath it, twisting and turning like a fish on a hook.

Babbitt roared, "Steady, stupid, steady! Get yourself ready to touch down!"

The cloud drifted along with the wind, descending slowly until it came to earth on a distant grassy spot, where it was transformed into a dazzling white cover over the green grass.

All that time, we stood on the edge holding our breath, mouths open, as we followed the white sheet with our eyes until it touched the ground; then we closed our mouths and recommenced breathing. But we quickly tensed up as we became aware that Second Sister was crying. It suddenly occurred to me that the commander had fallen to his death. Everyone's eyes were riveted on the patch of white, waiting for a miracle. Which is what we got: the sheet stirred and began to rise; a black object squirmed out from under it and stood up. He waved his arms; his excited shouts reached us on the mountaintop. A roar went up from the ledge.

Babbitt's face was bright red; the tip of his nose shone, as if smeared with oil. After tying his cords around him and strapping the bundle onto his back, he stood, limbered up his arms, and walked slowly backward. We couldn't take our eyes off him, but he was oblivious to his surroundings, eyes straight ahead. After he'd backed up a dozen yards or more, he stopped and closed his eyes; his lips were moving, as if he were uttering a charm. The charm completed, he opened his eyes and took off running. When he reached the spot where we were standing, he dove into the air, body straight, and began falling like a stone. For a moment, I was caught up in the illusion that he wasn't falling, but that the ledge was actually rising, along with the ground below. Then, all of a sudden, a pure white flower, the largest I'd ever seen, blossomed in the blue sky over the green grass. A roar greeted this big white flower as it drifted along, with Babbitt hanging steadily beneath it, like the weight on a scale. He hit the ground in a matter of seconds, right in the middle of our little herd of goats, which fled in all directions, like frightened rabbits. Suddenly, the big white flower collapsed in on itself, like a bubble, covering Babbitt and the shepherdess Niandi.

Sixth Sister shrieked in alarm as a layer of white closed in around her. When her goats fled in all directions, she gazed up into the pink face of Babbitt, as he hung beneath the white cloud. He was smiling. A god descending to the land of mortals! Or so she thought. As if in a trance, she watched him fall rapidly toward her, her heart filling with reverence and ardent love for him.

The rest of us stuck our heads out over the ledge to see what was going on down below. "This has sure been an eye-opener," said Huang Tianfu, who ran the coffin shop. "A god. I've lived seventy years, and I've finally seen a god descend to the land of mortals." Mr. Qin the Second, who taught at the local school, stroked his goatee and sighed. "There was something special about Commander Sima the day he was born. When he was my student, I knew he was headed for big things." Mr. Qin and Proprietor Huang were surrounded by township elders, all of whom were praising Sima Ku in similar language but different tones of voice and marveling over the eye-popping miracle that had just occurred. "You folks cannot imagine how many ways he differed from the others," Mr. Qin said loudly to drown out the discussion around him and make a show of his special relationship with Sima Ku, a man who could fly like a bird.

A shrill noise sliced through the air from somewhere beyond the crowd; it sounded a bit like a little whelp crying for the nipple, but even more like the cries of gulls circling boats on the river, which we'd heard many years earlier. Mr. Qin the Second's laughter stopped abruptly; the look of mirthful pride on his face vanished. We all turned to see where that strange noise had come from. It had, we discovered, come from Third Sister, Lingdi. But little of what made her "Third Sister" remained; when she uttered the strange, shrill noise that sent chills up our spines, she'd transformed almost completely into the Bird Fairy: her nose had hooked into a beak, her eyes had turned yellow, her neck had retreated into her torso, her hair had changed into feathers, and her arms were now wings, which she flapped up and down as she climbed the increasingly steep hillside, shrieking as if alone in the world and heading straight for the precipice. Sima Ting reached out to stop her, but failed, coming away with only a torn piece of cloth. By the time we snapped out of our bewilderment, she was already soaring through the air below the precipice — I prefer the word *soaring* to *plunging*. A thin green mist rose from the grass below.

Second Sister was the first to cry. The sound was disturbing. It was perfectly natural for the Bird Fairy to fly off a precipice, so what was she crying about? But then, First Sister, whom I'd always considered sneaky and cynical, began to cry. Inexplicably, even Eighth Sister, who couldn't see a thing, joined in. Her cries sounded a bit as if she were talking in her sleep and were filled with the passion of someone seeking permission to vent her emotions. One day, long after the event, Eighth Sister confided in me that the crunch of Third Sister hitting the ground sounded to her like the shattering of glass.

The excited crowd was stupefied, faces frosted, eyes glazed. Second Sister signaled a soldier to bring over a mule, which she mounted by grabbing the animal's short neck and swinging up onto its back. She dug her heels into the mule's belly, sending it into an uneasy trot. Sima Liang ran after the mule, but was stopped by a soldier before he'd taken more than a couple of steps. The soldier swept him up in his arms and sat him on the horse his father, Sima Ku, had just ridden up on.

Like a routed army, we headed down Reclining Ox Mountain. What were Babbitt and Niandi doing under the white cloud at that moment? As I rode my mule down the mountain path, I racked my brain trying to conjure up an image of Niandi and Babbitt inside the parachute. What I think I saw was: He was kneeling beside her, holding a stalk of bristlegrass in his hand and brushing the velvety tassel against her breasts, just as I had done not long before. She was lying on her back, her eyes closed, whimpering contentedly, like a dog when you rub its belly. See there, its legs rise into the air, its tail swishes back and forth on the ground. She's doing whatever it takes to please Babbitt! Not long before, she had nearly turned my backside raw because I'd tickled her with a stalk of grass. That thought angered me, and yet there was more to it than just anger. An erotic feeling was there as well, like flames licking at my heart. "Bitch!" I cursed, sticking my hands inside, as if to choke her. Laidi twisted around. "What's wrong with you?" she asked. "Babbitt," I muttered, "Babbitt, the American demon Babbitt has covered up Sixth Sister."

By the time we'd made our slow, winding way down the mountain, Sima Ku and Babbitt had freed themselves from their cords and were standing there, heads bowed, the ground in front of them covered by lush green grass; Third Sister lay heavily in the muddy ground, face-up. Splashes of mud and clods of uprooted grass dotted the area around her. The avian expression had left her face without a trace. Her eyes were open slightly; a sense of tranquillity had settled onto her still smiling face. Cold glints of light emerging from her eyes pierced my chest and went straight to my heart. Her face was ashen, her lips appeared covered with chalk. Threads of blood had seeped from her nostrils, her ears, and the corners of her eyes, and several alarmed red ants were darting across her face.

Second Sister limped over as fast as she could, fell to her knees beside Third Sister's body, and shrieked, "Third Sister, Third Sister, Third Sister . . ." She reached under her neck, as if to help her up. But the neck was as soft and pliable as a rubber band, and she merely stretched it out. The head lay in the crook of Second Sister's arm, like a dead goose. Second Sister quickly laid Third Sister's head back down on the ground and picked up her hand. It too was as soft and pliable as rubber. Second Sister cried and cried. "Third Sister, oh, Third Sister, why have you left us . . ."

First Sister neither cried nor shouted. She merely knelt beside Third Sister and looked up at the people standing around them. Her eyes were unfocused, her gaze narrow, shallow, diffuse. I heard her sigh and watched as she reached back and plucked a velvety pompon, a stately, gentle purple flower with which she wiped off the blood that had seeped out of Third Sister's nostrils, then her eyes, and finally her ears. Once she'd cleaned up the blood, she brought the purple flower up to her nose and sniffed it, every inch of it, and as she did so, I saw a strange smile spread across her face and a light in her eyes that belonged to a person in a certain realm of intoxication. I had the vague feeling that the Bird Fairy's transcendent, otherworldly spirit was being transferred to the body of Laidi by way of that purple velvety pompon of a flower.

Sixth Sister, who concerned me the most, elbowed her way through the crowd of onlookers and walked slowly up to Third Sister's body. She neither knelt nor cried. She just stood quietly, fidgeting with the tip of her braid, her head bowed, blushing one minute, ashen-faced the next, like a misbehaving little girl. But she already had the carriage and figure of a young woman; her hair was black and glossy, her buttocks rose up behind her, almost as if a bushy red tail were hidden there. She was wearing a white silk hand-me-down cheongsam from Second Sister, Zhaodi. With high slits on the sides, her long legs showed through. She was barefoot, and there were red scratches on her calves from the sharp-edged leaves of couch grass. The back of her cheongsam was soiled by crushed grass and wildflowers — spots of red here and there amid bright green stains . . . my thoughts leaped across and squirmed beneath the white cloud that had so gently covered her and Babbitt, bristlegrass . . . bushy tail . . . my eyes were like blood-sucking leeches, fastened to her chest. Niandi's high arching breasts, nipples like cherries, were magnified by the silk of her cheongsam. My mouth filled with sour saliva. From that moment on, whenever I saw a pair of beautiful breasts, my mouth would fill with saliva; I yearned to hold them, suck on them, I yearned to kneel before all the lovely breasts of the world, offer myself as their most faithful son . . . there where they jutted out, the white silk was marked by a stain, like dog slobber, and my heart ached, as if I'd been an eyewitness to the tableau of Babbitt biting my sixth sister's nipples. The blue-eyed whelp had gazed up at her chin, while she had stroked the golden hair of his head with the same hands that had so viciously attacked my backside, and all I'd done was gently tickle her, while he had actually bit her. This wicked pain deadened my reaction to Third Sister's death. But then, Second Sister's weeping unsettled me, while Eighth Sister's crying was the sound of nature, which called to mind the cherished memory of Third Sister's magnificence and her lofty actions that could make trees bend and leaves fall, that could cause the earth to tremble and the heavens to quake, and could incite ghosts to cry and demons to wail.

Babbitt took several steps forward, bringing into focus his reddened lips, so tender and soft, and his red face, which was overlain with white fuzz. He had white lashes, a big nose, and a long neck. Everything about him disgusted me. He spread out his arms. "What a shame," he remarked, "a terrible shame. Who could have imagined it . . ." All this he said in a peculiar foreign language that none of us understood, followed by some remarks in Chinese, which we did understand: "She was delusional, thinking she was a bird . . ."

The bystanders began talking among themselves, most likely about the relationship between the Bird Fairy and Birdman Han, possibly bringing Speechless Sun into the conversation, maybe even the two children. But I wasn't interested, and could not have heard what they were saying anyway, since there was a buzzing in my ear, coming from a hornets' nest on the cliff. Beneath the nest, a raccoon sat on its haunches in front of a marmot, a round, fleshy animal with tiny eyes set close together. Guo Fuzi, the village sorcerer, who was adept at planchette writing and catching ghosts, also had tiny, shifty eyes set close on either side of the bridge of his nose, and had earned the nickname "Marmot." He stepped out from the crowd and said, "Elder uncle, she's dead, and no amount of crying will bring her back to life. It's a hot day, so take her home, give her a funeral, and put her to rest in the ground." I didn't know what apron strings he relied upon to call Sima Ku "elder uncle," nor did I know who might be able to tell me. But Sima Ku nodded and wrung his hands. "Shit," he said, "what a terrible turn of events!"

Marmot stood behind my second sister, his tiny eyes shifting back and forth. "Elder aunt," he said, "she's dead, and it's the living who count. If you keep crying like that, now that you're with child, a real tragedy could result. Besides, was our aunty here a real person? When all is said and done, she wasn't, she was a fairy among birds that had been sent down to the land of mortals as punishment for pecking at the Western Mother's immortality peaches. Now that her allotted time is up, naturally she has returned to the fairyland where she belongs. You saw with your own eyes how she looked as she floated down from the precipice, as if drunk, as if falling asleep amid heaven and earth, floating so gently. If she were human, she could not have fallen with such ease and grace . . ." As Marmot spoke of heaven and earth, he tried to pull Second Sister to her feet. "Third Sister," she kept saying, "such a terrible death . . ."

"All right," Sima Ku said, with an impatient wave of his hand, "that's enough. Stop crying. For someone like her, life was a punishment. Death has brought her immortality."

"It's your fault," Second Sister complained. "You and your flyboy experiment!"

"I flew, didn't I?" Sima Ku said. "You women don't understand such momentous events. Staff Officer Ma, have some men carry her back home, then buy a coffin and take care of the funeral arrangements. Adjutant Liu, take the parachutes back up the mountain. Adviser Babbitt and I are going to fly again."

Marmot pulled Second Sister to her feet and said to the crowd, "Come, you people, lend a hand."

First Sister was still kneeling on the ground, sniffing her flower, the one stained with Third Sister's blood. Marmot said to her, "Elder aunt, there's no need to be so sad. She has returned to her fairyland, and that should make everyone happy . . ."

The words were barely out of his mouth when First Sister looked up, smiled mysteriously, and stared at Marmot. He muttered something, but did not have the nerve to say more. He hastily mixed with the crowd.

Laidi held up her purple floral pompon and got to her feet, a smile on her face. She stepped over the Bird Fairy's corpse, stared at Babbitt, and shifted her body under her loose black robe. Her movements were jumpy, like someone with a full bladder. She took a few mincing steps, threw away her floral pompon, and flung herself at Babbitt, wrapping her arms around his neck and flattening her body against his. "Lust," she muttered, as if feverish, "suffering . . ."

Babbitt had to struggle to break free of her grip. With sweat coating his face, he said, mixing foreign words with local, "Please, don't . . . it's not you I love . . ."

Like a red-eyed dog, First Sister spewed every vile comment she knew, then flung herself at Babbitt again. He awkwardly avoided the assault — once, twice, three times — eventually screening himself behind Sixth Sister. Unhappy at being his protection, she began spinning, like a dog trying to shake off a bell tied to its tail. First Sister spun right along with her, while Babbitt, bent at the waist, fought to keep Sixth Sister between him and the attacker. They spun so much it made me dizzy, and a kaleidoscope of images whirled in front of my eyes: arching hips, chests on the attack, the glossy backs of heads, sweaty faces, clumsy legs . . . My head swam, my heart was a tangle of emotions. First Sister's screams, Sixth Sister's shouts, Babbitt's heavy breathing, and the onlookers' ambiguous looks. Oily smiles decorated the soldiers' faces as their lips parted and their chins quivered. The goats, their full udders nearly touching the ground, headed home in a lazy column, my goat leading the way. The shiny coats of the horses and mules. Birds shrieked as they circled above, which must have meant that their eggs or hatchlings were hidden in the nearby grass. That poor, wretched grass. Flower stems broken by careless feet. A season of debauchery. Second Sister finally managed to grab a handful of First Sister's black robe. First Sister reached out to Babbitt with both hands. The filthy language pouring from her mouth made people blush. Her robe ripped at the seams, laying bare her shoulder and part of her back. Second Sister jumped up and slapped First Sister, who stopped struggling immediately; foamy drool had gathered at the corners of her mouth, her eyes were glazed. Second Sister slapped her over and over, harder and harder. Dark trickles of blood snaked out of her nostrils and her head slumped against her chest like a drooping sunflower, just before she fell headfirst to the ground.

Exhausted, Second Sister sat down in the grass, gasping for air. Her gasps soon turned to sobs. She pounded her own knees with her fists, as if setting up a rhythm for her sobs.

Sima Ku could not hide the look of excitement on his face. His eyes were fixed on First Sister's exposed back. Coarse, heavy breathing. He kept rubbing his trousers with his hands, as if they were stained by something that would never rub off.

3

The wedding banquet got underway in the newly whitewashed church at dusk. A dozen or more brilliant light bulbs hanging from the rafters turned the hall brighter than daytime. A machine in the tiny courtyard chugged noisily, sending mysterious currents of electricity through wires and into the bulbs, which emitted a strong light to drive out the darkness and attract moths, which were scalded to death the second they touched one of the bulbs and fell onto the heads of the Sima Battalion officers and gentry representatives from Dalan. Sima Ku was wearing his uniform; his face was radiant as he rose to his feet at the head table and cleared his throat. "For all you members of the militia and the local gentry," he said, "today's banquet is being held to celebrate the marriage of our esteemed friend Babbitt and my young sister-in-law Niandi. Such a joyous event deserves a heartfelt round of applause." Everyone clapped enthusiastically. Sitting in the seat next to Sima Ku, dressed in a white uniform, with a red flower stuck in his shirt pocket, was the beaming guest of honor himself, the young American. His blond hair, slicked down with peanut oil, was as glossy as if it had just been licked clean by dogs. Niandi, who sat in the chair beside him, was wearing a white gown, open at the neck to reveal the top half of her breasts. I nearly drooled. During the wedding ceremony earlier that day, Sima Liang and I had walked down the aisle behind her, carrying the long train of her gown, like the tail of a pheasant. She wore two heavy Chinese roses in her hair; a look of smug contentment showed on her heavily powdered face. Lucky Niandi, how shameless you were. The Bird Fairy's bones weren't even cold before you walked down the aisle with the American!

Sima Ku held out a glass that glowed red from the wine inside. "Mr. Babbitt came to us out of the sky; the heavens brought us our Babbitt. You all personally witnessed his flying demonstration, and he also rigged the electric lamps that shine above us." He stopped and pointed to the rafters. "That, folks, is electricity, stolen from the God of Thunder. From the moment Babbitt entered our midst, our guerrilla forces have enjoyed smooth sailing. Babbitt is our Good Fortune General, come to us with a bellyful of brilliant strategies. In a few moments, he'll reveal something truly eye-opening for us all." He turned and pointed to a white sheet covering the wall behind the podium from which Pastor Malory had once preached and which had later served Miss Tang of the demolition battalion when she spoke out for resistance against the Japanese. A veil of darkness shrouded my eyes — the electric lights were blinding me. "Now that the war has been won, Mr. Babbitt has said he wants to go home. To make sure that doesn't happen, we must do whatever it takes to keep him here, show him what is in our hearts. And that is why I've taken it upon myself to give him the hand of my young sister-in-law, more beautiful than the angels in Heaven, in marriage. Now a toast to the happiness of Mr. Babbitt and Miss Shangguan Niandi. Bottoms up!"

The guests got noisily to their feet, clinked glasses and — "Bottoms" — tipped back their heads — "Up!"

Niandi held out her glass, displaying the gold wedding ring on her finger, and clinked it against Babbitt's glass; then she clinked glasses with Sima Ku and Zhaodi. Unhealthy red spots showed on the pale cheeks of Zhaodi, who hadn't fully regained her strength following childbirth. "It's time for the bride and groom to drink up," Sima Ku said. "Link your arms, you two." Under his guidance, Babbitt and Niandi hooked arms and awkwardly drank the wine in their glasses, to the uproarious delight of the guests, who quickly toasted the newlyweds, before sitting down and entering the fray with their chopsticks; dozens of mouths chewing at the same time produced an irritating cacophony from greasy lips and sweaty cheeks.

Seated at our table, in addition to me, Sima Liang, Sha Zaohua, and Eighth Sister, were a bunch of little brats I didn't know. I watched them eat. Zaohua was the first to throw down her chopsticks and use her hands. With a drumstick in her left hand and a pig's foot in her right, she attacked them both, first one and then the other. In order to conserve energy, the children kept their eyes shut as they gnawed and chewed, taking a page out of Eighth Sister's book. Her cheeks looked to be on fire, her lips were like scarlet clouds; she was more beautiful than the bride. Once the children started grabbing food off the platters, their eyes snapped open; I was saddened by the sight of them tearing apart the corpses of dead animals.

Mother was opposed to Sixth Sister's marriage to Babbitt, but Sixth Sister said, "Mother, I've never told anyone that you killed Grandma." That silenced Mother, who looked like a withered autumn leaf, and she washed her hands of the wedding plans. The banquet proceeded along predictable lines: conversations between and among tables ended as drinking games got underway. The supply of liquor seemed unending, dishes streamed from the kitchen, with white-uniformed waiters trotting up to the tables, arms lined with platters of food. "Make room — here come braised meatballs — Make room — here come grilled capons — Make room — stewed chicken and mushrooms —"

The guests at our table were all "clean-plate generals." Make room — glazed pork loin — a glistening pork loin barely landed in the center of our table before several greasy hands reached out for it. Hot! They sucked in their breath like poisonous snakes. But that could not stay their hands, which reached back out and tore off chunks of meat; if the meat fell to the table, they picked it up and crammed it into their mouths. No stopping now. Stretching their necks, they swallowed — mouths open, frowning, teardrops squeezed out of the corners of their eyes. In no time, the platter was empty of skin and meat, nothing but silvery white bones. Then even they were snatched off the platter — time to gnaw at joints and tendons. Green lights emerged from the eyes of those who came away empty-handed and were forced to lick their fingers. Bellies swelled like little leather balls, skinny legs hung pitifully beneath the benches. Green bubbles rose from stomachs that made purring sounds. Make room — sweet-and-sour fish. A big-bellied, stumpy waiter with sagging jowls and flabby cheeks, dressed in white tails, came out carrying a large wooden tray with a white ceramic platter on which lay a huge, seared yellow fish. He was followed by a dozen other waiters, each taller than the one before and all dressed in white tails, carrying identical wooden trays with identical white ceramic platters on which lay similar huge, seared yellow fish. The last one out looked like a utility pole. He placed the tray in the center of our table and made a face at me. He looked familiar somehow. He had a crooked mouth, one of his eyes was closed, and his nose was creased with wrinkles. I'd seen that face somewhere, but where? Had it been at the wedding of Pandi and Lu Liren of the demolition battalion?

The side of the sweet-and-sour fish was scored with a knife from head to tail, the gaps filled with sour orange-colored syrup. One opaque eye was hidden beneath a bed of emerald green onions; its triangular tail hung miserably off the edge of the platter, as if still flapping slightly. Greasy little claws reached out in tentative probes, and since I did not have the heart to watch the fish disfigured, I looked away. Over at the head table, Babbitt and Niandi stood up, each holding a tall-stemmed glass of wine, their free arms linked. With a sort of feminine grace, they approached our table, where all eyes but mine were fixed on the disfigured corpse of the poor fish, the top half of which had been reduced to a bluish backbone. One little claw grabbed the backbone and gave it a shake, freeing the bottom half of its edible portions. Shapeless, steaming piles of fish lay on every other plate at the table. Like young wild beasts, the children dragged their kill to their dens to feast in leisure. Now only a bulging fish head, a handsome, slender tail, and the backbone that connected them remained. The white tablecloth was a mess, everywhere but in front of me, a spot of purity amid the litter, in the center of which stood a glass filled with red wine.

"Bottoms up, my dear little friends," Babbitt said genially, holding out his glass.

His wife also held out her glass; some of her fingers were bent, others were straight, like an orchid, a gold ring gleaming in the center. A cold white glare rose from the exposed upper half of her breasts. My heart was pounding.

My tablemates clambered to their feet, mouths crammed full of fish, their cheeks, the tips of their noses, even their foreheads, glistening with oil. Sima Liang, who was next to me, wolfed down his mouthful of fish and picked up a corner of the tablecloth to wipe his hands and mouth. I had smooth, fair hands, my outfit was spotless, and my hair had a glossy sheen. My digestive system had never been called on to process the corpse of a living animal, my teeth had never been told to chew the fibers of any vegetation. A line of oily claws held out their glasses harum-scarum and clinked them against those held by the newlyweds. I was the sole exception; I stood in a daze, staring at Niandi's breasts, gripping the edge of the table with both hands to keep from rushing over and suckling at the breast of my sixth sister.

A look of astonishment filled Babbitt's eyes. "Why aren't you eating or drinking?" he asked. "Haven't you eaten a thing? Not a bite?"

Niandi came briefly down off her cloud and regained some of what had made her my sixth sister. She rubbed the back of my neck with her free hand and said to her new husband, "My brother's the next thing to an immortal. He doesn't eat the food of common mortals."

The redolence emerging from her body threw my heart into a frenzy. In rebellion against my wishes, my hands reached out and grabbed her breasts. Her silk dress was slippery smooth. She yelped in alarm and flung her wine into my face. Her face was scarlet, and as she straightened the twisted bodice of her dress, she cursed: "Little bastard!"

The red wine slipped down my face, a nearly transparent red curtain lowering over my eyes. Niandi's breasts were like red balloons that crashed together noisily in my head.

Babbitt patted my head with one of his big hands. "Your mother's breasts belong to you, youngster," he said with a wink. "But your sister's breasts belong to me. I hope we become friends one day."

I drew back and glared hatefully at his comical, ugly face. The agony I felt at that moment was beyond words. Tonight, Sixth Sister's breasts, so glossy, so soft, so sleek, as if carved from jade, peerless treasures, would fall into the hands of that fair-skinned, down-covered American, to grab or stroke or knead at will. Sixth Sister's milky white breasts, filled with honey, a gastronomical treat unrivaled anywhere, land or sea, would be taken into the mouth of that ivory-toothed American, to bite or nibble or suck dry until only fair skin remained. But what incensed me was the fact that this is what Sixth Sister wanted. Niandi, you slapped me just for tickling you with a grassy tassel, and you flung wine in my face when I barely touched you. But you'll happily tolerate it when he strokes or bites you. It isn't fair. You bunch of sluts, why can't you understand the pain in my heart? No person on earth understands, loves, or knows how to protect breasts the way I do. And you all treat me like a jackass. I cried bitter tears.

Babbitt made a face and shrugged his shoulders. Then he took Niandi by the arm and headed over to toast the other tables. A waiter came up with a tureen of soup with egg drops and something that resembled dead man's hair floating on the top. My tablemates took their cue from the next table by scooping up the soup, the thicker the better, with white spoons, blowing on it to cool it a bit before sipping. At our table, the soup sprayed and splashed everywhere. Sima Liang poked me. "Try some, Little Uncle," he said. "It's good, at least as good as goat's milk." "No," I said. "None for me." "Then sit down. Everybody's looking at you." I looked around. No one was looking at me.

Steam rose from the center of every table, curling up near the electric lamps, where it turned to mist before dissipating. The tables were a jumble of plates and glasses, the guests' faces blurred, and the air inside the church stifling with the smell of alcohol. Babbitt and his wife were back at their own table. I watched as Niandi leaned over to Zhaodi and whispered something. What did she say? Was it about me? When Zhaodi nodded, Niandi leaned back, picked up a spoon and dipped it into the soup, then put it up to her mouth, wetted her lips, and drank it elegantly. Niandi had known Babbitt little more than a month, but she was already a different person. A month earlier, she'd been a common porridge-slurper. A month earlier, she'd been as noisy as anyone when she spat or blew her nose on the ground. I'd found her disgusting; but I'd admired her too. How could anyone change so quickly? Waiters came out carrying the main courses: there were boiled dumplings and some of those wormlike noodles that had ruined my appetite. There were also some colorful pastries. I can't bring myself to describe how the people looked when they ate. I was upset and I was hungry; Mother and my goat must have been waiting anxiously. So why didn't I get up and leave? Because after Sima Ku's proclamation, and after the meal, Babbitt was going to demonstrate once again the material and cultural superiority of the West. I knew he was going to show a moving picture, which, according to what I'd heard, was a series of live images projected on a screen by electricity.

Finally, the banquet ended, and the waiters came out with bushel baskets, spread out, and swept the tables clean of glasses and dishes, dumping it all noisily into the baskets. What went into the baskets was perfectly usable dinnerware; what they carried away were shards of glass and pieces of ceramic. A dozen or so crack troops ran in to lend a hand, each grabbing a tablecloth, folding it up, and running off with it. Then the waiters returned to spread out fresh tablecloths, on top of which they laid out grapes and cucumbers, watermelons and pears from Hebei; there was also something called Brazilian coffee, which was the color of sweet potatoes and gave off a strange odor — one pot after another, more than I could count. Then one cup after another, also more than I could count. The guests, still belching from all the food, came out to sit down again and take some tentative sips of the Brazilian coffee, as if it were some sort of Chinese medicine.

The soldiers carried in a rectangular table on which they placed a machine that was covered by a piece of red cloth.

Sima Ku clapped his hands and announced loudly, "The movie will begin in a few minutes. Let's welcome Mr. Babbitt, who will show us something special."

Babbitt stood up amid thunderous applause and bowed to the crowd. He then walked up to the table and removed the red cloth to reveal a mysterious, demonic machine. His fingers moved skillfully amid a bunch of wheels, big and small, until a rumbling noise emerged from the bowels of the machine. A beam of light knifed through the air and landed on the west wall of the church. It was met by a roar of approval, which was followed by the noise of stools being dragged across the floor. People turned to follow the light. At first it landed on the carved face of Jesus on the jujube cross that had recently been dug up and re-nailed to the wall. The features of the holy icon were unrecognizable. A yellow medicinal pore fungus called *lingzhi* now grew where the eyes had once been. As a devout Christian, Babbitt had insisted that the wedding take place in the church. During the day, the Lord had watched over the marriage rites for him and Niandi with pore-fungus eyes; now when night had fallen, he illuminated the Lord's eyes with an electric light, covering the pore fungus with a white mist. The beam of light began to descend, from Jesus' face to His chest, and from there to His abdomen, to His lower parts, which the Chinese woodcarver had covered with a lotus leaf, and down to the tips of His toes. Finally, the beam settled on a rectangular sheet of white cloth with wide black borders that hung on the gray wall. It was adjusted until it fit within the black borders, then shifted a bit more before holding steady. At that moment I heard the machine make a sound like rainwater cascading down from eaves.

"Turn off the lamps!" Babbitt shouted.

With a pop, the lamps hanging from the rafters went out, and we were thrown into darkness. But the beam of light from Babbitt's demonic machine intensified. Clusters of little white insects danced in the air and a white moth flitted erratically in the center of the beam, its shape suddenly magnified several times its original size against the white sheet. I heard cries of delight from the crowd; even I gasped. And there, in front of my eyes, were the electric images. Suddenly, a head appeared in the shaft of light. It belonged to Sima Ku. The light shone through his earlobes, in which the flow of blood was visible to us all. His head moved as he turned to face the spot where the light was coming from. His face flattened out and turned white as a sheet of paper, while blocking out a big section of the screen. Loud cries emerged from the darkness.

"Sit down!" Babbitt shouted irately, as a delicate white hand was thrust into the beam of light. Sima Ku's head sank beneath the light. The wall made a series of popping sounds, as dark specks flickered on the screen — the sight and sound of gunshots. Music then burst from a sound box hanging next to the screen. It sounded a little like a string instrument, the *huqin*, and a little like a wind instrument, the *suona*, but not exactly like either. It was thin and tinny, like mung bean noodles being squeezed through the holes of a sieve.

Some white, squiggly words appeared on the screen, several lines of them, some big and some small, rising from the bottom. More shouts from the crowd. Water, it's said, always flows downward, but these foreign words flowed in the opposite direction, disappearing into the blackness of the wall when they reached the top of the screen. A crazy thought popped into my head: Would they be found embedded in the church wall tomorrow morning? Water then appeared on the screen, flowing down a riverbed bordered by trees, noisy birds hopping around on the branches. Our mouths fell open in amazement; we forgot to shout. The next scene was of a man with a rifle slung over his back, his open-front shirt revealing a hairy chest. A cigarette dangled from his lips, smoke curling upward from the tip and streaming out from his nostrils. My god, what a sight! A black bear lumbered out from a stand of trees and went straight for the man. Shrieks from women and the sound of a pistol being cocked erupted in the church. The silhouette of a man burst into the beam of light. Sima Ku again. Revolver in hand. He had intended to shoot the bear, but its image on the screen behind him was shattered.

"Sit down, you damned fool!" Babbitt shouted. "Sit down! It's a movie!"

Sima Ku sat back down, but by then the bear already lay dead on the screen, a stream of green blood seeping from its chest. The hunter was sitting on the ground beside it, reloading.

"Son of a bitch!" Sima Ku shouted. "What a marksman!"

The man on the screen looked up, muttered something I couldn't understand, and then smiled contemptuously. Slinging his rifle over his back again, he stuck two fingers in his mouth and let out a shrill whistle, which echoed in the church. A horse-drawn wagon rumbled up along the riverbank. The horse had a proud, defiant look, but in a sort of stupid way. Its harness looked familiar, as if I'd seen it somewhere. A woman stood in the wagon behind the shaft, her long hair tossing in the wind; I couldn't tell what color it was. She had a big face, a jutting forehead, gorgeous eyes, and curled lashes as black and bristly as a cat's whiskers. Her mouth was enormous, her lips black and shiny. She looked immoral to me. Her breasts bounced and jiggled like crazy, like a pair of white rabbits caught by the tail. They were much bigger and fuller than any in the Shangguan family. She drove the wagon straight toward me at a gallop; my heart lurched, my lips tingled, my palms were sweaty. I jumped to my feet, but was pushed back down on the bench by a powerful hand on my head. I turned to look. The man's mouth was wide open; I didn't recognize him. The area behind him was packed with people, some even blocking the door. Others seemed to be hanging on the doorframe. Out in the street, people clamored to squeeze in.

The woman reined the horse in and jumped down off the wagon. She picked up the hem of her dress, exposing her milky white legs, and shouted, to the man, that I could tell. Then she took off running, still shouting. Sure enough, she was shouting at him. Ignoring the dead bear, he took his rifle off his back, threw it to the ground, and ran toward the woman. Her face, her eyes, her mouth, her white teeth, her heaving breasts. Then the face of the man, bushy eyebrows, eyes like a hawk, a glistening beard, and a shiny scar that separated his brow from his temple. Back to the woman's face. Then back to the man's. The woman's feet as she flicked off her shoes. The man's clumsy feet. The woman ran into the man's arms. Her breasts were flattened. She attacked the man's face with her large mouth. His mouth clamped over hers. Then, your mouth is outside, mine is inside. Two mouths coupling. Moans and chirps, all from the woman. Then their arms, draped around a neck or wrapped around a waist. The hands began to roam, over me, over you, until finally the two of them fell to the grassy carpet and began to writhe and tumble, the man on top one minute, the woman on top the next. They rolled around, over and over, for quite some distance, and then stopped. The man's hairy hand slipped under the woman's dress and grabbed one of her full breasts. My poor heart was being torn apart, and hot tears spilled out of my eyes.

The beam of light went out and the screen went dark. *Pop*, a lamp was lit next to the demonic machine. All around me people were gasping and panting. The hall was packed, including a bunch of bare-assed kids sitting on a table in front of me. From where he stood, alongside the machine, Babbitt looked like a celestial fairy in the light of the lamp. The spools of the machine kept turning, and turning. Finally, with a pop, they stopped.

Sima Ku jumped to his feet. "I'll be goddamned!" he said with a hearty laugh. "Don't stop now, play it again!"

4

On the fourth night, the movie-viewing was moved to the Sima compound's spacious threshing floor, where the Sima Battalion — officers and men — and the commanders' families sat in the seats of honor, village and township bigwigs sat in rows behind them, while ordinary citizens stood wherever they could find room. The large white sheet was hung in front of a lotus-covered pond, behind which the old, infirm, and crippled stood or sat, enjoying their view of the movie from the back, along with the sight of people watching it from the front.

That day was recorded in the annals of Northeast Gaomi Township, and as I think back now, I can see that nothing that day was normal. The weather was stiflingly hot at noon; the sun was black, sending fish belly-up in the river and birds falling out of the sky. A lively young soldier was felled by cholera while digging postholes and hanging the screen, and as he writhed on the ground in excruciating pain, a green liquid poured from his mouth; that was not normal. Dozens of purple snakes with yellow spots formed lines and wriggled their way down the street; that was not normal. White cranes from the marshes landed on soap-bean trees at the entrance to the village, flocks and flocks of them, their sheer weight snapping off branches, white feathers blanketing the trees. Flapping wings, necks like snakes, and stiff legs; that was not normal. Gutsy Zhang, who had gained his nickname owing to his status as the strongest man in the village, tossed a dozen stone rollers from the threshing floor into the pond; that was not normal. In midafternoon, a group of travel-weary strangers showed up. They sat on the bank of the Flood Dragon River to eat flatcakes as thin as paper and chew on radishes. When asked where they'd come from, they said Anyang, and when asked why they'd come, they said for the movies. When asked how they'd learned that movies were being shown here, they said that good news travels faster than the wind; this was not normal. Mother uncharacteristically told us a joke about a foolish son-in-law, and this too was not normal. At sunset, the sky turned radiant with burning colors that kept changing; this too was not normal. The waters of the Flood Dragon River ran blood red, and this too was not normal. As night began to fall, mosquitoes gathered in swarms that floated above the threshing floor like dark clouds, which was not normal. On the surface of the pond, late-blooming lotuses looked like celestial beings beneath the reddening sunset, and this was not normal. My goat's milk reeked of blood, and that truly was not normal.

Having taken my evening fill of milk, I ran like the wind over to the threshing floor with Sima Liang, drawn irresistibly to the movie, running head-on toward the sunset. We set our sights on the women carrying benches and dragging their children along and the oldsters with canes, since they were the ones we could easily overtake. Xu Xian'er, a blind man with a captivatingly hoarse voice, survived by singing for handouts. He was up ahead walking fast, making his way by tapping the ground in front of him. The proprietor of the cooking oil shop, an aged single-breasted woman known as Old Jin, asked him, "Where are you off to in such a hurry, blind man?" "I'm blind," he said. "Are you blind too?" An old man called White Face Du, a fisherman wearing his customary palm-bark cape, was carrying a stool made of woven cat-tail. "How do you expect to watch a movie, blind man?" he asked. "White Face," the blind man replied angrily, "to me you're a white asshole! How dare you say I'm blind! I close my eyes so I can see through worldly affairs." Swinging his pole over his head until it whistled in the wind, he came dangerously close to snapping one of White Face Du's egret-like legs. Du stepped up to the blind man and was about to hit him with his cattail stool, but was stopped just in time by Half Circle Fang, half of whose face had been licked away by a bear one day when he was up on Changbai Mountain gathering ginseng. "Old Du," he said, "what would people think if you started a fight

with a blind man? We all live in the same village. We win some argu-
ments and we lose others, but it's always a matter of someone's bowl
smashing into someone else's plate, and that's how it goes. Up there on
Changbai Mountain, it's no easy matter to run into a fellow villager, so
you feel as if you're with family!" All sorts of people crowded onto the
Sima threshing floor. Just listen, all those families at the dinner table
talking about Sima Ku's achievements, while gossipy women gossip
about the Shangguan girls. We felt light as a feather, our spirits soared,
and all we wanted was for movies to be shown forever.

Sima Liang and I had reserved seats right in front of Babbitt's machine. Shortly after we sat down and before the colors had finished
burning their way across the western sky, a rank, salty smell came to us
on the gloomy night winds. Directly in front of us was an empty circle
marked off by quicklime. Deaf Han Guo, a crooked-legged villager,
was kept busy driving township residents out of the circle with a
branch from a parasol tree. His breath reeked of alcohol and bits of
scallion clung to his teeth. Glaring with mantislike eyes, he swung his
parasol branch mercilessly and knocked a red silk flower right off the
head of the cross-eyed little sister of someone called Sleepyhead.
Little Cross-eyes had had relations with the quartermaster of every
military unit that had ever bivouacked in the village. At the time, she
was wearing a satin undershirt given to her by Wang Baihe, the Sima
Battalion quartermaster. Her smoky breath came from Quartermaster
Wang. With a curse, she bent down and picked up the flower, scooping
up a handful of dirt at the same time, which she flung into Deaf Han
Guo's mantislike eyes. The dirt blinded Han Guo, who threw down
his parasol branch and frantically spat out a mouthful of dirt as he
rubbed his eyes and cursed, "Fuck you, you cross-eyed little whore!
Fuck your mother's daughter!" Big-mouthed Zhao Six, a dealer in
steamed bums, said in a soft voice, "Deaf Han Guo, why keep running
around like that? Why not just come out and say fuck the cross-eyed
little bitch?" The words were barely out of his mouth when a little cypress stool slammed against his shoulder. Aiya! he yelped as he spun
around. The assailant was the cross-eyed girl's brother, Sleepyhead, a
skinny, haggard-looking man who parted his hair down the middle,
like a scar, leaving tufts hanging down both sides. Dressed in a dusty
gray silk shirt, he was quaking. His head was greasy, his eyes blinked
nonstop. Sima Liang told me on the sly that the cross-eyed girl and
her brother had a thing going. Where had he heard this juicy gossip?

"Little Uncle," he informed me, "my dad says they're going to shoot Quartermaster Wang tomorrow." "How about Sleepyhead, are they going to shoot him too?" I asked under my breath. Sleepyhead had called me a bastard once, so I had no use for him. "I'll go talk to my dad," Sima Liang said, "and have him shoot that little family rapist too." "Right," I agreed, venting my hatred. "Shoot that little family rapist!" Deaf Han Guo, tears streaming from his now nearly useless eyes, was flailing his arms in the air. Zhao Six grabbed the stool out of Sleepyhead's hands before he could be hit a second time and flung it in the air. "Fuck your sister!" he said bluntly. Sleepyhead, his fingers twisted into claws, grabbed Zhao Six by the throat; Zhao Six grabbed Sleepyhead by the hair, and the two of them grappled all the way over to the empty circle reserved for members of the Sima Battalion, each with a death grip on the other. The cross-eyed girl joined the fray to help her brother, but landed more punches on his back than anywhere. Finally seeing an opening, she slipped around behind Zhao Six, like a bat, reached up between his legs, and grabbed hold of his balls, a move that was met with a roar of approval from Comet Guan, a martial arts expert. "That's it, a perfect lower peach-pick!" With a scream of pain, Zhao Six let go of his opponent and bent over like a cooked shrimp. His body shrank; his face turned the color of gold in the darkening curtain of night. The cross-eyed girl squeezed with all her might. "Didn't I hear the word fuck?" she hissed. "Well, I'm waiting!" Zhao Six crumpled to the ground, where he lay, overcome by spasms. Meanwhile, Deaf Han Guo, his face awash in tears, picked up his parasol branch and, like the demon image at the head of a funeral procession, began flailing in all directions, not caring who he hit — wheat or chaff, royalty or commoner alike — wreaking havoc on anyone within striking distance. His branch whistled through the air, as women shrieked and children wailed. Those on the outer edges of the crowd pushed up closer to watch the fun, while those in danger of being hit ran for their lives, heading the other way. Shouts swept the area like a tidal wave, as clumps of people converged, trampling and shoving each other. I watched as the branch struck the cross-eyed girl squarely on her backside, sending her darting into the crowd, where the hands of avenging souls plus a few with no other purpose than to cop a feel found their mark and were met with howls of protest.

Pow! A gunshot. Sima Ku. A black cape thrown over his shoulders, and backed up by bodyguards, he strode angrily up to the crowd in the company of Babbitt, Zhaodi, and Niandi. "Stop that!" one of the soldiers shouted. "If you don't, there'll be no movie."

In fits and spurts the crowd quieted down. Sima Ku and his entourage took their seats. By then the sky had turned purple and total darkness was on its way. A thin crescent moon sent down enchanting light from the southwest corner of the sky: caught in its embrace, a single star twinkled brightly.

The horse company, the mule company, and the plainclothes soldiers had all shown up; formed into two columns, their weapons cradled in their arms or slung over their backs, they gazed at the array of women around them. A pack of lustful dogs streamed into the area. Clouds swallowed up the moon and darkness settled over the earth. Insects perched on trees set up a mournful din amid the noisy flow of the river.

"Turn on the generator!" Sima Ku ordered from where he sat off to my left. He lit a cigarette with his lighter and then extinguished the flame with a grand wave of his hand.

The generator had been set up in the ruins of the Muslim woman's home. Black images flickered and a flashlight sent out a beam of light. At last the machine came noisily to life, the pitch alternating between high and low sounds that quickly evened out. A lamp right behind our heads lit up. "Ao! Ao!" the crowd shouted excitedly. I watched as the people in front of me spun around to look at the lamp, which turned their eyes a sparkling green.

It was a repeat of the first night, with the light searching for the screen, illuminating the moths and grasshoppers caught in its beam and projecting their huge, darting bodies on the white cloth. Soldiers and civilians gasped in surprise. But there were many more differences from the first night: to begin with, Sima Ku didn't jump to his feet and let the beam of light shine through his ears. The darkness all around deepened, magnifying the intensity of the light. It was a humid night, with damp air from nearby fields sweeping over us. Wind whistled softly through the trees. The cries of birds gathered in the sky overhead. We could hear fish break the surface of the river, that and the snorts of mules tethered on the riverbank, animals that had transported the visitors from far away. Dog noises came from deep in the village. Green bolts of lightning flashed in the low curtain of sky off to the southwest, followed by rumbling thunder. A train loaded with artillery shells sped down the Jiaoji Line, the rhythmic clack of huge metal wheels on iron tracks wonderfully compatible with the flowing clicks of the projector. One distinct difference that night was my lack of interest in the movie playing on the screen. That afternoon, Sima Liang had said, "Little Uncle, my dad brought a new movie back from Qingdao with him, filled with images of women bathing naked." "You're lying," I said. "Honest. Little Du said the head of the plain-clothes soldiers went to get it on his motorcycle, and he'll be right back." But we wound up with the same old movie, and since Sima Liang lied to me, I pinched him on the leg. "I wasn't lying. Maybe they'll show this one first, and then show the new one. Let's wait." What happened after the bear was shot was old hat to me, and so was the scene where the hunter and the woman roll around on the ground. All I had to do was close my eyes to see every bit of it, which allowed me to turn my gaze to other people, sneaking looks here and there, and trying to see to what was going on around me.

Zhaodi, still weak from childbirth, was sitting in a red lacquered armchair specially brought out for her; a green wool overcoat was draped over her shoulders. On her left was Commander Sima, also in an arm-chair, his cape draped across the back of the chair. Niandi sat on his left, in a spindly rattan chair. She wore a white dress, not the one with the long train, but a tight-fitting one with a high collar. At first they all sat up straight, necks rigid, although from time to time Commander Sima's head tilted to the right so he could whisper something to Niandi. By the time the hunter was smoking his cigarette, Zhaodi's neck had begun to tire and a soreness had crept into her waist. She slipped down in her chair until her head rested on the back; I had only a vague glimpse of the glint from her hair ornaments and a faint whiff of camphor from her dress, but could easily hear the sound of her uneven breathing. When the big-breasted woman jumped down off the wagon and started running, Sima Ku shifted and Zhaodi was on the verge of falling asleep. Niandi, on the other hand, continued to sit up straight. Sima Ku's left arm started to move, very slowly, a fuzzy dark shape like the tail of a dog. His hand, I saw it, his hand came to rest on Niandi's leg. Her body stayed as it was, as if it weren't her leg being touched. The sight displeased me, not exactly angry and not exactly afraid. My throat was dry; and I felt a cough coming on. A bolt of green lightning, crooked as a gnarled branch, split a gray cloud that hung like worn-out cotton above the marsh. Sima Ku's hand darted in and back, lightning quick; he coughed like a little goat, and then shifted in his seat as he turned to look in the direction of the projector. I turned to do the same. Babbitt was staring idiotically at a small hole in the machine that was sending out the beam of light.

The man and woman on the screen were wrapped in each other's arms and kissing. Sima Ku's men were breathing heavily. Sima Ku jammed his hand roughly down between Niandi's legs. Slowly she raised her left hand, very slowly, until it was behind her head, as if she were touching up her hair. But she wasn't touching up her hair, she was removing a hairpin. Then the hand descended. She sat there as straight and proper as ever, seemingly absorbed in the movie. Sima Ku's shoulder twitched; he sucked in his breath — hot or cold, I couldn't tell. He slowly pulled his left hand back. Again he coughed like a little goat, an empty-sounding cough.

With a sigh, I turned back to the screen, but saw only fuzzy images. My palms were sweating, cold sweat. Should I let Mother in on the secret I'd discovered in the dark? No, I couldn't tell her. I hadn't revealed yesterday's secret, but she had guessed anyway.

The green bolts of lightning were like molten steel that lit up the sandy ridge occupied by Birdman Han's men, all its trees and all its huts and mud walls. They were like meandering liquid fingers that stroked the dark trees and the brown houses. Thunder grumbled like vibrating sheet metal covered with rust. The man and woman were rolling around on the grassy riverbank, and I was reminded of what I'd seen the night before.

The night before, Sima Ku had talked Mother and Second Sister into going to the church to watch the movie. During the scene where they were rolling around on the grassy ground, Sima Ku got up quietly and left. I followed him as he hugged the wall, looking more like a thief than a military commander; he must have been a thief at one time. He climbed the low southern wall into our yard, the very path my third brother-in-law, Speechless Sun, had taken; it was also a path the Bird Fairy knew well. I didn't have to climb the wall, since I knew another way in. Mother had locked the gate and hidden the key between two nearby bricks; I could find it with my eyes closed. But I didn't need that either, since there was a hole at the bottom of the gate that had been put there for dogs during Shangguan Lü's time. The dogs were gone; the hole remained. I was small enough to wriggle through, and so were Sima Liang and Sha Zaohua. So now I was inside the gate, in a small room that served as a passageway leading to the western part of the compound. Two steps and I was standing at the gate to the west wing. Everything was where it had always been: millstone, feeding trough for the mules, and Laidi's grass mat. It was there on that patch of grass that she'd lost her bearings and gone mad. In order to keep her from bursting in on Babbitt's wedding ceremony, Sima Ku had tied her by the wrist to the window frame and left her there for three days. I assumed that he wanted to liberate First Sister and help open her eyes. So what happened?

Sima Ku's frame seemed larger than ever in the hazy starlight. He didn't spot me as he groped his way in, since I was hiding in a corner. I heard a thump shortly after he entered the room — he'd bumped into a metal bucket that we'd put there as a chamber pot for Laidi. She giggled in the dark. A tiny flame lit the room up, and there was Laidi, lying on her straw mat, her hair spread out around her, teeth white as snow; her black robe couldn't cover her completely. Scary? She was nothing less than a demon. Sima Ku reached out and touched her face; that didn't frighten her. The cigarette lighter went out. Goats in the pen pawed the ground. Sima Ku's laughter. He said, "We're brother-in-law and sister-in-law, and there's nothing wrong with that, so why not give it a go? I thought you really wanted it. Well, here I am . . ." Laidi shrieked, a crazed sound that tore through the roof. "It's pretty much what you said that day — lust, suffering! You're a wave and I'm a boat. You're a drought, and I am rain. I'm your savior." The two of them gyrated together, as if submerged in water, as if clearing out a hollow filled with eels. Laidi's shrieks were more shrill than the Bird Fairy's ever were . . . Without a sound, I wriggled through the dog door and went back into the lane, cold sweat sticking to my body.

The movie was nearing its end when Sima Ku quietly reentered the church. Seeing that it was the commander, the people made room for him to return to his seat. As he walked by, he rubbed my head, and I detected the smell of Laidi's breasts on his hand. He whispered something to Second Sister once he was in his seat, and she appeared to laugh in response. The lights came on, bringing the viewers up short, as if for a moment they didn't know where they were. Sima Ku stood up and announced, "Tomorrow night the movie will be shown at the threshing floor. Your commander wants to bring benefits to this area through the introduction of Western culture." That brought the people back to reality, and the clamor that followed drowned out the sound of the projector. Later, after all the visitors had left, Sima Ku said to Mother, "Well, madam, what do you say? It was worth coming to see, wasn't it? The next thing I'm going to do is build a movie house for all of Northeast Gaomi. This Babbitt fellow can do just about anything, and you have me to thank for getting him as a son-in-law." "That's enough," Second Sister said. "Let's take Mother home." "You can stop wagging your tail," Mother said. "Nothing good comes of being proud, like dogs eating shit in a crowd."

Somehow or other, Mother found out what had happened that night with Laidi. The next morning Sima Ku and Second Sister came by with the grain ration, and as they were about to leave, Mother said, "I want to talk to my son-in-law about something." "Whatever it is," Second Sister said, "you can say it in front of me." "You go on," Mother insisted as she took Sima Ku into the next room. "What do you plan to do with her?" Mother asked him. "Do with who?" "Don't play dumb with me!" Mother said. "I'm not playing dumb," he said. "Choose the path you're going to take," Mother said. "What paths are you talking about?" Sima Ku asked. "I'll tell you," she said. "The first path is to marry her, either as first wife or as second wife or as one of two equal wives. You can work that out with my second daughter. The second is to kill her!" Sima Ku rubbed the sides of his trousers with both hands, although in a different frame of mind from the previous time he'd done the same thing. "I'll give you three days to make your choice. You can leave now."

Sixth Sister sat there without moving, as if nothing had happened. I heard Sima Ku cough, a sound that both thrilled and saddened me. On the screen, the man and woman were lying together under a tree, the woman's head resting on the man's chest. She was gazing up at the fruit on the tree, while the man was chewing on a blade of grass, lost in thought. The woman pushed herself up into a sitting position and turned to face him, the upper half of her bulbous breasts exposed above her dress. Her cleavage showed up purple, like an eel's hollow in the shallows of a river. This was the fourth time I'd seen that nest, and I yearned to wriggle into that hollow. But she moved slightly, and the hollow disappeared. She gave the man a shove and growled something at him. But he kept his eyes shut and continued chewing the blade of grass. Eventually, she slapped him and burst into tears. The sound of her crying wasn't much different than that of Chinese women. The man opened his eyes and spat the pulpy blade of grass into the woman's face. A strong gust of wind made the tree on the screen sway, sending pieces of fruit bumping against each other. The sound of rustling leaves drifted over from the riverbank, and I couldn't tell if the wind on the screen was rustling leaves on the river or wind from the river was rustling leaves on the screen. Another bolt of lightning sent a green light through the sky, followed by the rumble of thunder. The wind was picking up, and the viewers began to fidget. A swarm of sparkles flew through the beam of light. "It's raining," somebody shouted, just as the man was walking toward the wagon, the barefoot woman on his arm, her dress hanging crooked on her body. Sima Ku stood up abruptly. "Turn it off, that's it!" he said. "Water will ruin the projector!" He was blocking the light, bringing roars of disapproval from the crowd, so he sat back down. Sprays of water showed up on the screen. The man and woman jumped into the river. Another bolt of lightning snaked through the sky, its crackle hanging in the air for a long time and darkening the beam of light from the projector. A dozen or so black objects flew in, giving the impression that the lightning bolt had sent down a shower of turds. A violent explosion erupted from somewhere in the ranks of Sima Battalion soldiers. A thunderous blast, flashes of green and yellow light, accompanied by the pungent smell of gunpowder at about the same time. I wound up sitting on somebody's belly, and I felt something hot and wet on my head. I reached up and touched my face; it was sticky. The air was thick with the stench of blood. Screams and shouts erupted from panicky, blinded people. The beam of light shone on undulating backs, bloody heads, terrified faces. The man and woman frolicking in the American river had been blown to bits. Lightning. Thunder. Green blood. Pieces of flesh flying through the air. An American movie. A hand grenade. Golden flames snaking out of the barrel of a gun. Don't panic, brothers. Another series of explosions. Mother! Son! A living, severed arm. Intestines twisted around a leg. Raindrops bigger than silver coins. Eye-searing light. A night of mystery. "Get down on your stomachs, villagers, and don't move! Officers and men of the Sima Battalion, don't move! Lay down your weapons if you want to live! Lay them down or die!" The commands came from all directions, bearing down on us . . .

5

Before the concussion waves died out, seemingly countless burning torches bore down on us, as the soldiers of Lu Liren's independent

16th Regiment menacingly pushed their way toward us, black palm-bark capes draped over their shoulders, rifles with fixed bayonets at the ready, shouting in cadence. The torchbearers were civilians with white bandannas tied around their heads, mostly women with pageboy haircuts. Their blazing torches, made of old cotton wadding and rags soaked in kerosene, were held high to shine down on soldiers of the 16th Regiment. The crackle of gunfire emerged from the center of the Sima Battalion, sending a dozen or so 16th Regiment soldiers crumpling to the ground like kernels of grain. But soldiers behind them quickly took their places, and a dozen hand grenades flew through the air toward us, the explosions sounding like the sky had fallen and the earth split. "Give it up, men!" Sima Ku shouted. Weapons were thrown willy-nilly to the ground lit up by all those torches.

Sima Ku was holding Zhaodi in his bloody arms. "Zhaodi!" he screamed. "Zhaodi, my dear wife, wake up . . ."

A shaky hand grabbed my arm. I looked up and, in the light of the torches, saw Niandi's ashen face. She was also lying on the ground, pressed down by several broken bodies. "Jintong, Jintong . . ." She could barely get the words out. "Are you all right?" My nose ached and tears gushed from my eyes. "I'm okay, Sixth Sister," I sobbed. "How about you, are you okay?" She reached out with both hands. "Dear little brother," she pleaded, "help me. Take my hands." My hands were green and oily; so were hers. I grabbed hold of her hands, like catching live loaches, but they slipped out of my grip. By then, everyone else was lying on the ground; no one dared to stand up. The beam of light was still fixed on the white screen, where the clash between the American couple was reaching its climax. The woman was holding a knife above the snoring figure of the man. The young American, Babbitt, was shouting anxiously from alongside the projector, "Niandi, Niandi, where are you?" "Here I am, Babbitt, help me, Babbitt . . ." Sixth Sister reached a hand out to her Babbitt. She was wheezing, her face covered with tears and snot. Babbitt's tall, slender frame began to move as he struggled to reach Niandi. He was having trouble walking, like a horse stuck in the mud.

"Stand where you are!" someone bellowed as he fired into the air. "Don't move!"

Babbitt flattened himself out on the ground as if a sword had cut him down.

Sima Liang came crawling out of somewhere. A trickle of sticky blood was seeping out of his wounded ear onto his cheek and neck and into his hair. He lifted me up and felt me all over with his stiff fingers to see if I was all right. "You're fine, Little Uncle," he said. "Your arms and legs are still whole" Then he bent down and lifted the bodies off of Sixth Sister, then helped her to her feet. Her high-collared white dress was blood-spattered.

As the rain pelted down on us, we were herded into a mill house, the township's tallest building, which now served as a stockade. Thinking back now, I realize that we had plenty of opportunities to escape. The heavy rain put out the torches carried by 16th Regiment civilians, and the soldiers themselves stumbled along as they tried to protect themselves from icy raindrops that nearly blinded them. Two yellow flashlights up front were all that led the way. And yet, no one ran away. Prisoners and guards suffered equally. As we neared the dilapidated gate, the soldiers shoved us out of the way to get in.

The mill house shuddered in the deluge, and when lightning lit up the area, I saw water cascading in through the cracks in the sheet metal roof. A bright glistening cataract poured off the sheet metal eaves, sending a river of gray water down the ditch outside the gate into the street. Sixth Sister, Sima Liang, and I were separated as we slogged our way from the threshing floor to the mill house. Directly in front of me was a 16th Regiment soldier in a black palm-bark cape. His lips were too short to cover his yellow teeth and purple gums; his gray eyes were clouded. After a bolt of lightning had died out, he sneezed loudly in the dark, sending a strong whiff of cheap tobacco and radish right into my face, tickling my nose uncomfortably. Sneezes burst forth in the darkness all around me. I wanted to locate Sixth Sister and Sima Liang, but didn't dare call out to them, so I waited until the next brief flash of lightning to look for them amid the earthshaking peal of thunder that followed, filling the air with the smell of burning sulfur. I spotted Sleepyhead's gaunt, yellow face behind a little soldier. He looked like a graceful specter that had just climbed out of a grave. His face turned from yellow to purple, his hair looked like two pieces of felt, his silk jacket stuck to his body, his neck was stretched taut, his Adam's apple was as big as a hen's egg, and you could count his ribs. His eyes were graveyard will-o'-the-wisps.

Just before dawn the rain diminished and a gentler pitter-patter replaced the pounding on the sheet-metal roof. Lightning strikes had lessened a bit, and the frightful blues and greens had given way to softer yellows and whites. Thunder had moved off into the distance, while the winds blew in from the northeast, rattling the metal sheets on the roof and letting standing water pour in through the openings. As the bone-chilling wind turned our joints stiff, we all huddled together, friend and foe alike. Women and children were crying in the dark. I felt the eggs between my legs shrink, bringing stabbing pains to my intestines, and spreading to my stomach. My guts felt frozen, a mass of ice. If anyone had felt like leaving the mill house at that moment, no one would have stopped them. But none of us even tried.

A while later, some people showed up at the gate. By then I was numb, leaning against the back of someone, who was leaning against me. The splashing sounds of people wading through water came from beyond the gate, after which several swaying beams of light shone through the darkness. A bunch of men in raincoats, only their faces showing, stood in the gateway. "Men of the 16th Regiment," someone shouted, "fall in. You must return to headquarters." The shouts were hoarse, but I could tell that normal voice was loud and clear, capable of stirring people up. I knew who it was the second I laid eyes on him: the face above the raincoat and under the hat was that of the commander and political commissar of the demolition battalion, Lu Liren. Word of the elevation of his unit into an independent force had reached me that spring, and now here he was.

"Hurry it up," Lu Liren ordered. "All the other units have been given quarters, so it's time to head back, comrades, to soak your feet and drink some nice ginger tea."

The soldiers piled out of the mill house as fast as they could and lined up on the water-soaked street. Several men who looked like cadres raised hurricane lanterns and began shouting orders. "Company Three, follow me!" Company Seven, follow me!"

The soldiers marched off behind lanterns, and were replaced by soldiers in palm-bark capes who walked up cradling tommy guns. Their squad leader saluted. "Commander," he reported, "the security squad will stay behind to guard the prisoners." Lu Liren returned the salute. "Guard them well. Don't let any of them escape. I want a count first thing every morning. If I'm not mistaken," he said, turning to the mill house with a smile, "my old friend Sima Ku is in there."

"Fuck you and your ancestors!" Sima Ku cursed from behind a large millstone. "Jiang Liren, you despicable little runt, I'm right here!"

"I'll see you in the morning," Lu Liren said with a laugh before rushing off and leaving the leader of the security squad standing in the lamplight. "I know that some of you have weapons hidden on you," he said. "I'm in the light and you're in the dark, which makes me an easy target. But I strongly advise you to put such ideas out of your head, since I am the only one you'll hit. But" — here he made a sweeping motion with his hand at the dozen or so soldiers carrying tommy guns — "once those open fire, a lot more than one of you will fall. We treat our prisoners well. At daybreak tomorrow we'll sort you out. Those willing to join us will be welcomed with open arms. Those who aren't will be given money for the road and sent home."

The only sound in the mill house was the splash of water. The squad leader ordered his men to close the rotting gate. Light from his lantern streamed in through the holes and cracks and landed on several puffy faces.

Once the soldiers had departed, space opened up in the mill house, so I groped my way toward the spot where I'd heard Sima Ku just a moment before. I stumbled over hot, trembling legs and heard lots of cadenced, tuneful moans. The massive mill house was the creation of Sima Ku and his brother Sima Ting. After it was built, not a single bag of flour was ever milled there, because the blades of the windmill were blown away by violent winds the first night, leaving behind a few slivers of wood that rattled the year round. The building was big enough to accommodate a circus. An even dozen millstones the size of small hills stood obstinately on the brick floor.

Two days before, I'd come there with Sima Liang to look around, because he had suggested to his father that he convert the place into a movie theater. I shivered the minute I set foot in the mill house. A pack of ferocious rats rushed us, filling the immense building with their squeaks; they stopped just before they reached us. One big white rat with red eyes hunkered down at the head of the pack, raised its front claws, so fine they seemed carved from jade, and stroked its snowy white whiskers. Its beady eyes flashed as dozens of black rats formed a semicircle behind it, eyeing us gleefully, ready to charge. Fearfully, I backed up, my scalp tightening, cold chills running up and down my spine. Sima Liang shielded me with his body, even though he only came up to my chin. First he bent over, then he got down on his haunches and glared at the white rat. Not backing down a bit, the rat stopped stroking its whiskers and sat like a dog, mouth and whiskers twitching. Neither Sima Liang nor the rat was going to budge. What were those rats, especially the white one, thinking? And what was running through the mind of Sima Liang, a boy given to making me unhappy, but someone I was growing ever closer to? Was this a staring contest? A battle of wills, like a needle and wheat spike trying to see which was sharper? If so, who was the needle and who was the wheat spike? I actually thought I heard the rat say, This is our turf, and you're not welcome here. Then I heard Sima Liang say, This mill house belongs to the Sima family. My uncle and my father built it, so for me it's like going home. This is my place. The white rat said, The strong man is king, the weak man a thief. Sima Liang countered with, A thousand pounds of rat is no match for eight pounds of tomcat. To which the white rat replied, You're a boy, not a cat. I was in my last life, Sima Liang said, an eight-pound cat. How do you expect me to believe that? the white rat said. Sima Liang put both hands on the floor as his eyes slanted and a snarl split his mouth. Meow — meow — the shrill cry of a tomcat bounced off the mill house walls. Meow — meow — meeeow — the white rat, thrown into panicky confusion, fell back on all fours and was about to beat a hasty retreat when Sima Liang pounced and caught it in his hands. He squashed it before it had a chance to bite. The others fled in all directions. Me? Following Sima Liang's lead, I took out after them, screeching like a cat. But they were gone before I knew it. Sima Liang laughed and turned back to look at me. My god! They really were cat's eyes, giving off those devilish green lights. He tossed the dead white rat into the hole in the center of one of the millstones. We each grabbed one of the wooden handles and pushed with all our might; the thing refused to budge, so we gave up, and started prowling the mill house, moving from one millstone to the next, finding each of the others quite easy to turn.

"Little Uncle," Sima Liang said, "let's open our own mill." I didn't know what to say to that, since the only worthwhile things in my life were breasts and the milk they held. It was a glorious afternoon, with bright sunlight streaming in through the gaps in the sheet-metal roof and the lattice in the window and falling on the brick floor, which was a repository for rat and bat droppings; we spotted red-winged little bats hanging from the rafters, and another the size of a conical rain hat slipping through the air above them. Its squeaks sounded just right for its body, shrill and tapered, and made me shudder. Holes had been drilled in the centers of all the millstones, with China fir poles sticking up through the sheet-metal roof; the tips of the poles were the wheels on which the blades had once, and briefly, spun. Sima Ku and Sima Ting's assumption was: so long as there's wind, the blades will turn and the wheels will rotate, turning the China fir poles and the millstones below. But the Sima brothers' ingenious concept had been foiled by reality.

As I moved among the millstones looking for Sima Liang, I spotted several rats scurrying up and down the poles. Someone was on top of one of the millstones, eyes blazing. I knew it was Sima Liang. He reached down and grabbed my hand with his icy claw. With his help, I stepped on the wooden handle and climbed up. It was wet, with gray water emerging from the hole.

"Remember that white rat, Little Uncle?" he asked with an air of mystery. I nodded in the darkness. "It's right here," he said softly. "I'm going to skin it and make earmuffs for Granny." An anemic bolt of lightning knifed through the distant southern sky and threw some thin light into the mill house. I saw the dead rat in his hand. Its body was wet, its disgusting, skinny tail hung limp. "Throw it away," I said. "Why should I?" he asked unhappily. "It's disgusting. Don't tell me it doesn't disgust you." In the silence that followed, I heard the dead rat drop back into the millstone hole. "What do you think, Little Uncle, what are they going to do to us?" he asked dejectedly. Yes, what *were* they going to do to us? The splash of water beyond the gate signaled a change of the guard. The new guards were snorting like horses. "It's cold," one of them complained. "It doesn't feel like August here. Do you think the water's going to freeze?" "Don't be silly," another replied.

"Do you wish you were home, Little Uncle?" Sima Liang asked. The toasty brick bed, Mother's warm embrace, the nighttime wanderings of Big Mute and Little Mute, crickets in the oven platform, sweet goat's milk, the creaking of Mother's joints and her deep coughs, the silly laughter of First Sister out in the yard, the soft feathers of night owls, the sound of snakes catching mice behind the storeroom . . . how could I not with that? I sniffled. "Let's run away, Little Uncle," he said. "How can we, with guards at the door?" I said softly. He grabbed my arm. "See this fir pole?" he said as he laid my hand on the pole that went all the way up to the roof. It was wet. "We can shinny up, make a hole in the sheet-metal roof, and wriggle out." "What then?" I asked, unconvinced. "We jump to the ground," he said. "After that, we go home." I tried to picture us standing on the rusty, clattery sheet-metal roof, and felt my knees begin to knock. "It's too high," I muttered. "We'd break a leg jumping down from there." "Don't worry about it, Little Uncle, leave everything to me. I jumped down off this roof once this spring. There's a bunch of lilac bushes under the eaves. Their springy branches will break our fall." I looked up at the spot where the pole met the sheet metal; rays of gray light shone through; bright water slithered down the pole. "It'll be light soon, Little Uncle. Let's go," he urged anxiously. What could I do? I nodded.

"I'll go first and move the sheet metal out of the way," he said as he patted me on the shoulder to show he had everything under control. "Give me a boost." He wrapped his arms around the slippery pole, jumped up, and rested his feet on my shoulders. "Stand up," he urged, "stand up!" With my arms around the pole, I stood up, my legs shaking. Rats clinging to the pole squeaked as they jumped to the floor. I felt him press down with his feet as he plastered himself up against the pole like a gecko. In the muted light seeping in, I watched him shinny up the pole, slipping back every once in a while, until he finally made it to the top.

There he hit the sheet metal with his fist, making loud clangs and letting more rainwater in. It landed on my face, some of it entering my mouth and leaving the bitter taste of rust, not to mention tiny metal filings. He was breathing hard in the dark and grunting from exertion. I heard the sheet metal shift as a cascade of water hit me, and I held tightly to the pole to keep from being swept off the millstone. Sima Liang pushed with his head to make the hole bigger. It strained for a moment before giving way, and a raggedy triangle opened up in the roof, through which beams of gray starlight streamed. Amid the stars in the sky, I spotted several that hardly shone at all. "Little Uncle," he said from beyond the rafters, "wait there while I take a look around. Then I'll come down and help you up." With an upward surge, he stuck his head up through the new skylight to look around.

"Somebody's on the roof!" a soldier at the gate shouted. Bright tongues of light split the darkness as bullets ricocheted off the sheet metal with loud pings. Sima Liang slid down the pole so fast he nearly flattened me. He wiped the water from his face and spat out a mouthful of metal filings. His teeth were chattering. "It's freezing up there!"

The deep darkness just before dawn had passed, and the inside of the mill house began to turn light. Sima Liang and I were huddled

together; I could feel his heart beating fast against my ribs, like a feverish sparrow. I was weeping out of despair. Brushing my chin with the
top of his nice, round head, he said, "Don't cry, Little Uncle, they won't
dare hurt you. Your fifth brother-in-law is their superior officer."

There was now enough light to get a good look at our surroundings. The twelve enormous millstones, one of which Sima Liang and I
occupied, shimmered majestically. His uncle, Sima Ting, occupied another. Water dripped from the tip of his nose as he winked at us. Wet
rats covered the tops of the other millstones, huddled together, their
beady little eyes a glossy black, their tails like worms. They looked
pitiful and loathsome at the same time. Water puddled on the floor and
dripped in through the roof. The soldiers of the Sima Battalion stood
in tight little groups, their green uniforms, now black, sticking to their
bodies. The looks in their eyes and the expressions on their faces were
terrifyingly similar to those on the rats. For the most part, the civilian
prisoners were off by themselves, only a few choosing to mix with the
soldiers, like the occasional stalk of wheat in a cornfield. There were
more men than women, some of whom held whimpering children in
their arms. The women sat on the floor; most of the men were on their
haunches, except for a few who leaned against the walls. Those walls
had been whitewashed at one time, but now that they were wet, the
plaster rubbed off on the men's backs, changing their color. I spotted
the cross-eyed girl in the crowd. She was sitting in the mud with her
legs out in front, leaning against another woman. Her head was lolling
against her shoulder, as if her neck were broken. Old Jin, the woman
with one breast, was sitting on the buttocks of a man. Who was he? He
was sprawled in the water, facedown, white whiskers floating on the
surface, clots of black blood shifting in the water around them like
little tadpoles. Only Old Jin's right breast ever developed; the left side
of her chest was flat as a whetstone, which made the one breast seem
to stick up higher than normal, like a lonely hill on the plains. The
nipple was big and hard, nearly bursting through her thin blouse.
People called her "Oilcan," since they said that whenever her nipple
was aroused, you could hang an oilcan from it. Decades later, when I
finally had the chance to lie atop her naked body, I noticed that the
only sign of a breast on her left side was a little nipple the size of a bean,
like a mole announcing its existence. She was sitting on the dead man's
buttocks, rubbing her face, as if deranged; she'd rub her face, and then
rub her hands on her knees, as if she had just crawled out of a spider

hole and was tearing translucent cobwebs off her face. The other people were in a variety of postures and attitudes. Some were crying, others were laughing, while still others were mumbling with their eyes shut. One woman was rocking her head back and forth, like a water snake or a crane at water's edge. Married to Geng Da'le, the shrimp paste seller, she had a long neck and a small head, much too small for her body. People said she was a transformed snake, and her head sure looked like it. It stuck up out of a group of women whose heads all hung forward, and in the dank coldness of the mill house, with its muted light, the way her head swayed back and forth was all the proof I needed that she'd once been a snake and was now turning back into one. I didn't have the nerve to go take a look at her body, but even when I forced myself to look away, her image stayed with me.

A lemon-colored snake slithered down one of the China fir poles. It had a flat head like a spatula and a purple tongue that kept darting in and out of its mouth. Each time its head touched the top of the millstone, it went limp, turned a right angle, and slithered off in a new direction, heading straight for rats in the center of the millstone. The rats raised their claws amid a frenzy of squeaks. As the snake's head moved in a straight line, its thick body slithered smoothly down the pole, uncoiling as it went, as if the pole and not the snake were turning. When it reached the center of the millstone, the head abruptly rose at least a foot into the air and leaned backward, like a hand. The spot behind its head contorted, flattened out and widened, displaying a latticework pattern. The movement of the purple tongue quickened, a horrifying sight accompanied by a bone-chilling hiss. The rats made themselves as small as possible, squeaking all the while. One large rat stood up on its hind legs and bared its claws, like holding a book, then shifted its rear legs before leaping into the air, straight into the triangular opening of the snake's mouth. The snake closed its mouth, leaving the back half of the rat sticking out straight, its rigid tail still waving comically.

Sima Ku was sitting on an abandoned China fir pole, his head sagging onto his chest, his hair in total disarray. Second Sister lay across his knees, her head cradled in the crook of his arm, face-up, the skin of her neck pulled taut. Her mouth hung slack, a black hole in her ghostly white face. Second Sister was dead. Babbitt was sitting close to Sima Ku; his young face had the look of an old man. The upper half of Sixth Sister's body lay across Babbitt's knees, and it never stopped twitching. Babbitt stroked her shoulders with a hand made puffy by all the rain. Behind the decrepit gate, a skinny man was preparing to kill himself. His trousers had fallen down to his thighs, revealing underpants that were soiled by mud. He wanted to tie his cotton belt to the top of the doorframe, but couldn't reach that high, even when he jumped; he was so weak he barely left the ground. I saw by the way the back of his head protruded that it was Sima Liang's uncle, Sima Ting. Finally, too exhausted to try any longer, he reached down, pulled up his trousers, and retied his belt around his waist. He turned and gave the crowd of onlookers an embarrassed smile before plopping down in the mud and beginning to sob.

The morning winds blew in from the fields, like a wet cat with a glistening carp in its mouth, prowling arrogantly on the sheet-metal roof. The red morning sun climbed out of the hollows, filled with rainwater, dripping wet and exhausted. The Flood Dragon River was at flood stage, the crashing of its waves louder than ever in the morning quiet. We were sitting on the millstone, where our gaze was met by misty red sunbeams. The glass in the windows was spotless after a night of unremitting rain; August fields, obstructed by neither the building's roof nor trees, were right there in front of our eyes. Outside, the flow of rainwater had washed the street clean of dust and exposed the hard chestnut-colored ground below. The surface of the street shimmered as if varnished; a pair of not quite dead striped carp lay in the street, tails still flapping weakly. A couple of men in gray uniforms — one tall, the other short; the tall one skinny, the short one fat — were staggering down the street carrying a big bamboo basket filled with a dozen or more big fish, including striped carp, grass carp, even a silvery eel. Excited by the sight of the two fish on the street, they ran over — stumbled, actually, like a crane and a duck tied together. "Big carp!" the short, fat one said. "Two of them!" the tall, skinny one said. I could nearly make out their faces as they bent down to scoop up the fish, and I was pretty sure they were two waiters from the banquet after Sixth Sister and Babbitt's wedding, a couple of planted agents from the 16th Battalion. The men standing guard at the mill house watched them scoop up the fish. The platoon leader yawned as he walked up to the men. "Fat Liu and Skinny Hou, this is what's called finding balls in your pants and landing fish on dry ground." "Platoon Leader Ma," Skinny Hou said, "it's a tough assignment." "Not really, but I am hungry," Platoon Leader Ma replied. Fat Liu said, "Come over for some fish soup. A victory like ours deserves a reward of good food and drink for the soldiers." Platoon Leader Ma said, "You'll be lucky if those few fish are enough for you cooks, let alone the soldiers." "You're an officer, whatever your rank," Skinny Hou said. "And officers need to back up what they say with proof, they must temper their criticisms with political necessities. There is no room for irresponsible talk." "I was just joking. Don't take everything so serious!" "Skinny Hou," Platoon Leader Ma said, "in the few months since I last saw you, you've picked up the gift of gab!"

While they were squabbling, Mother walked slowly and heavily, but with determination, toward us, a red sunset at her back. "Mother —" I sobbed as I jumped down off the millstone. I wished I could have flown into her arms, but I slipped and fell in the mud at the foot of the millstone.

When I came to my senses again, the first thing I saw was Sixth Sister's agitated face. Sima Ku, Sima Ting, Babbitt, and Sima Liang were all standing beside me. "Mother's here," I said to Sixth Sister. "I saw her with my own eyes." I struggled out of Sixth Sister's grasp and ran toward the door, where I bumped into someone's shoulder. That rocked me for a moment, but then I took off again, cutting through the crowds of people. The gate stopped me. Pounding it with my fists, I cried out, "Mother — Mother —!"

A soldier stuck the black muzzle of his tommy gun in through a hole in the gate. "Pipe down! We'll let you out after breakfast."

Mother heard my shouts and began walking faster. She waded across the ditch at the side of the road and headed straight for the mill house. Platoon Leader Ma stopped her. "That's far enough, elder sister!"

But Mother reached up, pushed him out of the way, and kept walking without a word. Her face was encased in the red light, as if smeared with blood; her mouth was twisted in anger.

The guards quickly closed ranks, forming a line like a black wall.

"Stop right there, old lady!" Platoon Leader Ma ordered as he grabbed Mother's arm and would not let her proceed any farther. Mother strained to break his grip. "Who are you, and what do you think you're doing?" Platoon Leader Ma asked angrily. He jerked her backward, nearly causing her to fall.

"Mother!" I cried through the door.

Mother's eyes turned blue and her twisted mouth flew open, releasing a series of grunts. She broke for the door with no thought for anything else. But Platoon Leader Ma shoved her from behind, knocking her into the roadside ditch. Water splashed in all directions. Mother rolled once in the water and clambered to her knees. The water reached her navel. She crawled out of the ditch, drenched, muddy bubbles clinging to her hair. She'd lost one of her shoes, but hobbled forward on crippled bound feet.

"I said stop right there!" Platoon Leader Ma cocked his tommy gun and aimed it at her chest. "Are you trying to incite a jailbreak?" he fumed.

"Get out of my way!"

"What do you think you're doing?"

"I want to find my son!"

My crying got louder. Sima Liang, who was standing next to me, shouted, "Granny!"

Sixth Sister yelled, "Mother —"

Moved by our weeping, the women in the mill house began to sob. Their sobbing mixed with the sounds of men blowing their noses and the guards' grumblings.

Nervously, the guards made an about-face and pointed their weapons at the rotting gate.

"Stop that racket!" Platoon Leader Ma shouted. "You'll be out of here soon." Then he turned to Mother. "Go on home, elder sister," he said comfortingly. "As long as your son hasn't done anything wrong, you have my word we'll let him go."

"My child," she moaned as she ran around Platoon Leader Ma and headed for the gate.

Platoon Leader Ma jumped in front of her. "Elder sister," he said, "I'm warning you. One more step and I'll have no choice but to take action."

"Do you have a mother? Are you human?" She reached up and slapped him, and then set out again, rocking back and forth. The guards at the gate parted to make way for her.

Platoon Leader Ma, holding his cheek, shouted, "Stop her!"

The guards just stood there, as if they hadn't heard him.

Mother was at the doorway. I reached out through a hole in the door, waved, and shouted.

Mother pulled on the rusty lock, and I could hear her labored breathing.

The lock clanged loudly and a round of gunfire tore crisply through the door, sending chips of rotting wood raining down on me.

"Don't move, old lady!" Platoon Leader Ma screeched. "I won't miss the next time!" He fired another shot into the air.

Mother jerked the lock free and pushed the door open. I rushed up and buried my head in her bosom. Sima Liang and Sixth Sister were right behind me.

From behind us, someone shouted, "Make a break for it, men. It's our only chance!"

The men of the Sima Battalion rushed the door like a tidal wave, their hard bodies knocking us out of the way. I fell, and Mother fell on top of me.

Chaos reigned in the mill house — wails, shouts, and screams all merged together. As men of the 16th Regiment were sent tumbling, Sima Battalion soldiers grabbed their weapons and bullets began to fly, shattering glass. Platoon Leader Ma was knocked into the ditch, where he cut loose with his tommy gun, sending ten or more Sima Battalion troops crumpling to the ground like toy soldiers. Their comrades rushed him, pushed him down into the water, where they punched and kicked him ferociously, sending sprays of water everywhere.

Units of the 16th Regiment came running down the street, shouting and firing their weapons. Sima Battalion soldiers scattered, but were cut down by a merciless fusillade.

In the midst of all this activity, we flattened our backs against the mill house wall and pushed away everyone who came close to us.

An old 16th Regiment soldier fell to one knee beneath a poplar tree, held his rifle in both hands, closed one eye, and took aim. The rifle jerked upward, and a Sima Battalion soldier fell. More shots were fired, the spent cartridges falling into the water, where they sizzled and created steamy bubbles. The old soldier aimed again, this time at a big, swarthy soldier who had already run several hundred yards to the south. He was hopping through a bean field like a kangaroo, heading toward the bordering sorghum field. The old soldier unhurriedly pulled off another round, the crack hanging in the air when the runner fell head over heels in the field. The old soldier pulled back the bolt of his rifle, ejecting a shiny cartridge that arched end over end in the air.

Amid all that was going on, Babbitt caught my eye. He was like a brainless mule in a herd of sheep. With animals baa-ing all around him, he pushed and shoved, eyes big as saucers, clomped through the mud with heavy hooves, kicking the sheep out of his way as he went. Speechless Sun was like an ebony tiger, swishing his sword over his head as he led a dozen fearless swordsmen to block the sheep's way. Heads rolled, bloodcurdling screams blanketed the wilderness. Surviving sheep turned to run, seemingly lost, trying to escape any way they could. Babbitt froze and cast blank looks all around. He came to his senses as the mute charged him, and he bolted toward us as fast as he could run, gasping for breath, white foam filling the corners of his mouth. The old soldier took aim at him.

"Old Cao, hold your fire!" Lu Liren shouted as he bounded out of the crowd. "Comrades, don't shoot that American!"

The men of the 16th Regiment formed a human net, closing ranks as they drew nearer. The prisoners were still trying to get away, but they were like fish caught in the net, and before long they had all been herded onto the street in front of the mill house.

The mute charged into the gang of prisoners and drove his fist into Babbitt's shoulder, the force of the blow spinning him in a complete circle. Face-to-face with the mute again, he babbled something in his own language, which could have been loud curses and could have been a highly vocal protest. The mute raised his sword, which glinted in the sunlight. Babbitt raised his arms, as if to ward off the cold shards of light.

"Babbitt —" Sixth Sister jumped up from beside Mother and stumbled forward. But she fell before she'd taken more than a few steps, her left foot sticking out from under her right leg as she lay in the putrid mud.

"Somebody grab Speechless Sun!" Lu Liren commanded. Members of the mute's fearless squad grabbed his arm. Savage grunts tore from his throat as he lifted the soldiers holding him into the air like rag dolls. Jumping across the ditch, Lu Liren raised his arm. "Speechless Sun," he called out, "remember the policy on prisoners!" Speechless Sun stopped struggling when he saw Lu Liren, and his comrades let go. He stuck his sword in his belt, reached out and grabbed Babbitt's clothes with fingers like steel pincers, and dragged him away from the other prisoners, all the way up to where Lu Liren was standing. Babbitt said something to Lu Liren in his foreign tongue. Lu Liren responded briefly in the same language, punctuated by slashing gestures. Babbitt quieted down. Sixth Sister reached out to him and moaned, "Babbitt . . ."

Babbitt leaped across the ditch and pulled Sixth Sister to her feet. Her left leg hung limp, as if dead, and he had to hold her up with his arm around her waist. Her filthy dress, which looked like a wrinkled onionskin, crept up as her pale buttocks began slipping toward the ground. She hung on to Babbitt's neck, who hooked his arms under her armpits. The two of them, husband and wife, were standing — sort of. When Babbitt's sad blue eyes fell on Mother, he hobbled toward her, carrying Sixth Sister, who could no longer walk. "Mama," he said in Chinese, his lips quivering, large tears creeping out of his eyes.

Water sluiced down the ditch as Platoon Leader Ma shoved the corpse of a Sima Battalion soldier off of him and climbed slowly to his feet, like a gigantic toad. His raincoat was spattered with water, blood, and mud, the patterns on a toad's back. His legs were bent as he stood up, quaking fearfully, pitifully, sort of like a bear, if you didn't look closely, but like a hero if you did. One of his eyes had been gouged out and hung alongside his nose like a shiny marble. Two of his front teeth were missing and blood dripped from his steely chin.

A soldier with a first-aid kit rushed up to keep him from falling. "Commander Shangguan, this man is badly wounded!" she shouted, her slight frame bent over by the weight of his body.

At that moment, Pandi, with all her bulk, came running over ahead of two porters with a stretcher. A tiny army cap sat atop her head, the brim sticking out above her broad, full face; only her ears, which poked out from under her pageboy, retained the delicate beauty of a Shangguan girl.

Without a moment's hesitation, she jerked Platoon Leader Ma's eye loose and tossed it away; it rolled around on the muddy ground for a moment before coming to rest and staring up at us hostilely. "Commander Shangguan," Platoon Leader Ma said as he sat up on the stretcher and pointed at Mother. "Tell Battalion Commander Lu that this old lady broke down the gate . . ."

Pandi wrapped Platoon Leader Ma's face in gauze, round and round until he couldn't open his mouth. Then she stood in front of us and called out to Mother tentatively.

"I'm not your mother."

"I told you once," Pandi said, "that the river flows east for ten years and west the next ten. Look at the mud on your feet when you step out of the water."

"I've seen it," Mother said. "I've seen it all."

Pandi said, "I know everything that's happened in the family. You took good care of my daughter, Mother, so I absolve you of all guilt."

"I don't need your absolution. I've lived long enough."

"We've taken back our land, all of it," Pandi said.

Mother gazed up at the scattered clouds in the sky and muttered, "Lord, open Thine eyes and take a look at this world . . ."

Pandi walked up and, with no show of emotion, rubbed my head. I could smell the disagreeable odor of medicine on her hand. She didn't rub Sima Liang's head, and I assumed he wouldn't have allowed her to. He was grinding his feral little teeth, and if she'd tried to rub his head, he'd probably have bitten her finger off. She smiled sarcastically as she turned to Sixth Sister. "You've done well. The American imperialists are supplying our enemies with airplanes and artillery. They're helping our enemies slaughter people in the liberated areas."

With her arms wrapped around Babbitt, Sixth Sister said, "Let us go, Fifth Sister. You've already killed Second Sister. Is it our turn next?"

At that moment, Sima Ku dragged the body of Zhaodi out of the mill house, laughing hysterically. Moments earlier, when his soldiers had made their mad dash out of the building, he had stayed behind. Known for his meticulous dress, the buttons of his tunic always clean and shiny, Sima Ku had changed overnight. His face was like a bean that had swelled up in the rain and then baked dry in the sun, criss-crossed with white wrinkles. His eyes were lifeless, the hair on his large head spotted with gray. He dragged Second Sister's bloodless body up to Mother and fell to his knees.

Mother's mouth was twisted to one side, her cheekbones jerking up and down so violently she couldn't utter a single intelligible comment. Tears filled her eyes. She reached out to touch Second Sister's forehead, then cupped her daughter's chin in her hand and managed to say, "Zhaodi, my little girl, you and your sisters chose the men you went with and the paths you took. You wouldn't listen to your mother, so I couldn't save you. All of you . . . trusted to fate . . ."

Sima Ku let go of Second Sister's corpse and walked toward Lu Liren, who was surrounded by a dozen or more bodyguards as he walked toward the mill house. He stopped when he was a couple of paces from the other man. Two pairs of eyes were locked, seemingly in mortal combat, sparks flying, as if from crossed swords. No victor emerged after several rounds. Three dry laughs emerged from Lu Liren's mouth: "Ha ha! Ha ha! Ha ha ha!" They were met with three from Sima Ku: "Heh heh! Heh heh! Heh heh heh!"

"I trust you've been well since we last met, Brother Sima," Lu said. "It was a year ago that you drove me from the area. I'll bet you never imagined the same fate would befall you one day!"

"A six-month debt is quickly repaid," Sima said. "But Brother Lu, you've demanded too much interest."

"I am deeply pained over the tragic loss of your wife. But that is the nature of revolutions. When cutting out a tumor, some good cells must be sacrificed. But that cannot stop us from cutting out the tumor. I hope this is something you can understand."

"Don't waste your spittle," Sima Ku said. "You may kill me now!"

"Nothing so simple is planned for you."

"Then you'll forgive me if I take matters into my own hands."

He reached in and pulled out a silver-plated pistol, cocked the hammer, and turned to Mother. "I'm doing this to avenge your loss," he said as he put the pistol to his head.

Lu Liren roared with laughter. "So you're a coward, after all! Go ahead, kill yourself, you pathetic worm!"

Sima Ku's hand began to shake.

"Daddy!" It was Sima Liang.

Sima Ku turned to look at his son. Slowly his hand dropped to his side. He let out a self-mocking laugh and handed the pistol to Lu Liren. "Here, you take this."

Lu Liren took the pistol and hefted it in his hand. "This is a woman's toy," he said as he flipped it disdainfully to one of the men behind him, and then stomped his water-soaked, muddy feet on the ground. "Actually, once you handed over the weapon, your fate was no longer in my hands. My superiors will choose where you wind up — in Heaven or in Hell."

With a shake of his head, Sima Ku said, "I'm afraid you've got it all wrong, Commander Lu. There is no seat reserved for me in either Heaven or Hell. My seat exists between those two places, and when it's all over and done with, you will be in the same boat as me."

Lu Liren turned to the men beside him. "Take them away."

Guards moved up, nudged Sima Ku and Babbitt with their rifles, and said, "Get moving!"

"Let's go," Sima Ku said to Babbitt. "They can kill me a hundred times, but they won't touch a hair on your head."

Still holding Sixth Sister up, Babbitt walked up to Sima Ku.

"Mrs. Babbitt can stay behind," Lu Liren said.

"Commander Lu," Sixth Sister said, "I ask you to spare the two of us as a reward for helping Mother raise Lu Shengli."

Pushing up his glasses, with their broken rim, he said to Mother, "You talk some sense into her."

Mother shook her head and sat down on her haunches. "Give me a hand, children," she said to Sima Liang and me.

So Sima Liang and I hoisted Zhaodi's body up on Mother's back.

With her daughter on her back, Mother headed down the muddy road home, barefoot, with Sima Liang and me beside her, each holding up one of Zhaodi's stiffening legs to ease Mother's burden. The deep footprints she made in the muddy road with her crippled, once-bound feet were still discernible months later.

6

The Flood Dragon River had reached flood stage; by looking out the window from my bed, I could see murky yellow water roaring along at the crest of the dike. A detachment of soldiers stood atop the dike gazing at the river as they engaged in a loud discussion.

Out in the yard Mother was making flatcakes on a griddle, while Zaohua kept the fire going. Because the firewood was still wet, the flames burned dark yellow and filled the air with dense black smoke. The sun's rays were muted.

Sima Liang came inside, bringing with him the acrid smell of scholar tree. "They're planning to take my dad plus Sixth Aunt and her husband back to military headquarters," he said in a low voice. "Third Aunt's husband and the others are making a raft to sail downriver."

"Liang," Mother called out from outside. "Go down to the river with your uncle and aunt and keep the others there. Tell them I want to see them off."

The river flowed fast and dirty, carrying grain stalks, yam vines, dead animals, even — out in the deepest part — entire uprooted trees. The Flood Dragon River Bridge, three pylons of which Sima Ku had burned down, had disappeared under the raging water, its existence signaled only by swirling eddies and the loud crashing of waves. Scrub brush on both sides of the river had also disappeared, though every once in a while a branch poked through the surface, green leaves still attached. Gray-blue gulls skimmed the tips of waves, from time to time coming up with a small fish. The opposite bank looked like a black rope that kept popping in and out of view, dancing atop sprays of glistening water. No more than a few inches kept the river from swamping the dikes; in some spots, yellow tongues of water lapped seductively at the crests, formed eddies, and slithered over the outer edges.

When we reached the riverbank, Speechless Sun was holding his impressive organ in his hand and pissing into the water, the whiskey-colored liquid making bell-like sounds when it hit the surface. He smiled when he saw us, took out a whistle he'd fashioned from a cartridge, and entertained us with birdcalls: the throaty call of the thrush, the shallow moan of the oriole, and the sad wail of the lark. It was enchanting; even his warty face softened. After running through his repertoire, he flicked the saliva out of his whistle and, with a guttural *gr-ao*, thrust it toward me, obviously intending it as a gift. But I backed up fearfully and just looked at him. Speechless Sun, you demon, I'll never forget the look on your face when you were cutting down people with your sword! Again he reached out toward me, followed by another *gr-ao*, as a look of agitation spread across his face. I backed up. He came toward me. Sima Liang, who was standing behind me, said in softly, "Don't take it, Little Uncle. 'The whistling mute, confronted by a brute.' He uses that thing to call ghosts in the cemetery." *Gr-ao*! Beginning to get angry, Speechless Sun forced the brass object into my hand, before turning and walking over to a group of men who were making wooden rafts, ignoring us altogether. Sima Liang dug the whistle out of my hand and examined it carefully in the sunlight, as if expecting to have some secret revealed. "Little Uncle," he said, "I was born under the sign of the cat, not one of the twelve signs of the zodiac, so no ghost is a match for me. I'll hold on to this for you." He put the whistle into one of the many hidden pockets in his knee-length, liberally patched pants. A great many strange and interesting objects filled those pockets: a stone that changed color in the moonlight, a little saw used for cutting roof tiles, apricot pits in a variety of shapes, even a pair of sparrow talons and the skulls of two frogs. He also carried baby teeth — his, Eighth Sister's, and mine — which Mother had thrown into the yard behind the house; he'd retrieved every one of them, which was no mean feat, considering all the dog shit hidden in the tall weeds. But he said, "If you really want to find something, it'll jump right out of its hiding place." Now to the hidden treasures in his pants was added a demonic little whistle.

Like a column of ants, more than a dozen 16th Regiment soldiers were carrying pine logs down one of the lanes to the riverbank.

Crash! Bang! Sima Ting's watchtower was under siege. Speechless Sun led the assault, directing his men to take down the posts and fasten them together with thick wire. Zunlong the Elder, the village's handiest carpenter, was their technical supervisor. The mute was screaming at him like a wrathful gorilla, spittle flying everywhere. Zunlong stood at attention, arms at his sides, a clamp in one hand and a hatchet in the other. His scarred knees were pressed together; his calves, with their protruding veins, were straight and rigid; he was wearing wooden clogs.

At that moment, a guard with a rifle slung over his back came riding down the lane on a bicycle. After parking his bike, he scrambled up the dike; halfway there, one of his feet sank into a rat hole, and when he pulled it out, murky water seeped to the surface. "Look," Sima Liang said, "the dike's about to go." The soldier echoed his concern. "Look out!" he shouted. "There's a hole here." Panic-stricken soldiers stopped what they were doing and stared fearfully at the watery hole. A rare look of terror even appeared on the mute's face as he gazed out at the raging river, where the water flowed higher than the tallest building in the village. Taking out his sword and tossing it to the top of the dike, he stripped off his shirt and pants, until he was standing there dressed only in a pair of shorts that looked as if they were made of sheet metal. He turned to his men and grunted. Like a flock of startled woodcocks, they just gaped at him. Finally, one bushy-browed soldier shouted, "What do you want us to do? Jump into the river?" The mute ran up and grabbed him by the collar, pulling so hard that several black plastic buttons snapped off. In his excitement, the mute spat out a word — Strip! — everyone heard it.

Zunlong looked at the hole and at the eddies in the river. "You there, soldiers," he said, "it's a gopher hole, which means it widens out below. Your commander wants you to strip so you can go down and plug the holes. Go on, men, strip. If you don't do it now, it'll be too late."

Zunlong took off his patched jacket and threw it at the mute's feet. Taking their cue from him, the soldiers began to strip. One youngster merely took off his jacket, leaving his pants on. The mute, getting angrier by the minute, repeated his command: "Strip! Strip! Strip!" When cornered, dogs jump over walls, cats climb trees, rabbits bite, and mutes speak. Over and over he bellowed. "Commander," the young soldier stammered, "I'm not wearing undershorts!" The mute picked up his sword and laid the back of the blade across the soldier's neck, thumping it twice. The poor soldier paled and blubbered, "I'll strip, Grandpa Mute, how's that?" He bent down, untied his leggings, and took off his pants, revealing his lily-white backside and a nearly hairless prick, which he quickly covered with his hands. The mute turned to have the guard strip also, but the man ran down the dike, jumped on his bicycle, rocked back and forth a time or two, and sped away, shouting as he went, "The dike's about to go — the dike's about to go!"

While Zunlong knocked down a bean trellis at the foot of the dike and made a large ball out of the vines and pieces of lath, the mute put his clothes in a pile and tied them up with his leggings. Several soldiers helped him roll the bundle up to the top of the dike, where the mute picked it up and was about to jump into the river, when Zunlong pointed to a whirlpool. So he went over to his toolbox, took out a flat green bottle, and removed the cork. The smell of alcohol rose into the air. The mute took the bottle, tipped his head back, and poured the contents down his throat. With a thumbs-up, he waved at Zunlong and shouted, "Strip!" which everyone knew meant "good." Bundle in hand, he dove into the river, whose waters had already breached the dike. By then the gopher hole was the size of a horse's neck, releasing gushing water that snaked its way down the lane and turned into a full-blown stream of murky water that quickly reached our door. Our houses looked like miniature sand castles alongside the raging river. The mute disappeared in the river, the spot marked by bubbles and clumps of grass. Gulls skimmed the surface, their beady black eyes fixed with nervous anticipation on the spot where the mute had gone into the water. I could make out their bright red beaks and the black talons tucked under their bellies. With growing anxiety, we kept our eyes glued to the water as a glistening dark watermelon rolled once and was swallowed up. It resurfaced a few feet downriver. Then a scrawny black frog struggled to swim toward us from the middle of the muddy river, fighting the current. When it reached the relatively calm water near the bank, I could see the little wakes made by its scissoring legs. The soldiers, nervous looks frozen on their taut faces, stretched their necks to see what was happening. They looked like a line of condemned men awaiting the executioner's sword. The one who'd been forced to strip naked kept the family jewels hidden behind his hands as he too craned his neck to look. Zunlong, on the other hand, was staring at the hole in the dike. Seeing that no one was paying attention, Sima Liang picked up the mute's sword, a weapon that killed men as easily as slicing a melon, and furtively ran his thumb along the blade to test its sharpness.

"Okay!" Zunlong shouted. "The hole's been plugged!"

The savage gush of water from the hole was now a mere trickle. Like a huge black fish, the mute's head crashed through the surface, sending the gulls circling above the spot soaring skyward in fright. As he wiped the water from his face with one of his large hands, he spat out a muddy geyser. Zunlong ordered the soldiers to toss the ball of vines out into the river. The mute grabbed it with both hands, pressing it down into the water so he could climb on top, legs and all. He too dipped beneath the surface, but only for a moment; he sucked in a mouthful of air the moment his head reappeared. Zunlong reached out with a long branch to pull him in, but the mute waved him off and dipped back beneath the surface.

In the village the crash of a gong was followed by a bugled charge. Scores of armed soldiers rushed the riverbank from all the neighboring lanes. Lu Liren and his guards emerged from the mouth of our lane. The minute he reached the dike, he shouted, "Where's the danger?"

The mute's head popped up, and then quickly disappeared, a sign that he was exhausted. So Zunlong reached out again with his branch and pulled the mute to the river's edge, where soldiers dragged him up onto dry land. Rubber-legged, he sat on the bank.

"Commander," Zunlong said to Lu Liren, "if not for this man, the villagers would probably be feeding the turtles by now."

Lu walked up to the mute and gave him a thumbs-up. His skin a mass of goose bumps and his face covered with mud, the mute just smiled.

Lu Liren's men turned to shoring up the dike. Meanwhile, work on the rafts continued, since the prisoners had to be ferried across the river by noon, where they were to be met by escorts from headquarters. The soldiers who had shed their uniforms were relieved. The more praise that was heaped upon them, the more energetic they became, and they asked to stay to complete their mission, with or without uniforms. So Lu Liren had someone run back to camp to fetch a pair of pants for the little bare-assed soldier. He smiled at the young-ster and said, "Why be embarrassed just because you've got a hairless little pecker?" While he was giving orders, Lu turned to me and asked, "How's your mother? Shengli must be quite a handful." Sima Liang nudged me, but I didn't know what he wanted. So he spoke up: "Granny wants to come to see my father off and would like you to wait for her."

Meanwhile, Zunlong had thrown himself into his work, and within half an hour had built a raft several meters long. Since they had no oars, he recommended that they use wooden spades. Lu Liren gave the order. Then he replied to Sima Liang, "Go tell your granny that I've granted her request." He looked at his watch. "You two can leave now." But we didn't, because when we looked toward the house, we saw Mother walk out the door with a bamboo basket covered by a piece of white cloth over one arm and carrying a red earthenware teapot in her other hand. Zaohua walked out after her, a bunch of green scallions in her arms. Behind her came Sima Ku's twin daugh-ters, Sima Feng and Sima Huang; they were followed by the twin sons of the mute and Third Sister, Big Mute and Little Mute. Then came Lu Shengli, who had just learned to walk. Bringing up the rear was Shangguan Laidi, her face heavily powdered. The procession moved slowly. The twin girls kept looking at the bean vines and the morning glories growing among them, hoping to see dragonflies, butterflies, or cicada shells. The twin boys kept looking at trees lining the lane — scholar trees, willow trees, and mulberry trees, with their light yellow bark; they were looking for delectable snails. Lu Shengli kept her eyes peeled for puddles, and whenever she spotted one, she stomped down in the water and filled the lane with gales of innocent laughter. Laidi was walking like a proper young lady, but I was so far away I could see only her powdered face, not her features.

Lu Liren took a pair of binoculars from the neck of one of his guards and looked across the river. A soldier beside him asked with a sense of urgency, "Are they here?"

"No," he said without looking away. "Not a trace of them. All I see is a crow pecking at a pile of horse dung."

"Could something have happened to them?" the guard asked anxiously.

"I don't think so. They're all marksmen, and no one would dare try to stop them."

Suddenly, a group of dark-skinned men stood on the opposite dike; the sun's shifting reflection on the surface created the illusion that they were standing on the water, not the dike. "There they are," Lu Liren said. "Have the signalmen let them know we're here."

A young soldier stepped up, raised a short, stubby, strange-looking pistol, and fired it into the air. A yellow ball arced into the sky, froze there for a moment, and then fell in a sweeping curve, leaving a trail of white smoke and a sizzling sound before falling into the river. As it fell, some gulls were tempted to go after it, but a closer look sent them fleeing with shrill cries.

"Give another signal," Lu Liren said, when there was no response.

This time the soldier took out a red banner, tied it to the end of the branch Zunlong had discarded, and waved it in the air; the men on the other bank roared their approval.

"Good," Lu Liren said as he draped the binoculars around his neck. He turned to the young officer who had spoken with him a moment before. "Staff Officer Qian, run back and tell Chief of Staff Du to bring the prisoners, on the double." Staff Officer Du turned and ran down the dike.

Lu Liren jumped onto the raft and stomped on it to see how sturdy it was. "It won't break up out on the river, will it?" he asked Zunlong.

"Don't you worry, sir. Back in the autumn of 1921, the villagers ferried Senator Zhao across the river. I made the raft they used."

"These are important prisoners," Lu Liren said. "There can be no mistakes."

"Don't you worry, sir. If there are, you can cut off nine of my ten fingers."

"What good would that do? If the worst happened, even taking nine of *my* fingers would serve no purpose."

Mother led her procession up the dike, where she was met by Lu Liren. "Aunt," he said politely, "wait here for the time being. They're being brought over now." He bent down to put his face up close to Lu Shengli. Frightened, she started to cry, embarrassing Lu, who straightened his eyeglasses and said, "She doesn't even know her own daddy." "Fifth Son-in-law," Mother said with a sigh. "All this fighting, back and forth, when's it going to end?" Lu had an answer ready. "Don't worry, in two or, at the most, three years, you'll have the peaceful life you're looking for." Mother said, "I'm just a woman, and I ought to keep my thoughts to myself, but can't you find it in you to let them go? After all, you and they are part of the same family." "Dear Mother-in-law," Lu said with a smile, "that's not for me to decide. But how did you wind up with so many troublesome sons-in-law?" He laughed, a mirthful sound that lightened the mood on the dike. "Can't you ask your superiors to grant clemency?" "Please, Mother-in-law, don't trouble yourself over things like this."

A detachment of guards came down the lane escorting Sima Ku, Babbitt, and Niandi. Sima Ku's hands were tied behind his back with rope; Babbitt's were tied in front of him; Niandi's were free. When they passed by our house, Sima Ku walked up to the door. A guard blocked his way. Sima Ku spat at him and shouted, "Get out of my way, I'm going in to say good-bye to my family." Cupping his hands in front of his mouth, Lu Liren trumpeted down the lane, "Commander Sima, there's no need for that. They're all right here." As if he hadn't heard, Sima hunched his shoulders and, followed by Babbitt and Niandi, forced his way into the yard, where the three of them dawdled a while. Lu Liren kept looking at his watch, as the escort troops on the other side of the river waved a red banner back and forth. The signalman on this side waved his in response.

Finally, Sima Ku and his companions walked out of the yard and made their way up the dike. "Ready the raft!" Lu Liren ordered. A dozen or so soldiers responded by pushing the raft out into the roiling river. It bobbed to the surface and was turned parallel to the bank by the current. The soldiers held tightly to the rope handles to keep it from setting off downriver.

"Commander Sima, Mr. Babbitt," Lu Liren said, "we're a benevolent army. Humanity is our guiding principle, which is why I've permitted your family to see you off. Please be quick about it."

Sima Ku, Babbitt, and Niandi walked over to where we were standing. Sima was smiling; Babbitt looked worried. Niandi was in a somber mood, looking like a martyr, unafraid to die. "Sixth Sister," Lu Liren said softly, "you may stay behind." But Niandi shook her head, determined to follow her husband.

Mother took the cloth covering off of her basket, and Zaohua handed her a peeled scallion, which she broke in half and stuffed into a flatcake. Then she took a jar of bean paste from her basket and handed it to Sima Liang. "Hold it," she said. He took it and stood there staring at her. "Don't stare at me," she said, "look at your father." Sima Liang's gaze flew over to the face of Sima Ku, who looked down at his husky, dark-skinned son. A cloud of worry had settled on his face, something we hardly ever saw. His shoulder twitched. Was he going to reach down to touch his son? Sima Liang's lips parted. "Dad," he said softly. Sima Ku's yellow eyes seemed to spin; he forced back tears and swallowed them. "Don't forget, son," he said, "that no member of the Sima family has ever died in bed. I don't expect you to, either." "Dad, are they going to shoot you?" Sima Ku gazed at the murky river out of the corner of his eye. "Your father failed because he was too soft, too kind. So don't you forget that if you're going to be a bad man, you must kill without mercy, and if you're going to be a good man, you'll always have to walk with your head bowed to keep from stepping on ants. The one thing you must never become is a bat, neither bird nor beast. Can you remember that?" Biting his lip, Sima Liang nodded.

Mother handed a scallion-stuffed flatcake to Laidi, who merely stared back at her. "Feed it to him!" Blushing shyly, Laidi had obviously forgotten her mad passion of three days before; the shy look on her face proved that. Mother looked first at her, then at Sima Ku. Her eyes were like a golden thread that drew Laidi and Sima Ku's gaze together. Their looks spoke volumes. Laidi took off her black robe, under which she was wearing a purple jacket, purple-bordered pants, and purple cloth slippers. Her figure was graceful, her face thin and lovely. Sima Ku had harnessed her passion, but in doing so had created in her a sense of lovesickness. She was still a beautiful woman, well versed in coquettishness, an attractive widow. As he stared at her, he said, "Take good care of yourself." Laidi responded with a strange comment: "You're a diamond, he's a piece of rotten wood." She walked up to him, dipped the scallion-stuffed flatcake into the yellow paste Sima Liang was holding, and twisted it neatly in the air to keep the paste from dripping to the ground. She then held it up to Sima Ku's mouth. He threw back his head and then lowered it to take a savage bite of the flatcake, which he chewed with difficulty, making loud crunching noises. His cheeks swelled; a pair of large tears seeped from his eyes. He stretched his neck to swallow, sniffled loudly, and said, "Those scallions have a real bite!"

Mother handed me one of the flatcakes and another to Eighth Sister. "Jintong," she said, "feed it to Sixth Brother-in-law. Yunü, feed yours to Sixth Sister." As Laidi had done before me, I dipped the cake in the yellow paste and put it up next to Babbitt's mouth. His twisted lips parted as he bit off a tiny piece. Tears ran from his blue eyes. He bent down, placed his dirty lips on my forehead, and kissed me loudly. Then he walked over to Mother; I thought he was going to hug her, but since his hands were tied, all he could do was bend down and touch his lips to her forehead like a goat nibbling a tree. "I'll never forget you, Mama," he said.

Eighth Sister groped her way over to Sima Liang, reached out and dipped her flatcake in the bean paste, with Sima Liang's help. Holding it up in two hands, she raised her face. Her forehead looked like a crab's shell, her eyes were two deep, dark wells, her nose was straight and her mouth was wide, with tender lips like rose petals. My eighth sister, whom I'd always taken advantage of, was truly a pitiful little lamb. "Sixth Sister," she chirped, "Sixth Sister, this is for you."

As tears filled her eyes, Sixth Sister picked up Eighth Sister. "My poor, ill-fated little sister," she sobbed.

Sima Ku finished his flatcake.

All this time, Lu Liren was gazing at the river out of the corner of his eye. Now he turned and said, "It's time to board the raft."

"Not yet," Sima Ku said. "I'm still hungry. In olden days, when the court was about to execute a criminal, they made sure he'd eaten his fill first. You people of the 16th Regiment call yourselves a benevolent army, so the least you can do is allow me to fill up on scallion-stuffed flatcakes, especially since our mother-in-law made them with her own hands."

Lu Liren looked at his watch. "All right," he said, "go ahead and stuff yourself while we ferry Babbitt across the river."

The mute and six of his soldiers picked up their wooden spades and jumped gingerly onto the raft, which rocked in the water and twisted to one side as the waterline dipped below the surface and sheets of water spilled over the sides. Two soldiers with loosened leggings leaned back to bring the raft under control. Lu Liren was worried. "Old-timer," he said to Zunlong, "will it take two more?" "No, have two of the men with oars get off." "Baldy Han, Pan Yongwang, you two come back." Holding their wooden spades, they jumped off the raft, which rocked so severely that some of the soldiers nearly fell into the river. The mute, clad only in his underwear, growled, "Strip! Strip! Strip!" After that day, no one ever heard another *Gr-ao* from him again.

"Okay?" Lu Liren asked Zunlong. "Yes," he said as he took the spade out of one of the soldier's hands. "Yours is a benevolent army, and you've earned my respect. In the tenth year of the Republic I ferried a senator across the river. If you won't take offense, I'd be honored to serve you, even as a pack animal."

"Old man," Lu Liren said, clearly touched, "that's what I had in mind, but was too embarrassed to ask. With you at the helm, I know this raft is in good hands. Who's got liquor?"

An orderly ran up and handed Lu Liren a dented metal canteen. He unscrewed the top and held the canteen up to his nose. "Authentic sorghum liquor," he said. "Old man, I offer you a drink on behalf of my superiors." He handed the canteen to Zunlong with both hands. Stirred by this honor, Zunlong rubbed some of the mud off his hands before accepting the canteen and taking ten or more deep swallows before handing it back to Lu Liren. He wiped his mouth with the back of his hand, as a redness moved from his face down to his neck, and from there to his chest. "I've drunk your liquor, sir, which links our hearts together." With a smile, Lu Liren said, "Why stop at our hearts? Our livers are linked, and our lungs, even our intestines." Tears seemed to spurt from Zunlong's eyes as he leaped onto the raft, getting an immediate foothold at the rear. The raft rocked ever so slightly; Lu Liren nodded his approval, before walking up to Babbitt, looking down at his bound hands, and smiling apologetically. "I know this is hard on you, Mr. Babbitt. Commander Yu and Director Song asked for you by name, so you can expect courteous treatment." Babbitt raised his hands. "Is this what you call courteous treatment?" "In a way it is," Lu Liren said calmly, "and I hope you'll let it go at that. Now it's time to go."

Babbitt looked over at us, saying good-bye with his eyes before turning and jumping onto the raft. This time it rocked heavily, and he swayed with it. Zunlong reached out to steady him from behind with his spade.

Following Babbitt's lead, Niandi bent down and kissed me clumsily on the forehead, then did the same to Eighth Sister, running her thin fingers through Eighth Sister's soft, flax-colored hair. "My poor little sister," she said with a sigh. "I hope the old man above has a good life planned for you." She then nodded to Mother and the children lined up behind her, and turned to board the raft. "Sixth Sister, there's no need for you to go," Lu Liren reminded her, to which she responded mildly, "Fifth Brother-in-law, there's a popular saying that a steelyard's sliding weight doesn't leave its arm, and a good man doesn't leave his wife. You and Fifth Sister were inseparable, weren't you?" "I just want what's best for you," Lu Liren said. "So I'll do as you wish. You may board the raft."

Two of his guards picked up Niandi by the arms and placed her on the raft. Babbitt reached out to steady her.

The raft was sitting low and uneven in the water; parts were completely submerged, others were an inch or so above the surface. Zunlong said to Lu Liren, "Commander Lu, it's best if my guests are seated. That goes for the men with the oars too." So Lu Liren gave the order: "Sit down, all of you. Mr. Babbitt, for your own safety, please sit down."

Babbitt sat down on the raft — more accurately, he sat down in the water. Niandi sat down across from him, also in the water.

The mute and five of his soldiers sat down, three on each side of the raft. Zunlong was the only person standing, feet planted firmly at the rear of the raft.

The little red flag continued to wave on the opposite bank. "Send a signal," Lu Liren said to the signalman, "so they'll be ready to receive the prisoners."

The man took out his stubby pistol and fired three flares into the sky above the opposite bank, where the red flag stopped waving and a bunch of little black men began running around on the silvery surface of the river.

Lu Liren looked at his watch. "Launch the raft!"

The two soldiers loosened their grip on the ropes, as Zunlong pushed off with his spade and the soldiers began swishing their spades in the water. The raft eased out into the river and quickly turned sideways as the current dragged it downriver. As if flying a kite, the two soldiers on the dike fed out as much of the ropes as they could.

On the opposite bank the men stared anxiously at the raft. Lu Liren took off his glasses and gave them a quick wipe with his sleeve; he had a faraway look in his eyes, which were circled with white rims, like one of those birds that feed on loaches. He draped the cords that served as shafts for his eyeglasses over his ears, which had already been rubbed raw. Out on the river, the raft turned sideways; lacking experience in raft navigation, the soldiers wielded their spades this way and that, sending murky water splashing onto the raft and soaking the clothing of everybody aboard. Babbitt, his hands still bound, cried out fearfully; Sixth Sister held on to him for dear life. From where he

stood at the rear, Zunlong shouted, "Easy there, men, easy. Stop flailing like that, work together, that's the key!" Lu Liren fired a couple of
shots in the air, and the soldiers' heads jerked up. "Follow Zunlong's
cadence, work together!" Zunlong said. "Easy there, men, on my count:
one-two, one-two, one-two, nice and easy, one-two . . ."

The raft eased out into the middle of the river and spurted downstream. Babbitt and Sixth Sister let the waves wash over them. The
two soldiers holding the ropes shouted, "Commander, there's no more
rope to let out!" By then, the raft was a good hundred yards downstream, and the rope was taut as a wire. The soldiers wrapped the ends
around their arms; the ropes bit deeply into their flesh. They were
leaning so far backward they were nearly lying down, and their heels
began to slip in the mud; they were suddenly in danger of being
dragged down into the water. They screamed as the raft began to tip to
one side. "Hurry up, start running!" Lu Liren shouted. "Run, I said,
you bastards!" Stumbling at first, the two soldiers took off running, as
the men at the foot of the dike scrambled to get out of the way. A bit
of slack opened up, and the raft recommenced its rapid descent downstream. Zunlong kept shouting his cadence, as the soldiers on the sides
bent at the waist and rowed with all their might, their movements
gradually coming together, so that as the raft continued downstream, it
also moved closer to the opposite bank.

A moment earlier, when the raft was in danger of tipping over,
and all eyes were on the river, Sima Liang had put down his bowl and
said softly, "Dad, turn around." Sima Ku, who was still chewing his
flatcake, turned to face the river. Sima Liang ran up behind him, took
out a little bone-handled knife — the one Babbitt had given to me —
and began cutting the rope that bound his father's hands, concentrating on the part closest to his body, and not all the way through. While
he worked on the rope, Mother prayed loudly, "Dear Lord, show us
Thy mercy and see my daughter and son-in-law safely across the river,
dear merciful Lord." I heard Sima Liang whisper, "You can break the
rope now, Dad." He then turned, quickly slipped the knife back into
his pocket, and picked the bowl up again. Laidi continued feeding
Sima Ku. Meanwhile, the raft, which was now several hundred yards
downstream, eased up to the opposite bank.

Lu Liren walked over and glanced scornfully at Sima Ku. "You've
got quite an appetite."

Sima Ku muttered as he chewed, "My mother-in-law made them with her own hands and my sister-in-law is feeding me, so why wouldn't I eat? I'll never have another chance to eat this much food and in this manner again. How about some paste?"

Laidi squeezed the tip of the scallion out beyond the edge of the flatcake and dipped it in the bowl of paste Sima Liang was holding, then held it up to Sima Ku's mouth. He took an exaggerated bite and chewed hungrily.

Lu Liren shook his head scornfully and walked over to where we were standing. Mother picked up Shengli and held her in his arms. The baby cried and fought to get free; Lu Liren backed up awkwardly. "Brother Sima," he said, "I envy you, but I can't be like you."

Sima Ku swallowed the food in his mouth. "That's an insult, Commander Lu. You're the victor, which makes you king. You're the cleaver and I'm the meat. You can slice me up or chop me to pieces, and still you mock me."

"I'm not mocking you," Lu Liren said. "The truth is, when you get to headquarters, you'll have a chance to atone for your crimes. But if resistance is all you can manage, I'm afraid you won't like the outcome."

"I've lived a good life, with plenty of good food and good times, and I'm ready to die. But I'll have to leave my children in your hands."

"You can rest easy on that score," Lu Liren said. "If not for the war, you and I would be proper relatives."

"You're an intellectual," Sima Ku said, "and what you say sounds almost sacred. But being relatives like that can only come from sleeping with certain women." He laughed, yet I noticed that his arms didn't move.

The soldiers holding the ropes returned. On the opposite bank, the oarsmen-soldiers and the prisoner escorts were hauling the raft back upstream. After they'd gone some distance, they began rowing back toward us. This time they made good speed, now that they'd had practice, and were better coordinated with the two soldiers on this side. They sped across the river.

"Brother Sima," Lu Liren said, "mealtime's almost over."

Sima Ku belched. "That's enough for me. Thanks, Mother-in-law. You too, Sister-in-law and Yunü. Son, you've been holding that bowl all this time. Thank you. Feng, Huang, be sure to listen to your grandmother and aunt. In a pinch, go look up Fifth Aunt. Everything's going her way these days, while your father has fallen on hard times.

Little Uncle, grow up good and strong. You were your second sister's favorite. She often said that Jintong is going to be someone special someday, so show us she was right."

My nose began to ache out of sadness.

The raft nudged up to the bank; the head of the prisoner escort team, a confident-looking man, was seated in the middle. He jumped ashore and saluted Lu Liren, who returned the salute. They shook hands like old friends.

"Old Lu," the man said, "you fought well. Commander Yu is delighted, and Commissar Song knows all about it." He took a letter out of the leather pouch at his belt and handed it to Lu Liren, who took it and tossed a silver pistol into the man's pouch. "Here's a war trophy for little Lan." "I thank you for her," the man said. Lu Liren then said, "Hand it over." The man froze. "Hand what over?" "The receipt for the prisoners." The man fished around in his pouch for pen and paper and wrote out a hurried receipt, which he handed to Lu. "You're very meticulous," he said. Lu Liren laughed. "No matter how clever the trickster monkey is, he can't outwit the Buddha." "Then I must be the trickster monkey," the man said. "No, I am," Lu replied. They slapped hands and laughed. Then the man said softly, "Old Lu, I hear you got your hands on a movie projector. Headquarters knows about that too." "You folks have long ears," Lu said. "When you go back, tell your superiors we'll send it over with a projectionist once the floodwaters subside."

"Damn," Sima Ku said under his breath. "The tiger kills the prey just so the bear can eat."

"What did you say?" the escort officer asked, clearly displeased.

"Nothing."

"If I'm not mistaken, you'll be the famous Sima Ku."

"In person," Sima said.

"Well, Commander Sima," the man said, "we'll take good care of you as long as you cooperate. The last thing we want is to carry your corpse back."

With a laugh, Sima said, "I wouldn't dare do anything. You escorts are crack shots, and I'm not about to present myself as a human target."

"That's what I'd expect you to say. Okay, then, Commander Lu, that'll do it. After you, Commander Sima."

Sima Ku boarded the raft and sat down.

The leader of the escort team shook hands with Lu Liren again, turned, and jumped aboard. He sat at the rear, facing Sima Ku, his hand resting on his holstered pistol. "You don't have to be *that* cautious," Sima said. "My hands are tied, so if I jumped overboard, I'd drown. Sit up closer so you can help out if the raft starts to rock."

Ignoring Sima, in a soft voice the man said to the soldiers manning the oars, "Start rowing, and make it quick."

All the members of our family stood together on the bank, knowing something the others didn't know. We waited to see what would happen.

The raft eased out into the river and floated off. The two soldiers sped across the dike, gradually letting out the ropes wrapped around their arms. When the raft reached the middle of the river, it picked up speed, sending waves toward the banks. Zunlong, slightly hoarse by now, called out the cadence, as the soldiers bent to their oars. Gulls followed the raft, flying low. Where the water flowed the fastest, the raft began to rock violently, and Zunlong flipped over backward, right into the river. The leader of the escort team jumped fearfully to his feet and was about to draw his pistol when Sima Ku, having snapped his bindings to free his hands, threw himself at the man like a hungry tiger, sending both of them into the raging water. The mute and the other oarsmen panicked. One by one, they too fell into the river. The soldiers on the dike let go of their ropes, freeing the raft, which went sailing downstream like a big, black fish, tossed by the waves.

All this seemed to occur simultaneously, and by the time Lu Liren and his soldiers realized what had happened, there was no one left to man the raft.

"Shoot him!" Lu Liren demanded.

A head popped up out of the murky water every few moments, but the soldiers couldn't be sure it was Sima Ku, and didn't dare fire. Altogether nine men were in the water, which meant there was a one-in-nine chance that the exposed head belonged to Sima Ku. Besides, the river was tearing along like a runaway horse, so even if they fired, the odds of hitting their target were slim.

Sima Ku had gotten away. Having grown up on the banks of the Flood Dragon River, he was a practiced swimmer who could stay underwater for five minutes before coming up for air. Besides, all those flatcakes and scallions had given him plenty of energy.

Lu Liren was livid. A cold glint emanated from his dark eyes as his gaze swept past us. Sima Liang, still holding the bowl of bean paste, huddled up against Mother's legs, pretending to be scared witless. Cradling Shengli in her arms, Mother walked wordlessly down the dike, with the rest of us on her heels.

Several days later, we heard that only the mute and Zunlong had managed to make it back to dry ground. The rest, including the boastful leader of the escort team, simply vanished, and their bodies were never found. But no one doubted that Sima Ku had gotten away safely.

We were, however, more concerned about the fate of Sixth Sister, Niandi, and her American husband, Babbitt. During those days, as the flooded river continued to roar along, Mother went outside every night to pace the yard and sigh, the sound seeming to drown out even the roar of the river. Mother had given birth to eight daughters: Laidi had gone mad, Zhaodi and Lingdi were dead, Xiangdi had gone into prostitution and might as well be dead; Pandi had taken up with Lu Liren and, with bullets constantly flying around her, could die in a minute; Qiudi had been sold to a White Russian, which wasn't much better than being dead. Only Yunü remained at her side, but, unhappily, she was blind. Maybe her blindness was the only reason she remained at Mother's side. Now, if something were to happen to Niandi, nearly all the eight young beauties of the Shangguan family would be nothing but a memory. So amid Mother's sighs, we heard her utter loud prayers:

Old Man in Heaven, Dear Lord, Blessed Virgin Mary, Guanyin Bodhisattva of the Southern Sea, please protect our Niandi and all the children. Place all the heavenly and worldly miseries, pains, and illnesses on my head. So long as my children are well and safe . . ."

A month later, after the waters had receded, news of Sixth Sister and Babbitt came to us from the opposite bank of the Flood Dragon River: There had been a horrific explosion in a secret cave deep in Da'ze Mountain. Once the dust had settled, people entered the cave and found three bodies huddled together, two women and a man. The man was a young blond foreigner. Although no one was prepared to say that one of the women was our sixth sister, when Mother heard the news, a bitter smile spread across her face. "It's all my fault," she said, before breaking into loud wails.

7

In the late fall, Northeast Gaomi's most beautiful season, the flood had finally passed. The sorghum fields were so red they seemed black, and reeds, which grew in profusion, were so white they seemed yellow. The early-morning sun lit up the vast fields that were covered by the first frost of the year. Soldiers of the 16th Regiment moved out silently, taking with them their herds of horses and mules; after tramping across the badly damaged footbridge above the Flood Dragon River, they disappeared over the dike on the northern bank, and we saw no more of them.

Once the 16th Regiment had departed, their commander, Lu Liren, took up the newly created posts of Northeast Gaomi county head and commander of the county militia. Pandi was appointed commander of the Dalan Army District, with the mute serving as its district team leader. His first assignment was to remove everything from the Sima mansion — tables, chairs, stools, water vats, jugs, everything — and distribute it among the local villagers. But that very night, everything found its way back to the mansion gate. Next the mute delivered a carved bed frame to our front yard. "I don't want that," Mother said. "Take it away!" "Strip! Strip!" the mute said. So Mother turned to Commander Pandi, who was darning socks at the time, and said, "Pandi, get this bed out of here." "Mother," Pandi said, "it's a trend of the times, so don't fight it." "Pandi," Mother said, "Sima Ku is your second brother-in-law. His son and daughter are here in my care. What will he think when he returns one day?" Pandi put down her darning, picked up her rifle, slung it over her back, and ran outside. Sima Liang followed her out the door; when he returned, he said, "Fifth Aunt's gone to the county government office." He added that a two-man sedan chair had brought a VIP, with eighteen armed bodyguards, to the office. County Head Lu welcomed him with all the courtesies of a student greeting his mentor. Word had it that he was a famous land reformer, who was reputed to have come up with a slogan in Shandong's Northern Wei area: "Killing a rich peasant is better than killing a wild rabbit."

The mute sent men over to take the bed away.

Mother sighed in relief.

"Granny," Sima Liang said, "let's get away from here. I think something bad is going to happen."

"Good luck is always good," Mother said, "and you cannot escape bad luck. Don't worry, Liang, even if the man above sent Heavenly Generals and Celestial Troops down to Earth, what more could they do to a bunch of widows and orphans?"

The VIP never appeared in public. Two armed sentries stood at the Sima mansion gate, where county officials with rifles slung over their backs shuttled in and out. One day, after taking our goats out to pasture, we met the mute's district team and several county and military officials on our way home. They were walking down the street with Huang Tianfu, the coffin shop proprietor, Zhao Six, the steamed bun vendor, Xu Bao, who ran the cooking oil extracting mill, single-breasted Jin, who owned the oil shop, and the local academy teacher, Qin Two, in custody. The distressed prisoners walked with hunched shoulders and bent backs. "Men," Zhao Six said, screwing his neck around, "what are you doing this for? I'll forget what you owe me for the steamed buns, how's that?" One of the officers, a man with a Mount Wulian accent and a mouthful of brass-capped teeth, slapped Zhao. "You prick!" he screeched. "Who owes you anything? Where did your money come from?" The prisoners did not dare say another word as they shuffled along with bowed heads.

That night, as a freezing rain fell, a shadowy figure climbed the wall into our yard. "Who's there?" Mother whispered. The man rushed up and knelt on the path. "Help me, Sister-in-law," he said. "Is that you, Sima Ting?" "It's me," he said. "Help me. They're going to hold a big assembly tomorrow and put me in front of a firing squad. We've been fellow villagers for all these years, and I'm asking you to save my life." Mother opened the door, and Sima Ting slipped quickly inside. He was trembling in the darkness. "Can I have something to eat? I'm starving!" Mother handed him a flatcake, which he grabbed out of her hand and gobbled down. Mother sighed. "It's my brother's fault," he said. "He and Lu Liren have become mortal enemies, even though we're all related." "That's enough," Mother said. "I don't want to hear any more. You can hide out here, but I am, after all, his mother-in-law."

At last the mysterious VIP showed his face. He was seated in a tent, writing brush in hand. A large inkstone carved with a dragon and a phoenix lay on the table in front of him. He had a pointed chin and a long, narrow nose; he was wearing a pair of black-rimmed glasses, behind which his tiny black eyes glistened. His fingers were long, thin, and ghostly pale, like the tentacles of an octopus.

The greater half of the Sima family's threshing floor was thronged with poor-peasant representatives from Northeast Gaomi Township's eighteen villages. They were ringed with sentries every four or five paces, members of the county and military district production teams. The VIP's eighteen bodyguards were lined up on the stage, faces hard as steel, murderous looks in their eyes, like the Eighteen Arhats of legend. Not a sound from the area below the stage, not even the crying of children old enough to know better. Those too young to know better had nipples stuffed in their mouths at the first whimper. We sat around Mother. In contrast with the anxious villagers sitting nearby, she was surprisingly calm, absorbed in strips of hemp lying on her exposed calf, which she twisted into shoe soles. The white strips rustled as they turned on one leg and merged into identical strands of twisted rope on the other. That day a freezing northeast wind brought cold air over from the icy Flood Dragon River and turned the people's lips purple.

Before the assembly was called to order, a disturbance occurred as the mute and members of the military district team marched Zhao Six and a dozen or so other men up to the edge of the threshing floor. They were bound and wore placards with black lettering over which red Xs had been drawn. When the villagers spotted them, they lowered their heads and said nothing.

People tucked their heads between their legs to keep the VIP from actually seeing their faces as his black eyes swept the crowd. But Mother kept twisting hemp, her eyes never leaving the work in front of her, and I sensed that the sinister gaze rested on her for a long time.

Lu Liren, wearing a red headband, addressed the audience, spittle flying everywhere. He had been suffering migraine headaches, and nothing worked to stop them, although the headband lessened the pain a little. When he was finished, he asked the VIP for instructions. The man slowly got to his feet. "Welcome Comrade Zhang Sheng, who will instruct us on what to do," Lu Liren said as he began to clap. The villagers sat dumbfounded, wondering what was going on.

The VIP cleared his throat and began to speak, slowly drawing out each and every word. His speech was like a strip of paper dancing in the cold northeast wind, and over the decades that followed, whenever I saw one of those white funeral paper cutouts that are filled with incantations to ward off evil spirits, I was reminded of that speech.

When the speech ended, Lu Liren stepped up and ordered the mute and his men, plus several officers with holstered Mausers, to drag the prisoners up to the stage like a string of pinecones. The men filled the stage and blocked the villagers' view of the VIP. "Kneel!" Lu Liren commanded. Quick-witted men fell to their knees. Dull-witted ones were kicked to theirs.

Below the stage, people glanced at one another out of the corners of their eyes. A few of the bolder ones stole a glance at the stage, but the sight of all those men kneeling, snot dripping off the tips of their noses, drove their heads back down.

A skinny man in the crowd stood up on shaky legs and announced in a hoarse, quaking voice, "District Commander...I...I have a grievance..."

"Good!" Pandi shouted excitedly. "There's nothing to be afraid of. Come up onto the stage!"

The crowd turned to look at the man. It was the one called Sleepyhead. His gray silk robe was ripped and torn; one sleeve hung by a thread, exposing his swarthy shoulder. His hair, once neatly combed and parted, had turned into a crow's nest. He quaked in the cold wind as he looked around fearfully.

"Come up and speak your piece!" Lu Liren said.

"It's no big deal," Sleepyhead said. "I'll tell you from down here, all right?"

"Come up!" Pandi said. "You're Zhang Decheng, aren't you? I recall that your mother was once forced to go around with a basket begging for food. You have suffered bitterly and your hatred is deep. Come up and tell us about it."

Bowlegged Sleepyhead made his way through the crowd up to the front of the stage, which, made of rammed earth, was a meter or so high. He jumped, but only managed to further dirty his robe. So a soldier bent down, grabbed his arm, and jerked him into the air, his legs curling beneath him as he cried out in pain. The soldier deposited him on the stage; he landed on unsteady legs, which swayed as if he were standing on springs until he was finally able to steady himself. Raising his head, he looked out over the crowd below and was startled by gazes that hid countless emotions. His knees knocked as he bashfully stammered out something that no one could hear, let alone understand, then turned to climb down. Pandi grabbed him by the shoulder and dragged him back, nearly causing him to lose his footing. Looking increasingly pathetic, he said, "Please let me go, District Commander. I'm a nobody, please let me go." "Zhang Decheng," she said truculently, "what are you afraid of?" "I'm a bachelor, stiff when I'm lying down and straight when I'm standing up. I've got nothing to be afraid of." Pandi said, "Well, since you're afraid of nothing, why don't you speak up?" "I told you, it's no big deal," he said. "So let's just forget it." "Do you think this is some sort of game?" "Don't get mad, District Commander. I'll talk. What happens happens."

Sleepyhead walked up in front of Qin Two and said, "Mr. Two, you're an educated man. That time I went to study with you, all I did was fall asleep, right? So why did you smack my hand with a ruler until it looked like a warty toad? Not only that, you gave me a nickname. Remember what you said?" "Answer him!" Pandi roared. Mr. Qin Two looked up until his goatee stuck out straight and muttered, "That was a long time ago. I've forgotten." "Of course you don't remember," Sleepyhead said, with rising excitement and increasing clarity. "But I'll never forget! What you said, old master, was 'Zhang Decheng, in my book you're a sleepyhead.' That is all it took for me to be saddled with the name Sleepyhead from then on. That's what men call me and what women call me. Even snot-nosed kids call me Sleepyhead. And because I'm stuck with a rotten name like that, I still don't have a wife at the age of thirty-eight! What girl would marry a man called Sleepyhead? That name ruined me for the rest of my life." Poor Sleepyhead was so upset by then that his face was awash with snot and tears. The county official with the brass-capped teeth grabbed a handful of Qin Two's gray hair and jerked his head back. "Speak up!" the man demanded. "Is what Zhang Decheng said true?" "Yes, yes it is," Qin Two replied as his goatee quivered like a goat's tail. The official shoved Qin Two's head forward until his face was in the dirt. "Let's hear more accusations," he said.

Sleepyhead wiped his eyes with the back of his hand, squeezed a gob of snot with his fingers, and flung it away; it landed on the tent. Scowling in disgust, the VIP took out a white handkerchief to clean his glasses. "Qin Two," Sleepyhead continued, "you're an elitist. Back when Sima Ku was going to school, he stuffed a toad down your chamber pot and climbed up on the roof to sing a bad song about you. Did you smack him? Yell at him? Give him a nickname? No, no, and no!"

"This is wonderful!" Pandi said excitedly. "Zhang Decheng has brought a serious problem out into the open. Why didn't Qin Two have the guts to punish Sima Ku? Because of Sima Ku's wealthy family. And where did their wealth come from? They ate buns made of white flour, but never worked a field of wheat. They wore silk, but never raised a silkworm. They were drunk every day, but never distilled a drop of liquor. Fellow villagers, these rich landlords have fed on our blood, sweat, and tears. Redistributing their land and wealth is simply taking back what's rightfully ours."

The VIP applauded lightly to show his appreciation for Pandi's impassioned speech. All the county and district officials, as well as the armed guards, joined in the applause.

Sleepyhead wasn't finished. "Sima Ku is only one man, but he had four wives, while I have none. Is that fair?"

The VIP frowned.

Lu Liren said, "We don't need to go into that, Zhang Decheng."

"No?" Sleepyhead argued. "That's the source of my bitterness. I may be Sleepyhead, but I'm a man, aren't I? I've got a man's tool hanging between my legs . . ."

Lu Liren walked up to Sleepyhead to stop the performance and raised his voice to drown out Sleepyhead's monologue. "Fellow villagers," he said, "Zhang Decheng's words may be a little coarse for our ears, but his meaning is clear and undeniable. Why can some men take four, five, or more wives, while somebody like Zhang Decheng here can't even find one?"

Debates broke out below the stage, and many eyes turned to Mother, whose face darkened; but there was no sign of anger or hate in her eyes, which were as serene as a placid lake in autumn.

Pandi nudged Sleepyhead. "You can go back down now."

He took a couple of steps and was about to climb down off the stage when he was reminded of something. He turned and walked up to Zhao Six, grabbed him by the ear, and gave him a resounding slap. "You son of a bitch," he growled. "Today's your day too. You probably forgot the time you used the authority you received from Sima Ku to mistreat me!"

Zhao twisted his neck and drove his head into Sleepyhead's belly. With a yelp, Sleepyhead fell to the ground and rolled off the stage.

The mute rushed up and kicked Zhao Six to the ground. Then he stepped down on Zhao's neck, twisting the poor man's face out of shape. He was gasping for breath, but even then he cried out like a man possessed, "You'll never get me to admit a thing, never! Where's your conscience? Your crimes are unspeakable . . ."

Lu Liren bent down to ask the VIP what to do. The man banged his red inkstone on the table, the sign for Lu Liren to read from a slip of paper: "Rich peasant Zhao Six has lived by exploiting others. During the war against Japan, he fed their fellow travelers. When Sima Ku governed the area, he supplied food to bandit soldiers. Now that land reform is underway, he has spread ugly rumors in open defiance of the People's Government. If a die-hard element like him is not killed, the people's anger will never be quelled. In the name of the Northeast Gaomi County People's Government, I hereby sentence Zhao Six to death, judgment to be carried out at once!"

Two of the soldiers picked up Zhao Six and dragged him off like a dead dog. When they reached the weedy edge of the pond, the men backed away to let the mute step up and put a bullet in the back of Zhao's head. His body lurched into the water. With the smoking gun still in his hand, the mute walked back onto the stage.

The terrified prisoners on stage began banging their heads on the ground. By then they'd all soiled themselves. "Spare me, spare me . . ." The cooking oil shop proprietress, Old Jin, crawled on her knees up to Lu Liren and wrapped her arms around his legs. "County Head Lu," she sobbed, "spare me. I'll give everything to the villagers — my oil, my sesame seeds, all my family property, I won't keep anything, not even a chicken-feed trough — just don't take my life. I'll never do business that exploits people again . . ." Lu Liren tried to break free of her grasp, but she held on for dear life until an official came up and pried her fingers away. She then crawled toward the VIP. "Take care of her!" Lu Liren commanded. The mute raised his pistol and struck her in the temple. Her eyes rolled up into her head as she fell backward, her single breast pointing at the gloomy sky.

"Who else wants to pour out their bitterness?" Pandi shouted down at the crowd.

Someone began to wail. It was the blind man, Xu Xian'er, who propped himself up on a yellow bamboo staff.

"Lift him up onto the stage," Pandi said.

No one did. So he made his way toward the stage by tapping his staff on the ground; people jumped out of his way. Then two officials hopped down and hoisted him up onto the stage.

Filled with hatred, Xu Xian'er banged the ground with his staff, punching holes in the loose dirt.

"Speak your piece, Uncle Xu," said Pandi.

"Commander," Xu Xian'er said, "can you really exact revenge for me?"

"Don't worry. You see what we did for Zhang Decheng just now."

"Then I'll say it," he said, "I'll say it. That bastard Sima Ku drove my wife to her grave, and my mother died of anger because of it. He owes me two lives." Tears fell from his blind eyes.

"Take your time, uncle," Lu Liren said.

"In the fifteenth year of the Republic, 1926, my mother spent thirty silver dollars to get me a wife, the daughter of a beggar woman in West Village. She sold a cow and a pig, plus two pecks of wheat, and all she got was thirty silver dollars. Everyone said my wife was pretty, but that word — pretty — spelled disaster. Sima Ku was only sixteen or seventeen at the time, but even at that age he was no good. Since his family had money and power, he made a habit of coming over to my house to sing and play his two-stringed *huqin*. Then one day he took my wife to see a local opera, and after he brought her home, he had his way with her. My wife swallowed opium and died, which upset my mother so much she hanged herself . . . Sima Ku, you owe me two lives! I want the government to right the wrong for me . . ."

He fell to his knees.

A district official came over to pull him to his feet, but he said, "I won't get up if you won't avenge me . . ."

"Uncle," Lu Liren said, "Sima Ku will not escape the net of justice, and when we catch him, we will redress this injustice."

"Sima Ku is a sparrow hawk, the king of the skies," the blind man said. "You'll never catch him. So I ask the government to repay one life with another. Execute his son and daughter. Commander, I know you're related to Sima Ku, but if you are a true dispenser of justice, you'll honor my request. If you let personal feelings get in the way, then Xu the blind man will go home and hang himself, so Sima won't be able to get to me when he returns."

"Uncle," Lu Liren managed to blurt out, "every grievance has its target, every debt has its creditor. A person must be held responsible for his deeds. Since Sima Ku caused the deaths, only Sima can be held accountable. The children are blameless."

Xu struck the ground with his staff. "Fellow villagers," he called out, "did you hear that? Don't let yourselves be fooled. Sima Ku has run away, Sima Ting is in hiding, and the children will be grown before you know it. County Head Lu is related to them, which counts for a great deal. Fellow villagers, alive Xu Xian'er is only this staff, and dead he is little more than food for the dogs. Compared to you, I am nothing, but, fellow villagers, do not be fooled by these people . . ."

Pandi blew up: "Old blind man, your demands are unreasonable!"

"Miss Pandi," Xu the blind man said, "you and the rest of the Shangguans are impressive. When the Jap devils were here, your eldest brother-in-law, Sha Yueliang, was in charge. Then during the reign of the Kuomintang, your second brother-in-law, Sima Ku, ran roughshod over the area. Now you and Lu Liren are in charge. You Shangguans are flagpoles that cannot be cut down, boats that cannot be overturned. Someday, when the Americans rule China, your family will boast a foreign son-in-law . . ."

Sima Liang's face had turned ghostly white; he was clutching Mother's hand. Sima Feng and Sima Huang hid their faces in Mother's armpits. Sha Zaohua was crying. So was Lu Shengli. So, too, after a while, was Eighth Sister, Yunü.

Their crying drew the attention of people both on and below the stage. The gloomy VIP looked down at us.

Xu Xian'er may have been blind, but he knelt right at the feet of the VIP. "Sir," he howled tearfully, "stand up for this old blind man!" He banged his head on the ground as he howled, until his forehead was covered with dirt.

Lu Liren looked at the VIP, pleading with his eyes; the VIP returned his look with an icy stare that was as sharp as a knife. Lu's face was beaded with sweat that dampened his headband, making it look like a wound on his forehead. No longer calm and at ease, he alternated between looking down at his feet and gazing out at the crowd below, the courage to make eye contact with the VIP long gone.

Pandi had also lost the poise of a district commander. Her face was bright red, her lower lip trembled. "Blind old Xu," she shouted in the tone of a countrywoman, "you're trying to stir up trouble! What has my family ever done to you? That slutty wife of yours seduced Sima Ku and took him out into the wheat field. Then when they were caught, she swallowed opium because she couldn't face decent folk. Not only that, people said you used to bite her all night long, like a dog. She showed people the scars on her chest, did you know that? You were the cause of your wife's death. What Sima Ku did was wrong, but most of the blame falls on you! So if anybody is to be shot, I say we start with you!"

"You heard that, didn't you, exalted sir?" Blind Xu said. "Cut down the wheat stalks, and a wolf appears."

Lu Liren quickly stepped in to mediate for Pandi. He tried to pull Xu Xian'er away, but Xu turned to jelly and would not be moved. "Uncle," Lu said, "you are right to demand the execution of Sima Ku, but not of his innocent children."

Xu Xian'er argued, "What were Zhao Six's crimes? All he did was sell a few buns. It was a personal dispute with Zhang Decheng, wasn't it? But you folks said shoot him, and that's what you did. Esteemed County Head, I won't rest until you execute Sima Ku's descendants."

Someone below the stage said softly, "Zhao Six's aunt was Xu Xian'er's mother, which makes them cousins."

An unnatural smile was frozen on Lu Liren's face as he walked hesitantly up to the VIP and, looking embarrassed, said something to him. The man caressed the glossy inkstone in his hand as a murderous look spread across his gaunt face. He glared at Lu Liren and said icily, "Do you really expect me to deal with something this insignificant?"

Lu took out a handkerchief to mop his sweaty brow, then reached back and tightened the headband, turning his face waxen. He walked up to the front of the stage and announced in a loud voice, "As the government of the masses, we carry out the wishes of the people. So now I leave it up to you. All those in favor of executing Sima Ku's children, raise your hands."

Infuriated, Pandi asked him, "Have you lost your mind?"

The villagers below the stage bowed their heads. No raised hands and no sound.

Lu Liren cast a questioning glance at the VIP.

With a sneer, the VIP said to Lu Liren, "Try again, but this time ask how many are in favor of *not* executing the children of Sima Ku."

"All those in favor of not executing Sima Ku's children, raise your hands."

They kept their heads down; no raised hands and no sound.

Mother slowly rose to her feet. "Xu Xian'er," she said, "if it's a life you demand, then you can have mine. But your mother didn't hang herself, she died of a blood hemorrhage that had its origin during the bandit era. My mother-in-law took care of her funeral arrangements."

The VIP stood up and walked to the open space behind the

stage. Lu Liren quickly followed. There the VIP spoke to Lu softly but rapidly, raising his soft white hand and slicing it downward, like a knife. Then he walked off, surrounded by his bodyguards.

Lu Liren remained standing there, his head bowed, like a piece of petrified wood, for a long moment before snapping out of it. Finally, he headed back, walking as if his legs were made of lead, and stared down at us with madness in his eyes. His eyeballs seemed frozen in their sockets. He looked pathetic up there. Finally, he opened his mouth to speak:

"I hereby sentence Sima Liang, son of Sima Ku, to death, to be carried out immediately! And I sentence Sima Feng and Sima Huang, daughters of Sima Ku, to death, also to be carried out immediately!"

Mother's body rocked, but only for a moment. "I dare any of you to even try!" she said as she took the two girls in her arms. Sima Liang alertly threw himself to the ground and began crawling slowly away from the stage. The crowd shielded him.

"Speechless Sun, why aren't you carrying out my orders?" Lu Liren roared.

"Your damned mind is addled," Pandi cursed, "giving an order like that!"

"My mind's not addled, it's clear as can be," Lu said as he pounded his head with his fist.

Hesitantly, the mute climbed down off the stage, followed by two soldiers.

Once he'd crawled to the rear of the crowd, Sima Liang jumped to his feet and ran past two sentries as he scrambled up the dike.

"He's getting away!" a soldier up on the stage shouted.

A sentry unshouldered his rifle, pulled back the bolt, sending a bullet into the chamber, and fired into the air. By then, Sima Liang was already well hidden in the bushes on top of the dike.

The mute and his men walked up to us. His sons, Big and Little Mute, gaped at him with lonely, haughty looks in their eyes. He reached out with an iron claw; Mother spat in his face. He pulled back his claw and wiped the spittle off his face, then reached out again. Mother spat a second time, but with less force; the spittle landed on his chest. With a twist of his neck, he looked back at the people on the stage. Lu Liren was pacing back and forth, his hands clasped behind his back. Pandi was resting on her haunches, her face buried in her hands. The faces of the county and district officials and those of the armed soldiers seemed set in clay, like temple idols. The mute's rock-hard jaw twitched out of habit. "Strip!" he said. "Strip, strip . . ."

Mother stuck out her chest and demanded shrilly, "Kill me first, you bastard!" Then she threw herself at him and clawed at his face.

The mute reached up and rubbed his face, then raised his hand to his eyes to see if anything was stuck to his fingers. That went on for a moment before he put his fingers up to his nose and sniffed them to see if he could detect any special odor. He then stuck his tongue out and licked his fingers to see if there was any special taste. That was followed by a series of grunts as he reached out and shoved Mother, who settled weightlessly to the ground. We threw ourselves on top of her, crying the whole time.

The mute picked us up, one at a time, and flung us out of the way. I landed on the back of some woman; Sha Zaohua landed on my belly. Lu Shengli landed on the back of an old man; Eighth Sister landed on the shoulder of an older woman. Big Mute was hanging from his father's arm, and no amount of shaking could loosen his grip. He bit his father on the wrist. Little Mute had his arms wrapped around his father's leg and was gnawing on his bony knee. With one kick, the mute sent that son head over heels, right into the head of a middle-aged man. Then he swung his arm with all his might, sending Big Mute flying into the lap of an old woman, a chunk of his father's flesh in his teeth.

Picking up Sima Feng in his left hand and Sima Huang in his right, he strode off, taking high steps, as if walking through mud. When he reached the front of the stage, he flung the two girls up onto it, one after the other. They both screamed for their grandmother and jumped down off the stage, only to be caught by the mute, who tossed them back up. By then, Mother had struggled to her feet and was staggering toward the stage; she fell before she'd taken more than a couple of steps.

Lu Liren stopped pacing and said dismally, "All you poor peasants, I ask you, am I or am I not a man? Can you not imagine how I feel about having to shoot these two little girls? My heart aches. They're only children, after all, and relatives of mine to boot. But for that very reason, I have no choice but to swallow my tears and sentence them to death. Come out of your stupor, my friends. By executing Sima Ku's children, we avoid taking the wrong path. On the surface, we'll be executing two children. And yet it's not children we'll be executing, but a reactionary, backward social system. We will be executing two symbols! Rise up, friends. You're either revolutionary or counterrevolutionary, there's no middle ground!" He was shouting so loudly he was over-come by a coughing fit. His face paled and tears gushed from his eyes. A county official stepped up and began thumping him on the back, but Lu waved him off. Once he'd caught his breath, he bent over and spat out a gob of mucus. Sounding like a man suffering from consumption, he managed to gasp, "Carry out the sentence!'

The mute hopped up onto the stage, grabbed the two girls, and carried them over to the pond, where he dropped them to the ground and backed up ten or fifteen paces. The girls wrapped their arms around each other; their long, thin faces seemed coated with gold powder. They looked at the mute with terror in their eyes as he took out his pistol and raised it heavily. His wrist bled and his hand shook from the exertion of raising the pistol, as if it weighed twenty pounds. Then — *pow* — a shot rang out. His hand jerked up from the recoil as blue smoke spewed from the muzzle; then his arm dropped weakly. The bullet passed over the girls' heads and thudded into the ground in front of the pond, sending mud flying.

A woman came sailing down the weedy path along the base of the dike, a sloop in the wind, clucking loudly like a mother hen driving her brood of chicks ahead of her. The moment she appeared beneath the dike, I saw it was First Sister, who had been excused from the meeting on the basis of being mentally disturbed. As the widow of the traitor Sha Yueliang, she should have been high on the list of those to be executed, and if people had known about her one-night stand with Sima Ku, she'd have been shot twice. Seeing her throw herself into the net had me worried sick, but she ran up to the pond and planted herself in front of the two girls. "Kill me," she shouted like a madwoman, "kill me! I slept with Sima Ku, and I am their mother!"

The mute's chin twitched again, a sure sign that troubling waves were billowing in his heart. He raised his pistol and said gloomily, "Strip — strip — strip —"

Without a second thought, First Sister undid the buttons of her blouse and exposed her perfect breasts. The mute stared straight ahead, his eyes snapping into place; his chin twitched so violently it seemed about to fall off. Cupping his hand under his chin to keep it in place, he opened his mouth and sputtered, "Strip — strip — strip!" First Sister obediently removed her blouse; she was naked from the waist up. Her face was dark, but her body glistened like fine porcelain. On that gloomy morning, she stripped to the waist and engaged the mute in a battle of wills. He walked up to her on bowed legs, looking like a baked snowman, crumbling piece by piece — first an arm, then a leg, intestines coiling on the ground like a snake; a red heart beating in his cupped hands. All those scattered parts came back together with great difficulty when he knelt at First Sister's feet and wrapped his arms around her waist. His big head rested against her belly.

Lu Liren and the others were stunned to witness this remarkable change, their mouths agape, as if filled with hot, sticky sweets. It was impossible to tell what they were thinking as they observed the scene beside the pond.

"Speechless Sun!" Lu Liren called out weakly, but the mighty Speechless Sun ignored him.

Pandi jumped down off the stage and ran to the pond, where she picked the jacket up off the ground and draped it around First Sister. She had hoped to drag First Sister away, but the lower half of First Sister's body had already merged with the mute, and how could Pandi pull her away from that? So she picked up the mute's pistol and hit him on the shoulder. He looked up at her; his eyes were awash with tears.

What happened then remains a puzzle even now. At the moment when Pandi was facing the tear-washed, trancelike face of the mute; at the moment when Sima Feng and Sima Huang stood up hand in hand, still terrified, and began looking around for their grandmother; at the moment when Mother came to her senses and began muttering as she ran toward the pond; at the moment when Xu Xian'er rediscovered his conscience and said, County Head, don't kill them — my mother didn't hang herself, and Sima Ku isn't the only one responsible for the death of my wife; at the moment when a pair of dogs got into a fight in the ruins behind the house of the Muslim woman; at the moment when the sweet recollection of the game I played with Laidi in the horse trough came to me, and my mouth filled with the taste of ashes and the fragrance of elasticity of her nipple; at the moment when everyone was trying to guess where the VIP had come from and where he'd gone; at that moment two men on horseback rode in from the southeast like a whirlwind. One of the horses was white as snow, the other black as charcoal. The rider on the white horse was all in black, including a black bandanna covering the lower half of his face and a black hat. The man on the black horse was all in white, including a white bandanna covering the lower half of his face and a white hat. Both carried a pair of pistols. They were expert horsemen; they leaned slightly forward, legs hanging straight down. As they approached the pond they fired several shots in the air, so frightening the armed soldiers, not to mention the county and district officials, that they all threw themselves to the ground, facedown. The two riders whipped their horses as they circled the pond, their mounts leaning to form beautiful arcs. Then each fired another shot before whipping their mounts again and riding off, the horses' tails fluttering in the air behind them. They vanished in front of our eyes, truly a case of coming on the winds of spring and leaving on the winds of autumn. They seemed like an illusion, though they were real enough. Slowly we regained our composure, and when we looked down we saw Sima Feng and Sima Huang laid out beside the pond, each with a bullet hole between the eyes. Everyone was paralyzed with fear.

8

On the day of the evacuation, shouting and bawling residents of Northeast Gaomi Township's eighteen villages led their livestock, carried their chickens, supported their elders, and carried their very young up to the alkaline soil and weed-covered northern bank of the Flood Dragon River, their nerves on edge. The ground was covered with a layer of white alkali, like a coat of frost that wouldn't melt. The leaves of grasses and reeds unaffected by the alkali were yellow, their cottony tassels waving and fluttering in the cold winds. Crows, always attracted by commotions below, wheeled and filled the sky with the ear-shattering noise of poets — *Aah*! *Wah*! Lu Liren, now demoted to deputy head of the county, stood before the stone sacrificial table of the huge crypt of a Qing dynasty scholar, shouting himself hoarse as he addressed the people mobilized to evacuate the area: "Now that bitter winter has settled in, Northeast Gaomi Township is about to turn into a vast battlefield, and not to evacuate is suicide." Branches of the black pines were packed with crows, some of which even perched on the stone men and horses. *Ahh*! They cawed. *Wah*! The sounds not only infected the tone of Lu Liren's speech, but increased the people's sense of dread and solidified their determination to flee from danger.

With the firing of a gun, the evacuation got underway. The dark mass of people moved out with a clamor. Donkeys brayed and cows lowed, chickens flapped into the air and dogs leaped, old ladies cried and children whooped, all at once. A skilled young officer on a white pony raised a red flag that hung dejectedly from the staff and rode back and forth across the bumpy, alkali-covered road leading to the northeast. Leading the procession was a contingent of mules carrying county government files, dozens of them plodding ahead listlessly under the watchful eyes of young soldiers. Behind them came a camel left over from Sima Ku's time. It carried a pair of metal boxes atop the long, dirty fur of its hump. It had spent so many years in Northeast Gaomi that it was more oxen than camel. Behind it came a dozen or so porters transporting the county printing press and a lathe for the production team repair shop. They were all swarthy, robust young men wearing thin shirts with padded shoulders, shaped like lotus leaves. From the way they swayed as they walked, their brows furrowed and their mouths open, it was easy to see how heavy their loads were. Bringing up the rear was the chaotic mass of locals.

Lu Liren, Pandi, and a host of county and district officials rode up and down the roadside on their mules and horses, trying their best to bring order to the mass evacuation. But the people were shoulder to shoulder on the narrow road, while more spacious roadsides beckoned. More and more of them left the road for the sides, as the route grew wider and wider. The expanded procession tramped noisily heading northeast. It was pandemonium.

We were carried along by the crowd, sometimes on the road, sometimes not; there were times we didn't know if we were on the road or not. Mother had draped a hemp strap around her neck and was pushing a cart with wooden wheels; the handles were so far apart she was forced to spread her arms out. A pair of rectangular baskets hung from the sides of the cart. The basket on the left carried Lu Shengli and our quilts and clothing. Big Mute and Little Mute were in the basket on the right. Sha Zaohua and I, both carrying baskets, walked alongside the cart, one on each side. Blind little Eighth Sister held on to Mother's coat and stumbled along behind her. Laidi, vacillating between clarity and confusion, walked ahead, leaning forward as she pulled the family cart with a strap over her shoulder, like a willing oxen. The sound of the creaking wheels grated on our ears. The three little ones in the cart kept looking at all the commotion around them. I could hear the crunching of my feet on the alkali ground and could smell its pungent odor. At first it seemed like fun, but after a few miles, my legs began to ache and my head grew heavy; my strength was ebbing and sweat dripped from my underarms. My little white milk goat, which was strong as an ox, trotted respectfully behind me. She knew what we were doing, so there was no need to tether her.

Strong winds from the north sliced painfully into our ears that day. Little clouds of white dust jumped up in the boundless wilderness all around us. Formed of alkali, salt, and saltpeter, the dust stung our eyes, burned our skin, and fouled our mouths. People forged ahead into the wind, their eyes mere slits. The porters' shirts were sweat-soaked and covered with alkali, turning them white from head to toe. Once we entered the marshy lowland, keeping the cart's wheels turning became a real problem. First Sister struggled mightily, the strap digging deeply into her shoulder. Her labored breathing was like a death rattle. And Mother? Tears flowed from her melancholy eyes, merging with the sweat on her face and creating a patchwork of purple ravines. Eighth Sister hung on to Mother, rolling around like a heavy bundle as our cart dug ruts in the road. But they were quickly trampled and torn up by carts, pack animals, and the people behind us. There were refugees everywhere, a great mass of faces — some familiar, others not. The going was treacherous — for the people, for the horses, and for the donkeys. The only ones having a relatively easy time were the chickens in old women's arms and my goat, which pranced along, even stopping from time to time to nibble on the dead leaves of reeds.

The sunlight raised a painful glare on the alkali ground cover, so bright we had to close our eyes. The glare shimmered along the ground like quicksilver. Wilderness that spread out before us seemed like the legendary Northern Sea.

At noon, as if in the grips of an epidemic, the people began sitting down in groups without being told to do so. Deprived of water, their throats were smoky and their tongues were so thick and brackish they no longer functioned properly. Hot air spurted from their nostrils, but their backs and bellies were cold; the northern winds tore through sweaty clothes, turning them hard and stiff.

As she sat on a cart handle, Mother reached into one of the baskets and took out some windblown steamed buns, which she broke into pieces and handed to us. First Sister took a single bite and her lip split, oozing blood that stained the bun. The little ones in the cart, with their dusty faces and dirty hands, looked to be seven parts temple demon and three parts human. Hanging their heads, they refused the food. Eighth Sister nibbled on one of the dry buns with her dainty white teeth. "For all this you can thank your daddies and mommies,"

Mother said with a sigh. "Let's go home, Grandma," Sha Zaohua
pleaded. Without answering, Mother looked up at the crowds of people
on the hill and sighed once more. Then she looked at me. "Jintong,"
she said, "you're going to start eating differently from today on." She
reached into her bundle and took out an enamel mug stamped with a
red star. Then she walked over to my goat, bent down, and cleaned the
dirt off of one of its teats. When the goat balked, Mother told me to
hold it. After wrapping my arms around its cold head, I watched her
squeeze the animal's teat until a white liquid began dripping into the
mug. I could tell that the goat was not comfortable, for it was used to
having me lie down and drink directly from its teats. It kept moving its
head and arching its back like a cobra. All this time, Mother muttered
a terrifying phrase over and over: "Jintong, when will you start eating
regular food?" In days past, I'd tried a variety of foods, but even the
best of them gave me a stomachache, after which I'd start vomiting until all that came up was a yellow liquid. I looked at Mother with shame
in my eyes and launched a severe self-criticism. Because of my eccentric behavior, I'd brought Mother, not to mention myself, no end of
trouble. Sima Liang had once promised to cure me of this eccentricity,
but he hadn't shown his face from the day he'd run away. His cunning
little face flashed before my eyes. The lights that emanated from the
gunmetal blue bullet holes in the foreheads of Sima Feng and Sima
Huang made my skin crawl. I conjured up the sight of them lying side
by side in their tiny willow coffins. Mother had pasted little red pieces
of paper over the holes, turning bullet holes into little beauty marks.
After filling the mug half full, Mother stood up and found the milk
bottle the female soldier named Tang had given her for Sha Zaohua
years earlier. She twisted off the top and poured the milk in, then
handed me the bottle and watched me eagerly and somewhat apologetically. Although I hesitated before accepting the bottle, I didn't
want to let Mother down, and at the same time wanted to take my first
step toward freedom and happiness. So I stuck the yolk-colored rubber nipple into my mouth. Naturally, it couldn't compare with the real
things on the tips of Mother's breasts — hers were love, hers were poetry, hers were the highest realm of heaven and the rich soil under
golden waves of wheat — nor could it compare with the large, swollen,
speckled teats of my milk goat — hers were tumultuous life, hers were
surging passion. This was a lifeless object; though it was slippery, it
wasn't moist. But what I found downright scary was that it had no

taste. The mucous membranes of my mouth felt cold and greasy. But for Mother's sake, and for my own, I forced back the feelings of disgust and bit down on it. It spoke to me as a stream of milk, tinged with the acrid taste of alkaline soil, squirted awkwardly over my tongue and up against the walls of my mouth. I took another mouthful and reminded myself, This is for Mother. Another mouthful. This is for Shangguan Jintong. I kept taking in mouthfuls and swallowing them. This is for Shangguan Laidi, for Shangguan Zhaodi, for Shangguan Niandi, for Shangguan Lingdi, for Shangguan Xiangdi, for all the Shangguans who have loved me, cared for me, and helped me, and for that lively little imp, Sima Liang, who hasn't a drop of Shangguan blood flowing through his veins. I held my breath and, with this new tool, took the life-sustaining liquid into my body. Mother's face was bathed in tears when I handed the bottle back to her. Laidi laughed gleefully. "Little Uncle's grown up," Sha Zaohua said. Forcing myself to endure the spasms in my throat and the secret pain in my gut, I took several steps forward, as if everything were perfectly all right, and pissed with the wind, spiritedly trying to see how high and how far I could send the stream of golden yellow liquid. I saw the bank of the Flood Dragon River laid out not far from where I stood; and there, vaguely, were the steeple of our village church and the towering poplar in the yard of Fan the Fourth. After traveling all morning, we'd managed such a pitifully short distance.

Pandi, who had been demoted to district chairwoman of the Women's Salvation Society, rode in from the west on an old horse that was blind in one eye and had a numbered brand on its right flank. The animal kept its neck cocked at a strange angle and made a dull thudding sound as it ran up to us awkwardly on tired old hooves. Pandi hopped nimbly off the horse, even with her swollen belly. As I stared at her belly, I tried to see the child inside, but my eyes failed me, and all I saw were a few dark red spots on her gray uniform. "Don't stop here, Mother," Pandi said. "We've got water boiling up ahead. That's where you should eat lunch." "Pandi," Mother said, "I tell you, we don't want any part of your evacuation." "You must, Mother," Pandi said anxiously. "It'll be different when the enemy returns this time. In the Bohai District, they slaughtered three thousand people in one day. The Landlord Restitution Corps even killed their own mothers." "I don't believe anyone could kill their own mothers," Mother said. "I don't care what you, say, Mother," Pandi insisted. "I'm not going to let you go back. That's walking straight into the net, sheer suicide. And if you're not concerned about yourself, at least be concerned about all these kids." She took a little bottle out of her knapsack, unscrewed the cap, and dumped out some little white pills, which she handed to Mother. "These are vitamin pills," she said. "Each one supplies more nutrition than a head of cabbage and two eggs. When you've worn yourself out, take one of these, and give one to each of the children. After this stretch of alkaline soil, the road gets better, and the local folks of the Northern Sea will welcome us with open arms. So let's go, Mother. This is no place to rest." She grabbed a handful of horse's mane, stepped into the stirrup, and swung up into the saddle. As she galloped off, she shouted, "Fellow villagers, get on the road. There's hot water and oil and salted vegetables and scallions waiting for you at Wang Family Mound!"

At her urging, the people got to their feet and continued on their way.

Mother wrapped the pills in a bandanna and tucked them away in her pocket. Then she draped the strap around her neck and picked up the handles of the cart. "Come on, kids, let's go."

The evacuation procession lengthened until we couldn't see either end, front or back. We walked until we reached Wang Family Mound, but there was no hot water there, nor any oil, and certainly no salted vegetables or scallions. The donkey company had left by the time we reached the village; the ground was littered with patches of straw and donkey droppings. People lit bonfires to cook dry food, while some of the boys dug up wild garlic with spiked tree branches. As we were leaving Wang Family Mound, we saw the mute and a dozen or so of his production team members coming toward us to reenter the village. Instead of dismounting, he took two half-cooked sweet potatoes and a red-skinned turnip out from under his shirt and tossed them into one of the baskets on our cart. It nearly cracked open the head of Little Mute. I took special note of the grin he flashed at First Sister. He looked like a snarling wolf or a tiger.

When the sun fell behind the mountain, we dragged our lengthening shadows into a bustling little village, where dense white smoke poured out of every chimney. Exhausted citizens lay strewn all over the streets, like scattered logs. A group of spirited officials in gray were hopping up and down amid the local villagers. At the head of the village, people crowded around the well to fetch water. The crowd was made even denser by the addition of livestock; the taste of fresh water roused the villagers. My goat snorted loudly. Laidi, carrying a large bowl — apparently a rare ceramic treasure — tried to jostle her way up to the well, but was pushed back time and again. An old cook who worked for the county government recognized us and brought us a bucket of water. Zaohua and Laidi rushed over, got down on all fours, and banged heads as they began lapping up the water. "Children first!" Mother scolded Laidi, who paused just long enough for Zaohua to bury her face in the bucket. She lapped up the water like a thirsty calf, the only difference being that she held the sides with her filthy hands. "That's enough. You'll get a bellyache if you drink too much," Mother said as she pulled her away from the bucket. Zaohua licked her lips to get every last drop, as her moistened insides began to rumble. After drinking her fill, First Sister stood up; her belly stuck way out. Mother scooped up some water for Big Mute and Little Mute. Eighth Sister sniffed the air and made her way over to the bucket, where she knelt down and buried her face in the water. "Want to drink a little, Jintong?" Mother asked me. I shook my head. She scooped up another bowlful of water as I let go of the goat, which would have run over to the water long before if I hadn't wrapped my arms around its neck. The goat drank thirstily from the bucket and didn't look up once as the water sloshed down its throat and swelled its belly. The old cook showed his feelings, not with words, but with a long sigh, and when Mother thanked him, he sighed again, even louder.

"What took you so long to get here, Mother?" Pandi asked critically. Mother didn't give her the satisfaction of responding. Instead she picked up the handles of the cart and led us, goat and all, twisting and turning through the crowd, into a small courtyard ringed by a rammed-earth wall; we suffered no end of curses and complaints as we wound our way through tiny spaces amid the crowd of people. Pandi helped Mother take the little ones off the cart in order to leave the cart and goat outside the courtyard, where the donkeys and horses were tethered. There were no baskets and no hay, so the animals fed on the bark of the trees. We left the cart in the lane, but took the goat inside with us. Pandi gave me a look, but didn't say anything, since she knew that that goat was my lifeline.

Inside the house, a dark shadow swayed in the bright lamplight. A county official was bickering loudly about something. We heard Lu Liren's hoarse voice. Armed soldiers were loitering in the courtyard, nursing their sore feet. Stars twinkled in the deepening night. Pandi led us into one of the side rooms, where a weak lantern projected ghostly shadows onto the walls. An old woman, dressed in funeral clothes, lay in an open coffin. She opened her eyes when we entered. "Do me a favor, kind people, and put the lid on my coffin," she said. "I want this space to myself." "What's this all about, old aunty?" Mother asked her. "This is an auspicious day for me," the old woman replied. "Do that for me, will you, kind people?" "Try to make the best of it, Mother," Pandi said. "It's better than sleeping in the street."

We did not sleep well that night. The bickering in the main room continued late into the night, and the moment it stopped, gunfire erupted out on the street. That disturbance was followed by a blazing fire in the village, the flames licking skyward like red silk banners, lighting up our faces and that of the old woman lying comfortably in her coffin. At sunrise she was no longer moving. Mother called out to her, but she didn't open her eyes. A check of her pulse showed that she had died. "She's a semi-immortal," Mother said as she and First Sister placed the lid on.

The next few days were even harder on us, and by the time we reached the foot of Da'ze Mountain, Mother's and First Sister's feet were rubbed raw. Big and Little Mute had both developed coughs, while Shengli had a fever and diarrhea. Reminded of the pills Fifth Sister had given her, Mother took out one and gave it to Shengli. Poor Eighth Sister was the only one who wasn't sick. It had been two full days since we'd last seen Pandi or, for that matter, any county or district officials. We'd seen the mute once, as he carried a wounded soldier on his back, a man whose leg had been blown off, and whose blood dripped off his torn, useless pant leg. He was sobbing. "Do a good deed, Commander, finish me off, the pain's killing me, oh dear Mother . . ."

It must have been on our fifth day on the road when we saw a tall, white, tree-covered mountain rise up out of the north. A little monastery sat on its peak. From the bank of the Flood Dragon River, behind our house, this mountain was visible on clear days; but it had always shown up dark green. Seeing it close up, its shape and clean, crisp smell made me realize how far from home we had traveled. As we walked along a broad gravel-paved road, we met a detachment of troops on horseback coming toward us; the soldiers were dressed the same as those of the 16th Regiment. It was clear, as they passed us, heading in the opposite direction, that our home had become a battlefield. Foot soldiers were the next to come down the road, followed by a detachment of donkeys pulling artillery pieces, the muzzles sporting bouquets of flowers; soldiers perched on the big guns had smug, confident airs. After the artillery detachment passed, stretcher bearers and two columns of wagon troops came down the road; the wagons were loaded with sacks of flour and rice, plus bales of hay. We hugged the roadsides timidly to let the troops pass.

Some of the foot soldiers stepped out of line with their Mausers and asked what was going on. At this point, Wang Chao, the barber, who had joined the procession with his smart-looking rubber-tired cart, ran into trouble, as one of the wooden-wheeled provisions carts broke an axle. The driver flipped the cart over, removed the axle, and examined it closely until his hands were black with grease. His son was no more than fifteen or sixteen, with sores on his face and an ulcerated mouth. He was wearing a shirt with no buttons and a belt made of hemp. "What happened, Dad?" he said. "The axle's broken, son." Father and son took the wheel off of the axle. "Now what, Dad?" His father walked to the side of the road and wiped his greasy hands on the rough bark of a poplar tree. "Nothing we can do," he said. Just then a one-armed soldier in a thin army uniform, rifle over his back and a dogskin cap on his head, stepped out of the line of carts ahead and ran over.

"Wang Jin!" he shouted angrily. "What are you doing out of line? What's the idea? Are you trying to make our Iron and Steel Company lose face?"

"Political Instructor," Wang Jin said with a frown, "we broke an axle."

"You couldn't let it happen a little earlier or a little later, could you? You had to wait till we were going into battle, didn't you? I told you to check your cart carefully before we left, didn't I?" He slapped Wang Jin angrily.

"Ouch!" Wang Jin yelped as he lowered his head; blood trickled out of his nose.

"Why did you hit my father?" the gutsy youngster asked the political instructor.

The political instructor froze. "I didn't do it intentionally," he said. "But you're right, I shouldn't have bumped him. But if the provisions don't get there in time, I'll have you both shot."

"We didn't break the axle on purpose," the youngster said. "We're poor and we had to borrow this cart from my aunt."

Wang Jin pulled some ratty cotton filling out of his sleeve and stuffed it up his bloody nose. "Political Instructor," he muttered, "please be reasonable."

"Reasonable?" the political instructor said menacingly. "Getting provisions up to the front lines is reasonable. Not getting them there is unreasonable. I've had enough of your prattling. You're going to transport these two hundred and forty pounds of millet up to Taoguan Township if you have to lug it on your backs!"

"Political Instructor, you're always saying how we need to be practical and realistic. Two hundred and forty pounds of millet . . . he's just a boy . . . please, I beg you . . ."

The political instructor looked up into the sunny sky, then down at his watch, and surveyed the area. His gaze fell first on our wooden-wheeled cart, then on Wang Chao's rubber-tired cart.

Wang Chao was a bachelor, a practiced barber who had made plenty of money, some of which he spent on his favorite food, pig's head. Well fed, he had a square face, big ears, and a healthy complexion. Nothing like a farmer. In his cart he carried a box with his barber's tools and an expensive quilt wrapped with a dog's pelt. The cart was made from the wood of a scholar tree, coated with tung oil that made the wood shine. It was a good-looking, good-smelling cart. Before setting out, he'd pumped up the tires, so that the cart bounced lightly on the hard surface of the road, hardly disturbing its contents. A strong man, he was never without a flask of liquor, from which he drank regularly as he moved spryly, singing little ditties and having a grand old time. Among us refugees, he was royalty.

The political instructor's dark eyes rolled in his head as he headed over to the side of the road with a smile on his lips. "Where are you people from?" he asked pleasantly.

No one answered him. Then his glance shifted to the face of Wang Chao and his smile vanished, replaced by a look as formidable as a mountain and as forbidding as a remote monastery. "What do you do for a living?" he asked, his eyes fixed on Wang Chao's big, oily face.

Wang Chao rather stupidly looked away, tongue-tied.

"By the looks of you," the political instructor said, "if you're not a landlord, you're a rich peasant, and if you're not a rich peasant, you're a shop owner. Whatever you are, you certainly don't make a living by the sweat of your brow. No, you're a parasite who lives by exploiting others!"

"You've got me all wrong, Commander," Wang Chao protested. "I'm a barber, a man who makes a living with his hands. I live in two run-down rooms. I've got no land, no wife, and no kids. If I eat my fill, no one in the family goes hungry. I eat for today, and let tomorrow take care of itself. They checked my background at the district and gave me a label as an artisan, which is the same as a middle peasant, basic work."

"Nonsense!" the one-armed man said. "As I see it, you may have a clever mouth, but a parrot can't talk its way through Tong Pass. I'm commandeering your cart!" He turned to Wang Jin and his son. "Take down the millet and load it on this cart."

"Commander," Wang Chao said, "this little cart cost me half a lifetime of savings. You're not supposed to appropriate poor people's possessions."

The one-armed man replied angrily, "I gave one of my arms in the cause of victory. Just how much is one little cart worth? Our front-line troops are waiting for these provisions, and I don't want to hear any protests from you."

"You and I are from different districts, sir," Wang Chao said. "And different counties. So what authority do you have to commandeer my cart?"

"Who cares about county or district," the one-armed man said. "This is support for the front lines."

"No," Wang Chao, "I can't let you do that."

The one-armed man knelt down on one knee, took out a pen, and removed its cap with his teeth. Then he laid a slip of paper across his knee and scribbled something on it. "What's your name?" he asked. "And which county and district are you from?"

Wang Chao told him.

"Your county head, Lu Liren, and I are old comrades-in-arms. So here's what we'll do. After the battle's over, you give this to him, and he'll see that you get a new cart."

Wang Chao pointed to us and said, "That's Lu Liren's mother-in-law, sir. That's his family."

"Madam," the one-armed man said, "you'll be my witness. Just tell him that the situation was critical, and that Guo Mofu, political instructor of the Eighth Militia Company of the Bohai District, borrowed a pushcart belonging to the villager Wang Chao, and ask him to take care of it for me."

Then he turned back to Wang Chao. "That'll do it," he said as he pressed the slip of paper into Wang's hand. Then he turned and said angrily to Wang Jin, "What are you standing around for? If we don't get these provisions there in time, you and your son will taste the whip, and me, Guo Mofu, I'll taste the bullet!" He turned to Wang Chao. "Unload your cart, and be quick about it!"

"What am I supposed to do, sir?" Wang Chao said.

"If you're worried about your cart, you can come along with us. Our porter company has enough food for one more man. Once the battle's over, you can take your cart with you."

"But, sir, I just escaped from there," Wang Chao said tearfully.

"Are you going to make me take out my pistol and put a bullet in you?" the enraged political instructor demanded. "We're not afraid to spill blood and make sacrifices for the revolution. I can't believe you're making such a fuss over a little cart."

"Aunt," Wang Chao said pathetically. "You're my witness."

Mother nodded.

Wang Jin and his son gleefully walked off with Wang Chao's rubber-tired cart, as the one-armed man nodded politely to Mother, before turning and running off to catch up with his men.

Wang Chao sat down on his quilt, a pained look on his face, mumbling to himself. "Talk about bad luck! Why does everything happen to me? Who did I offend?" Tears slid down his fat cheeks.

We finally made it to the foot of the mountain, where the gravel road spoked off into ten or more narrow paths that wound their way up the mountainside. That evening, the refugees gathered in groups where all sorts of dialects were spoken, to pass on conflicting reports. We suffered through the night huddled amid the underbrush at the foot of the mountain. Dull explosions, like peals of thunder, sounded both to the north and the south, as artillery shells tore through the darkness in sweeping arcs. The air turned cold and damp as the night deepened, and bitter winds snaked out of mountain crevasses, violently shaking the leaves and branches of our shelter and setting fallen leaves rustling. Foxes in their dens cried mournfully. Sick children moaned like unhappy cats; the coughs from old folks sounded like gongs being struck. It was a terrible night, and when dawn broke, we would find dozens of frozen corpses lining the mountain hollows — children, old folks, even young men and women. Our family owed its survival to the unusual low trees, with their golden leaves, that protected us. They were the only trees whose leaves had not fallen. We lay together on the thick, dry grass beneath the trees, huddled under the one quilt we'd brought. My goat lay up against my back and shielded me from the wind. The hours after midnight were the worst. The rumble of artillery fire to the south only increased the stillness of the night; people's moans cut deeply into our hearts and made us tremble. A melody much like the familiar "cat's meow," our local drama, sounded in our ears. It was a woman's sobs. Amid the overwhelming silence, the sounds sliced into the rocks, cold and damp, and dark clouds stuck to the icy quilt that covered us. Then the rain came, freezing rain; raindrops fell on our quilt, they fell on the rustling yellow leaves, they fell on the mountainside, they fell on the refugees' heads, and they fell on the thick coats of baying wolves. Most of the raindrops turned to ice before they hit the ground, where they formed a hard crust.

I was reminded of that night years before when Elder Fan Three had led us away from sure death, his torch held high, flames the red of a roan colt dancing in the air. That night I'd been immersed in a warm sea of milk, holding on to a full breast with both hands and feeling myself fly up to Paradise. But now the frightful apparition began, like a golden ray of light splitting the darkness, or like the beam of light from Babbitt's film projector; thousands of icy droplets danced in the light, like beetles, as a woman with long, flowing hair appeared, a cape like sunset draped over her shoulders, its embedded pearls glittering and casting shimmers of light, some long and some short. Her face kept changing: first Laidi; then the Bird Fairy; then the single-breasted woman, Old Jin; and then suddenly the American woman . . .

"Jintong!" Mother was calling me. She brought me out of my hallucinations. In the darkness, she and First Sister were massaging my arms and legs to bring me back before I fell into the abyss of death.

The sound of someone crying emerged from the underbrush in the hazy sunlight of early morning. People faced with the stiffened corpses of loved ones gave vent to their grief with loud wails. But thanks to the yellow leaves on the trees above us and the tattered quilt that covered us, all seven of our hearts were still beating. Mother handed each of us one of the pills Pandi had given her. I said I didn't want mine, so Mother shoved it into the mouth of my goat. After chewing up the pill, the goat turned its attention to the leaves of the underbrush; they, like the branches from which they hung, were covered by a filmy layer of ice, which also hung from boulders on the mountainside. There was no wind, but a freezing rain continued to fall, making a loud tattoo on the branches. The surface of the mountain glistened like a mirror.

One of the refugees, leading a donkey with a woman's corpse draped over its back, was trying to make his way up one of the mountain paths. But the going was so treacherous that the donkey slipped on the ice, and every time it got to its feet, it hit the ground again. The man wanted to help, but he invariably fell down too. It did not take long for their plight to result in the corpse slipping off the animal's back and into a ditch. Just then a golden-pelted wildcat emerged from one of the mountain hollows carrying a child in its mouth as it bounded awkwardly from one boulder to another, struggling to keep its balance as it moved. A woman whose hair was in disarray was chasing the wildcat, shrieking and wailing as she ran, but she too kept losing her footing on the icy rocks. Unfazed, every time she fell, she scrambled to her feet and continued the chase, for which she paid a heavy price: chin split open, teeth knocked out, a gash on the back of her head, broken fingernails, a sprained ankle, a dislocated shoulder, and traumatized internal organs. And still she kept going, until the wildcat slowed down enough for her to grab it by the tail.

Danger lurked for everyone: if they tried to move, they fell; if they didn't try, they froze to death. And since freezing to death was not an option, they kept falling, and soon lost sight of their evacuation goal. The mountaintop monastery had by then turned white and gave off a frigid glare. So did the trees halfway up the mountain. At that height, the freezing rain turned to snow. Lacking the nerve to climb to the top, the people merely kept moving at the foot of the mountain. We looked up and spotted the body of Wang Chao the barber hanging from a rubber tree; he had looped his belt over a low-hanging branch, the weight of his body nearly breaking it off from the trunk. The toes of his shoes were touching the ground, his pants were down around his knees, and his padded jacket was tied around his waist to salvage his image, even in death. One look at that purple face and protruding tongue, and I turned away in disgust. But too late to keep the image of his dead face from appearing often in my dreams from that day on. No one gave him a second thought, although several simple-looking people were fighting over his quilt and the dog pelt that covered it. In the midst of their grappling, a tall young man suddenly screamed in pain; a ratty little man beside him had bitten off a chunk of one of his protruding ears. The fellow spat the earlobe into his hand, looked it over, and handed it back to it owner, before picking up the heavy quilt and dog pelt. To keep from falling, he took little hops over to the side of an old man, who promptly whacked him on the head with a forked stick used to keep a cart from rolling away. The little fellow hit the ground like a sack of rice. The old man picked up the quilt, backed up against a tree, holding on to his prize with one hand and brandishing his forked stick with the other. Some foolhardy young devils entertained thoughts of taking the quilt away from the old man, but a mere tap of his forked stick sent them tumbling to the ground. The old man was wearing a long robe cinched at the waist with a length of coarse cloth from which hung his pipe and tobacco pouch. His long white beard was dotted with icy globules. "Come on if you're willing to die!" he shouted shrilly as his face seemed to lengthen and green lights shot from his eyes. His would-be attackers fled in panic.

Mother reached a decision: Turn back!

Picking up the handles of the cart, she wobbled off in a southwestern direction. The ice-covered axle creaked and groaned. But we set an example for others, who, without a word, fell in behind us — some even passed us in their hurry to get back to their homes.

Shards of ice crackled and exploded beneath the wheels, but were quickly replaced by the freezing rain that continued to fall. Before long, ice the size of buckshot pierced our earlobes and stung our faces. The vast countryside set up a loud cacophony. We headed back much the same way as we'd come: Mother pushing the cart from behind, while First Sister pulled from the front. First Sister's shoes split open in the back, exposing her chapped, frozen heels, and forced her to walk as if she were performing a rice-sprout dance. Every time Mother tipped the cart over, First Sister went down with it. The rope was pulled so taut that she fell head over heels more than once, until she cried out with every step she took. Zaohua and I were crying too, but not Mother. Her eyes had a blue cast as she bit down on her lip for strength. She moved cautiously, but with courage and steely determination. Her tiny feet were like two little spades that dug solidly into the ground. Eighth Sister followed silently behind, holding on to Mother's clothes with a hand that looked like a rotten, water-soaked eggplant.

We were in a hurry to get home, and by noontime we'd reached the broad, poplar-lined gravel road. Although the sun hadn't broken through the clouds, the sky was bright and the road seemed paved with glazed tiles. Snowflakes gradually replaced the hailstones, turning the road, the trees, and the surrounding fields white. We saw many corpses along the way, human and animal, and an occasional sparrow or magpie or wild hen. But no dead crows. Their black feathers were nearly blue against the white backdrop, and glossy. They feasted on the dead, making quite a racket.

Then our luck improved. First, next to a dead horse we found half a sack of chopped straw mixed with broad beans and bran. That filled my goat's belly, and what was left was used to cover the feet of Big and Little Mute to protect them against the wind and snow. Once the goat had eaten its fill, it licked snow for the moisture. I knew what it meant when it nodded in my direction. After we were back on the road, Zaohua said she smelled roasted wheat in the air. Mother told her to follow the smell to its source. In a little hut overlooking a cemetery, we discovered the body of a dead soldier; lying beside him were two sacks filled with roasted wheat. We'd grown used to seeing dead people, and were no longer afraid. We spent the night in that hut.

First, Mother and First Sister dragged the dead young soldier outside. He'd killed himself by holding his rifle against his chest and putting the muzzle into his mouth, and then, after removing his worn sock, pulling the trigger with his toe. The bullet had blown off the top of his head; rats had eaten his ears and nose and had gnawed his fingers down to the bone, until they looked like willow twigs. Hordes of rats glared red-eyed as Mother and First Sister dragged him outside. Even though she was exhausted, Mother wanted to give thanks for the food, so she knelt on the frozen ground and, using the soldier's bayonet, dug a shallow hole to bury his head. A little dugout like that meant next to nothing to a bunch of rats who survived by digging holes, but it brought comfort to Mother.

The hut was barely big enough to accommodate our little family and its goat. We blocked the door with our cart, with Mother sitting closest to the door, armed with the soldier's brain-spattered rifle. As night fell, clusters of people tried to squeeze into our little hut; there were plenty of thieves and no-accounts among them, but Mother frightened them all away with her rifle. One man with a big mouth and malevolent eyes challenged her: "You know how to shoot that?" he said as he tried to force his way in. Mother poked at him with the rifle. She didn't know how to shoot it. So Laidi took it away from her, pulled back the bolt, ejecting a spent cartridge, then pushed the bolt forward, sending a bullet into the chamber. Then she aimed the rifle above the man's head and pulled the trigger. A column of smoke rose to the ceiling. Watching the way Laidi handled the weapon made me think of her glorious history as she followed Sha Yueliang from battlefield to battlefield. The big-mouthed man crawled away like a whipped dog. Mother looked at Laidi with gratitude in her eyes, before getting up and moving inside so the new guard could take her place.

That night I slept like a baby, not waking up until red sunbeams had lit up the snowy white world. I wanted to get down on my knees and beg Mother to let us stay in this ghostly little hut, stay here next to this towering cemetery, stay in this snow-covered pine grove. "Let's not leave this happy spot, this lucky spot." But she picked up the handles of her cart and led us back on the road. The rifle lay alongside Shengli, under our tattered quilt.

There was half a foot of snow on the road; it crunched beneath our feet and the wheels of our cart. No longer falling as often, we were able to make pretty good time. The glare of the sun was blinding, making us look especially dark by contrast, no matter what we were wearing. Mother was bolder than usual that day, maybe because of the presence of the rifle in the basket and Laidi's ability to use it. She turned into a bit of a tyrant at around noon, when a retreating soldier, a straggler from the south, the sling around his arm giving the illusion that he was wounded, decided he'd search our cart. Mother slapped him so hard his gray cap flew off. He took off running without even stopping to retrieve his cap, which Mother picked up and clapped onto the head of my goat. The goat wore its new cap proudly; the cold, hungry refugees around us parted their lips and, with what energy they had left, managed an array of laughter that actually sounded worse than weeping and wailing.

Early the next day, after my morning meal of goat's milk, my spirits soared; my thoughts were lively and my perceptions keen. As I looked around, I discovered the county government's printing machine and the document-filled metal cases lying abandoned by the side of the road. Where were the porters? No way of knowing. And the mule company? Gone too.

There was plenty of activity on the road, as columns of stretcher bearers headed south with their moaning cargo of wounded soldiers. The bearers panted from exhaustion, their faces bathed in sweat; they kicked snow into the air with their ragged movements. A woman in white was staggering along behind the stretcher bearers when one of them stumbled and fell, dumping the shrieking soldier he was carrying onto the ground. The man's head was swathed in bandages, leaving only the black holes of his nostrils and his pale lips visible. A soldier carrying a leather case on her back rushed up to curse the careless porter and console the wounded soldier. I recognized her at once: it was the woman named Tang, Pandi's comrade-in-arms. She cursed the militiamen in the coarsest language and spoke gently to the wounded soldiers. I saw deep wrinkles on her forehead and crow's feet at the corners of her eyes; a once vivacious young soldier had turned into a haggard, matronly woman. But she didn't even look at us, and Mother didn't seem to recognize her.

The line of stretchers seemed never-ending. We hugged the side of the road so as not to slow down their procession. Finally, the last stretcher passed, leaving the icy roadway a mess from all the tramping it had withstood. Melted snow was now nothing but dirty water and mud; unmelted snow was spotted with fresh blood, giving it the horrifying look of rotting skin. My heart clenched as my nostrils filled with the smell of melting snow and the stench of human blood. That and the repulsive smell of sweaty bodies. We got back on the road, with considerably more trepidation now; even the milk goat, which had been prancing along proudly with its army cap, trembled fearfully, like a new recruit on his first day in battle. The rest of the people paced up and down on the road, unable to decide whether to keep going or to head back. The road to the southwest led to a battlefield, that was a given, and would take us straight into a forest of weapons and a hailstorm of gunfire; everyone knew that bullets don't have eyes, that artillery shells aren't given to apologies, and that soldiers are tigers down off the mountain, none of them vegetarians. People cast questioning glances back and forth, but no answers were forthcoming. Without looking at anyone, Mother forged ahead with her cart. When I turned to look, I saw that some of the refugees had turned and were heading to the northeast, while others fell in behind us.

9

We spent the first night after the fighting in the same place we'd spent the first night of the evacuation: the same little courtyard and the same little side room, complete with the coffin in which the old woman had lain. The only difference was that nearly all the buildings in the tiny village had been leveled; even the three-room hut where Lu Liren and members of the county government had lived was now nothing but a pile of rubble. We entered the village just before nightfall, when the setting sun was a blood-red ball. The street was littered with broken bodies; twenty or more mangled corpses had been stacked neatly in an open square, as if connected by an invisible thread. The air was hot and dry; a number of trees with charred limbs appeared to have been struck by lightning. *Clank!* First Sister stubbed her toe on a helmet with a hole in it. I stumbled and fell after stepping on a bunch of spent cartridges that were still warm to the touch. The smell of burnt rubber hung in the air, mixed with the pungent odor of gunpowder. The black barrel of a lonely cannon poked out from a pile of broken bricks, pointing up at cold stars flickering in the sky. The village was quiet as death; we felt as if we were walking through the legendary halls of Hell. The number of refugees following us home had slowly dwindled until finally there were no more — we were alone. Mother had stubbornly brought us here. Tomorrow we would cross the alkaline-blanketed northern bank of the Flood Dragon River, then the river itself, and from there to the place we called home. We'd be home. Home.

Amid the ruins of the village, only that little two-room hut remained standing, as if it had continued to exist just for us. We pulled away the fallen beams and posts that blocked the door and went inside. The first thing we saw was the coffin, which brought home the realization that after nearly twenty days and nights, we were right back where we had spent that first night. "The will of Heaven!" Mother said tersely.

As soon as it was light outside, Mother got busy putting the kids and our belongings — rifle included — on the cart.

Suddenly the road was swarming with people, most in army uniforms, and all equipped with leather belts from which wood-handled grenades hung. Spent cartridges lay here and there on the ground, and in the roadside ditch artillery casings lay alongside dead horses with their bellies blown open. Mother abruptly reached into the cart for the rifle and flung it into the icy water in the ditch. A man carrying two heavy wooden cases on a shoulder pole looked at us in astonishment. He laid down his load and retrieved the rifle.

As we neared Wang Family Mound, a blast of hot air hit us in the face, as if from a huge smelting oven. Smoke and mist hung over the village, trees at the entrance were covered with soot, and hordes of flies that seemed out of place swarmed from the rotting innards of dead horses to the faces of dead humans.

To avoid trouble, Mother turned onto a path that skirted our village; the badly rutted path made the going difficult for our cart, so she put it down, took the oil jug off the handle, dipped a feather into the oil, and spread it on the axle and the hubs of the wheels. Her puffy hands looked like baked sorghum cakes. "Let's go into that stand of trees to rest awhile," Mother said after she finished oiling the cart. After so many days on the road, Shengli and Big and Little Mute had gotten used to doing what they were told without so much as a whimper. They knew that riding in the cart cost them their right to object to anything. The freshly oiled wheels now sang out loudly. Not far off the path was a desiccated patch of sorghum with dried-out buds on the dark tassels, some pointing to the sky, others sagging to the ground.

As we drew up to the trees, we discovered a hidden artillery blind with dozens of cannon barrels, looking like the necks of aging turtles. Tree branches had been used as camouflage; the wheels were mired deeply in the ground. A row of cases lay on the ground behind the big guns, the open ones revealing artillery shells neatly stacked and looking quite pampered. The gun crews, all wearing camouflage headgear, were squatting or standing under trees, drinking water out of enamel bowls. A cauldron with iron handles sat on a rack over an open fire behind them. Horsemeat was cooking in the cauldron. How did I know it was horsemeat? I spotted a horse hoof, ringed with long hairs, like goat whiskers, poking up over the top, a horseshoe glinting in the sunlight. The cook was putting the branch of a pine tree into the fire. Flames licked skyward as the liquid in the cauldron roiled and steamed, causing the pitiful horse's leg to tremble nonstop.

A man who looked like an officer came running up and gently urged us to turn around and head back. Mother replied with cold self-assurance. "Captain," she said, "if you force us to leave, we have no choice. But we will just have to find another way around the place." "Don't you fear for your lives?" the man said, clearly puzzled. "You're not afraid of losing your family to artillery fire? You don't know how powerful these guns are." "We've come this far not because we're afraid of death, but because death is afraid of us," Mother replied. The man stepped aside. "You're free to go where you want."

We moved on, traveling through an alkaline wilderness. We had no choice but to follow along behind Mother. Actually, we were following along behind Laidi. Throughout our arduous journey, Laidi pulled the cart like an uncomplaining beast of burden and, when necessary, stopped to fire the rifle at anyone who threatened our safety when we stopped for the night, for which she earned my admiration and respect.

The deeper we went into the wilderness, the harder the going on the heavily trampled road. So we moved off the road and onto the alkaline ground. Unmelted snow made the ground look like a head with scabies, the occasional clump of dead grass like tufts of hair. Though danger seemed to lurk in the area, noisy flocks of larks still flew overhead and a cluster of wild rabbits the color of dead grass set up a skirmish line before a white fox, attacking it with high-pitched whoops. Having suffered bitterly and nursing deep hatred for the fox, they mounted a heroic charge. Behind them, a bunch of wild goats with finely chiseled faces moved up in fits and starts, and I couldn't tell if they were backing up the rabbits or just curious.

Something in the grass glittered in the sunlight. Zaohua ran over, picked it up, and handed it to me across the cart. It was a metal mess kit. Inside were little golden-fried fish. I handed it back to her. She picked up one of the fish and offered it to Mother, who said, "None for me. You eat it." Zaohua ate the fish daintily, like a cat. Big Mute reached out from the basket with his dirty little hand and grunted, "Ao!" Little Mute did the same. Both boys had square, gourdlike faces, eyes high up on their heads, which made their foreheads seem smaller than normal. Their noses were flat, with long grooves that led to wide mouths and short, upturned upper lips that failed to hide their yellow teeth. Zaohua looked over at Mother to see what she should do. But Mother was looking off into the distance. So Zaohua picked up two of the fish and gave them each one. Now the mess kit was empty, except for a few scraps of fish and little spots of oil. She licked it clean. "Let's rest awhile," Mother said. "We don't have far to go before we should be able to see the church."

I lay on my back on the alkaline ground and gazed up into the sky. Mother and First Sister took off their shoes and knocked them against the handles of the cart to empty them of alkaline soil. The heels of their feet looked like rotten yams. All of a sudden, a frightened flock of birds swooped down close to the ground. Had they seen a hawk? No, it was a pair of black, double-winged airships buzzing through the sky from the southeast. The sound they made was like a thousand spinning wheels turning at the same time. At first they were flying high up in the air, traveling slowly, but when they were directly over-head, they went into a dive and picked up speed. They flew with the grace of winged calves, plunging at full speed, propellers buzzing loudly, like hornets circling the head of a cow. As they flew past, nearly scraping the top of our cart, one of the goggled men behind the glass smiled at us like an old friend. I thought he looked familiar, but before I could get a good look, he and his smile sped past me like a bolt of lightning. A violent gust of swirling wind, carrying a cloud of fine dust sucked up loose grass, sand, and rabbit pellets, and flung them into us like a hail of bullets. The mess kit in Zaohua's hand flew into the air. Panic-stricken, I jumped up, spitting dirt out of my mouth, as the sec-ond airship bore down on me even more savagely, spitting two long tongues of flame from its belly. Bullets kicked up dirt all around us. Trailing black smoke behind them, the airships tacked to one side and flew into the sky above the sandy ridge. Flames continued to spurt from under their wings in bursts, the sound like barking dogs, sending more puffs of yellow dirt up into the air. They dove and dipped like swallows skimming the surface of water, swooping down recklessly and then abruptly soaring upward again, sunlight dancing off the glass and turning the wings a bright steel blue. Dust gray soldiers on the sandy ridges were thrown into a panic, leaping and shouting. Yellow flames spat into the sky around them, announcing the insistent crack of gun-fire, like continuous gusts of wind. The airships were like gigantic startled birds wheeling through the sky, the sound of their engines like a crazed form of singing. One of them abruptly stopped wheeling as thick black smoke belched from its belly; it gurgled, it rocked, it spun, and then it plunged straight down into the wilderness, gouging out a furrow in the mud below. The wings shuddered briefly before a crack-ling ball of fire consumed its belly, creating an earsplitting blast that rocked all the wild rabbits in the vicinity. The other bird banked sharply high above with a cry of anguish, and flew off.

At that moment, we saw that half of Big Mute's head had disappeared and that a fist-sized hole had appeared in Little Mute's belly. Not yet dead, he showed us the whites of his eyes. Mother grabbed a handful of alkaline dirt and pressed it up against the hole, but too late to hold back the sizzling green liquid and white intestines that squirmed out. She rammed more and more dirt up into the hole, but couldn't stop the flow. Little Mute's intestines began filling up the basket. My goat's front legs buckled, drawing a series of strange-sounding complaints; then its belly contracted violently and its back arched, as it threw up a mouthful of half-eaten grass. First Sister and I both bent over and vomited. Mother, her hands smeared with fresh blood, stood there gaping in bewilderment at the mass of intestines. Her lips were quivering; suddenly, her mouth flew open, releasing a jet of red liquid, followed by loud, grief-stricken wails.

Shortly after that, volleys of black artillery shells tore into the sky like flocks of crows from the artillery blind in the little stand of trees, heading straight for our village. Blue flashes of light turned the sky above the grove the color of lilacs. The sun was a dull, colorless gray. After the first volley, the ground trembled, followed by the shrieks of the shells overhead; then came the muted thuds of explosions, sending columns of white smoke into the air above our village. Finally, the shooting stopped, producing a momentary silence that was quickly shattered when guns on the opposite bank of the Flood Dragon River sent their answer our way with even bigger shells; some landed among the trees, others fell in the open wilderness. And so it went, like a series of family visits. Waves of hot air swept across the wilderness. After an hour or so, the stand of trees went up in flames as the guns fell silent. But not those from our village, as their shells fell farther and farther off in the distance. All of a sudden, the sky above the sandy ridge was blue with flying shells that whistled through the air and landed on our village. The volleys dwarfed those that had come from the trees, both in numbers and impact. I've described the volleys from the grove as flocks of crows. Well, those that burst from behind the sandy ridge were like neat formations of little black pigs, with loud oinks and twitching tails until they chased each other straight into our village. When they landed, they were no longer little black pigs, but big black panthers, tigers, wild boars, biting everything they touched with fangs like ripsaws. As the artillery battle raged, the airships returned; but this time there were twelve of them, flying in pairs, wingtip to wingtip. From high up in the sky, they dropped their eggs, creating holes over the landscape. And then? A column of tanks rumbled out of our village. At the time I didn't know those clumsy machines with long, trunk-like gun barrels were called tanks. Once the column reached the alkaline wilderness, the tanks spread out, followed by helmeted foot soldiers, trotting at a crouch and firing into the air. *Pow pow pow. Pow pow pow. Pow pow pow pow pow pow pow.* Hit-or-miss. We dashed over to one of the artillery craters, where some of us sat and others flattened out on the ground, yet calmly, as if unafraid.

The caterpillar tracks under the tanks sped along, one link following the other, carrying the tank ahead with a loud rumble. Ruts and humps didn't faze them; their trunks kept pointing forward. They raced along, wheezing, sneezing, spitting, a column of outrageous tyrants. Tiring of spitting their phlegm, they began spitting fireballs, the trunks recoiling with each burst. All they had to do was spin back and forth a time or two to flatten out a ditch, sometimes burying khaki-colored little men in the process. Everywhere they passed was now a mass of newly plowed soil. They rolled up to the sandy ridge, where bullets rained down on them — *pow pow*. They just bounced off. But not off the soldiers behind them, who crumpled in droves. A platoon of men ran out from behind the sandy ridge with sorghum-stalk torches, which they flung beneath the tanks. Explosions sent some of the tanks leaping off the ground and men rolling on the ground in front of them. A few of the tanks died, others were wounded. More men on the sandy ridge reacted like rubber balls, rolling down the sides to do battle with the helmeted soldiers. Jumbled shouts, incoherent screams. Flying fists, well-aimed kicks, choke holds, squeezed groins, bitten fingers, grabbed ears, gouged eyes. Silvery swords went in, red swords emerged. No form of battle went untried. A little soldier was losing to a bigger one, so he picked up a handful of sand and said, "Elder brother, you and I are distant cousins. The wife of a cousin on my father's side is your kid sister. So please don't use that rifle butt on me, okay?" "All right," the bigger soldier said, "I'll spare you this time, since I've sat in your house and enjoyed a few drinks. That wine decanter at your place is finely crafted. Those things are called Mandarin Duck decanters." Without warning, the little soldier flung his sand into the bigger soldier's face, blinding him temporarily. He then ran around behind the man and cracked his head open with a hand grenade.

There was so much happening that day that I'd have had to grow ten pairs of eyes to see it all and ten mouths to tell it. Helmeted soldiers charged in waves, the dead piling up like a wall; and still they couldn't break through. Then they brought over flamethrowers that spurted death and crystallized the sand on the ridge. And more airships came, dropping great flatcakes and meat-filled buns, as well as bundles of colorful paper money. Exhausted by nightfall, both sides stopped to rest, but only for a short while, before the battle recommenced, so heated that sky and earth turned red, the frozen ground softened, and wild rabbits died in droves, their lives ending not by weapons but from fright.

The rifle fire and artillery barrages were unending; flares lit up the sky so brilliantly we could barely open our eyes.

As dawn broke, the helmeted soldiers threw up their arms in surrender.

On the first morning of 1948, the five members of our family, plus my goat, cautiously crossed the frozen Flood Dragon River and crawled up the opposite bank. Sha Zaohua and I helped First Sister drag the cart to the top, where we stood and gazed out at the patches of shattered ice, where artillery shells had landed, and at the water gushing out of the holes; as we listened to the crisp sound of ice cracking, we were thankful that none of us had fallen in. Sunlight fell on the battleground north of the river, where the smell of gunpowder lingered on; shouts, whoops of delight, and an occasional burst of gunfire kept the place alive. Fallen helmets looked like toadstools, and I was reminded of Big and Little Mute, whom Mother had placed in a bomb crater, where they lay uncovered, even by dirt. I told myself to turn and look toward our village, which had somehow avoided being reduced to rubble — a true miracle. The church was still standing, as was the mill house. Half of the tiled buildings in the Sima compound had been leveled, but our buildings were still standing, marred only by a hole from one of the artillery shells in the roof of the main house. We exchanged glances as we walked into the yard, as if we were all strangers. But then there were hugs all around, before we broke down and cried, Mother leading the way.

The sound of our crying was abruptly drowned out by the precious weeping of Sima Liang. We looked up and spotted him crouching in an apricot tree, looking like a wild animal. A dog pelt was draped over his shoulders. When Mother reached out to him, he leaped out of the tree like a puff of smoke and threw himself into her arms.

Chapter  Five

1

The first snowfall of the era of peace blanketed the corpses, while hungry wild pigeons hobbled about on the snow, their unhappy cries sounding like the ambiguous sobs of widows. The next morning, the sky took on the appearance of translucent ice, and when the sun rose red in the eastern sky, the space between heaven and earth looked like a vast expanse of colored glaze. A carpet of white covered the land, and when the people emerged from their houses, their breath a steamy pink, they tramped through the virgin snow on the eastern edge of the open fields, their possessions on their backs, leading their cattle and sheep behind them as they headed south. Crossing the crab- and clam-rich Black Water River, they were setting out for the baffling, fifty-acre highlands, and Northeast Gaomi Township's remarkable "snow market" — a marketplace erected on the snowy ground — for their snow-bound business transactions, ancestral sacrifices, and celebrations.

This was a rite for which people knew they had to keep all their thoughts bottled up inside, for the minute they opened their mouths to make them known, catastrophes would rain down on them. At the snow market, you engaged your senses of sight, smell, and touch to comprehend what was going on around you; you could think, but you mustn't speak. Exactly what might befall you if you broke the speech proscription was something no one ever questioned, let alone answered; it was as if everyone knew, but participated in a tacit agreement not to divulge the answer.

Northeast Gaomi Township's survivors of the carnage — mostly women and children — all dressed up in their New Year's finest and headed through the snow toward the highlands, their noses pricked by the icy smell of the snow at their feet. The women covered their noses and mouths with the sleeves of their thickly lined coats, and although it might appear that they were trying to ward off the biting smell of the snow, I was pretty sure it was to keep them from saying anything. A steady crunching sound rose from the white land, and while the people observed the practice of not speaking, their livestock didn't. Sheep bleated, cows mooed, and those few aging horses and crippled mules that had somehow made it through the battles whinnied. Rabid wild dogs tore at the corpses along the way with their unyielding claws and howled at the sun like wolves. The only village pet to escape the ravages of rabies, the blind dog belonging to the Taoist priest Men Shengwu, followed its master bashfully through the snow. A three-room hut in front of a brick pagoda on the highlands was home to 120-year-old Men Shengwu, a practitioner of a magical art form known as eschewing grain. Rumor had it that he had not eaten human food for ten years, surviving exclusively on morning dew, like cicadas that live in trees.

In the eyes of the villagers Taoist Men was half man, half immortal. He moved about secretively with light, nimble steps; his head was bald and shiny, like a light bulb, his white beard bushy thick. He had lips like a little mule's and teeth so bright they glittered like pearls. Both his nose and his cheeks were red, his white eyebrows as long as a bird's wing feathers. Every year he appeared in the village on the day of the Winter Solstice to carry out his special responsibility of choosing the "Snow Prince" during the annual snow market — or more appropriately, the Snow Festival. This Snow Prince was required to fulfill sacred duties at the snow market, for which he received considerable material rewards, which is why all the villagers hoped that their sons would be chosen.

I — Shangguan Jintong — was chosen as that year's Snow Prince. After visiting all eighteen villages of Northeast Gaomi Township, Taoist Men had selected me, proof that I was no ordinary boy. Mother wept tears of joy. When I was out on the street, women looked at me with reverence. "Snow Prince, oh Snow Prince," they'd call out sweetly, "when is it going to snow?" "I don't know when it's going to snow, how could I?" "The Snow Prince doesn't know when it's going to snow? Ah, you don't want to give away Nature's secrets!"

Everyone was looking forward to the first snowfall, especially me. At dusk two days earlier, dense red clouds filled the sky; on the following afternoon, snow began to fall. Starting out as a mere dusting, it grew into a full-fledged snowstorm, with flakes the size of goose feathers and then downy little balls. Huge drifts of falling snow, one on top of the other, blotted out the sun. Out in the marshes, foxes and a variety of canines cried out, while the ghosts of wronged individuals roamed the streets and lanes, wailing and weeping. Wet, heavy snow pounded the paper coverings of people's windows. White animals crouched on windowsills, beating the lattices with their bushy tails. I was too restless to sleep that night, my eyes filled with many strange sights; I won't say what they were, because they would sound too mundane to someone who didn't see them.

It was barely light outside when Mother got out of bed and boiled a pot of water to wash my face and hands. As she cleaned my hands, she said she was tending to the paws of her little puppy. She even trimmed my nails with a pair of scissors. Once I was all cleaned up, she stamped my forehead with her thumbprint in red, like a little trademark. Then she opened the door, and there was Taoist Men standing in the doorway. He'd brought along a white robe and cap, both made of glossy satin, softly pleasing to the touch. He'd also brought me a white horsetail whisk. After outfitting me, he told me to take a few steps around the snow-covered yard.

"Marvelous!" he said. "This is a true Snow Prince!"

I could not have been prouder. Mother and Eldest Sister were obviously pleased. Sha Zaohua gazed at me with a look of adoration. Eighth Sister's face was adorned with a beautiful smile, like a little flower. The smile on Sima Liang's face was more like a sneer.

Two men carried me on a litter with a dragon painted on the left side and a phoenix on the right. Wang Taiping, a professional sedan bearer, led the procession; he preceded his older brother, Wang Gongping, also a professional sedan bearer. Both brothers spoke with a slight stammer. Some years earlier, they'd tried to avoid conscription into the army, Taiping by cutting off the first finger of his own hand, Gongping by smearing red croton oil over his testicles to make it appear as if he had a hernia. When the village head, Du Baochuan, saw through their hoax, he pointed his rifle at them and gave them a choice between being shot and going up to the front lines as stretcher bearers, carrying wounded soldiers on their backs, and transporting munitions. They stammered incoherently, so their father, Wang Dahai, a mason who had fallen from a scaffold during the construction of the church and wound up crippled, chose for them. The two men carried their loads with a quick, steady gait that earned for them high marks from their superiors, and when they were demobilized, their commander, Lu Qianli, wrote references for them. But then Du Baochuan's younger brother, Du Jinchuan, who had gone to war with them, died of a sudden illness, and the two brothers carried his body home, a full fifteen hundred li, experiencing untold hardships along the way. When they arrived, Du Baochuan accused them of killing his brother and greeted them with resounding slaps; unable to say anything without stammering uncontrollably, they took out the reference letters from their regiment commander. Du Baochuan snatched them out of their hands and ripped them up on the spot. Then, with a wave of his hand, he said, "Once a deserter, always a deserter." All they could do was swallow their bitter feelings. Their tempered shoulders were hard as steel, their legs well trained for their profession. Riding on a litter carried by them was like being in a boat floating downstream. Waves of light tumbled across the snowy wasteland.

A stone bridge stood on pine pylons across the Black Water River. It swayed beneath us, making the roadway growl at our feet. After we had crossed, I turned and saw the lines of footprints on the snowy wasteland. I spotted Mother and Eighth Sister, and all the small children of the family, plus my goat, coming up behind me.

The sedan-bearing brothers carried me all the way to the highland, where I was welcomed by the spirited looks and tightly shut mouths of people who had arrived before us, men, women, and children. The adults wore somber expressions; the children all had mischievous glints in their eyes.

Led by Taoist Men, the brothers carried me up to a square earthen platform smack in the center of the highland, where a pair of benches stood behind a large incense burner with three joss sticks. They placed the litter between the benches, so I could dangle my legs as I sat. The silent cold nipped at my toes like a black cat and chewed on my ears like a white one. The sound of burning incense was like that made by worms as the curling ash fell into the burner and rumbled like a collapsing house. Its fragrance crawled up the left nostril of my nose like a caterpillar and out the right. Taoist Men burned a bundle of spirit money in a bronze brazier at the foot of the platform. The flames were like golden butterflies with wings covered with golden powder; the paper was like black butterflies fluttering up into the sky until they were worn out, and then settling down onto the snow, where they quickly died. Taoist Men then prostrated himself before the platform of the Snow Prince and signaled the Wang brothers to lift me up again. I was handed a wooden club wrapped in gold paper, its head formed into a tinfoil bowl — the Snow Prince's staff of authority. After choosing me as the Snow Prince, Taoist Men had told me that the founder of the snow market was his teacher, Taoist Chen, who had received his instructions from Laozi, the founder of Taoism himself, and that once he'd carried out his instructions, he'd risen up to Heaven to become an immortal, living on a towering mountaintop, where he ate pine nuts and drank spring water, flying from pine trees to poplars, and from there to his cave. Taoist Men explained in great detail the duties of the Snow Prince. I'd already carried out the first — receiving the veneration of the multitudes — and was at that moment carrying out the second, which was an inspection of the snow market.

This was the Snow Prince's divine moment, as a dozen men in black-and-red uniforms stepped forward; although they held nothing in their hands, they assumed the posture of musicians with trumpets, *suonas*, bugles, and brass cymbals. The cheeks of some puffed out as if they were trumpeting loudly. Once every few paces, the cymbalist raised his left hand to shoulder height and pretended to strike his cymbal with his right hand; the silent clangs were carried far off in the distance. The Wang brothers bounced and swayed on springy legs as the citizenry ceased their silent transactions and stood straight, eyes gaping, arms at their sides, to watch the procession of the Snow Prince. The colors of those familiar and unfamiliar faces were enhanced by the glare of the snow: reds like dates, blacks like charcoal briquettes, yellows like beeswax, and greens like scallions. I waved my staff of authority in the direction of the crowd, momentarily sending them scurrying in confusion; their hands now swung wildly in the air and their mouths were open, as if screaming. But no one dared or was willing to make a sound. One of the sacred duties bestowed upon me by Taoist Men was to stop up the mouth of anyone who dared make a sound with the tip of my staff, then to jerk it back quickly, pulling the person's tongue out with it.

I spotted Mother, First Sister, and Eighth Sister in the crowd of people releasing their silent screams. I also saw others, such as Sha Zaohua and Sima Liang. My goat had been fitted with a mask over its mouth; fashioned out of white cotton in the shape of a cone, it was held on by a white cotton strap looped around the ears, for the proscription against making a sound was heeded not only by the Snow Prince's family, but by its goat as well. I waved my staff in the direction of my family, all of whom greeted me in return by raising their arms. Sima Liang made circles with both hands and raised them to his eyes, as if looking at me through binoculars. Zaohua's face was radiant, like a fish deep in the ocean.

All variety of things were sold at the snow market. The first stop by my silent honor guard was the shoe market. Only straw sandals were displayed, all made of softened cattails, the kind of footwear that Northeast Gaomi residents wore throughout the winter. Hu Tiangui, the father of five brothers who had survived the war and then been sent into forced labor, stood holding a willow branch, icicles hanging from his chin, white cloth wrapped around his chin; wearing only a tattered burlap sack, he was bent over, two grimy fingers extended as he bartered with Qiu Huangshan, a master sandal-maker. Qiu stuck out three fingers and laid them over Hu's two. Hu stubbornly reextended his two fingers; Qiu quickly countered with three. Back and forth they went — three, four, five times — until Qiu pulled back his hand and, with a pained look to show his frustration, untied a pair of inferior sandals made of the green tips of cattails from his string of wares. Hu Tiangui's open mouth was a silent expression of his angry reaction. He thumped his chest, looked heavenward, and then pointed to the ground. What he meant by all this was unclear. With his staff he dug through the pile of sandals, settling upon a superior pair the color of beeswax with thick, sturdy soles, made from cattail roots. Qiu pushed Hu's staff away, stuck out four fingers, and held them unflinchingly under Hu's nose. Once again Hu looked heavenward and pointed to the ground, his burlap sack shifting with each movement. He bent down and untied the pair of sandals he'd selected, gave them a squeeze, and shifted his feet; his tattered shoes, with rubber soles that were barely attached to the tops, now lay on the ground in front of him. Supporting himself by his staff, he slipped his trembling feet into the new sandals, then took a crumpled bill out of his patchwork pocket and tossed it at the feet of Qiu Huangshan. With rage written all over his face, Qiu uttered a silent curse and stomped angrily on the ground; but he picked up the frayed bill, flattened it out, held it by one corner, and waved it in the air for the benefit of people nearby. Some shook their heads sympathetically, while others wore silly grins. Inching his way along with the help of his staff, Hu Tiangui walked off on legs that were stiff as boards. I was disgusted with Qiu Huangshan, he with the skillful mouth and nimble fingers, and deep down hoped that his anger would get the best of him, causing him to blurt out something; that way, with my temporary authority, I could jerk that long tongue out of his mouth with my staff. But he cleverly saw what I was thinking and tucked the pink bill into a pair of sandals hanging from his carrying pole. When he took down the sandals, I saw they were nearly stuffed full of brightly colored paper money. One by one he pointed to the sandal-makers around him, who looked at me with fawning expressions and then slowly pointed to the money in his sandals. Once he'd finished, he reverently flung the sandals to me; they bounced off my gut and landed on the ground in front of me. Several of the bills, with images of dumb fat sheep seemingly waiting to be sheared or slaughtered, fell out. As I moved forward, several more pairs of sandals stuffed with money came flying my way.

In the food market, Fang Meihua, the widow of Zhao the Sixth, was anxiously frying stuffed buns in a flat-bottomed wok. Her son and daughter sat on a straw mat with a blanket wrapped around them, their four eyes rolling nonstop. She had set up a number of rickety tables in front of her stove, and at the moment, six burly reed-mat peddlers were squatting in front of the tables eating buns and garlic. The tops and bottoms of the fried buns were a crusty brown color; they were so hot you could hear them sputter in the men's mouths, and so oily that red grease spurted out with each bite. None of the other bun sellers or flatcake peddlers had any customers; glaring enviously at the spot in front of Widow Zhao's stand, they stood there banging the sides of their woks.

As my litter passed, Widow Zhao stuck a bill on a bun, took aim at my face, and casually tossed it over. I ducked just in time, and the bun struck Wang Gongping squarely in the chest. Flashing me a look of apology, Widow Zhang wiped her hands on an oily rag. Her eyes were deep-set in her ashen face, ringed with dark purple circles.

A tall, skinny man sidled over from the stand where live chickens were sold; the frightened hens were cackling nervously. The woman who ran the stand nodded repeatedly. The man had a peculiar walk: stiff as a board, he strode rhythmically, his shoulders shrugging with each step as if he were about to take root in the ground. It was Heavensent

Zhang, whom people had nicknamed "Old Master Heaven." A practitioner of the strange occupation of escorting the dead back to their hometowns, he had the gift of getting them back on their feet to walk home. Anytime a resident of Northeast Gaomi died away from home, Zhang was hired to bring the person back. And anytime an out-of-towner died in Northeast Gaomi Township, he was hired to take him back. How could anyone not venerate a man who had the ability of getting a corpse to walk over as many mountains and rivers as it took to get home? A strange smell emanated from the man's body, and even the meanest dog tucked its tail between its legs, turned, and ran off when he drew near. Taking a seat on the bench in front of the widow's wok, he extended two fingers. In the flurry of hand signals that passed between him and the woman, it quickly became clear that he wanted two trays of her buns, a total of fifty — not just two and not just twenty. So the widow hurried to serve this big-bellied customer, her face brightening, as green glares converged from neighboring stands. I hoped they'd say something, but even jealousy lacked the power to open their mouths.

Heavensent sat quietly, eyes riveted on the widow as she worked, his hands resting tranquilly on his knees; a black cloth sack hung from his belt, but what it held no one knew. In the late autumn he'd taken on a big job — delivering a New Year's scroll peddler who had died in Northeast Gaomi County's Aiqiu Village back to his home in the far-off Northeast. After agreeing to the fee, the man's son left his address and went on ahead to prepare to receive his father. Given all the mountain ranges Heavensent would have to cross, people doubted that he'd ever make it back. But he had, and by the looks of him, he'd only just returned. Was that money in his cloth bag? His straw sandals were tattered, exposing swollen toes and bony ankles.

As Sleepyhead's younger sister, Cross-eyed Beauty, walked past my litter with a large head of cabbage, she cast me a flirtatious look. Her hands were red from the freezing cold, and as she passed in front of Widow Zhao's stand, the widow's hands began to quake violently. Their gazes met, and mortal enemies' eyes turned red. Not even the sight of the woman who had killed her husband was enough for Widow Zhao to violate the snow market ban on speaking. Yet I could see that her blood was boiling. Widow Zhao possessed the quality of letting nothing, not even rage, keep her from her work. After filling a large white ceramic bowl with the first rack of buns, she placed it in front of Heavensent, who stretched out his hand. It took Widow Zhao a moment to figure out what he wanted. She smacked her forehead apologetically, then reached into a jar, removed two large purple pungent stalks of garlic, and laid them in front of him. She then filled a small black bowl with sesame-flavored chili sauce and placed it too before Heavensent as a special treat. The reed-mat peddlers looked on with disgruntled expressions, censuring her for toadying up to Heavensent Zhang, who slowly and contentedly peeled the garlic as he waited for the buns to cool. Then he placed the white, unpeeled stalks on the table in a row by size, like a column of soldiers, now and then reaching down to switch one or two to make a perfect column. He didn't start eating — more like inhaling — the buns until my litter had been carried way over to the cabbage market.

A tiny hut stood silently at the base of the pagoda, one devoted to no particular god or deity. The subtle fragrance of burning incense wafted out the door. A large wooden cauldron standing in front of the incense burner was filled with virgin snow. Behind it was a wooden stool — the "Snow Prince" throne. Taoist Men lifted the gauze curtain that separated the silent hut from the outside, walked in, and covered my face with a piece of white satin. I knew from his instructions that while carrying out this duty I was not to remove the veil. I heard him slip quietly out of the hut, so that only the sounds of my soft breathing, my faint heartbeat, and the tiny sizzle of burning incense remained. Gradually, I heard the gentle crunch of snow as people walked toward me.

A girl with dainty steps walked in. All I could see through my veil was the outline of a large girl whose body reeked of burnt pig bristles. Not likely a girl from Dalan, and quite possibly from Sandy Ridge Village, where a family ran a handicraft business of making brushes. But wherever she came from, the Snow Prince was obliged to be impartial. So I stuck my hands into the snow in the cauldron to cleanse them of impurities. Then I stretched them out to her. The custom was for all women wanting to bear a child in the coming year and those who wanted milk to fill their young, healthy breasts to lift up their blouses and expose their breasts to welcome the outstretched hands of the Snow Prince. It happened just as it was supposed to: two spongy mounds of flesh pressed toward my icy hands. My head spun as warm currents of joy passed through my hands and quickly suffused my body. The woman panted uncontrollably as her breasts brushed my fingertips and then, like a pair of heated doves, flew away.

I'd barely felt the first pair of breasts, and now they were gone. My disappointment gave way to desire as I thrust my hands back into the snow to cleanse and purify them once again. I waited impatiently for the arrival of the next pair, which I was not going to let get away so easily. When they came, I grabbed them and wouldn't let go. They were small and exquisite, neither too soft nor too firm, like steamed buns fresh from the oven. Even though I couldn't see them, I knew they were snowy white, smooth, and glossy, their tiny tips like button mushrooms. As I grasped them, I said a silent prayer of good wishes. One squeeze: May you have pudgy male triplets. Two squeezes: May your milk gush like a fountain. Three squeezes: May your milk be as wonderfully sweet as morning dew. She moaned softly before pulling away, to my considerable disappointment. My feelings plummeted, and shame set in. To punish myself, I buried my hands in the snow until my fingertips touched the slick bottom. I didn't pull them out until the numbness reached halfway up my arms. The Snow Prince raised his purified hands in benediction to the women of Northeast Gaomi Township. I was feeling glum until a sagging, shifting pair of breasts brushed up against my hands. They cackled like stubborn hens as fine bumps rose up on the skin. I pinched the two weary nipples, then pulled my hands back. Rusty puffs of air from the woman's mouth penetrated the gauzy veil and struck me on the face. The Snow Prince does not discriminate. May your wishes be fulfilled. If you desire a son, may you have a boy; if you desire a daughter, may you have a girl; and may you possess all the milk you desire. Your breasts will be healthy always, but if it is a return to your youth that you desire, the Snow Prince cannot help you.

The fourth pair of breasts were like explosive quails, with brown feathers, unyielding beaks, and short, powerful necks. Those unyielding beaks kept pecking at the palms of my hands.

Two hornets' nests seemed hidden in the fifth pair of breasts, for they began to buzz the moment I touched them. The surface heated up from all the insects trying to break out, making my hands tingle as they bequeathed their blessings.

That day I fondled at least a hundred and twenty pairs of breasts, gaining layer upon layer of feelings and impressions of women's breasts, like turning the pages of a book. But the unicorn shattered all those crisp impressions. She was like a thrashing rhino, an earthquake rumbling through the storehouse of my memory, a wild bull crashing into a garden.

I had stretched out my hands, by then swollen and all but desensitized, intent on carrying out the duties of the Snow Prince as I awaited the next pair of breasts. I heard a familiar giggle, but there were no breasts. Red face, red lips, tiny dark eyes — all of a sudden, the face of this flirtatious young woman floated into my mind's eye.

My left hand touched the fullness of a large breast; my right hand touched nothing, and at that moment I knew that single-breasted Old Jin had arrived. After coming perilously close to being shot following a mass-struggle session, this flirtatious widow, who ran a sesame oil shop, married the poorest man in the village, a homeless beggar named One-eyed Fang Jin, and was now the wife of a poor peasant. Her husband had one eye; she had a single breast. It was a match made in heaven. Old Jin wasn't really old, but word of her unique style of making love had made the rounds among the village men, and had even reached my ears on several occasions, although I didn't understand much of what I heard. As I was cupping her breast with my left hand, she grabbed my right hand and brought it over, until her unusually full breast weighted down both hands. Under her guidance, I felt every inch of it. It was a lonely mountain peak spread across the right side of her chest. The top half an easy, relaxing slope, the bottom half was a droopy hemisphere. Hers was the warmest breast I'd ever felt, like a vaccinated rooster, so hot it nearly sparked. It was smooth and glossy, and would have been more so if not for the heat. The end of the droopy hemisphere jutted out like an overturned bowl for wine, tipped by a slightly upturned nipple. It was hard one second, soft the next, like a rubber bullet; several drops of a cool liquid stuck to my hand, and I was reminded of something said to me by a diminutive villager who had traveled to the south to sell silk: he said lusty Old Jin was like a papaya, a woman who oozed white fluids the moment she was touched. Since I'd never seen a papaya, I could only imagine that they were an ugly fruit with a deadly attraction. The discharge of the Snow Prince's sacred duties was gradually taken off course by Old Jin's single breast. My hands were like sponges, soaking up the warmth of her breast, and it seemed to me that my fondling brought her contentment as well. Grunting like a little pig, she grabbed my head and buried it in her bosom, where her overheated breast burned my face, and I heard her mutter softly, "Dear boy . . . my own dear boy . . ."

The snow market rule was broken.

A single utterance invited disaster.

*   *   *

A green Jeep was parked in the square in front of Taoist Men's house. Four security police in khaki uniforms with white cotton insignia over the breast pockets piled out and, with nimble precision, burst through Taoist Men's door; they reappeared moments later with handcuffed Taoist Men in tow. As he was bundled up to the Jeep, he cast a sorrowful look my way, but said nothing. He meekly climbed into the Jeep.

Three months later, the leader of the reactionary sect, Men Shengwu, Taoist Men, who had regularly secreted himself on a high mountain slope to fire signal shots to secret agents, was shot beneath Enchanted Bridge in the county seat. His blind dog ran after the Jeep in the snow, only to have his head blown apart by a sharpshooter riding in the car.

2

I sneezed, and woke myself up. Golden light from the kerosene lamp coated the glistening walls. Mother was sitting beneath the lamp rubbing the golden pelt of a weasel, a pair of shears lying across her knees. The weasel's bushy tail jumped and leaped in her hand. A grimy, monkey-faced man in a brown army greatcoat sat on a stool in front of the *kang*. He was scratching the scalp under his gray hair with crippled fingers.

"Is that you, Jintong?" he asked tentatively as a look of pity shone from his black eyes.

"Jintong," Mother said, "this is your . . . it's your elder cousin Sima . . ."

It was Sima Ting. I hadn't seen him in years, and just look what those years had done to him! Sima Ting, the township head who had stood atop the watchtower all those years ago, lively and full of energy, where had he gone? And his fingers, red as ripe carrots, where were they?

Back when the mysterious horseman had shattered the heads of Sima Feng and Sima Huang, Sima Ting had jumped out of the horse trough beside the west wing of our house, like a carp leaping out of the water, as the crack of gunfire split his eardrums. He stormed around the mill house like a spooked donkey, circling it over and over. The clatter of horse's hooves rolled through the lane like a tidal wave. I have to run away, he was thinking. I can't hang around here waiting to be killed. With wheat husks clinging to his head, he clambered over our low southern wall and landed in a pile of dog shit. As he lay sprawled on the ground, he heard a disturbance somewhere in the lane, and scrambled on his hands and knees over to an old haystack, which he discovered he shared with a laying hen with a bright red comb. The next sounds he heard, only seconds later, were a heavy thud and the crash of a splintering door. Immediately after that, a gang of men in black masks came outside and headed straight for the wall. They trampled the weeds and grass at the base of the wall in their thick-soled cloth shoes. All were armed with black repeater rifles. Moving with the assurance of fearless bandits, they negotiated the wall like a flock of black swallows He wondered why they had covered their faces, but when he later learned of the deaths of Sima Feng and Sima Huang, a glimmer of light filtered into his clouded mind, clearing up things he hadn't understood until then. The men spilled into the yard. Caring only for his head and letting his rear end take care of itself, he squirmed into the haystack to await the outcome.

"Number Two is Number Two, and I'm me," Sima Ting said to Mother in the lamplight. "Let's be clear on that, Sister-in-law."

"Then he'll call you Elder Uncle. Jintong, this is your elder uncle, Sima Ting."

Before I drifted off to sleep again, I watched Sima Ting take a shiny gold medal out of his pocket and hand it to Mother. "Sister-in-law," he said in a muffled, bashful voice, "I've made amends for my crimes."

After crawling out of the haystack, Sima Ting slipped out of the village in the dark of night. Half a month later, he was dragooned into a stretcher unit, where he was paired with a dark-faced young man. During one of the battles, he lost three fingers of his left hand in an explosion. But he did not let the pain stop him from carrying a squad leader who had lost a leg to the hospital on his back.

I listened to him prattle on and on, relating all his strange adventures, like a young man spinning yarns to divert attention from his errors. Mother's head rocked in the lamplight, a golden sheen on her face. The corners of her mouth were turned up slightly in what looked like a sneer.

When I woke up early in the morning, a foul smell assailed my nostrils. I saw Mother in a chair, leaning against the wall, fast asleep. Sima Ting was squatting on a bench next to the *kang*; he too was asleep, looking like a perched eagle. The floor in front of the *kang* was littered with yellow cigarette butts.

Ji Qiongzhi, who would later be my homeroom teacher, came down from the county government and started a Woman's Remarriage Campaign in Dalan Town. She brought with her a bunch of female officials who acted like a herd of wild horses; they called a meeting of all the township widows to publicize a campaign to have them remarry. Under their active mobilization and organization, just about all the widows in our village found husbands.

The only widows to become obstacles to this campaign were those of the Shangguan family. No one dared to seek the hand of my eldest sister, Laidi, since all the local bachelors knew she'd been the wife of the traitor Sha Yueliang, had been exploited by Sima Ku, who'd fled the revolution, and that she'd also been the wife of the revolutionary soldier Speechless Sun. Even in death, these three men were no one to get on the bad side of. Mother fell within the age limit set by Ji Qiongzhi, but she refused to remarry. The moment the official stepped foot in the door to try to talk Mother around, she was sent away with a barrage of curses. "Get out of my house!" Mother yelled. "Why, I'm older than your mother!"

But, strangely enough, when Ji Qiongzhi herself came over to give it a try, Mother spoke to her genially: "Young lady," she said, "who do you plan to have marry me?"

"Someone younger than you would not be a good match, aunty," Ji Qiongzhi said, "and about the only man in your age group is Sima Ting. Even though there are blemishes in his history, he set everything straight with his meritorious service. Besides, you two have a special relationship."

With a wry smile, Mother said, "Young lady, his younger brother is my son-in-law."

"What does that matter?" Ji Qiongzhi said. "You're not related by blood."

The wedding ceremony for forty-five widows took place in the decrepit old church. I attended, in spite of the anger I felt. Mother took her place among the widows, with what looked like a pink tinge to her puffy face. Sima was standing with the men, scratching his head with his crippled hand the whole time, maybe to cover his embarrassment.

On behalf of the government, Ji Qiongzhi gave each of the new couples a towel and a bar of soap. The township head presented them with marriage certificates. Mother blushed like a young maiden as she accepted the towel and certificate.

Wicked thoughts burned in my heart. My face was hot with a sense of shame for Mother. There was only dust on the spot on the wall where the jujube Jesus had once hung. And on the platform where Pastor Malory had baptized me stood a bunch of brazen men and women. They seemed to be cowering, their glances evasive, like a gang of thieves. Even though Mother's hair had turned gray, here she was, about to marry the elder brother of her own son-in-law. One of the female officials scattered some withered China rose petals from a yellow gourd ladle in the direction of the hapless new couples. Some landed on Mother's gray hair, which was slicked down with elm sap, falling like dirty rain, or shriveled bird feathers.

Like a dog whose soul had taken flight, I slunk out of the church. There, on the ancient street, I saw Pastor Malory, a black robe draped across his shoulders, slowly wandering along. His face was mud-spattered; tender yellow buds of wheat were sprouting in his hair. His eyes, looking like frozen grapes, shone with the light of sorrow. In a loud voice, I reported to him that Mother had married Sima Ting. I saw his face twitch in agony, and watched as his frame and the black robe began to break up and dissolve into curls of black, stinking smoke.

Eldest Sister was in the yard, her snowy white neck bent down as she washed her lush black hair. In that position, her lovely pink breasts were singing like a pair of silky-voiced orioles. When she straightened up, crystalline beads of water coursed down the valley between her breasts. With one hand, she coiled the back of her hair as she narrowed her eyes and looked at me, a smirk on her face. "Are you aware," I said, "that she's marrying Sima Ting?" Again that smirk; she ignored me. Mother walked into the house hand in hand with Shangguan Yunü, shameful rose petals still stuck to her hair. Dejected Sima Ting was right behind them. Eldest Sister picked up her basin and flung the water into the air, where it spread into a luminous fan. Mother sighed, but said nothing. Sima Ting handed his medal to me, either to win me over or to prove his worth, but I just stared at him solemnly. A look of hypocrisy was frozen on his smiling face. He averted his eyes and covered his embarrassment with a cough. I flung the medal away. It flew over the rooftop like a bird, trailing a gold-colored ribbon behind it. "Go pick that up!" Mother said angrily.

"No," I replied defiantly.

Sima Ting said, "Let it be, forget it. There's no need to keep that around."

Mother slapped me.

I fell backward and rolled around on the ground.

Mother kicked me.

"Shame on you!" I spat out venomously. "You have no shame!"

Mother's head slumped from her weighty sorrow and a loud wail burst from her mouth; she turned and ran tearfully into the house. Sima Ting sighed before squatting beneath the pear tree to have a smoke.

Several cigarettes later, he stood up and said, "Go in and talk to your mother, nephew. Get her to stop crying." Then he took the marriage certificate out of his pocket, tore it into strips, and tossed them to the ground just before walking out of the yard, stooped over, an old man, like a candle guttering in the wind.

3

At the height of the age of bluster, Sima Ku gave his revered mentor, the nearsighted Qin Er, a pair of rhinestone eyeglasses. Now, with the counterrevolutionary gift perched on his nose, Qin was sitting at a brick rostrum holding an open volume of Chinese literature, his voice trembling as he lectured to us, Northeast Gaomi Township's first freshman class, a group whose ages varied dramatically. The heavy eyeglasses slid halfway down the bridge of his nose; a single drop of oily green snot hung from the tip of his nose, threatening to drop to the floor, but somehow hanging on. *Big goats are big* — he intoned. Even though it was already the sixth month, among the hottest of the year, he sat there wearing a lined, black, full-length robe and a black satin skullcap with a red tassel. *Big goats are big* — we shouted out the words, trying to mimic his tone of voice. *Little goats are little* — he intoned sorrowfully. The room was stifling, dark and dank, and we sat there, barefoot and shirtless, our bodies covered with greasy sweat, while our teacher, dressed for winter, his face pale and his lips purple, looked as if he were freezing. *Little goats are little* — our voices resounded in the room, which smelled like stale urine, like a neglected goat pen. *Big goats and little goats run up the hill* — *Big goats and little goats run up the*

hill — *Big goats run, little goats bleat* — *Big goats run, little goats bleat* —
given my profound knowledge of goats, I knew that big goats, with
their sagging teats, couldn't run; why, they could barely walk. For little
goats to bleat was entirely possible, and, for that matter, to run. Big
goats grazed lazily in the pasture, while little goats ran around bleating.
I was tempted to raise my hand to ask the venerable teacher his opinion, but I didn't dare. A discipline ruler lay in front of him, its sole purpose to smack the palms of disobedient students' hands. *Big goats eat
a lot* — *Big goats eat a lot* — *Little goats eat a little* — *Little goats eat a
little* — those were true statements. Of course big goats eat more than
little goats, and little goats eat less than big goats. *Big goats are big* —
little goats are little — with that, we went back and started over from the
beginning. The teacher intoned on and on tirelessly, but classroom order began to fall apart. One of the students, Wu Yunyu, was a tall,
husky eighteen-year-old son of a farm laborer. He was already married
to the widowed proprietor of a bean curd shop, who was eight years his
senior and in the last stage of pregnancy. He was about to become
a daddy. The soon-to-be daddy took a rusty pistol from his waistband and took aim at the red tassel of Qin Er's cap. *Big goats run* — *Big
goats* — *pow! Ha ha ha ha, run* — The teacher looked up, his gray ovine
eyes peering down over the top of the rhinestone lenses. He was so
myopic he probably couldn't see a thing. So he went back to reading.
Little goats bleat — *pow*! Wu Yunyu fired off another imaginary shot,
and the red tassel on the old teacher's cap fluttered. Laughter filled
the room. The teacher picked up his ruler and smacked the table.
"Quiet!" he demanded, like a judge. The recitation recommenced.
Guo Qiusheng, the seventeen-year-old son of a poor peasant, left his
seat at a crouch and tiptoed up to the rostrum, where he stood behind
the teacher, bit his lower lip with his ratlike front teeth, and made gestures of stuffing shells into a mortar, the barrel of which was the top of
the teacher's bony skull. Over and over he fired his imaginary weapon.
Chaos took over in the classroom, with all of us rocking back and forth
laughing. Xu Lianhe, a big boy, pounded his desk, while the smaller
but fatter Fang Shuzhai tore out the pages of his book and flung them
into the air, where they fluttered like butterflies.

The old teacher banged the table over and over, but that didn't
quiet things down. He kept peering over his eyeglasses, trying to determine the cause of all the commotion; meanwhile, Guo Qiusheng
was furiously acting out his violently humiliating performance behind

Qin Er, eliciting strange yells from all the idiotic boys over the age of fifteen. Then Guo Qiusheng's hand brushed against the ear of the old teacher, who spun around and grabbed the offending hand.

"Recite your lesson!" the stately old teacher demanded.

Guo Qiusheng stood at the rostrum with his hands at his side, trying to look the part of the obedient student. But the smirk on his face betrayed him. He pointed his lips to turn his mouth into what looked like a belly button. Then he shut one eye and twisted his mouth as far as it would go to one side. He clenched his teeth, making his ears wiggle.

"Recite your lesson!" the teacher roared angrily.

Guo Qiusheng began: *Big girls are big, little girls are little, big girls chase the little girls away.*

Amid the crazed laughter that followed, Qin Er stood up by gripping the edge of the table. His gray beard quivered as he muttered: "Bad boy! Bad boys cannot be taught!" He groped for his ruler, grabbed Guo Qiusheng's hand, and pressed it down on the table. "Bad boy!" *Pa.* The ruler landed savagely on the hand of Guo Qiusheng, who cried out hoarsely. The teacher looked him in the eye and raised the ruler over his head; but his arm froze when he saw the insolent look of a proletarian thug on Guo's face, those steely black eyes glinting with a hateful defiance. A look of defeat crept into the teacher's rheumy gaze, and he let his arm drop weakly to his side, ruler in hand. He mumbled and took off his eyeglasses, which he placed in a metal case, wrapped with a piece of blue cloth, and put into his pocket. He also tucked the offending ruler, with which he'd once punished Sima Ku, into his robe. That done, he removed his skullcap, bowed to Guo Qiusheng, then turned and bowed to the class, and finally announced in a mournful voice that evoked both pity and disgust:

"Gentlemen, I, Qin Er, am a thickheaded old fool, no better than the mantis who thought it could stop a wagon, someone who has overrated his own abilities, a man who has outlived his usefulness and has shamed himself by hanging on to life. I have deeply offended you, and can only beg for your forgiveness!"

He then clasped his fists in front of his midriff and respectfully shook them several times, before crouching over like a cooked shrimp and leaving the classroom with light, unsteady steps. Once he was outside, we heard the muddled sound of his coughing.

Thus ended our first class of the day.

Our second class was music.

Music — our instructor, Ji Qiongzhi, who had been sent down by the county government, laid the tip of her pointer on the blackboard, where large words had been written in chalk, and said in a high-pitched voice — "For this class in music, there will be no textbook. Our text-books will be here" — she pointed to her head, her chest — "and here" — she pointed to her diaphragm. She turned to write on the blackboard as she continued, "There are lots of ways to make music — on a flute or fiddle, humming a tune or singing an aria — it's all music. You may not understand now, but you will someday. Singing is a form of chanting, but not always. Singing is an important musical activity and, for a remote village like this, will be the most important aspect of our music lessons. So today we will learn a song," she went on as she wrote on the blackboard. From where I sat, looking out the window, I could see the counterrevolutionary's son, Sima Liang, and the traitor's daughter, Sha Zaohua, both of whom had been refused permission to attend classes and were assigned to tending sheep, gazing wistfully at the schoolhouse. They were standing in knee-high grass, backed by a dozen or more thick-stemmed sunflowers, with their broad green leaves and brilliant yellow flowers. All those yellow faces mirrored the melan-choly in my heart. Seeing the flashing eyes brought tears to mine. As I took measure of the window, with its thick willow lattices, I imagined myself turning into a thrush and flying outside to bathe in the golden sunlight of a summer afternoon and perch on the head of one of those sunflowers, alongside all the aphids and ladybugs.

The song we were being taught that day was "Women's Libera-tion Anthem." Our teacher bent over at the waist as she scribbled the last few lines at the bottom of the blackboard. The fullness of her up-raised backside reminded me of a mare's rump. A feathered arrow, its tip smeared with sticky peachtree sap, made its lopsided way past me and hit her upraised backside. Evil laughter swept through the class-room. The archer, Ding Jingou, who sat right behind me, waved his bamboo bow triumphantly a time or two before quickly hiding it from sight. Our music teacher retrieved the arrow from its target and smiled as she looked it over, then flung it down on the table, where it stuck straight up after quivering briefly. "Nice shooting," she said calmly as she laid down her pointer and shed her military jacket, which was white from countless washings. With the jacket gone, her white short-sleeved, V-necked blouse, with its turned-down collar, dazzled our eyes. It was tucked into her trousers, which were cinched by a wide leather belt that had turned black and shiny with age. She had a thin waist, high, arching breasts, and full hips. Her military trousers had also turned white from countless washings. Finally, she had on a pair of fashionable white sneakers. To make her appearance more appealing, she cinched her belt even tighter right in front of us. She smiled and displayed all the charm of a lovely white fox; but the smile disappeared as quickly as it had come, and she now displayed the ferocity of a white fox. "You've just driven away Qin Er. What heroes!" With a smirk she removed the arrow from the table and jiggled it with three fingers. "What a remarkable arrow," she said. "Is it Li Guang's? Or maybe Hua Rong's. Anyone dare to stand up and put a name to this?" Her lovely black eyes swept the classroom. No one stood up. She grabbed her pointer. *Pow*! She smacked the table. "I'm warning you," she said, "in my classroom you'll wrap all your little hoodlum tricks in a piece of cotton and take them home to your mothers" — "Teacher, my mother's dead!" Wu Yunyu shouted — "Whose mother is dead?" she asked. "Stand up." Wu Yunyu stood up, trying to look unconcerned. "Come up to the front, where I can see you." Wu Yunyu, wearing a greasy snakeskin cap down low over his wispy head — as it was all year round, even, it was said, when he slept at night or bathed in the river — strutted up to the front of the classroom. "What's your name?" she asked with a smile. Wu Yunyu told her his name with blustery airs. "Students," she said, "my name is Ji Qiongzhi. I was orphaned as a baby and spent my first seven years living in a garbage heap. I then joined a traveling circus. There isn't a hoodlum or delinquent type I haven't seen. I learned to do stunt cycling, walk a tightrope, swallow a sword, and spit fire. Then I became an animal trainer, starting with dogs and moving to monkeys, bears, and finally tigers. I can teach a dog to jump through a hoop, a monkey to climb a pole, a bear to ride a bicycle, and a tiger to roll over. At the age of seventeen, I joined a revolutionary army. I've battled the enemy, my sword entering white and exiting bright red. At twenty, I was sent to the South China Military Academy, where I learned sports, painting, singing, and dancing. At twenty-five I married Ma Shengli, head of intelligence at the Public Security Bureau and a champion wrestler whom I can fight to a draw." She brushed back her short hair. She had a dark, healthy, revolutionary face; pert breasts that strained proudly against her shirt; a valiant nose, fierce, thin lips, and teeth as white as limestone. "I, Ji Qiongzhi, am not afraid of tigers," she said as dryly as plant ash, as she glared contemptuously at Wu Yunyu. "So do you think I'm afraid of you?" At the same time she was voicing her contempt, she reached out with her pointer, inserting the tip under the edge of Wu's cap, and, with a flick of the wrist, tore it off his head, like flipping a flatcake on a griddle, with an audible *whoosh*. It all happened in a mere second. Wu covered his head with both hands, the scalp looking like a rotten potato; his arrogant expression disappeared without a trace and was replaced by a look of stupidity. Still holding his head, he looked up, searching for the object that kept his disfigurement hidden. It was high up in the air, dancing and spinning on the tip of her pointer, round and round like a circus performer's prop; the sight of his cap spinning so artfully, so captivatingly, drove the soul right out of Wu Yunyu's body. Another flick of her wrist, and the cap soared into the air, only to settle back onto the tip of the pointer and spin some more. I was dazzled. She flung it into the air again. But this time, she guided the ugly, smelly thing so that it landed at Wu Yunyu's feet. "Put that crummy hat back on your head and get your ass back in your seat," she said with a look of disgust. "I've eaten more salt than you have noodles," she said as she picked the arrow up off the table. Her glare landed on one of the students. "You! I'm talking to you," she said icily. "Bring me that bow!" Ding Jingou stood up nervously, walked to the platform, and obediently laid the bow on the table. "Back to your seat!" she said, picking up the bow. She tried it out. "The bamboo's too soft, and the bowstring's next to useless! The best bowstrings are made from a cow's tendon." Fitting the feathered arrow onto the horsehair string, she pulled it back lightly and took aim at Ding Jingou's head. He scrambled under his desk. Just then a fly buzzed in on the light streaming through the window. Ji Qiongzhi took careful aim. *Twang*, went the horsehair string. The fly dropped to the floor. "Anyone need more proof?" she asked. Not a peep from any of the students. She smiled sweetly, forming a dimple on her chin. "Now we can begin. Here are the lyrics to our song":

In the old society, this is how it was:
A dark, o so dark dry well, deep down in the ground.
Crushing the common folk, women at the bottom, at the very, very
    bottom.
In the new society, this is how it is:
A bright, o so bright sun shines down on the peasants.
Women have been freed to stand up, at the very, very top.

4

My ability to memorize lyrics and my musical talent stood out among the students in Ji Qiongzhi's music class. As I was singing "with women at the very very bottom," Mother held up a towel-wrapped bottle filled with goat's milk, stood outside the window, and called out repeatedly:

"Jintong, come have your milk!"

Her shouts and the smell of the milk diverted my attention, but when class was nearly over, I was the only one who finished the song without missing a beat. There were forty students in the class, and I was the only one Ji Qiongzhi commended. After asking my name, she had me stand up and sing "Women's Liberation Anthem" from start to finish. Now that class was over, Mother handed me my milk through the window. When I hesitated taking it, she said, "Drink it, son. Mother's proud to see how well you're doing."

There was muted laughter in the room.

"Take it, child. What's there to be embarrassed about?" Mother said.

Ji Qiongzhi walked up beside me. Leaning on her pointer as she looked out the window, she said in a friendly voice, "I see it's you, aunty. I ask you please not to do anything to disrupt the class from now on." Gazing into the classroom, Mother replied respectfully, "Teacher, he's my only son, and, unfortunately, he hasn't eaten real food since he was a baby. When he was small, he lived on my milk, and now he gets by with goat's milk alone. This morning the goat didn't give enough for a meal, and I want to make sure he has enough to get through the day." Ji Qiongzhi smiled and said, "Take it. Don't make your mother stand there holding it." My face was burning as I took the bottle from her. Ji Qiongzhi said to Mother, "But he needs to eat real food. You don't expect him to drag a milk goat along when he goes to high school and college, do you?" She was probably trying to picture a college student walking into a classroom with a goat on a tether. But then she laughed, a hearty laugh without a hint of ill will, and asked, "How old is he?" "Thirteen, born the year of the rabbit," Mother answered. "He worries me too, but he can't keep other food down. It gives him such a terrible bellyache that he breaks out in a sweat, and that scares me every time it happens." "That's enough, Mother," I said unhappily. "Please don't say any more. And I don't want the milk." I handed her the bottle through the window. Ji Qiongzhi flipped my ear with her finger. "Don't be like that, student Shangguan. You can gradually overcome your problem, but for now drink your milk." I turned and saw all those shining eyes and felt deeply ashamed. "Now listen to me," Ji said. "You are not to laugh at other people's weaknesses." She walked out of the classroom.

Facing the wall, I drank down the milk as fast as I could, and handed the bottle out through the window. "Mother," I said, "please don't come here anymore."

During the break between classes, Wu Yunyu and Ding Jingou were on their best behavior, sitting expressionless on their stools. The fat kid Fang Shuzhai took off his belt, stepped up onto his desk, and looped his belt over a rafter to play the hangman's game. Then, in the high-pitched voice of a widow, he began to sob and voice her grief: *Dog Two, Dog Two, how could you do that? With your arms outstretched, you return to your maker, and leave your little woman to sleep alone night after night. A worm gnaws at my heart, so I must hang myself. I'll see you down in the Yellow Springs.*

He sobbed and he grieved until, there on his fat little piggy cheeks, two lines of tears appeared. His nose was running, the stuff dripping down into his mouth. "I can't go on living!" he wailed as he stood on his tiptoes and stuck his head through the loop he'd made with his belt. Grabbing hold of the noose with both hands, he leaned forward and jumped. "I can't go on living!" he shouted. He jumped again. "I've lived long enough!" The laughter in the room had a strange quality. Wu Yunyu, who was still nursing his anger, placed both hands on his desk, stuck out his leg, and knocked Fang Shuzhai's desk out from under him, leaving him hanging there. He shrieked as he grabbed the rope with both hands and hung on for dear life, his squat, pudgy legs flailing in the air, but more and more slowly by the second. His face began to turn purple, he was foaming at the mouth, and a death rattle sounded deep in his throat. "He's dead!" several of the younger children screamed in terror as they ran out of the classroom. Out in the yard they stomped their feet and continued to scream: "He's dead! Fang Shuzhai hanged himself!" Fang Shuzhai's arms were hanging limply at his sides by now and his legs were no longer flailing. With a jerk, his body stretched out long. A loud fart wriggled out of the crotch of his pants like a snake, while out in the yard, the other students were running around crazily. Ji Qiongzhi came out of the faculty office along with several men whose names and the subjects they taught I didn't know. "Who's dead? Who is it?" they asked on their way into the classroom, tripping on all the construction debris that hadn't yet been cleared away. A bunch of excited and panicky students led the way, stumbling when they turned to look behind them. Leaping like a gazelle, Ji was inside the classroom in seconds. She looked confused as she went from bright sunlight into a dark room. "Where is he?" she demanded. Fang Shuzhai's body lay fell heavily on the floor like a slaughtered pig. His belt had snapped in two.

Ji knelt down and turned him face-up. She frowned and scrunched up her lips to block her nostrils. Fang Shuzhai stank to high heaven. She reached down and put her finger under his nose and then savagely pinched the ridge between his nose and mouth. Just then, Fang Shuzhai reached up and grabbed her hand. Still frowning, she got to her feet and kicked Fang Shuzhai. "Stand up!"

"Who kicked that desk over?" There was anger in her look and in her voice as she stood facing the class. "I couldn't see." "I couldn't see." "I couldn't see." "Well, then, who did see? Or which of you kicked it over? How about showing some guts for once." We held our heads way down low. Fang Shuzhai was sobbing. "Shut up!" she said, smacking the table. "If you're really that eager to die, there's nothing to it. I'll teach you some surefire ways a little later. I don't believe that none of you saw who kicked the desk over. Shangguan Jintong, you're an honest boy, you tell me." I let my head droop even lower. "Raise your head and look at me," she said. "I know you're scared, but you have my word there's nothing to be scared of." I looked up and gazed into that revolutionary face, with those beautiful eyes, and I was immersed in a feeling like an autumn wind. "I believe you have the courage to expose bad people and evil deeds," she said crisply, "a necessary quality for the youth of new China." I tilted my head slightly to the left, only to be confronted by an intimidating glare from Wu Yunyu. My head fell back down onto my chest.

"Wu Yunyu, stand up for me," she said calmly. "It wasn't me!" he bellowed. She just smiled and said, "Why are you so edgy? Why shout?" "Well, it wasn't me," he muttered, tapping the top of his desk with his fingernails. "Wu Yunyu," she said, "any person of worth takes responsibility for his actions." He abruptly stopped tapping the desk and slowly raised his head, his expression turning mean. He threw his book to the floor, wrapped his slate board and slate pencil in a piece of blue cloth, tucked it under his arm, and said with a sneer, "So what if I kicked that desk over? I'm not going to stick around this shitty school! I never wanted to be here in the first place, but you talked me into it." He walked arrogantly toward the door. He was tall and big-boned, the perfect image of a coarse, unreasonable individual. Ji Qiong-zhi stood in the doorway, blocking his way. "Get out of the way!" he said. "What do you think you're doing?" Ji smiled sweetly and said, "I'm going to show a thieving punk like you" — she struck him in the knee with a flying kick with her right foot — "that if you do something evil" — Wu Yunyu groaned in pain and crumpled to the floor — "that you'll be punished!" Wu took the wrapped slate board from under his arm and flung it at Ji Qiongzhi. It hit her in the chest. Protecting her injured breast with her arms, she moaned. Wu Yunyu stood up and said in a blustery voice that belied his fear, "You don't scare me. I'm a third-generation tenant farmer. Every member of my family — aunts, uncles, nieces, nephews — is a poor peasant. I was born by the side of the road where my mother was begging for food!" Rubbing her sore breast, Ji Qiongzhi said, "I hate dirtying my hands on a mangy dog like you." She laced the fingers of her hands and bent them back. *Crack*! *Crack*! Her knuckles popped. "I don't care if you're a third-generation tenant farmer or a thirtieth-generation tenant farmer, I'm still going to teach you a lesson!" With a blur, her fist landed on Wu's cheek. He yelped and staggered from the blow. The next blow landed in his ribs, followed by another kick in the ankle. He lay spreadeagled on the floor, crying like a baby. Ji then grabbed him by the neck and lifted him to his feet, smiling as she looked into his ugly face. As she backed him to the door, she drove her knee into his belly and gave him a shove. Wu Yunyu lay face-up on a pile of bricks. "You," Ji Qiongzhi an-nounced, "are hereby expelled from this school."

5

They stopped me on the path between the school and the village, each holding a springy mulberry switch, the bright sunlight casting a waxy sheen onto their faces. The gentle warmth of the sun's rays brought special luster to Wu Yunyu's snakeskin cap and swollen cheek, Guo Qiusheng's sinister eyes, Ding Jingou's funguslike ears, and the black teeth of Wei Yangjiao, who had a reputation in the village of being particularly crafty. I planned to get past them by hugging the side of the path, but Wei Yangjiao blocked my way with his mulberry switch. "What do you think you're doing?" I asked timidly. "What are we doing, you little bastard?" The whites of his crossed eyes leaped in their sockets like moths. "We're teaching a lesson to the bastard son of a redheaded foreign devil!" "I didn't do anything to you," I complained. Wu Yunyu's switch landed on my backside, creating hot currents of pain. Then the others joined in: four mulberry switches landed on my neck, my back, my backside, my legs. By then I was howling, so Wei Yangjiao took out a bone-handled knife and waved it under my nose. "Shut up!" he demanded. "If you don't stop crying, I'll cut out your tongue, gouge out your eyes, and slice off your nose!" Sunlight glinted coldly off the blade; properly terrified, I shut my mouth.

I was pinned down under their knees while they attacked the backs of my legs with their switches, like wolves ganging up on a sheep and driving it into the wildwoods. Water flowed silently down the ditches on either side of the path, bubbles bursting on the surface and releasing a stink that grew stronger as dusk settled in. I kept turning back to plead, "Let me go, big brothers," but that only made them hit me harder, and whenever I cried out, Wei Yangjiao was there to shut me up. I had no choice but to quietly take the beating, go where they wanted to take me.

After crossing a footbridge made of dried stalks, they stopped me in a field of castor flowers. By then my backside was wet — blood or urine, hard to tell. Red rays of sunset were draped across their bodies as they stood in a line. The tips of their mulberry switches were torn and ragged, and so green they looked black. The plump fanlike leaves of the castor plants were home to big-bellied katydids that chirped bleakly, and the strong odor of castor flowers brought tears to my eyes. Wei Yangjiao turned to Wu Yunyu and asked fawningly, "What are we going to do with him, big brother?" As he rubbed his swollen cheek, he muttered, "I say we kill him!" "No," Guo Qiusheng said, "we can't do that. His brother-in-law is deputy county head, and his sister's also an official. If we kill him, our lives are as good as over." "We can kill him," Wei Yangjiao said, "and dump the body into the Black Water River. Within days, he'll be food for ocean turtles, and nobody will be the wiser." "You can count me out if you plan to kill him," Ding Jingou said. "His brother-in-law, Sima Ku, who's killed lots of people, might show up, and he'd capable of wiping out our whole families."

I listened to them discuss my fate and future like a disinterested observer. I wasn't afraid, and never entertained the thought of running away. I was in a state of suspended animation. I even had time to look far off in the distance, where I saw the blood-red meadows and golden Reclining Ox Mountain off to the southeast, and the boundless expanse of dark green crops due south. The banks of the Black Water River, as it snaked its way east, were hidden behind tall grain and reappeared behind the shorter stalks; flocks of white birds formed what looked like sheets of paper as they flew over waters I couldn't see. Incidents from the past flashed into my head, one after another, and I suddenly felt as if I'd been living on this earth for a hundred years already. "Go on, kill me," I said. "You can kill me. I've lived long enough!"

Looks of astonishment flashed in their eyes. After exchanging glances among themselves, they all turned back to me, as if they hadn't heard me right.

"Go on, kill me!" I said resolutely, before starting to cry. Sticky tears ran down my face and into my mouth, salty, like fish blood. My plea had put them in an awkward position. Again they exchanged glances, letting their eyes talk for them. So I upped the ante: "I beg you, gentlemen, finish me off now. I don't care how you do it, just make it fast, so I won't suffer much."

"You think we don't have the guts to kill you, is that it?" Wu Yunyu said, cupping my chin in his rough fingers and staring me in the eye.

"No," I said, "I'm sure you do. All I'm asking is that you make it quick."

"Men," Wu Yunyu said, "he's put us in a sticky situation, and killing him is about the only way out. We can't back down now, no matter what happens. It's time to finish him off."

"You do it, then," Guo Qiusheng said. "I'm not going to."

"Is that mutinous talk I hear?" Wu said as he grabbed Guo by the shoulders and shook him. "We're four locusts on a string, so nobody better think about taking off. If you even try, I'll make sure people know what you did to that goofy girl in the Wang family."

"Hold on," Wei Yangjiao said. "Quit arguing. All we're talking about is killing him. If you want to know the truth, I'm the one who killed that old woman in Stone Bridge Village. No reason, I just wanted to try out this knife of mine. I used to think that killing someone would be hard to do, but now I know how easy it is. I jammed the knife into her rib cage, and it was like burying it in a cake of bean curd. *Slurp*. Even the handle went in. She was dead by the time I pulled the knife out.' She didn't make a sound." He rubbed the blade of his knife against his pants and said, "Watch me." Taking aim at my belly, he thrust the knife. I shut my eyes happily, and it seemed to me that I could actually see green blood gush from my belly right into their faces. They ran over to the ditch, where they scooped up water to wash off the blood. But the water was like nearly translucent red syrup, and instead of washing their faces clean, it actually made them dirtier than ever. As the blood gushed, my guts slithered out, slipping along the path over to the ditch, where they were caught up in the flow. With a cry of alarm, Mother jumped into the ditch to scoop up my guts, coiling them around her arm, one loop after another, all the way back to where I was standing. Weighted down by my guts, she was breathing hard and looking at me with sorrow in her eyes. "What happened to you, child?" "They killed me, Mother." Her tears fell on my face as she knelt down and stuffed my guts back into my belly. But they were so slippery that she no sooner got one section in than it slithered right back out, and she wept in frustration and anger. Eventually, she managed to stuff them all back in; she then took a needle and thread from her hair, and sewed me up like a torn overcoat. I felt a strange shooting pain in my belly and felt my eyes snap open. Everything I'd seen up till that moment was an illusion. The real situation was: They'd kicked me to the ground, taken out their impressive peckers, and were pissing in my face. The wet ground was spinning, and I felt as if I were flailing in a pool of water.

"Uncle — Little Uncle —!"

"Uncle — Little Uncle —!"

Shouts from Sima Liang and Sha Zaohua — one low, the other high — rose from behind the patch of castor plants. I opened my mouth to answer them, only to have it fill up with piss. My assailants hurriedly put away their hoses, pulled up their pants, and vanished into the castor patch.

Sima Liang and Sha Zaohua stood by the footbridge, calling out blindly, like Yunü often did. Their shouts hung above the field for a long time, filling my heart with sadness and stopping up my throat. I struggled to my feet, but before I'd managed to straighten up, I fell on my face. I heard Zaohua call out excitedly, "There he is!"

Together they lifted me up by my arms; I was as unsteady as one of those knock-over dolls. When Zaohua got a good look at my face, her mouth cracked open and — *wah* — she began to bawl. Sima Liang reached down to feel my backside — I yelped in pain. He looked at his hand, red with blood and green from the mulberry switches. His teeth chattered. "Little Uncle, who did this to you?" "They did . . ." "Who are they?" "Wu Yunyu, Wei Yangjiao, Ding Jingou, and Guo Qiusheng." "Let's go home, Little Uncle," he said. "Grandma's worried half to death. You out there, Wu Wei Ding Guo, you four bastards, I want you to listen and listen good. You may be able to hide today, but not tomorrow; you might get past the first of the month, but not the fifteenth. You touch another hair of my little uncle, and they'll be hoisting a flagpole at your house!"

Sima Liang's shouts still hung in the air when Wu, Wei, Ding, and Guo jumped out of the field of castor plants, laughing loudly. "Well, I'll be damned. Where did this runt with all the big talk come from? Isn't he afraid of losing his tongue?" They picked up their mulberry switches and, like a pack of dogs, charged us. "Zaohua, you take care of Little Uncle," Sima Liang shouted as he pushed me away and rushed to meet the charge of the attackers, all bigger than him. They were shocked by this fearless, almost suicidal charge, and before they could raise the switches, Sima Liang drove his head into the belly of cruel, foul-mouthed Wei Yangjiao, who bent over double and fell to the ground, where he curled up into a ball, like an injured hedgehog. The other three attackers brought their switches down on Sima Liang, who protected his head with his arms and took off running, with them hot on his heels. Compared to the weakling Shangguan Jintong, the little wolf Sima Liang was a more interesting specimen. They shouted excitedly — the chase was on, the battle was launched on the lethargic grassland. If Sima Liang was a little wolf, Wu, Guo, and Ding were massive and savage but very clumsy mongrels. Wei Yangjiao was a hybrid — half wolf and half mongrel — so he had been Sima Liang's first target. Knocking him out of commission removed the leader of the pack. Sima ran fast for a while, then slowed down, using a tactic designed to deal with zombies, changing directions often to keep them from catching up to him. Several times they lost their footing when they had to change direction. The knee-high grass parted and closed back up as they passed through it, scaring tiny wild rabbits out of their burrows; one couldn't get out of the way fast enough, and was squashed under Wu Yunyu's heavy foot. Sima Liang did more than merely run; every once in a while he turned and charged his pursuers. By zigging and zagging, he'd open up enough distance between them that he could turn and make a lightning attack on one. He picked up a dirt clod and flung it in Ding Jingou's face; he took a bite out of Wu Yunyu's neck; and he employed the Cross-eyed Beauty tactic against Guo Qiusheng, grabbing the object hanging between his legs and pulling it hard. All three bullies were wounded, but Sima Liang had received plenty of blows to the head in the process. They were slowing down. Sima Liang retreated to the footbridge. His pursuers formed up ranks; they were gasping for breath, spittle flying like an old bellows, as they cautiously took out after him as a group again — by then, Wei Yangjiao had caught his breath and rejoined his pals. He was like a cat on the prowl. Bending down low, he began to crawl, feeling his way with his hands, his bone-handled knife lying coldly on the ground. "You motherfucker! Bastard son of a restitution corps landlord! I'll kill you or know the reason why!" He cursed softly as he groped along; the white moths of his crossed eyeballs hopping around like hatching eggs. Seeing her chance, Sha Zaohua bounded over like a leaping deer, picked the knife up off the ground, and held it out to me in both hands. Wei Yangjiao stood up and reached out his hand. "Hand it over, you seed of a traitor!" he growled threateningly. Saying nothing, Zaohua backed into me as she shrank from Wei Yangjiao, never taking her eyes off his callused paws. Several times he lunged forward, but quickly backed off at knifepoint. By then, Sima Liang had retreated all the way to the footbridge. "Wei Yangjiao, you fucking asshole!" Wu Yunyu swore loudly. "Come over here and kill this bastard son of a restitution corps landlord! Get your ass over here!" Wei Yangjiao hissed at Zaohua, "I'll be back to take care of you!" He tried to pull up a castor plant to use as a weapon, but it was too thick, so he just broke off one of its branches and, waving it in the air, charged the footbridge.

Zaohua stuck close to protect me as we staggered up to the narrow footbridge. Water in the ditch flowed rapidly below, as schools of tiny carp were swept along. Some leaped over the bridge, others landed on it and flopped around angrily, their sleek bodies arching in the air. My crotch felt sticky, and everywhere else I'd been beaten — back, buttocks, calves, neck — felt as if it were on fire. A sweet yet bitter flavor, like rusty iron, filled my heart; with each step I took, my body rocked and a moan escaped between my lips. My arm was draped across Sha Zaohua's bony shoulder, and although I tried to straighten up to lessen the pressure on her, I couldn't do it.

Sima Liang was loping down the path to the village. Whenever his pursuers got a bit too close, he sped up, and when they slowed down, so did he. He maintained a distance close enough to keep them interested, but not so close that they could catch him. Mist rose from the fields on both sides of the path, dyed red from the setting sun; frogs filled the ditches with dull croaks. Wei Yangjiao whispered something to Wu Yunyu, after which the three of them split up. Wei and Ding crossed the ditch and ran to opposite ends of the field. Wu and Guo continued the chase, but at a leisurely pace. "Sima Liang," they shouted, "Sima Liang, a true warrior doesn't run away. Stay where you are if you've got the balls, and let's do battle."

"Run, big brother," Sha Zaohua shouted. "Don't let them trick you!"

"You little bitch!" said Wu Yunyu, as he turned and shook his fist at her. "I'll beat the shit out of you!"

Sha Zaohua stepped in front of me and held out the knife. "Come on," she said bravely. "I'm not afraid of you!"

As Wu pressed up closer, Zaohua kept pushing me back with her rear end. Sima Liang came up and called out, "Scabby head, if you so much as touch her, I swear I'll poison that stinky bean-curd-peddling old lady of yours!"

"Run, big brother!" Sha Zaohua screamed. "Those two mongrels, Wei and Ding, have circled around behind you."

Sima Liang stopped in his tracks, not knowing if he should advance or retreat. Maybe he stopped for a reason, since both Wu Yunyu and Guo Qiusheng also stopped. Meanwhile, Wei Yangjiao and Ding Jingou emerged from the field, crossed the ditch, and were crawling along the path. Sima Liang stood there looking very much at ease, wiping his sweaty forehead. That was when I heard Mother's shouts coming on the wind from the village. Sima Liang jumped down into the ditch and ran down a narrow path dividing the two crops — sorghum and corn. "Okay, men," Wei Yangjiao shouted excitedly, "let's get him!" Like a flock of ducks, into the ditch they went, slogging in pursuit of their prey. Leaves of the sorghum and corn stalks hid the path from view, so we had to rely on the rustling sounds and barking shouts to follow their progress. "You wait here for Grandma, Little Uncle, while I go help Brother Liang." "Zaohua," I said, "I'm scared." "Don't be, Little Uncle. Grandma will be here in a minute. Grandma!" she shouted. "They're going to kill Brother Liang. So shout!" "Mother — I'm over here! Here I am, Mother —"

Zaohua bravely jumped down into the ditch; the water came up to her chest. She splashed, creating green ripples, and I was worried she might drown. But she climbed up the other side, knife in hand, her skinny legs getting bogged down in the mud. She left her shoes behind as she turned onto the narrow path and disappeared from sight.

Like an old cow protecting its young, Mother ran up, rocking from side to side, and by the time she reached me, she was out of breath. Her hair was like golden threads, her face was coated with a warm yellow sheen. "Mother —" I shouted. Tears gushed from my eyes. I didn't think I could stand any longer. I stumbled forward and tumbled into Mother's hot, moist bosom.

"My son," Mother said through her tears, "who did this to you?"

"Wu Yunyu, and Wei Yangjiao . . ." I was sobbing.

"That bunch of thugs!" Mother said through clenched teeth. "Where did they go?"

"They're chasing Sima Liang and Sha Zaohua!" I pointed out the path.

Clouds of mist poured from the path; a wild animal called out from deep in the mysterious path; from farther away came the sounds of fighting and shrieks from Zaohua.

Mother looked back toward the village, which was already cloaked in heavy mist. Taking me by the hand, she decided to go down into the ditch, where the water was warm as axle grease as it rushed up through my pant legs. Mother's heavy frame and tiny feet made the going hard in all that mud. But by clinging to weeds on the side, she managed to make it to ground level.

Still holding my hand, she then turned onto the narrow path. We had to walk at a crouch to keep the sharp edges of the leaves from scratching our faces and our eyes. Creepers and wild grass nearly covered the path, the sharp nettles pricking the soles of my feet. I moaned sorrowfully. Having soaked in the water, my wounds hurt like hell, and the only thing that kept me from crumpling to the ground was Mother's iron grip on my arm. The light was fading, and the strange beasts out in the deep, serene, and seemingly endless croplands around us were stirring. Their eyes were green, their tongues bright red. Snorts emerged from their pointy noses, and I had this vague feeling that I was about to enter Hell; could that person clutching my hand, panting like an ox, and charging ahead single-mindedly really be my mother? Or was it a demon that had taken her form and was leading me down to the depths of Hell? I tried jerking my hand out of the painful grip, but all that accomplished was that she held it tighter than ever.

At last the frightful path opened out into light. To the south the sorghum field, like a boundless dark forest; to the north a wasteland. The sun was about to set, and the crickets on the vacant land raised a chorus of chirps. An abandoned brick kiln welcomed us with its fiery redness. Behind several piles of unfired bricks, Sima Liang and Sha Zaohua were engaged in a fierce guerrilla war with the four bullies. Each side was dug in behind a row of adobe bricks, which they threw at their enemy. Since they were smaller and weaker, Sima Liang and Zaohua were at a disadvantage, barely able to throw the missiles with their skinny arms. Wu Yunyu and his three buddies were flinging so many pieces of broken brick that Sima Liang and Sha Zaohua didn't dare poke their heads over the top of their pile.

"Stop it right now!" Mother screamed. "You bullying bunch of swine!"

Caught up in the intoxication of battle, the four assailants paid no attention to Mother's angry outburst. They kept hurling missiles, all the while sneaking around their pile of bricks to outflank Sima Liang and Sha Zaohua. Pulling the girl along with him, Sima darted over to the abandoned kiln. A piece of tile hit Zaohua in the head. She staggered with a yelp of pain and seemed about to fall. The knife was still in her hand. Sima Liang picked up a couple of bricks, jumped into the open, and flung them at the enemy, who quickly took cover. Mother put me down in the sorghum field, hidden from view, spread out her arms, and charged the battlefield, moving as if she were performing a rice-sprout dance. Her shoes stuck in the mud, exposing her pitifully small feet; her heels left holes in the mud from which water seeped.

Sima Liang and Zaohua showed themselves at the end of the wall of bricks. Hand in hand, they half ran, half stumbled in the direction of the kiln. By then the blood-red moon had already climbed quietly into the sky; Sima Liang and Sha Zaohua's purple shadows spread out across the ground. The four bullies' shadows stretched out far longer. Zaohua was slowing Sima Liang down, and when they reached the open ground in front of the kiln, a brick hurled by Wei Yangjiao knocked Sima Liang to the ground. Zaohua ran straight at Wei with the knife, but missed when he sidestepped the attack; Wu Yunyu came up and kicked her to the ground.

"Stop right there!" Mother shouted.

Like vultures spreading their wings, the four attackers bared their arms and began kicking Sima Liang and Sha Zaohua, over and over again. She cried out piteously; he didn't make a sound. They rolled on the ground, trying to avoid the feet of the attackers, who, in the moonlight, seemed caught up in a strange dance.

Mother stumbled and fell, but got stubbornly back to her feet and grabbed the shoulder of Wei Yangjiao and wouldn't let go. Known for being sinister and cunning, he drove his elbows back into her, catching her on both breasts. With a loud yelp, she backed off, lost her balance, and sat down hard on the ground. I threw myself down on the ground and buried my face in the mud; it seemed to me that black blood was gushing from my eyes.

And still they kicked Sima Liang and Zaohua in an explosion of savage fury. At that moment, a hulking figure with a mass of unkempt hair, an unruly beard, a face covered with soot, and dressed all in black emerged from the kiln. His movements were stiff as he crawled out and got clumsily to his feet; raising a fist that seemed as big as a pile driver, he swung at Wu Yunyu and shattered his collarbone. This one-time hero sat on the ground and cried like a baby. The other three hardy souls stopped dead. "It's Sima Ku!" Wei Yangjiao shouted in alarm. He turned to run away, but when he heard the angry roar from Sima Ku, like an explosion out of the earth, he and the others froze in their tracks. Sima Ku raised his fist again; this time it crunched into Ding Jingou's eye. The next punch drove the bile up and out of Guo Qiusheng's mouth. Before the next punch was launched, Wei Yangjiao fell to his knees and began banging his head on the ground, kowtowing and begging for his life: "Spare me, old master, spare me! Those three forced me to join in. They said they'd beat me up if I didn't, knock the teeth right out of my mouth . . . please, old master, spare me . . ." Sima Ku hesitated for just a moment before delivering a kick that sent Wei Yangjiao rolling backward. He scrambled to his feet and ran off like a frightened jackrabbit. It didn't take long for his barking voice to break the silence over the road leading to the village: "Go catch Sima Ku — the leader of the restoration corps landlords, Sima Ku, is back — go catch him —"

Sima Ku helped Sima Liang and Sha Zaohua to their feet, then did the same for Mother.

Mother's voice quaked. "Are you human or are you a ghost?"

"Mother-in-law —" Sima Ku sobbed, but didn't go on.

"Dad, is it really you?" Sima Liang blurted out.

"Son," Sima Ku replied, "I'm proud of you."

Sima Ku turned back to Mother. "Who's left at home?"

"Don't ask any questions," Mother said anxiously. "You must get away from here."

The frantic beating of a gong and crisp rifle fire came from the village.

Sima grabbed hold of Wu Yunyu and said, slowly so there'd be no misunderstanding, "You piece of shit, you tell that bunch of turtles in the village that if anyone lays a hand on any relative of mine, I, Sima Ku, will personally wipe his family off the face of the earth! Do you understand me?"

"I understand," Wu Yunyu said eagerly. "I understand."

Sima Ku released his grip and let Wu fall back onto the ground.

"Hurry, go on now!" Mother slapped the ground with her hand to get him moving.

"Dad," Sima Ku sobbed, "I want to go with you . . ."

"Be a good boy," Sima Ku said, "and go with your grandma."

"Please, Dad, take me with you."

"Liang," Mother said, "don't get in your father's way. He has to get out of here."

Sima Ku knelt in front of Mother and kowtowed. "Mother," he said sorrowfully, "the boy is going to have to stay with you. Since I could never repay the debt I owe you in this lifetime, you'll have to wait till my next lifetime!"

"I failed the two girls, Feng and Huang," Mother replied tearfully. "Please don't hate me."

"It wasn't your fault. And I've already exacted vengeance."

"Go on, then, go on. Run fast and fly far. All vengeance does is lead to more of the same."

Sima Ku got to his feet and ran back into the kiln. He reemerged a moment later wearing a straw rain cape and carrying a machine gun; shiny ammunition clips hung from his belt. In a flash, he vanished into the sorghum field, making the stalks rustle loudly. Mother called out after him:

"Hear what I have to say — run fast and fly far, and don't stop to do any more killing."

Silence returned to the sorghum field. The moonlight cascaded down like water. A tide of human sounds rushed toward us from the village.

Wei Yangjiao led a ragtag bunch of local militia and district public security forces up to the kiln. Carrying lanterns, torches, rifles, and red-tasseled spears, they put on a show of surrounding the kiln. A public security officer named Yang, who had been fitted with a prosthetic leg, lay up against a pile of bricks and said through a megaphone, "Sima Ku, give yourself up! There's no way out!"

Officer Yang kept it up for a while, with no response from inside the kiln. So he took out his pistol and fired twice at the dark opening of the kiln. The bullets produced echoes when they hit the inside walls.

"Bring me some grenades!" Officer Yang called out. A militiaman crawled up on his belly, like a lizard, and handed him two wood-handled grenades. Yang pulled the pin on one, tossed it in the direction of the kiln, then flattened out behind the bricks waiting for it to go off, which it did. Then he tossed the second one, with the same result. Concussion waves rolled far off into the distance, but still not a sound emerged from the kiln. Yang picked up his megaphone again. "Sima Ku, throw out your weapon, and we won't harm you. We treat our prisoners well." The only response was the soft chirping of crickets and the croaking of frogs in the ditches.

Yang found the nerve to stand up, the megaphone in one hand and his pistol in the other. "Follow me!" he called out to the men behind him. A couple of brave militiamen, one with a rifle, the other with a red-tasseled spear, fell in behind Yang, whose prosthetic leg clicked with each lurching step he took. They entered the old kiln without event and reemerged a few moments later.

"Wei Yangjiao!" Officer Yang bellowed. "Where is he?"

"I swear I saw Sima Ku come out of that kiln. Ask them if you don't believe me."

"Was it Sima Ku?" Officer Yang turned his glare on Wu Yunyu and Guo Qiusheng — Ding Jingou was lying unconscious on the ground. "No mistake?"

Wu Yunyu glanced uneasily at the sorghum field and stammered, "I think it was . . ."

"Was he alone?"

"Yes."

"Was he armed?"

"I think . . . a machine gun . . . ammunition clips all over his body . . ."

The words were barely out of Wu Yunyu's mouth when Officer Yang and all the men he'd brought with him hit the ground like mowed grass.

6

A class education exhibit was set up in the church. No sooner had the students reached the front door than they burst into tears, as if on command. The sound of hundreds of students — Dalan Elementary had by then become the key elementary school for all of Northeast Gaomi Township — all crying together rocked the street from one end to the other. The newly arrived principal stood on the stone steps and announced in a heavy accent, "Quiet down, students, quiet down!" He took out a gray handkerchief, with which he first wiped his eyes and then blew his nose loudly.

Once the students had stopped crying, they followed their teachers in single file into the church and lined up on a square drawn on the floor in chalk. The walls were covered with colorful ink drawings, all with explanations written beneath them.

Four women with pointers stood in the corners.

The first one was our music teacher, Ji Qiongzhi, who had been punished for beating up a student. Her face was a waxy yellow, her spirit obviously broken. Her once radiant eyes were now cold and lifeless. The new district head, a rifle slung over his shoulder, stood at Pastor Malory's pulpit while Ji pointed to the drawings behind her and read the descriptions beneath them.

The first dozen or so drawings described Northeast Gaomi Township's natural environment, its history, and the state of society prior to Liberation. After that came the drawing of a nest of venomous snakes with red forked tongues. A name was written on each snake's head, and on one of the largest heads was the name of Sima Ku and Sima Ting's father. "Under the cruel oppression of these bloodsucking snakes," Ji Qiongzhi intoned with apathetic fluency, "the residents of Northeast Gaomi Township were caught in an abyss of suffering, living lives worse than beasts of burden." She pointed to a drawing of an old woman with a face like a camel. The woman is carrying a decrepit basket and a begging bowl; a scrawny little monkey of a girl is holding on to the hem of her jacket. Black leaves with broken lines indicating they are falling from the upper left-hand corner of the drawing show how cold it is. "Countless numbers of starving people had to leave their native homes as beggars, only to be attacked by landlords' dogs that left their legs torn and bloody." Ji Qiongzhi's pointer moved to the next drawing: A black, two-paneled gate is opened slightly; above the gate hangs a gilded wooden plaque inscribed with two words: Felicity Manor. A tiny head in a red-tasseled skullcap is poking out through the gate opening — obviously the little brat of a tyrannical landlord. What I found strange was the way the artist had drawn this landlord brat: with his rosy cheeks and bright eyes, what should have been a loath-some image was actually quite fetching. A huge yellow dog had its teeth sunk into the leg of a little boy. At this point, one of the girls be-gan to sob; she was a student from Sandy Ridge Village, a second-grade "girl" of seventeen or eighteen. All the other students turned to look at her, curious to see why she was crying. One of them raised his arm and shouted a slogan, interrupting Ji Qiongzhi's account. Still, holding her pointer, she stood waiting patiently, a smile on her face. The one who had shouted the slogan then began to wail fearfully, al-though no tears appeared in his bloodshot eyes. I looked around; all the students were crying, waves of sound rising and falling. The prin-cipal, who was standing where he could be seen by all, had covered his face with his handkerchief and was thumping himself on the chest with his fist. Shiny dribbles of slobber ran down the freckled face of the boy next to me, Zhang Zhongguang, and he too was thumping himself on the chest, one hand after the other, either from anger or grief, I couldn't tell. His family had been labeled tenant farmers, but prior to National Liberation, I'd often seen this son of a tenant farmer in the Dalan marketplace tagging along behind his father, who made a living from gambling; the boy would be eating a chunk of barbecued pig's head wrapped in a fresh lotus leaf, until his cheeks, and even his forehead, would be spotted with glistening pork grease. Now slobber ran down the chin from that open mouth, which had consumed so much fatty pork. A full-bodied girl to my right had a tender, yellow, budlike extra finger outside the thumb of each hand. I think her name was Du Zhengzheng, but we all called her Six-Six Du. Those hands were now covering her face as she emitted sobs like the cooing of doves, and those darling little extra digits fluttered over her face like the curly tails of little piglets. Two gloomy rays of light emerged from between her fingers. Naturally, I saw a lot more students whose faces were damp with real tears, tears so precious no one was willing to wipe them away. I, on the other hand, couldn't squeeze out a single one, nor could I figure out how those few badly drawn ink drawings could tear at the students' hearts like that. I didn't want to be too obvious, though, since I'd noticed that Six-Six Du's sinister glare kept sweeping over my face, and I knew she hated my guts. We shared a bench in the classroom, and as we were sitting there one evening, doing our lessons by lamplight, she had touched my thigh with one of her extra fingers on the sly, without pausing in her recitation. Well, I had jumped to my feet in a panic, disrupting the entire class, and when the teacher yelled at me, I blurted out what had happened. It was a stupid thing to do, no doubt about it, since boys are supposed to welcome this sort of contact by girls. Even if you don't like it, you don't make a big deal out of it. But I didn't realize that until decades later, and when I did, I shook my head, wondering why I hadn't . . . But at the time, those caterpillar-like digits scared and disgusted me. When I exposed her, she looked for a hole to crawl into from shame; fortunately, it was an evening study session, and in the muted lamplight only a watermelon-sized halo of light lit up the area in front of each student. She hung her head low, and amid the obscene snickers around her, stammered, "It was an accident, I just wanted to use his eraser . . ." Like a complete idiot, I said, "She meant it, all right. She pinched me." "Shangguan Jintong, shut up!" So in addition to being ordered to be quiet by our music and literature teacher, Ji Qiongzhi, I had made an enemy out of Du Zhengzheng. One day later, I found a dead gecko in my school bag, and I figured she must have put it there. And now today, as this somber event was unfolding around me, I was the only one whose face was dry — no slobber and no tears. That could mean big trouble. If Du Zhengzheng chose this moment to get even . . . I didn't even want to think about it. So I covered my face with my hands and opened my mouth to make crying sounds. But I couldn't cry, I just couldn't.

Ji Qiongzhi raised her voice to drown out the sounds of crying: "The reactionary landlord class lived a life of luxury and excess. Why, Sima Ku alone had four wives!" Her pointer banged impatiently against one of the drawings, which was a portrait of Sima Ku, but with the head of a wolf and the body of a bear, his long, hairy arms wrapped around four alluring female demons: the two on the left had snake heads; the two on the right had bushy yellow tails. A clutch of little demons stood behind them, obviously the fruit of Sima Ku's loins. They included Sima Liang, the hero of my youth. But which one was he? Was he the cat spirit, with triangular ears on both sides of his forehead? Or was he the rat spirit, the pointy-mouthed one in the red jacket, claws reaching up out of the sleeves? I felt Du Zhengzheng's cold glare sweep past me. "Sima Ku's fourth wife, Shangguan Zhaodi," Ji Qiongzhi said in a loud but passionless voice as she pointed to a woman with a long fox tail, "feasted on so many delicacies from land and sea that the only thing left for her to eat was the delicate yellow skin of a rooster's leg. So a mountain of Sima roosters was slaughtered in order to indulge her extravagant desire!" That's a lie! When did my second sister ever eat the yellow skin of a rooster's leg? She never ate chicken. And there was never a mountain of slaughtered Sima roosters! The slander they were heaping onto my second sister filled me with anger and a sense of betrayal. And tears of complex origins gushed from my eyes. I wiped them away as fast as I could, but they kept coming.

Now that she'd completed her indoctrination duties, Ji Qiongzhi moved to one side, breathing heavily from exhaustion. Her place was taken by a woman who had just been sent down from the county government, Teacher Cai. She had thin brows over single-fold eyelids and a clear, melodic voice. Her eyes brimmed with tears before she even began speaking. This portion of the lesson had a fury-spewing topic: *Monstrous Crimes of the Landlord Restitution Corps.* Cai carried out her task scrupulously, pointing to each heading and reading it aloud, like a vocabulary lesson. The first drawing was of a crescent moon partially hidden behind dark clouds in the upper right-hand corner; in the upper left-hand corner were some black leaves trailing black lines. But this drawing was of an autumn, not a winter wind. Beneath the dark clouds and crescent moon, buffeted by icy autumn winds, the head of all of Northeast Gaomi evils, Sima Ku, in his military overcoat and bandolier — mouth open, fangs bared, blood dripping from his lolling tongue — held a bloody knife in one claw that poked out from his loose left sleeve and a revolver in his right, badly drawn flames spewing from the barrel, which had just fired several bullets. He was wearing no pants; his army overcoat hung all the way down to the top of his bushy wolf's tail. A pack of savage, ugly beasts was right on his heels. The neck of one of them was stretched out straight; it was a cobra spitting red venom — "This is Chang Xilu, a reactionary rich peasant from

Sandy Ridge Village," Teacher Cai said as she pointed to the head of the cobra. "And this one," she said as her pointer touched a wild dog, "is Du Jinyuan, the despotic landlord of Sandy Ridge Village." Du Jinyuan was dragging a spiked club (dripping blood, naturally). Next to him was Hu Rikui, a soldier of fortune from Wang Family Mound; he looked more or less human, but with the long, narrow face of a mule. The reactionary rich peasant Ma Qingyun from Two County Hamlet was a big, clumsy bear. All in all, a pack of armed savage beasts, murderous looks on their faces as they made their assault on Northeast Gaomi Township under Sima Ku's leadership.

"The Landlord Restitution Corps engaged in frenzied class warfare, and in a matter of only ten days, using every imaginable cruel means at their disposal, killed 1,388 people." Cai touched the images of one scene of brutal murder by landlord restitution members after another, drawing wails of grief from the students. It was like a magnified dictionary of shocking torture scenes that combined text and vivid drawings. The first few drawings showed traditional execution methods — decapitation, firing squad, and the like. But they gradually became more creative: "Here you see live burials," Teacher Cai said. "As its name implies, the victim is buried alive." Dozens of ashen-faced men were standing at the bottom of a large pit. Sima Ku stood at the edge of the pit, directing the gangster members of the restitution corps as they tossed in dirt. "According to the testimony of a survivor, old Mrs. Guo," Teacher Cai read the text below the drawing, "the restitution corps bandits tired themselves out from their work, and forced the revolutionary cadres and ordinary citizens to dig their own pits and bury each other. When the dirt reached their chests, the victims had trouble breathing. Their chests seemed about to explode, as the blood rushed to their heads. At that point, the restitution corps bandits fired their weapons at their victims' heads, sending blood and brain three feet into the air." The face of Teacher Cai, who was feeling lightheaded to begin with, was white as a sheet. The students' wails shook the rafters, but my eyes were dry. According to the time indicated at the bottom of the drawings, when Sima Ku was leading the restitution corps on the murderous frenzy in Northeast Gaomi Township, I was with Mother and revolutionary cadres and other activists on their retreat along the northeast coast. Sima Ku, Sima Ku, was he really that cruel? Teacher Cai rested her head against the drawing of the live burial. A little restitution corps member was raising a shovelful of dirt over his head, looking as if he was about to bury her. Translucent beads of sweat covered her face. She began to slide toward the floor, bringing the drawing down with her. Now she was sitting on the floor, leaning against the wall, the drawing covering her face. Gray flakes of the wall fluttered down onto the white paper.

This turn of events brought to an end the students' wails. Several district officials came running up and carried Teacher Cai out the door. The district chief, a middle-aged man with regular features, but moles all over the side of his face, kept his hand on the wooden butt of the rifle slung across his back as he said sternly, "Students, comrades, we now invite the elderly poor peasant from Sandy Ridge Village, Mrs. Guo, to report on her personal experiences. Send in Mrs. Guo!"

We turned to look at the battered little door that led from the church to what had been Pastor Malory's residence. Quiet, quiet, quiet that was abruptly shattered by a drawn-out wail that entered the church from the yard out front. A pair of officials opened the door by backing into it and entered, supporting Mrs. Guo, a gray-haired old woman who was covering her mouth with her sleeve and sobbing piteously. Everyone in the church joined her tearful outburst for a full five minutes, until she wiped away the tears, shook out her sleeve, and said, "Don't cry, children. Tears can't bring the dead back to life, and we must go on living."

The students stopped crying and gaped at her. To my ears, what she said was so simple, yet held profound significance. She seemed somehow reserved as she asked in a sort of confused manner, "What am I supposed to say? There's no need to talk about the past." She turned as if to leave, but was stopped by the director of the Sandy Ridge Women's League, Gao Hongying, who ran up to her and said, "Old aunty, you agreed to address us, didn't you? You can't back out now." Gao was visibly upset. The district head said genially, "Old aunty, just tell them how the members of the Landlord Restitution Corps buried people alive. We need to educate our youngsters that the past cannot be forgotten. As Comrade Lenin said, 'To forget the past is a form of betrayal.'"

"Well, since even Comrade Lenin wants me to talk, that's what I'll do." Mrs. Guo sighed. "There was a full moon that night, so bright I could have embroidered in its light. There aren't many nights like that. When I was a girl, an old-timer told me he recalled a white moon like that way back during the Taiping Rebellion. I couldn't sleep, worrying that something bad was about to happen, so I got up to go borrow a shoe pattern from the mother of Fusheng in West Lane and, while I was at it, talk to Fusheng about finding a wife, since I had a niece who had reached marrying age. As I was walking out the door, I spotted Little Lion, carrying a big, shiny sword, with Jincai's mother and wife and his two kids, the older one only seven or eight years old, and the younger one, a girl, barely two. The older kid was walking with his grandmother, scared and crying. Jincai's wife was carrying the little girl, who was also scared and crying. Jincai himself had a sword cut, a big, gaping, bloody wound on his slumping shoulder that scared me half to death. Three mean-looking fellows I thought I knew were walking behind Little Lion, also with swords, and I tried to hide so they wouldn't see me, but it was too late, and that bastard Little Lion spotted me. Now Little Lion's mother and I are some sort of cousins, so he said, 'Isn't that my aunt over there?' 'Little Lion,' I said, 'when did you get back?' He said, 'Last night.' 'What are you doing?' I asked him. 'Nothing,' he said. 'Just looking for a place for this family to sleep.' That didn't sound good, so I said, 'They're our neighbors, Lion, no matter how bad things get.' He said, 'There are no bad feelings, not even between them and my dad. In fact, my dad and his dad are sworn brothers. But he hung my dad up from a tree and demanded money from him.' Jincai's mother said, 'He didn't know what he was doing, so forgive him for the sake of the older generation. I'll get down on my knees and kowtow to you.' 'Mother,' Jincai said, 'don't beg.' Little Lion said, 'Jincai, you're starting to sound like a man, so no wonder they made you head of the militia.' 'You won't last more than a few days,' Jincai said. 'You're right,' Little Lion said, 'I imagine I'll last ten days or a couple of weeks. But tonight's all the time I'll need to take care of you and your family.' I tried to take advantage of my age by saying, 'Let them go, Little Lion. If you don't you're no nephew of mine.' He just glared at me and said, 'Who the hell is your nephew? Don't pull any of that relation stuff on me! The time I accidentally squashed one of your little chicks that year, you split my head open with a club.' 'Lion, what kind of human being are you?' He turned and asked the men with him, 'Boys, how many have we killed today?' One of them said, 'Counting this family, exactly ninety-nine.' 'You old woman, you're such a distant aunt that you'll have to sacrifice yourself so I can make it an even number.' That made my hair stand on edge. That bastard was talking about killing me! I ran into the house, but could I really get away from them? Family meant nothing to Little Lion. When he thought his wife was having an affair, he buried a live grenade in the stove ashes, but his mother got up early to clean out the stove and she was the one who dug out the grenade. I'd forgotten that incident, and now I was going to suffer, all because of my big mouth. They dragged Jincai and his family, plus me, over to Sandy Ridge Village, where one of them starting digging a big pit. It didn't take him long in that sandy ground. The moon was so bright we could see everything on the ground — blades of grass, flowers, ants, slugs — clear as day. Little Lion walked up to the edge of the pit to take a look. 'Make it a little deeper, men,' he said. 'Jincai's as big as a fucking mule.' So the man continued, and wet sand flew. Little Lion asked Jincai, 'Got anything to say?' 'Lion,' Jincai said, 'I'm not going to beg. I killed your dad, but if I hadn't done it, somebody else would have.' 'My dad was a frugal man who sold seafood along with your dad. He saved up a little money and bought a few acres of land. Unfortunately for your dad, somebody stole his money. You tell me, what was my dad's crime?' 'He bought land, that was his crime!' 'Jincai, tell me the truth, who wouldn't like to buy some land? How about your dad, for instance? And you your-self.' 'Don't ask me,' Jincai said. 'I can't answer that question. Is the pit deep enough?' The man said it was. Without another word, Jincai jumped into it. Only his head showed above the ground. 'Lion,' he said, 'I want to shout something.' 'Go ahead,' Lion said. 'We've been friends since we were bare-assed naked kids, so you deserve special treatment. Go ahead, shout whatever you want.' Jincai thought for a moment, then raised his good arm and shouted at the top of his lungs, 'Long live the Communist Party! Long live the Communist Party! Long long live the Communist Party!' Just three shouts. 'That's it?' Little Lion said. 'That's it.' 'Come on,' Lion said, 'let's hear some more. That's some voice you've got.' 'No,' Jincai said, 'that's it. Three times is enough.' Little Lion nudged Jincai's mother. 'All right,' he said. 'Now you, aunty.' Jincai's mother fell to her knees and banged her head on the ground, but Little Lion merely took the shovel out of the other man's hands and used it to push her into the sandy pit. The other men pushed Jincai's wife and kids in. The kids were bawling. So was their mother. 'Stop that!' Jincai demanded. 'Shut your mouths and spare me the shame.' His wife and kids stopped crying. Then one of the men pointed to me and said, 'What about this one, Chief? Toss her down there too?' Before Little Lion could answer, Jincai shouted,

'Little Lion, you said this pit was for my family. I don't want any outsiders down here.' 'Don't worry, Jincai,' Little Lion said, 'I understand
you perfectly. For this old woman, we'll —' He turned to the others.
'Men, I know you're tired, but dig another pit to bury this one.'

"The men split into two groups, one to dig a pit for me, the other
to fill in the pit with Jincai's family. Jincai's daughter began to cry.
'Mommy, the sand's getting in my eyes.' So Jincai's wife wrapped her
wide sleeves around the girl's head. Jincai's son struggled to climb out
of the pit, but was knocked back down by one of the shovels. The boy
began to bawl. Jincai's mother, on the other hand, sat down, and was
quickly buried in sand. She was gasping for air. 'Communist Party, ah,
the Communist Party!' she grumbled. 'We women are dying by your
hand!' 'So you finally got it, now that you're about to die!' Little Lion
said. 'Jincai, all you have to do is shout "Down with the Communist
Party" three times, and I'll spare a member of your family. That way
there'll be someone to tend your grave in the future.' Jincai's mother
and wife both pleaded with him, 'Go ahead, Jincai, do it, and hurry!'
His face nearly covered with sand, Jincai glared fiercely. 'No, I won't
do it!' 'Okay, you've got backbone,' Little Lion said admiringly as he
took the shovel from one of his men, scooped up sand, and flung it into
the pit. Jincai's mother wasn't moving. The sand covered his wife up
to her neck; it had already buried his daughter and all but the head of
his son, who reached up with his hands to keep struggling to get
out. Black blood was seeping out of his wife's nose and ears, while the
words 'Agony, oh, such agony' poured out of the black hole that was
her mouth. Little Lion paused in his work and said to Jincai, 'Well,
what do you say now?' Panting like an ox, Jincai, whose head had
swelled up like a basket, said, 'No problem, Little Lion.' 'Because we
were childhood friends,' Little Lion said, 'I'll give you one more
chance. All you have to do is shout "Long live the Nationalist Party,"
and I'll dig you out.' With wide, staring eyes, Jincai stammered, 'Long
live the Communist Party . . .' Infuriated, Little Lion recommenced
flinging sand into the pit. Jincai's wife and kids were quickly buried,
but there was still some movement just below the surface, which showed
they weren't all dead yet. All of a sudden, we were shocked to see Jincai's swollen head stick up in a terrifying manner. He could no longer
speak, and blood was seeping from his nose and his eyes. The veins on
his forehead were as big as silkworms. So Little Lion started jumping
up and down to pack down the sand. Then he squatted down in front

of Jincai's head. 'Well, what do you say now?' he asked; Jincai could no longer answer. Little Lion tapped him on the head with his finger and said, 'Say, men, want to try some human brains?' 'Who'd want to eat that stuff?' they said. 'It'd make me puke.' 'Some people have eaten it,' Little Lion said. 'Detachment Leader Chen, for one. Add some soy sauce and strips of ginger, he said, and it tastes like jellied bean curd.' The man who was digging the other pit climbed out and said, 'It's ready, sir!' Little Lion walked over to take a look. 'Come over here, my distant aunty, and tell me what you think of this crypt I made for you.' 'Lion,' I said, 'Lion, show a little mercy and spare this old life.' 'What does someone as old as you have to live for? If I let you go, I'll just have to find someone to take your place, since I need an even hundred.' So I said to him, 'Then finish me off with your sword. Being buried alive is just too horrible!' All that turtle-spawn son of a bitch said was, 'Life is nothing but suffering. But when you die, you go straight to Heaven,' before he kicked me down into the pit. That's when a bunch of people came shouting their way out of Sandy Ridge Village, with Sima Ku, the junior steward of Felicity Manor. I'd taken care of his third wife in the past, and all I could think was, my savior has arrived, swaggering up to us in riding boots. He'd aged a lot in the years since I'd last seen him. 'Who are you?' he asked. 'Me? I'm Little Lion!' 'What are you up to?' 'Burying people.' 'Burying who?' 'The head of the Sandy Ridge militia, Jincai, and his family.' Sima Ku walked up to where I was. 'Who's that down there?' 'Second Master, save me!' I shouted. 'I took care of your third wife. I'm the wife of Guo Luoguo.' 'Ah, it's you,' he said. 'How did you fall into his hands?' 'I talked when I shouldn't have. Show me some mercy, Second Master.' Sima Ku turned to Little Lion. 'Let her go,' he said. 'If I do that, Team Leader, I won't get an even hundred.' 'Forget the number. Just kill those who deserve to be killed.' One of his men reached down with his shovel, so I could climb out of the pit. You can say what you want, but Sima Ku is a reasonable man, and if not for him, that bastard Little Lion would have buried me alive."

The officials dragged and pushed old woman Guo out of the room.

Ashen-faced Teacher Cai picked up her pointer and returned to the spot where she had collapsed and recommenced her descriptions of torture. Even though tears filled her eyes as she droned on in a desolate tone of voice, the students were no longer crying. My gaze swept the faces of all those people who had been pounding their chests and stomping their feet, now showing the effects of exhaustion and impatience. All those drawings, reeking of blood, had turned insipid, sort of like flatcakes that have soaked in liquid for days then laid out to dry. Compared to what we'd heard from old woman Guo, whose personal experience had given her the voice of authority, the drawings and explanations had lost their appeal to our emotions.

7

They dragged me out of school.

A crowd had gathered on the street, clearly waiting for me. A pair of grimy-faced militiamen walked over and tied me up with a length of rope that was long enough to wrap around me more than a dozen times and still have enough for one of the armed guards to hold on to as he dragged me along. The other man followed, nudging me along with the muzzle of his rifle. Everyone along the way gawped at me as I passed by. Then, from the far end of the street another group of bound individuals came staggering toward me. It was my mother, my first sister, Sima Liang, and Sha Zaohua. Shangguan Yunü and Lu Shengli, who weren't tied, kept rushing up to Mother, only to be pushed aside by one of the burly militiamen. We met at the district headquarters — Felicity Manor — where we exchanged looks. There was nothing I could say, and I'm sure they felt the same way.

Escorted by the militiamen, we passed through several courtyards, all the way to the far end, where they crowded us into the southernmost room. The window on the southern wall was one big hole, its latticework and paper covering smashed and torn, as if to open up the activities inside to public scrutiny. I spotted Sima Ting, cowering in a corner, his face black and blue, front teeth missing. He gazed sadly at us. The furthermost little garden was just beyond the window, ringed by a high wall, one section of which had been broken through, as if to make a special gate. Guards patrolled the area, their uniforms billowing in the southern winds coming from the fields beyond.

That night, the district official hung four gas lamps in the room, and had a table and six chairs moved in. He also brought along some leather whips, clubs, rattan switches, steel wire, ropes, a bucket, and a broom. In addition to these, he installed a bloodstained slaughter rack for hogs, a butcher knife, a short flaying knife, iron meat hooks, and a bucket for catching blood. Everything you needed for a slaughterhouse.

Escorted by a squad of militiamen, Inspector Yang walked into the room, his prosthetic leg crackling. He had sagging jowls and rolls of fat under his armpits that made his arms stick out from his body, like a yoke hanging down from his neck. He sat behind the table and leisurely began preparations for the interrogation. First he took a Mauser that glistened blue from his back pocket, cocked it, and laid it on the table. Then he told one of the militiamen to hand him a bullhorn, which he laid beside the pistol. Next came a tobacco pouch and a pipe, which he laid beside the bullhorn. Finally, he bent down, removed his prosthetic leg — shoe, sock, and all — and placed it on a corner of the table. The leg was a terrifying pink under the gleaming white lamplight, but was marred by a series of black scars on the calf. The shoe and the sock were both badly worn. The thing rested on the table like one of Inspector Yang's loyal bodyguards.

Other district officials sat somberly on either side of Inspector Yang, pens poised over notebooks. Militiamen stood their rifles against the wall, rolled up their sleeves, and picked up whips and clubs. Like yamen guards, they lined up in rows across from each other, breathing heavily.

Lu Shengli, who had surrendered voluntarily, was grasping Mother's leg and weeping. Teardrops hung on the tips of Eighth Sister's long eyelashes, even though she was smiling. She was bewitching even under the most trying circumstances, and I began to feel guilty about keeping her from Mother's breasts when we were young. Mother was staring at the lamps, expressionless.

Inspector Yang filled his pipe and struck a match against the rough surface of the table. It lit with a pop. His lips smacked noisily as he drew on the pipe to get the tobacco burning. Then he tossed the match away and covered the bowl with his thumb before sucking deeply and noisily and expelling the white smoke through his nostrils. He removed the burnt ashes by knocking the pipe bowl against the leg of his stool. After laying the pipe on the table, he picked up the bullhorn, placed it up to his mouth, so that the open end faced the masses outside the window. "Shangguan Lu, Shangguan Laidi, Shangguan Jintong, Sima Liang, Sha Zaohua," he announced in a gravelly voice, "do you know why we've brought you here?"

We all turned to look at Mother, who was still staring at the lamp.

Her face was so puffy the skin was nearly translucent. Her lips twitched a time or two, but she said nothing. She merely shook her head.

Inspector Yang said, "Shaking your head is no way to answer my question. Based upon revelations by the masses and a full investigation by the authorities, we have gathered a mass of evidence. Over a long period of time, the Shangguan family, under the leadership of Shangguan Lu, concealed the whereabouts of Northeast Gaomi Township's number one counterrevolutionary, a man whose blood debts are incalculable, the public enemy Sima Ku. In addition, during one recent night, a member of the family vandalized the class education exhibition hall and filled the church blackboard with reactionary slogans. For these crimes alone, your entire family can be shot. But in line with current policy, we're prepared to give you a chance, a last chance, to save your lives. We want you to reveal the hiding place of the evil bandit, Sima Ku, so that this feral wolf can be brought to justice without delay. Second, we want you confess to vandalizing the class education exhibition hall and writing reactionary slogans, even though we already know who the guilty party is. We expect complete honesty, and for that you can expect leniency. Do you understand what I'm saying?"

We reacted with silence.

Inspector Yang snatched up his pistol and banged it against the table, without so much as lowering the bullhorn, which was still pointed at the window. "Shangguan Lu," he bellowed, "did you hear what I said?"

In a steady voice, Mother said, "This is a frame-up."

"A frame-up," the rest of us echoed her.

"A frame-up, you say? We are not in the business of framing innocent people, nor in the business of letting guilty ones off the hook. String them all up."

We fought and we cried, but all that did was delay the inevitable. They tied our hands behind us and strung us up from the rafters of Sima Ku's house. Mother hung from the southernmost end, followed by Shangguan Laidi, Sima Liang, and me at the other hand. Sha Zaohua was behind me. My arms hurt, but that was bearable; the pain in my shoulder joints, on the other hand, was excruciating. Our heads slumped forward, our necks stretched out as far as they would go. It was impossible to keep our legs straight, impossible not to straighten out our insteps, and impossible to keep our toes from pointing straight down to the floor. I couldn't stop whimpering, but Sima Liang didn't make a sound. Shangguan Laidi was moaning, but Sha Zaohua kept silent. The weight of Mother's body stretched the rope as taut as a wire; she was the first to start sweating and the one who sweated the most. Nearly colorless steam rose from her scraggly hair. Shengli and Yunü held on to her legs and swung back and forth, so the militiamen pulled them away like a pair of baby chicks. They rushed back and were pulled away again. "Inspector Yang," the men said, "want us to string these two up too?" "No!" Inspector Yang said firmly. "We do things by the book."

Without meaning to, Shengli pulled off one of Mother's shoes. Her sweat ran all the way down to the tip of her big toe, and from there fell like rain to the floor.

"Ready to talk?" Inspector Yang asked us. "Come clean, and I'll take you down at once."

Straining to lift her head and catch her breath, Mother said rasply, "Let the kids down . . . I'm the one you want . . ."

"We'll make them talk!" he announced to the window. "Beat them, and I mean hard!"

The militiamen picked up their whips and clubs and, with terrifying shouts, began to beat us systematically. I shrieked in pain, and so did First Sister and Mother. Sha Zaohua reacted with stony silence, and had probably passed out. As for Inspector Yang and the district officials, they pounded the table and shouted insults the whole time. Several of the militiamen dragged Sima Ting over to the slaughter rack, where they began beating him on his buttocks with a metal club, each stroke followed by a cry of agony. "Second Brother, you son of a bitch, get over here and confess to your crimes! You can't beat me like this, not after all I've done . . ." The militiaman swung his club over and over, without a word, as if pounding a piece of rotten meat. One of the officials smacked a leather water bag with his whip, while a second militiaman beat a burlap bag with his whip. Shouts and loud cracks, some real and others not, filled the room with a jumble of noises; the whips and clubs danced in the bright light of the gas lamps.

After about the time it takes for a class to end, they untied the rope fixed to the window lattice, and Mother crumpled to the floor. Then they untied another, and First Sister crumpled to the floor. The rest of us followed. A militiaman carried over a bucket of water and flung cold water on our faces with a ladle, bringing us around immediately. Every joint in my body was numb.

"Tonight has just been a warning!" Inspector Yang bellowed. "I want you to think good and hard. Are you going to talk or aren't you? If you talk, your previous crimes will be forgiven. If you don't, then the worst is yet to come." He picked up his prosthetic limb, put away his pipe, and holstered his pistol, then ordered the militiamen to guard us well before turning and hobbling out the door in the company of his bodyguards, creaking with each step.

The militiamen bolted the door and hunkered down by the wall to smoke, their rifles cradled in their arms. We huddled up next to Mother, whimpering and unable to say a word. She stroked our heads with her puffy hand. Sima Ting was moaning from the pain.

"Hey," one of the militiamen said, "tell him what he wants to know. Inspector Yang can make a stone statue confess. How many days do you think your flesh-and-blood bodies can hold out? You'll be lucky to make it past tomorrow."

One of the others said, "If Sima Ku is the man they say he is, he should give himself up. These days he can hide in the green curtain of crops. But come winter, he'll be out in the open."

"That son-in-law of yours is one strange tiger. Late last month, a squad of police had him surrounded in a patch of reeds at White Horse Lake, but he got away and managed to kill seven or eight pursuers with one burst of his machine gun. Even the squad leader was wounded in the leg."

The militiamen seemed to be hinting at something, I wasn't sure what. But they had let slip news about Sima Ku: after showing himself at the brick kiln, he had disappeared like a pebble in the ocean. We'd wanted him to fly high and far, but he'd stayed close to Northeast Gaomi, raising chaos and bringing us nothing but trouble. White Horse Lake was just south of Two County Hamlet, no more than three or four miles from Dalan.

8

At noon the next day, Pandi rode up from the county seat. Filled with anger, she was intent on making the district officials pay for what they'd done. But she had calmed down by the time she walked out of the office of the district chief, who came with her to see us. Not having seen her for six months, we didn't know what she was doing at county headquarters. She'd lost a lot of weight, but the dried milk stains on her blouse showed that she was nursing. We glared at her. "Pandi," Mother asked, "what have we done wrong?" Pandi looked at the district chief, who was staring out the window. As her eyes filled up with tears, she said, "Mother . . . be patient . . . trust the government . . . the government would never hurt the innocent . . ."

At the same time that Pandi was trying awkwardly to console us, out in the Scholar Ding family graveyard in the dense pine grove beyond White Horse Lake, Cui Fengxian, a widow from Sandy Mouth Village, was rhythmically pounding the tombstone over the grave of Scholar Ding, with its carved commendation for his heroic deeds. The crisp sounds merged with the *du-du-du* of a woodpecker at work on a tree. The fanlike white tail feathers of a gray magpie slipped through the sky above the trees. After pounding on the marker for a while, Cui Fengxian sat before the altar to wait. Her face was powdered, her clothes neat and clean; a covered bamboo basket hung from her arm, all of which gave her the appearance of a newly married young woman on a trip to her parents' home. Sima Ku stepped out from behind the grave marker, causing her to jump back in fright. "You damned ghost!" she cursed. "You scared me half to death." "Since when is a fox spirit like you afraid of ghosts?" "So that's how it is," she said, "still as sharp-tongued as ever." "What do you mean, that's how it is? Everything is wonderful, never better." He added, "Those local turtle-spawn bastards think they'll capture me, do they? Ha ha, dream on!" He patted the automatic rifle draped across his chest, the chrome-plated German Mauser in his belt, and the Browning pistol in its holster. "My mother-in-law wants me to leave Northeast Gaomi. Why would I want to do that? This is my home, the place where my ancestors are buried. I'm intimate with every blade of grass, every tree and mountain and river. This is where I get my enjoyment, and it also has a flaming fox spirit like you, so, I ask you, why would I want to run away?" Off in the reedy marshes a startled flock of wild ducks took to the air, and Cui Fengxian reached out and clapped her hand over Sima Ku's mouth. He wrenched her hand away and said, "Nothing to worry about. I've taught the Eighth Route Army a lesson over there. Those ducks were frightened off by vultures." Cui dragged him farther back into the graveyard, where she said, "I've got important news for you."

They threaded their way through a thicket of brambles on their way into a large vault. "Aiya!" Cui Fengxian yelped as a bramble pricked her finger. Sima Ku slipped his machine gun over his head and lit a lantern, then reached back and grabbed her hand. "Did it break the skin?" he asked. "Let me see." "It's fine," she replied as she tried to pull her hand back. But he'd already stuck the finger in his mouth and was sucking hard. She moaned. "You're a damned vampire." Sima Ku spat her finger out, covered her mouth with his, and grabbed hold of her breasts with his large, coarse hands. She writhed passionately and let her basket fall to the ground, sending brown eggs rolling around on the brick floor. Sima Ku picked her up and laid her on top of the broad crypt cover . . .

Sima Ku lay naked atop the crypt cover, his eyes half closed as he licked the tips of his dirty yellow mustache, which hadn't been trimmed for a long time. Cui Fengxian was massaging the large knuckles of his hand with her soft fingers. All of a sudden, she laid her burning face against his bony chest, which had the smell of a wild animal, and began to bite him. "You're a demon," she said, a note of hopelessness in her voice. "You never come to me when things are going well, but as soon as you're in trouble, you come and wrap your tentacles around me . . . I know that any woman who gets tangled up with you is in for a bad time. But I can't control myself. You wag your tail, and I run after you like some bitch . . . tell me, you demon, what evil power do you have that makes women follow you, even when they know you're leading them into a pit of fire, one they'll jump into with their eyes wide open?"

Sima Ku smiled even though her comment had saddened him. He took her hand and pressed it against his chest, where she could feel the strength of his heartbeat. "You have to believe in this, my heart, my true heart. I give my heart to women."

Cui Fengxian shook her head. "You only have one heart. How can you give it to different women at the same time?"

"However many I give it to, it's still genuine. And also this," he said with a lecherous laugh as he moved her hand down his body. Cui Fengxian wrenched her hand free and pinched him on the lips. "What am I going to do with a monster like you? Even when you're chased to the point where you have to sleep in your grave, you've still got time to play your silly games!"

With a laugh, Sima Ku said, "The harder they try, the more I feel like playing. Women are true treasures, treasures among treasures, more precious than anything." He reached out for her breasts again.

"You lecher," she said, "that's enough. Something has happened at your house." "What?" he asked as he continued fondling her. "They've taken them all into custody — your mother-in-law, your eldest and youngest sisters-in-law, plus your son, your little brother-in-law, the daughters of your eldest and fifth sisters-in-law, and your older brother. They have them locked up in the family compound. They string them up from the rafters nightly and beat them with whips and clubs . . . it breaks your heart, and I don't think they'll be able to hold out more than another day."

Sima Ku's hands froze in front of Cui Fengxian's chest. He jumped down off the crypt cover, picked up his automatic rifle, and bent down to scramble out of the vault. Cui Fengxian wrapped her arms around him and pleaded, "Don't go. You're just asking to be killed."

Once he'd calmed down, he sat beside a coffin and bolted down one of the boiled eggs. Sunlight filtering in through the brambles fell on his puffy cheek and the gray temple hair. The egg yolk caught in his throat; he coughed, and his face began to turn purple. Cui Fengxian thumped him on the back and massaged his neck until the food finally slipped down his gullet. Her face was bathed in sweat. "You frightened me half to death!" she said breathlessly as two large tears dropped onto Sima Ku's cheek and rolled down. He sprang to his feet, his head nearly hitting the vault ceiling, as flames of anger seemed to leap from his eyes. "You sons of bitches, I'll flay the skin off your bones!"

"Please don't go," Cui Fengxian pleaded as she wrapped her arms around him. "Yang the Cripple has set a trap for you. Even a long-haired old woman like me can see what he's up to. Use your head. By storming in there alone, you'll fall right into his trap."

"So what should I do?"

"Heed the words of your mother-in-law and get as far away from here as possible. I'll go with you if I won't be a burden, even if I wear out the soles of my feet."

Sima Ku took her hand and said emotionally, "I'm a lucky man to have met so many good women, each of them willing to throw in her lot with me, heart and soul. What else could a man ask for in this life? But I can't bring any more harm to you. You go now, Fengxian, and don't come looking for me anymore. Don't be sad when you hear that I'm dead. I've had a good life . . ."

With tears in her eyes, she nodded and removed an ox-horn comb from her head, with which she lovingly combed Sima Ku's tangled, gray-specked hair, removing bits of grass, broken snail shells, and tiny bugs. She kissed his forehead wetly and said in a calm voice, "I'll wait for you," before picking up her basket and crawling out of the vault. Parting the brambles as she went, she left the graveyard. Sima Ku sat there without moving until long after she'd disappeared from view, his eyes fixed on the sunlit, gently swaying brambles.

The following morning, Sima Ku crawled out of the vault, leaving his weapons behind, and walked over to White Horse Lake, where he took a bath. Then, like a man out on a nature stroll, he walked around the lake, looking here and there, striking up a conversation with birds in the reeds one minute and racing with roadside rabbits the next. He walked along the edge of the marshy land, stopping every few minutes to pick red and white wildflowers, which he held up to his nose and breathed in their fragrance. He then made a wide sweep around the pastureland, where he looked off into the distance at Reclining Ox Mountain, which was gilded in the rays of the setting sun. As he was crossing the footbridge over the Black Water River, he jumped up and down, as if trying to gauge how sturdy it was. It swayed and moaned. Feeling mischievous, he opened his pants and exposed himself, then looked down and liked what he saw; he let loose a stream of steaming urine into the river. As it hit the water with loud, rhythmic splashes, he howled: Ah — ah — ah ya ya — the sound soaring over the vast wilderness and circling back to him. Over on the riverbank, a cross-eyed little shepherd cracked his whip, which grabbed Sima Ku's attention. He looked down at the boy, who returned his look, and as they held each other's gaze, they both began to laugh. "I know who you are, boy," Sima Ku said with a giggle. "Your legs are made of pear wood, your arms are made of apricot wood, and your ma and I made your little pecker with a mud clod!" Angered by the comment, the boy cursed, "Fuck your old lady!" This vile curse threw Sima Ku's heart into turmoil; his eyes moistened as he sighed deeply. The shepherd cracked his whip again to drive his goats into the sunset. He cast a long shadow as he sang in his high-pitched childish voice: "In 1937, the Japs came to the plains. First they took the Marco Polo Bridge, then the Shanhai Pass. They built a railway all the way to our Jinan city. The Japs they fired big cannons, but the Eighth Route soldier cocked his rifle, took aim, and — *crack*! Down went a Jap officer, his legs stretched out as his soul flew into the sky . . ." Even before the song ended, hot tears spilled out of Sima Ku's eyes. Holding his burning face in his hands, he squatted down on the stone bridge . . .

Afterward, he washed his tear-streaked face in the river, brushed the dirt from his clothes, and walked slowly along the dike, which was overgrown with garish flowers. As dusk grew deeper, the birds' calls were bleak and chilling; the palette of colors in the sky was one gigantic smear, and the odors of the surrounding flowers, some heavy, others subtle, intoxicated Sima Ku, while the sometimes bitter and sometimes spicy grassy smells roused him from his inebriation. Heaven and earth both seemed so remote, eternity seemed to pass in the blink of an eye, thoughts that brought him profound anguish. Egg-laying locusts covered the gray footpath on the crest of the dike; they burrowed their soft abdomens in the hard, muddy ground, leaving the tops of their bodies sticking straight up, a scene of suffering and joy at the same time. Sima Ku squatted down, picked up one of the locusts. Studying its long, undulating, disjointed abdomen, he was reminded of his boyhood days and of his first love — a fair-skinned young woman with plucked eyebrows who was the mistress of his father, Sima Weng. How he had loved to rub his gristly nose against her breasts . . .

The village was just up ahead; kitchen smoke curled into the air, and the smell of humans grew heavy. He bent down to pick a wild chrysanthemum and breathe in its fragrance to clear his head of bygone images and put a stop to all fanciful thoughts. He then strode purposefully over to a newly opened breach in the southern wall of his family's compound. A militiaman who had been hiding in the hole jumped out, cocked his rifle, and shouted, "Halt! Don't come any closer!" "This is my house," Sima Ku retorted coldly.

Momentarily stunned, the guard fired a shot into the air and screamed wildly, "It's Sima Ku! Sima Ku is here!"

Sima Ku watched the militiaman run away, dragging his rifle behind him, and murmured, "What's he running for? Really!"

Inhaling another whiff of the yellow flower and humming the anti-Japanese ditty the shepherd had sung, he was determined to make a dignified entrance. But the first step he took landed in thin air, and he tumbled into a hole that had been dug in front of the breach for the sole purpose of catching him. A squad of county policemen who were keeping watch day and night in the field beyond the wall quickly emerged from their hiding places. The black holes of dozens of rifle barrels were pointed at the trapped Sima Ku, whose feet had been cut by sharpened bamboo sticks. "What do you men think you're doing?" he reviled them as he was racked by pain. "I came to give myself up, so why set a wild boar trap to catch me?"

The chief investigator reached down, pulled Sima Ku up to level ground, and snapped handcuffs on him.

"Release the members of the Shangguan family!" he bellowed. "I'm here to answer for my actions!"

9

To satisfy the demands of Northeast Gaomi residents, the public trial of Sima Ku was held in the square where he and Babbitt had shown their first open-air movie. Originally his family's threshing ground, it contained a tamped-earth platform that now barely rose above the ground around it; it was the spot where Lu Liren had once led the masses in the land reform campaign. In preparation for the arrival of Sima Ku, district officials had sent armed militiamen to the spot the night before to dig up hundreds of square feet of dirt in order to re-build the platform until it was as high as the Flood Dragon River dikes, and to dig a trench that ran in front and along the sides of the platform, which was then filled with oily green water. Once that was done, they authorized the expenditure of enough money to purchase a thousand catties of millet, which was then exchanged for two wag-onloads of tightly woven, golden yellow matting from a marketplace ten miles out of town, with which they erected a huge tent over the platform, and then covered it with colorful sheets of paper on which were written a variety of slogans, some angry and others jubilant. The leftover matting was spread over the platform itself and its sloping sides, giving it the appearance of golden cascades. The district chief, in the company of the county head, came personally to inspect the interrogation site. Standing on the sleek, easy-on-the-feet platform, which rose like an opera stage, they gazed out at the roiling blue waters of the Flood Dragon River as it flowed east, a cold wind billow-ing their sleeves and pant legs until they took on the appearance of sausage links. The county head rubbed his red nose as he turned to ask the district chief loudly, "Who's responsible for this masterpiece?"

Unable to tell if the county head was being sarcastic or compli-mentary, the district chief replied ambiguously, "I was involved in the planning, but he was in charge of the work." He pointed to an official from the District Propaganda Committee standing off to one side.

The county head glanced over at the beaming official and nodded. Then, lowering his voice, but not enough to keep the people behind him from hearing, he said, "This looks more like a coronation than a public trial!"

Inspector Yang hobbled up at that moment and bowed respectfully to the county head, who sized him up and said, "The county recognizes your outstanding service in arranging the capture of Sima Ku. But your scheme entailed the torture of members of the Shangguan family, for which you have been censured."

"Bringing the murdering devil Sima Ku to justice is what counts," Inspector Yang responded passionately, "and for that I'd have gladly given my good leg!"

The public trial was scheduled for the morning of the eighth day of the twelfth lunar month. Residents cloaked in the cold glare of early-morning stars and capped by the chilly countenance of the moon began pouring into the site to be part of the excitement. By dawn the square was black with people, some of whom stood behind railings thrown up on the banks of the Flood Dragon River. When the sun made its shy appearance, casting its rays on the people's frosty eyebrows and beards, pink mist rose from their mouths. Other people had lost sight of the fact that it was the morning when they normally ate bowls of fruity rice porridge, but not the members of my family. Mother tried to infect us with her feigned enthusiasm, but Sima Liang's constant weeping had us in a foul mood. Like a little mother, Eighth Sister felt around for a sponge she'd picked up on the sandbar and dried Sima Liang's copious tears. He wept without making a sound, which made it worse than if he'd been bawling loudly. First Sister stayed close by Mother, who was running around busily, and asked over and over, "Mother, if he dies, will I be expected to die with him?"

"Stop talking nonsense!" Mother reprimanded her. "You wouldn't be expected to do that even if the two of you had been properly married."

By the tenth or twelfth time she asked the same question, Mother lost patience and said pointedly, "Laidi, does face mean anything to you? When you hooked up with him, it was nothing more than a brother-in-law taking up with his sister-in-law, a shameful act in any-one's book."

First Sister was stunned. "Mother," she said, "you've changed."

"Yes, I've changed," Mother said, "and yet I'm still the same. Over the past ten or more years, members of the Shangguan family have died off like stalks of chives, and others have been born to take their place. Where there's life, death is inevitable. Dying's easy; it's living that's hard. The harder it gets, the stronger the will to live. And the greater the fear of death, the greater the struggle to keep on living. I want to be around on the day my children and grandchildren rise to the top, so I expect all of you to make a good showing for my sake!"

Her eyes, wet with tears, yet spitting fire, swept across our faces, resting finally on me, as if I were the repository of all her hopes. That made me incredibly fearful and restive, since, with the exceptions of an ability to memorize school lessons and sing the "Women's Liberation Anthem" with a degree of accuracy, I couldn't think of a thing I was particularly good at. I was a crybaby, I was scared of my own shadow, and I was a weakling, sort of like a castrated sheep.

"Get yourselves ready," Mother said, "so we can give him a proper send-off. He's a bastard, but he's also a man worthy of the name. In days past, a man like that would come around once every eight or ten years. I'm afraid we've seen the last of his kind."

We stood as a family on the river dike and watched the people around us slink away. Many sideward glances were cast our way. Sima Liang tried to move up closer, but Mother grabbed hold of his arm. "Stay right here, Liang. We'll watch from a distance. If we're too close, it'll just give him something else to worry about."

The sun rose high in the sky as truckloads of armed, helmeted soldiers crept across the Flood Dragon River Bridge and through the breach in the dike. They wore the looks of men confronted by a powerful enemy. After the trucks came to a stop beside the tent, the soldiers jumped to the ground in pairs and dispersed rapidly to form a blockade line. Two soldiers then climbed out of one of the trucks and opened the tailgate. Out stepped Sima Ku, wearing a pair of shiny handcuffs, in the custody of a squad of soldiers. He stumbled when he was pushed to the ground, but was immediately picked up by a tall, robust soldier who was obviously handpicked for this assignment. Sima

Ku, his swollen legs covered with thick blood, stumbled along with his captors, leaving putrid-smelling footprints in the dirt. They led him over to the tent and up onto the raised platform. Out-of-town witnesses who were seeing Sima Ku for the first time, and had assumed him to be a murderous demon, half man–half beast, a monster with fangs and a ferocious, green face, later said that seeing him in person had been a disappointment. This middle-aged man with his shaved head and big, sad eyes didn't look threatening at all. In fact, he struck them as a guileless, good-natured fellow, and had them wondering if the police had arrested the wrong man.

The trial quickly got underway, beginning with the magistrate's reading of Sima Ku's crimes and ending with the pronouncement of the death sentence. Soldiers then led him down off the platform. He hobbled as he walked, causing the soldiers to stumble as they held his arms. The procession halted at the edge of the pond, the infamous execution site. Sima Ku turned to face the dike. Maybe he spotted us, and maybe he didn't. Sima Liang called out, "Daddy," but Mother quickly clapped her hand over his mouth.

"Liang," she whispered in his ear, "be a good boy, and do as I say. I know how you feel, but it's important that we don't make your daddy feel any worse than he does now. Let him face this last challenge free from worries."

Mother's words worked like a magic charm, transforming Sima Liang from a mad dog into a tame sheep.

A pair of powerful-looking soldiers grabbed Sima Ku's shoulders and forced him to turn around to face the execution pond, whose thirty-year accumulation of rainwater had the appearance of lemon oil, in which his gaunt face and scarred cheeks looked back at him. With his back to the squad of soldiers and facing the pond, he saw countless women's faces reflected in the water, their smell floating up from the surface, and he was suddenly overcome by a sense of his own frailty; turbulent waves of emotion overwhelmed the calmness in his heart. He wrenched himself from the grip of the soldiers to turn back around, throwing a fright into the director of the Judicial Department of the County Security Bureau, as well as the executioners, who were known for their ability to kill without batting an eye.

"I won't let you shoot me in the back!" he shouted shrilly.

Facing the stony stares of his executioners, he felt stabs of pain from the scars on his cheeks. Sima Ku, for whom face was so important, was overcome with regret as the events of the day before surfaced in his mind.

When the legal representative had handed down the article of execution, Sima Ku had received it joyfully. The representative had asked if he had any last requests. Rubbing his stubble, he'd said, "I'd like to have a barber shave my head," to which the representative had replied, "I'll take that back to my superiors."

The barber arrived, carrying his little case, and approached the condemned cell with obvious trepidation. After haphazardly shaving his head, he turned his razor to the beard. But about halfway, he nicked Sima Ku on the cheek, drawing a screech from the victim, so frightening the barber that he leaped back toward the cell door and placed himself between the two armed guards.

"That guy's hair is pricklier than hog bristles," the barber said as he showed the guards the nicked razor. "The blade's ruined. And his beard's even worse. It's like a wire brush. He must concentrate his strength at the roots of his beard."

So the barber gathered up his stuff and was about to leave, when he was stopped short by a curse from Sima Ku: "You son of a bitch, what do you think you're doing? Do you expect me to go to meet my ancestors with half my face shaved?"

"You, there, condemned man," the barber shot back. "Your beard's tough enough already, and then you go concentrating your strength there."

Not knowing whether to laugh or to cry, Sima Ku said, "Don't blame the toilet when you can't do your business. I have no idea what you mean by concentrating my strength somewhere."

"The way you keep grunting, if that isn't concentrating your strength, what is it?" the barber replied cleverly. "I'm not deaf, you know."

"You bastard!" Sima Ku said. "I'm groaning from all the pain."

One of the guards said to the barber, "You've got a job to do. So suck it up and finish shaving him."

"I can't," he said. "Go find a master barber."

Sima Ku sighed and said, "Shit, where in the world did you find this piece of rubbish? Take off these handcuffs, men, and I'll shave myself."

"Not on your life!" one of the guards said. "If you used that as a ploy to attack us and run off, or kill yourself, it would be on our heads."

"Fuck your old lady!" Sima Ku bellowed. "I want to see whoever's in charge." He banged his handcuffs noisily against the window bars.

A security officer came running over. "What do you think you're doing, Sima Ku," she demanded.

"Look at my face," Sima said. "He shaved half and then stopped because he said my beard's too tough. Does that make sense to you?"

"No," she said as she slapped the barber's shoulder. "Why won't you finish shaving him?"

"His beard's too tough. And he keeps concentrating his strength in the roots . . ."

"Fuck your ancestors, with all that talk about concentrating strength!"

The barber held up his damaged razor in defense of his position.

"How about acting like a man, friend?" Sima Ku said to her. "Take off these handcuffs, and I'll shave myself. It's the last favor I'll ever ask."

The officer, who had participated in Sima's capture, hesitated momentarily before turning to one of the guards and saying, "Take them off."

With a sense of foreboding, the guard did as he was told, then jumped back out of harm's way. Sima Ku rubbed his swollen wrists. When he stuck out his hand, the officer took the razor from the barber and handed it to Sima, who took it and gazed at her dark, grapelike eyes, which were topped by bushy eyebrows. "Aren't you afraid I'll attack you, or run off, or kill myself?"

"If you did," she said with a smile, "then you wouldn't be Sima Ku."

With a sigh, Sima said, "I never dreamed it would take a woman to really understand me!"

She smiled scornfully.

Sima stared at the woman's hard, red lips, and then let his gaze move down to her chest, which arched upward under her khaki uniform. "You've got nice breasts, little sister," he said.

Grinding her teeth in anger, she said, "Is that all you can think about the day before you're going to die?"

"Little sister," Sima replied somberly, "I've screwed a lot of women in my life, and my only regret is that I've never screwed a Communist."

Furious, she slapped him, so loud and so hard that dust rained down from the rafters. He smiled impishly and said, "I've got a young sister-in-law who's a Communist. She has a firm political stance and nice, firm breasts . . ."

As her face reddened, the officer spat in Sima's face and said in a low growl, "Be careful, you mangy mongrel, or I might cut your balls off!"

Sima Ting cried out, his voice filled with sadness and anger, rousing Sima Ku from his anguished thoughts. What he saw was a squad of militiamen dragging his elder brother up to the crowd of onlookers. "I'm innocent — innocent! I've rendered great service, and I broke off relations with my brother a long time ago!" No one paid any attention to Sima Ting's tearful pleas. Sima Ku sighed, as threads of guilt filtered into his heart. When the chips were down, the man was a good and loyal brother, even if you couldn't trust some of the things he said.

Sima Ting's legs were so rubbery he couldn't stand. A village official demanded, "Tell me, Sima Ting, where's the Felicity Manor treasure vault? If you don't tell me, you can walk down the same road as him!" "There's no treasure vault. During land reform, they dug down three feet and didn't find anything," Sima Ku's wretched brother pled his case. Sima Ku grinned and said, "Quit your bitching, Elder Brother!" "It's all your fault, you bastard!" Sima Ting complained. Sima Ku just shook his head with a wry smile. "Stop this nonsense!" a security bureau officer rebuked the village officials, resting his hand on the butt of his holstered pistol. "Take that man away! Don't you give a damn about policy?" As they dragged Sima Ting away, the village official said, "We figured this might be a good opportunity to get something out of him."

The man in charge of the execution raised a little red flag and announced in a loud voice, "Ready —"

The firing squad raised their weapons, waiting for the command. An icy grin spread across Sima Ku's face as he stared down the black muzzles of the rifles aimed at him. A red glare rose above the dike, and the smell of women blanketed heaven and earth. Sima Ku shouted:

"Women are wonderful things —"

The dull crack of rifle fire split Sima Ku's head like a ripe melon, sending blood and brain in all directions. His body stiffened for a brief moment, and then toppled forward. At that moment, like the climactic scene in a play, just before the curtain drops, the widow Cui Fengxian from Sandy Mouth Village, wearing a red satin jacket over green satin pants, a spray of golden-yellow silk flowers in her hair, flew down from the top of the dike and lay on the ground beside Sima Ku. I assumed she would begin to wail over the corpse, but she didn't. Maybe the sight of Sima Ku's shattered skull drove the courage out of her. She took a pair of scissors from her waistband, which I thought she was going to plunge into her breast to accompany Sima Ku in death. But she didn't. In the midst of all those staring eyes, she plunged the scissors into Sima Ku's dead chest. Then she covered her face, shattered the stillness with shrieks of grief, and staggered off as fast as her feet would take her.

The crowd of onlookers stood there like wooden stakes. Sima Ku's decidedly inelegant last words had bored their way into their hearts, tickling them as they crawled around mischievously. Are women really wonderful things? Maybe they are. Yes, women definitely are wonderful things, but when all is said and done, they aren't really "things."

Chapter Six

1

On the day of Shangguan Jintong's eighteenth birthday, Shangguan Pandi took Lu Shengli away with her. Jintong sat on the dike gazing unhappily at swallows soaring above the river. Sha Zaohua came out of the woods and handed him his birthday present — a little mirror. The dark-skinned girl already had nicely developed breasts; her dark, slightly crossed eyes looked like pebbles on the river bottom and were filled with the glow of passion. "Why don't you keep it for Sima Liang when he gets back?" Jintong said. She reached into her pocket and took out a larger mirror. "This one's for him." "Where'd you get so many mirrors?" Jintong asked, obviously surprised. "I stole them from the co-op," she said in a soft voice. "I met a thief wizard at the Wopu Market who took me on as her apprentice. After I finish my apprenticeship, if there's anything you need, just tell me, and I'll steal it for you. My teacher stole a watch off the wrist of a Soviet adviser and a gold tooth right out of his mouth." "But that's against the law." "She said minor thievery is against the law, but not big-time stealing." Taking Jintong's fingers in her hand, she said, "You've got soft, slender fingers. You'd make a good thief." "No, not me. I don't have the nerve. But Sima Liang does, he's got guts and he's always vigilant. He's your man. You can teach him when he gets back." As Zaohua put away the big mirror, she said "Liangzi, Liangzi, when will you be coming back?" sounding like a grown-up woman.

* * *

Sima Liang had disappeared five years earlier. We buried Sima Ku the day after he was shot, and Sima Liang took off that night. A cold, dank wind from the northeast made the chipped pots and jugs on the wall sing out gloomily. We sat dully in front of a solitary lantern, and when the wind blew out the flame, we sat in the darkness. No one spoke; we were all caught up in the scene surrounding Sima Ku's burial. Lacking a coffin, we had to wrap his body in a straw mat, like a leek in a flatcake, good and tight, and truss it up with rope. A dozen or so people carried his body over to the public cemetery, where we dug a hole. Then we stood at the head of the grave, where Sima Liang fell to his knees and kowtowed once. There were no tears on his finely wrinkled face. I wanted to say something to make this dear friend of mine feel better, but couldn't think of a thing. On the road home, he whispered, "I'm going to take off, Little Uncle." "Where to?" I asked him. "I don't know." At the moment the wind blew out the lantern flame, I thought I saw a dark, hazy image slip out the door, and I was pretty sure that Sima Liang had left, though there wasn't a sound. Just like that, he was gone. With a bamboo pole, Mother probed the bottom of every dry well and deep pond in the area, but I knew she was wasting her time, since Sima Liang was not the type to kill himself. Mother then sent people into neighboring villages to look for him, but all she got were conflicting reports. One person said he'd spotted him in a traveling circus, while someone else said he'd seen the body of a little boy by the side of a lake, his face pecked clean by vultures; a group of conscripts back from the Northeast said they'd seen him near a bridge over the Yalu River. The Korean War was heating up then, and U.S. warplanes came on daily bombing runs.

I looked into the little mirror Zaohua had given me, getting my first good view of my features. At eighteen, I had a shock of yellow hair, pale, fleshy ears, brows the color of ripe wheat, and sallow lashes that cast a shadow over deep blue eyes. A high nose, pink lips, skin covered with fine hairs. To tell the truth, I'd already gotten an idea of what I looked like by looking at Eighth Sister. With a sense of sadness, I was forced to admit that Shangguan Shouxi was definitely not our father, and that whoever he was, he looked like the man people sometimes talked about in hushed conversations. We were, I realized, the illegitimate offspring of the Swedish man of the cloth, Pastor Malory, a couple of bastards. Frightful inferiority feelings gnawed at my heart. I dyed my hair black and darkened my face, but there was nothing I could do about the color of my eyes, which I'd have liked to gouge out altogether. I recalled stories I'd heard about people who committed suicide by swallowing gold, so I rummaged around in Laidi's jewelry box until I found a gold ring dating back to Sha Yueliang's days. I stretched out my neck and swallowed the thing, then lay down on the *kang* to await death, while Eighth Sister sat on the edge of the *kang* spinning thread. When Mother returned from work at the co-op and saw me lying there, she caught her breath in surprise. I expected her to feel a sense of shame, but what I saw instead was a look of terrifying anger. She grabbed me by the hair and jerked me into a sitting position, then began slapping me, over and over, until my gums bled, my ears rang, and I saw stars.

"That's right, Pastor Malory was your father, so what? Wash that stuff off your face and out of your hair, then go out in the street with your head held high, and announce: My father was the Swedish Pastor Malory, which makes me an heir to royalty, and a damned sight better than the likes of you turtles!" All the while she was slapping me, Eighth Sister sat quietly spinning her threads, as if none of this had anything to do with her.

I sobbed the whole time I was squatting in front of the basin washing my face, turning the water black. Mother stood behind me, cursing under her breath, but I knew I was no longer the target of those curses. When I was finished, she ladled out some clean water and poured it over my head as she began to cry. The water ran down my nose and chin and into the basin on the floor, slowly turning the water clear again. While she dried my hair, Mother said: "Back then there was nothing I could do, son. You are what you are, so stand up straight and act like a man. You're eighteen years old, no longer a child. Sima Ku had his faults, plenty of them, but he lived his life like a man, and that's worth emulating."

I nodded obediently, but suddenly remembered the gold ring. Just as I was about to tell her what I'd done, Laidi ran breathlessly into the house. She'd begun working at the district match factory, and was wearing a white apron stenciled with the words: Dalan Starlight Match Factory.

"He's back, Mother!" she announced nervously.

"Who?" Mother asked.

"The mute," First Sister said.

Mother dried her hands and looked into First Sister's haggard face. "I'm afraid it's your fate, Daughter."

The mute, Speechless Sun, "walked" into our front yard. He had aged since the last time we'd seen him; flecks of gray poked out from under his army cap. His rheumy eyes were more clouded than ever, and his jaw looked like a rusty plow. He was dressed in a new yellow uniform with a high-collar tunic, buttoned at the throat, a row of glittering medals on his chest. His long, powerful arms ended in a pair of gleaming white gloves, his hands resting on squat, leather-trimmed stools. He was sitting on a red Naugahyde pad that was attached to him. His wide trouser legs were tied together at his waist, below which were two stumps. That was the image the mute, whom we had not seen for years, presented to us now. Stretching the squat stools out in front with his powerful arms, he heaved his body forward and moved closer, the pad strapped to his hips glistening red in the light.

With five lurching movements, he brought himself up to within about ten feet of us, far enough that he didn't have to strain to look up at us. Dirty water splashed as I rinsed my hair and flowed to the ground in front of him. Putting his hands behind him, he lurched backward, and at that moment it dawned on me that a person's height depends mainly on his legs. The upper half of Speechless Sun's body looked thicker, bulkier, and more menacing than ever. Even though he'd been reduced to a torso, he retained an awesome fearfulness. He looked us in the eye, a welter of mixed emotions showing on his dark face. His jaw quivered, much as it had years ago, as he grunted over and over the same word: "Strip, strip, strip . . ." Two lines of diamondlike tears slipped down his cheeks from gold-tinged eyes.

Raising his hands in the air, he made a series of gestures to the accompaniment of "Strip strip strip," and I realized we hadn't seen him since he'd traveled to the Northeast to inquire into the whereabouts of his sons, Big and Little Mute. Covering her face with a towel, Mother ran tearfully into the house. Understanding her meaning at once, the mute let his head sag down on his chest.

She returned with two bloodstained caps, which she handed to me and signaled me to give him. Forgetting all about the gold ring I'd swallowed, I walked up to him. Gazing up at my rail-thin body as I stood before him, he just shook his head sadly. I bent over, but quickly changed my mind and squatted down in front of him, handed him the caps, and pointed to the northeast. Images of that sad journey rushed into my head, with the mute carrying the wounded soldier on his back away from the front lines and, far worse, the horrifying sight of the two little mutes lying dead and abandoned in the artillery shell crater. He took one of the caps from me, raised it to his face, and smelled deeply, the way a hunting dog might sniff out the odors of a killer on the run or a corpse. He placed the cap between his stumps and grabbed the other one out of my hand, smelling it the same way before tucking it away with its mate. Then, without bothering to see if it was all right, he lurched into the house and examined every corner of every room, from the living spaces to the milling room and the storeroom. He then went back outside to look over the outhouse in the southeast corner of the compound. He even stuck his head inside the chicken coop. I followed him everywhere he went, captivated by how nimbly and uniquely he moved from place to place. In the room where First Sister and Sha Zaohua slept, he sat on the floor beside the *kang*, gripping the edge with both hands, a sight that saddened me. But what happened next proved how wrong I was to feel sorry for him. Still gripping the edge of the *kang*, he pushed himself up until he was hovering above the ground, displaying the kind of strength I'd only seen in sideshow performances. As his head rose above the edge, his arms flexed noisily, and he flung himself up onto the *kang*, landing awkwardly, although it took only a moment for him to seat himself properly.

Now seated on First Sister's bed, he looked like the head of the family, or a true leader, and as I stood at the head of the bed, I felt like an uninvited visitor in someone else's room.

First Sister was in Mother's room, and I could hear her crying. "Get him out of there, Mother," she said through her tears. "I didn't want him when he had legs. Now that he's only half a man, I want him even less."

"It's easy to invite a deity into one's life, child, but hard to get one to leave."

"Who invited him in?"

"I was wrong to do that," Mother said. "I gave you to him sixteen years ago, and now our nemesis is here to stay."

Mother handed a bowl of hot water to the mute, who showed a bit of emotion as he took it and gulped it down.

"I was sure you were dead," Mother said. "I'm surprised to see you're still alive. I failed in my attempt to look after the children, and my grief is greater than yours because of it. You were their parents, but I was their guardian. It looks like you served the government well, and I hope you're being well taken care of. Sixteen years ago, I followed our feudal customs in arranging your marriage. That is no longer how people get married in the new society. You are an enlightened representative of the government, while we are a family of widows and orphans, and you should leave us to live as best we can. Besides, Laidi didn't really marry you. That was my third daughter's doing. I beg you, leave us alone. Go let the government take care of you the way you deserve."

Ignoring Mother completely, the mute poked his finger through the paper window and looked into the yard through the hole. Meanwhile, First Sister had found a pair of tongs dating back to her grandmother's days and burst into the room holding them in two hands. "You mute bastard!" she growled. "You stump of a man, get the hell out of our house!" She went after him with her tongs, but he merely reached out and grabbed them in the air. No matter how hard she tried, she couldn't get them out of his grasp, and in the midst of this desperately unequal contest of strength, a smug grin spread across the mute's face. Weakly, First Sister let go of the tongs and covered her face with her hands. "Mute," she said tearfully, "whatever it is you're thinking, forget it. I'd marry a pig before I'd marry you."

A crashing of cymbals erupted out in the lane, followed by the shouts of a mob, led by the district chief, as they walked through our gate. He was followed by a dozen or more party cadres and a bunch of schoolchildren carrying bouquets of flowers. The district chief walked into the house, bent at the waist, and loudly congratulated Mother.

"For what?" Mother asked coldly.

"For heaven's blessings, aunty," he said. "Let me explain."

Out in the yard, the children waved their flowers in the air and shouted, "Congratulations! Great honor and hearty congratulations!"

"Aunty," the district chief said, "we have reviewed land reform material and have concluded that you were wrongly categorized as upper middle peasants. The decline in your family situation in the wake of all your troubles makes you poor peasants, and so we have reclassified you. That is the first piece of joyful news. We have also studied documents from the 1939 Japanese massacre, and have concluded that your mother-in-law and your husband had a record of resisting the Japanese invaders, and should be honored with the title of martyrs. They deserve to recoup their original status, and your family deserves to enjoy the benefits of revolutionary descendants. That is the second piece of joyful news. In line with these redressings and rehabilitations, the local middle school has decided to accept Shangguan Jintong as a student. In order to make up for the time he lost, he will be assigned a tutor, and your granddaughter, Sha Zaohua, will also be given the opportunity for an education. The county theatrical company is now taking students, and we will do everything within our power to see that she is among them. That is the third piece of joyful news. The fourth piece of joyful news, of course, is that the first-class hero of the volunteer resistance movement, your son-in-law, Speechless Sun, has returned home covered in glory. The fifth piece of joyful news is that the veteran's convalescent hospital has taken the unprecedented step of recruiting your daughter, Shangguan Laidi, as a top-ranked nurse. She will be given a monthly salary but will not have to actually show up at the hospital. The sixth piece of joyful news is truly joyful. And that is a celebration of the reunion of the resistance hero and the wife from whom he was separated. The district government will arrange the ceremony. Aunty, as a revolutionary grandmother, you are about to be rewarded with six joyful events!"

Mother stood there, wide-eyed and mouth agape, as if she'd been struck by lightning. The bowl in her hand crashed to the floor.

Meanwhile, the district chief signaled one of the officials, who separated himself from the crowd of schoolchildren and walked up, followed by a young woman carrying a bouquet of flowers. The official handed the district chief a white envelope. "The martyr's descendant certificate," he whispered. The district chief took it from him and presented it to Mother with both hands. "Aunty, this is the martyr's certificate." Mother's hands shook as she took it from him. The young woman stepped forward and laid her bouquet of white flowers in the crook of Mother's arm. Then the cadre handed the district chief a red envelope. "Certificate of employment," he said. The district chief took the envelope and handed it to First Sister. "This is your certificate of employment," he said. First Sister stood there with her sooty hands clasped behind her back, so the district chief reached out, took one of her arms, and placed the red envelope in her hand. "You deserve this," he said. The young woman placed a bouquet of purple flowers under First Sister's arm. The official then handed the district chief a yellow envelope. "School enrollment notice," he said. The district chief handed me the envelope. "Little brother," he said, "your future looks bright, so study hard." As the young woman handed me a bouquet of yellow flowers, her eyes were filled with extraordinary affection. The gentle fragrance of the golden flowers reminded me of the gold ring that still rested in my stomach. I wouldn't have swallowed the damned thing if I'd known all this was going to happen! The official handed a purple envelope to the district chief. "The theatrical company." The district chief held out the purple envelope and looked around for Sha Zaohua, who popped out from behind the door and took it from him. He shook her hand. "Study hard, girl," he said, "and become a great actress." The young woman handed Zaohua a bouquet of purple flowers. As she took the flowers, a shiny medal fell to the floor. The district chief bent down to pick it up. After reading what was written on it, he handed it to the mute, who was seated on the *kang*. I felt a surge of happy excitement as the mute pinned it to his own chest. Obviously, our family could now boast a master thief. Finally, the district chief took the last envelope — a blue one — from the official and said, "Comrade Speechless Sun, this is a wedding certificate for you and Shangguan Laidi. The district has already taken care of the details. All you two have to do is put your fingerprints on it sometime in the next few days." The young woman reached out and placed a bouquet of blue flowers in the mute's hand.

"Aunty," the district chief said, "do you have anything to say? Don't be shy. We're all one big, happy family!"

Mother cast a troubled look at First Sister, who stood there holding her bouquet of red flowers, the side of her mouth twitching all the way over to her right ear. A few glistening tears leaped from the corners of her eyes and landed on her flowers, like dew covering their petals.

"In the new society," Mother said tentatively, "we should listen to our children . . ."

"Shangguan Laidi," the district chief, "do you have anything to say?"

First Sister looked at us and sighed. "It's my fate, I guess."

"Wonderful!" the district chief said. "I'll send some people over to put the house in order so we can hold the ceremony tomorrow!"

The night before Shangguan Laidi was formally married to the mute, I passed the gold ring.

* * *

The dozen or so doctors at the county hospital were organized into a medical group that, under the direction of a specialist from the Soviet Union, finally weaned me from my milk diet and aversion to regular food using the theories of Pavlov. Freed of that burdensome yoke, I entered school. My studies took off, and before much time had passed, I'd become the top first-year student at Dalan Middle School. Those were the most glorious days of my life. I belonged to the most revolutionary family around, I was smarter than anyone, I had an enviable physique and a face that made all the girls lower their eyes in shyness, and I had a voracious appetite. In the school cafeteria, I'd gobble down a huge piece of cornbread impaled on a chopstick and a thick green onion in my other hand while I was talking and laughing with the other kids. By the sixth month at school I'd jumped two grades and become the third-year class representative in my Russian class. I was admitted into the Youth League without having to apply and was quickly selected as a member of the branch propaganda committee, whose major function was to sing Russian folk songs in Russian. I had a strong voice, rich as milk and bold as a thick green onion, and I invariably drowned out all the voices around me. In short, I was the brightest star at Dalan Middle School during the latter half of the 1950s, and the favorite of Teacher Huo, a pretty woman who had once served as interpreter for visiting Russian experts. She often sang my praises in front of the other students, saying I had a gift for languages. In order to raise my proficiency in Russian, she arranged for a pen pal, a ninth-grade girl in a Soviet city, the daughter of a Soviet expert who had worked in China. Her name was Natasha. We exchanged photos. She gazed out at me with a slight look of surprise in her staring eyes, and lush, curling lashes.

2

Shangguan Jintong felt his heart race and the blood rush to his head; the hand holding the photo trembled uncontrollably. Natasha's full lips turned up slightly to reveal almost blindingly white teeth, and the warm, gentle fragrance of orchids seemed to rise up into his eyes, as a sweet sensation made his nose ache. He gazed at the flaxen hair that spread out over her silky shoulders. A low-cut scoop-collared dress that belonged either to her mother or to an elder sister hung loosely from her pert little breasts. Her long neck and décolletage left nothing to the imagination. For some mysterious reason, tears glistened in his eyes, producing a glazed effect. As he took in the nearly unobstructed view of her breasts, the sweet smell of milk permeated his soul, and he imagined he heard a call from the distant north — grassy steppes as far as the eye could see, a dense forest of melancholy birch, a little cabin deep in the woods, fir trees blanketed with snow and ice . . . lovely scenes moved past his eyes like a sequence of still images. And in the middle of each image stood the young Natasha, a bouquet of purple flowers cradled in her arms. Jintong covered his eyes with his hands and wept with joy, the tears coursing down through his fingers.

All that night, Jintong hovered between sleep and wakefulness, as Natasha paced back and forth before him, the hem of her dress sweeping across the floor. In fluent Russian, he poured out his heart to her, but her expression went from happiness to anger, which took him from the heights of arousal to the depths of despair. And yet a single tantalizing smile pulled him right back up again.

At daybreak, the boy in the lower bunk, a fellow by the name of Zhao Fengnian, who was the father of two boys, complained, "Shangguan Jintong, I know you speak wonderful Russian, but you've got to let others get some sleep."

Suffering from a splitting headache, after letting go of Natasha's captivating image, Jintong apologized caustically to Zhao Fengnian, who noticed his ashen face and blistered lips. "Are you sick?"

In agony, he shook his head, suddenly feeling as if his thoughts were like a car negotiating a slippery mountain slope, when it suddenly loses control and tumbles down the mountainside. At the grassy base of the mountain, where purple blossoms bloom all around, the beautiful Natasha scoops up the hem of her dress and runs silently toward him . . .

He grabbed the bunk bed post and banged his head against it over and over.

Zhao Fengnian summoned the political instructor, Xiao Jingang, the onetime member of an armed working brigade, a man with a true proletarian background. He'd once sworn that he'd put Teacher Huo before a firing squad for wearing short skirts, which he considered morally degenerate. His shadowy eyes, set in a face like hardened steel, threw an instant chill into Jintong's roiling brain, and he felt as if he was being pulled up out of quicksand.

"What's going on with you, Shangguan Jintong?" Xiao Jingang asked sternly.

"Xiao Jingang, you flat-faced oaf, mind your own business!" In order to allow the man's sternness help him break free from Natasha's grip, all he could think of was to make the man good and angry.

Xiao smacked him on the side of the head. "You little fuckhead!" he swore. "Who the hell are you to talk to me like that? I won't let some snot-nose darling of Huo Lina get away with that!"

At breakfast, as he sat looking down at his bowl of corn porridge, Jintong's stomach lurched, and he knew that his frightful aversion to all food except mother's milk had taken hold again. So he picked up the bowl and, calling up the remnants of clear thought in his murky brain, forced himself to start drinking the porridge; but the moment the liquid came into view, a pair of living breasts seemed to rise out of the bowl, which fell from his hands and shattered on the floor, the hot porridge splashing on his legs. He didn't feel a thing.

His frightened classmates immediately dragged him over to the clinic, where the school nurse cleaned his legs and rubbed ointment on the burns, then told his classmates to take him back to the dormitory.

There he ripped up Natasha's photograph and tossed the pieces into the river behind the school; he watched as Natasha, now in shreds, flowed downstream into a swirling eddy, where she came together again and, like a naked mermaid, floated on the surface, the wet locks of her hair draping over her hips.

His classmates, who had followed him down to the river, watched as he spread his arms and dove into the water, after shouting something. Some of them ran down to the river's edge, while others ran back to school for help. As he sank below the surface, Jintong saw Natasha swimming like a fish amid the waterweeds. He tried to call to her, but water rushed into his mouth and stifled his shout.

The next time Jintong opened his eyes, he was lying on Mother's *kang*. He tried to sit up, but Mother held him down and stuffed the nipple of a bottle of goat's milk into his mouth. Dimly, he recalled that the old goat was long dead, so where had the milk come from? Since he couldn't get his stubborn brain working, he wearily closed his eyes. Mother and First Sister were talking about exorcism, but the thin sound of their voices seemed to come from a bottle far away. "He must be possessed," Mother said. "Possessed?" First Sister asked. "By what?" "I think it's an evil fox spirit." "Could it be that widow?" First

Sister asked. "She worshipped a fox fairy when she was alive." "You're right," Mother replied. "She shouldn't be coming for Jintong . . . we barely had a chance to enjoy a few good days . . ." "Mother," First Sister said, "these so-called good days have been torture for me. That half-man of mine is crushing me to death . . . he's like a dog, but a useless one. Mother, don't blame me if I do something." "Why would I blame you?" Mother said.

Jintong lay in bed for two days, as his mind slowly cleared. Natasha's image kept floating before his eyes. When he washed up, her weeping face appeared in the basin. When he looked in the mirror, she smiled back at him. Every time he closed his eyes, he heard the sound of her breathing; he could even feel her soft hair brush up against his face and her warm fingers move over his body. His mother, frightened by her son's erratic behavior, followed him everywhere, wringing her hands and whimpering like a little girl. His gaunt face stared back at him from the water in their vat. "She's in there!" "Who is?" his mother asked. "She is?" "Who is she?" "Natasha! And she's unhappy." She watched as her son thrust his hand into the vat. Nothing there except water, but her excited son muttered words she couldn't understand. So she dragged him away and covered the vat. But Jintong fell to his knees in front of a basin and began speaking in tongues to the spirit of the water inside. As soon as his mother dumped the water out of the basin, Jintong pressed his lips up against the window, as if to kiss his own reflection.

Tears glistened on his mother's face. Jintong saw Natasha dancing in those tears, jumping from one to the next. "There she is!" he said, a moronic look on his face, pointing at his mother's face. "Don't go, Natasha."

"Where is she?"

"In your tears."

Mother hurriedly dried her tears. "Now she's jumped into your eyes!" Jintong shouted.

Finally, his mother understood. Natasha appeared anywhere there was a reflection. So she covered everything that held water, buried the mirrors, covered the windows with black paper, and would not let her son look into her eyes.

But Jintong saw Natasha take shape in the darkness. He had moved from the stage of trying everything possible to avoid Natasha to a frenzied pursuit of her; she, meanwhile, had moved from the stage of being everywhere to hiding from place to place. Calling out, "Listen to me, Natasha," he ran headlong into a dark corner. She crawled into a mouse hole under a cabinet; he stuck his face up to the hole and tried to crawl in after her. In his mind, he actually made it, and followed her down a winding path, calling out, "Don't run away from me, Natasha. Why are you doing this?" Natasha crawled out through another hole and disappeared. He looked everywhere for her, finally spotting her stuck to the wall, after stretching herself out thin as a sheet of paper. He ran up and began stroking the wall with both hands, as if he were caressing her face. Bending at the waist, Natasha slipped under his arms and crawled up the stove chimney, her face quickly covered with soot. Kneeling at the foot of the stove, he reached out to wipe the soot from her face, but it wouldn't come off. Instead, his own face was streaked with soot.

Not knowing what else to do, Mother fell to her knees, kowtowed, and summoned the great exorcist Fairy Ma, who had not practiced his craft for many years.

The man of spirits came in a long black robe, his hair hanging loose around his shoulders. He was barefoot, both feet stained bright red. Holding a peachwood sword in one hand, he murmured things no one could understand. The moment he saw him, Jintong was reminded of all the strange tales he'd heard about the man and, as if he'd swallowed a mouthful of vinegar, felt his head shudder; a crack opened up in his confused mind, and Natasha's image vanished, for the moment at least. The fairy had a dark purplish face with bulging eyes that gave him a feral look. He coughed up a mouthful of phlegm and spat it out like the wet stool of a chicken. Waving his wooden sword in the air, he performed a strange dance. Soon tiring, he stood beside the water basin and, uttering a spell, spat into the basin; then, holding the sword in both hands, he began stirring the water, which slowly turned red. That was followed by another dance. Growing tired again, he went back to stirring the water, until it was the color of fresh blood. Throwing down his sword, he sat on the floor, breathing heavily. He dragged Jintong up beside him and said, "Look into the basin and tell me what you see." Jintong detected a sweet-smelling herbal odor as he stared at the mirrorlike surface of the water, stunned by the face that looked back at him. How had Jintong, so full of life, turned into a haggard, wrinkled, and very ugly young man? "What do you see?" the fairy pressed him. Natasha's bloody face rose slowly out of the basin and merged with his. She slipped out of her dress and pointed to the bloody wound on her breast. "Shangguan Jintong," she cursed, "how could you be so heartless?" "Natasha!" Jintong shrieked as he buried his face in the water. He heard the fairy say to Mother and Laidi, "He's fine now. You can carry him back to his room."

Leaping to his feet, Jintong threw himself on the mountain fairy. It was the first time in his life he had actually attacked someone. What courage it took to attack someone who dealt with ghosts and demons! All for the sake of Natasha. With his left hand he grabbed the fairy's gray goatee and pulled with all his might, stretching the man's mouth until it was a black oval. Vile-smelling saliva slithered down his hand. Cupping her injured breast in one hand, Natasha sat on the fairy's tongue and looked admiringly at Jintong. Spurred on by the look, he tugged harder on the goatee, this time using both hands. The fairy's body bent over painfully, until he looked like the picture of the Sphinx in their geography text. Moving awkwardly, he struck Jintong on the leg with his wooden sword. But Jintong felt no pain, thanks to Natasha, and even if he had, he wouldn't have let go, because Natasha was in the man's mouth. The thought of what would happen if he let go made him shudder: The fairy would chew Natasha to pulp and swallow her into his digestive tract. The fairy's intestines were filthy things! Hurry, Natasha, get away from there! he shouted anxiously. But she remained seated on the fairy's tongue, as if she were deaf. The man's goatee was getting more slippery by the minute, for the blood from Natasha's breast had seeped into his whiskers. He kept tugging, hand over hand, her blood staining Jintong's fingers. The fairy tossed his sword away, reached out with both hands, grabbed Jintong's ears, and pulled with all his might. Jintong's lips parted and he heard shrieks from Mother and First Sister. But nothing was going to make him let loose of the fairy's goatee. The two combatants circled the yard, round and round, followed closely by Mother and First Sister. Something on the ground tripped Jintong, who stopped his hand-over-hand motion just long enough for the fairy to bite down on one of them. His ears felt as if they were about to be wrenched off the sides of his head; the back of his hand had been bitten to the bone. He screamed in pain, but that was nothing compared to the pain in his heart. Everything was a blur. Frantic, he thought of Natasha. The fairy had swallowed her, and she was now in his stomach, crumbling in his digestive juices; the prickly walls of his stomach were kneading her mercilessly. The blurred vista before him darkened until it was black as the belly of a cuttlefish.

Speechless Sun, who had gone out to buy a bottle, came into the yard. With the keen eye and rich experience of a soldier, he immediately figured out what was going on. Calmly as can be, he set the bottle down at the base of the side room wall. "Jintong's in trouble!" Mother shouted. "Save him!" Speechless Sun effortlessly maneuvered himself up behind the fairy, lifted both little stools into the air, and brought them down together into the man's calves; he dropped like a stone. Speechless Sun's stools swirled in the air a second time and came down on the fallen man's arms; Jintong's ears were set free. Sun's stools came crashing into the fairy's ears; he spat out Jintong's hand and began rolling in agony on the ground. He reached out to pick up his sword and clenched his teeth. Speechless Sun roared; the man shuddered. By then, Jintong was wailing and struggling to charge the fairy again, determined to rip open the man's belly and rescue Natasha. But Mother and First Sister had their arms wrapped around him and were holding him back. The fairy took off, giving the crouching tiger, Speechless Sun, a wide berth.

Very gradually, Jintong recovered his equilibrium, but not his appetite. So Mother went to see the district chief, who immediately sent someone out to buy goat's milk. Jintong spent most of the time lying in bed, only occasionally getting up to stretch his legs. His eyes were as lifeless as ever. Every time he thought of poor Natasha and her bleeding breast, tears sluiced down his cheeks. Lacking the will to speak, he broke his silence infrequently by muttering to himself; but the minute anyone approached him, he shut up.

One hazy morning, as he lay in bed staring at the ceiling, his tears over Natasha's injured breast barely dry, he felt his nose stop up and his brain begin to turn mushy; a need to go back to sleep swept over him. All of a sudden, a shrill, hair-raising scream tore from Laidi and the mute's room, driving away all thoughts of sleep. Cocking his ear to hear what it was all about, the only thing he heard was a buzzing in his ears. He was about to close his eyes when another shrill scream, this one longer and more horrifying, came on the air. His heart raced and his scalp tightened. Driven by curiosity, he crawled out of bed and tiptoed over to the door to the eastern room, where he peeked in through a crack. Speechless Sun, stripped naked, was a big, black spider, wrapped around Laidi's soft, thin waist. Slobber covered his protruding lips as he sucked first on one of Laidi's nipples, then the other. Her neck stretched out long over the edge of the bed, her upturned face white as the outer leaf of a cabbage. Her full breasts, the same ones Jintong had seen as she lay in the mule trough all those years before, were like yellowing steamed buns, lying spongily above her rib cage. There was blood on the tips of her nipples and bite marks on her chest and upper arms. Speechless·Sun had turned Laidi's body, once so fair and silky, into something that looked like a scaled fish. Her long legs lay bare on the bed.

When Jintong began to sob, Speechless Sun picked up a bottle at the head of the bed and flung it toward the door, sending Jintong running out into the yard, where he picked up a brick and threw it at the window. "Mute!" he shouted. "You're going to die a horrible death!"

The words were barely out of his mouth when exhaustion overcame him. Natasha's image floated before his eyes and quickly dissolved like a puff of smoke.

The mute's powerful fist smashed through the window; Jintong backed off in terror, all the way to the parasol tree, where he watched the fist draw back inside the room and a stream of yellow piss emerge through the hole and drip into a bucket beneath the window, placed there for that very purpose. Grinding his teeth in anger, Jintong walked over to the side room, where a strange figure came up to him. The person walked at a crouch, dragging his long arms behind him. Beneath his shaved head and bushy gray eyebrows, the large black eyes were circled by fine wrinkles and were so forbidding it was hard to look into them. Purple welts — some large, some small — covered his face, and his ears were scarred and ragged, burned in places and bitten by frostbite in others, looking like the shriveled ears of a monkey. He was wearing a gray, high-collared, ill-fitting tunic that reeked of mothballs. A pair of bony hands with chipped and cracked nails hung at his sides and shook uncontrollably. "Who are you looking for?" Jintong asked in a loathsome voice, assuming it was one of the mute's comrades-in-arms. The man bowed deferentially and replied, his tongue stiff, his mouth forming the words awkwardly:

"Home . . . Shangguan Lingdi . . . I'm . . . Birdman . . . Han . . ."

3

Birdman Han gave me a terrible shock on the day he walked back into our house. I dimly recalled something involving a bird fairy in my past, but that was all about some romantic dealings with the mute, that and the incident where the fairy had jumped off a cliff. But I had no memory of this strange brother-in-law. I glided off to one side to let him out into the yard, just as Laidi, a white sheet around her waist, and naked from there up, ran out into the yard. The mute's fist tore through the paper window covering, followed by the upper half of his body. "Strip!" he said. "Strip!" Laidi, in tears, stumbled and fell. Her sheet had been stained red by blood from down below. And that is how she appeared in front of Birdman Han — tormented and half-naked, blood dripping down her legs.

Mother returned, with Eighth Sister in tow and driving a goat ahead of them. She didn't seem overly surprised by First Sister's unsightly appearance, but the minute she spotted Birdman Han, she crumpled to the ground. It wasn't until much later that Mother told me she realized at once that he had returned to demand his due, and that we would have to come up with the principal and interest for the birds we'd eaten fifteen years before, before he'd been taken forcibly to Japan, where he'd escaped and led a primitive existence.

The arrival of Birdman Han would bring to an end the wealth and rank we had obtained by sacrificing Mother's eldest daughter. But that did not stop her from preparing a sumptuous welcoming meal. This strange bird that had dropped from the sky sat trancelike in our yard as he watched Mother and Laidi busy themselves at the stove. Moved by Birdman's unusual tale of fifteen years hiding out in Japan, Laidi temporarily forgot her suffering at the hands of the mute, who maneuvered himself out into the yard and looked Birdman over provocatively.

At the table, Birdman handled his chopsticks so awkwardly he couldn't pick up a single piece of meat. So Mother took them from him and urged him to eat with his hands. He raised his head. "She . . . my . . . wife?" Mother cast a hateful glance at the mute, who was gnawing on a chicken head. "She," Mother said, "has gone far away."

Mother's kind nature would not allow her to refuse Birdman's request to live with us, not to mention the urgings of the district chief and the head of the Civil Administration: "He has no place else to go, and it's up to us to satisfy the needs of someone who has returned to us from Hell. Not only that . . ." "You don't need to say any more," Mother interrupted. "Just send over some people to help us put the side room in order for him."

And with that, Birdman Han moved into the two rooms in which the Bird Fairy had once lived. Mother reached up into the dusty rafters and took down the insect-scarred drawing of the Bird Fairy and hung it on the northern wall. When Birdman saw the drawing, he said, "I know who killed my wife, and one of these days I'll get my revenge."

The extraordinary love affair between First Sister and Birdman Han was like a marshland opium poppy — toxic yet wildly beautiful. That afternoon, the mute went off to the co-op to buy some liquor. While First Sister washed a pair of underwear beneath the peach tree, Mother sat on the *kang* making a duster out of the feathers of a rooster. She heard a noise at the door and saw Birdman Han, who was once again hunting birds, walk lightly into the yard, a beautiful little bird perched on one of his fingers. He went up to the peach tree and stared down at Laidi's neck. The bird chirped fetchingly, making its feathers tremble. The swirling chirps incited the fine hairs of her passion. Deep-seated feelings of remorse settled in Mother's heart. That bird was nothing less than the incarnation of Birdman Han's pain and suffering. She watched as Laidi raised her head and gazed at the bird's beautiful blood-red chest and black, heartbreaking eyes, no bigger than sesame seeds. Mother saw Laidi's cheeks redden and her eyes grow wet, and she knew that the bird's passionate cries were raising the curtain on the one thing she'd worried about. But she was powerless to stop it from happening, for she knew that when the emotions of a Shangguan girl were stirred, not even a herd of horses could alter the course of events. In the grip of despair, she squeezed her eyes shut.

Laidi, her heart moved to its core, her hands still soapy, slowly rose to her feet, amazed that such a tiny bird, no bigger than a walnut, could be the source of such captivating chirps. Even more important, she felt that it was sending her a mysterious message, an exciting yet fearful temptation the likes of a purple water lily floating on a pond in the moonlight. She struggled to resist the temptation, standing up so she could go inside; but her feet felt as if they'd taken root and her hands moved toward the bird as if they had a mind of their own. A flick of Birdman's wrist sent the tiny bird into the air; it perched on Laidi's head. She felt its delicate claws dig into her scalp and its chirps bore into her head. Gazing into the kindly, anxious, fatherly, and beautiful eyes of Birdman Han, she was swallowed up by a powerful sense of being wronged. He nodded to her, turned, and headed back to his rooms. The tiny bird flew off her head to follow him inside.

Standing there dazed, she heard Mother call from the *kang*. But rather than turn around, she burst into tears and, with no sense of shame, ran into the side room, where Birdman Han awaited her with open arms. Her tears wetted his chest. He let her pound him with her fists, even stroking her arms and the ridge down her back while she was hitting him. Meanwhile, the tiny bird perched on the altar table in front of the drawing, where it chirped excitedly. Little stars like drops of blood seemed to emerge from its tiny beak.

Laidi calmly removed her clothes and pointed to the scars from the mute's abuse. "Look at that, Birdman Han," she complained, "just look at that. He killed my sister, and now he's trying to do the same to me. And he'll make it. He's worn me out." Bursting into tears again, she threw herself down onto his bed.

This was Birdman Han's first real look at a woman's body. Surprise showed on his face as he thought about women, the supernatural objects his dismal experience had kept from him all his life, and it was the most beautiful thing he'd ever seen. He was moved to tears by her long legs, her rounded hips, her breasts, which were flattened against the bedding, her slender waist, and the fair, glossy, jadelike skin all over her body — fairer even than her face, in spite of the scars. After being suppressed for fifteen torturous years, while he avoided falling into the hands of his captors again, his youthful desires ignited slowly. Growing weak at the knees, he knelt alongside Laidi and covered the soles of her feet with hot, tremulous kisses.

Laidi felt blue sparks sizzle up from her feet and quickly cover her body. Her skin grew taut as a drum, and then went slack. She rolled over, spread her legs, arched her body, and wrapped her arms around Birdman Han's neck. Her experienced mouth drew the virginal Birdman to her. She broke off her passionate kiss to say breathlessly, "I want that mute bastard, that demonic stump of a man to die, I want him to rot, I want birds to peck out his eyes!"

In order to block out their cries of passion, Mother slammed shut the door and began beating a badly worn pot out in the yard. At the time, schoolchildren were searching up and down the lanes for all sorts of used metal objects to take to the smelting ovens — pots, spatulas, cleavers, door latches, thimbles, even nose rings from oxen. But our family, enjoying the prestige of the martial hero Speechless Sun and the legendary Birdman Han, was spared from having to give up our utensils. Mother waited impatiently for Birdman and Laidi to finish their lovemaking. Owing to her feelings of sympathy and remorse over the abuse Laidi had received at the hands of the mute, and to feelings of sympathy over the agonies Birdman Han had suffered in a foreign land, as well as her gratitude for the delicious birds he had supplied fifteen years before, not to mention the cherished memory of and respect for Lingdi, she assumed the role of protector in the illicit relationship between the two lovers without even being aware of it. Although she anticipated the tragic consequences that were bound to follow, she was determined to do what she could to guard their secret and, at the very least, delay the inevitable. But the inescapable truth was that once a man like Birdman Han was exposed to the passions and affections of a woman, no power on earth could restrain him. He was a man who had survived fifteen years in the woods, like a wild animal; he was a man who had existed on the swings between life and death every day for fifteen years, and in his eyes a stump of a man like the mute had no more value than a wooden stake. For Laidi, a woman who had known Sha Yueliang, Sima Ku, and Speechless Sun, three totally different men, a woman who had experienced the heat of battle, wealth, and fame, and known the mad apex of joy with Sima Ku and the demeaning nadir of physical abuse at the hands of Speechless Sun, Birdman Han offered total satisfaction. His deeply grateful touch brought her the gratification of a father's love; his clumsy innocence in bed brought her the gratification of a sexual mentor; and his greedy consumption of forbidden fruit and unbridled passion brought her sexual gratification and the gratification of vengeance against the mute. And so, every coupling was accompanied by hot tears and sobs, with no hint of lewdness, filled with human dignity and tragedy. When they made love, their hearts overflowed with unspoken words.

The mute, a liquor bottle hanging around his neck, lurched down the crowded street. Dust flew as one gang of laborers pushed carts filled with iron ore from east to west, while another gang pushed carts of the same color from west to east. Mixed with the two crowds, the mute was leaping forward, a great leap forward. All the laborers gazed respectfully at the glittering medal pinned to his chest and stopped to let him pass, something he found enormously gratifying. Although he only came up to the other men's thighs, he was the most spirited individual among them. From that moment on, he spent most of his daylight hours out on the street. He would leap from the eastern end of the street all the way to the western end, take a few refreshing drinks from his bottle, and then leap all the way back. And while he was engaged in his great leap forward, Laidi and Birdman Han would be performing their own great leap forward on the ground or in bed. Dust and grime covered the mute's body; his stools had been worn down an inch or more, and a hole had opened up in the rubber mat attached to his backside. Every tree in the village had been cut down to stoke the backyard furnaces; a layer of smoke hung over the fields. Jintong had fallen in with the sparrow eradication corps, marching under bamboo poles with red strips of cloth and accompanied by the clang of gongs, as they stalked the sparrows in Northeast Gaomi Township from one village to the next, keeping them from finding food or a spot to perch, until they dropped to the streets from exhaustion and hunger. A range of stimuli had cured him of his lovesickness, and he had gotten over his obsession with mother's milk and revulsion of food. But his prestige had plummeted. His Russian teacher, Huo Lina, to whom he was devoted, had been declared a rightist and sent to the Flood Dragon River labor reform farm, two miles from Dalan. He saw the mute out on the street, and the mute saw him, but they merely acknowledged one another with a wave before moving on.

The raucous season of rejoicing, with flames lighting up the sky, came quickly to an end, replaced in Northeast Gaomi Township by a new and dreary age. One drizzly autumn morning, twelve trucks with artillery pieces rumbled down the narrow road from the southeast into Dalan. When they entered the village, the mute was lurching around on the wet ground, all alone. He had exhausted himself during the recent days of leaping, and had turned listless. His eyes were lifeless, and because of all the liquor he'd consumed, his legless torso had grown bloated. The arrival of the artillery company reinvigorated him. Inappropriately, apparently, he moved out into the middle of the road to block the convoy. The soldiers stood there blinking in the rain and looking at the strange half-man in the middle of the road. An officer, wearing a pistol on his hip, jumped out of the cab of his truck and cursed angrily, "Tired of living, you stupid bastard?" Incredibly, since the road was slick, he was truncated, and the truck tires were tall, the mute had leaped out into the road, well out of sight of the driver, who had seen a brown streak in front of the truck and slammed on the brakes, not quite in time to keep his bumper from touching the mute's broad forehead. Although it didn't break the skin, it raised a large purple welt. The officer wasn't finished cursing when he saw the hawkish glare in the mute's eyes and felt his heart clench; at that moment, his eye was drawn to the medal pinned to the mute's tattered uniform. Drawing his feet together, he bowed deeply and shouted, "My apologies, sir. Please forgive me!"

This gratifying reaction put the mute in high spirits. He moved to the side of the road to let the convoy pass. The soldiers saluted as the trucks passed by slowly, which he returned by touching the beak of his soft cap with the tips of his fingers. The trucks left a chewed-up road behind them. A northwest wind blew, rain slanted down, and the road was veiled by an icy mist. A few surviving sparrows slipped through the gaps in the rain, while some water-soaked dogs standing under a roadside propaganda tent were captivated by the sight of the mute's movements.

The passage of the artillery company signaled the end of the season of rejoicing. The mute slinked home in dejection. As before, he banged on the door with one of his stools; it opened on its own, creaking loudly. He had lived in a world of silence so long that Birdman Han and Laidi had been able to keep their adultery hidden from him. For months, he had spent most of his daylight hours out on the street near the smelting ovens, and then dragged himself home to sleep like a dead dog. Come morning, he'd be out the gate again, with no time for Laidi.

The restoration of the mute's hearing may well be attributed to his encounter with the truck bumper. The touch on his forehead must have loosened whatever was stopping up his ears. The creaking of the door stunned him; then he heard the patter of rain on leaves and the snores of his mother-in-law as she slept. She had forgotten to latch the door. But what utterly shocked him were the moans of pain and pleasure from Laidi's room.

Sniffing the air like a bloodhound, he detected the clammy odor of her body and lurched over to the eastern side room. The rain had leaked through his rubber cushion, soaking his backside, and he felt stabbing pains around his anus.

Recklessly, the door had been left open, and a candle burned inside. In the drawing, the Bird Fairy's eyes shone coldly. One look, and he spotted Birdman Han's long, hairy, and enviably sturdy legs. Birdman's buttocks were pumping up and down; beneath him, Laidi's buttocks arched upward. Her breasts sagged and jiggled; her tousled black hair shifted on Birdman Han's pillow, and she was clutching the bed sheet. The intense moans that had so aroused him were coming from the mass of black hair. The scene was lit up as if by an explosive green flame. He howled like a wounded animal and flung one of his stools; it glided off Birdman's shoulder, bounced off the wall, and landed next to Laidi's face. He threw the other stool; this one hit Birdman in the rump. He turned and glared at the drenched mute, who was shivering from the cold, and grinned smugly. Laidi's body flattened out and she lay there panting as she reached down to cover herself with the blanket. "You've seen us, you mute bastard, so what?" She sat up and cursed the mute, who propped himself up on both hands, froglike. He bounded across the threshold, and from there to the feet of Birdman Han, where he lunged forward with his head. Birdman's hands flew to his groin to protect the organ that just moments ago had been such a masterful performer; with a shriek he doubled over and yellow beads of perspiration dotted his face. The mute charged again, harder this time, scissoring Birdman's shoulders with his powerful arms, like the tentacles of an octopus; at the same time, he wrapped his callused hands, the steel traps in which his strength was concentrated, around Birdman's throat. Birdman crumpled to the floor; his mouth opened in a fearful grimace, and his eyes rolled back in his head.

Laidi snapped out of her state of panic, picked up the stool lying next to her pillow, and jumped out of bed, naked. As soon as her feet touched the floor, she attacked the mute's arms with the stool, but with no more effect than if she were hitting the trunk of a tree. So she then swung at his head, creating a thump like hitting a ripe melon, before dropping the stool and picking up the heavy door bolt, which she swung in the air and brought down on the mute's head. He groaned, but his body remained upright. After the second hit, the mute let loose of Birdman's throat, wobbled for a moment, then crashed headlong to the floor. Birdman slumped over on top of him.

The clamor in the side room woke Mother, who shuffled up to the door; it was over by then, and the outcome was sorrowfully obvious. She saw Laidi, naked, leaning weakly against the door, then watched as she dropped the bloody door bolt and walked out into the downpour, as if in a trance. The rain skittered off her body, her ugly feet sloshing through muddy puddles on the ground. She squatted down in front of the water basin and washed her hands.

Mother went over and dragged Birdman off of the mute and, with her shoulder under his arm, helped him over to the bed. With a sense of disgust, she covered him with the blanket. She heard him moan, which meant that this legendary hero was in no danger of dying. Walking back over to the mute and lifting him up like a sack of rice, she noticed two streams of black liquid running from his nostrils. After placing her finger under his nose to detect any sign of life, she let her hand drop; the mute's still warm corpse was sitting up straight, no longer ready to topple over.

After wiping her bloody finger on the wall, Mother walked back to her room, her mind a fog, and lay down in her clothes. Episodes from the mute's life drifted in and out of her mind, and when she recalled how the young mute and his brothers had straddled the wall, pretending they were the kings of the world, she laughed out loud. Out in the yard, Laidi scrubbed her hands over and over, the soapy lather covering the ground around her. That afternoon, Birdman walked outside, one hand around his throat, the other cupped around his crotch. He picked Laidi up off the ground, her body icy cold; she wrapped her arms around his neck and giggled idiotically.

Somewhat later, a young military officer with pink lips and sparkling white teeth, in the company of the district chief's secretary, walked into the yard carrying a basin covered with red paper. They called out, and when no one answered, went straight to Mother's room.

"Aunty," the secretary said to her, "this is Commander Song of the heavy artillery company. He's here to pay a courtesy call on Comrade Speechless Sun."

"My apologies, aunty," Commander Song said bashfully. "One of our trucks nearly ran Comrade Sun over, and raised a lump on his forehead."

Mother sat up in bed with a start. "What did you say?"

"The road was slick," Commander Song said, "and the bumper of one of our trucks hit him in the head.

"After he returned home," Mother said tearfully, "he groaned awhile and then died."

The young company commander paled. He was nearly in tears when he said, "Aunty, we slammed on the brakes, but the road was slick . . ."

When the medical expert came over to examine the body, Laidi, neatly dressed and carrying a small bundle, said, "I'm leaving, Mother.

I'll take things as they come, but I cannot let those soldiers take the blame."

"Go tell the authorities," Mother said. "It's always been the rule that a pregnant woman has to give birth before . . ."

"I understand. In fact, I've never in my life understood anything as clearly as this."

"I'll raise your child for you."

"I have no more worries, Mother."

She walked over to the side room, where she reported, "There's no need for an investigation. I hit him with a stool and then killed him with the bolt of a door. He was choking Birdman Han when I did it."

Birdman walked into the yard carrying a string of dead birds. "What's going on?" he asked. "The world now has one less half-man piece of garbage, and I'm the one who killed him."

The police handcuffed Laidi and Birdman Han and placed them under arrest.

Five months later, a policewoman brought a baby boy to Mother, scrawny as a sick cat, and reported that Laidi was to be shot the next day. The family was free to retrieve the body, but if they chose not to, it would be sent to the hospital to be dissected. The policewoman also told Mother that Birdman Han had been sentenced to life imprisonment and that he would soon begin serving his sentence at Tarim Basin, in the Uighur Autonomous Region, far from Northeast Gaomi. The family would be permitted a last visit.

By then Jintong had been expelled from school for destroying trees on campus, while Zaohua had been expelled from the drama troupe for stealing.

"We're going to retrieve the body," Mother said.

"I don't see why," Zaohua said.

"She committed a capital crime, and deserves a bullet. But it wasn't a heinous crime."

More than ten thousand people turned out for Shangguan Laidi's execution. A truck brought the condemned prisoner to the execution ground at the Bridge of Sorrows. Birdman Han was in the truck with her. In order to avoid any last-minute vocal outbursts, the execution team had sealed both their mouths.

Not long after Laidi's execution, the family received word of Birdman Han's death. On his way to prison, he had managed to break free and died under the wheels of the train.

4

In order to reclaim tens of thousands of acres of Northeast Gaomi Township's wasteland, all of Dalan's able-bodied young men and women were mobilized into teams at the state-run Flood Dragon River Farm. On the day the work assignments were handed out, the director asked me, "What are you good at?" At the time, I was so hungry my ears were buzzing, and I didn't hear him clearly. His lips parted, exposing a stainless steel tooth right in the middle, as he asked me again, louder this time, "What are you good at?" I'd just spotted my teacher, Huo Lina, on the road carrying a load of manure, and I recalled her saying that I had a natural talent for the Russian language. So I said, "I speak Russian well." "Russian?" he said with a sneer, his stainless steel tooth glinting in the sunlight. "How well?" he asked derisively. "Good enough to be an interpreter for Khrushchev and Mikoyan? Can you handle a Sino-Soviet communiqué? Listen to me, young man. People who have studied in the Soviet Union tote manure around here. Do you think your Russian is better than theirs?" All the young laborers awaiting assignments had a good laugh over that. "I'm asking you what you do at home, what you do best." "At home I tended a goat, that's what I did best." "Right," the director said with a sneer. "Now, that's what you're good at. Russian and French, or English and Italian, none of those are worth a thing." He scribbled something on a slip of paper and handed it to me. "Report to the animal brigade. Tell Commander Ma to assign you."

On my way over, an old laborer told me that Commander Ma Ruilian was the wife of the farm director, Li Du, in other words, the "first lady." When I reported for duty, knapsack and bedding over my back, she was out at the breeding farm giving a demonstration on crossbreeding. Tied up in the yard were several ovulating female animals: a cow, a donkey, a ewe, a sow, and a domestic rabbit. Five breeding assistants — two men and three women — in white gowns, masks over their mouths and noses, and rubber gloves, were holding insemination utensils, standing like attack troops ready for battle. Ma Ruilian had a boyish haircut; her hair was as coarse as a horse's mane. She had a round, swarthy face; long, narrow eyes; a red nose; fleshy lips; a short neck; a thick chest; and full, heavy breasts like a pair of grave mounds. Shit! Jintong cursed to himself. Ma Ruilian my ass! That's Pandi! She must have changed her name because of the rotten reputation the

name Shangguan had earned. That being the case, Li Du had to be Lu
Liren, who was once called Jiang Liren, and maybe before that something else Liren. The fact that this name-changing couple had been
sent here must have meant they were out of favor. She was wearing a
short-sleeved cotton shirt of Russian design and a pair of wrinkled
black trousers over high-topped sneakers. She was holding a Great
Leap cigarette in her hand, the greenish smoke curling around her fingers, which looked like carrots. She took a drag on her cigarette. "Is
the farm journalist here?" A sallow-faced middle-aged man wearing
reading glasses ran out from behind the horse-tethering rack, bent at
the waist. "I'm here," he said. "Here I am." He was holding a fountain
pen poised over an open notebook, ready to write. Commander Ma
laughed loudly and patted the man on his shoulder with her puffy
hand. "I see the chief editor himself has come." "Commander Ma's
unit is where the news is," he said. "I wouldn't trust anyone else to
come." "Old Yu here is a real zealot!" Ma Ruilian complimented him
as she patted him on the shoulder a second time. The editor paled and
tucked his neck down between his shoulders, as if afraid of the cold.
Later on, I learned that this fellow, Yu Zheng, who edited the local
newsletter, had been the publisher and editor of the provincial Party
Committee newspaper until he was labeled a rightist. "Today I'm going to give you a headline story," Ma Ruilian said, giving the urbane Yu
Zheng a meaningful look and taking a deep drag on the stub of her cigarette, nearly burning her lips. Then she spat it out, tearing the paper
and sending the few remaining shreds of tobacco floating in the air —
this little trick of hers was enough to frustrate anyone scavenging cigarette butts on the ground. As she exhaled the last of the smoke, she
asked her assistants, "Ready?" They responded by raising their insemination utensils. The blood rushed to her face as she wrung her
hands and clapped uneasily. She then took out a handkerchief to dry
her sweaty palms. "Horse sperm, who has the horse sperm?" she asked
loudly. The assistant holding the horse sperm stepped forward and
said, "Me, I've got it," the words muffled by the mask over his mouth.
Ma Ruilian pointed to the cow. "Give it to her," she said, "inseminate
her with the horse sperm." The man hesitated, looking first at Ma
Ruilian and then at his fellow assistants, lined up behind him, as if he
wanted to say something. "Don't just stand there," Ma Ruilian said.
"Strike while the iron's hot if you want to get things done!" With a
mischievous look, the assistant said, "Yes, ma'am," and carried the

horse sperm over behind the tethered cow. As her assistant inserted the insemination utensil into the cow, Ma Ruilian's lips were parted and she was breathing heavily, as if the instrument were being inserted in her and not in the cow. But immediately afterward, she issued a stream of rapid commands: She ordered that the bull's sperm envelop the sheep's egg and that the ram's sperm merge with the rabbit's egg. Under her direction, the donkey's sperm was inserted into the sow and the boar's seed injected into the donkey's womb.

The editor of the farm newsletter's face was lusterless, his mouth hung slack, and it was impossible to tell if he was about to burst into tears or burst out laughing. One of the assistants — the one holding the ram's sperm — a woman with curled lashes above small but bright, jet black eyes with very little white showing — refused to carry out Ma Ruilian's order. She tossed her insemination utensil into a porcelain tray and removed her gloves and mask, revealing the fine hairs on her upper lip, a fair nose, and a nicely curved chin. "This is a farce!" she said angrily.

"How dare you!" Ma Ruilian snarled as she smacked her palms together, her eyes sweeping across the woman's face. "Unless I'm mistaken," she said darkly, "you have been capped." She reached up as if taking a hat off her head. "Not a cap you can remove at will. No, you're an ultra-rightist, and that will be with you forever, a rightist who will always wear the cap. Am I right?" The woman's head slumped weakly to her chest, as if her neck were a frost-laden blade of grass. "You're right," she said, "I am a lifelong ultra-rightist. But, as I see it, these are unrelated issues, one scientific and one political. Politics are fickle, always shifting, where black is white and white is black. But science is constant." "Shut your mouth!" Ma Ruilian jerked and sputtered like an out-of-control steam engine. "I am not going to let you spread your poison in my breeding farm! Who are you to be talking about politics? Do you know the name of politics? Do you know what it eats? Politics are at the heart of all labor! Science divorced of politics is not true science. There is no science that transcends politics in the proletariat dictionary. The bourgeoisie has its bourgeois science, and the proletariat has its proletarian science." "If proletarian science," the woman responded, risking it all, "insists on crossbreeding sheep and rabbits in the hope of producing a new species of animal, then as far as I'm concerned, that so-called proletarian science is nothing more than a pile of dog shit!"

"Qiao Qisha, how can you be so arrogant?" Ma Ruilian's teeth were chattering from anger. "Take a look at the sky and then look down at the ground. You should understand the complexity of things. Calling proletarian science dog shit makes you an out-and-out reactionary! That comment alone is enough for us to throw you in jail, even put you in front of a firing squad! But seeing how young and beautiful you are . . ." Shangguan Pandi, now Ma Ruilian, softened her tone. "I'm willing to let it go this time, but I demand that you carry out your breeding mission! If you refuse, I wouldn't care if you were the flower of the medical college or the grass of the agricultural college. I can break that horse with the gigantic hooves, so don't think I can't do the same with you!"

The well-meaning newsletter editor spoke up: "Little Qiao, do as Commander Ma says. This is, after all, a scientific experiment. Over in Tianjin District, they successfully grafted cotton onto a parasol tree, and rice onto reeds. I read that in *The People's Daily*. This is an age of breaking down superstitions and liberating thought, an age of creating human miracles. If you can produce a mule by mating a donkey with a horse, who can say you won't produce a new species of animal by mating a sheep with a rabbit? So go ahead, do as she says."

The flower of the medical college and ultra-rightist, Qiao Qisha, felt her face turn beet red, and indignant tears swam in her eyes. "No," she said obstinately, "I won't do it. It flies in the face of common sense!"

"You're being foolish, little Qiao," the editor said.

"Of course she's foolish. Otherwise, she wouldn't be an ultra-rightist!" Ma Ruilian shot back, offended by the editor's concern for Qiao Qisha.

The editor lowered his head and held his tongue.

One of the other assistants walked up. "I'll do it, Commander Ma. Sheep sperm into a rabbit is nothing. I don't care if you want me to inject Director Li Du's sperm into the sow's womb."

The other assistants broke up laughing, while the newsletter director managed to cover up his laughter by pretending to cough. "Deng Jiarong, you bastard!" Ma Ruilian cursed, enraged. "This time you've gone too far!"

Deng removed his mask, exposing his insolent horselike face. With a reckless sneer, he said, "Commander Ma, I don't have a cap, permanent or not. I come from three generations of miners, as red and upright as they come, so don't try to intimidate me the way you did with little Qiao." He turned and walked off, leaving Ma Ruilian to vent her anger on Qiao Qisha. "Are you going to do it, or aren't you? If you don't, I'll take back your grain coupons for the rest of the month."

Qiao Qisha held back, and held back, until she could hold back no longer. Tears coursed down her cheeks and she cried openly. She picked up the insemination utensil in her gloveless hand, stumbled over to the rabbit — it was a black animal tethered by a piece of red rope — and held it down to keep it from struggling free.

At that moment, Pandi, now Ma Ruilian, spotted me. "What are you doing here?" she asked coldly. I handed her the note from the farm management director. She read it. "Go to the chicken farm," she said. "They're short one laborer." Then she turned her back on me and said to the newsletter editor, "Old Yu, go turn in your story. You can leave out the unnecessary parts." He bowed. "I'll bring the galleys over for you to check," he said. Then she turned to Qiao Qisha. "In ac-cordance with your wishes, Qiao Qisha, your transfer out of the breed-ing station is approved. Get your things and report to the chicken farm." Finally, she turned back to me. "What are you waiting for?" "I don't know where the chicken farm is," I said. She looked at her watch. "That's where I'm headed now, so come with me."

She stopped when the whitewashed wall of the chicken farm came into view. We were on the muddy path leading to the chicken farm, which ran past the munitions scrapyard; the little ditch alongside the road ran red with rust, and the fenced-in yard was overrun by weeds that covered the caterpillar tracks of crumbling tanks, their rust-ing cannons pointing into the blue sky. Tender green morning glory vines were wrapped around the remaining half of a heavy artillery piece. A dragonfly rested on the muzzle of an antiaircraft gun. Rats scampered in and out of the gun turret. Sparrows had made a nest in one of the cannons to raise their fledglings, feeding them emerald-colored insects. A little girl with a red ribbon in her hair sat dully on the blackened tire of a gun carriage, watching a couple of little boys bang rocks against the controls of one of the tanks. Ma Ruilian, who had been staring at the scrapyard desolation, turned to me. No longer the commander who was ordering people around at the breeding station, she said, "How's everyone at home?"

I turned away and stared at the antiaircraft gun, the morning glo-ries appearing like little butterflies, in an attempt to hide my anger. What kind of question was that, coming from someone who'd gone and changed her name?

"There was a time when your future couldn't have been brighter," she said. "We were happy for you. But Laidi ruined everything. Of course, it wasn't all her fault. Mother's foolishness also . . ."

"If you have nothing more for me," I said, "I'll report to the chicken farm."

"Well, I see you've developed a temper since I last saw you!" she said. "That's encouraging. Now that our Jintong is twenty, it's time to sew up the crotch of his pants and throw away the nipple."

I swung my bedding over my shoulder and headed off to the chicken farm.

"Stop right there! There's something you need to understand. Things have not gone well for us these past few years. Every time we open our mouths, people accuse us of rightist leanings. We've had no choice." She took the slip of paper out of her pocket and reached into a little bag hanging around her neck for a pen. After scribbling something, she handed the slip to me and said, "Ask for Director Long and give him this." I took it from her. "Is there anything else? If so, let's hear it." She hesitated for a moment, then said, "Do you have any idea how hard it's been for old Lu and me to get to where we are today? Please don't cause us any trouble. I'll do what I can for you in private, but in public . . ."

"Don't say it. When you decided to change your name, you ended your relationship with the Shangguan family. You're no sister of mine, so don't give me any of that 'I'll do what I can for you in private.'"

"Terrific! Next time you see Mother, tell her that Lu Shengli is doing fine."

Paying her no more attention, I started walking, following the rusty, symbolic fence that had gaps big enough to allow a cow in to graze among the relics of war, heading for the white wall of the chicken farm and feeling quite pleased with how I'd handled myself. I felt as if I'd won a decisive battle. Go to hell, Ma Ruilian and Li Du, and go to hell all you rusty gun barrels, like a bunch of turtles sticking your heads out of your shells. All you mortar chassis, all you artillery gun shields, all you bomber wings — you can all go to hell. I rounded some towering plants and found myself at the edge of a field covered with a sort of fishnet between two rows of red-roofed buildings. Inside, thousands of white chickens were in constant, lazy movement. A single large rooster with a bright red comb was perched high up, a king surveying his harem, crowing loudly. The clucking of the hens was enough to drive a person crazy.

I handed the slip given to me by Ma Ruilian to a one-armed woman, Director Long. One look at her cold face told me that this was no ordinary woman. "You've come at the right time, youngster," she said after reading the note. "Here are your duties. Every morning you will rake up the chicken droppings and deliver them to the pig farm. Then you'll go to the feed processing plant and bring the coarse chicken feed we'll need back with you. In the afternoons, you and Qiao Qisha, who will be here soon, will deliver the day's output of eggs to the farm management office, and from there you'll go to the grain storehouse and bring back enough fine chicken feed for the next day. Got it?" "Got it," I replied as I stared at her empty sleeve. She sneered when she saw where I was looking. "There are only two rules around here. One, no lying down on the job, and two, no sneaking food."

The moon lit up the sky that night as I lay on some flattened cardboard boxes in the storage room of the chicken farm dorm, finding it hard to sleep amid the soft murmuring of hens. I was next to the women's dorm, which held a dozen or so chicken tenders. Their snores came though the thin wall, along with the sound of someone talking in her sleep. Cheerless moonlight streamed in through the window and the gaps in the door, illuminating the words on the boxes:

AVIAN FLU VACCINE
KEEP DRY AND OUT OF SUNLIGHT
FRAGILE, DO NOT STACK
THIS SIDE UP

Slowly, the moonlight slipped across the floor, and I heard the roar of East Is Red tractors out in the early summer fields, driven by members of the night-shift tractor detail cultivating virgin land. The day before, Mother had walked me to the head of the village, holding in her arms the baby left behind by Birdman Han and Laidi. "Jintong," she said, "remember that the tougher the job, the harder you have to work at living. Pastor Malory used to say that he'd read the Bible from cover to cover, and that's what it all came to. Don't worry about me. Your mother is like an earthworm — I can live wherever there's dirt." I said, "Mother, I'm going to watch what I eat so I can send you the surplus." "I don't want you to do that," she said. "As long as my children eat their fill, that's enough for me." When we reached the bank of the Flood Dragon River, I said, "Mother, Zaohua has become an expert at . . ." "Jintong," Mother said in frustration, "During all these years, not a single girl in the Shangguan family has taken advice from anyone."

Sometime in the middle of the night, a commotion broke out in the chicken house. I jumped to my feet and stuck my face up against the window, where I saw chickens seething under the tattered net like foam-capped waves. A green fox was leaping amid them in the watery moonlight, an undulating ribbon of green satin. Raising the alarm, the women next door rushed outside half dressed, one-armed Commander Long in the lead, armed with a black pistol. The fox had a fat hen in its mouth and was scampering along the base of the wall, the hen's foot scraping the ground. Commander Long fired; flames shot from the muzzle of her pistol. The fox stopped in its tracks and dropped the hen. "You hit it!" one of the women shouted. But the glossy eyes of the fox swept the women's faces. Its long face was haloed in moonlight; it wore a sneer. The women were stunned by that mocking grin, and Commander Long's arm fell weakly to her side. But then she steeled herself and fired another round. It didn't come close, did, in fact, raise a puff of dirt in the vicinity of the women. With no more concerns, the fox picked up the hen and slipped nonchalantly through the metal ribs of the enclosure, the women watching its exit as if in a trance. Like a puff of green smoke, the fox disappeared among the war relics in the scrapyard, where the grass grew tall and will-o'-the-wisps dotted the landscape — a fox paradise.

The following morning, my eyelids felt weighted down as I pulled a full cartload of chicken droppings over to the pig farm. When I turned the corner of the scrapyard, I heard a shout behind me. I turned and saw the rightist Qiao Qisha running briskly toward me. "The director sent me to help you," she said indifferently. "You push from behind," I said, "and I'll pull."

The two wheels of the heavy cart kept getting stuck in the soft earth of the narrow road, and each time that happened, I had to turn and tug with all my might, my arched back nearly touching the ground. At the same time, she pushed with everything she had. Once the wheels were free, she'd look over at me before I turned around. The sight of her jet black eyes, the fine hairs on her upper lip, her fair nose and nicely curved chin, as well as her expression, which was filled with hidden meaning, reminded me of the fox in the chicken coop. That look lit up a dark place in my brain.

The pig farm was about a mile from the chicken farm, and the road passed by a fertilizer pit for the vegetable garden unit. My teacher, Huo Lina, walked past us carrying a load of manure, her slim waist compressed by the weight of her load until she seemed about to snap in two. At the pig farm, we delivered our chicken droppings to the woman in charge, Ji Qiongzhi, my former music teacher, who dumped the slimy, stinking mess into the pig troughs.

One of the members of the food processing team was an athletic fellow who could high-jump nearly two meters using the latest flop method. Naturally, he was a rightist. He displayed a great deal of concern for Qiao Qisha, and was extremely friendly to me, one of those cheerful rightists, unlike the ones who went around scowling the day long. Wearing a towel draped around his neck and a pair of goggles, he worked happily on the pulverizer, which filled the air with dust. The leader of his team was another special case, an illiterate man named Guo Wenhao who created clapper-talk lyrics that were sung all over the farm. On our very first trip with coarse fodder made of yams, he entertained us with one of his lyrics:

"There's this animal farm leader, Ma Ruilian, who has a new vocation. She carries out experiments at the breeding station, mating a sheep and rabbit with high elation. She angered her assistant, Qiao Qisha, and hit her in the belly, ha ha ha. A horse and a donkey produce a mule, but a rabbit sheep would be a new creation. If a sheep can marry a rabbit, a boar can take Ma Ruilian for gestation. With anger in her breast, she told Li Du with detestation. Tolerant Director Li counseled hesitation. These rightists, he said, don't understand cessation. Little Qiao went to medical school, Yu Zheng uses a newsletter for his narration. Ma Ming studied in the American nation, Zhang Jie's dictionary is a clarification. Even rightist Wang Meizan, whose head knows no sensation, is a great athlete, cause for celebration . . ."

"You there, rightist!" Guo Wenhao shouted. Wang Meizan brought his legs together. "Yo!" he responded. "Load the Qiao girl up with fodder." Wang replied, "Will do, Leader Guo."

Wang Meizan loaded our cart with fodder, as Guo Wenhao asked me over the roar of the pulverizer, "Are you a Shangguan?" "Yes," I said, "I'm the little Shangguan bastard. "A bastard can become a great man. You Shangguans are an incredible family. Sha Yueliang, Sima Ku, Birdman Han, Speechless Sun, Babbitt. You're really something . . ."

On our way back to the chicken farm with the feed, Qiao Qisha blurted out, "What's your name?"

"Shangguan Jintong. Why do you ask?"

"No reason," she said. "We work together, so we might as well know each other's name. How many sisters do you have?"

"Eight. No, seven."

"What about the eighth?"

"She turned traitor," I replied with annoyance. "That's all you need to know."

Every night the same fox came to harass the chickens, and every other night it stole off with one of the hens. On off nights, it didn't steal a hen not because it couldn't, but because it didn't want to. Its nightly activities fell into two categories: nights when it was hungry, and nights when it merely wanted to cause a disturbance. This drove the women chicken tenders to distraction, and cost them lots of sleep. Commander Long fired at least twenty bullets at the fox, but never harmed a hair of its fur. "That fox is a demon for sure," one of the women said. "It can recite a charm to ward off bullets."

"Nonsense!" a tall woman nicknamed "Wild Mule" disagreed sharply. "No mangy fox can turn into a demon."

"If that's true, how come Commander Long, who was a sharpshooter in the militia, keeps missing?" asked the other woman.

"I think it's intentional. The fox is a male, after all," Wild Mule said salaciously. "Maybe a handsome green visitor comes to her bed late at night, when everything's quiet."

Commander Long stood under the tattered netting silently listening to the women's talk, fiddling with her pistol, apparently lost in thought. The wanton laughter roused her from her ruminations; tapping her gray cap with the muzzle of the pistol, she strode into the chicken coop, skirting the laying pens, and planted herself in front of Wild Mule, who was gathering eggs. "What did you say just now?" she demanded angrily. "I didn't say anything," Wild Mule replied calmly, a brown egg in the palm of her hand. "I heard you!" Commander Long raged as she tapped the wire with her pistol. "Exactly what did you hear?" Wild Mule asked provocatively. Commander Long's face turned the color of the egg Wild Mule was holding. "I'll never forgive you for that!" she sputtered as she turned and walked away, enraged. Wild Mule looked at her back and said, "If your heart is pure, not even the devil can scare you! Don't be fooled by her serious appearance, fox. She's lusting, all right. The other night, you think I didn't see with

my own eyes?" "Wild Mule," one of the more prudent women counseled, "that's enough. Where do you find all this energy on the six
ounces of noodles you're given to eat?" "Six ounces of noodles? Fuck
her and her six ounces of noodles!" She pulled a pin out of her hair,
poked a hole in each end of the egg she was holding, and quickly
sucked it dry. Then she put the outwardly whole egg with the others.
"Anyone who wants to report me, go ahead. My dad's found me a husband in the Northeast, and I'm leaving next month. There are enough
potatoes up there to form mountains. How about you, planning on reporting me?" she asked Jintong, who was shoveling chicken droppings
by the window. "You're the most likely one, a fragrant baby rooster,
just the type favored by our armless leader. An old cow like her, with
bad teeth, has to graze on tender grass!" Jintong was totally befuddled
by the verbal assault. Holding his shovel out in front of him, he said,
"Want some of this chicken shit?"

That afternoon, when they reached the vegetable unit's fertilizer
pit with their load of four crates of eggs, Qiao Qisha asked Jintong to
stop. He slowed down and lowered the cart handles to the ground.
"Have you seen them?" Qiao Qisha asked when he turned around.
"They all steal eggs, even Commander Long. You've seen the one
called Wild Mule, what good shape she's in? Those women get more
nutrition than they need." "But these eggs have been weighed," Jintong said. "Are we supposed to go hungry, even when we're delivering
a load of eggs? I'm about to drop from hunger." Picking up two of the
eggs, she darted into the fenced-off enclosure and disappeared behind
two tanks. A few moments later, she reappeared with what looked like
two whole eggs and put them back into the load. "Qiao Qisha," Jintong said worriedly, "that's like a cat covering up its own shit. When
they weigh this load at the farm, they'll know what's happened." She
laughed. "Do you think I'm stupid?" she said as she picked up two
more eggs and motioned to him. "Come with me," she said.

Jintong followed her into the enclosure, where white pollen floated
above tall artemesia stalks, filling the air with a dizzying fragrance. She
squatted down beside a tank and removed something wrapped in oilpaper from a gap between the tractor tread and a wheel. Her crime kit. It
included a tiny drill bit, a hypodermic needle, a piece of rubberized fabric dyed the color of an eggshell, and a little pair of scissors. After drilling
a tiny hole in one of the eggs, she inserted the hypodermic needle and
slowly drew out the contents. "Open your mouth," she said, and emp-

tied the contents down Jintong's throat, making him her accomplice. Once that was done, she drew water out of an upturned steel helmet lying next to the tank and inserted it into the shell. Finally, she cut out a small piece of fabric to cover the hole. All this with practiced efficiency. "Is this what they taught you at the medical school?" Jintong asked. "That's right," she said with a smile. "Egg theft!"

When the eggs were weighed, they had actually gained an ounce or so.

The egg-stealing drama was brought to a ruthless end in a couple of weeks. Midsummer rains signaled the hens' molting season, and egg production dropped precipitously. One day they stopped at the same spot with their load of a crate and a half of eggs, and entered the enclosure through the wet fence; the artemesia buds were filled with seeds, and a watery mist hung over the military relics. The rusting hulks gave off a thick, bloodlike odor. A frog was resting on one of the tank wheels, its sticky green skin creating a sense of unease in Jintong. When Qiao Qisha squirted the egg into his mouth, he suddenly felt nauseous; with his hand around his throat, he said, "This egg tastes rotten, and it's cold." In a couple of days, you'll be lucky to get cold, rotten eggs. The curtain is about to drop on our little drama." "That's right," Jintong said, "the hens are about to molt." "You're a silly kid," she said. "I wonder if you have some sort of intuition about me." "You?" Jintong shook his head. "What kind of intuition would that be?" "Forget I said anything. There's enough going on with your family already, and I'd only complicate things more." "I don't get what you're talking about," Jintong said. "I'm confused." "Why haven't you asked anything about my background?" she said. "I'm not planning on marrying you, so why should I?" She froze for a moment, then smiled. "Spoken like a true Shangguan. Always a hidden meaning. Who says you have to marry me to ask about my background?" "My teacher, Huo Lina, said that asking a girl about her background is rude." "Are you talking about that manure carrier?" "She speaks beautiful Russian," Jintong said. With a sneer, Qisha said, "I hear you were her prize student." "I guess so." In a display of grandstanding, Qisha responded by reciting a long monologue in perfect Russian, clearly more than Jintong could handle. "Did you get all that?" "I think it was a sad folktale about a little girl . . ." "Is that the best Huo Lina's prize student can do? A three-legged cat, a paper tiger, a dim lantern, an empty pillowcase." She picked up the four refilled eggs and headed back. "I studied with her less than six months," Jintong defended himself. "You expect too much from me." "I don't have time to expect anything from you," she replied. The wet artemesia plants had brushed up against her blouse, which stuck to her breasts, made full from the sixty-eight eggs she'd eaten, in stark contrast to her skinny frame. Feelings of tenderness and melancholy swept over Jintong, as a sensation of familiarity with this beautiful rightist worked its way into his head like an army of ants. Instinctively, he reached out to her, but she bent down and stepped nimbly through the wire fence. A moment later, the sound of Commander Long's grim laughter came on the air from the other side of the fence.

Commander Long turned one of the refilled eggs over and over in her hand. Jintong, his knees knocking, stared at that hand. Qiao Qisha, on the other hand, was gazing haughtily at the gun barrels pointing into the overcast sky, as if launching silent screams. A fine rain formed translucent beads on her forehead and then slid down the sides of her nose. Jintong saw in her eyes the calmly contemptuous look so common among all the Shangguan girls when faced with a bad situation. At that moment, he had a pretty good sense of her background and, at the same time, understood why she'd asked so many questions about his family during the weeks and months they'd been working together.

"A genius!" Commander Long sneered. "A credit to your education." Then, without warning, she flung the refilled egg at Qiao Qisha, hitting her squarely in the forehead. The shell broke, causing Qisha's head to wobble, and drenching her face with dirty water. "Follow me to the farm headquarters," Commander Long said. "There you'll get the punishment you deserve." "This has nothing to do with Shangguan Jintong," Qisha said. "All he's guilty of is not reporting me. The same as my not reporting the others, who not only steal and eat eggs, but the hens as well."

Two days later, Qiao Qisha forfeited half a month's grain rations and was reassigned to the vegetable unit as a manure carrier, to work alongside Huo Lina. There the two Russian speakers were often seen brandishing their manure spades in one another's face and cursing in Russian. Jintong kept his job at the chicken farm, where less than half the laying hens had survived. The dozen or so women were reassigned as night-shift field workers, leaving Commander Long and Jintong to tend the surviving molting hens in the once-busy farm. As for the fox, it continued its incursions; battling the marauder became Commander Long and Jintong's primary duty.

One summer night, when dark clouds swallowed up the moon, the fox returned and was heading out the gate with a featherless hen in its mouth and a swagger in its step. Commander Long got off her usual two shots, which had evolved into a sort of farewell ritual. Amid the intoxicating smell of gunpowder, the two of them stood facing each other. The croaking of frogs and cries of birds came on the wind from distant fields as the moon broke through the clouds and oiled the two combatants' bodies in its light. Hearing a grunt from Commander Long, he saw that her face had grown long and scary; the glare of her teeth turned a terrifying white. And there was more: a bushy tail swelled the seat of her pants like an expanding balloon. Commander Long was a fox! A horrifying clarity burst in his head. She was a female fox, the mate of that other one, and that was why her shots always missed. The frequent green visitor that Wild Mule said entered the sleeping quarters in the hazy moonlight was that transformed fox. The noxious odor of fox filled the air, and he gaped as he watched her come toward him, the smoking pistol still in her hand. Flinging away his club, he ran screeching back to his quarters and put his shoulder to the door as soon as he was inside. He heard her go into the adjoining room; she was alone. Moonlight struck the wall, which was nailed together with old slats. She scraped the wall with her claws and murmured softly. All of a sudden, she knocked a gaping hole in the wall and entered his room, completely naked, once again in human form. Only a horrible scar, like the tightly closed opening of a burlap bag, remained where her arm had once been. Her breasts protruded hard and heavy, like the weights of a scale. She fell to her knees at Jintong's feet and wrapped her arm around his legs. Muttering like a teary old woman, she said, "Shangguan Jintong, take pity on a wretched woman!"

Jintong fought to step out of her grip, but she reached up and grabbed his belt, tugging so hard she snapped it and pulled down his pants. When he bent down to pull them up, she wrapped her arm around his neck and her legs around his waist. In the grappling that ensued, she somehow managed to undress him. Once that was done, she tapped him on the temple; his eyes rolled back into his head and he lay flat on the floor like a beached fish. Commander Long nibbled every inch of Jintong's body, but was unable to release him from his terror. Enraged by her failure, she ran back into the adjoining room, grabbed her pistol, tucked the barrel between her legs, and shoved two yellow bullets into the chamber. Then, pointing the weapon at a spot below his belly, she said, "There are two paths open to you. You can get it up, or I'll shoot it off." The glare in her eyes was all the proof he needed to know that she was serious. The iron-hard breasts were bouncing around on her chest. Once again Jintong watched as her face lengthened and a bushy tail emerged behind her, slowly, until it reached the floor.

Over the drizzly days that followed, Commander Long did everything possible, from encouragement to threats, day or night, to make a man out of Jintong. In the end, she failed, and by then she was spitting blood. In the final moments before she turned her gun on herself, she wiped the blood from her chin and said sadly, "Long Qingping, ah, Long Qingping, you're still a virgin at the age of thirty-nine. Everyone knows what a hero you are, but no one realizes that you're also a woman, and that your life has been wasted . . ." She coughed and hunched her shoulders; her dark face paled, and, with a loud cry, she spit out a mouthful of blood, driving the soul right out of Jintong, who stood with his back flattened up against the door. Tears ran down Long Qingping's face as, with a look of resentment in her eyes, she crawled on her knees to him, raised her pistol, and put the muzzle against her temple. Not until that moment did Jintong finally comprehend the seductiveness of a woman's body. Raising her elbow to reveal the fine hairs under her arm, she sat down on her heels, as a cloud of golden smoke burst in front of his eyes. The cold spot between his legs suddenly swelled with heated blood. The inconsolable Long Qingping pulled the trigger — if, at that moment, she had glanced back, the tragedy would have been averted — and Jintong saw a puff of burnt ocher smoke emerge from her temple hair as the dull crack of a pistol sounded. Her body rocked briefly before she crumpled onto the floor. Jintong rushed up and turned her over, exposing the black hole in her temple, circled by tiny blue particles of gunpowder; dark blood oozed from inside her ear and ran down his fingers. Her eyes were open, still showing traces of her grief. The skin of her chest was still twitching, like ripples on a pond.

Jintong held her in his arms, overcome by remorse, and granted her final wish as her life slipped away. Finally, he climbed off her, utterly spent; the sparks of light in her eyes died as her lids descended. A pall of gray settled in his head as he gazed at her now lifeless body.

Outside, a torrential rain fell, a blinding gray that entered the room in waves and swallowed up both their bodies.

5

Shangguan Jintong was taken into the chicken coop for interrogation. His bare legs seeped in rainwater that cascaded in over the eaves, flooded the compound, and crashed against the roof. Ever since that moment between him and Long Qingping, the rain had been unending, letting up briefly, only to start up again harder than ever.

The water nearly reached his knees. Wrapped in a black raincoat, the security section chief was squatting on his chair. Two days and nights of questioning had produced no results. The man was a chain-smoker; the water around him was peppered with water-soaked cigarette butts and the air was suffocating with acrid smoke. Rubbing his bloodshot eyes, the section chief yawned from exhaustion, as did the official recorder. Then he picked up a notebook from the wet desktop and stared at the smudged writing. Reaching out and grabbing Jintong by the ear, he barked, "Did you rape her first and then kill her?" Jintong stood there weeping, but with no more tears to shed. "I didn't kill her," he repeated, "and I didn't rape her . . ."

"You don't have to tell me," the section chief said, running out of patience. "But a medical expert from the county will be here soon, and he's bringing attack dogs with him. Tell me now, and that will count as a voluntary confession."

"I didn't kill her," he said one more time, sleepily, "and I didn't rape her."

The section chief took out a pack of cigarettes, crushed it, and tossed it into the water. As he rubbed the sleep from his eyes, he said to the recorder, "Go to the farm headquarters building, Sun, and place a call to the County Security Bureau. Tell them to get over here as soon as possible." He sniffed the air. "The body's starting to stink, and if they don't come soon, our investigation will be ruined."

"Boss," the man said, "are you crazy? I tried calling the day before yesterday and couldn't get through. The rain has washed away telephone poles."

"Shit!" the section chief cursed as he jumped down off of his chair, put on his rain cap, and waded over to the door, where he stuck out his head to look around. A roaring curtain of water drenched his shiny back as he ran over to the site of Jintong and Commander Long's illicit liaison. Out in the yard, clean and dirty water merged, with dead chickens floating on the surface. The few surviving hens were perched atop the wall — heads tucked down, clucking piteously. Jintong had a splitting headache and his teeth were chattering. His mind was a blank, except for the movements of Commander Long's nakedness. After impulsively entering her dying body, he had experienced terrible remorse, but now all he felt toward her was loathing and disgust. He struggled to break free of her likeness, but, as with Natasha years before, it stuck doggedly in his mind. The difference was that Natasha was a beautiful young image, while Commander Long was a repulsive, demonic one. At the moment he was dragged out to be interrogated, he made up his mind not to reveal the ugly details of what had happened. I didn't rape her, and I didn't kill her. She tried to force herself on me, and when I resisted, she killed herself. That's all he would reveal under the pressures of the relentless questioning.

The security chief returned and shook the water off of his neck. "Damn!" he exclaimed. "She's all bloated. Like a debristled hog. Disgusting." He pinched his throat.

Off in the distance, the cafeteria's red-brick chimney came crashing to the ground, still belching black smoke, and took the building itself — roof, windows, venetian blinds, and all — with it, sending gray water towering into the air with a roar.

"The building's down," the security chief exclaimed. "Now what? Forget the fucking interrogation — now we won't even be able to eat!"

The collapse of the cafeteria opened up an unobstructed view of the fields. It also created the terrifying sight of an ocean of water, all the way to the horizon. The dikes of the Flood Dragon River poked through the surface here and there, but the water within them rose above the level beyond. The rain fell unevenly to earth, as if dumped by a gigantic watering can moving rapidly across the sky. Directly below the watering can the downpour set up a roar, with torrents of water creating a mist over the land; everywhere else, sunlight lit up the gentle flow of floodwaters. Situated in the lowest spot of the Northeast Gaomi marshy lowland, the Flood Dragon River Farm was irrigated by water from three separate counties. Soon after the cafeteria collapsed, every farm structure, from those with rammed-earth walls to tile-roofed buildings, crumbled into the rushing water, except for the grain storage building, which had been planned and constructed by a rightist named Liang Badong. A few sections of the chicken coop, built with bricks from the graveyard, managed to remain upright, but the water had already reached the windows. Benches and stools floated on the water, which was up to Jintong's navel as he too began to float in his chair.

Cries of distress sounded everywhere, as people struggled against the flood. "Head for the river dikes!" someone shouted.

The security section recorder kicked out the window and fled, followed by the curses of the section chief. He turned to Jintong. "Follow me," he said.

So Jintong followed the squat section chief out into the yard, where the man had to move his arms back and forth in the water to keep standing. Jintong looked behind him and spotted a clutch of chickens perched on the roof, alongside the wicked fox. Long Qingping's corpse floated out of the room and followed him. When he sped up, so did the corpse, and when he made a turn, the corpse followed suit. Long Qingping's corpse nearly made him soil himself out of fright. Finally, her tangle of hair was caught in the wire fence around the war relics, and Jintong was free of her. The artillery barrels poked out of the muddy water; of the tanks, only the turrets and guns showed above the surface, like enormous turtles sticking their necks out of the water. When the two men drew up to the tractor unit, the chicken farm collapsed.

In the tractor unit garage, people had crowded onto a pair of red Russian combines, and more were trying to climb aboard; by doing so, they sent others sliding down into the water.

A surge of water washed away the security section chief, gaining for Jintong his freedom. He and several rightists headed, hand in hand, toward the Flood Dragon River under the leadership of the high-jumper Wang Meizan, with the civil engineer Liang Badong bringing up the rear. Huo Lina, Ji Qiongzhi, Qiao Qisha, and others he didn't know walked between the two men, joined by Jintong, who half walked and half swam into their midst. Qiao Qisha reached out to him. The women's wet blouses stuck to their bodies, almost as if they were naked. By force of habit, however disgusting, he cast fleeting glances at the chests of Huo Lina, Ji Qiongzhi, and Qiao Qisha. They carried Jintong back to the dreamland of his youth, and drove Long Qingping's image out of his head. He felt himself turning into a butterfly crawling out of Long's blackened corpse to dry his wings in the sun and flit among a garden of breasts that emitted a strange redolence.

Jintong found himself wishing he could trudge through this water forever, but the Flood Dragon River dike dashed his hopes. Farm workers huddled atop the dike were hugging their shoulders as the floodwaters flowed slowly down the trough and sent a soft mist into the air. There were no swallows, there were no gulls. Off to the southwest, Dalan was shrouded in the whiteness of rain; everywhere they looked they saw the chaos of water.

When the red-tiled grain storage shed finally fell, the Flood Dragon River Farm became nothing but a gigantic lake. Sounds of weeping rose from the dike — leftists were crying, and so were rightists. Director Li Du, a man they seldom saw, was shaking his gray head — Lu Liren's head, that is — and shouting shrilly, "Don't cry, comrades. Be strong. As long as we remain united, we can overcome any difficulty . . ." All of a sudden, he clutched his chest and began to crumple. The head of the management section tried to catch him, but he fell onto the muddy ground in a heap. "Is there a doctor here? Anyone with medical knowledge, come, quickly!" the man bellowed.

Qiao Qisha and a male rightist ran up. They checked the victim's pulse and raised his lids to look at his eyes. Then they pinched the trough under his nose and the spot between his thumb and index finger, but that did no good. "He's gone," the man said matter-of-factly. "Heart attack."

Ma Ruilian opened her mouth and released wails from Shangguan Pandi's throat.

As night fell, the people huddled to stay warm. An airplane with flashing green lights appeared in the sky, rekindling hope below. But it flew past, like a comet, and never returned. At some time in the middle of the night, the rain stopped, and hordes of frogs croaked an earsplitting chorus. A few stars twinkled tentatively in the sky, looking as if they were about to fall to earth. During a brief respite from the croaking frogs, the wind whistled through tree branches floating past us. Out of nowhere, someone dove into the water and immediately turned belly-up, like a large fish. No one screamed for help; no one even seemed to notice. Before long, someone else jumped in, and this time, the reaction on the dike was, if anything, even more callous.

Starlight shone down on Qiao Qisha and Huo Lina as they walked up to Jintong. "I want to tell you about my background in a roundabout fashion," Qiao Qisha said. She then turned to Huo Lina and spoke to her in Russian for several minutes. Huo Lina matter-of-factly interpreted for her. "When I was four, I was sold to a White Russian woman. No one could tell me why this woman wanted to buy a Chinese girl." Qiao Qisha continued in Russian, with Huo Lina interpreting. "One day the Russian woman died of alcohol poisoning and I was left to roam the streets, until I was taken in by a railroad station manager. He and his family treated me like their own daughter. Since they were well-off, they paid for me to go to school. After Liberation, in 1949, I was admitted to a medical school. But then, during the great airing of views, I said that there are bad poor people, just as there are good rich people, and I was labeled a rightist. I believe I am your seventh sister."

Qisha shook Huo Lina's hand to thank her. Then she took Jintong by the hand and led him to one side, where she said softly, "I've heard things about you. I studied medicine. Your teacher told me that you had sex with the woman before she killed herself. Is that right?" "It was after she did it," Jintong said haltingly. "That's despicable," she said. "The security section chief was a fool. This flood saved your life. You know that, don't you?" Jintong nodded. "I saw her corpse float away, and so they have no evidence against you," the woman claiming to be my seventh sister said in a flat voice. "Be firm. Deny ever having sex with her — if we manage to survive the flood, that is."

Qiao Qisha's prediction came true. The flood had come to Jintong's aid. By the time the chief investigator of the County Security Bureau and a medical examiner arrived in a rubber raft, half the people lay unconscious on the Flood Dragon River dike, while the remainder had survived by eating rotting grass they'd fished out of the river, like starving horses. The moment the men climbed out of the raft, they were surrounded by hungry, hopeful people. They responded by flashing their badges, unholstering their pistols, and announcing that they were there to investigate the rape and murder of a heroic woman. A chorus of angry curses erupted. The scowling investigator demanded to see the survivors' leader, and was directed to Lu Liren, who lay on the muddy ground, his gray uniform torn apart by his bloated body. "That's him." Holding his nose, the investigator made a wide turn around the decaying, fly-specked body of Lu Liren, searching out the farm's security section chief, who had reported the crime by telephone. He was told that the man had floated down the river on a plank three days earlier. The investigator stopped in front of Ji Qiongzhi; the chilled looks they exchanged revealed the complex emotions of a divorced couple. "The death of a person means about as much as the death of a dog these days, doesn't it?" she said. "So what's to investigate?" The investigator glanced out at the corpses floating in the murky water, some animal and others human, and said, "Those are two separate matters." So they went looking for Shangguan Jintong and began to grill him, applying a range of psychological tactics. But Jintong held firm, refusing to divulge this final secret.

Several days later, after tramping through a sea of knee-high mud, the conscientious chief investigator and the medical examiner found Long Qingping's body, which had been snagged by the wire fence. But as the examiner was photographing the body, it exploded like a time bomb, its rotting skin and sticky juices fouling the water over a wide area. All that remained snagged on the fence was a skeleton. The medical examiner retrieved the skull, with its bullet hole, and examined it from every angle. He arrived at two conclusions: the muzzle was up against the temple when the shot was fired, and while it looked like suicide, murder was a possibility.

They prepared to take Jintong back with them, but were quickly surrounded by rightists. "Take a good look at this boy," Ji Qiongzhi said, taking advantage of her special relationship with the chief investigator. "Does he look like someone who's capable of rape and murder? That woman was a terrifying demon. This boy, on the other hand, was my student."

By that time, the chief investigator had himself nearly been driven to suicide by hunger and the pervasive stench. "The case is closed," he said, fed up with the whole matter. "Long Qingping took her own life." With that, he and the medical examiner climbed into their rubber raft to return to headquarters. But the raft no sooner left the bank than it spun around and was swept downriver.

6

In the spring of 1960, when the countryside was littered with the corpses of famine victims, members of the Flood Dragon River Farm rightist unit were transformed into a herd of ruminants, scouring the earth for vegetation to quell their hunger. Everyone was limited to an ounce and a half of grain daily, minus the amount skimmed off the top by the storekeeper, the manager of the dining hall, and other important individuals. What remained was enough for a bowl of porridge so thin they could see their reflection in it. But that didn't release them from their duties of rebuilding the farm. Also, with the help of soldiers from the local artillery unit, they cultivated acres of muddy land with millet. Poison was added to the fertilizer to keep away the thieves. It was so potent that the ground was carpeted with dead crickets, worms, and assorted other insects unknown to the rightist Fang Huawen, who was a trained biologist. Birds that fed on insects flopped over stiff, and critters that came to feed on their corpses hopped into the air and were dead before they hit the ground.

In the spring, when the millet crop was knee high, all sorts of vegetables were ready to be picked, and the rightists out in the field crammed whatever they could find into their mouths as they worked. During rest periods, they sat in trenches, regurgitating the leafy mess in their stomachs to chew it up as finely as possible. Green saliva gathered at the corners of their mouths, on faces so bloated the skin was translucent.

No more than ten farm workers were spared from dropsy. The new director, called Little Old Du, was one of them; the granary storekeeper, Guo Zilan, was another, and everyone knew they were pilfering horse feed. Special Agent Wei Guoying did not suffer, since his wolfhound warranted a supply of meat. Another man, by the name of Zhou Tianbao, was also spared. As a child he'd blown off three of his fingers with a homemade bomb; years later, he'd lost an eye when his rifle blew up in his face. Put in charge of farm security, he slept during the day and prowled every corner of the farm at night, armed with a Czech rifle. He was housed in a tiny sheet-metal hut in a corner of the military hardware scrapyard, from which the fragrant odor of meat being cooked often emerged late at night. The smell made sleep all but impossible for people in the area. One night, Guo Wenhao crept over to the hut and was about to peek in the window when he felt the thud of a rifle butt. "Damn you," Zhou Tianbao cursed, the light from his one good eye cutting through the darkness. "A counterrevolutionary! What are you doing, sneaking around like this?" The muzzle of Zhou's rifle dug into Guo's back. "What's cooking in there, Tianbao?" Guo asked mischievously. "How about giving me a taste?" "I doubt that you have the guts," Zhou grumbled softly. "The only thing with four legs I won't eat is a table," Guo said. "And the only two-legged thing I won't eat is a person." Zhou laughed. "That's human meat I'm cooking." Guo Wenhao turned and ran.

Word that Zhou Tianbao was eating human flesh quickly made

the rounds, throwing everyone into a panic. People slept with one eye open, terrified that Zhou would come get them for his next meal. In order to quell the rumor, Little Old Du called a meeting to announce that he had looked into the matter, and that Zhou Tianbao was cooking and eating rats he found in abandoned tanks. He told everyone, especially the rightists, to quit acting like stinking intellectuals and learn how to open up new sources of food, like Zhou Tianbao, in order to save up grain during lean years and make it possible to support people throughout the world who are worse off than us. Wang Siyuan, a graduate of an agricultural college, suggested growing mushrooms on rotting wood; Little Old Du gave him the go-ahead. Two weeks later, the mushroom plan led to the poisoning of more than a hundred people; some suffered no more than a bout of vomiting and diarrhea, but others were temporarily deranged, as if they were speaking in tongues. The security section thought it was an act of sabotage, but the health department attributed it to food poisoning. As a result, Little Old Du was censured, and the rightist Wang Siyuan was reclassified as an ultra-rightist. Most of the victims were treated in time and were soon out of danger. Huo Lina, on the other hand, could not be saved. In the aftermath of her death, a rumor spread that she had been involved with a dining hall worker everyone called Pockface Zhang, and that she always got larger helpings of food than the others. Someone said that on a Sunday night, during the movie, the two of them were seen slipping out in the dark into some tall grass.

Huo Lina's death hit Jintong especially hard, and he refused to believe that someone from a good family who had gone to school in Russia would give herself to anyone as ugly and as coarse as Pockface Zhang for a little extra soup. What happened later on to Qiao Qisha proved him wrong. For when a woman is so undernourished that her breasts lie flat on her chest and her periods stop coming, self-respect and chastity cease to exist. Poor Jintong was to witness the entire incident, from start to finish.

During the spring, some plow oxen were delivered to the farm. Before long, they discovered there weren't enough females for mating purposes, so they castrated four of the bulls to fatten them up for food. Ma Ruilian was still in charge of the livestock unit, but with significantly less power, now that Li Du was dead. So when Deng Jiarong walked off with all eight of the detached testicles, all she could do was glare at his back. When she detected the salivating fragrance of the testicles on Deng Jiarong's grill wafting out of the breeding station, she told Chen San to bring some back. Deng demanded a quantity of horse feed in return, to which Ma Ruilian reluctantly agreed, exchanging a catty of dried bean cakes for one of the testicles.

Jintong was given the job of walking the oxen at night to keep them from lying down and reopening the wounds. It was murky at dusk, and at the farm's eastern irrigation ditch, he led the animals into a stand of willows, where he tied them to trees. Five nights in a row he had walked them, until his legs felt weighted down with lead. As he sat leaning against one of the trees, his eyelids grew heavy, and he was about to fall asleep when the soul-stirring, sweet and fresh aroma of freshly baked and still warm buns assailed his nose. His eyes snapped open. What he saw was the cook, Pockface Zhang, walking backward with a steamed bun on a skewer, waving it in the air like bait. And that's exactly what it was. Some three or four feet away, Qiao Qisha, the flower of the medical school, was following him, her eyes fixed greedily on the bun. Weak light from the setting sun haloed her puffy face, as if coating it with the blood of a dog. She walked with difficulty, gasping for breath and reaching out with her hand. More than once she nearly touched it, but Pockface Zhang pulled it back each time, grinning maliciously. She whimpered like an abused puppy. But whenever her frustration nearly forced her away, the fragrance of the bun brought her back, as if in a trance. Qiao Qisha, who, at a time when everyone was given six ounces of grain a day, could still refuse to inseminate a rabbit with sheep's sperm, had lost her faith in politics *and* science, now that the ration had dwindled to one ounce a day; animal instinct drove her toward the steamed bun, and it didn't matter who was holding it. She followed it deep into the stand of willows. That morning, Jintong had spent his rest period helping Chen San cut hay, for which he'd received three ounces of dry bean cakes. That had given him enough self-control to resist the temptation to join the bun parade. Evidence would later show that during the famine of 1960, Zhang traded food for sex with nearly every female rightist at the farm. Qiao Qisha was the last stronghold he breached. The youngest, most beautiful, and most obstinate woman among the rightists turned out to be no harder to conquer than any of the others. In the blood-red rays of the dying sun, Jintong watched the rape of his seventh sister.

What was a waterlogged catastrophe for the farm was a wonderful time for the willows. Red aerial roots sprouted on their black trunks, like the antennae of an ocean creature, which bled when they were broken off. The great canopies were like enraged madwomen, their hair flying. Tender, supple, watery leaves, normally a soft yellow, now pink in color, sprouted on all the limbs. Jintong had the feeling that both the branches and the leaves must be truly delectable, and while the episode ran its course in front of him, his mouth was stuffed with willow twigs and leaves.

Finally, Pockface Zhang tossed the bun to the ground. Qiao Qisha rushed up and grabbed it, stuffing it into her mouth before she even straightened up. Pockface Zhang moved behind her, lifted her skirt, pulled her filthy red panties down to her ankles, and skillfully lifted out one leg. After parting her legs, he took out his organ, unaffected by the famine of 1960, and stuck it in. Like a dog stealing food, she forced herself to tolerate the painful posterior attack as she gobbled down the food, continuing to swallow even when it was gone. The pain in her crotch was nothing compared to the pleasure the food brought. And so, while Pockface Zhang was madly pumping from behind, making her body rock, she never stopped attacking her food. Tears wet her eyes, a biological reaction from choking on the bun, totally devoid of emotion. Maybe, once she'd finished swallowing the food, she became aware of the pain in her backside, because when she straightened up, she turned to look behind her. The dry bun had gone down hard, stretching her throat, so she thrust out her neck like a duck. Pockface Zhang was still inside her, so he wrapped his arm around her waist and, with the other hand, took a flattened bun out of his pocket and tossed it on the ground in front of her. She stepped forward and bent down again, with him still attached, one hand on her hip, the other pushing down on her shoulder. This time, as she ate the bun, she allowed him unconditional freedom to proceed as he wished, with no interference.

Jintong chewed ferociously on the willow twigs and leaves, a delicacy that somehow had gone unnoticed. At first they were sweet, but when he ate them later, that sweetness was soon replaced by a puckery bitterness that made it impossible to swallow. There was a reason people didn't eat them. He kept chewing as his eyes filled with tears. Through the haze of his tears he saw that the drama in front of him had played itself out and that Pockface Zhang had left the scene, leaving Qiao Qisha standing there looking around as if she didn't know where she was. Then she too walked off, her head banging against low-hanging willow branches.

With his arms around one of the trees, Jintong rested his weary head against the bark.

The long spring season was nearly over; the millet was ripe, a sign that the days of hunger were coming to an end. In order to make sure the workers had the strength to bring in the millet harvest, the authorities sent a load of bean cakes to the farm, enough for everyone to get four ounces. But just as Huo Lina had died from eating mushrooms, Qiao Qisha's system would not be able to handle all the extra food, and she too would die.

She stood in the line of people waiting for their ration, which was distributed by Pockface Zhang and one of the cooks. Holding a rice container, she was in line directly ahead of Jintong. He saw Pockface Zhang wink at her when he handed over her ration, but she was too captivated by the fragrance of the food to make much of it. Fights broke out over minor disparities in the distribution, and Jintong had the vague and painful feeling that Qisha would get more than she was entitled to. Orders had come down that four ounces were to last two days, but everyone took their ration home and consumed every last crumb immediately. That night there was a constant stream of people running over to the well for water. The food in their stomachs swelled, and Jintong enjoyed the all-but-forgotten pleasure of feeling full. He belched and farted constantly, the smell of bean cakes emerging from both ends. There was a line at the toilet the next morning; the bean cakes had wrought havoc on the systems of people who had gone hungry for too long.

No one knew just how much Qiao Qisha had eaten, no one but Pockface Zhang, who wasn't talking. And Jintong had no desire to soil the reputation of his seventh sister. He'd noticed that her belly poked out like a water vat. Sooner or later, he was thinking, every one of them would die from starvation or overeating anyway, so why worry about it?

The cause of her death was clear, so no investigation was called for. And since the body would not keep long in the late-summer heat, the order came down to bury her at once. There was no coffin and, of course, no ceremony. A few of the female rightists planned to dress her in the nicest clothes she owned, but the sight of her grotesquely distended belly and the foul bubbly foam on her lips drove them back in disgust. So some of the male rightists scrounged up a tattered piece of canvas once used by the tractor unit, wrapped her up in it and fastened the ends with wire, then loaded her onto the back of a cart and carried her over to a grassy spot near the war relic scrapyard, where they dug a hole and buried her next to Huo Lina and in front of the skeleton of Long Qingping, all but the skull, which had been taken away by the medical examiner.

7

Night fell as Jintong walked into the house he hadn't seen for a year. The son left behind by Laidi and Birdman Han was standing in a canopied cradle that hung from the parasol tree, holding on to the sides. Although he was dark and very thin, he was healthier than most children of the time. "Who are you?" Jintong asked as he put down his bedroll. The dark-eyed youngster blinked and gazed at Jintong curiously. "Don't you recognize me? I'm your uncle." "Gramma . . . yao yao . . ." The boy's speech was muddled; slobber ran down his chin.

Jintong sat down in the doorway to wait for Mother to come out. This was his first trip home since being sent to the farm, and he was told he didn't have to return there if he didn't want to. The thought of all those thousands of acres of millet enraged him, because once the harvest was in, the farm workers were scheduled for a real meal. And that is when Jintong and several other young men had been cut from the workforce. A few days later, his rage lost its meaning, because just as the rightists were driving their red Russian combines out to the fields to begin the harvest, a hailstorm mercilessly pounded the ripe millet into the mud.

The little boy ignored him as he sat in the doorway. Parrots with emerald green feathers flew down from the parasol tree and circled the cradle. The bright-eyed little boy followed them as they flitted around totally unafraid. Some landed on the edge of the cradle, others perched on his shoulders and pecked him on the ears, while he mimicked their hoarse cries.

Jintong sat dully in the doorway, his eyelids drooping. He was thinking about the boat ride over, and the surprised look in the eyes of the ferryman, Huang Laowan. The Flood Dragon River Bridge had been washed away by the flood the year before, so the People's Commune had begun operating a ferry. A talkative young soldier from somewhere down south had accompanied him on the ride across the river. The man waved a telegram under the nose of Huang Laowan and pressed him to get underway. "Let's shove off, uncle. See here, I'm supposed to be back in my unit by noon today. At times like this, a military order can topple a mountain!" Huang Laowan's reaction to the hurried soldier was stone-cold silence. With a shrug of the shoulders, he perched on the bow of the ferryboat like a cormorant, gazing out at the rushing river water. A while later, a pair of officials who were returning to the commune from town came aboard and sat on opposite sides of the ferry. "Say, old Huang, let's get underway!" one of them urged. "We have to be back to pass on the essence of our meeting." "In a minute," Huang said in a muffled voice. "I'm waiting for her."

She jumped aboard carrying a balloon lute and sat down across from Jintong. She was powdered and rouged, but not enough to conceal her sallow complexion. The officials eyed her wantonly. "What village are you from?" one of them asked in a superior tone.

Raising her head, she stared at the man. Her gloomy eyes, which had been downcast from the moment she boarded the ferry, suddenly emitted a wild glare of hostility, causing Jintong's heart to shudder; the look in the eyes of this sallow-faced woman left him with the feeling that she could conquer any man she chose, and could never be conquered by any man. The skin on her face sagged and her neck was deeply wrinkled, but Jintong noticed her slender fingers and polished nails, a good indication that she wasn't nearly as old as her face and neck made her appear. As she glared at the official, she hugged the lute to her chest, as if it were an infant.

Huang Laowan got up and walked to the stern, where he picked up a bamboo pole and pushed the ferry out of the shallows, then turned it around and headed out into the river, leaving whitecaps in its wake as it slid forward like a big fish. Swallows skimmed the surface; the chilled stench of water weeds rose all around them. The passengers sat there morosely. But the official who'd spoken to the woman could not abide the silence. "Aren't you that Shangguan who . . ." Jintong responded with a look of indifference; he knew what the man had left unsaid, so he replied in the manner he'd gotten used to, "That's right, I'm Shangguan Jintong, the bastard." The straightforward response and self-belittling attitude created an awkward moment, as the arrogance so common to people on the public payroll came under attack. That put him off stride, and class struggle, with clear insinuations, was his way back. The official studiously avoided looking at Jintong, keeping his eyes instead on Huang Laowan's bamboo pole. "They say those secret U.S./Chiang Kai-shek agents are all from Northeast Gaomi Township, men who once served Sima Ku. I tell you, those with the blood of the people on them were all trained by an American adviser. Huang Laowan, can you guess who that adviser was? No? I'm told you've seen him before. He's none other than the tyrant who threw in his lot with Sima Ku in Northeast Gaomi County, the man who showed all the movies, Babbitt! And they say that his stinking old lady, Shangguan Niandi, even threw a banquet for secret agents and gave each of them a fancy embroidered slipper sole!"

The woman with the lute stole a glance at Jintong; he could feel her eyes on him and saw her fingers quivering on the instrument's sound box.

The commune official was just getting started. "Young man," he said, "now's the chance for you soldiers to do something for your country. The day you catch one of those secret agents is the day you stand tall among your countrymen!"

The young soldier whipped out his telegram. "I knew something big was up," he said, "which is why I put off my wedding and am rushing back to my unit."

When the ferry drew up to the opposite bank, the young soldier was the first to jump off. The woman with the lute held back, as if she wanted to speak to Jintong. "Come with us to the commune," the official said sternly.

"Why?" she said nervously. "Why should I?"

He ripped the lute out of her hands and shook it. Something rattled around inside. He turned red with excitement, his wormlike nose began to twitch. "A transmitter!" he bleated. "Either that or a gun!" The woman rushed up to grab it away from him, but he stepped to the side, and she grabbed only air. "Give it to me!" she demanded. "Give it to you?" He sneered. "What's hidden inside?" "A woman's personal item." "A woman's personal item? Why hide something like that in there? Come with me to the commune, madam citizen." A fierce look appeared on the woman's gaunt face. "I asked you nicely to give it to me, son. You can beat the mountain to frighten tigers all you want. I've seen this sort of daylight robbery plenty of times. People who live off of others are nothing new to me." "What do you do?" the official asked, his confidence beginning to fade. "That's none of your business. Now give me back my lute!" "I'm not authorized to do that," he said. "I'd like you to come with me to the commune." "You steal from people in broad daylight! You're worse than the Japs!" The official turned and ran in the direction of the commune headquarters — the onetime compound belonging to the Sima family. "Thief!" the woman shouted as she ran after him. "You thug, you lousy bedbug!"

Feeling that this woman was somehow tied to the Shangguan family, Jintong ran down the fate of his sisters in his mind. Laidi was dead, and so were Zhaodi, Lingdi, and Qiudi. Though he hadn't seen Niandi's body, he knew she was dead too. Pandi had changed her name to Ma Ruilian, and even though she was still alive, she might as well be dead. That left only Xiangdi and Yunü. The woman's teeth were yellow and her head looked bulky. The corners of her mouth sagged when she yelled at the official, and a green light emerged from her eyes, like a cat defending her young. It had to be Xiangdi, the one who had sold herself — Fourth Sister, who had sacrificed so much for the family. What then had she hidden inside her lute?

Jintong was pondering the mystery of the lute when Mother, by then little more than skin and bones, rushed into the house. When he heard the door being bolted, he looked up in time to see her rush in from the side room. He called out to her and burst into tears at the same moment, like an abused little boy. Seemingly surprised to see him, she managed to not say a word. Instead, with her hands over her mouth, she turned and ran outside, straight to the water-filled wooden basin beneath the apricot tree, where she fell to her knees, grabbed the rim with both hands, stretched out her neck, opened her mouth, and threw up. A bowlful of still dry beans gushed out, sending water splashing out of the basin. When she caught her breath, she raised her head to look at her son, her eyes filling with tears. She tried to say something before she bent over and threw up again. Jintong looked at the frightening sight of his mother with her neck thrust out and her shoulders hunched down, as her body reacted to the spasms deep down inside. Once the retching had stopped, she reached into the water and scooped up the dried beans, a satisfied look spreading across her face. Finally, she stood up, walked over to her tall yet weak son, and wrapped her arms around him. "Why didn't you come home before this?" she asked in a slightly reproachful tone. "It's only a couple of miles." Before he could reply, she continued, "Shortly after you left, I found work operating the commune mill, the one at the Sima compound. They tore down the windmill, so now it's turned by hand. Du Wendou got me the job. The pay is half a catty of dried yams a day. If not for this job, I wouldn't be here to greet you this time. Nor would Parrot."

That is when Jintong found out that Birdman Han's son was called Parrot. He was still in his cradle, bawling loudly. "Go pick him up, and I'll make lunch for the two of you."

Mother rinsed off the dried beans she'd scooped out of the basin and put them into a large bowl, nearly filling it. Noting the look of surprise on his face, she said, "I do what has to be done, son. Don't laugh at me. I've done many bad things in my life, but this is the first time I've ever stolen anything."

He rested his head on his mother's shoulder and said sadly, "Don't say that, Mother. That's not stealing. Even if it were, there are far worse things than stealing."

Mother took a garlic mortar out from under the stove and crushed the beans in it, then added cold water to make it pasty. "Go ahead, son, eat it," she said as she handed him the bowl. "I don't dare light a fire, or they'll come to see what I'm cooking, and I can't let that happen."

"What made you think of doing this?" Jintong asked sadly as he gazed at her gray, slightly tremulous head.

"At first I hid them in my socks, but they caught me and made me feel lower than a dog. Then everyone began eating beans. Once, I was milling beans and tossed some into my mouth; my stomach felt heavy on the road home and I could hardly walk. I knew they could kill me, and that frightened me. I stuck a chopstick down my throat and brought them back up in the yard when it was raining, and so I just let them be. In the morning, I saw they'd all turned white in the rain, and Parrot was on his hands and knees eating them, remarking how sweet they tasted and asking what they were. Big as he was, he'd never even seen beans. He stuffed some into my mouth, and they were sweet and sticky, delicious. When they were all gone, Parrot clamored for more, and that's when I got the idea. At first I had to use a chopstick to make myself throw up . . . oh, the feeling . . . but now I'm used to it, and all I have to do is lower my head . . . your mother's stomach has turned into a grain sack . . . but I'm afraid today was the last time. All the women I work with at the mill have been doing the same thing, and the man in charge has noticed how much food turns up missing each day. He's threatened to muzzle us . . ."

The conversation then turned to Jintong's experiences on the farm over the preceding year, and he told Mother everything, including sex with Long Qingping, the death of Qiudi and Lu Liren, and how Pandi had changed her name.

Mother sat silently until the moon crept from the eastern sky and cast its light into the yard and through the window. "You didn't do anything wrong, son," she said at last. "That young woman Long's soul found peace, and we will count her as a member of the family. Wait until the times get better, and we will bring her and your seventh sister's remains home."

Mother picked up Parrot, who was rocking back and forth from sleep, and carried him to the bed. "There was a time when there were so many Shangguans we were like a herd of sheep. Now there are few of us left."

Jintong forced himself to ask, "What about Eighth Sister?"

With a sigh, she gave him an embarrassed look, as if begging for forgiveness.

Even at the age of twenty, Yunü was still like a little girl, a frightened, timid little girl. She'd always been like a chrysalis, spending her life in a cocoon, never wanting to cause the family any trouble. During the gloomy, rainy months of summer, she listened sorrowfully to the sound of Mother out in the yard throwing up. Thunder rolled off in the distance, the wind rustled leaves on the trees, the burnt odor of crackling lightning was in the air, but the sounds weren't loud enough to cover up the retching noise outside, and none of the smells masked the stench of her vomit. The sound of the beans falling into the water went straight to the girl's heart. How she wished it would stop, but at the same time she wanted it to continue forever. She was disgusted by the smell of Mother's stomach juices and blood, but at the same time grateful for it. When Mother crushed the beans in the mortar, she felt as if it were her heart being mashed. And when Mother handed her the bowl of beans, with their raw, cold, sticky odor, hot tears rolled out of her sightless eyes and her lovely mouth twitched with each spoonful of the gooey mix. The enormous sense of gratitude in her heart went unspoken.

The previous year, on the morning of the seventh day of the seventh month, as Mother was leaving for the mill, Yunü had blurted out, "What do you look like, Mother?" Reaching out with her fair hands, she'd said, "Let me feel your face — please."

With a sigh, Mother said, "Foolish little girl, bad as the times are, is that all you want?"

Mother brought her face up to Eighth Sister's hands and let her stroke it with her soft fingers, which had a damp, cold odor. "Go wash your hands, Yunü. There's water in the basin."

After Mother left, Eighth Sister climbed down off the bed. She heard Parrot singing happily in his cradle, mixed with the chirps of birds, the sound of snails dragging slime across the bark of trees, and swallows making a nest in the eaves. Sniffing the air, she followed the smell of clear water over to the basin, where she bent down. Her lovely face was reflected in the water, just as Natasha's image had once found Jintong's eyes, but she couldn't see it. Not many people had seen the face of this Shangguan girl. She had a high nose, fair skin, soft, yellow hair, and a long, thin neck, like that of a swan. When she felt the cold water on the tip of her nose, and then her lips, she buried her face in it. The rush of water up her nose made her choke, bringing her back to reality, and she jerked her head up out of the water. There was a buzzing in her ears, her nose ached and felt swollen. As soon as she smacked her ears with her hands to clear out the water, she heard the chirping of parrots in the tree and the cries of Parrot Han for his eighth aunt. She walked over to the tree, where she reached up and rubbed his drippy nose. Then, without a word, she groped her way out the gate.

Mother reached up and wiped away the tears with the back of her hand. "Your eighth sister left because she thought she was a burden," she said softly. "Your eighth sister was sent to us by her father, the Dragon King. But her time was up, and now she has returned to the Eastern Ocean to continue her life as the Dragon Princess . . ."

Jintong wanted to console Mother, but could not find the words. He merely coughed to mask the pain in his heart.

Just then there was a knock at the door. Mother trembled briefly, before hiding the mortar and saying to Jintong, "Open the door. See who it is."

Jintong opened the door. It was the woman from the ferry boat. She was standing timidly at the door holding her lute. "Are you Jintong?" she asked in a tiny, mosquito-like voice.

Shangguan Xiangdi had come home.

8

Five years later, on a winter morning, as Xiangdi lay waiting to die, she suddenly climbed out of bed. Her nose had rotted away, leaving behind only a black hole, and she was blind in both eyes. Nearly all her hair had fallen out, and all that remained were a few rust-colored wisps here and there on her shriveled scalp. After groping her way over to the standing cabinet, she climbed onto a stool and took down her lute, the box of which had been smashed. She then groped her way outside. Sunlight warmed the body of this woman whose rotting flesh smelled like mildew. She looked up at the sun, without seeing it. Mother, who was in the yard weaving rush mats for the production team, stood up. "Xiangdi," she said anxiously, "my poor daughter, what are you doing out here?"

Xiangdi sat huddled at the base of the wall, her scaly legs sticking out straight. Her belly was exposed, but modesty had long since played no role in her life, and she was no longer bothered by the cold. Mother ran inside for a blanket, which she draped over Xiangdi's legs. "My precious daughter, all your life, you ...." She wiped her eyes dry of the few tears that may have been there, and went back to weaving mats.

The shouts of grade-school children sounded nearby: "Attack attack attack all class enemies! Carry out the Great Proletarian Cultural Revolution!" Their hoarse slogans traveled up and down the streets and lanes. Childlike drawings and badly written but intense slogans in colored chalk adorned all the walls in the neighborhood.

Xiangdi said in a muffled voice, "Mother, I've slept with ten thousand men and earned a great deal of money. With it I bought gold and jewels, enough to keep food on your table for the rest of your lives." She rubbed her hand across the box of her lute, which the commune official had smashed, and said, "It was all in here, Mother. Look at this night-luminescent pearl. It was a gift from a Japanese client. If you sew it into a cap and wear it at night, it lights the way like a lantern ... I traded ten rings and a small ruby for this cat's eye ... this pair of gold bracelets was a gift from Old Master Xiong, who took my maidenhead." One by one she removed the precious memorabilia that had been inside the lute. "There's no need to worry, Mother, not with all this. This emerald alone is enough to buy a thousand catties of flour, and this necklace is at least worth a donkey ... Mother, on the day I entered the fire pit of prostitution, I vowed that I would give my sisters a good life, since sleeping with one man is no different than sleeping with a thousand of them. This is what I traded my body for. I carried this lute with me everywhere I went. I had this longevity locket made especially for Jintong. Make sure he wears it . . . Mother, put these things where thieves cannot find them, and don't let the Poor Peasants Association take them from you . . . what you have here is your daughter's blood and sweat . . . are you hiding them?"

Mother's face was now awash in tears. She wrapped her arms around Xiangdi's syphilitic body and sobbed, "My precious daughter, you've shredded my heart . . . all that we've been through, no one had it worse than my Xiangdi . . ."

Jintong had just returned from having his head split open by a gang of Red Guards while he was out sweeping the streets. Now he stood beneath the parasol tree, all bloody, listening to Fourth Sister's heartbreaking tale. Red Guards had nailed a row of placards to the gate of their compound, with notices such as: Traitor's Family, Landlord Restitution Corps Nest, and Whore's House. But as he listened to his dying sister, he had the urge to change the word "Whore's" to "Filial Daughter's" or "Martyr's." Up till now he had kept his distance from his sister because of her sickness; how he wished he hadn't done that. He walked up to her, took her cold hand in his, and said, "Fourth Sister, thank you for the locket . . . I'm wearing it now."

The glow of happiness shone in Fourth Sister's blind eyes. "Really? It doesn't give you a bad feeling? Don't tell your wife where you got it . . . let me touch it . . . see if it fits."

During Xiangdi's final moments on earth, all the fleas on her body left her, sensing, I guess, that there would be no more blood from her.

A smile, an ugly smile, rose on her lips and she said, her voice faltering, "My lute . . . let me play something . . . for you . . ."

She strummed the strings a time or two before her hand fell away and her head slumped to the side.

Mother wept for a moment only; then she stood up and said, "My precious daughter, your suffering has come to an end."

Two days after we buried Xiangdi, just as things were calming down, a team of eight rightists from the Flood Dragon River Farm brought the body of Shangguan Pandi up to our gate. A man with a red armband, their leader, pounded on the gate. "You, Shangguans, come claim your body!"

"She's not my daughter," Mother told the leader.

The leader, a member of the tractor unit, knew Jintong, so he handed him a slip of paper. "This is your sister's letter. In the spirit of revolutionary humanism, we've brought her home to you. You can't imagine how heavy she is — carrying her body has just about worn out these rightists."

Jintong nodded apologetically to the rightists before unfolding the slip of paper. On it were the words: I am Shangguan Pandi, not Ma Ruilian. After participating in the revolution for over twenty years, this is how I've ended up. When I die, I beg the revolutionary masses to take my body back to Dalan and turn it over to my mother, Shangguan Lu.

Jintong walked up to the door leaf on which the body lay, bent over, and removed the white paper covering her face. Pandi's eyeballs bulged and her tongue stuck halfway out. Quickly covering her face again, he threw himself at the feet of the eight rightists and said, "I beg you, please, carry her over to the graveyard. There's no one here who can do it."

Mother began to wail loudly.

After burying his fifth sister, Jintong walked into the lane, dragging a shovel behind him, where he was stopped by a gang of Red Guards. They placed a paper dunce cap on his head. He shook his head, and the cap fell to the ground; he saw that his name had been written on it, with a red X through it. The black and red ink had run together, like blood. Beneath his name were the words "Necrophiliac and Murderer." When the Red Guards began beating him on the buttocks with a club, he set up a howl, even though his padded pants kept the blows from hurting much. One of the Red Guards picked up the cap, ordered him to squat down like the comic opera character Wu Dalang, and put the cap back on his head, then pounded it down so it would stay. "Hold it on!" a fierce-looking Red Guard demanded. "The next time it falls off, we'll break your legs!"

Holding the cap on with both hands, Jintong stumbled down the lane. At the gate of the People's Commune, he saw a line of people, all wearing dunce caps. There were Sima Ting, his belly bloated, the taut skin nearly transparent; the grade-school principal; the middle-school political instructor, plus five or six commune officials minus their usual swagger, and a bunch of people who had once been forced by Lu Liren to kneel on the earthen platform in front of all the people. Then Jintong saw his mother. Next to her was little Parrot Han, and next to him was Old Jin, the woman with one breast. The words "Mother Scorpion,

Shangguan Lu" were written on Mother's cap. Parrot Han wasn't wearing a cap, but Old Jin was, along with an old shoe that hung around her neck, as a sign of wantonness. With drums and gongs shattering the stillness, the Red Guards began the public parading of the "Ox-Demons and Snake-Spirits." It was the last market day before New Year's, and the streets were packed with shoppers. People squatted on both sides of the street with piles of straw sandals, cabbages, and yam leaves, salable agricultural by-products. Everyone wore black padded jackets, shiny with a winter of snivel and greasy smoke. Many of the older men cinched up their pants with belts of hemp, and the general appearance of the people wasn't much different from the Snow Festival fifteen years earlier. Half the people who had attended the Snow Festival had died during the three years of famine, and the survivors were now old men and women. A scant few of them could still recall how graceful and elegant the Snow Prince, Shangguan Jintong, had looked at that last Snow Festival. At the time, none of them could have imagined that he would one day become a "Necrophiliac and Murderer."

The Ox-Demons and Snake-Spirits walked on woodenly as Red Guards smacked them in the buttocks with clubs, more symbolic than real. The clanging of gongs and the beating of drums rocked the earth, the shouted slogans made eardrums throb. Crowds of people pointed fingers and engaged in animated discussions. As they walked, Jintong felt someone step on his right foot, but he let that pass. When it happened a second time, he looked up and saw that Old Jin's eyes were on him, though her head was bowed and strands of yellow hair covered her reddened ears. "Goddamned 'Snow Prince,'" he heard her say. "With all the living girls waiting for you, you had to do it to a corpse!" Pretending he hadn't heard her, he kept his eyes fixed on the heels of the person ahead of him. "Come see me when this is over," he heard her say, throwing him into confusion. Her inappropriate teasing disgusted him.

Sima Ting, who was hobbling along, tripped over a brick and fell to the ground. The Red Guards kicked him, but got no reaction. So one of the smaller ones stepped on his back and jumped up and down. We all heard a dull sound like a balloon popping and saw rivulets of yellow liquid ooze from his mouth. Mother knelt down and turned his head to face her. "What's the matter, uncle?" His eyes opened just enough to show white, and with one last look at Mother, those eyes closed for the last time. The Red Guards dragged his body over to the ditch by the road. The procession continued.

Jintong spotted a graceful figure in the crowd, and recognized her at once. She was wearing a black corduroy overcoat, a brown scarf, and a blindingly white mask over her mouth and nose, so that all that showed were her dark eyes and lashes. Sha Zaohua! He nearly shouted out her name. She'd gone away right after First Sister was shot; during the seven years that had passed since then, he'd heard a rumor about a female thief who'd stolen Princess Sihanouk's earring, and he knew it had to be Zaohua. From her appearance alone, she looked to have grown into a mature young woman. Among the black-clad citizens in the marketplace, those wearing scarves and face masks were the first group of urban youngsters to be sent down to the countryside, and Zaohua had the most urban airs of any of them. She was standing in the doorway of the co-op restaurant looking in his direction. The sun's rays fell on her face, and he saw that her eyes shone like a pair of glittering marbles. Her hands were in the pockets of her overcoat; she was wearing a pair of blue corduroy pants, cut in the fashionable style of the day, which Jintong caught a glimpse of when she moved over to the doorway of the general store. A shirtless old man came running out of the restaurant and straight into the procession of Ox-Demons and Snake-Spirits, with two men, who were not locals, in hot pursuit. The old man was so cold his skin was nearly black; his coarse white padded pants were hitched up all the way to his chest. As he weaved in and out among the people in dunce caps he crammed a flatcake into his mouth, nearly choking on it. The two men caught him, and he burst into tears, covering what was left of the food with snot and saliva. "I was hungry!" he sobbed. "Hungry!" The two men frowned in disgust at the sight of the wet, dirty remnant of the cake on the ground. One of them picked it up with two fingers and studied it disgustedly, but appeared to think it would be a pity to throw it away. "Don't eat it, young fellow," someone in the crowd urged him. "Take pity on him." The man flung the cake down at the old man's feet and snarled, "Go ahead, eat it, you old bastard, and I hope you choke on it!" He took out a handkerchief to wipe his fingers and walked off with his companion. The old man picked up the wet, sticky cake and carried it over to a nearby wall, where he rested on his haunches and slowly finished it off.

Sha Zaohua was moving in and out of the crowd. A uniformed petroleum worker in a dogskin cap made his way conspicuously toward them. His eyes were scarred, and a cigarette hung from his lips as he edged sideways through the crowd. Everyone eyed him with envy, and the greater his sense of self-importance, the brighter his eyes became. Jintong recognized him and was moved by the sight. Clothes make the man; saddles make the horse. A worker's uniform and a dogskin cap had turned the village bully Fang Shixian into a new man. Few people in the crowd had ever seen one of those coarse blue uniforms, thick with padding, the cotton bulging between stitches, and obviously very warm. A youngster who looked like a dark monkey, in lined pants with a torn crotch from which cotton batting had migrated outside, like the tail of a sheep, and a padded jacket whose buttons had long since departed, leaving his belly exposed, followed on Fang Shixian's heels, his hair looking like a rat's nest. The people in the procession pushed and shoved to keep warm, when the youngster suddenly jumped into the air, swept the dogskin cap off of Fang's head, clapped it onto his own, and scampered through the crowd like a cunning dog. Shouts erupted as the pushing and shoving increased. Fang Shixian reached up and felt his head; it took him a moment to realize what had happened, before he too began to shout and took off in pursuit of the youngster, who wasn't running particularly fast, as if waiting for his pursuer. Fang followed him, cursing the whole time, his eyes fixed not on the road ahead, but on the sunlight glinting off the dog hairs of his cap; he crashed into people, who pushed back and spun him around. The unfolding drama captured the attention of everyone on the street, even the Red Guard little generals, who temporarily put aside class struggle, abandoning their Ox-Demons and Snake-Spirits in order to push through the crowd and enjoy the spectacle. The youngster ran up to the gate in front of the People's Commune steel mill, where some girls were selling roasted peanuts, something that was not permitted; always on the alert, they were ready to flee at any time. Even though it was the middle of winter, steam rose from the surface of the nearby pond owing to all the red liquid waste the mill dumped into it. The youngster took off the cap and flung it into the pond. Momentarily stunned, the people quickly regained their voices, shouting their gloating approval of what he'd done. The cap floated in the water, refusing to sink below the surface, and all Fang Shixian could do was stand at the edge of the pond and curse, "You little bastard, just wait till I get my hands on you!" But by then the little bastard was long gone, and Fang just paced back and forth, gazing out at his cap and blinking furiously, tears sliding down his cheeks. "Say, young man, go home and get a bamboo pole. That'll do it," someone shouted. "Ten dogskin caps would have sunk by the time you got back," someone else said. As if to prove him right, the cap had already begun to slip beneath the surface. "Strip and go fetch it," someone said. "Whoever gets it owns it!" Suddenly panicked, Fang tore off his uniform, until he was standing there dressed only in a pair of shorts; he stepped tentatively into the water, which quickly submerged him up to the shoulders. Finally, however, he managed to retrieve his cap. But while he was in the water, and everyone's attention was focused on him, Jintong saw the youngster appear out of nowhere, scoop up Fang's uniform, and disappear down a lane, where a slender figure flicked out of sight. By the time Fang climbed out of the pond, cap in hand, all that greeted him at the water's edge were a pair of shoes and socks with holes in them. "Where are my clothes?" he shouted, the shouts quickly turning to agonizing wails. By the time he realized that his clothes had been stolen and that the theft of his dogskin cap had been a ruse, that he'd been tricked by a pro, he shouted, "My god, my life is over!" Still holding his cap, he jumped into the pond. Shouts of "Save him!" erupted all around, but no one was willing to strip down and jump in after him. What with the freezing wind and the ice on the ground, even though the water itself was heated, going in would be easier than getting out. So while Fang Shixian thrashed around in the water, the people merely commented on the thief's scheme: "Brilliant!" they said. "Just brilliant"

Had Mother forgotten that she was being paraded in public? Whatever the answer, this elderly woman who had raised a houseful of daughters and was mother-in-law to many renowned young men flung down her dunce cap and hobbled toward the pond on bound feet. "How can you people just stand there when a man's drowning?" she castigated the crowd. She picked up a broom from a nearby peddler. At the pond's edge she shouted, "You there, nephew Fang, have you gone mad? Quick, grab hold of the broom and I'll pull you out!"

The brackish water had apparently changed Fang's mind about ending it all, so he grabbed hold of the broom and, like a plucked chicken, dragged himself up onto dry ground. His lips had turned purple, and his eyes barely moved in their sockets; he couldn't speak. Taking off her jacket, Mother wrapped it around his shoulders, which immediately turned him into a comic figure. The people didn't know whether to laugh or to cry. "Put your shoes on, young nephew," Mother said, "then run home as fast as you can. Work up a good sweat, if you don't want to die from the cold." Unfortunately for him, his fingers were frozen stiff, and he couldn't get his shoes on, so a few of the onlookers, moved by Mother's kindness, managed to help him into his shoes. Then they picked him up and carried him off at a trot, his stiff legs dragging along behind.

Dressed only in a thin blouse, Mother hugged her shoulders to keep warm as she watched them drag Fang Shixian away. She was the recipient of admiring glances from many people. But Jintong was not one of them. It was Fang Shixian, after all, the man who the year before had been in charge of the farmers' security unit. Every day, as the commune members headed home, he was the one who searched them and their baskets. On her way home one day, Mother had picked up a yam on the road and put it into her straw basket. Fang Shixian found it and accused her of theft. When Mother denied the accusation, the son of a bitch had slapped her, bloodying her nose; the blood had dripped onto the lapel of her shirt, the same white shirt she was wearing now. An idler like him, who strutted around just because he was categorized as a poor peasant, why not let him drown? His feelings for her at that moment bordered on loathing.

At the gate to the commune slaughterhouse Jintong spotted Zaohua standing in front of a red board with a slogan in yellow letters, and he was sure that she'd been involved in Fang Shixian's misfortune. The youngster must have been her apprentice. If she was capable of stealing a diamond ring off the finger of Princess Monica under tight security at the Yellow Sea Restaurant, she certainly wasn't interested in a worker's uniform. No, that had been a payback for the bad man who had slapped her grandmother. Jintong's view of Zaohua underwent an immediate change. As he saw it, thievery was a disgrace, and had been since time immemorial. But now he considered what Zaohua had done was right. There was no honor in being a common thief, of course, but someone like Zaohua, a thief for all ages, was worthy of high praise. In his eyes, the Shangguan family had raised yet another glorious banner to flap in the wind.

The little Red Guard leader, who was upset over what Mother had done, picked up a battery-powered bullhorn, a rarity those days, but well suited to and necessary for revolutionary activities, and, in the style of the leader of Northeast Gaomi Township's land reform decades earlier, announced in a sickly, shaky voice, "Revolutionary — comrades — Red Guards — comrades-in-arms — low and middle poor peasants — do not be misled — by the phony kindness — of the old-line historical counterrevolutionary — Shangguan Lu — who is trying to divert the direction of our struggle —"

This Red Guard leader, Guo Pingen, was in fact the abused son of the eccentric Guo Jingcheng, a man who had broken his wife's leg and then warned her not to cry. When people passed by their house, they often heard the sound of someone being beaten and a woman's muffled moans. A good-hearted man by the name of Li Wannian once decided to try to put a stop to it, but had no sooner opened the door than he was struck by a rock that came flying out. Guo Pingen had inherited his father's cruel, ruthless ways. As the Cultural Revolution progressed, he had already injured the kidney of a teacher by the name of Zhu Wen with a vicious kick.

His exhortation completed, he slung the bullhorn over his back, walked up to Mother, and aimed a well-placed kick into her knee. "Kneel!" he demanded. With a yelp of pain, Mother got down on her knees. He then grabbed her by the ear and demanded, "Get up!" She'd barely gotten to her feet when he sent her to the ground again with another kick and stepped on her back. All his beatings were administered to give concrete meaning to the popular revolutionary slogan: "Knock all class enemies to the ground, then step on them."

The fires of rage burned in Jintong's heart as he watched his mother being beaten; he ran up to Guo Pingen with balled fists, but was brought up short by Guo's sinister glare. Two deep creases ran from mouth to chin on the face of this revolutionary leader, who was little more than a boy himself, which gave him the appearance of a prehistoric reptile. Jintong unclenched his fists, as if by instinct. His heart shuddered, and he was about to ask Guo what he thought he was doing when the young Red Guard raised his hand, and Jintong's question emerged instead as a wail: "Mother . . ." He fell to his knees beside his mother, who raised her head with difficulty and glared at him. "Stand up, my useless son!"

Jintong got to his feet, while Guo Pingen signaled the Red Guards with their clubs, their gongs, and their drums to round up the Ox-Demons and Snake-Spirits and recommence the parade through the marketplace. Resorting once again to his bullhorn to exhort the marketgoers to shout slogans along with him, the effect of his strangely altered voice was like feeding them poison. They frowned, but no one answered the call.

Meanwhile, Jintong stood there caught up in a fantasy: A sunlit day. Armed with the legendary Dragon Springs sword, he has Guo Pingen, Zhang Pingtuan, Mousy Fang, Dog Liu, Wu Yunyu, Wei Yangjiao, and Guo Qiusheng dragged up onto the stage, where he forces them to kneel and face the glinting tip of his sword.

"Get back there, you little bastard!" one of the little Red Guard generals growled as he drove his fist into Jintong's belly. "Don't you dare think of running away!"

Jintong's fantasy had brought tears to his eyes, but the fist in the belly brought him back to reality, which seemed worse than ever. The road ahead was an impenetrable haze. But at that moment, a dispute broke out between Guoping's faction and the "Golden Monkey Rebel Regiment," under the leadership of Wu Yunyu. And what began as a battle of words soon led to pushing and shoving, and, finally, to war.

Wu Yunyu started it with a kick, which Guo answered with a punch. Then they tore into each other. Guo ripped off Wu's cap, his prized possession, and scratched his scabby head bloody. Wu stuck his fingers into Guo's mouth and pulled with all his might, opening a cut in one corner. As soon as the factions of Red Guards saw what was happening, they turned it into a gang war, and in no time clubs were cutting through the air, bricks were flying, leaving the participants bloody but determined to fight to the death. Wu Yunyu's subordinate Wei Yangjiao stabbed two combatants in the gut with the steel tip of his red-tasseled spear; blood and some sticky gray oozed from the wounds. Guo Pingen and Wu Yunyu backed off to direct their troops in battle. At that moment, Jintong saw the veiled young woman he recognized as Zaohua pass in front of Guo Pingen, her hand seeming to brush his face as she passed; a moment later he set up a loud agonizing wail, a gash appearing on his cheek, almost as if he'd grown a second mouth. Blood gushed from the wound, a terrifying sight. He turned and ran in the direction of the commune clinic; nothing else mattered to him at that moment. Seeing that the battle had turned deadly and that blood might wind up on their hands, the peddlers packed up their goods and disappeared down a myriad of lanes.

One of the two combatants with belly wounds died on the way to the clinic, while the other needed a blood transfusion before he was out of danger. The blood came from the veins of the Ox-Demons and

Snake-Spirits. Upon his subsequent release from the clinic, none of the Red Guard units wanted anything to do with him, since his poor-peasant blood had lost its purity; now the blood of class enemies — landlords, rich peasants, and historical counterrevolutionaries — flowed in his veins. According to Wu Yunyu, Wang Jinzhi was now a class enemy himself, like a grafted fruit tree, possessor of the five evils. Poor Wang had been a member of the fighting propaganda unit of the Wind and Thunder Faction. Given the cold shoulder and incapable of dealing with loneliness, he formed his own faction, the "Unicorn Struggle Team," complete with official seal, banner, and armbands; he even talked those in charge of the commune public address system into giving him five minutes of airtime, all the news items for which he personally selected. They ran the gamut from developments in the Unicorn faction to historical anecdotes relating to Dalan, interesting tidbits, sex scandals, items of general interest, and so on. The show ran three times a day — morning, noon, and night. Before the PA began to broadcast, representatives from all the various factions sat lined up on a bench to await their turn. Unicorn was given the last slot, so when his five minutes were up, "The Internationale" was played, and that ended the broadcasting day.

In an age when there were no radio dramas and no musical programs, the Unicorn five-minute program served as entertainment for the citizens of Northeast Gaomi Township. Whether tending their pigs, sitting down to eat, or lying in bed, the people would prick up their ears in anticipation. One night, the Unicorn announcer said, "Low and middle poor peasants, revolutionary comrades-in-arms, according to an authoritative source, the individual who attacked the onetime leader of the Wind and Thunder Faction, Guo Pingen, leaving a gash in his cheek, was the infamous thief Sha Zaohua. Thief Sha is the daughter of the traitor Sha Yueliang, who ran rampant for years in Northeast Gaomi Township, and Shangguan Laidi, who murdered a public servant and was herself executed for the crime. In her youth, thief Sha met a strange man at Southeast Lao Mountain, from whom she learned martial arts. She can fly over eaves and walk up walls, she is a master of sleight-of-hand who can pick a pocket or walk off with a purse right under your eyes, and you'll never know it. According to my authoritative source, thief Sha sneaked back to Northeast Gaomi Township three months ago, and has already established secret contacts in every village and hamlet. Using intimidation and coercion, she has enlisted the services of underlings who report to her on everything and serve as a little army of spies. The youngster who stole the dogskin cap of poor peasant Fang Shixian at the Dalan marketplace was one of thief Sha's accomplices. Thief Sha has plied her evil trade in large towns. She has many aliases, but the most commonly heard is Swallow Sha. Her purpose in sneaking back to Northeast Gaomi this time is to avenge the deaths of her father and mother, and the gash on Guo Pingen's cheek signals the first stage of her class retaliation. Even crueler, even more terrifying incidents can be expected in the days to come. It has been reported that one of the tools of her trade is a bronze coin she placed on a railroad track to be run over by a passing train. It is thinner than paper and so sharp it can cut a hair in half by blowing on it. When it cuts skin it takes ten minutes for the wound to bleed and twenty for the victim to feel the pain. Thief Sha hides this weapon between her fingers, and with an unnoticeable flick can sever a man's carotid artery, bringing instant death. Thief Sha's skills are unmatched. When she was studying with her master, she tossed ten coins into a pot of boiling oil, then reached in with bare fingers and removed every single one without so much as singeing her skin. Her movements are so fast, and so precise, they are barely visible. Revolutionary comrades-in-arms, low and middle poor peasants, the enemies who use guns have been eliminated, but the ones who use coins remain among us, and they can be counted on to fight us with ten times the deceit and a hundred times the frenzy." *Time's up, time's up!* That was what the listeners heard over the PA all of a sudden. "I'm almost done, almost done." *No, that's it. The Unicorn can't talk over "The Internationale"!* "Can't we go on a little longer?" But the strains of "The Internationale" abruptly poured out of the PA.

The following morning, the PA broadcast the Golden Monkey Rebel Regiment's detailed renunciation of Unicorn's Sha Zaohua myth, and then laid all the crimes at the feet of Unicorn. The mass organizations broadcast a joint declaration retracting Unicorn's broadcast privileges and ordered the faction's leaders to disband within forty-eight hours and to destroy the official seal and all propaganda materials.

Even though the Golden Monkey Rebel Regiment denied the existence of a super-thief named Sha Zaohua, they nonetheless assigned secret agents and sentries to watch the Shangguan family. Not until the following spring, during the Qingming Festival, when a police van from the County Security Bureau came to take Jintong away, did Wu Yunyu, who by then had risen to the position of chairman of the Dalan Revolutionary Committee, relieve the agents and sentries, who were pretending to be wok menders, knife sharpeners, and shoe repairmen, of their duties.

When they were clearing out the Flood Dragon River Farm, a diary kept by Qiao Qisha was discovered. In it she recorded in detail the illicit relationship between Shangguan Jintong and Long Qingping. As a result, the County Security Bureau arrested Jintong on charges of murder and necrophilia and, even before the investigation began, sentenced him to fifteen years in prison, which he began to serve at a labor reform camp on the edge of the Yellow Sea.

Chapter  Seven

1

During the first spring of the 1980s, Jintong, having served his time, sat in an out-of-the-way corner of a bus station waiting room, feeling shy and confused as he waited for the bus to Dalan, the capital of Northeast Gaomi Township.

The fifteen long years now behind him truly seemed like a bad dream. He thought back until his head ached, but all he could conjure up were memory fragments, all linked to bright light that stung his eyes like shards of glass imbedded in mud. He recalled the moment when handcuffs were first snapped on his wrists, and the reflected light that seared his eyes just before darkness enshrouded him and he heard his mother's shouts in the distance: "What right do you have arresting my son? My son is a good man, he's never hurt anyone" . . . and then he recalled the frightful days spent in the lockup awaiting sentencing, how every night by the muted light in his cell he had been forced to perform oral sex on the bearded guard . . . and he recalled the unbearable heat beating down on the labor camp salt works, creating even more blinding light. The guards wore sunglasses; the inmates were not permitted to. Wherever he looked the salty, corrupting, blinding light brought tears to eyes that were exposed to the salty air . . . then he recalled scenes of gathering kindling in the freezing cold of winter, sunlight sparkling on the snow-covered ground and glinting off the guards' rifle barrels. The deafening crack of rifle fire straightened him up, and as he looked into the sun he saw a dazzlingly dark figure wobble and fall to the ground. He later learned that it was an inmate who had tried to escape, only to be shot by a guard ... his thoughts then took him back to a summer when bursts of lightning the size of basketballs lit up the skies over the fields. Terrified, he fell to his knees. "Heavenly Father," he prayed, "spare me. I did nothing wrong, please don't strike me dead ... let me go on living ... let me live out my sentence and regain my freedom ... I want to see my mother once more" ... another blast of thunder rent the sky, and when he came to, a goat lay beside him, struck dead by lightning, the smell of burnt flesh hanging in the air ...

Outside, the predawn sky was still dark. The dozen hanging lights in the waiting room were mere decorations; the little bit of light inside was supplied by a pair of low-wattage wall lamps. The ten or so black benches were monopolized by trendy youngsters who lay there snoring and talking in their sleep, one with his knees bent and his legs crossed, his bell-bottom trousers looking as if they were made of sheet metal. Hazy morning sunlight gradually filtered in through the windows and lit up the place, and as Jintong examined the clothes of the sleepers arrayed around him, he knew that he had reentered the world in a new age. In spite of the patches of spittle, the filthy scraps of paper, even the occasional urine stain, he could see that the floor was constructed of fine marble. And even though the walls provided rest for plenty of fat but weary black flies, the wallpaper pattern was bright and eye-catching. For Jintong, who had just emerged from a rammed-earth hut in the labor reform camp, everything around him was fresh and new, completely alien, and his unease deepened.

Finally, the early-morning sun lit up the foul-smelling waiting room, and passengers began to stir. A pimply-faced young man with a mass of wild hair sat up on his bench, scratched his toes and feet, closed his eyes as he took out a flattened filter cigarette, and lit it with a plastic lighter. After taking a deep drag, he coughed up a mouthful of phlegm and spat it on the floor. He slipped his feet into his shoes and rubbed the sticky mess into the floor. Turning to the young woman lying beside him, he patted her on the rear. She moaned seductively as she squirmed herself awake. "Here's the bus," he said louder than he needed to. Slowly she sat up, rubbed her eyes with her reddened hands, and yawned grandly. When it finally occurred to her that her companion had tricked her, she gave him a few symbolic thumps and moaned once more, before stretching out on the bench again. Jintong studied the young woman's fat face, her stubby, greasy nose, and the white, wrinkled skin of her belly, which poked out from under her pink shirt. With an air of impertinence, the man slipped his left hand, on which he wore a digital watch, under her blouse and caressed her flat chest, eliciting a feeling in Jintong that he had been left behind by time, and it gnawed at his heart like a silkworm feasting on mulberry leaves. For the first time, apparently, a thought occurred to him: My god, I'm forty-two years old! A middle-aged man who never had a chance to grow up. The young man's display of affection reddened the cheeks of this covert observer, who looked away. The unforgiving nature of age spread a layer of deep sadness over his already gloomy mood, and his thoughts spun wildly. I've lived on this earth for forty-two years, and what have I accomplished? The past is like a hazy path leading into the depths of a wilderness; you can only see a few feet behind you, and ahead nothing but haze. More than half my life is over, a past utterly lacking in glory, a sordid past, one that disgusts even me. The second half of my life began the day I was released. What awaits me?

At that moment he spotted a glazed porcelain mural on the opposite wall of the waiting room: a muscular man in a fig leaf was embracing a bare-breasted woman with a long ponytail. The looks of longing on the faces of the young couple — half human and half immortal — gave rise to a sad emptiness in his heart. He had experienced this feeling many times before, while lying on the ground at the Yellow Sea labor reform camp and looking up into the vast blue sky. While his herd of sheep grazed in the distance, Jintong often gazed up at the sky, within sight of the row of red flags that marked the inmates' boundary line, and patrolled by mounted armed guards who were followed by the mongrel offspring of army dogs belonging to former soldiers and local mutts that interrupted their lazy rounds by howling meaninglessly at the foamy whitecaps on the sea just beyond the dike.

During the fourteenth spring of his imprisonment, he became acquainted with one of the grooms, a bespectacled man named Zhao Jiading who was incarcerated for attempting to murder his wife. A gentle man, he had been an instructor at a college of politics and law before his arrest. Without holding back any of the details, he related to Jintong how he had planned to poison his wife: his well-conceived plan was a work of art, and yet his wife somehow survived the attempt. Jintong repaid him by relating the details of his case. When he finished, Zhao said emotionally, "That's beautiful, sheer poetry. Too bad our laws can't tolerate poetry. Now if at the time I'd . . . no, just forget it, that sounds stupid! They gave you too heavy a sentence. But of course you've already served fourteen of your fifteen years, so there's no need to complain about it now."

When the labor reform camp leadership proclaimed that his time was up and he was free to go home, he actually felt abandoned. With tears in his eyes, he pleaded, "Can't I spend the rest of my life right here, sir?" The official who had given him the news looked with disbelief and shook his head. "Why would you want to do that?" "Because I don't know how I'm going to survive out there. I'm useless, worse than useless." The official handed him a cigarette and lit it for him. "Go on," he said with a pat on the shoulder, "it's a better world out there than in here." Never having learned to smoke, he took a deep drag and nearly choked to death. Tears gushed from his eyes.

A sleepy-eyed woman in a blue uniform and hat walked past him, lackadaisically sweeping up the cigarette butts and fruit peels on the floor. The look on her face showed how much she hated her job, and she made a point of nudging the people sleeping on the floor with her foot or broom. "Up!" she'd shout. "Get up!" as she swept puddles of piss onto them. Her shouts and nudges forced them to sit or stand up. Those who stood stretched and yawned, while those who remained sitting on the floor wound up getting hit by her dustpan or her broom, and they too jumped to their feet. And the minute they did that, she swept the newspaper they'd been lying on into her dustpan. Jintong, who was huddled in a corner, did not manage to escape her tirade. "Move aside!" she demanded. "Are you blind?" Employing an alertness tempered over fifteen years at the camp, he jumped to the side and watched her point unhappily at his canvas traveling bag. "Whose is that?" she snarled. "Move it!" He picked up the bag that held all his possessions, not putting it down until she'd passed her broom across the floor a time or two; he sat back down.

A pile of trash lay on the floor in front of him; the woman dumped the contents of her dustpan on the pile, then turned and walked off. The mass of flies resting on the garbage she had disturbed buzzed in the air for a moment before settling back down. Jintong looked up and spotted a line of gates along the wall where the buses were parked, each topped by a sign with a route number and destination. People were lined up behind some of the metal railings waiting to have their tickets punched. By the time he located the gate for bus number 831, with a destination of Dalan and the Flood Dragon River Farm, a dozen or more people were already in line. Some were smoking, others were chatting, and still others were just sitting blankly on their luggage. Studying his ticket, he noted that the boarding time was 7:30, but the clock on the wall showed it was already 8:10. A touch of panic set in as he wondered if his bus had already left the station. Tattered traveling bag in hand, he quickly joined the line behind a stone-faced man carrying a black leather bag and took a furtive look at the people in line ahead of him. For some reason, they all looked familiar, but he couldn't put a name to any of them. They seemed to be observing him at the same time, their looks running from surprise to simple curiosity. Now he didn't know what to do. He longed to see a friendly face from home, but was afraid of being recognized, and he felt his palms grow sticky.

"Comrade," he stammered to the man in front of him, "is this the bus to Dalan?" The man eyed him up and down in the manner of the officials at the camp, which made him as anxious as an ant on a hot skillet. Even to himself, let alone others, Jintong saw himself as a camel amid a herd of sheep, a freak. The night before, when he'd seen himself in the blurry mirror on the wall of a filthy public toilet, what had looked back at him was an oversized head covered with thinning hair that was neither red nor yellow. The face was as mottled as the skin of a toad, deeply wrinkled. His nose was bright red, as if someone had pinched it, and brown stubble circled his puffy lips. Feeling the man's eyes scrutinizing him, he felt debased and dirty; the sweat on his palms was now dampening his fingers. The man's response to his question was limited to pointing with his mouth to the red lettering on the sign above the gate.

A four-wheeled cart pushed by a fat woman in a white uniform walked up. "Stuffed buns," she announced in a childishly high-pitched voice. "Hot pork and scallion buns, right out of the oven!" Her greasy red face had a healthy glow, and her hair was done up in a tight perm, with countless little curls like the backs of the woolly little Australian sheep he'd tended. Her hands looked like rolls straight from the oven, the pudgy fingers like sausages. "How much a pound?" a fellow in a zip-up shirt asked her. "I don't sell them by the pound," she said. "Okay, how much apiece?" "Twenty-five fen." "Give me ten." She removed the cloth covering — once white, but now almost completely black — tore off a piece of newspaper hanging on the side of the cart, and picked out ten buns with a pair of tongs. Her customer flipped through a wad of bills to find something small enough to give her, and every eye in the crowd was glued to his hands.

"The peasants of Northeast Gaomi have done well for themselves the past couple of years!" a man with a leather briefcase said enviously. Zip-up Shirt stopped wolfing down a bun long enough to say, "Is that a greedy look I see, old Huang? If it is, go home and smash that iron rice bowl of yours and come with me to sell fish." "What's so great about money?" Briefcase Man said. "To me, it's like a tiger coming down from the mountain, and I don't feel like getting bitten." "Why worry about stuff like that?" Zip-up Shirt said. "Dogs bite people, so do cats, even rabbits when they're scared. But I never heard of money biting anyone." "You're too young to understand," Briefcase Man said. "Don't try that wise old uncle routine on me, old Huang, and you can stop slapping your face to puff up your cheeks. It was your township head who proclaimed that peasants were free to engage in business and get as rich as they can." "Don't get carried away, young man," Briefcase Man said. "The Communist Party won't forget its own history, so I advise you to be careful." "Careful of what?" "A second round of land reform," Briefcase Man said emphatically. "Go ahead, do your reform," Zip-up Shirt shot back. "Whatever I earn, I spend on myself — eating, drinking, and having a good time — since true reform is impossible. You won't find me living like my foolish old grandfather! He worked like a dog, wishing he didn't have to eat or shit, just so he could save up enough to buy a few acres of unproductive land. Then came land reform and — whoosh — he was labeled a landlord, taken down to the bridge, where you people put a bullet in his head. Well, I'm not my grandfather. I'm not going to save up my money, I'm going to eat it up. Then, when your second round of land reform is launched, I'll still be a bona fide poor peasant." "How many days since your dad finally had his landlord label removed, Jin Zhuzi?" Briefcase Man asked. "And here you are, acting so pompous!" "Huang," Zip-up Shirt said, "you're like a toad trying to stop a wagon — you overestimate yourself. Go home and hang yourself! You think you can interfere with government policy? I doubt it."

Just then a beggar in a tattered coat tied with red electric wire walked up with a chipped bowl holding a dozen or so coins and a few filthy bills; his hand shook as he held the bowl out to Briefcase Man.

"How about it, elder brother, something for me . . . maybe to buy a stuffed bun?" The man backed up. "Get away from me!" he said angrily. "I haven't even had my breakfast yet." When the beggar glanced over at Jintong, a look of disdain shone in his eyes. He turned away to seek out someone else to beg from. Jintong's depression deepened. Even a beggar turns away from you, Jintong! The beggar walked up to the fellow in the zip-up shirt. "Elder brother, take pity on me, a few coins, maybe a stuffed bun . . ." "What's your family standing?" Zip-up Shirt asked him. "Poor peasant," the beggar replied after a brief pause. "For the last eight generations." Zip-up Shirt laughed. "Coming to the rescue of poor peasants is my specialty!" He tossed his two remaining stuffed buns and greasy paper wrapping into the bowl. The beggar crammed one into his mouth, the greasy paper sticking to his chin.

Suddenly there was a commotion in the waiting room. A dozen or so obviously jaded ticket-takers in blue uniforms and caps emerged from their lounge with ticket punches, the cold glare in their eyes a sign of their loathing for the waiting passengers. A crowd fell in behind them, pushing and shoving their way up to the gates. A man with a battery-powered bullhorn stood in the corridor and bellowed, "Line up! Form lines! We don't start punching tickets till there are neat lines. All you ticket-takers, please note — no lines, no tickets!" The people crowded up to the ticket-takers anyway. Children began to cry, and a dark-faced woman with a little boy in her arms, a baby girl on her back, and a pair of roosters in her hand loudly cursed a man who pushed up against her. Ignoring her, he lifted a cardboard box filled with light bulbs high over his head and kept forging his way up front. The woman kicked him in the backside — he didn't so much as turn around.

Jintong wound up getting pushed backward, until he was last in line. Summoning what little courage remained, he gripped his bag tightly and plunged forward. But he had barely begun when a bony elbow thudded into his chest; he saw stars and, with a groan, slumped to the floor.

"Line up! Form lines!" the man with the bullhorn bellowed over and over. "No lines, no tickets!" The ticket-taker for the Dalan bus, a girl with crooked teeth, pushed her way back through the crowd with the help of her clipboard and ticket punch. Her cap was knocked askew, sending cascades of black hair out. Stomping her foot angrily, she shouted, "Go ahead, shove away. Maybe a couple of you will get trampled in the process." She stormed back to the lounge, and by then the two hands of the clock came together at the 9.

The people's passion cooled off the minute the ticket-taker went on strike. Jintong stood on the fringe of the crowd, gloating secretly over this turn of events. He felt sympathy for the ticket-taker, viewing her as a protector of the weak. By then, the other gates had opened, and passengers were pushing and shoving their way along the narrow passageway between two barricades, like a rebellious waterway forced between sandbars.

A muscular, well-dressed young man of average height walked up carrying a cage with a pair of rare white parrots. His jet black eyes caught Jintong's attention, while the caged white parrots reminded him of the parrots that had circled the air above the son of Birdman Han and Laidi decades earlier on his first trip home from the Flood Dragon River Farm. Could it be him? As Jintong observed him closely, Laidi's cold passion and Birdman Han's resolute innocence began to show in the man's face. Jintong's astonishment led to a sigh. How big he's gotten! The dark little boy in a cradle had grown into a young man. That thought reminded him of his own age, and he was quickly immersed in the doldrums of a man past his prime. Listlessness, that great emptiness, spread through him, and he envisioned himself as a withered blade of dry grass rooted in a barren land, quietly coming to life, quietly growing, and now quietly dying.

The young man with the parrots walked up to the ticket gate to look around; several of the passengers called out greetings, which he acknowledged in a cocky manner, before looking down at his watch. "Parrot Han," someone in the crowd yelled out. "You're well connected, and you're good at talking to people. Go tell that young woman to come back here." "She wouldn't punch your tickets, because I hadn't arrived." "Stop bragging! We'll believe you when you get her out here." "Now line up, all of you, and quit shoving! What good does shoving do? Line up, I say, line up!" He ordered them around, half in jest, forcing them into a straight line, all the way back to the benches in the waiting room. "If I catch anyone pushing and shoving, disrupting this line, well, I'll take his mother and . . . understand?" He made an obscene gesture. "Besides, everyone will get on, early or late. And if you can't get inside, you can climb up onto the luggage rack, where the air is fresh and the view is great. I wouldn't mind sitting there. Now wait here while I go get that girl."

He was as good as his word. She came out of the lounge, still angry, but with Parrot Han at her side peppering her with sweet talk. "Dear little aunty, why get upset over the likes of them? They're the dregs of society, punks and sluts, twisted melons and sour pears, dead cats and rotten dogs, rotten shrimp paste, all of them. Fighting with them just brings you down to their level. Even worse, getting angry leads to physical swelling, and poor uncle would die if he saw that, wouldn't he?" "Shut up, you stinking parrot!" she said as she rapped him on the shoulder with her ticket punch. "No one will ever try to palm you off as a mute!" Parrot Han made a face. "Aunty," he said, "I've got a pair of beautiful birds for you. Just tell me when you want them." "You're quite the smooth talker, like a teapot without a bottom! Beautiful birds, you say? Ha! You've been promising that for a year, and I haven't seen so much as a single feather!" "I mean it this time. I'm going to show you a real bird for a change." "If you had a heart, you'd forget about your so-called beautiful birds and give me that pair of white parrots." "I can't give you these," he said. "These are breeders. Just arrived from Australia. But if it's white parrots you want, next year I'll give you a pair, or I'm not your own Parrot Han!"

When the narrow gate opened, the crowd immediately tried to squeeze through. Parrot Han, cage in hand, stood beside the ticket-taker. "You see, aunty," he said. "How can anyone dispute the poor quality of the Chinese? All they know how to do is push and shove, even when that actually slows things down." "The only thing your Northeast Gaomi Township can produce is bandits and highwaymen, a bunch of savages," she said. "I wouldn't advise you to try to catch all the fish in the river with one net, aunty. There are some good people there. Take, for instance —" He stopped in midsentence as he saw Shangguan Jintong walking bashfully toward him from the end of the line.

"If I'm not mistaken," he said, "you're my little uncle."

Timidly, Jintong replied, "I . . . I recognized you too."

Parrot Han grabbed Jintong's hand and shook it eagerly. "You're back, Little Uncle," he said, "finally. Grandma has almost cried herself blind thinking about you."

The bus was by then so packed that some people were actually hanging out the windows. Parrot Han walked around to the rear of the bus and climbed the ladder up to the luggage rack, where he drew back the netting, secured the caged parrots, and then reached down for Jintong's traveling bag. Somewhat fearfully, Jintong followed his bag up to the luggage rack, where Parrot Han pulled the netting over him. "Little Uncle," he said, "hold tight to the railing. Actually, that's probably unnecessary. This bus is slower than an old sow."

The driver, a cigarette dangling from his mouth and a mug of tea in his hand, walked lazily up to the bus. "Parrot," he shouted, "you really are a birdman! But don't blame me if you fall off there and wind up as roadkill." Parrot Han tossed a pack of cigarettes down to the driver, who caught it in the air, checked the brand, and put it in his pocket. "Not even the old man in the sky can handle someone like you," he said. "Just drive the bus, old-timer," Parrot Han said. "And do us all a favor by not breaking down so often!"

The driver pulled the door shut behind him, stuck his head out the window, and said, "One of these days this beat-up old bus is going to fall apart. I'm the only one who can handle it. You could change drivers if you wanted, but then it wouldn't even leave the station."

The bus crept out onto the gravel road to Northeast Gaomi Township. They met many vehicles, including tractors, coming from the opposite direction, carefully passing the slow-moving bus, the wheels sending so much dust and gravel into the air that Jintong didn't dare open his eyes. "Little Uncle, people say you got a raw deal when they sent you up," Parrot Han said, looking Jintong in the eye. "I guess you could say that," Jintong said mildly. "Or you could say I deserved it." Parrot handed him a cigarette. He didn't take it. So Parrot put it back in the pack and glanced sympathetically at Jintong's rough, callused hands. "It must have been pretty bad," he said, looking Jintong in the face again. "It was okay once I got used to it." "There have been a lot of changes over the past fifteen years," Parrot said. "The People's Commune was broken up and the land parceled out to private farmers, so everyone has food on their table and clothes on their back. The old houses have been torn down under a unified program. Grandma couldn't get along with that damned old lady of mine, so she moved into the three-room pagoda that used to belong to the old Taoist, Men Shengwu. Now that you're back, she won't be alone."

"How . . . how is she?" Jintong asked hesitantly.

"Physically she's fine," Parrot said, "except for her eyesight. But she can still look after herself. I'm not going to hide anything from you,

Little Uncle. I'm henpecked. That damned woman of mine comes from a hooligan proletarian family, and doesn't know the first thing about filial piety. She moved in, and Grandma moved right out. You might even know her. She's the daughter of Old Geng, who sold shrimp paste, and that snake woman — she's no woman, she's a damned snake temptress. I'm putting all my energy into making money, and as soon as I've got fifty thousand, I'm kicking her ass out!"

The bus stopped on the Flood Dragon River bridgehead, where all the passengers disembarked, including Jintong, with the help of Parrot Han. His eye was caught by a line of new houses on the northern bank of the river, and by a new concrete bridge not far from the old stone one. Vendors selling fruit, cigarettes, sweets, and the like had set up their stalls near the bridgehead. Parrot Han pointed to some buildings on the northern bank. "The township government moved its offices and the school away, and the old Sima family compound has been taken over by Big Gold Tooth — Wu Yunyu's asshole son — who built a birth control pill factory, and makes illicit liquor and rat poison on the side. He doesn't do a damned thing for the people. Sniff the air," he said, raising one hand. "What do you smell?" Jintong saw a tall sheet-metal chimney rising above the Sima family compound, spewing clouds of green smoke. That was the source of the stomach-churning smell in the air. "I'm glad Grandma moved away," Parrot Han said. "That smoke would have suffocated her. These days the slogan is 'Eight Immortals Cross the Sea, Each Demonstrating His Own Skills.' No more class, no more struggles. All anyone can see these days is money. I've got two hundred acres of land over in Sandy Ridge, and plenty of ambition. I've set up an exotic bird breeding farm. I've given myself ten years to bring all the exotic birds in the world here to Northeast Gaomi Township. By then, I'll have enough money to secure influence. Then, with money and influence, the first thing I'm going to do is erect a pair of statues of my parents in Sandy Ridge . . ." He was so excited by his plans for the future, his eyes lit up blue and he thrust out his scrawny chest, like a proud pigeon. Jintong noticed that when they weren't selling something, the vendors on the bridgehead were watching him and Parrot Han, who never stopped gesticulating. His feelings of inferiority returned, accompanied by regrets that he hadn't gone to see slutty Wei Jinzhi the barber for a shave and a haircut before leaving the labor reform camp.

Parrot Han took some bills out of his pocket and stuffed them into Jintong's hand. "It's not much, Little Uncle, but I'm just starting out and things are still pretty tight. Besides, that stinking old lady of mine still has a string tied to my money, and I don't dare treat Grandma the way she deserves, not that I could. She nearly coughed up blood raising me. Things couldn't have been harder for her, and that's something I won't forget even when I'm old and my teeth fall out. I'll make things right for her once I carry out my plans." Jintong put the bills back into Parrot Han's hand. "Parrot," he said, "I can't take that." "Not enough?" That embarrassed Jintong. "No, it's not that . . ." Parrot put the bills back into Jintong's sweaty hand. "So, you look down on your useless nephew, is that it?" "After what I've become, I don't have the right to look down on anyone. You're special, a thousand times better than your absolutely worthless uncle . . ." "Little Uncle," Parrot said, "people don't understand you. The Shangguan family is made up of dragons and phoenixes, the seed of tigers and panthers. Too bad the times were against us. Just look at you, Little Uncle — you've got the face of Genghis Khan, and your day will come. But first go home and enjoy a few days with Grandma. Then come see me at the Eastern Bird Sanctuary."

Parrot walked over and bought a bunch of bananas and a dozen oranges from one of the vendors. He put them into a nylon bag for Jintong and told him to take them to Grandma. They said good-bye on the new bridge, and as Jintong looked down at the glistening water, he felt his nose begin to ache. So he found an isolated spot, where he put down his bag, and went to the river's edge, where he washed the dirt and grime off his face. He's right, he was thinking. Since I'm home, I've got to grit my teeth and make my mark — for the Shangguan family, for Mother, and for myself.

Calling upon his memory, he made his way back to the old family home, where so many exciting events had occurred. But what spread out before him was a vast stretch of open land, where a bulldozer was just then knocking down the last remnants of the wall that had encircled the house. He thought back to what Parrot had said while they were on the top of the bus: the three counties of Gaomi, Pingdu, and Jiaozhou each gave up a tract of land for a new city, the center of which was to be the town of Dalan. So the spot where he was standing would soon become a thriving city, and his house was planned as the site for a seven-story high-rise that would house the Dalan Metropolitan Government offices.

Streets had already been widened, paved with gravel over clay, and bordered by deep ditches, in which workers were in the process of burying thick water mains. The church had been razed, and a sign that read "Great China Pharmaceutical Company" hung above Sima's house. A fleet of beat-up old trucks was parked on the onetime church grounds. All the millstones from the Sima family mill house were lying here and there in the mud, and on the spot where the mill had once stood a circular building was going up. Amid the rumbling of a cement mixer and the biting odor of heated tar, he passed by teams of surveyors and gangs of laborers, most of them drunk on beer, as he walked out of a construction site that had once been his village and onto the dirt path that led to the stone bridge over the Black Water River.

As he was crossing the bridge to the southern bank of the river, he spotted the stately seven-story pagoda on the hill; the sun was just setting, and its fiery red rays seemed to set the bricks ablaze and turn the bits of straw between them to cinders. A flock of doves circled the structure, a single column of white smoke rose from the kitchen of the hut in front. The fields lay in a deathly silence broken only by the roar of heavy equipment at the work site. Jintong felt as if his head had been pumped dry, except for the hot tears slipping into the corners of his mouth.

In spite of the pounding of his heart, he forced himself to walk toward the sacred pagoda. Long before he reached it, he saw a white-haired figure standing in front of the pagoda, leaning on a cane fabricated out of an old umbrella handle and watching his progress. His legs felt so heavy he could barely put one foot in front of the other. His tears continued to flow unobstructed. Like the straw in the building, Mother's white hair looked as if it had caught fire. With a muffled shout, he fell to his knees and pressed his face up against her bony knees, deformed from a lifetime of physical labor. He felt like a man at the ocean bottom, where sounds and colors and shapes ceased to exist. From somewhere deep in his memory, the smell of mother's milk rose, overwhelming all his senses.

2

Not long after returning home, Jintong fell seriously ill. At first, it was only a weakness in his limbs and soreness in his joints. But that was followed by vomiting and diarrhea. Mother spent all she'd accumulated over the years by collecting and selling scrap to pay doctors from all over Northeast Gaomi. But none of the injections or medicines made any difference in his health. One day in August, he took her hand and said, "Mother, all my life I've brought you nothing but trouble. Now that my life is about over, you won't have to suffer any longer . . ."

She squeezed his hand. "Jintong, I won't permit you to talk like that! You're still young. I may be blind in one eye, but I can still see good days ahead. The sun is bright, the flowers smell like heaven, and we have to keep moving into the future, son . . ." She spoke with all the energy she could muster, but sad tears had already dripped onto his bony hand.

"Mother, talk all you want, but it won't do any good," Jintong said. "I saw her again. She had stuck a plaster over the bullet hole in her temple and was holding a piece of paper with her and my names on it. She said she'd gotten our marriage certificate and was waiting for me to marry her."

"Dear daughter," Mother said through her tears to the empty space before her. "Dear daughter, you did not deserve to die, I know that, and you're like my very own daughter. Jintong spent fifteen years in prison over you, and his debt has been paid in full. So I beg you to show some mercy and forgive him. That way this lonely old woman will have someone to look after her. You're a sensible girl. As the saying goes, life and death are different roads, and you must take one or the other. Forgive him, dear daughter. This blind old woman begs you on her knees . . ."

As his mother prayed, Jintong saw Long Qingping's naked body in the sunlit window, her ironlike breasts covered with rust. She opened her legs wantonly, and out came a clump of round, white mushrooms. But when he looked closer, he saw that it was a cluster of rounded infant heads, not mushrooms, and that they were all joined together. Each tiny head had a complete face and was covered with downy yellow hair: tall noses, blue eyes, paper-thin earlobes, like the skin of beans soaked in water. All the infants were crying out to him, the sound soft and weak, but clear as a bell. Daddy! Daddy! The sound struck terror in his heart, so he closed his eyes. The infants broke free and rushed toward him, landing on his face and body, where they tugged at his ears, stuck their fingers in his nose, and clawed at his eyes, all the while calling out Daddy. He squeezed his eyes shut even tighter, but that did not block out the sight of Long Qingping scraping her rusty breasts with sandpaper, the sound grating on his ears. She stared at him with a mixture of melancholy and rage, still scraping her breasts until they looked as if they'd been turned on a lathe, shiny and brand-new, emitting a cold glint that gathered around the nipples and, like freezing rays, bore straight into his heart. He shrieked, and passed out cold.

When he regained consciousness, he saw a candle burning on the windowsill and an oil lamp hanging on the wall. Gradually, the tortured face of Parrot Han materialized in the flickering light. "What happened, Little Uncle?" The voice seemed to come from far away, and he tried to answer, but couldn't make his lips move. Wearily, he shut his eyes to block out the candlelight.

"Take my word for it," he heard Parrot say. "He's not going to die. Not long ago, I read a fortune-telling book. Little Uncle has the face of someone for whom wealth and good fortune await, someone who will live a long life."

"Parrot," Mother said, "I've never begged for anything in my life, but now I'm begging you."

"Grandma, when you talk like that you might as well be cursing me."

"You know lots of people, so I'm asking you to get a cart and take your uncle to the county hospital."

"There's no need for that, Grandma. Our town facilities enjoy big-city standards. Local doctors outshine those at the county hospital. Since Dr. Leng has already seen him, there's no need to go anywhere else. He graduated at the top of his class at the Union Medical College and studied abroad. If he says there's no cure, then there's no cure."

With a look of dejection, Mother said, "Parrot, we don't need your fine words. You'd better go. If you're late getting home, you'll have to answer to that wife of yours."

"Sooner or later I'm going to be free of those shackles. Here, Grandma, take this twenty yuan and buy something Little Uncle would like to eat."

"Keep your money," she said. "Now go. There's nothing your Little Uncle wants to eat."

"Maybe he doesn't, but you need to eat. Raising me to manhood took a lot out of you, Grandma. We suffered under government oppression and were so poor we barely got by. After they took Little Uncle away, you put me on your back and went out begging, knocking on doors all over Northeast Gaomi. Thoughts of what you had to do cut into my heart like a dagger and I can't help but weep. We were the lowest of the low. If not, I'd never have married that shrew. Don't you agree, Grandma? But those hellish days are about to come to an end. I've requested a loan for my Eastern Bird Sanctuary, and the mayor has approved it. If this works out, I have my cousin, Lu Shengli, to thank. She's manager of the Dalan Bank of Industry and Commerce. She's young and talented, and what she says goes. Grandma, don't worry, I'll go talk to her. If she won't help us with Little Uncle's illness, who will? She's another family member you raised to adulthood. Yes, I'll go talk to her. She's made quite a name for herself. She has a car and a driver, and she eats like a queen: two-legged pigeons, four-legged turtles, eight-legged crabs, curvy prawns, prickly sea cucumbers, poisonous scorpions, and nonpoisonous crocodile eggs. That cousin of mine can no longer be bothered by duck and chicken and pork and dog meat. I know it may sound bad, but the gold necklace around her neck is as thick as a dog leash. She wears platinum and diamond rings on her fingers and a jade bracelet on her wrist. Her eyeglasses have gold frames and natural crystal lenses, she wears Italian designer fashions and French perfume whose fragrance will stay with you the rest of your life . . ."

"Parrot, take your money and go!" Mother cut in. "And don't go talk to her. The Shangguan family doesn't rate a rich relative like that."

"That's where you're wrong, Grandma. I could take Little Uncle to the hospital in a cart, but getting anything done these days depends on contacts. The difference in treatment between a patient I bring in and one my cousin brings in is night and day."

"That's the way it's always been," Mother said. "Whether your uncle lives or dies is in the hands of fate. If luck is with him, he's bound to live. If not, even if the magical doctors Hua Tuo and Bian Que came back to Earth, they couldn't save him. Now go on, and don't upset me."

Parrot had more to say, but Mother angrily banged the tip of her cane on the floor and said, "Parrot, please do as I say. Take your money and go!"

Parrot left. Jintong, still in a sort of half-sleep, heard Mother outside the house wailing. A night wind rustled the dry grass on the pagoda. A bit later, he heard her busying herself at the stove, sending the odor of herbal medicine into his room. It seemed to him as if his brain had shrunk down to a mere sliver, and the medicinal odor squeezed its way into that sliver, as if through a sieve. Ah, that sweet taste is cogongrass, the bitter taste is soul-returning grass, the sour taste is clover, the salty taste is dandelion, the spicy taste is Siberian cockle-bur. Sweet, bitter, sour, salty, and spicy, all five tastes, plus purslane, pinellia tuber and Chinese lobelia, mulberry bark, peony skin, and dried peach. Apparently, Mother had gotten nearly every herbal med-icine available in Northeast Gaomi and was cooking it all in a big pot. The combined odor, with its mixture of life and of soil, poured into his brain as if from a powerful faucet, washing away the filth and slowly opening up his mind. He thought about the lush green grass outside, the flower-covered open fields, and cranes that roamed the marshland. A cluster of golden wild chrysanthemums summoned pollen-laden bees to them. He heard the heavy breathing of the land and the sound of seeds dropping to the ground.

Mother came in and bathed him with cotton soaked in the herbal mixture. She could see he was embarrassed. "Son," she said, "you could live to be a hundred, but in my eyes you'll always be a little boy." She cleaned him from head to toe, even the dirty spaces between his toes. Evening winds entered the room as the smell of the herbal concoction grew heavier. He'd never felt more refreshed or cleaner than at that moment. He heard Mother sobbing and muttering out behind the house, alongside a wall of empty liquor bottles. He began to sleep and, for the first time, was not startled awake by a nightmare. He slept till dawn. When he opened his eyes in the morning, his nose filled with the smell of fresh milk. But it was different from the mother's milk and goat's milk he'd lived on before, and he tried to determine the source: the feeling he'd experienced years earlier, when, as the Snow Prince, he'd blessed all those women by caressing their breasts, flooded into his mind. The greatest sense of longing came from the last breast he'd ca-ressed that day, the one belonging to the proprietor of the sesame oil shop, Old Jin, the woman with only one breast.

Mother was delighted to see that he appeared to be on the mend. "What would you like to eat, son?" she asked. "Whatever it is, I'll make it. I went into town and borrowed some money from Old Jin. She'll bring a cart over one of these days and take away all those bottles in back for repayment."

"Old Jin . . ." Jintong's heart was pounding. "How is she?"

With her one good eye — even it was failing — she looked at her son, puzzled by how uneasy he seemed, and let out an exasperated sigh. "She's turned into the 'queen of trash' of the entire area. She owns a car and has fifty employees who melt down used plastic and rubber. She's doing fine financially, but that man of hers is worthless. She has a bad reputation, but I had no choice but to go see her. She's as generous as ever, a woman in her fifties, and, strangely, she even has a son . . ."

As if slapped in the face, Jintong bolted upright, like someone who has seen the merciful, bright red face of God. A happy thought came to him: My feelings weren't wrong after all. He was sure that the one-eyed breast of old Jin was heading toward his room and that the sandpapered breasts of Long Qingping were retreating. "Mother," he blurted out with a degree of bashfulness, "could you step outside before she comes?"

Momentarily at a loss, she regained her composure and said, "Son, you've managed to send away the death demon, so I'll do anything you ask. I'm going now."

Jintong lay back down, filled with excitement, and was quickly immersed in that life-giving aroma. It came from his memory, not from anywhere outside, bursting upon him. He closed his eyes and saw her fuller yet still smooth face. Her eyes were as dark as ever, moist and seductive, every movement intended to snatch away a man's soul. She was moving quickly, like a comet, and that breast of hers, left unscarred by time, jiggled under her cotton shirt, as if straining to get out. Very slowly, the spiritual aroma emanating from his heart and the material aroma emanating from Old Jin's breast drew together like a pair of mating butterflies. They touched and quickly merged. He opened his eyes, and there, standing by his bed, was Old Jin, just as he had imagined her.

"Little brother," she said emotionally as she bent down and took his brittle hand in hers, her dark eyes awash with tears, "my dear little brother, what is wrong with you?"

Feminine tenderness melted his heart. Arching his neck like a newborn puppy that has yet to open its eyes, he nibbled at her breast with his feverish lips. Without a moment's hesitation, she lifted her shirt and lowered her overflowing breast, full as a muskmelon, onto his face. His mouth sought out the nipple; the nipple sought out his mouth. Once his trembling lips encircled her and she entered his mouth trembling, they were both boiling hot and moaning madly. Powerful jets of sweet, warm milk hit the membranes of his mouth and converged at the opening of his throat, where it coursed down into a stomach that had retched up everything it held. At the same time, she felt the morbid infatuation for this onetime beautiful little boy she had stored up for decades leave her body along with the milk . . .

He sucked her dry, then, like a baby, fell asleep with the nipple in his mouth. She stroked his face tenderly and gently pulled the nipple away. His mouth twitched, but she could see the color returning to his sallow face. Mother was standing by the door, watching sadly. But what she detected in the weather-worn face of the old woman was neither rebuke nor jealousy; rather, it was self-rebuke and gratitude. Old Jin stuffed her breast back under her shirt and said resolutely, "I wanted to do it, aunty. It's something I've wanted to do all my life. He and I had a bond in a previous life."

"Since that's the case," Mother said, "I won't thank you."

Old Jin took out a roll of bills. "Old aunty, the other day I calculated wrong. That pile of bottles out back is worth more than I gave you."

"Sister-in-law," Mother said, "I don't think Brother Fang will be happy when he finds out."

"As long as he's got a bottle around, he's happy. I'm awfully busy these days, and I can only come once a day. When I'm not around, give him something light and watery."

Under the ministrations of Old Jin, Jintong quickly regained his health. Like a molting snake, he shed a layer of dead skin. For two whole months, the only nutrition he received was from Old Jin; on those frequent occasions when his stomach rumbled, all he had to do was think about regular, coarse food for darkness to settle around him and his intestines to knot up painfully. His mother's brow, smoothed out after he had been pulled back from the brink of death, now began to knit again. Every morning he stood in front of the wall of bottles behind the house, the wind whistling in the bottlenecks, like a child waiting for its mother or a woman waiting for her lover, eyes cast anxiously in the direction of the road that led from the bustling new city, through the open fields, to where she stood, nearly bursting with anticipation.

One day Jintong waited from dawn to dusk for Old Jin, but she didn't show. He stood until his legs were numb and his eyes began to glaze over, so he sat down and leaned up against the wall of whistling bottles. At dusk, the chorus of music sounded mournful, only deepening his sense of dejection. Tears slipped unnoticed down his cheeks.

Supporting herself on her cane, Mother stood beneath the darkening sky looking scornfully at him, her expression a mixture of pity over his misfortunes and anger over his inability to overcome them. She watched him for a while without saying a word, then turned and walked back into the house, accompanied by the taps of her cane on the ground.

The following morning, Jintong picked up the family sickle and a basket and walked over to the nearby trench. At breakfast, he'd eaten a pair of mushy yams, staring wide-eyed as if someone were stripping the skin from his body. Now his stomach ached badly and he had a sour taste in his throat. He had to fight not to throw up as he followed his nose to the delicate fragrance of wild peppermint. He recalled that the co-op's purchasing station was willing to buy peppermint. Naturally, earning some extra money wasn't the only reason he wanted to gather peppermint; even more importantly, he thought it might help him break his addiction to Old Jin's milk. The stuff grew from halfway down the slope all the way to the water's edge, and its odor was invigorating. He even found that he could see more clearly. He breathed in deeply, wanting to fill his lungs with the fragrance of peppermint. Then he began cutting it down, using skills he'd honed during his fifteen years in the labor reform camp and quickly leaving a trail of fallen peppermint stalks, with their white sap and fine hairs.

As he moved down the slope, he discovered a hole the size of a rice bowl. His initial fright over the discovery quickly turned to excitement as it occurred to him that it must be a rabbit hole. Presenting Mother with a wild rabbit would bring a little joy into her life. He began by sticking the handle of his sickle into the hole and shaking it. Something moved down there — he heard it — which meant the hole was occupied. So he sat down, gripping his sickle tightly, and waited. The rabbit stuck its head up out of the hole until its furry mouth showed. Jintong swung his sickle, but the rabbit pulled its head back just in time. The next time, however, he felt the sickle cut deeply into the rabbit's head; jerking it back, the rest of the animal appeared, still twitching, and landed at his feet. The tip of the sickle had entered the rabbit's eye, from which trickles of blood emerged and ran down the glistening blade of the weapon. The little marble-like eyes were barely visible through tiny slits. Suddenly chilled to the bone, Jintong threw down the sickle, scrambled up to the top of the slope, and looked around like a boy in deep trouble who needs help.

Mother was there already, right behind him. "Jintong, what are you doing?" she asked in a voice that crackled with age. "Mother," he blurted out in agony, "I killed a rabbit . . . oh, the poor thing . . . what have I done? Why did I have to kill it?"

"Jintong," Mother said in a stern voice she'd never used with him before, "you're forty-two years old, and still you act like a little sissy! I haven't said anything to you these past few days, but I can't hold back any longer. You know I can't be here with you forever. After I'm gone, you'll have to shoulder the family responsibilities and get on with your life. You can't go on like this."

Looking down at his hands in disgust, Jintong wiped off the rabbit blood with dirt. His face was burning, stung by Mother's criticism, and he wasn't happy.

"You have to go out into the world and do something. It doesn't have to be anything big."

"What can I do, Mother?" he said dejectedly.

"Here's what you can do. Be a man and take that rabbit down to the Black Water River. Skin it, gut it, and clean it, then take it home and cook it for your mother. I haven't tasted meat in six months at least. Maybe you'll have trouble skinning and gutting the rabbit, worrying about being cruel. But isn't it just as cruel for a grown man to be sucking at a woman's breast? Don't ever forget that a woman's milk is her lifeblood, and sucking it dry is ten times crueler than killing a rabbit. If you think like that, you'll be able to do it, and it will give you a satisfying feeling. Killing an animal doesn't bring a hunter remorse over taking a life, it brings him pleasure. And that's because he knows that all the millions of beasts and birds in this world were put here by Jehovah to satisfy human needs. Humans are the pinnacle of existence, people represent the soul of this earth."

Jintong nodded vigorously as he felt something hard settle slowly in his chest. His heart, which up till then had seemed to be floating on water, felt as if it were starting to sink.

"Do you know why Old Jin stopped coming?"

Jintong looked into Mother's face. "Was it you . . ."

"Yes, it was me! I went to talk to her. I couldn't stand by while she ruined my son."

"You . . . how could you do that?"

She continued, ignoring his tone. "I told her that if she really loves my son, she can sleep with him, but I won't allow you to suckle at her breast anymore."

"Her milk saved my life!" Jintong shouted shrilly. "If not for her milk, I'd be dead now, rotting away, food for the worms!"

"I know that. Do you think I could ever forget that she saved your life?" She thumped the ground with her cane. "I've been a fool all these years, but I finally understand that it's better to let a child die than let him turn into a worthless creature who can't take his mouth away from a woman's nipple!"

"What did she say?" he asked anxiously.

"She's a good woman. She told me to go home and tell you that there will always be a pillow for you on Old Jin's bed."

"But she's a married woman . . ." Jintong's face had grown pale.

Mother threw down a challenge, her voice quaking with madness. "If you don't show a little spunk, you're no son of mine. Go see her. I don't need a son who refuses to grow up. What I want is someone like Sima Ku or Birdman Han, a son who's not afraid to cause me some trouble, if that's what has to be done. I want a man who stands up to piss!"

3

With newfound valor, he crossed the Black Water River, as Mother had told him to, and went to see Old Jin. With Mother's help, this was to be the start of his life as a real man. But as he set out on the road to the newly created city, his courage left him like a tire with a slow leak. The high-rises, with mosaic inlays on the sides, were impressive in the sunlight, while at a number of work sites, the yellow arms of cranes swung massive prefabricated forms into place. Insistent jackhammers thudded against his eardrums, arc welders on steel girders near the sandy ridge lit up the sky more brightly than the sun. White smoke curled around a tower, and his eyes began to wander. Mother had given him directions to Old Jin's recycling station, which was near the bay where Sima Ku had been shot all those years ago. Some of the buildings alongside the wide asphalt street had been finished, others were in the process of going up. No sign remained of the Sima family compound. The Great China Pharmaceutical Company was gone. Several large excavators were digging deep trenches in the ground. Where the church had once stood, a bright yellow, seven-story high-rise towered over its surroundings like a golden-toothed member of the nouveau riche. Red characters, each the size of an adult sheep, proclaimed in glittering fashion the power and prestige of the Dalan Branch Office of the China Bank of Industry and Commerce.

Old Jin's recycling station was spread out over a large area, behind a plaster board fence. The scrap was separated by type: empty bottles formed a great wall that dazzled the eyes, a mountainous prism of broken glass; old tires were stacked in heaps; a mound of old plastic rose higher than a rooftop; smack in the middle of discarded metal stood a howitzer minus its wheels. Dozens of workmen, towels covering the lower half of their faces, were scampering all over the place like ants. Some were lugging tires, others were doing the sorting, while still others were loading or unloading trucks. A black wolfhound was tied to the base of a wall with the chain from an old waterwheel, still wrapped in red plastic. It appeared far more ferocious than the mongrels at the labor reform camp; its fur looked as if waxed. Lying on the ground in front of the dog were a whole roasted chicken and a half eaten pig's foot. The watchman had a mass of unruly hair, rheumy eyes, and a deeply wrinkled face; on closer examination, he looked like the militia leader of the original Dalan Commune. A large furnace stood in the yard for melting plastic. Strange-smelling black smoke was belching out of a squat sheet-metal chimney; dust skittered along the ground. A group of scrap vendors was gathered around a large scale, arguing with the old man in charge of the scale. Jintong recognized him as Luan Ping, a salesclerk at the old Dalan Co-op. A white-haired old man rode into the station on a three-wheeled cart; it was Liu Daguan, onetime head of the local branch of the Post and Telecommunications Bureau. Once known for the way he strutted around, he was now in charge of Old Jin's workers' dining hall. Feeling his nerve slipping away, Jintong stood in the yard looking helpless. But a window in the simple two-story building in front of him was pushed open, and there stood the capitalist, single-breasted Old Jin in a pink bathrobe, holding her hair in one hand and waving to him with the other. "Adoptive son," he heard her shout brazenly, "come on up!"

It seemed to him as if everyone in the yard turned to watch him walk toward the building, head down, their stares making every step an awkward one. What about my arms? Should I cross them? Let them hang straight down? Stick them in my pockets, maybe, or clasp them behind my back? Finally, he decided to let them hang at his sides, shoulders hunched, and walk the way he'd been trained during his fifteen years at the camp, like a whipped dog, slinking along with its tail between its legs, head bowed but always looking from side to side, moving as rapidly as possible alongside a wall, like a thief. When Jintong reached the bottom of the stairs, Old Jin shouted from the second floor, "Liu Daguan, my adoptive son's here. Put on a couple more dishes." Out in the yard, someone — he didn't know who — sang a nasty little ditty: "If a child wants to grow up strong, he needs twenty-four wanton adoptive mothers . . ."

As he climbed the wooden staircase, the heavy aroma of perfume floated down to him. He looked up timidly and saw Old Jin standing at the top of the stairs, her legs spread, a mocking smile on her powdered face. He stopped and clenched the metal banister with his sweaty palm.

"Come on up, adoptive son," she welcomed him, her mocking smile now gone.

He forced himself to keep going, until a soft hand gripped his wrist. In the dark hallway it felt as if the odor of her body were dragging him along to a den of seduction, a brightly lit, carpeted room where the walls were papered; colorful balls made of paper hung from the ceiling. In the center of the room stood a desk, on which a fountain-pen holder rested. "That's all for show. I don't read or write much."

Jintong stood rooted to the floor, unwilling to look her in the eye. All of a sudden, she laughed and said, "I can't believe this is happening. This has to be an all-time first."

He looked up and met her seductive gaze. "Adoptive son," she said, "don't let your eyeballs drop out and injure your feet. Look at me. With your head up you're a wolf; with your head down you're a sheep. The most uncommon thing in the world is a mother arranging sex for her own son, and I'm impressed she even thought of it. Do you know what she said to me?" Old Jin made her voice sound like his mother's: "'If you're going to save someone, dear sister-in-law, go all the way; if you're seeing off a guest, take them to their door. You saved him with your milk, but you can't feed him for the rest of his life, can you?' She was right, since I'm over fifty already." She patted the robe over her breast. "This treasure of mine won't hold up for long, no matter how I use it. When you stroked it thirty years ago, it was, in the popular phrase of a few years back, 'high-spirited and full of life, militant and ready for a good fight.' But now it's more a case of 'the phoenix past its prime is no match for a chicken.' I owe you from a previous life. I don't want to think about why, nor is it important for you to know. All that's important is the fact that this body of mine has simmered for thirty years, until it's cooked through and through. Now it's up to you to feast on it any way you want."

Jintong stared at her single breast as if in a trance, greedily breathing in its fragrance and that of the milk it held, not even seeing the full thighs she exposed for his benefit. Out in the yard, the man in charge of the scale shouted, "This guy wants to sell this to us, Boss." He held up some thick cable. "Do we want it?" Old Jin stuck her head out the window. "Why bother me?" she said unhappily. "Go ahead, take it." She slammed the window shut. "Damn! I'll buy anything someone has to sell. Don't look so surprised. Eight out of ten of people with things to sell are thieves. I'll get whatever's being used at the work site. I've got welding rods, tools in their original packages, steel ribs, cement. I don't turn anyone away. I pay scrap prices, then turn around and sell it as new, and there's my profit. I know this will all fall apart one of these days, so I use half of every yuan I make to feed those bastards down there and spend the other half any way I want. I'll tell you straight out that at least half of those clever, fancy men out there have visited my bed. Know what they mean to me?" Jintong shook his head. "All my life," she said, patting her breast again, "this is what has gotten me where I wanted to go. Those idiot brothers-in-law of yours, from Sima Ku to Sha Yueliang, fell asleep with this nipple in their mouths, and not one of them meant a thing to me. In my lifetime, the only person who's ever set my soul on fire is you, you little bastard! Your mother told me you've only been with a woman once, and that was a corpse, and she figured that's the source of what's bothering you. So I told her not to worry, that there's at least one thing I'm good at. Send your son to me, I said, and I'll turn him into a man of steel."

Old Jin opened her robe seductively. She was wearing nothing underneath. The white parts were white as snow, the black parts black as coal. His face bathed in sweat, Jintong sat down weakly on the carpet.

She giggled at the sight. "Scared you, didn't I? There's nothing to be scared of, adoptive son. Breasts may be a woman's treasure, but there are even greater treasures. You can't eat steaming bean curd if you hurry it. Stand up and let me fix what's wrong with you."

She dragged him into her bedroom like a dead dog. The walls were ablaze with color; a large bed sat on deep pile carpeting near the window. She undressed him as if he were a naughty little boy. Beyond the sunlit window, the yard was alive with men walking around. Recalling Birdman Han's movements, Jintong cupped his hands over his crotch and squatted down. He saw his reflection in a floor-to-ceiling dressing mirror — it was so disgusting it nearly made him puke. Old Jin doubled up with laughter — she sounded so young, so wanton, the laughter flying out into the yard like a dove. "My god, where did you learn that? I'm no tiger, you know, and I won't bite that thing off!" She nudged him with her foot. "Get up, it's bath time!"

She led Jintong into the bathroom, where she turned on the light and pointed to a pink bathtub beneath a crystal fixture with a frosted bulb, bordered by tiled walls, a coffee-colored Italian commode, and a Japanese water heater. "I bought all this from scrap dealers. Half the people in Dalan are thieves these days. I don't have running hot water, so I need to heat my own bath water." She pointed to four water heaters arrayed around the tub. "I spend half my day soaking in the tub. I never took a single hot bath the first half of my life, so I'm making up for that now. But you're worse off than I, son, and I don't imagine the labor reform camp supplied hot water for baths." While she talked, she reached out and turned on all four heaters, from which hot water gushed into the tub and steam quickly filled the room. Old Jin pushed him in, but he shrieked and jumped back out. She pushed him in again. "Tough it out," she said. "It'll cool down in a minute." So he gritted his teeth, as all the blood in his body seemed to rush to his head. He felt a prickly sensation all over. Neither truly painful nor totally numbing, it fell somewhere between agony and bliss. He went limp, his body slipping weakly under the water, as the four jets pummeled his skin with watery arrows. Through the steamy air he saw Old Jin slip out of her robe, climb in like a big white sow, and cover him with her soft, lustrous body. The steam was suddenly perfumed. Picking up a bar of fragrant bath soap, she washed his head, his face, and his body, which was quickly covered with a rich lather. He submitted weakly, and when her nipple brushed against his skin, he nearly died of ecstasy. The dirt and grime fell away as the two of them moved and shifted in the tub; his hair, his stubbly beard, were cleansed of filth. An ordinary man would have thrown his arms around her, but he just lay there and let her scrub and pinch him all over.

After they emerged from the bath, she flung the rags he'd worn home from the camp out the window and dressed him in clean underwear. Then she helped him into a Pierre Cardin suit she'd readied for the occasion. After completing the outfit with a tie, with which she struggled for a moment, she combed his hair, adding some Korean hair oil, trimmed his beard, and splashed on some cologne. She then led him over to the dressing mirror, where a tall, handsome, impressive-looking Chinese man in Western garb looked back at him. "My dear," Old Jin exclaimed, "you look like a movie star!" He blushed and turned away. But he'd liked what he'd seen. It wasn't the Shangguan Jintong who had survived on stolen eggs at the Flood Dragon River Farm, and it surely wasn't the Shangguan Jintong who had tended livestock in a labor reform camp.

Old Jin led him over to a sofa at the foot of the bed and handed him a cigarette, which he refused. Fearfully he accepted the tea she held out to him. She leaned against the folded comforter on the bed, spread her legs casually, and covered herself with her bathrobe, as she leisurely blew smoke rings from a cigarette she'd lit for herself. With the powder washed off in the bath, wrinkles and a few dark freckles showed on her face. When she closed her eyes to keep out the smoke, crow's feet fanned out in the corners. "I've never seen a more innocent man in my life," she said with a squint. "Am I just an ugly old hag?"

Unable to bear the penetrating glare that squeezed out from her slitted eyes, he lowered his head and laid his hands on his knees. "No," he said, "you're not old, and you're not ugly. You're the most beautiful woman in the world."

"I thought your mother was lying to me," she said, sounding demoralized. "But I see it was true, every bit of it." She stubbed her cigarette out in an ashtray and sat up. "The incident with that woman, did it really happen?" He stretched his neck, unused to being confined by a starched collar and a tie; his face was sweaty. As he rubbed his knees, he felt he was on the verge of crying.

"That's all right," she said. "I was just asking. You're such a little idiot."

At noon, a dozen or so men in Western suits and leather shoes joined them for lunch. Holding his hand, she introduced him to her guests. "This is my adoptive son. Looks like a movie star, doesn't he?" The men gazed at him with their clever eyes. One of them, a man with slicked-down hair and wearing a gold Rolex, the band intentionally loose around his wrist, said with a salacious wink, "Old Jin, you're an old cow feasting on tender new grass!" Jintong recalled that Old Jin had introduced this middle-aged man as the chairman of some commission or other.

"Up your mother's ass!" Old Jin swore. "This son of mine is the Golden Boy at the feet of the Queen Mother of the West, a gentleman in every respect. Not like you horny dogs. You're attracted to women like mosquitoes are drawn to blood. You'll sink your teeth into them even if you get swatted flat in the process."

"Old Jin," a bald man piped up, "you're the one we want to sink our teeth into." His jowls flapped when he talked, so badly he often had to cup his hands around his cheeks to keep his mouth from twisting out of shape. "Such tasty flesh!"

"Old Jin, you're taking a page out of Empress Wu's book," said a husky young man with naturally wavy hair and eyes like a goldfish. "You've got yourself a little pretty boy!"

"You all have your second and third wives, but I can't . . ." Old Jin stopped short. "Just shut your foul mouths. If you don't watch out, I'll make sure people find out about all your sneaking around."

A heavy-browed, hollow-cheeked man held out his wineglass and walked up to Jintong. "Elder brother Shangguan Jintong, here's to you and your release from the camp."

Now that his secret was out, Jintong felt like crawling under the table.

"He was framed!" Old Jin shouted indignantly. "Jintong is an honest man who would never do what he was charged with."

The men began whispering among themselves. Then they stood up and, one after the other, toasted Jintong. Since he'd never drunk alcohol before, it took little to set his head spinning. The men's faces took on the appearance of sunflowers waving in the wind, and he had the baffling feeling that he ought to clear something up with these people. He held out his cup and said, "I did it . . . with her, but her body was still warm . . . eyes still open . . . she smiled . . ."

"Now that's a real man!" he heard one of the sunflowers say, which made him feel better, just before he fell facedown into the food on the table.

He awoke to find himself stark naked on Old Jin's bed. She was there beside him, also naked, leaning against the comforter, a glass of wine in her hand; she was watching a video. It was the first color TV Jintong had ever seen — at the camp he'd seen a tiny bit of TV on a black-and-white set, which was astonishing enough, but the color picture had him doubting his own eyes. Especially since a naked man and woman were cavorting right there on the screen. Feelings of guilt weighed his head down. He heard Old Jin giggle. "You can stop pretending, son. Raise your head and take a good look. You need to see how people do it." Jintong raised his head and stole another look or two. Chills ran up and down his spine.

Old Jin leaned over and switched off the video. White dots filled the screen until she turned off the TV. When she adjusted the bedside lamp, a soft yellow light painted the walls. The light blue window curtains cascaded down to the bed mat like a waterfall. Old Jin smiled and began teasing him with her feet.

His throat was as dry as an abandoned well; the top half of his body was hot as cinders, the lower half was like a stagnant pond. His eyes were fixed on her full breast, which hung down to her navel and sagged slightly to the left. His lips parted as he moved over to take it into his mouth, but Old Jin moved it away and, at the same time, shifted provocatively. Irritated by her rejection, he grabbed her soft shoulders to roll her over. She turned toward him, her breast flashing into view like a frightened wild goose, but was quickly moved back out of sight. Before long, they were engaged in a wrestling match, one struggling to find the breast, the other fighting him off, until they were worn out. Finally, Old Jin was too weary to deny him any longer, and he buried his head in her bosom, with no thoughts for anything else, taking the nipple into his mouth with such force it's a wonder he didn't swallow up the whole breast. Once she'd surrendered her nipple, all the fight in her vanished. With moans of pleasure, she dug her fingers into his hair as he proceeded to suck her dry.

Jintong slept like a baby after emptying her of her milk. Old Jin, her heart on fire, tried every trick she knew to wake the man-child up, but he snored on.

The next morning, she awoke with a weary yawn and glared at Jintong. Her nursemaid brought over her baby for a feeding, and Jintong saw the infant, not yet a month old, in the nursemaid's arms, staring at him with hatred in his eyes. "Not now," Old Jin said to the woman, rubbing her breast. "Go get him a bottle of milk at the dairy farm."

Once the nursemaid had made a tactful exit, Old Jin cursed, "Jintong, you bastard, you sucked so hard you drew blood." He smiled apologetically and stared at the hand cupping her treasure. The demon of desire reappeared, and he began to make his move. But this time she stood up and took her breast into the other room.

That night, Old Jin wore a thick padded coat over a specially made canvas bra; she cinched her waist with a wide, brass-studded belt of the type used by martial arts masters. She had trimmed the bottom of the coat to just above her hips; tufts of cotton trailed from the un-hemmed opening. She was naked from the waist down, except, inter-estingly, for a pair of red high-heeled shoes. The moment Jintong saw how she was dressed he felt as if his insides were on fire, and he was quickly and impressively aroused to the point where his erection bumped into his belly. She was about to bend over like an animal in heat, but Jintong, too filled with desire to wait, threw her down on the rug like a tiger pouncing on its prey, and took her then and there.

Two days later, Old Jin introduced her new general manager, Shang-guan Jintong, to the workers. He was dressed in a tailored Italian suit, with a Lacrosse silk tie and a camel-colored serge overcoat. The outfit was topped by a French beret, worn at a rakish angle. He stood with his hands on his hips, like a rooster that's just hopped off of a hen's back — weary yet haughty, as he faced the motley crowd of workers in Old Jin's network. He made a brief speech, both the words and manner styled af-ter the way the guards at the labor reform camp had reprimanded the inmates. He saw a mixture of envy and hatred in their eyes.

With Old Jin as his guide, Jintong traveled to every corner of Dalan, where he was introduced to people who had dealings — direct and indirect — with the recycling station and the various sales outlets. He took up smoking foreign cigarettes and drank foreign liquor, learned the ins and outs of mah-jongg, and mastered the arts of play-ing host, passing out bribes, and evading taxes; once he even took the delicate hand of a young waitress in the Gathering Dragons Guesthouse restaurant in front of a dozen or more guests; flustered, she dropped the glass she was holding, smashing it to pieces. He took out a wad of bills and stuffed them into the pocket of her white uni-form. "A little something for you," he said. She thanked him in a flir-tatious voice.

Every night, like a farmer who never tires, he cultivated Old Jin's fer-tile soil. His inexperience and clumsiness brought her special pleasure and a new kind of excitement; her shouts often woke the fatigued workers as they slept in their shacks.

One evening, a one-eyed old man strolled into Old Jin's bedroom, his head cocked. Jintong shuddered when he saw him and pushed Old Jin to the side of the bed before scrambling to cover himself with the blanket. He recognized the man at once: it was Fang Jin, at one time in charge of the People's Commune production brigade, Old Jin's legal husband.

Old Jin sat there with her legs crossed. "Didn't I just give you a thousand yuan?" she asked, a sharp edge to her voice.

Fang Jin sat down on the Italian leather sofa in front of the bed, where he had a coughing fit and spat a gob of phlegm onto the beautiful Persian rug at his feet. The glare of hatred in his good eye was hot enough to light a cigarette. "I didn't come for money this time," he said.

"Then what do you want?" she asked irately.

"Your lives!" Fang Jin pulled a knife our from under his jacket, jumped up from the sofa with an agility that belied his age, and threw himself onto the bed.

With a shriek of horror, Jintong rolled to the far edge of the bed and wrapped the blanket around him. He was too petrified to move after that. He then watched in terror as the cold gleam of Fang Jin's knife pressed toward his chest.

Like a fish flopping on the ground, Old Jin placed herself between Fang Jin and Jintong, so that the tip of the knife was aimed at her chest. "If you're not the illegitimate child of a first wife, you'll stab me first!" she said coldly.

Grinding his teeth, Fang Jin said, "You whore, you stinking whore . . ." Despite the savagery of his words, the hand holding the knife began to tremble.

"I'm no whore," Old Jin said. "Sex is how a whore earns her living. But me, I actually pay for it. I'm a rich woman who's opened a brothel for her own pleasure!"

Fang Jin's gaunt face twitched like waves on the ocean. Beads of snot hung from the sparse ratlike whiskers on his chin. "I'll kill you!" he said shrilly as he thrust his knife at Old Jin's breast. But she spun out of the way, and the knife stuck into the bed.

With a single kick, she knocked Fang off of the bed. After whipping off her martial arts belt, slipping out of her short robe, taking off her canvas bra, and kicking off her shoes, she slapped her belly wantonly, the hollow sound nearly frightening Jintong out of his skin. "You old coffin shell," she shouted. "Can you do it? Climb on up if you can. If not, get the fuck out of here!"

Fang Jin was sobbing like a baby by the time he rose to a stooped position. With his eyes on Old Jin's jiggling pale flesh, he pounded himself on the chest and wailed in agony, "Whore, you whore, one of these days I'm going to kill you both . . ."

Fang Jin ran away.

Peace returned to the room. The roar of a power saw came from the carpentry shop, merging with the whistle of a train entering the station. At that moment, Jintong heard the dreary sound of the wind whistling through the empty liquor bottles at home. Old Jin sprawled in front of him, and he saw her single breast splayed in all its ugliness across her chest, the dark nipple looking like a dried sea cucumber.

She gave him an icy stare. "Can you do it like this?" she said. "No, you can't, I know that. Shangguan Jintong, you're dog shit that won't stick to a wall, you're a dead cat that can't climb a tree. I want you to get your balls out of here, just like Fang Jin!"

4

Except for the fact that her head was on the small side, Parrot Han's wife, Geng Lianlian, was actually quite a stunning woman, especially her figure. She had long legs, nicely rounded hips, a soft, narrow waist, slender shoulders, full breasts, and a long, straight neck — from the neck down there was absolutely nothing to complain about, since she'd inherited it all from her water-snake mother. Thoughts of her mother reminded Jintong of that stormy night in the mill years earlier, back during the civil war. Her head, small and flat as the blade of a shovel, had swayed in the early-morning rain and mist, and she truly looked to be three parts human and seven parts snake.

After Old Jin fired him, Jintong wandered the streets and lanes of the increasingly prosperous Dalan City. He didn't have the nerve to go home to see his mother. He'd sent her his severance pay, even though he'd spent nearly as much time lined up at the post office to wire the money as it would have taken to go over to the pagoda, and even though she'd have to go to the same post office to get the money, and even though the clerk there would be puzzled by his action, that's how he did it.

When his steps took him to the Sandy Ridge district, he discovered that the Cultural Bureau office had set up two monuments on the ridge. One commemorated the seventy-seven martyrs who had been buried alive by the Landlord Restitution Corps, the other commemorated the courageous fight against the German imperialists by Shang-guan Dou and Sima Daya, who had given their lives in the cause nearly a century before. The text, in virtually incomprehensible classi-cal prose, made Jintong's head swim and his eyes glaze over. A group of boys and girls — college students, by the look of them — was gath-ered around the monuments, discussing them animatedly before hud-dling together for group photos. The girl with the camera was wearing skintight blue-gray pants, the flared bottoms covered with white sand, and uneven rips at the knees, under an incredibly bulky yellow turtle-neck sweater that hung from her armpits like the sagging neck of a cow. A heavy Chairman Mao pin was pinned to her chest, and a cam-era vest with pockets of all sizes was draped casually over her sweater. She was bent at the waist, raising her backside in the air like a horse doing its business. "Okay!" she said. "Don't move. I said don't move!" Then she began looking for someone to take their picture. Her gaze fell on Jintong, who was still wearing the outfit Old Jin had given him. The girl said something in a foreign language, which he didn't under-stand. But he sensed at once that she'd mistaken him for a foreigner. "Say, girl, if you speak to me in Chinese, I'll understand you!" She gulped, probably surprised by his heavy local accent. For someone from a distant land to come to China and actually learn the Northeast Gaomi dialect was really something! is what he assumed she was thinking, and even he heaved a sigh. How wonderful it would be if a real foreigner could speak like someone from Northeast Gaomi. But, of course, there was such a person — the sixth son-in-law of the Shangguan family, Babbitt. Not to mention Pastor Malory, who had spoken better Chinese than Babbitt. "Sir," the girl said with a smile, "would you mind taking our picture?" Infected by her vitality, Jintong forgot for the moment his current situation, shrugged his shoulders, and made a face the way he'd seen foreigners do in the movies. He was quite convincing. Taking the camera from her and watching as she showed him which button to push, he said Okay, followed by a few comments in Russian. That produced the desired effect; the girl stared at him with obvious interest, before turning and running over to the monuments, where she leaned on her friends' shoulders. He looked into the viewer like an executioner, cutting all the girl's friends out of the shot and zeroing in on her. *Click*. He pressed the button. "Okay," he said. A moment later he was standing alone in front of the monuments, watching the youngsters as they walked off. An aura of youth lingered in the air, and he breathed in it greedily. He had a bitter taste in his mouth, as if he'd just eaten an overripe persimmon, a stiff tongue, and a bellyful of disapproval.

Resting his hand on the monument, he was hopelessly mired in fanciful thoughts, and if his nephew's wife, Geng Lianlian, hadn't come to his rescue, he might have withered right there on the marble monument like a dead bird. She rode up from town on a green sidecar motorcycle. Jintong had no idea why she stopped by the monuments, but he gazed appreciatively at her lovely figure. "Are you my uncle, Shangguan Jintong?" she asked.

He blushed in acknowledgment.

"I'm Geng Lianlian, the wife of Parrot Han," she said. "I know he's had nothing but terrible things to say about me, as if I were some kind of female tiger."

Jintong nodded ambiguously.

"I hear Old Jin showed you the door," she said. "That's no big deal, since I've come to hire you for our Eastern Bird Sanctuary. I'm sure you'll be satisfied with your duties, salary, and benefits, so you needn't even ask."

"I'm worthless, I can't do anything."

She smiled. "We'll give you something you *can* do," she said, taking him by the hand before he could respond with more self-deprecating comments. "Come with me," she said. "I've spent a good part of the day running all over town looking for you."

She seated Jintong in the sidecar along with a giant macaw tethered by a chain. It gave him a mean look and screeched. Lianlian reached over and tapped the bird before undoing the chain. "Old Yellow," she said, "fly back and notify the manager that Uncle's on his way."

The bird hopped awkwardly onto the edge of the sidecar and from there down to the sandy ground. Like a child learning to walk, it stumbled forward a few paces, spread its stiff wings, and rose into the air. After climbing thirty or forty feet, it wheeled and buzzed the motorcycle. "Old Yellow," Lianlian said, looking up at the circling bird, "go on now. No more funny stuff. I'll give you some pistachios when I get home." With a cry of delight, the parrot skimmed the treetops and flew off to the south.

Lianlian stepped down on the starter, then climbed onto the motorcycle, twisted the handlebar, and careened off down the street, the wind billowing her hair — his too. They sped down a newly paved road, quickly reaching a marshy area, where the Eastern Bird Sanctuary occupied a fenced-in area of at least two hundred acres. The garish entrance gate, which looked like a memorial arch, was guarded by two watchmen with Sam Browne belts across their chests and toy pistols on their hips. They saluted Lianlian as she drove past.

Just inside the gate was a man-made mountain of stones from Taihu, fronted by a pond with a fountain that was surrounded by cranes that looked real, but weren't. The macaw that had flown back ahead of them was resting alongside the pond. When it saw Lianlian, it fell in behind her, hopping awkwardly.

Parrot Han, made up like a circus clown and wearing white gloves, ran out from a little building with beaded curtains over the door. "Well, Uncle, we finally got you to come. I always said that as soon as things picked up around here I'd start paying back my debts." He waved a glittering silver baton as he spoke. "Heaven and earth may be vast, but not as vast as Grandma's kindness. And so, the first debt I owe is to her. Sending her a sack filled with meat wouldn't please her, nor would the gift of a gold cane. Finding work for her son, on the other hand, would please her no end."

"Okay, that's enough," Lianlian said, like a supervisor speaking to a subordinate. "Have you got the mynah bird trained? You swore you could do it."

"Don't you worry, my dear wife!" Parrot acted the part of a clown, bowing deeply. "It'll be able to sing ten songs, you've got my word on that."

"Uncle," Lianlian said turning back to Jintong, "we can talk about your new job, but first let me show you around."

As the new director of public relations for the Eastern Bird Sanctuary, Jintong was sent by Lianlian to a spa for ten days, where he was tended to by a Thai masseuse. Then he went to a beauty salon for ten facials. He emerged totally rejuvenated, a new man. Lianlian spared no expense, dressing him in the latest fashions, drenching him in Chanel cologne, and assigning a young woman to attend to his daily needs. All these extravagances made Jintong uneasy. Rather than give him any concrete job, Lianlian concentrated on filling his head with bird knowledge and taking him through blueprints for the sanctuary expansion plans. By the time they finished, he was convinced that the future of the Eastern Bird Sanctuary was in fact the future of the city of Dalan.

One night, when all was quiet, sleep eluded Jintong as he tossed and turned on his springy Simmons mattress. As he took stock of his life up that point, he realized that the life he was enjoying at the bird sanctuary was nothing short of a miracle. Exactly what does this small-headed woman have in mind for me? Rubbing his chest and underarms, now nicely fleshed out, he finally fell asleep, and almost immediately dreamed that peacock feathers had grown on his body. Fanning his tail feathers, like a gorgeous wall, he saw thousands of little dancing spots. All of a sudden, Geng Lianlian and several mean-looking women came up and began pulling out the tail feathers to give as gifts to rich and powerful friends. He complained to them in peacock-talk. Uncle, Lianlian said, if you won't let me pluck your feathers, what good are you to me? She grabbed a handful of his colorful tail feathers and pulled — Jintong shrieked, and woke himself up. His face was covered with a cold sweat, and he immediately noticed a dull pain in his rear. There was no more sleep for him that night. As he listened to birds fighting off in the marshland, he reflected upon his dream, trying to analyze just what it meant, a trick he'd learned back in the labor reform camp.

The next morning, Lianlian invited him to breakfast in her office. Sharing this honor was her husband, the master bird trainer, Parrot Han. The moment Jintong stepped through the door he was greeted by a "Good morning" from a black mynah on a golden perch. The bird ruffled its feather as it "spoke," and he wondered if his ears had deceived him. He walked around to see if he could find the source of the sound. "Shangguan Jintong," the mynah bird said. "Shangguan Jintong." The bird's greeting shocked and elated him. He nodded in its direction. "Good morning," he said. "What's your name?" The bird ruffled its feathers and said, "Bastard! Bastard!" "Did you hear that, Parrot?" Lianlian said. "This is what you've been teaching your little pet!" Parrot slapped the mynah. "Bastard!" he cursed. "Bastard!" the dizzy mynah echoed him. "Bastard!" Obviously embarrassed, Parrot turned to Lianlian. "Damn," he said, "have you ever seen the likes of this bird? It's like a little child. You can try to teach him proper language till you're blue in the face, but it's no use. Then say a bad word, and he picks it up at once."

Lianlian treated Jintong to some fresh milk and a partially cooked ostrich egg. She had the appetite of a bird, while Jintong had the appetite of a pig. She drank a cup of wonderfully fragrant Nestlé's coffee. "Uncle," she said, "an army trains for a thousand days to fight for one. The time has come for you to display your skills."

Jintong gulped in surprise, which led to a series of hiccups. "Um," he stammered, "what can, what can I do . . ."

Noticeably disgusted by the hiccups, she fixed her callous gray eyes on his mouth. Because of the callousness, her normally tender eyes were suddenly unbelievably intimidating, reminding him of her mother and of those marshland snakes that could swallow a wild goose. That thought cured his hiccups.

"You can do lots of things!" Rays of tenderness shot from her gray eyes, returning them to their enchanted beauty. "Uncle," she said, "do you know the one thing needed for us to turn our plans into reality? Of course you do, it's money. The sauna resort cost money. The big-breasted Thai masseuse cost money. Do you know how much that ostrich egg you just ate cost?" She held out five fingers. "Fifty? Five hundred? Five thousand! Everything we do costs money, and for the Eastern Bird Sanctuary to prosper, we need a lot of it. Not eighty or a hundred thousand, and not two or three hundred thousand, but millions, tens of millions! And for that we need the support of the government. We need bank loans, and the government owns the banks. The bank managers do the mayor's bidding, and who does the mayor listen to?"

She smiled, looked at Jintong, and answered her own question. "You, that's who!"

More hiccups.

"Take it easy, Uncle. Listen carefully. The new mayor of Dalan isn't just anybody, it's none other than your very own mentor, Ji Qiongzhi, and the first person she inquired about as mayor was you. Just think, Uncle, after all these years, you're still in her thoughts. Emotions don't get any deeper than that."

"So I go see her and say, mentor Ji, I'm Shangguan Jintong, and I'd like you to lend my niece several million yuan for her bird sanctuary, is that it?" Jintong said.

Lianlian laughed hard. Gently pounding Jintong on the shoulder, she said, "Silly Uncle, my silly Uncle, you sure have earned your reputation as an innocent man. I'll teach you how to do it."

Over the next couple of weeks, Lianlian put Jintong through the sort of day-and-night training that Parrot used on his birds, instructing him on what a powerful woman likes to hear. On the day before Ji Qiongzhi's birthday Lianlian conducted a dress rehearsal in her bedroom. Dressed in a sheer white nightgown, she played the part of Mayor Ji, a cigarette in one hand and a glass of fine wine in the other, a love potion on the pillow, and embroidered slippers on her feet. Jintong, wearing a tailored suit and French cologne, was holding an array of peacock feathers in one arm and a trained parrot in the other as he gently pushed open the leather-trimmed door —

— The moment he stepped into the room, Ji Qiongzhi's prestige and manner froze him in his tracks. Unlike Lianlian, she wasn't dressed in a revealing nightgown. Instead, she was wearing an old army uniform, buttoned all the way up to the neck. And she wasn't smoking a cigarette or holding a glass of wine. Needless to say, there was no love potion on the pillow. In fact, she didn't receive him in her bedroom. She was smoking a Stalin-era pipe filled with reeking coarse tobacco, and was guzzling tea from an oversized mug with chipped porcelain and the words "Flood Dragon River Farm" stamped on one side. Seated in a beat-up rattan chair, she had her feet, encased in smelly nylon socks, on the desk in front of her. She was reading a mimeographed document when he entered. She tossed it aside when she saw him. "Bastard! Lousy bedbug!" Jintong's legs nearly buckled, and he all but threw himself to his knees in front of her. Taking her feet off the desk, she slipped into her shoes, caving in the backs, and said, "Come here, Shangguan Jintong. Don't be frightened, that wasn't meant for you."

In line with Lianlian's instructions, Jintong should have bowed deeply at that moment, and then, with tears in his eyes, gazed at her soft bosom, but for only about ten seconds. Longer than that would give the impression of unwelcome intentions; less than that implied disrespect. Then he was to say, "My dear teacher, Ji Qiongzhi, do you still remember that useless student you once had?"

But she'd called him by name before he could open his mouth and looked him over from head to toe, the same liveliness in her eyes as before. He felt prickly all over, and wished he could drop what he was carrying and get away as fast as his feet would carry him. She sniffed the air. "How much cologne did Geng Lianlian spray on you?" she asked mockingly.

She got up and pushed open a window to let in the cool night air. Off in the distance, arc welders raised sparks on steel girders high above the ground, like holiday fireworks. "Have a seat," she said. "I have nothing to offer you, except a glass of water." She picked up a mug with a missing handle from the tea cart, studied the gunk at the bottom, and said, "Maybe not. It's filthy, and I'm too lazy to go wash it out. I'm getting old. Time is unforgiving. After running around all day, my legs have swelled up like leavened bread."

"When she brings up her age and complains about getting old, Uncle, you mustn't agree with her. Even if her face looks like a dried-up gourd, what you have to say is" — now he parroted the exact words Geng Lianlian had coached him to say: "Teacher, except that you've filled out a little, you look just the same as when you were teaching us songs all those years ago. You look like a woman of twenty-seven or twenty-eight, certainly no more than thirty!"

With a sneer, Ji said, "Geng Lianlian told you to say that, didn't she?"

"Yes." He blushed.

"Jintong, you can't sing a song well just by memorizing the lyrics. I assure you that that sort of ass-kissing is wasted on me. Under thirty, indeed! That's crap! I don't have to be told that I'm getting old. My hair's turning gray, my eyesight's getting worse, my teeth are threatening to fall out, and my skin sags. There's more, but I'd rather not talk about it. People out there praise me to the sky to my face, but curse me behind my back, silently if not out loud. That old deadbeat! The old witch! Since you owned up to it, I'll overlook it today. I could just as easily have thrown you out. But have a seat. Don't just stand there."

Jintong handed her the array of peacock feathers. "Teacher Ji, Geng Lianlian asked me to give you these and told me to say, 'Teacher, these fifty-five peacock feathers are a birthday gift that mirrors your own beauty.'" "More crap!" Ji said. "A peacock is beautiful. But a peahen is uglier than a roosting chicken. Take those feathers back to her. And what's that, a talking parrot?" She pointed at the cage he was holding. "Uncover it and let me have a look." Jintong removed the red silk cover and tapped the cage. The sleepy parrot inside ruffled its wings and said angrily, "How are you, how are you, Teacher Ji?" Ji Qiongzhi smacked the cage, throwing such a scare into the bird that it hopped up and down, its pretty feathers banging loudly against the cage. With a sigh, Ji said, "How am I? No damned good, that's how."

She refilled her pipe and sucked on it like a toothless old man. "Birdman Han planted a dragon seed," she said, "but all he got for his efforts was a flea! Why did Geng Lianlian send you here?"

Jintong stammered, "She asked me to invite you to take a tour of the Eastern Bird Sanctuary."

"That's not the real reason," Ji said as she picked up her mug of tea and took a drink. She banged it down on the table and said, "What she really wants is a bank loan."

5

On one glorious spring day, Ji Qiongzhi elevated Jintong's status in the eyes of others by leading a delegation of Dalan's most influential officials and, by special invitation, the managers of the Construction Bank, the Bank of Industry and Commerce, the People's Bank, and the Bank of Agriculture on an inspection tour of the Eastern Bird Sanctuary. Lu Shengli, a woman of majestic bearing, dressed very simply that day, but any discerning individual could see that this very simplicity was in itself a fashion statement, and that her "simple" clothes were all designer imports.

Forty or more expensive sedans pulled up at the gate of the Eastern Bird Sanctuary, where a pair of red palace lanterns three meters in diameter, filled with more than a hundred silver-throated skylarks, hung. Parrot Han had trained the birds to start singing as soon as they heard the sound of automobile engines. The lanterns vibrated with the skylarks' songs, natural music of unsurpassed and unforgettable beauty. The arched roof of the gate was home to more than seventy nests of golden swifts, also trained by the magical hand of Parrot Han. A wooden plaque standing alongside the gate gave the English name of the swifts and a Chinese and English detailed description of the birds. Of special note was the fact that the nearly transparent nests were famous for their high nutritional value; a single nest sold for 3,000 yuan. For this occasion, Geng Lianlian had secretly installed several hundred audio speakers on nearby trees, which flooded the area with taped birdcalls. Just inside the gate, four wooden plaques proclaimed: Birds Call Flowers Sing, one gigantic word on each plaque. At first, the observers assumed that the word "sing" was a mistake, but they quickly realized that it was the perfect choice, since the flowers of the Eastern Bird Sanctuary did in fact appear to be singing as they swayed along with the nearly deafening birdcalls. A flock of well-trained wild chickens performed a welcoming dance in the middle of the courtyard, pairing off as couples one minute and spinning in the air the next, in perfect cadence with the music. These can't be wild chickens! They're nothing less than a flock of young gentlemen (for the sake of aesthetic continuity, Parrot Han had trained only male birds), a flock of young dandies forming a multicolored chorus line that dazzled the observers' eyes. Geng Lianlian and Jintong led the visitors into the sanctuary's performance hall, where Parrot Han, wearing ceremonial dress with embroidered red flowers, waited impressively, baton at the ready. Once the visitors were inside, a young female attendant threw a switch, flooding the hall with light, and twenty tiger-skin parrots on a horizontal perch directly opposite the entrance sang out in unison: Welcome welcome, hearty welcome, welcome welcome, hearty welcome! The visitors responded with ecstatic applause. Before the sound had died out, a flock of little siskins flew out, each carrying a folded pink slip in its beak, which they dropped into the hands of the visitors. Opening their slips, the visitors read the following: Greetings to your honorable personages! Your advice and guidance will be much appreciated. The recipients clicked their tongues in amazement. Next came two mynahs dressed in red jackets and little green hats; waddling up to a microphone at the center of the stage, one of them announced haughtily, Ladies and gentlemen, how do you do! The second mynah translated into fluent English. Thank you for honoring us with your presence. We welcome your precious advice — more translation. The director of the Municipal Trade Bureau, who knew English well, commented, Pure Oxford English. Now, for your enjoyment, we offer a solo rendering of "The Women's Liberation Anthem," sung by Hill Mynah. A hill mynah in purple dress bird-walked up to the microphone and bowed to the audience, so deeply that they could see the two yellow flaps on the back of her head. She said, today I'm going to sing a historical song, which I respectfully dedicate to Mayor Ji. I hope you all enjoy it. Thank you. Another deep bow exposed for the second time the two flaps, as ten canaries hopped out onto the stage to sing the opening bars in their lovely voices. The hill mynah began to rock as her voice rose in song:

In the old society, this is how it was:
A dark, o so dark dry well, deep down in the ground.
Crushing the common folk, women at the bottom,
At the very, very bottom.
In the new society, this is how it is:
A bright, o so bright sun shines down on the peasants.
Women have been freed to stand up,
At the very, very top.

The song ended amid thundering applause. Lianlian and Jintong sneaked a look at Ji Qiongzhi to gauge her reaction. She sat there calmly, neither clapping nor shouting her approval. Lianlian began to squirm. "What's with her?" she asked softly, giving him a nudge with her elbow. He shook his head.

Lianlian cleared her throat to get everyone's attention. "I now invite our honorable guests to the dining room. Since the Eastern Bird Sanctuary is a new enterprise and has limited funds, we can offer only a modest meal. Our chef has prepared a 'hundred bird banquet' in your honor."

The pair of avian masters of ceremony rushed up to the microphone to announce in unison, "Hundred bird banquet, hundred bird banquet, delicacies galore. From ostrich to hummingbird. Mallard and blue horse chicken. Red-crested crane and long-tailed turtledove. Bustard and ibis, hawfinch and mandarin duck, pelican and lovebird. Yellow roc, thrush, and woodpecker. Swan, cormorant, flamingo . . ."

Ji Qiongzhi walked out before the mynahs could list all the birds on the menu, her face hard as iron. Her subordinates fell in behind her with demonstrable reluctance. She had no sooner entered her car than Lianlian stomped her foot in anger and cursed, "What a witch! A goddamned deadbeat!"

The next day, the relevant portions of a meeting of the Municipal Government were sent to Geng Lianlian. "A bird sanctuary?" Ji Qiongzhi was quoted as saying. "They'll not see a penny of government money as long as I'm mayor of this city!"

Lianlian giggled at the news. "That old fart. We'll keep riding the donkey and singing our song, and see what happens." She then directed Jintong to send the gifts they'd already prepared to the homes of the people who had come to the show, Ji Qiongzhi not included. The gifts included a pound of swallow's nest and a bouquet of peacock feathers. For the most important visitors — that is, bank managers — an additional pound of swallow's nest.

Jintong hesitated. "I . . . can't do something like that."

Within the space of a second, Lianlian's gray eyes turned into those of a snake. "Can't do it," she said icily. "Then I'm afraid I'll have to ask Uncle to look for work elsewhere. Who knows, maybe that precious teacher of yours will find you an official position somewhere."

"We can have Uncle be a gateman or something," Parrot Han volunteered.

"Shut your mouth!" Lianlian hissed. "He may be your uncle, but he isn't mine. I'm not running an old folks' home here."

"I'd advise you not to kill and eat the donkey after the milling's finished," Parrot muttered.

Lianlian flung her coffee cup at Parrot's head. Yellow rays shot from her eyes, her lips parted savagely, and she said, "Get out of here, get the hell out, both of you! Anger me, and I'll feed you to the eagles!"

Feeling his soul fly off in terror, Jintong cupped his hands in front of his chest. "It's all my fault, Niece, I should die a thousand deaths. I'm not human, I'm the scum of the earth. Don't take it out on my nephew. I'll leave. You fed and clothed me, and I'll pay you back, even if I have to become a garbage collector or scavenge empty bottles for their deposit."

"That's some drive you've got," Lianlian mocked him. "You're a damned idiot. Anybody who spends his life hanging by his mouth on women's nipples is lower than a dog. If I'd been you, I'd have hanged myself from a crooked tree long ago. Pastor Malory planted a dragon seed, but all he harvested was a flea. No, you're no flea. A flea can at least jump high into the air. At best you're a stinking bedbug, and maybe not even that. You're like a louse that's gone hungry for three years!"

Cupping his hands over his ears, Jintong fled the Eastern Bird Sanctuary, but no matter how fast he ran, Lianlian's razor-sharp verbal barbs cut him to ribbons. In his confusion, he ran into a field of reeds, all yellow and withered, since they hadn't been cut down the year before; the new reeds had already grown half a foot. He burrowed deep into the field, and was, for the moment, cut off from the outside world. The dry plants rustled in the wind; the bitter odor of new plants rose from the muddy ground at his feet. His heart was nearly breaking, and as he tumbled to the ground, he began to wail piteously, pounding his cumbersome head with his muddy hands. Like a little old lady, he cried out between sobs, "Why did you let me be born, Mother? How could you raise a worthless piece of garbage like me? You should have stuffed me down a toilet right after I was born. Mother, I've lived my life like something that's neither human nor demon! Adults picked on me, children picked on me, men picked on me, women picked on me, the living picked on me, the dead picked on me . . . Mother, I can't go on, it's time for me to depart this world. Old man in Heaven, open your eyes, strike me dead with a bolt of lightning! Mother Earth, open up and swallow me down. Mother, I can't take it any longer! She cursed and reviled me right to my face . . ."

Once he'd cried himself out, he lay down on the muddy ground. But that was so uncomfortable he had to get right back up. He blew his nose, red from crying, and wiped his tear-streaked face. It had been a good cry, and he felt much better. His attention was caught first by a shrike's nest in the reeds, and then by a snake slithering out between them. He froze for a moment, but then congratulated himself for not giving the snake a chance to crawl up his pant leg. The shrike's nest took his thoughts back to the Eastern Bird Sanctuary. The snake shifted those thoughts to Geng Lianlian, and his heart slowly filled with rage. He gave the nest a hard kick, but since it was tied to the reeds by horsetail grass, not only did it stay where it was, but he nearly lost his balance. He ripped the nest loose, threw it to the ground, and stomped on it with both feet. "Lousy goddamned bird sanctuary! Son of a bitch! Here's what you get! I'll stomp you out of existence! Son of a bitch!" All that stomping gave him courage and increased his anger, so he bent down and broke off a reed, accidentally cutting his palm with the razor-sharp leaf. Ignoring the pain, he raised the reed high over his head and took out after the snake, which he found slithering amid the purple buds of young reeds; it was racing along the ground. "Geng Lianlian," he shouted as he raised the reed over his head again, "you venomous snake! You messed with the wrong person, and now your life is mine!" He swung the reed with all his might. He wasn't sure if he hit the snake on the head or on the body, but he was sure he hit it somewhere, because it immediately curled up, raised its black-streaked head, and began hissing. It stared at him with its malicious gray eyes. He shuddered and his hair stood on edge. He was about to strike out with his reed again when the snake slithered toward him. With a cry for his mother, he threw down the reed and ran out of the patch as fast as his legs would carry him, oblivious to the cuts on his face from the sharp leaves brushing against him. He stopped to catch his breath only when he was sure the snake hadn't followed him. There was no strength in his limbs, his head was swimming, and he felt weak all over; and his empty stomach grumbled. Off in the distance, the arched gate of the Eastern Bird Sanctuary sparkled in the bright sunlight. The honking of cranes soared up to the clouds. In days just past, this would be lunchtime. The sweet fragrance of fresh milk, the smell of bread, and the redolence of quail and pheasant sought him out all at once, and he began to regret his impulsiveness. Why did I leave? What would it have cost me to hand out a few gifts? He slapped himself. It didn't hurt, so he did it again. This time it stung a little. He hauled off and slugged himself, and leaped into the air, it hurt so much. His cheek throbbed. Shangguan Jintong, you're a bastard who's let his obsession over face cause nothing but suffering! he cursed himself loudly. His feet carried him in the direction of the Eastern Bird Sanctuary. Go on. A true man knows how to stand tall when he should and bend when he must. Apologize to Geng Lianlian, admit you were wrong, and beg her to take you back. What good does face do when you've sunk this low? Face? That's a luxury for the well-to-do, not for the likes of you. Just because she called you a stinking bedbug doesn't make you one. Or, for that matter, a louse. He berated himself, he begrudged himself, he grieved for himself, he forgave himself, he felt his own pain, he enlightened himself, he talked himself around, he taught himself a lesson, and before he knew it, he was standing at the gate of the Eastern Bird Sanctuary.

He paced irresolutely. Every time he got up the nerve to go in, he held back at the last minute. When a true man says he's setting out, a team of four horses can't hold him back. If there's no place for me here, there'll be one somewhere. A good horse doesn't turn and eat the grass it's trampled on. I do not lower my head even if I die from hunger; I stand tall before the wind as I die from the cold. I'll fight over a good showing, but not over bread. We may lack food, but we don't lack will. Everyone has to die sometime, and we must leave a name for history. He recited one cliché after another to strengthen his resolve, but he'd taken no more than a few steps before he returned to the gate. Jintong faced a dilemma. He hoped against hope that he might bump into Parrot Han or Lianlian there at the gate. But then he heard Parrot Han call out something, and he ran behind a tree. And so he remained, just outside the gate, until the sun went down. Gazing up at the house, he saw soft light streaming out of Lianlian's window, and melancholy set in. He continued gazing, but nothing came to mind, and in the end he turned and dragged himself off in the direction of town.

It was the smell of food that drew him instinctively to the night snack market in town. Originally the site of a martial arts training center, it was now the place where tasty snacks were sold. When he arrived, the shops were still open, their neon lights flashing on and off. Shop owners lolled about in their doorways, spitting watermelon seed husks effortlessly into the street as they waited in vain for customers. The scene on the cobblestone street, was more welcoming, the asphalt glistening with water, both sides alight with warm red electric lamps. Proprietors of roadside stands were dressed in white uniforms and high hats, their faces shone. A plaque at the entrance proclaimed:

SILENCE IS GOLDEN
HERE YOUR MOUTH IS FOR EATING, NOT FOR TALKING
YOUR COMPLIANCE WILL BE REWARDED

He never dreamed that the snow market regulations would find their way to this little snack market. Pink mist rose above the street, thanks to the red lamps, framing the shop owners as they signaled passersby with their eyes and their hands, lending the area a mysterious, furtive aura. Clusters of boys and girls in bright clothes, arm in arm, shoulder to shoulder, cuddling together and passing looks, but scrupulously observing the no-talking ban, were part of a grand spectacle, sharing in the strange, joyous mood of what was neither a game nor a joke, resembling tiny clutches of birds, staggering along, pecking here and there, buyers and sellers alike caught up in the seriousness of the moment. The moment Jintong stepped onto this street of silence, he experienced the rush of returning to his roots, and momentarily forgot his hunger and the humiliation of that morning. It felt to him that the silence had broken down all barriers between the people

Sometime after midnight, damp, cold winds from the southeast covered him like the skin of a snake. He had walked from one place to another, eventually winding up back in the night market, which had closed up for the night. The red lamps had been turned off, leaving only a few dim streetlights shining down on the street, now cluttered with feathers and snakeskins. Sanitation workers were sweeping up the garbage; some young hooligans were engaged in a wordless fistfight. They stopped when they saw him and simply stared. The hooligans exchanged glances, one of them gave a signal with his eyes, and they swarmed around Jintong. Before he knew what was happening, he found himself on the ground being freed of his suit, his shoes, everything but his underwear. Then, with a loud whistle as a sign, his tormentors vanished like a school of fish in the ocean.

Jintong went off looking for the thieving hooligans, up one dark lane and down another, half naked and barefoot. Maintaining the silence was no longer a concern to him, as he cursed one minute and wailed the next. The sauna-softened soles of his feet took a beating from the shards of brick and tile on the ground, while the freezing night air cut into his skin, made tender by the Thai masseuse. At that moment he realized that people who have spent years in Hell aren't especially bothered by its agonies, but such is not the case with those who have lived in more heavenly circumstances. Now he felt as if he'd been consigned to the lowest level of Hell, that he was as miserable as he'd ever been. Thoughts of the scalding water in the sauna baths made the bitter cold seem as if it had penetrated the marrow of his bones. Thinking back to the days of passion spent with Old Jin, he reminded himself that he had been naked then too; but that was being naked for fun. And now? Walking the streets late at night, he felt like a zombie.

Dogs had been outlawed in the city by municipal order. A dozen or more abandoned dogs — fascist-like German shepherds, mastiffs with the bearing of lions, loose-skinned Shar-Peis, and other breeds — had come together to form a pack, making its home in garbage heaps. Sometimes they were so stuffed with food they poisoned the air with their farts; at other times they were so hungry they could barely drag themselves along. The dogcatchers of the Municipal Environmental Protection Bureau were their mortal enemies. Not long before, Jintong had heard that the son of Zhang Huachang, the MEP Bureau chief, had been singled out from the hundreds of children at a kindergarten, taken off by a pack of savage dogs, and eaten. At the time, Zhang's son was playing on a carousel when a black wolfhound soared like an eagle from a high chain bridge, landing precisely in the seat occupied by the poor little boy; it grabbed his neck in its jaws as a motley collection of mongrels emerged from hiding places as a protective unit for the wolfhound. They swaggered unhurriedly past the petrified kindergarten teachers and carried the bureau chief's son off with them. The famous radio personality, Unicorn, ran a series of broadcasts about this frightful incident on the local radio station, concluding with the astonishing view that the dog pack was disguised members of a society of criminals. Back when Jintong had been neatly dressed and was eating like a king, the news had made no impression on him. But now he could think of nothing else. The city was just then promoting "Love your city, keep it clean month," and garbage collection had become a priority, so the dogs had been reduced to skin and bones. Dogcatchers were armed with imported automatic rifles with laser gunsights, forcing the dogs to spend the days down in the sewers, not daring to show themselves above ground, emerging only at night to scavenge for food. They'd already killed and eaten the Shar-Pei belonging to the owners of a furniture shop, and Jintong, with his inviting naked flesh, was in danger of becoming the next course.

The mastiff pressed toward him on paws as big as human fists, its fangs glinting between upturned lips, growls emerging from deep in its throat. A pair of wolfhounds that could have been twins were right behind it, one on each side as a protective escort, sinister looks on their long, thin faces. A ragtag assortment of mutts brought up the rear.

They were about to attack; the fur on their backs was standing straight up. Slowly Jintong retreated, after bending down and picking up two black rocks. His first impulse had been to turn and run; but then he recalled the advice Birdman Han had once given him: When you're face-to-face with a wild animal, the worst thing you can do is run. No two-legged animal can outrun a four-legged one. Your only hope is to stare it down.

The dogs pressed forward, confident that this big piece of tender meat in front of them was on the verge of cracking up, getting closer and closer to total paralysis. His steps began to falter as his legs turned increasingly rubbery and his body swayed from side to side; the rocks were about to slip from his hands, and the foul sweat of fear oozed from his pores.

Jintong's eyes were glazing over; the rocks fell to the ground. He knew that the moment of his liberation from worldly concerns had arrived. But how could he end his days on earth in the stomachs of a pack of dogs? Wearily, he thought of his mother, and he thought of Old Jin, who, with her single breast, would take on any man alive and never come out second best. He didn't have the energy to let his thoughts continue. Once he was seated on the steps, his sole wish was that the dogs would finish him off quickly. He hated the thought of leaving behind a leg, or something like that. Gobble up every scrap, lick up every drop of blood, and let Shangguan Jintong's disappearance be a complete mystery.

A wayward calf came to Jintong's rescue, a miraculous scapegoat. The calf, fat and oily, its hide like fine satin, had broken free from a nearby butcher shop. Its flesh obviously surpassed that of Jintong, for the dogs abandoned their assault on Jintong the instant they laid eyes on the fat little calf. He watched as the calf, frightened out of its wits, ran right in amid the pack of dogs. With a single leap, the mastiff sank its fangs into the calf's neck. With a mournful lowing, it was thrown onto its side, and the wolfhounds went for its belly, ripping it open in a flash. The rest of the dogs joined in the kill, nearly picking the calf up off the ground as they tore it limb from limb.

Jintong took off running, avoiding dark lanes. This time, by god, if I run into those dogs, there won't be a calf to come to my rescue. It's out in the open for me. I'm bound to have better luck if I go where people are and try to scare up some rags to cover my body. If all else fails, I'll go home to Mother. If necessary, I'll follow in her footsteps and become a scavenger, since I've had my share of the good life these past few years with Old Jin and Geng Lianlian. If I die now, at the age of forty-two, so what?

No place was more "out in the open" than the town's market square, with its movie theater, bordered by a museum on one side and a library on the other. All three buildings were fronted by tall steps, with blue glass walls that rose up into the sky and rotating electric lights. He'd often driven past this theater in Lianlian's car, but had never realized how big it was. Now, as Prince Jintong, down on his luck, strolled alone through the square, it seemed enormous, taking up the entire vista. The square was laid with octagonal concrete tiles. His feet were killing him. He took a look at one of the soles; there were at least ten blisters the size of grapes, some of which had already popped and were oozing a clear liquid. The blood blisters hurt the worst. When he spotted several piles of animal droppings, the thought that they might be dog shit filled him with dread.

A gust of wind carried several white plastic bags tumbling through the air around him; he ran after them in spite of his aching feet, catching one and racing after another, leaving bloody footprints all the way to the edge of the square. The second bag was snagged on the branch of a holly tree, so he sat down, and remained sitting even though the cold wind and tiles sent stabbing pains up his rectum. As he wrapped the plastic bags around his feet, he noticed that many others were caught in the tree, and in a mad but joyous frenzy he took them all down and wrapped them around his feet. He stood up and started walking again, happy to see that his soles were springier and more comfortable, and that the shooting pains were hardly noticeable. The scraping sound of his plastic feet traveled into the distance.

The rumble of heavy machinery came to him from the bank of the Flood Dragon River. Here in the renamed Osmanthus District residents were home in bed sleeping peacefully. All the lights in the district were off, except for a few lighted windows in the newly built Osmanthus Mansions southeast of where he stood, the most luxurious building in town. Finally, he decided to head over to the pagoda and be with his mother. This time he wouldn't leave her side again, no matter what. If that made him a hopeless case, so be it. He might not be able to dine on ostrich eggs, or bathe in a sauna, but he wouldn't have to worry again about sinking so low that he walked the streets alone, half naked, plastic bags for shoes.

As he passed shop after shop along the way, he was drawn to a brilliant window display; he stopped — though he shouldn't have — in front of six fashionably dressed mannequins, three male and three female, standing in the window. What caught his attention, besides the golden or jet black hair, the sleek and intelligent foreheads, the high noses, the curled lashes, the expressions of tenderness in the eyes, and the soft, red lips of the female mannequins, were, of course, the high, arching breasts. The more he looked, the more the mannequins seemed to come alive; the sweet smell of women's breasts seeped through the window glass and warmed his heart. He didn't return to his senses until his head bumped up against the cold glass. Fearing that his madness was upon him again, and that this time it would not go away, he forced himself to turn and walk off while he remained clearheaded. But he did not get far before circling back and raising his hands in supplication. "Please, Lord, let me touch them! I need to touch them. I'll never ask for anything again, as long as I live."

Flinging himself toward the mannequins, he felt the glass shatter, but there was no sound. When he reached out to touch the breasts, the mannequins tumbled to the floor. He landed on top of them, his hand cupped around a rigid breast, and a horrifying realization came to him. My god, there's no nipple!

A salty, acrid liquid washed into his eyes and his mouth as he fell into a bottomless abyss.

6

Toward the end of the 1980s, the Cultural Affairs Office of the Municipal Bureau of Culture decided to build an amusement park on the high ground currently occupied by the pagoda. The director led a red bulldozer, a dozen or more reassigned policemen armed with billy clubs, an official witness from the Municipal Notary Office, and TV and newspaper reporters to surround the house in front of the pagoda. There he read aloud the government's proclamation for the benefit of Jintong and his mother: "After careful study, it has been determined that the house in front of the pagoda is public property belonging to Northeast Gaomi Township, not the private property of the Shangguan family. Their house has been sold at fair value, the money given to their kin, Parrot Han. The Shangguan family is in violation of the law by occupying said house, and must vacate the premises within six hours. If they do not, they will be guilty of squatting on public property. Do you understand what I have just read?" the director asked truculently.

Seated calmly on her bed, Mother replied, "Your tractors will have to go through me."

"Shangguan Jintong," the director said, "your aged mother has lost her mind, I'm afraid. Go talk to her. A wise individual submits to circumstances. You do not want to make an enemy of the government."

Jintong, who had spent three years in a mental institution for crashing through the shop window and destroying a mannequin, woodenly shook his head. A scar stood out on his forehead, and his glassy eyes showed the depth of his mental defect. When the director took out his mobile phone, Jintong fell to his knees, holding his head in his hands and pleading, "Please, no electric shocks . . . no shocks . . . I'm a mental defect . . ." "The old one's losing her mind," the director said, "and the young one's already lost his. What now?"

"We have this on tape," the government witness said, "so if they won't move on their own, we'll just have to move them!"

The director signaled the police, who dragged Jintong and his mother out of the house. With her white hair flying, she fought like an old lion, but all Jintong did was beg, "Please don't shock me . . . no shock . . . I'm a mental defect . . ."

When his mother tried to fight her way over to the straw huts, the police bound her hand and foot. She was so enraged she foamed at the mouth before finally passing out.

The police tossed the few pieces of broken furniture and tattered bedding out into the yard. Then the red bulldozer raised its enormous scoop, with its row of steel teeth, and rumbled up to the little house; smoke belching from its smokestack. In Jintong's mind, it was coming for him, and he pressed himself up against the damp base of the pagoda to await death.

At this critical moment, Sima Liang, who had not been seen in years, dropped from heaven into their midst.

7

In fact, ten or fifteen minutes earlier, I had spotted the olive green helicopter circling in the air above Dalan. Like a gigantic dragonfly, it skimmed across the sky, dropping lower and lower, at times nearly scraping the pointed dome of the pagoda with its drooping belly. Swirls of wind from the rotors created a buzzing in my ears as the helicopter swooped down, tail high in the air. A large head peeked out through the brightly lit cockpit window and looked down at the ground. The person moved out of sight before I got a good look at his face. The bulldozer roared, its tracks clanking as it raised its toothed scoop and moved up to the house like a bizarre dinosaur. The old Taoist, Men Shengwu, dressed in his customary black robe, appeared like an apparition in front of the pagoda, and just as quickly vanished. All I could think to do was shout, "Don't shock me, I'm a mental defect, isn't that enough?"

The helicopter returned, this time leaning to one side and spitting yellow smoke. A woman's figure leaned out of the cockpit and shouted, her voice barely audible over the earsplitting *thunk-thunk-thunk* of the rotors, "Stop . . . can't raze that . . . historic buildings . . . Qin Wujin . . ."

Qin Wujin was the grandson of Mr. Qin Er, who had taught Sima Ku and me. He was in charge of the Cultural Relics Office, but was more interested in development than preservation, and was at that moment examining a large celadon bowl belonging to our family. How bright his eyes were. His jowls twitched; the shout from the helicopter overhead had obviously given him a start. As he looked up into the sky, the helicopter circled back and shrouded him in a blast of yellow smoke.

Eventually, it landed in front of the pagoda. Even after it was safely on the ground, the flat blades of its rotor continued their witless revolutions — *thunk-thunk-thunk* — each turn slower than the one before, until they finally shuddered to a stop, and the beast sat there staring wide-eyed. A hatch opened in its belly, framed by light from the cockpit, and down the ladder came a man in a leather coat, followed by a woman in a bright orange windbreaker over a muted orange woolen skirt. Her calf muscles tensed at each step. She had a dignified, rectangular face under a dense swirl of shiny black hair. I recognized her at once: it was the daughter of Lu Liren and my sister Pandi — Lu Shengli, the former manager of the city's Bank of Industry and Commerce. She had just been elevated to the position of mayor, following the death of the incumbent mayor, Ji Qiongzhi, who had died of a cerebral hemorrhage — from rage, according to some people. Shengli had inherited my fifth sister's physique, but was more dignified than her mother, proving that each generation surpasses the former. She walked with her head held high, her chest thrust forward, like a thoroughbred racehorse. A middle-aged, big-headed man followed her down the ladder. He wore a designer suit and a wide tie.

The man was turning bald, but had the face of a mischievous little boy, with spirited eyes that held great mystery. A bulbous nose sat atop a handsome little mouth with full lips, and his large, fair, and fleshy earlobes hung down heavily like turkey wattles. I'd never seen a man with a face like that before, nor a woman, of course. With regal looks like that, such individuals were the type fated to be emperors, to be lucky in love, to enjoy the company of three wives, six consorts, and seventy-two concubines. It could be Sima Liang, but I didn't dare believe it. At first he didn't see me, which was fine with me, since he surely could not acknowledge my presence. Shangguan Jintong was a former mental patient, a man with a sexual hang-up. Right behind him came a woman of mixed blood who was both taller and bigger than Lu Shengli. She had deep-set eyes and blood-red lips.

Lu Shengli kept glancing at the man, a bewitching smile creasing her customary stern expression. Her smile was more precious than diamonds and more terrifying than poison. The Cultural Affairs director waddled over with our celadon bowl. "Mayor Lu," he said, "how wonderful to have you come observe our work." "What are you planning to do?" she asked. "We're going to build a theme park around this ancient pagoda as a tourist attraction for Chinese and foreigners." "Why wasn't

I informed?" "It was approved by your predecessor, Mayor Ji." "Since it was her decision, we'll have to go back to the drawing table. The pagoda is under the city's protection, and I don't want you knocking down the house in front. We are going to reinstate the snow market activities. How much amusement do you think you'll get out of throwing up a few lousy electronic games, crummy bump'em cars, and chintzy game tables? What's amusing about that? Comrade, vision is required if we're going to attract foreign visitors and relieve them of their spending money. I've called upon the city's residents to learn from the pathbreaking spirit of the Eastern Bird Sanctuary, to walk where others have not trod before and to produce something new and different. What do we mean by reforms? What does it mean to open up? It means to think and act boldly. There may be things you cannot think of, but nothing you cannot do. The Eastern Bird Sanctuary is in the process of implementing their 'Phoenix Plan.' By crossbreeding ostriches, golden pheasants, and peacocks, they plan to produce a bird that so far exists only in legend — a phoenix." Having grown addicted to orating, the more she spoke, the more frenzied she grew, like the hooves of a horse that cannot stop running. The government witness and the policemen all stood transfixed. The reporter from the municipal TV station, a man with a well-deserved reputation as subordinate to the head of the Radio and Television Bureau, Unicorn, had his camera trained on Mayor Lu Shengli and the honored guests. Reporters from local newspapers abruptly snapped out of their trance and began running around, kneeling and standing to snap pictures of the dignitaries.

Finally, Sima Liang spotted Mother, who was lying in front of the pagoda, bound hand and foot. He stumbled backward and his head rocked from side to side. Tears all but spurted from his eyes. Then he fell to his knees, slowly at first, quickly prostrating himself just as his kneecaps touched the ground. "Grandma!" he said with a loud wail. "Grandma . . ."

There was nothing contrived about his weeping, as his tear-streaked face proved, that and the snivel running from his nose. With her failing eyesight, Mother tried to focus on him. Her lips quivered. "Is that you, little Liang?"

"Grandma, dear Grandma, it's me, Sima Liang, the boy you nursed as an infant." Mother tried to roll over. "Cousin," Sima Liang said as he got to his feet, "why have you trussed my grandmother up like that?" "It's all my fault, cousin," Lu Shengli said awkwardly. Then she turned to Qin Wujin and hissed through clenched teeth, "You sons of bitches!" Qin's knees began to knock, but he managed to hold on to our celadon bowl. "Just wait till I'm back in my office — no, I'm not going to wait. You're fired! Now go back and write a self-criticism." She bent down and started untying Mother; when she encountered a knot she couldn't undo, she loosened it with her teeth. It was a touching scene. After helping Mother to her feet, she said, "I'm sorry I came so late." Mother had a puzzled look on her face. "Who are you?" "Don't you recognize me, Grandma? I'm Lu Shengli." Mother shook her head. "You don't look like her." She turned back to Sima Liang. "Liang, let me touch you. I want to see if you've filled out." Mother stroked Sima Liang's head. "You're my little Liang, all right," she said. "People may change over the years, but not the shape of their skull. That's where your fate is determined. You have plenty of meat on your bones, my child. You seem to have done well for yourself. At least you're eating well." "Yes, Grandma, I'm eating well," Sima Liang sobbed. "We've risen out of our hardships, and from now on you can relax and enjoy the good life. Where's my Little Uncle? How is he doing?"

Sima Liang and I were nearly face-to-face. Should I continue with the mental case act or should I let him see me clearheaded? After a separation of nearly forty years, seeing me as a mental case would be hard for him to take, and I decided that my childhood friend deserved to see me as a normal, intelligent human being. "Sima Liang!" "Little Uncle!" We embraced. His cologne made my head swim. After stepping back, I gazed into his shifty eyes. He sighed, like a man of great wisdom, and I spotted the marks of my tears and snivel on the shoulder of his neatly pressed suit. Then I saw Lu Shengli thrust out her arm as if she wanted to shake my hand; but the minute I stuck mine out, she pulled hers back, which both embarrassed and enraged me. Shit, Lu Shengli, you've forgotten your past, you've forgotten history! And forgetting history means betrayal. You've betrayed the Shangguan family, and a representative of — who can I represent? No one, I guess, not even myself. "How have you been, Little Uncle? The first thing I did after I arrived is ask around about you and Granny." Like hell! Lu Shengli, you inherited the wild imagination of Shangguan Pandi, who once ran the Flood Dragon River Farm's livestock section, but you didn't inherit her sincerity and openness. The Eurasian woman who came with Sima Liang walked up to shake my hand. I had to hand it to Sima Liang, the way he returned with this mixed-blood woman, who looked like the actress in the movie Babbitt had shown years before, on his arm, to bring glory to his ancestors. Apparently not affected by the cold, the woman was wearing a thin dress and thrusting her breasts out toward me. "How are you?" she said in halting Chinese. "I never imagined that our Little Uncle would wind up like this," Lu Shengli said sadly. But Sima Liang just laughed. "Leave everything to me," he said. "I'll make sure this problem goes away. Madam Mayor, I am building the city's most spectacular hotel, right downtown. I'll put in a hundred million. I'll also put up the money to preserve the pagoda. As for Parrot Han's bird sanctuary, I'm waiting for a report now to see whether or not I'll invest in that as well. You are the true descendant of the Shangguan family, and you have my complete support as mayor. But I hope I never again see Grandma tied up like that." "You have my word," Lu Shengli said. "Every courtesy will be extended to her and to the rest of her family from now on."

The contract-signing ceremony for a joint venture hotel between the Dalan Municipal Government and the tycoon Sima Liang was held in the Osmanthus Mansions conference room. After the signing, I followed him up to the Presidential Suite. I could see my reflection on the mirrorlike floor. Hanging on the wall was a lamp in the shape of a naked woman carrying a water jug on her head, her nipples like ripe cherries. "Little Uncle," Sima Liang said with a laugh, "you don't need to look at that. I'll show you the real thing in a minute." He turned and shouted, "Manli!" The mixed-blood woman came into the room. "I'd like you to give my Little Uncle a bath and get him into some new clothes." "No, Liang," I objected, "no." "Little Uncle," he said, "we are like brothers. Whatever comes, good or bad, we share and share alike. Whatever you desire — food, clothing, entertainment — all you have to do is tell me. If you hold back out of a false sense of politeness, it's the same as slapping me in the face."

Manli led me into the bathroom. She was wearing a short dress with spaghetti straps. With a seductive smile, she said in terrible Chinese, "Whatever you want, Little Uncle, I'm here to provide. Mr. Sima's orders." With that, she began peeling off my clothes, just as single-breasted Old Jin had done years before. I sputtered feeble objections, but wound up letting her have her way. My tattered clothes wound up in a black plastic bag; once I was undressed, I covered my nakedness with my hands. She pointed to the tub. "Please," she said.

As I sat in the tub, she turned on the faucets, which sent sprays of hot water from openings all around the tub, gently massaging me as layers of filth were washed away. Meanwhile, Manli, who had put on a shower cap and shed her dress, stood there, her nude figure right in front of my eyes, but only for a moment, before climbing into the tub and straddling me. She began to rub and knead me all over, turning me this way and that, until I finally screwed up the courage to wrap my lips around one of her nipples. She made a clucking sound, then stopped. Another outbursts of clucks, then she stopped again. She sounded like a motor that won't start. It had taken her only a minute to discover my weakness, and her breasts quickly sagged in dejection. The excitement gone, she scrubbed me front and back, then combed my hair and draped a fluffy bathrobe around me.

8

"So, what do you say, Little Uncle?" Sima Liang was sitting on a leather sofa, a cigar from the Philippine island of Luzon in his hand and a smile on his lips. "How do you feel?" "I feel wonderful," I said gratefully. "Better than I've ever felt before." "Your day of salvation has come, thanks to me," he said. "Now, get dressed. There's something I want to show you."

We rode to the commercial center of Dalan in a stretch limo, which pulled up in front of a newly decorated lingerie shop. A crowd had gathered around the Cadillac, as if it were a rare dragon boat, by the time we'd stepped out and walked up to a gigantic shop window filled with mannequins. Above the door, the shop's name — Beautify You Lingerie — was written in a florid script; beneath that, the shop's motto: Distinctive Fashions in Ladies' Undergarments. "Well?" Sima Liang asked me. "It's wonderful!" I said excitedly. "That's good, because you're going to run this shop." What a shock! "I can't handle anything like this," I protested. Sima Liang smiled. "You're an expert in women's breasts, so who could possibly be more qualified than you at selling brassieres?"

Sima led me through the silent automatic door into the spacious shop, where decorating work was still going on. All four walls were mirrored from one end to the other; the ceiling was a metal material that also reflected images. The foreman of the cleanup crew rushed up and bowed to us. "Now's the time to make any changes you might have in mind, Little Uncle," Sima said. "I don't much care for the name 'Beautify You,'" I said. "You're the expert. What would you like to call it?" "Unicorn," I said without a moment's hesitation. "Unicorn: The World in Bras." After a momentary pause, Sima laughed and said, "But they always come in pairs!" "Unicorn," I repeated. "I like it." "You're the boss," Sima said, "and what you say goes." He turned to the fore-man. "Have a new sign made right away. Beautify You has now be-come Unicorn. Hm, Unicorn, Unicorn. Not bad. It's distinctive. See, Little Uncle, I said you were the man for the job. If you held a gun to my head, I couldn't have come up with a more stylish name than that for this shop."

"Women won't let you fondle their breasts just because you feel like it," the head of the Municipal Broadcasting and Television Bureau said as he stirred his Nescafé coffee with a tiny silver spoon. His gray hair, proof of a long, hard life, was combed back neatly. His face was dark, but not dirty; his teeth were yellow, but brushed; his fingers were stained yellow, but the skin was soft. He lit an expensive China-brand cigarette and looked at me out of the corner of his eye. "Are you of the opinion," he asked, "that you can do whatever you want so long as you have the backing of a rich businessman like Sima Liang?"

"No, of course not." Somehow I managed to keep my anger in check and appear as respectful as possible. "Bureau Chief," I said to this man who had made such a name for himself during the Cultural Revolution and was still as powerful as ever, "whatever it is you want to say to me, please just say it."

"Heh-heh," he sneered. "This son of Sima Ku — a counterrevo-lutionary with the blood of Northeast Gaomi's villagers on his hands — has become Dalan's most honored guest on the basis of a few measly coins he's put together. Like they say, 'If you've got money, you can get the devil to turn the millstone!' Shangguan Jintong, what were you before this? A necrophiliac and a mental patient. Now you're a CEO!" Class hatred turned the eyes of this man they called the Unicorn bright red. He squeezed his cigarette so hard liquefied tar oozed out. "But I didn't come here today to dispense revolutionary propaganda," he said grimly. "I'm here in the cause of fame and wealth."

I listened without interrupting. What difference could it make to Shangguan Jintong, who had suffered abuse all his life? "You know," he said, "and you won't ever forget, that time when you and your mother were paraded through the Dalan marketplace, how I suffered in the name of revolution. That's right, I still recall what it felt like to be slapped by you. Well, I created the Unicorn Struggle Team and had my own program, called *The Unicorn*, over the Revolutionary Committee PA system, which I utilized to air a number of instructive broadcasts regarding the Cultural Revolution. Anyone around the age of fifty knows who Unicorn was. In the thirty years since, I've consistently used the pen name Unicorn, publishing eighty-eight celebrated articles in national magazines and newspapers. The people associate the name Unicorn with me. But now you've linked my name with women's undergarments. You and Sima Liang are so wildly ambitious, you don't care who you hurt. What you're doing is nothing short of insane class vengeance and a brazen defamation of my good name. I am going to expose you in print and take you to court, a double-barreled attack using the weapons of public opinion and the law. It's a fight to the death."

"Be my guest."

"Shangguan Jintong, don't assume that just because Lu Shengli is mayor, you have nothing to fear. My brother-in-law is a vice minister in the provincial Party Committee, a higher rank than mayor. Besides, I know all about her checkered past, and it would not take much for Unicorn to pull her down off her pedestal."

"Go right ahead. I have nothing to do with her."

"Naturally," he went on, "Unicorn has only the best of intentions, and you and I are, after all, fellow residents of Dalan. All I'm asking is that you do right by me."

"Please, get to the point, revered Bureau Chief."

"What I mean to say is, I think we can settle this privately."

"How much?"

He extended three fingers. "I'm not interested in extorting money, so let's keep it at thirty thousand. That's peanuts for someone like Sima Liang. I'd also like you to get Mayor Lu Shengli to appoint me as deputy chairman of the Standing Committee of the Municipal Board. If not, there'll be hell to pay."

I felt cold all over. "Bureau Chief," I said as I got to my feet, "you'll have to talk to Sima Liang about the financial arrangements.

The lingerie shop has just opened and we haven't earned a cent yet. And since I'm ignorant where official matters are concerned, there's nothing I can say to Lu Shengli."

"Shit, so that's his game, is it?" Sima Liang said with a smile. "He didn't even check around to see what Sima Liang is all about! I'll take care of that bastard, Little Uncle. I'll see that he winds up swallowing his own teeth. He thinks he knows a thing or two about blackmail, how to fleece the well-to-do, does he? Well, our 'Unicorn' has met his master this time around!"

A few days later, Sima Liang came to me. "You're in business, Little Uncle. Now, let's see what you can do. I've already taken care of that chump Unicorn. Don't ask how. He won't cause any trouble from now on. It's the dictatorship of the propertied class where he's concerned. So go have a good time and make yourself proud. Don't worry about whether you make or lose money in the process. It's time for the Shangguan family to make a real splash. As long as I've got money, you've got money. So go for it! Money stinks, it's nothing but dog shit! I've already made arrangements for someone to deliver everything Grandma will need on a regular basis. Now I have to go away on an important business trip and won't be back for a year or so. I'll put in a telephone for you. That way I can call if anything comes up. Please don't ask where I'm going or where I've been."

Business was booming at Unicorn: The World in Bras. The city was expanding rapidly, and another bridge was built over the Flood Dragon River. Where the Flood Dragon River Farm once stood was now home to a pair of large cotton mills, a chemical fiber factory, and a synthetic fiber factory; the area was now a celebrated textile district.

9

On the night of March 7, 1991, as a light rain fell outside, Shangguan Jintong, CEO of Unicorn: The World in Bras, was in a highly emotional state; thoughts thronged his mind as he paced the floor in the shop happily after the lights had been turned off for the night. Upstairs, the salesgirls were giggling. The money was rolling in. Finding himself understaffed, he'd advertised on TV; the following day, more than two hundred young women showed up to apply for jobs. Still excited, he rested his head against the shop window to watch the goings-on outside, also to clear his head and settle down. Shops on both sides of the street had closed for the day, their neon signs flashing in the drizzle. The number 8 bus, a newly established route, shuttled back and forth between Sandy Ridge and Eight-Sided Well.

While Jintong was standing there, a bus pulled up and stopped under the parasol tree in front of the Hundred Bird Restaurant. A young woman stepped down onto the curb, looking slightly lost for a moment. But then she spotted Unicorn: The World in Bras, and walked across the street, where Jintong waited in the darkened interior. She was wearing a raincoat the color of a duck's egg, but was bareheaded. Her hair, which was nearly blue, was combed straight back to reveal a broad, shiny forehead. Her pale face seemed shrouded in the gloomy mist, and Jintong concluded that she was a recently widowed woman. He was, as he later learned, right on target. For some reason, the woman's approach threw fear into him; he had the strange feeling that the gloom she exuded had penetrated the thick display window and was spreading throughout the shop. Before even reaching the place, she'd turned it into a mourning hall. Jintong felt like hiding, but it was too late — he was like an insect paralyzed by the stare of a predatory toad. This woman in the raincoat had just that sort of penetrating stare. Undeniably, they were beautiful eyes, beautiful but frightening. She stopped directly in front of Jintong. He was in a dark place and she was in the light, which meant she should not have been able to see him standing there in front of a stainless steel display rack; but she obviously could, and she obviously knew who he was. Her aim was clear. All that looking around as if lost while she stood beneath the parasol tree a moment before had only been an act, intended to confuse him. Later on she would say that God had led her straight to him, but he didn't believe her, figuring it was all part of a planned scheme, especially after learning that the woman was the widowed eldest daughter of the Broadcasting Bureau chief, Unicorn, who, he was convinced, was behind it all.

Like lovers meeting, she stood before him, separated only by a pane of glass with teary raindrops slipping down one side. She smiled, revealing a pair of dimples that had aged into wrinkles. Even through the glass, he could smell her sour widow's breath, which sent waves of sympathy crashing into his heart. Jintong gazed upon the woman as if she were a long-lost friend, and tears gushed from his eyes; even more tears gushed from her eyes, soaking her pale cheeks. He could think of no reason not to open the door, so he did. As the rain suddenly fell harder, and as the smell of cold, moist air and muddy soil poured into the shop, she threw herself into his arms as if it were the only natural thing to do. Her lips sought out his; his hands slipped under her raincoat, and he grasped her bra, which felt as if it was made of construction paper. The smell of cold earth in her hair and on her collar snapped him out of his trance, and he quickly jerked his hands away, wishing he'd never let them stray in the first place. But, like the turtle that's swallowed the golden hook, he wished in vain.

He could think of no reason not to take her into his private room.

He locked the door behind him, but, finding that somehow inappropriate, quickly rushed back and unlocked it before pouring her a glass of water and offering her a seat. She preferred to stand, and he rubbed his hands nervously. How he loathed himself, both for his provocative action and for his bad behavior. If he could have absolved himself from sin and gone back a half hour in time by cutting off a finger, he'd have done it without a moment's hesitation. But that was not possible; even a missing finger would not bring him absolution. The woman he'd kissed and fondled was standing in his private room covering her face with her hands and sobbing, tears oozing from between her fingers and dripping onto her raincoat. Not content to stifle her sobs, she was nearly bawling, her shoulders heaving. Jintong forced himself to contain his disgust toward this woman, who carried the smell of a cave animal, and led her over to a red Italian leather swivel chair. But she'd barely sat down before he jerked her back to her feet and helped her out of her wet raincoat, soaked from a mixture of rain, sweat, snivel, and tears. That is when he discovered that she was a truly ugly woman: pushed-in nose, protruding lips, and pointy chin — the face of a weasel. So how had she seemed so appealing standing in front of the display window? Somebody is out to trick me, but who? But the real surprise still awaited him; for the minute he removed her raincoat, he nearly cried out in alarm. All this woman, whose skin was covered with dark moles, was wearing was a Unicorn: The World in Bras blue brassiere with the price tag still attached. Seemingly embarrassed, she covered her face. Flustered, Jintong rushed to cover her with the raincoat in his hands, but she shrugged it off. So he locked the door, pulled down the curtains, and made her a cup of instant coffee. "Young woman," he said, "I deserve nothing less than death. Please don't cry. There's nothing that bothers me more than a woman crying. If you'll stop crying, you can drag me to the police station tomorrow morning, or you can slap me sixty-three times, or I'll get down on my knees and bang my head on the floor sixty-three times . . . if you so much as sniffle, I'm overcome with guilt, so I beg you . . . beg you . . ." He took out a handkerchief and dried her face, which she permitted, raising her head like a little bird. Play the role, Shangguan Jintong, he was thinking, play it to the hilt. You're like a pig that remembers the food but not the beatings, so do what you must to get her away from here. Then you can go to the nearest temple, light incense, and give thanks to the Bodhisattva. The last thing you want is to spend another fifteen years in a labor reform camp.

Once he'd dried her face, he held the coffee cup in both hands. "Here, drink this, young lady, please." She gave him another flirtatious look; it hit him like ten thousand arrows piercing his heart, opening up ten thousand little holes that were home to ten thousand wriggly worms. With the look of someone who was lightheaded from crying, she leaned against Jintong and took a sip of coffee. The crying stopped, but she was still sniffling, like a little girl, and Jintong, who'd spent fifteen years in a labor reform camp and another three in a mental institution, was starting to get angry over her performance. "Young lady," he said as he tried to drape her raincoat over her shoulders, "it's getting late, time for you to be going home." Her lips parted in a grimace, the coffee cup in her hand followed the contours of her breast and abdomen as it crashed to the floor. *Wah*! She was crying again, this time louder than ever, as if she wanted the whole city to bear witness to her grief. Flames of rage ignited in his heart, but he didn't dare let so much as a spark emerge. Happily, there were a couple of chocolate drops wrapped in gold foil on the table, like a pair of tiny bombs; he picked up one, peeled off the foil, and stuffed the dark candy into her mouth. "Young lady," he said, clenching his teeth to keep his tone passably gentle, "don't cry. Eat the candy . . ." She spit it out; it landed on the floor, where it rolled around like a little turd, dirtying the wool carpet. On and on she cried. Jintong peeled the foil off of the second piece of chocolate, and stuffed it too into her mouth. In no mood to be an obedient soul, she was about to spit it out, when he covered her mouth with his hand. So she doubled up her fist and tried to slug him. He ducked, putting his face directly opposite the blue bra, beneath which her milky white breasts jiggled. Jintong's anger melted away, replaced by feelings of pity. Now that reason had taken flight, he wrapped his arms around her ice-cold shoulders. Then came the kissing and petting, the melted chocolate drop serving to fuse their lips together.

A long, long time passed. He knew there was no way he could get rid of this woman before sunup, especially now that they'd kissed and held each other tightly; accompanying an increase in mutual feelings was a greater sense of responsibility. "What have I done to make you dislike me so?" she asked through her tears.

"Nothing," Jintong protested. "It's me I dislike. You don't know me. I've served time in prison and in a mental institution. Bad things await any woman who gets close to me. I don't want to bring harm to you, young lady."

"You don't need to say anything," she said as she covered her face and sobbed. "I know I'm not good enough for you . . . but I love you, I've loved you in secret for the longest time . . . there's nothing you need to do except allow me to stay with you for a while . . . make me a happy woman."

With that she turned and walked across the room, paused briefly, and opened the door.

Deeply touched, Jintong cursed himself for his pettiness and for having such bad thoughts about the woman. How could you let someone with such a pure heart, a widow who's suffered so much, walk away in the grip of sadness? What makes you so great? Does an old lecher like you deserve a woman's love? Can you really let her leave in the middle of the night, in the rain? What if she catches her death of cold? Or what if she meets up with one of those gangs of hooligans?

He rushed out into the corridor and caught up with her. Still teary-eyed, she put her arms around his neck and let him carry her back to his room. The smell of her oily hair made him wish he'd let her go after all, but he forced himself to lay her out on his bed.

With eyes like a little sheep, she said, "I'm yours. Everything I have is yours."

10

Jintong could not have felt worse as he applied his fingerprint to the marriage certificate, but he did it anyway. He knew he didn't love this woman, hated her, in fact. First, he had no idea how old she was. Second, he didn't know her name. And third, her background was a complete mystery. As they walked together out of the civil administrator's office, he asked her, "What's your name?"

She grimaced angrily as she opened the red marriage certificate binder. "Take a good look," she said. "It's written right there."

There it was, in black and white: Wang Yinzhi and Shangguan Jintong, having expressed their desire to marry, and having satisfied all the requirements of the Marriage Laws of the People's Republic of China . . .

"Are you related to Wang Jinzhi?" he asked her.

"He's my father."

Everything went black — Jintong swooned.

Like an idiot, I've boarded a ship of thieves, but what can I do? Getting married is easy; getting unmarried is not. Now I'm more convinced than ever that Wang Jinzhi is behind all this. Damn that Unicorn, just because he suffered at the hands of Sima Liang, he dreamed up this sinister scheme to punish me. Where are you, Sima Liang?

With tears still wetting her eyes, she said, "Jintong, I know what you're thinking, and you're wrong. I love you. This has nothing to do with my father. In fact, he's even threatened to disown me because of it. He asked me what I saw in you, reminding me that it was public knowledge that you served time for necrophilia and spent several years in a mental institution. So what if you have a nephew who is rolling in money or a niece who is mayor? he said. We may be poor, but not in spirit or integrity . . . it's all right, Jintong," she continued, looking at him through the mist in her eyes, "we can go file for divorce if you want, and I'll pick up the threads of my life . . ."

Her tears fell on his heart. Maybe I was letting my suspicions get the better of me. What's wrong with knowing that someone loves you?

Wang Yinzhi was a managerial genius. She set to work revising Jintong's business strategy by building a factory behind the shop to produce top-quality "Unicorn" brassieres. Suddenly little more than a figurehead, Jintong spent most of his time in front of the TV set, where he was treated to ubiquitous ads for Unicorn Bras:

"Wear a Unicorn and life starts anew."

"In a Unicorn fortune smiles on you."

A third-rate actor was waving a bra in front of the camera:

"Put on a Unicorn and your hubby will flip.

Take it off and your fortunes will slip."

Disgusted by what he saw, Jintong turned off the TV and began pacing back and forth along the rut he'd created in the lush wool carpet. His pace quickened, his excitement rose, his thoughts grew confused, like a starving, penned-up goat. Soon tiring, he sat down and turned the TV back on with the remote control. *The Unicorn Hour* was in progress. The program featured interviews and biopics of Dalan's most influential women. Lu Shengli and Geng Lianlian had both been featured.

The familiar theme music, the pleasant strains of Fate knocking at the door, preceded the voice of the announcer: "This program is brought to you by Unicorn Lingerie. Wear a Unicorn and life starts anew. The unicorn is the beast of love. It warms my heart day and night." The Unicorn logo filled the screen. The image: a cross between a rhinoceros and a nippled breast.

"Today's guest is Wang Yinzhi. Thanks to Ms. Wang's aggressive marketing, the young men and women of Dalan take great pride in wearing Unicorn products. No longer limited to women's lingerie, the line now features caps and socks, and everything in between." The microphone moved over to the heavily lipsticked mouth of Unicorn's general manager, Wang Yinzhi.

"Madam General Manager, my first question to you is, how did you come up with the unusual name 'Unicorn' for your shop, your factory, and your line of clothing?" Her smile exuded confidence. One look at her told you she was educated, intelligent, rich, and powerful — a woman to be reckoned with. "It's rather a long story," she replied. "More than three decades ago, my father adopted the pseudonym Unicorn. According to him, the unicorn is a magical beast that resembles, to some degree at least, a rhinoceros. It is the 'magic horn of the heart' that signifies a coming together in ancient texts. Lovers, spouses, friends, aren't they all a magic horn of the heart? That is why I chose it for the name of our shop. Turning it into a product name was the next logical step. Magic horn of the heart, yes, magic horn of the heart, doesn't the sound just carry you off into a world of blissful emotions? But I'm afraid I've gotten carried away myself, and all our magic horn of the heart friends out there don't need me to offer an explanation."

Why don't you just shut up! Jintong sputtered indignantly. How dare you take the credit for that! I'll "Unicorn" you one day!

Seated across from the hostess, a woman with protruding front teeth, Wang Yinzhi talked on and on. "Of course, my husband played a significant role in the early days of the business, but then he fell ill and is now convalescing, leaving it up to me to fight on alone. The unicorn is a true fighter in the wild, and I consider it my duty to carry on the unicorn's fighting spirit." "What, may I ask," the bucktoothed hostess asked, "is your goal?" "To turn Unicorn into a nationally known product line within three years, an international one within ten, and, ultimately, the world leader in apparel."

Jintong flung the remote control at the televised image of Wang Yinzhi. Have you no shame at all? The remote control bounced off of the TV set and landed on the floor. Meanwhile, on the screen, Wang Yinzhi, her falsies protruding like little umbrellas beneath her thin blouse, captivating a vast audience of youngsters, talked on and on. "Madam General Manager, in recent years, young women in the West have gotten caught up in a breast liberation movement. They say that brassieres are no different than the harmful corsets women wore in the seventeenth century. What's your opinion?" "It's ignorance, pure and simple!" Wang Yinzhi said categorically. "Those corsets were made of canvas and bamboo splints, like a suit of armor, so of course they were harmful. I'd say you can equate the European women's love affair with the corset with the way Chinese women bound their feet. But you can't compare either the corset or bound feet with a modern bra, especially our Unicorn product. A brassiere meets the needs of beauty and health. At Unicorn we take both aspects into account, doing everything possible to satisfy both aesthetic and biological requirements."

Jintong picked up a teacup to fling at the TV set, but at the last moment he aimed it at the paper-cushioned wall; it hardly made a sound as it bounced harmlessly onto the carpeted floor, sending a few mildewed tea leaves and some red tea splashing onto the wall and the TV set.

A single limp tea leaf stuck to the 29-inch TV screen, like a beard just beneath her mouth. "May I ask, Madam General Manager, are you wearing a Unicorn bra?" the bucktoothed hostess asked, trying to be witty. "Of course I am," she said as she reached up and shifted her false breasts — seemingly subconsciously, but actually quite intentionally. A bit of free advertising there. "How about your home life, Madam General Manager. Would you say it's happy?" "Not really," she replied candidly. "My husband suffers from a psychosis. But he's a good and decent man."

That's crap! He jumped up off the sofa. This is all a plot against me. Honeyed words to my face, then you stab me in the back. You've got me under house arrest. The camera caught Wang Yinzhi at an angle that showed her sinister smile, as if she knew that Jintong was home watching her on TV.

He got up, turned off the TV, and began pacing the floor anxiously like a caged simian, hands clasped behind his back, anger mounting by the second. Psychosis? You're the one with the goddamned psychosis! You say I can't manage the business? I'm saying I can! You daughter of a whore, you just won't let me. You're not a real woman. You're a stone woman, a hermaphroditic toad spirit! Overcome by a welter of emotions, an exhausted Shangguan Jintong lay down on his faux antique carpet on that spring evening in 1993 and began to sob uncontrollably.

By the time his tears had soaked a spot the size of a bowl, his Filipina servant entered. "Dinner's ready, sir," she said as she placed a basket of food on the table, then took out a bowl of glutinous rice, a platter of stewed lamb and turnips, another of tiny shrimp and celery, and a bowl of sweet-and-sour soup with snakehead fish. She handed him a pair of imitation ivory chopsticks and urged him to eat.

Jintong had no appetite for the steaming food arrayed in front of him. Turning to the servant, his eyes puffy from crying, he shouted in anger, "What am I? Tell me that!"

The poor girl was so frightened she just stood there with her arms hanging loosely at her side. "I don't know, sir . . ."

"You damned spy!" He flung his chopsticks down on the table. "You're working undercover for Wang Yinzhi, you damned spy!"

"I don't understand, sir, I don't know what you mean . . ."

"You put slow-acting poison in this food. You want to see me dead!" He picked up the dishes and dumped their contents on the table. Then he flung the bowl of soup at the servant. "Get out of my sight, you spying bitch!"

She ran out of the room howling, her clothes wet and sticky.

Wang Yinzhi, you counterrevolutionary, you enemy of the people, you bloodsucking insect, you damned rightist, capitalist-roader, reactionary capitalist, degenerate, class outsider, parasite, petty scoundrel tied to the post of historical disgrace, bandit, turncoat, hooligan, rogue, concealed class enemy of the people, royalist, filial daughter and virtuous granddaughter of old man Confucius, feudalism apologist, advocate for the restoration of the slave system, spokeswoman for the declining landlord class . . . Calling up every degrading political term he'd learned over several turbulent decades, he launched a verbal attack against Wang Yinzhi. Tonight you and I are going to have it out once and for all. Either the fish dies or the net breaks. Only one will be left standing. When two armies clash, victory goes to the most heroic!

Wang Yinzhi opened the door, a ring of golden keys in her hand, and stood in the doorway. "Here I am," she said with a scornful smile. "Let's see what you're made of."

Mustering up his courage, Jintong said, "I'm going to kill you!"

"Well," she said with a laugh, "a spark of life, finally. If you really have the guts to kill anyone, you've earned my respect."

She walked unafraid into the room, gave the filth on the floor a wide berth, and stopped in front of Jintong. She smacked him on the head with her key ring. "You ungrateful bastard!" she cursed. "I'd like to know what you're so unhappy about. You live in the finest hotel in town, you've got a servant to prepare your meals. Stick out your arms and you'll be clothed, open your mouth and you'll be fed. You live like an emperor, so what the hell else do you want?"

"I want . . . my freedom," Jintong muttered.

She froze for just a moment, before bursting out laughing. "I don't restrict your freedom," she said after she'd had a good laugh. "In fact, you can leave right this minute. Go!"

"Who are you to tell me to go? It's my shop, and if anyone's going to get out of here, it's you, not me."

"Like hell!" Wang Yinzhi said. "If I hadn't taken over the business, you'd have gone under even if you had a hundred shops. And you have the nerve to say this shop is yours! You've lived off me for a year already, which is all anyone could expect. Now it's time to give you back your precious freedom. There's the door. This room is reserved for someone else tonight."

"I'm your lawful husband, and I'm not leaving until I'm good and ready."

"Lawful husband," Wang Yinzhi repeated mawkishly. "Husband. Do you think you're worthy of the term? Have you fulfilled your husbandly duties? Are you really up to it?"

"Yes, if you'd do as I say."

"How dare you!" Wang Yinzhi exploded. "What do you take me for, a whore? You think you can order me around any way you want?" As her face turned bright red, and her ugly lips began to twitch, she flung the keys in her hand at his forehead. A sharp pain drilled its way into his brain and a hot, sticky liquid soaked his eyebrows. He reached up to touch it and pulled back a bloody finger, just as a couple of men he knew burst into the room. One was wearing a police uniform, the other was in a judge's robe. The policeman was Wang Yinzhi's younger brother, Wang Tiezhi; the judge was her brother-in-law, Huang Xiao-jun. They went straight for Jintong. "What do you say, Brother-in-law?" the policeman said as he drove his shoulder into him. "Anyone who takes advantage of a woman isn't much of a man, wouldn't you say?" The judge kneed him in the back. "My sister's been good to you. Don't you have a conscience?"

But just as Jintong was about to speak up in defense, a punch in the stomach drove him to his knees and sour liquid shot out of his mouth. Then the policeman leveled him out with a mighty karate chop in the neck. This brother-in-law, the judge, was a onetime military official who'd been a scout for ten years and had such a powerful hand he could break three bricks with a single chop. Jintong was grateful he'd held back a bit; if he hadn't, he'd have been lucky to keep his head on his shoulders. Cry, he told himself. They won't hit a man who's crying. Crying is what weak people do. Crying is a plea for mercy, and real men never ask for mercy. But they kept hitting him, even as he knelt on the carpet, weeping and sniveling.

Wang Yinzhi was also crying, really crying, like a woman abused. "Don't cry, Sis," the judge said. "He's not worth it. Get a divorce. There's no need for you to throw away your youth. "You, there," the policeman said, "I suppose you think the Wang family is an easy mark for you. Well, your niece the mayor has been suspended from duties and is under investigation. Your days of bullying people owing to connections are about to come to an end."

The policeman and the judge picked Jintong up, carried him out of the room and down the dark corridor, past the brightly lit shop and outside, where they dumped him next to a rubbish heap. Like people said during the Cultural Revolution, he was swept onto the rubbish heap of history. A couple of sick cats in the rubbish heap meowed plaintively. He nodded apologetically. We're in the same wretched boat, cats, so I can't help you.

Jintong hadn't seen his mother for at least six months, ever since Wang Yinzhi had kept him under house arrest, and he longed to see the light shining in that window and smell the enchanting aroma of lilacs beneath it. Last year at this time Wang Yinzhi had been a gloomy woman pacing beneath his window. Now he was the gloomy one, as the raucous laughter of the two brothers-in-law emerged from that window. She was too well connected in Dalan, with protectors everywhere, and he was no match for her. It's another rainy night, but colder. Tears slither down the glass of the display; but this time they're mine, not hers. How many nights in a person's life does he find himself with no home to return to? This time last year I was fearful of letting her wander late at night all alone; tonight that's exactly what I'm doing.

Before he realized it, his hair was soaked by the rain and his nose was stopped up, a sure sign of a cold. He was also hungry, and regretted flinging that wonderful soup at the maid instead of eating it himself. But now that he thought back, her fit of anger wasn't altogether unreasonable. Any woman with a useless husband has no choice but to take over. Maybe, he was thinking, there's still a chance. She hit me, but I didn't hit her back. I was wrong to throw the soup, but I got down on my hands and knees and licked some of it up as part of the punishment the two men dished out. I'll go over first thing in the morning and apologize — to her and to the Filipina servant. For now, I should be snoring away on the mattress at home. Maybe suffering a bit will do me good.

He recalled the overhang in front of the People's Cinema, which was as good a place as any to get out of the rain, so he started walking. His decision to apologize to Wang Yinzhi in the morning went a long way toward putting his mind at ease, and he noticed the starlit edges of the misty sky. You're fifty-four years old; the dirt is already up to your neck, so it's time to stop making trouble for yourself. What difference does it make to you if Wang Yinzhi has slept with one or a hundred men? A cuckold is a cuckold.

11

Tears wetted my cheeks, all puffy from slapping myself, but the only reaction I got from Wang Yinzhi was a sneer. No indication that this cold-blooded woman had any intention of forgiving me as she fiddled with her key ring and watched my performance.

"Yinzhi, as the saying goes, one day of married life means a hundred days of tangled emotions. I'm begging you to give me another chance."

"The problem is, we haven't had our one day of married life."

"How about that night of March 7, 1991? That should count."

I watched as she thought back to the night of March 7, 1991. Suddenly her face reddened, as if I'd humiliated her. "No," she said indignantly, "it doesn't! That was an indecent act, an attempted rape!"

Shocked and angered by her characterization, I asked myself how I could have been worried about losing a woman who could turn on me like that? Shangguan Jintong, after a lifetime of tears and snivel, isn't it time you took a stand for a change? She can have the shop, she can have everything, except for my freedom. "All right, then, when shall we file for divorce?"

She took out a slip of paper. "Sign this, and it's done. Naturally," she added, "as a fair and decent person, I'm giving you thirty thousand yuan as a settlement. Sign here." I did. As she handed me a bankbook in my name, I asked her, "Don't I need to appear in court?" "Everything's been taken care of," she said as she tossed me the divorce papers, which had already been filled out. "You're free," she said.

Now that the final curtain had fallen on this drama, I really did feel as free and easy as I'd ever felt before. Before the night was over I was back home with Mother.

In the days before Mother died, Dalan's mayor, Lu Shengli, was found guilty of accepting bribes and sentenced to death, with a one-year reprieve. Found guilty of paying bribes, Geng Lianlian and Parrot Han were put in chains and thrown into prison. Their "Phoenix Plan" had been a gigantic hoax, and the loans of millions to the Eastern Bird Sanctuary, guaranteed by Lu Shengli, as mayor, were, for the most part, used as bribes; what little remained was simply squandered. The interest on the loans was never recovered, let alone the loans themselves, but the banks did nothing for fear that the sanctuary would go belly-up; that, in fact, was a worry shared by all of Dalan City. Eventually, this farce of a sanctuary closed its doors, the birds all gone, weeds covering the feathers and bird droppings all over the compound, the workers off to their next employment. But it continued to exist on the books of all the local banks, as the interest mounted.

Sha Zaohua, who had been missing for years, returned from wherever she'd been; she'd taken good care of herself, and looked like a woman in her thirties. But when she went to the pagoda to see Mother, she received a cold reception. In the days that followed, she carried a torch for Sima Liang, who had returned to town. She produced a glass marble, which she said was an expression of his love for her, and a mirror, which was to be her gift to him. She said she'd saved herself all these years for him. But in his penthouse apartment at Osmanthus Mansions, Sima Liang had too much on his mind to give any thought to rekindling the love affair with Zaohua. Yet she followed him everywhere, which nearly drove him crazy. "My dear cousin," he bellowed one day, "just what do you think you're doing? I've offered you money, clothes, jewelry, but you don't want any of those. What do you want?" Pulling her hand off of the hem of his jacket, he sat down hard on his sofa, angry and frustrated, accidentally knocking over a flower vase with his foot; a dozen or more purplish red roses lay strewn limply over the now water-soaked table. Zaohua, who was wearing a diaphanous black dress, got down on her knees on the wet carpet and stared up into Sima Liang's face. He couldn't help but look at her out of the corner of his eye. She had a small head and a long neck on which only a few fine lines spoiled the perfect texture. Given his vast experience with women, he knew that the neck was the one place that always gave away a woman's age. How had Zaohua, a woman in her fifties, kept her neck from looking like either like a length of sausage or a piece of dried-out wood? From there his gaze moved down to the hollows just below her shoulders and the cleavage above the scoop neck of her dress, and nowhere did she have the appearance of a woman in her fifties; rather, she looked like a flower that had been kept in cold storage for half a century, or a bottle of fine liquor that's been buried for fifty years at the base of a pomegranate tree. A chilled flower is just waiting to be picked; a bottle of old liquor demands to be drunk. Sima Liang reached out and touched her gently on the knee; she moaned and her face flushed bright red, like a brilliant sunset. Throwing herself into his arms, she wrapped her arms around his neck and thrust her heated bosom into his face, rubbing her breasts back and forth until an oily substance ran from his nose and tears oozed from his eyes. "Sima Liang, I've waited for you more than thirty years." "Don't give me that," he said. "Thirty years. Do you know what that makes me guilty of?" "I'm a virgin." "A thief *and* a virgin? If that's true, I'll jump out that window!" Zaohua began to cry, stung by his comment. But then, as anger got the better hand, she jumped to her feet, shed her dress, and lay down on the carpet in front of him. "Sima Liang, come, you be the judge. If I'm not a virgin, *I'll* jump out that window!"

Before walking out of the room, Sima Liang looked down at the aging virgin and said glibly, "Well, I'll be damned, sure and truly damned. You are a virgin." Sarcasm aside, a pair of tears filled the corners of his eyes. As for Zaohua, who still lay on the carpet, her eyes were moist with joy and infatuation as she looked up at him.

When Sima Liang returned to the room, Zaohua was seated on the windowsill, stark naked, obviously waiting for him. "Well, am I a virgin or aren't I?" she said coldly.

"Cousin," Sima Liang replied, "you can forget the act. Remember, I've spent most of my life around women. Besides, if I were to marry you, what difference would it make if you were a virgin or not?"

Zaohua responded with a shriek that caused Sima Liang to break out in a cold sweat. A blue glare, like poisonous gas, emerged from her eyes. He sprang toward her just as she tipped backward; the last thing he saw were the reddened heels of her bare feet, heading down.

With a sigh, Sima Liang turned to me as I rushed into the room, drawn to the bloodcurdling shriek. "Did you see that, Little Uncle? If I follow her out the window, I won't be a worthy son of Sima Ku. But the same is true if I don't. What should I do?"

I opened my mouth to say something, but nothing came out.

Grabbing an umbrella some woman had left in his penthouse, he said, "If I die, Little Uncle, you take care of my body. If I don't, then I'll live forever."

He flicked open the umbrella, and with a loud "Shit!" leaped out the window and fell like a ripe fruit.

Nearly blind with fright, I stuck the upper half of my body out the window and yelled, "Sima Liang — Sima Liang —" But he was too busy falling to pay attention to me. People below craned their necks to witness the spectacle, ignoring the body of Sha Zaohua, which was splattered like a dead dog on the cement in front of them, and watching as Sima Liang parachuted right through the canopy of a plane tree and into a cluster of holly trees, trimmed as neatly as Stalin's mustache, sending what looked like green sludge out in waves. The people on the ground crowded around the trees just in time to see Sima Liang emerge as if nothing had happened, patting the seat of his pants and waving to the crowd. His face was a riot of colors, like the glass windows of the church we went to as children. "Sima Liang," I shouted tearfully. He pushed his way through the crowd, walked up to the building's entrance, and hailed a yellow cab. He opened the door and jumped in before the purple-clad doorman could react. The cab sped away with a burst of black exhaust, turned the corner, and entered the stream of traffic; then it was gone.

I heaved a great sigh, as if awakening from a nightmare. It was a bright, sunny, intoxicating, and lazy day, the sort that seems filled with hope but is rife with traps. Sunlight glistened off of Mother's seven-story pagoda at the edge of town.

"Son," Mother said weakly, "take me to church. It'll be the last time . . ."

With my nearly blind mother on my back, I walked for five hours down the lane behind the Beijing Opera dormitory that wound past the polluted stream by the chemical dye plant, until I found the recently restored church. Tucked away among a row of squat houses, it was simple and a bit run-down, no longer the imposing place it had once been. The front of the church and both sides of the lane were packed with bicycles decorated with colorful ribbons. An old woman sat at the gate entrance, looking like a cross between a ticket-taker and a lookout for secret activities occurring inside. She gave us a friendly nod and let us pass through the gate. The yard was packed with people; there were even more inside the church itself, all of them listening to a sermon delivered by a wizened old pastor who slurred his words. His wrinkled hands were folded on the pulpit, illuminated by a ray of sunlight. The parishioners included old people and small children, but the majority consisted of girls and young women, all seated on benches and making notations in open Bibles in their laps. An old woman who recognized Mother made room for the two of us against the wall, beneath the canopy of an aged locust tree, covered with white blossoms like oversized snowflakes. The air was stifling. A loudspeaker attached to the trunk of the tree spread the old pastor's words throughout the gathering. Hard to say whether the crackles and static stemmed from the age of the loudspeaker or of the pastor. We sat quietly and listened as he droned on and on, exhorting the parishioners to good deeds and a pure life.

When the sermon ended, a chorus of Amens emerged from the teary-eyed crowd, followed by the strains of a pipe organ off to the side, playing a closing hymn familiar to the worshippers. Those who could sing did so loudly; those who couldn't hummed along as best they could. That ended the service; some of the parishioners stood and stretched, while others remained seated to talk softly among themselves.

Mother sat on the bench, hands on her knees, eyes closed, as if she'd fallen asleep. Not a whisper of wind, yet the white blossoms suddenly fell from the tree above us, as if the electricity to the magnet holding them on to the branches had been switched off. Their fragrance filled the courtyard as great quantities of them fell onto Mother's hair, her neck, her earlobes, her hands, her shoulders, and the ground all around her.

Amen!

The old pastor, having completed his sermon, shuffled over to the door of the church and, bracing himself by holding on to the doorframe, gazed at the wondrous floral spectacle before him. He had a mass of unruly red hair, deep blue eyes, a red nose, and a heavy yellow beard. Metal caps covered some of his teeth. Startled by the sight, I stood up. Was this the legendary father I'd never known? The old woman who knew Mother hobbled over on bound feet to make the introductions. "This is Pastor Malory, our old pastor's eldest son. He has come to us from Lanzhou to head up the church. This is Shangguan Jintong, the son of Shangguan Lu, a parishioner of very long standing."

Actually, her introductions were unnecessary, because even before she spoke our names, God had already revealed our origins to one another. This bastard son of Pastor Malory and a Muslim woman, my half brother, wrapped his hairy arms around me and held me tight. With tears filling his eyes, he said:

"I have been waiting for you for a very long time, my brother!"